Strange Cargo

A WESTERN LIGHTS BOOK

Strange Cargo

JEFFREY E. BARLOUGH

ACE BOOKS, NEW YORK

An Ace Book
Published by The Berkley Publishing Group
A division of Penguin Group (USA) Inc.
375 Hudson Street
New York, New York 10014

PRINTING HISTORY
Ace trade paperback edition / August 2004

Library of Congress Cataloging-in-Publication Data

Barlough, Jeffrey E.
    Strange cargo / Jeffrey E. Barlough.— Ace trade pbk. ed.
        p.   cm.
    ISBN 0-441-01160-8
    1. Young women—Fiction.   2. Glacial epoch—Fiction.   3. Good and evil—
Fiction.   I. Title.

PS3552.A67246S76 2004
813'.54—dc22   2004046157

PRINTED IN THE UNITED STATES OF AMERICA

10   9   8   7   6   5   4   3   2   1

TO MY AUNT AND UNCLE

Ida and Joseph Zizda

IN MEMORY

Our birth is but a sleep and a forgetting:
The Soul that rises with us, our life's Star,
Hath had elsewhere its setting,
And cometh from afar.

WORDSWORTH

CONTENTS

CHAPTER ONE

Fairlight Station

In one of the drearier seasons of the year, in a year concerning which we need not be too precise, a dog was heard barking at the top of a coastal light-tower near the village of Paignton Swidges, one dreary afternoon.

The tower was called Fairlight, and it stood at the east end of the sea-channel that lies between the coast and the offshore islands, some dozen miles from the old cathedral city of Nantle. The dreary afternoon was little more than the continuation of a dreary morning, the dreariness deriving from a rumpled sky of dirty gray clouds — massive, far-spreading, impenetrable. What was worse, a thick fog was approaching now from the open ocean. Great gliding billows of it could be seen sailing forward of the wind like ghostly warships of the air. Already the noisy gulls soaring and dipping round the lighthouse had taken notice of the coming chill. At any moment the fog-bell would begin to sound, and then the great monster of a light in the lantern room would wick on and throw its saving beams out to sea, to guide the merchantmen passing through the treacherous mouth of the channel.

The old rubblestone tower rises aloft like the fabled bean-stalk of our nursery days, though considerably hardier in form and composition and a deal more weather-beaten. In the lantern room itself, at the top of the tower, the assistant keeper is busy about his labors. All the dreary morning Mr. Jobberley had spent polishing up the brass fittings in the room, in his slow, sluggish, desultory way. This accomplished, he had begun the task of cleaning the silver reflectors ranged behind the lantern, wiping the accumulated soot and brine from their delicate faces and from the five oil-lamps that constituted the light. And always it seemed there were more things that needed doing, in and about the lantern room, and about the tower itself and the keeper's lodge and the outbuildings, daily and nightly duties without end to keep the beacon shining and the fog-bell ringing.

Aiding the old wickie in his efforts — or keeping him company, more like, for he does little apart from sitting on his haunches with his tongue a-wag—is a genial, rough-coated, biscuit-colored dog of the collie variety. Undaunted by the shiftless habits of his companion, Mr. Jobberley remains stubbornly at his post, absorbed in the slow, sluggish pursuit of his vocation. He knows he must complete the task at hand, and soon, for the keeper will be ascending the iron staircase shortly to light the lamps.

As he bends his mole-like body over the mirrors, observing the distorted reflection of his gray, grizzled face in their parabolic surfaces, an odd sort of howl reaches his ears, followed almost at once by an excited barking — the voice of the collie dog, who had gotten up and removed himself to the circular railed gallery outside. Mr. Jobberley calls to his companion to desist — "Leave off yer yapping," or some such phrase — but the dog sees fit to ignore him.

Then the brow of the wickie rolls itself up, as something like a shadow descends upon him and upon the entire chamber, darkening it. No, not so much a shadow, he thinks — more like a large, weighted mass, something taking up sufficient space to dim the light in the windows. Mr. Jobberley takes a step back to absorb the view from the mirrors, and his eyes grow very round indeed as they see what is reflected there.

"Lord save us," he whispers, to no one in particular.

With his fists he rubs at those eyes in disbelief, burnishing them nearly as hard as he had the silvered glass of the mirrors. He casts a trembling glance over his shoulder, then staggers out the door and onto the gallery for a clearer look.

Just beyond the door stands the collie dog, growling and barking at the thing that is hovering in the air no more than twenty feet from the rail. Mr. Jobberley takes a long, steady stare at the thing — an enormous, open-mouthed stare of the blankest astonishment. He draws a greasy hand across his beard, his cheeks, his seal-skin cap, his goggle-eyes threatening to burst from his head apoplectically.

In a panic he retreats inside and makes for the spiral staircase. He descends in a mad rush toward the keeper's lodge, his frantic cries echoing through the hollow length of the tower. Above him the voice of the collie dog breaks off, and the wickie can hear the tread of nailed feet upon the iron steps as the animal comes racing after him.

"Matthew! Matthew Mulks! O Lord, O Lord, dear Matthew!" are among the many exclamations escaping the lips of Mr. Jobberley.

To his great relief his boots touch solid ground at last, and he barrels his way through the connecting door into the keeper's residence. There he is met by a limber, upright, straight-shouldered girl of sixteen or seventeen in a blue stuff dress. She is a dark girl with dark eyes and darker curls, and her immediate concern appears to lie more with the welfare of the collie dog than that of Mr. Jobberley.

"What have you done to Christian?" the girl demands, suspiciously, as she kneels to comfort the dog and examine him for injuries.

"Nothing it is I've done to that creature o' yern, Miss Goody Two Shoes," is the hasty and impertinent reply of Mr. Jobberley. "It's what I seen, I tell ye, and what yer Christian there himself has seen, that's stirred him up so. Where be Matthew, then? Where be yer uncle?"

"In the oil house," replies the girl.

Mr. Jobberley is about to go in search of the keeper of the light when that gentleman obligingly makes his appearance, striding in at the door from the brisk cold outside.

Mr. Mulks was a tall, strong man with a broad forehead and bulging temples, shrewd dark eyes like the girl's, and a flat nose planted on a weathered potato of a face. He was dressed in a heavy coat and trousers of brown fustian, a patterned neck-shawl and worn top-boots, and was a younger man by some years than his assistant Mr. Jobberley.

"I've heard you shouting your head off, Hake," said Mr. Mulks, a trifle irritably. He closed the heavy door behind him. "What mischief is it you've gotten into now? Are you done polishing the reflectors? For it's near time to light up the old lass."

"I've scraped all the silver and mirrors I'll be scraping today," said Mr. Jobberley, obviously much troubled. "I ain't mounting to that crow's-nest again, Matthew. Not today, nor not tomorrow, at any rate. Nor never!"

"What in botheration's the matter with you, man?"

"It's what I seen from the tower, Matthew. It's what I seen flying in the air *aside* the tower — sich a thing as has no business to be flying in air at all!"

"Children and fools have merry lives," sighed Mr. Mulks. He folded his arms on his chest. "Very well, then, what did you see, Hake? Hurry it up now. The clouds are grown dropsical and there's fog in the channel."

"Clouds, aye!" exclaimed Mr. Jobberley, wiping his lips. "Out of the clouds it come — hugeous it were — dropped from the sky and hangs afloat in air aside the gallery rail, like a gull on the vertical draft. It were something awful — something evil — it were something *fantastic*, Matthew!"

The keeper of the light stood for some moments in silence, looking very grave and sober, as he revolved in his mind how to answer. He had had trouble with Hake Jobberley before, and more than a few times, as had others before him. The old fellow had long since formed the habit of drink, garnering for himself a reputation as a drone and a tosspot. A job such as theirs made one prey to liquor's temptations, for loneliness and melancholy were often part and parcel of a wickie's existence; but Mr. Matthew Mulks would have none of it on *his* watch. He was the keeper of Fairlight station. His was the responsibility to warn the crews away from the rocky, ship-killing shoals that littered the mouth of the channel. It was a virtuous call-ing, a noble one even, and Mr. Mulks clung to it fiercely like bark to a tree.

Yet he had to confess that there was that in Mr. Jobberley's voice, in his fervent manner and air of general desperation, which had more the ring of truth than of liquor.

"What is it you think you saw, Hake?" he asked. "What did you see fly-ing beside the tower?"

"A flying bottle of gin, most like," sniffed the girl.

"That'll be enough, Jenny," admonished her uncle. "Well, Hake?"

"It ain't only what I saw, Matthew, it were what the dog saw, too," said Mr. Jobberley, gaining courage. "Ye both heard the yapping of the creature. Why, it were the dog there as saw the thing afore I! Like a shadow it come over me as I were at work upon the mirrors. That were when I saw its pic-ture in the glass, and turned round and saw the thing for myself. A prodi-gious huge kind of thing it were, Matthew! A kind of structure, squarish in shape, made of stone and mortar and timbering, with a high gable, and a steep-pitched roof and a weather-vane, and lattice windows, and a door, and a brick chimbley — the whole of it riding there in the sky as easy as ye please. And inside the latticed panes I seen two fellows a-watching me — it were that near the tower, Matthew! Then it was I run for the winding-stair, and the dog come bounding after. And that's the truth of it, Matthew, as I'll vow. Ye'll not report me again, will ye? By the Lord, ye'll not report me, Matthew, not at my time of life?"

Again Mr. Mulks was silent for a while. Then he said —

"Very well, Hake, I'll not report you. I'll take you at your word for the present. And so, too, will you, Jenny. Though I'll have you know, Hake, that in coming across from the oil house I had myself a fine view of the tower, and there was nothing to be seen but clouds and the fog coming down-channel fast and thick."

"But it were there, Matthew, it *were*!" insisted Mr. Jobberley, struggling to contain himself. "I ain't maddish!"

"It doesn't matter," the girl said to her uncle. She rose, having succeeded in calming her dog. "What of the toad that crawled over his coverlet, late in the night, and turned itself into a grisly paw to choke him? What of that, and a hundred other like tales? I tell you he's not to be trusted, Uncle."

It was clear that Mr. Jobberley was not a particular favorite of Miss Jenny Mulks's.

"Not a nip I've had this entire week, Matthew, as I'll vow by high heaven," said the wickie. "Do I smell of the spirits now — do I? I ask ye!"

And he pushed his face up close to that of his taller superior, the better for Mr. Mulks to examine him by. The keeper was forced to admit that his assistant did smell, chiefly of grease and paraffin oil and tobacco, and half-a-dozen other things, but that alcohol was not one of them.

"We'll discuss it more once our work is done, and there's an end of it," declared Mr. Mulks. "Now, you'll get yourself at once to the bell, Hake, and set the mechanism a-going. Jenny, you'll help me with the old lass. Come, the time is stealing on!"

The girl nodded and followed her uncle into the tower, leaving the dog and Mr. Jobberley behind. When they came to the lantern room, the keeper looked about him with a show of caution. But of course there was nothing there except for the lantern and the mirrors, and the dreary sky, and the gray sea, and the fog creeping into the channel.

What of the grand sweep of coastline curving away to the north and west toward the city of Nantle, and Falaise beyond it? Gone, swallowed up in the gloom. There was not a wilder or a lonesomer spot in all the country round, from Paignton Swidges to the slopes of Howler's Hill, than Fairlight on its craggy headland there above the sea.

What had Mr. Mulks expected to find in the lantern room? What was the prodigious huge kind of thing with timbers and lattice windows and a weather-vane that Mr. Jobberley had seen floating beside the tower? Had it been something real, or just another of the wickie's wild imaginings?

Neither the keeper nor his niece had time to make head or tail of it now, for the short day was drawing in and the fog was drawing on; and so they got themselves about the tricky business of vaporizing the oil in preparation for lighting the lamps.

In the lodge below, Mr. Jobberley threw himself into a chair and dropped his face into his hands. For a full five minutes he remained thus. Then on a sudden he lifted his head, as memory of the keeper's charge came back to him.

"I must toll the bell," he mumbled, his eyes roving distractedly about the room. "I must toll the bell —"

The collie dog meanwhile had settled himself very comfortably in the chimney-corner, looking every bit the lazy canine beside the stiff iron dogs of the fireplace. Over the mantelpiece hung a square bit of board inscribed with the single word VIGILANCE in grim black letters. Anything but vigilant now himself, he seemed much recovered from the late excitement. More than likely he had already puzzled it all out in his mind, and for a moment or two Mr. Jobberley envied him.

"Aye, ye know the verity of it, don't ye, old dog?" said Hake, getting to his feet.

The dog lifted his ears but otherwise offered no reply. In the flicker of the turf-fire he seemed possessed of a kind of sphinx-like serenity — the mystagogus of the light-tower he was, who, if he could have spoken, might have supplied proof of the wild imaginings of Mr. Jobberley.

"Ye seen it, too, just as I seen it," nodded the wickie. "Ye know Hake Jobberley ain't daft, ain't the fool drunkard he was upon a time. Aye, ye know the truth, old dog. Ye know what it were ye seen there. As I'm a Christian man, and ye're yerself in name a Christian creature — *if a house could be made to fly in this weary world, then that were it!*"

CHAPTER TWO

In Chambers

"I don't believe it," said the prim young woman with the keen steady gaze, who stood with arms crossed and one foot impatiently tapping on the boarded floor. "I still simply don't believe it. I *won't* believe it!"

"But my dear Susan," said the young man beside her, very smart and spiffish, and quite plainly her husband, "we've been over this ground before. We have all agreed we must respect my late grandfather's wishes. It was his intent that his estate be divided thus, and so it shall be. His will was duly executed and attested by our good friend Mr. Liffey here, who has been our family's solicitor since the year dot."

As he spoke, his glance shifted to an elderly gentleman who sat at the desk before which the couple was standing, in the cramped but snug little space of an office which the gentleman called his chambers. The gentleman had a short beard as white as his hair, and as neatly clipped, and fleshy ears as pink as his face, and kindly brows from beneath which a pair of gentle blue eyes shone out.

"Mrs. Cargo," said the elderly gentleman of the law, "we all of us can be assured that Mr. Joseph Cargo was in perfect soundness and recollection of mind, if not in the best of bodily health, when his last will and testament was prepared. I myself as his executor am witness that its provisions reflect his true intent as regards the distribution of his estate among his heirs."

"Heirs? And which heirs are those, sir?" returned the young wife, sternly. "What other heirs can there be but my husband Frederick and myself, and Miss Veal here?"

At mention of her name, the fourth member of the party, who occupied an elbow-chair beside Mrs. Cargo, nodded in dignified acknowledgment.

She was a stoutish, middle-aged, matronly lady with a pale, drab oblong of a face. There was a tall, square wig, very stiff and solid and perfectly black, sitting on her head. Her clothing was of the same pattern — stiff, solid, black — and in her lap she held a reticule that resembled a netted fish.

"There are no other relations surviving, no direct family but Frederick," Mrs. Cargo went on. "Of course we do not begrudge Grandfather Cargo his few trifling bequests to his house servants, his bailiff, his lodge-keeper. But to squander away a quarter of his fortune on a person who is utterly unknown to us! A person of whose whereabouts we have little knowledge, apart from brief mention in the will that he resides at Nantle, a place very distant from our own fine town of Cargo, and no doubt very different, and in all probability not at all to our liking. Really, Mr. Liffey, is this customary for gentlemen of the late Mr. Cargo's means and position?"

"It is not unusual for gentlemen with large sums to bestow, to make bequests to persons unconnected to them by blood or marriage, in gratitude for some prior kindness or bond of friendship that may have existed between them," said the attorney. "For it is, in due consideration of law, the testator's choice how he makes disposition of his bounty."

"Yes, but a full quarter of that bounty, Mr. Liffey? It's intolerable!"

"One quarter of the *cash* component of that bounty. You must remember, Susan, that the estates real — comprising the mansion-house, farm buildings, and pasturage at Tiptop Grange, and the extensive lands and tenantries adjoining thereto — are by force of law entailed and descend to your husband as the surviving male heir of Joseph Cargo. You and Fred will receive the balance of his fortune, irrespective of the other dispositions of the will."

"Yes, but a quarter of the cash, sir!" protested the young woman, with a little stamp of her foot. "What did Frederick's grandfather tell you of this Squailes person, this interloper from Nantle, this nobody? What reason could he have had for making such a lunatic settlement?"

"As I have earlier stated, he told me nothing. His bailiff, Mr. Grindlestone, was more in line of such confidence. And there was his neighbor, Mr. Merripit, who attested and subscribed the will, together with myself and the notary."

"But Mr. Grindlestone is dead. He died in the spring of a gouty stomach," said the lady in the wig.

"And Mr. Merripit is dead as well," Mrs. Cargo said. "Burst a blood vessel while mounting his horse."

"And so they can be of no help to us," smiled Fred, speaking the obvious — "unless you propose we get ourselves up a little *séance*."

"I repeat, it's intolerable," said his quick-spoken little wife, with another stamp of her foot. "Frederick, you must agree that it's intolerable. More than that, it's *beastly*!"

"My grandfather was a hard man, that I'll admit," said Fred, crisply smoothing and stroking his glossy mustaches as he spoke. His was a neat, trim figure, rather short like his wife's, with neat, short hair to match, a sportsman's clean-cravatish formality of dress, and a liking for fancy waistcoats. "Hard upon his tenants he was, hard upon his associates and his few relations. He did not suffer fools gladly, as the saying is. He was not a man for sentiment, the old potentate! I'm sure he had his reasons for remembering this Mr. Squailes, though we're not apt to learn what they were until we've spoken to the man ourselves. It's a pity my grandmother didn't live longer, for she may have had some knowledge of the fellow."

"Mr. Cargo was a forthright and, might I add, a knowing man," said Mr. Liffey. "As his solicitor it was my obligation to attend to his interests, not to pry into his personal concerns. The will was drawn up from his exact instructions on the date you see there." And he touched a hand to the legal instrument itself, which lay upon the desk in the full glory of white parchment and red ink lines and handsome law-scrivenery. "I regret now that he did not share with me his confidence as regards Mr. Squailes, or his purpose for settling such a sum upon that gentleman."

"Whoever that gentleman may be," reminded Miss Veal, ominously, "for unknown persons should *not* be sponging on deceased persons."

"It's beastly and unnatural," declared Mrs. Cargo.

"Oh, it's not so beastly, Susan," smiled her husband, "for we shall have Tiptop Grange, and I for one am heartily glad of that."

"I agree with Fred," said Mr. Liffey. "You and your husband will both be very comfortably off, as will you, Miss Veal. You have seen the figures I have prepared. Mr. Cargo was a very wealthy man. Moreover he left no encumbrances, no bond debts, no liabilities or obligations. He was a shrewd man with a penny."

"And a brute to treat his grandson so!" retorted Mrs. Cargo, her eyes flashing. "Think, Mr. Liffey, of all the many hours we passed at the Grange — Fred and I, and Miss Veal, too — in his final illness, the time we three spent in caring for him, and he already with one foot in Charon's boat. It's intolerable! But perhaps, somehow, the will can be set aside? Yes, yes — perhaps we may contest it! There must be some legal means, some suit or other, by which we may oust this nobody from Nantle?"

"I've no doubt the will shortly will be proved in the Prerogative Court. To challenge its validity we must file a bill of contest, an objection to probate of the will, and from there we must get into Chancery," said the attorney, with a grave folding of his hands. "As to the likelihood of a judgment in a testamentary suit's being both favorable and timely in that esteemed chamber, well, oh dear, oh dear —" And he smiled at her in a pitying way and shook his head.

"I believe I know something of this High Court of Chancery," said Fred. "We might batter away at Grandfather's will before the Lord Chancellor there, like Quixote running tilts against his windmills, for years before we would see any of the money — if we saw any money at all! The skirmishes and special motions in putting a case through the Court, the filing of affidavits, the mussling and tussling, and all those damned attorneys to make their crushing costs of us — oh, I do apologize, Mr. Liffey, I did not mean to give offense."

"No offense taken, Fred," returned the lawyer, benevolently.

"I don't regard you as paint from that same Chancery brush, for you have always been as good a friend to us as the sun in winter. You see, Susan, how relinquishing a quarter of the cash to Mr. Squailes, as my grandfather directed, would leave much more in our own hands — the remaining three-quarters, in fact — rather than in the vile hands of the Court. As Chancery suitors we might very well lose everything, the lawyers' costs consuming not only Mr. Squailes's share of the money but ours as well. Dear, we might even lose Tiptop Grange!"

"The law is a ravenous beast," stated Miss Veal, touching offended fingers to her wig to steady it.

"If it could be proved that your interests were harmed by the bequest to Mr. Squailes, that might be a leg for us to stand on, but you all are handsomely provided for," explained Mr. Liffey. "In like wise, if it were shown that this Mr. Squailes had exerted undue influence upon Mr. Cargo in the apportionment of the estate, either through fraud or extortion or other means, that might be another leg. Apart from these, however, I fear we have no other means. We cannot object simply to a perceived inequality in the provisions, for this would interfere with Mr. Cargo's right to dispose of his bounty as he chooses. We might go round and round in the Court for a donkey's years before receiving a judgment, one which might not work to our favor. Is it worth the risk?"

"The law is a blight," decreed Miss Veal, with solemn indignation.

"But lawsuits spring from the graves of rich men every day," said Mrs. Cargo.

"Indeed, Susan," said her husband, "but who is it who profits by them?"

At this point a servant entered with the tea and muffins, and so some few minutes were made over to their disposal. The attorney had made arrangement for them, not only in kindness to his clients, but in the hope that they might have a moderating effect upon Mrs. Cargo, who was ever the more spirited of the conjugal pair. As for Miss Veal, she accepted her ration with a lofty acquiescence. She had already a comfortable income of her own, which was about to become even more comfortable thanks to Joseph Cargo, in recognition of her service to Fred's late parents as their dear close friend and confidante.

The heirs of Mr. Cargo had gathered that morning in the attorney's offices, a top set of chambers in fashionable Thavies Square, overlooking the esplanade — fashionable, so far as fashion went in a retiring little seaside town like Cargo — to discuss matters *à propos* the inheritance, which had been perturbing their slumbers for some days now.

"Have you enough cream there for your tea, Miss Veal?" said Mr. Liffey, as they settled down to the good things before them.

"Yes, thenk yaw," replied the lady in the wig.

"Sugar?"

"No, thenk yaw. I am told laced tea is bad for the head."

"Capital fare," said Fred, champing on a muffin. "Who's your pastry man, sir?"

"Tovey, at the cake-house yonder," answered the attorney. "He's our regular."

"Absolute wizard with a muffin."

"It is good, isn't it?"

"Tell me, how is his plum duff?"

"Superb."

"Ah. And the tea is delightful as well. Warms one up tremendously."

Which was a fine thing, no doubt, for it was a bitter cold day, one of the coldest of the season; though with Mrs. Susan Cargo in chambers one was always assured of a little heat. Her husband, an easy man to please, was perfectly satisfied with his grandfather's will, for he knew the inheritance would allow him to enjoy the pleasures of Tiptop Grange, to bask among his grandfather's horses and hounds, his sherry and port wine, for the remainder of his days. His cup of happiness was filled. What cared he for a lost quarter of the cash, when he had a fortune already?

But in this, as in most things, Mrs. Cargo held a different view. She rose from her chair and approached the attorney's desk, ready to resume the inquisition.

"What success have you had in tracing this Squailes person?" she asked.

"None, I'm afraid," said Mr. Liffey.

His plan as regards the tea and muffins had fallen to the ground, for Mrs. Cargo seemed anything but mollified.

"What else do you know of him? Could he have been a business associate of Grandfather Cargo's?"

"I know nothing of him. I've told you that."

"Nor do I," said Fred, vaulting into the breach, for which the attorney was thankful. "But of course I suppose that doesn't count for much, for I knew so little of Grandfather's dealings; he left me quite in the dark about them. He was a tight-fisted, pippin-squeezing old rascal, who knew his own mind and did not look to others for advice or consolation. I don't think he confided in anyone, really, not even in old Grindlestone. And at the end he was under laudanum and could tell us nothing."

"I've had our clerks examine the records back for many years, but there is no mention of a man called Jerry Squailes, or anybody else called Squailes, in any of the matters we undertook for your grandfather."

"Well, what do you suggest we do, sir? I confess I'm quite out of my orbit here."

"Your grandfather was rather clear as to his intent. Should Mr. Squailes be found to be deceased, the money will pass to his heirs or assigns, and due diligence is to be exercised by the executor to find them. The bequest will revert to the family Cargo — in short to you, Fred, with a sum to Miss Veal — if it is determined that Mr. Squailes has died without a wife or lawful issue."

"With neither hen nor chick, as the saying is," Fred smiled, hooking his thumbs in the pockets of his fancy waistcoat.

"It is a difficult business. Of course I wrote off immediately to a colleague in Nantle, but to no avail, for he has been unable to locate anyone there by the name of Squailes. The municipal authorities have no record of the man, nor do any of the parish registers. Nantle is the seat of a bishopric, you know, and the records in such places are quite complete. But our Mr. Squailes would seem to have eluded their notice."

"Perhaps he no longer lives there?" Fred suggested. "Or perhaps he's dead, with no wife or issue?"

"If he had died there, his name should have appeared in the register of burials," the attorney pointed out.

"Ah, true," Fred nodded. He thought a moment and then snapped his fingers. "Unless he were a pauper? A nobody, dead without a name?"

"Why should Mr. Cargo have left his fortune to a nobody without a name?" asked Miss Veal, with a puzzled stare.

Another moment of thought, another snap of the fingers from Fred. "Perhaps he's *changed* his name!" he exclaimed.

"There is something rather more sinister afoot here, I think," said his wife. "I fail to see any purpose for Frederick's grandfather to have made such a lunatic settlement, unless this Squailes person had somehow gotten the whip hand of him. Didn't you tell us, Mr. Liffey, that a will might be upset if it were shown that a beneficiary had exercised undue influence? Perhaps that is the case with this Squailes. Perhaps he *forced* Grandfather Cargo to make him a legatee?"

Her husband burst out in a hearty chuckle. "That would be one for the books, Susan — somebody making my grandfather do something he didn't want to do!"

"But surely we must consider the possibility?"

"We have run across no letters among his correspondence from anyone called Squailes, nor any letters mentioning such a man. We have searched and searched, my dear. You would think something might have turned up."

"Perhaps he destroyed them?" said Miss Veal.

"Exactly my thought, Aspasia," nodded Susan. "Your grandfather must have had his secrets, Frederick. Would he have left trace of them to be found after his death?"

"Every man has his secrets, my dear," said Fred — which, we observe, was perhaps *not* the wisest thing for a husband to say to a wife, considering how the eyes of Mrs. Cargo narrowed at the remark. But this particular husband landed nimbly on his feet, yielding the floor to the trusted family solicitor. "What then are we to do, sir? How shall we proceed?"

"What I was about to propose," said Mr. Liffey, folding his hands upon the will, "is that I myself should go to Nantle to uncover what I can of this Mr. Squailes. Should I fail to unearth him, his share of the fortune is to remain in trust for a period not to exceed seven years. If by that time he has not come forward, or if he should be found to be deceased with no widow and no lawful issue, the money will revert to the surviving beneficiaries."

"Seven years!" exclaimed a horrified Miss Veal, clutching at her wig.

"Beastly!" said Mrs. Cargo.

"Wherefore I have a little proposal of my own to offer, sir," said Fred.

"Yes?" returned Mr. Liffey, peering at the young heir from under his kindly brows.

"I propose that I accompany you. More to the point, I insist upon it. The trip to Nantle will be a strenuous one. A sea voyage down the long coast by packet-boat is most assuredly involved, for you'll not want to go overland. The coaches tending that way are not of the best, and the routes circuitous and fraught with peril. What's more I believe the road from Cargo to Crow's-end is blocked by avalanche, and will remain so for some time. As for the mastodon trains — well, surely that would be a disagreeable experience for a gentleman of your years. Moreover, sir, can the firm spare you for so long? Perhaps I should go alone in your place?"

"Frederick!" cried his wife, stamping her little foot hard.

"I have complete faith in the ability of young Mr. Hawkins to handle the reins while I am away," said Mr. Liffey, in reference to his junior partner in the law, a gentleman of no fewer than sixty-odd winters himself. "And we have our clerks as well — sturdy, industrious, capable young fellows, most bound for Clive's Inn. So you see, Fred, I shall be little missed. As for the voyage, I shall endure its little discomforts as best I can. My man John will travel with me, of course, as per usual."

"As will I, too, for there may be danger along the way," Fred declared, with a brisk little tug at his waistcoat. "In this, sir, I am resolved."

"I do not like it," intoned the lady in the wig.

"Whyever not, Miss Veal?"

"Such time and effort expended upon a nobody. It really is too much. Myself I'll have none of it, thenk yaw!"

"He must be more than a nobody, Miss Veal, if my grandfather saw fit to provide for him. Dear old Grandfather! I'll miss him, though you know I hardly ever saw him. The old rascal!"

"You'll miss him, after he treated you so?" returned his wife, her foot impatiently tapping. "There are times I simply cannot make you out, Frederick. Have you no respect for yourself or your family? If he were truly deserving of your regard, he should have named *you* his executor."

"But my dear, he left us nearly all," Fred pointed out. "Tiptop Grange — his holdings in land all about the county — the bulk of his fortune — these are hardly trifles! Are they not enough for you?"

"That is not my concern. We must stand upon principle. Consider all we did for your grandfather there at the Grange, the care we provided him in his last illness when he could not leave his bed."

"It was the servants who cared for him."

"But at whose *express command* did they care for him? Who saw to it that his meals were given to him, that he received his pipe, his sherry, his mulled port of an evening? His spectacles, his books, his paper? Who saw to it that he received his medicines? Who saw that his every need was instantly met? That he was waited upon at all hours? Who did this?" demanded Mrs. Cargo, flinging her eyes at her beloved.

"Why, you did, my dear."

"Who saw to it that the housemaids kept his bedchamber tidy and smelling sweet, in those awful days when he suffered such fits of coughing we thought it must bring the walls down round our ears? Who saw that his door was guarded in his quieter moments and that his peace was not disturbed? Who did this?"

"You did."

"Who sent for the doctor whenever the doctor was required?"

"You did."

"Who read to him at his bedside whenever his strength failed him? And who wrote out his last letters for him?"

"Why, *I* did, dear."

"Do you see? *Beastly*!" Susan exclaimed. "Now you'll be running off to Nantle with Mr. Liffey, leaving me alone in that enormous house and Aspasia on her own as well. Have you so little consideration for us, Frederick?"

"But one can never be alone at Tiptop Grange," her husband answered, cheerfully. "Haven't you staff aplenty there to keep you company?"

A little pause followed; then —

"You have never understood me," said Susan, her eyes smoldering.

"On the contrary," returned her husband. He stuffed his hands into his pockets and paced up and down a few times before the chimney-piece, his watch-chain and seals jingling a little as he went. "What then do you propose, my dear?"

"What do *you* propose to do if you succeed in finding Mr. Squailes?" she countered.

"Why, offer him the money, I suppose," he replied after a little thought, and a glance at Mr. Liffey.

"We must find him, make certain of his identity, and advise him of his good fortune," stated the attorney.

"You'll not try to dissuade him?" Susan asked.

"Dissuade him from accepting a fortune?" said her husband.

"Dissuade him upon a point of conscience, Frederick. This is a person who, to the best of anybody's knowledge, has played no part in your grandfather's life. Why has he refused to be found? To squander away a groat upon such a being would be worse than ludicrous."

"Perhaps he has not read of Grandfather's death."

"Such a person could not in his entire life spend his share of the money. Why should he deserve so much?"

"But my dear, you know the same might be said of us," smiled Fred.

"Beastly!" cried his wife, in open revolt. "You are his heir. It is *your* fortune, Frederick, it is *your* inheritance. You are in every way deserving of it. You are the last of the stock, the one person in this world entitled to carry on the name of Cargo. You have a right to your proper share of his fortune; it is in point of fact your birthright. And this Squailes person need not enter into it."

"Now, Susan, I fear I must protest —" said Mr. Liffey, rising.

"I'll hear no protests, sir. As you insist upon going to Nantle to find this man, and Frederick *will* insist upon following you, then I myself shall follow the both of you. I am convinced this man Squailes must have exercised some wicked hold upon the mind of Grandfather Cargo, and am set upon knowing what it was. It is my duty as your wife, Frederick, to guard your interests, as you seem so little inclined to guard them yourself. Am I not correct in this, Aspasia?"

"You are," said the lady in the wig, looking very dignified and confident.

"And you shall come with us, Aspasia, as my companion."

All semblance of either dignity or confidence was struck from the lady's face.

"*I shall?*" returned Miss Veal, looking startled — no, appalled — for this sudden proposal of Susan's had quite taken her by surprise. The thought of a lengthy sea voyage to unknown shores was a prospect of such little appeal to her that she dropped both her jaw and her reticule. She already had declared she wanted none of it, wanted no part in tracking down a nobody. But the die had been cast by Susan, and Miss Veal, who had been rewarded in the will for her devotion to the family Cargo, could not refuse. As if in some dim, dark dream she heard herself replying —

"I suppose it is the very least I can do, thenk yaw."

"It is settled, then," declared Mrs. Cargo. "We shall leave for Nantle as soon as our passage can be secured."

Mr. Liffey, having listened with growing alarm, tried to persuade Mrs. Cargo of the rashness of her decision, but the young woman would not be moved. As for Fred, he found himself trapped between forces he could not command — his affection for his deceased if unsentimental grandfather on the one hand, and the stern glance of his wife on the other. But even as the attorney strove to dissuade Mrs. Cargo, her husband began to see more clearly the logic of her argument.

He was, indeed, the last of the Cargoes of Cargo, until such time as Providence deigned to bless him and his wife with children; it was and would be then his moral duty to provide for those children; and now here was this man Squailes, this interloper from Nantle, this nobody, conspiring to strip him of his inheritance, his birthright, and by such means snatch the very breadcrumbs from the mouths of his unborn children.

How beastly! How unnatural!

And so it *was* settled, without further discussion and over learned counsel's objections.

The conjugal pair and Miss Veal then departed the chambers of Mr. Liffey, leaving the old gentleman to gaze upon his desk, his papers, and the will of Joseph Cargo with a troubled air.

More than a few times he ran a hand across his beard, and shuffled the pages of the will, and poked up the fire as he lingered over his tea.

And still he lingered, and as he lingered, he thought.

He thought of days gone and past, of his long years of dutiful attention to the interests of Joseph Cargo, and of growing white in the service of the family.

He thought of the young heir, such an agreeable fellow, and the young heir's rather less agreeable wife, and of Miss Veal.

And he thought of the late Joseph Cargo himself, screwed up in his cold stone bed there in the crypt at St. Loope's, freed of all earthly cares and even more unfeeling than he'd been in life.

Of such things Mr. Liffey thought, and more besides, all of which caused him to wonder how he had gotten into such a situation as he now found himself.

"Oh dear, oh dear!" he murmured.

CHAPTER THREE

In Other Chambers

When Mr. Arthur Liffey finally quitted his top set of chambers in Thavies Square, it was early evening.

A minute's walk in the frosty street brought him to the cab-stand, where he quickly found himself a hansom. He had lapsed again into his reflective mood of the morning and said little to the driver as he boarded, apart from telling him the address at which he wanted to be set down.

Safely closeted behind the double doors of the cab, Mr. Liffey gazed upon the chilly world gliding past but noted it not. Through a wintry landscape glistening in the light of the few lamps that marked the way, the cab rumbled on. The road was loose and sloppy under the wheels, the houses passing by streaked and dotted with old snow. It looked as if everything in the town had been constructed of a sort of grimy architectural fruitcake, the whole of it smeared over with a cheerless dull frosting and plunged into a deep freeze.

The fine town of Cargo lay upon the coast some distance north of Crow's-end. Cargo was nothing compared to that other, more well-known place, that great metropolis atop its mighty headland overhanging the sea. The fine town of Cargo was a backwater, on a little bay with no breakwater. And like all such towns fronting the coast, it was regularly visited by rains, sleets, and snows, and subject to the whims and fancies of wandering mists and dense, enveloping fogs.

It was while they were driving through a particularly miry quarter that Mr. Liffey became conscious of a strange whim or fancy of his own, which suggested to him that he had company of some kind there in the cab. Glancing beside him, he saw nothing. The adjoining seat was vacant; still, he had the distinct impression that there was someone there — that the seat, however empty, *was* occupied. He was aware, too, of a kind of fierce and angry scrutiny, directed towards himself, and emanating from his invisible companion there in the cab.

Yet every evidence of his eyes told him there was no one.

He shook his head to clear it, and was peering out again at the gloom when a snarling whisper was hurled into his ear.

"Traitor!"

He cried out in alarm. It was terrifying, knowing that something malignant was so near at hand, and invisible, and about to lay hold of him. Frantically he beat on the trap in the roof to gain the attention of the cabman.

The driver, red-nosed and brown-whiskered, stopped the cab, and descended from his perch with every appearance of concern.

"Please, I need a little air," the attorney gasped, putting his head out and drawing in deep breaths. "Please, a little air —"

"Stomach-sick o' the motion, is that it, sir?" ventured the driver. "Aye, vell, it happens sometimes vith the old vuns. Ve'll remain for a spell, then, till ye're right vell recovered."

"Yes, yes, that's it, thank you," the lawyer said. Agreeing was so much easier than explaining about unseen companions and voices in one's ear. "I shall be better in a moment or two — please give me a moment or two —"

The driver beamed self-congratulation at his diagnosis. A few minutes later, with his passenger's consent, he drove on again toward their destination, leaving the attorney to his thoughts, and *only* his thoughts, or so Mr. Liffey fervently hoped.

The old gentleman maintained a wary watch on the seat beside him, but there were no further disturbances along the route. In a short time they pulled up before the lawyerly residence. The attorney was aided in alighting by the driver, who, though he wore a gruff exterior shaped by the harshness of the climate and the nature of his trade, was possessed of an interior of softer mettle. He responded with a grin and a tip of his hat to his passenger, who had rewarded him with a larger fare than was required, for his help in getting out; after which horse, cab, and cabman vanished into the night.

Mr. Liffey was met by his manservant, who relieved him of his cloak and hat. He then betook himself to his bedchamber for a rinse of his hands and a change into more leisurely dress. This accomplished, he retired to the sitting-room, where his man John had lit a fire and placed the current number of the *Coast Intelligencer* on the arm of his wing-chair. A half-hour of reading followed, which Mr. Liffey found of only marginal use in relieving his anxiety. Supper then being announced, he went downstairs to the dining-room.

It was a quiet meal he had there in the glow of the wax-lights, in a temper of mind that could hardly be described as easy. His eyes were on his plate, but all the while he was chewing he was thinking, and expending considerable effort at both, for he was chewing and thinking very hard.

After a time the very quiet of it got to him. He heard his servants enjoying their own meal in the kitchen below stairs, in the company of much good humor; and so Mr. Liffey took up his bottle of sherry and went to join them. His present mood notwithstanding, such an action was not unusual for him, for despite his being a lawyer, Mr. Liffey was a kind, just, and honorable man. And so he shared his wine with his servants there in the gleaming orderliness of the kitchen, and joined in their mirth, which he found to be just the thing for cheering up a chilly soul on a chilly night; and so his own spirits recovered something of their accustomed tone.

In due course he returned to his sitting-room, and spent an hour or two more in his wing-chair with a book in his lap and his feet propped against the fender. Gradually, as the time passed, the reading came harder, and the salutary effect of draining a bumper with his servants faded. His attention began to wander. Every now and again he found himself looking up and glancing about the room, for what reason exactly he couldn't say.

After a while his man John entered with a velvet step, to ask if there was anything more he might need before retiring.

"No, John, nothing more, except perhaps for a little carbonate of soda. I've tucked away a bit too much this evening, I'm afraid."

This item the servant brought him, whereupon he offered Mr. Liffey a polite nod, and quietly and efficiently evaporated.

Once again the attorney's eyes went drifting about the room. Here and there they roamed, as they had roamed their troubled way about his lawyerly chambers in Thavies Square. He thought he must have a sweep in to examine the chimney, for the wind had been making some odd noises in it of late. Although strangely, when he had mentioned this earlier to John, he had received only a blank look in reply, as if to say, *What odd noises?*

On impulse he rose, and going to an old cabinet standing against the wall, took from it several small painted portraits in miniature, each mounted in a gilded frame. There was a portrait of his good-humored father in the blush of youth, and one of his pretty, blue-eyed mother, and one of his brother George. Three pictures from the past they were, three glimpses of happy times gone by. Three portraits of those who had been dear to him in this life, and who had long since turned to dust.

There was a fourth picture, too, one in an oval frame and most delicately rendered. It was a portrait of a lambent beauty with almond-colored hair, a laughing face, and lips as red as any two cherries. This last image the old man held before him for some time. As he gazed upon her of long years a-gone, a wistful smile played about his white beard, and crinkled up his old eyes, which had grown strangely moist and shiny. Then a frown as of some remembered sorrow darkened his brow. The light came and went in his pink face, and came and went, until an expression of grim determination at last settled over it. Without further thought, he returned his treasures to their place and resumed his seat.

Some few minutes more he spent gazing into the fire. He was about to poke it up a little, when the sinister fancy that had come upon him in the cab came upon him again, and he felt the weight of eyes observing him from behind.

He peered cautiously round the wing of his chair, and saw, or thought that he saw, a black thing — a swollen, disfigured mass of a black thing — crouching in the corner. He stared at it for some time, not knowing what it was. At one turn it appeared solid, like a pile of charcoal, at the next more like an ugly shadow or a column of black vapor. His uneasy mind, however, suggested to him it was the figure of a man huddling there.

"Who is it?" said Mr. Liffey, in a halting voice. "Who is there? Why do you watch me?"

Of course, no one answered him; he would have been staggered if someone had. To his rather profound amazement, he found himself rising from his chair and advancing with small, measured steps toward the corner. As he drew near it, the black thing seemed to retreat, dissolve, and spread itself out flat against the wainscot. On closer inspection, he saw that it was nothing more than a shadow, thrown by the curiously wrought china cupboard that stood beside it.

Now did the old man put himself down for an arrant fool. It was just an illusion, a nervous fancy! Surely his mind was going now.

But what to make of the awful illusion in the hansom cab?

He heard the longcase clock in the passage sound the hour, which for Mr. Liffey was a very late hour indeed; and so he put away his book, and wished his man John a good-night, and with a chamber candle in hand climbed the stairs to his bedroom. On entering the room, he made certain to lock and bolt the stout oak door of it after him, nervous fancy or no.

Ten minutes on found his preparations complete, his nightcap on his head, and his body in his feather bed. He put out the candle and drew the curtains of the four-poster, for as we have noted, it was a chilly night. New snow had begun to fall, as evidenced by the muffled stillness in the road outside. Every now and again a carriage or solitary rider could be heard passing by, the plod of the horses' shoes and rumble of the wheels sounding faint and far away. For an hour or more Mr. Liffey tried very hard to render himself unconscious, and he very nearly succeeded.

He was roused from the attempt by a sort of rattling or clattering noise. It went on with occasional lapses for some minutes, until Mr. Liffey found any hope of sleep irretrievably dashed. He sat up in his bed, pulled back the curtain, and lit the candle. Peering out, he found nothing amiss; yet the rattling and clattering persisted. He got into his slippers and dressing-gown, and candle in hand went looking for the cause of the disturbance.

Where was it? *What* was it?

He examined the chimney-glass, but that was not it. He examined his small table-mirror, but that was not it. He examined his washing-stand with its basin and ewer, but that was not it. He looked into the alcove, into his dressing-room, into the wardrobe, but the noise was not there. His interest was attracted next to the two windows with their heavy cloth hangings. He stepped to the nearer window and found that the noise was louder there. He reached forth and drew the cover aside.

To his astonishment he beheld the shutters of the window, as well as the window-glass itself, rattling noisily in their casings. Indeed, the contents of both windows appeared to be rattling in unison with a weird, unearthly vibration. It was like a prolonged earthquake, but with only the windows and shutters affected, the rest of the house remaining perfectly still.

No illusion or nervous fancy this, unless it was the windows that were nervous!

Gaining courage, Mr. Liffey extended a hand toward the shutters, to confirm the testimony of his eyes and ears. The moment his fingers made contact, however, the rattling in both windows ceased and did not start up again.

Glancing uneasily round, the attorney drew the hangings across the windows and returned to his bed. He was on the point of crawling into it when he heard another, rather different kind of noise. It was more of a stretching, straining, splintering kind of noise, as of timbers slowly yielding under a force of pressure. At first he saw nothing unusual. But the odd straining and cracking sounds persisted, and now there were some metallic clicks as well, as of a door-handle being jostled.

He turned to the locked and bolted door of his room, and was astounded to see it being bent slowly inward, as though a great weight were pressing on it from the corridor without.

The old man tumbled back a step. He had never known oak, or any other hardwood for that matter, to be so pliant, so plastic. It was as though the force acting upon the door was pressing itself *into* the door, and creating an impression of its form in the wood. That form was slowly emerging now from the surface of the wood, like a tomb effigy sprouting from a sarcophagus. It was a form dimly human in shape, but dark and malignantly so — an unholy, evil sort of shape, aiming, it appeared, to burst clear through the door and into the room.

Mr. Liffey went cold to the very roots of his white hair. He stood gazing at the door with a fearful fascination. It could not be much longer, he knew, before the stout oak timbers gave way under the force being applied to them. Nevertheless he managed to regain a semblance of his lawyerly presence of mind. He caught up the fire-shovel from the grate and crept towards the door. With his pulse throbbing in his ears, he called out to the intruder —

"Who is it? What are you? What do you want here?"

For answer he heard only the echo of his own thin voice. Then the straining and cracking and splintering abruptly ceased. The door was relieved of the force upon it, the imprint of the intruder frozen on its surface.

Mr. Liffey went about the room inspecting it for other irregularities, but he found none. Then he placed a cane chair against the door, wedging it under the handle so that the door, though fast locked and bolted, could not be opened without considerable noise and effort. Lastly he examined the door itself and the half-formed image in the wood. A resemblance to certain sculptings in stone upon the tomb-lids in the church of St. Loope was immediately apparent. With a faint shudder, the attorney crawled back into his bed and drew the curtain tight.

"Confound it all, I shall go," he murmured, as he gathered the bedclothes round his chin. "I shall go to Nantle — I *must* go. My duty's clear. And it will do me good to get free of these haunted chambers. Oh dear, oh dear . . ."

When Mr. Liffey awoke in the morning, he found the door of the room quite normal in every respect. Not the slightest trace remained of the unholy excrescence that had sprouted from it in the night. He wondered whether it could have been another illusion, the product of an excited imagination and perhaps a bit too much wine and mirth-making with the household staff. But there before him was the cane chair wedged under the door-handle, just as he had left it. He removed the chair and opened the door a crack. Peeping into the passage, he found it empty of sight and sound, apart from the distant voices of the servants early astir.

In spite of the early hour Mr. Liffey knew he could sleep no more. He got up a little fire in the grate, drew the hangings from the windows, and opened the shutters — windows and shutters which were *not* rattling — to find Cargo still in darkness. He applied himself then to his morning's toilet.

He was bent over his basin of soap and water when it came upon him again, that strange and sinister feeling of an unseen presence close at hand. Abruptly he glanced up, for out of the tail of one eye he thought he'd seen someone standing in the open door. But the doorway, like the passage without, was empty.

It was while he was drying his face in his towel that he felt something take firm hold of his shoulder, and heard again the angry snarl in his ear. He dropped the towel in alarm and found himself looking into his table-mirror, where he caught a glimpse of something dark and ghoulish leaning over him. The moment his eyes fell upon the thing, however, the grip on his shoulder was released, and as he turned round, his frightened glance fell upon —

Nothing.

CHAPTER FOUR

Blue Lady, Black Monkey

On an evening not so very different from that just described, a young woman sat writing at the little limewood desk in her sitting-room. It was a sitting-room not unlike that of Mr. Liffey's, although it was many miles from Cargo. It was a pleasant, fire-lit sitting-room in a handsome, solid, stone-built house in the heart of old Pinewick, on the outskirts of the great metropolis of Crow's-end.

The woman had been busy with her pen and paper for some little while, when an interruption caused her to break off her work. Her maid had entered to inquire as to the suitability of certain items of clothing, which she proceeded to enumerate, and whether Miss Wastefield intended to take them with her on the trip? If so, then she — the maid — would see to it now that the items were packed away with the others.

The young woman sat for a moment in thought, before answering in both the affirmative and the negative — that yes, she would like this item to be taken along, and that item, this bonnet and that shawl, for instance, and that one, too, but only this one and only that one, and a few other things, as for example her black kid gloves, but none of the rest.

"For we must travel as lightly as possible, you understand, Lucy. We shall be sore burdened as it is."

"Yes, miss."

"And so that should be most all of it."

"Yes, miss."

Saying which the maid disappeared through the door and resumed her preparations, while the young woman dipped pen into ink and bent again to her task, which it seemed was not an easy one.

"I can offer you nothing more in the way of an explanation at present," she wrote. "Truly, I am sorry that it must be so, but I have no choice. The cloud that has descended upon our home will not be lifted without action on my part. I regret that I cannot enlighten you as to the nature of the trouble that afflicts us, but believe me, it is better for you this way. Neither can I tell you where I am going, nor do I wish for you to inquire after me. If I am successful, I promise you that upon my return I shall tell you all. Until such time you must have faith in me. There is nothing else to be done. And so for the present, adieu."

This interesting message she signed simply, *Jane.*

She then read the letter through, slowly and carefully, making a few minor emendations in the process. Satisfied, she pressed the writing over the blotting-pad, folded the paper neatly, and sealed it with a wafer. The outside she inscribed with a gentleman's name and address. She then rang for another servant, to whom she entrusted the letter, instructing him to convey it to the indicated party in two days' time, *but no sooner.*

"If you please, miss, I've finished the packing," the maid announced, coming in again at the door. "Is there anything more I can do for you, miss?"

The young woman shook her head. "You'll go off to bed now, Lucy. It's best we both have an early night, for we must be up and away by dawn."

"If you please, miss, you'll not tell your Lucy where we're bound for?"

"No. I dare not run the risk of it just yet. The night has ears as well as eyes — too many eyes. We must go swiftly and secretly in the morning. Mellors will drive us in the carriage."

The maid stood chafing her hands in silent worry, and biting her lip, and casting uneasy glances at the large, chain-bound trunk that stood nearby.

"Must it come with us, miss?" she asked.

Her mistress replied that, however regrettably, it must; for it was the object cause and purpose of their journey. Still the maid had her doubts and misgivings, which, asking pardon for making so free, she expressed now in rather certain terms.

"As I've told you, we'll not speak of it," returned her mistress, a trifle crossly. "How little you know of the matter. How little you know of my fears and sorrows, Lucy!"

"What little I do know, miss," said Lucy, bravely, "is that its coming into this house was certain sure the cause of the master's death from his apoplopsy. Asking pardon, miss, but it's said that misfortunes never come single —"

"It was I who was the cause of my father's death," the young woman declared, in a voice of suppressed emotion. "It was my doing, Lucy, only mine, do you hear? Were it not for my carelessness, my poor father would be living today. Have I taken you aback by my confession? Well, then, you see just how little you know of the matter."

The maid held her tongue while gazing in surprise at her mistress.

This young mistress of hers was a woman of considerable personal beauty. She had the sweetest of hazel eyes, and bountiful hair splashed through with gold, and a pretty dimple in the middle of her chin. She was not so short but not so tall, and marvelously well-formed. But there her resemblance to other pretty young women ended, for the unnamed burden she carried hung about her all too visibly, like the shadow of the cloud hanging over her house there at Pinewick.

"Forgive me, Lucy, for I'm very tired," she said, touching a hand to her brow.

"There's been trouble for you, miss, nothing but trouble since the arrival of it," said her maid, stealing another fearful glance at the trunk. "That I know, for you can't hide such a thing from your Lucy. If you please, miss, will you not confide in me?"

"We'll speak no more of it. My poor father died a needless death, but there's nothing can be done about it now. But there *is,* thank God, a way out of the thicket at last — a way to dispose of the foul, wretched thing — and it lies at our journey's end."

"I hope it's so, miss, truly I do."

"And now it is past time you were in bed."

"If you please, miss — you'll not want a quiet game of piquet, then, as we often have of an evening? For I can easily place the card-table and make the tea —"

"No, Lucy, it's too late for that. My eyes are tired, and our hours of sleep will be few enough as it is. Off you go then."

"Yes, miss," said Lucy, and dropping a little curtsy she retired to her sleeping-closet, which was *en suite* with her mistress's boudoir.

Having cleared away the materials from her writing-desk, the young woman took from a pocket of her dress another letter, which she opened and read over with the most concentrated attention. And though she had read those same words over again and again, so many times these past weeks that she knew them by rote, still she read them over another time, and another — words written by a gentleman of whom she knew little but for his name, which was Gilbert Thistlewood. The letter had been sent to her father after his death, and it enclosed the promise of assistance she had been seeking. It was her way out of the thicket.

She returned the precious document to her dress and walked to the door, and from there to her boudoir, which lay at the end of a short hall. The luggage her maid had prepared was waiting for her there, all of it in apple-pie order — dear, efficient Lucy! — and ready for loading into the carriage. Before entering the apartment, however, she glanced behind her at the trunk in the sitting-room. As her eyes fixed themselves upon it, a stream of emotions crossed her pretty face, darkening the shadow that lay across it, and sank her once more deep into thought.

Her trance was broken by an outburst of chirping from her boudoir. A thing like a hairy baby sprang from a little basket-bedstead on the floor, and scampered up the side of her dress and into her arms.

The young woman was a trifle startled, but pleasantly so. No baby but a small black monkey, the animal hopped onto her shoulder and clung to her, chirping and chattering. She swept a loving hand over the tiny creature and, crossing to the well-stuffed divan, settled down with it by the fireside.

"And how are you tonight, my little one?" she smiled, gently smoothing the animal's coat and its long curling tail. The monkey chirped and cooed in response. Tiny fingers played with the slender strands of her hair; eyes like shiny black beads peeped into hers. Then the monkey yawned — it had been dozing there in its little bed — and threw up its eyebrows, and yawned again, showing her its white teeth, and cooed a little more, and chirped a little more, as it snuggled in her arms.

"It is good that you can't understand," the woman said softly. "It's better that you know nothing of it. The day that wretched thing came into my life" — here she cast a glance at the door, though from her place on the divan she no longer could see through to the sitting-room — "that day was an evil day. To think of my birthday as an evil day! And because of it my father died before his time. To be freed of it now we must make this long journey. But we shall survive, you and I, and Lucy, too. And when all is done, we shall rejoice that the wretched thing is no more with us, and return to Pinewick with happy hearts!"

She looked down into the face of her little pet. Already its eyelids were drooping. "You have been full of your monkey tricks today, but now they've exhausted you. You are my own dear Juga, my own little one, as you have been for so many years. It is good you cannot know. I would not burden you with my troubles for the world."

Shortly after this the monkey fell asleep, child-like, in her arms. For a while she sat quietly, listening to the voice of the mantel-clock, while absently fingering one of the curious earrings she wore. It was made of a coiled sea shell. She'd found the pair of them at a stall in Crow's-end, and for all their oddness had been drawn to them at once. Listening to the clock now, with one shelly bauble between a thumb and finger, images began to drift one by one into her brain. They were faint at first, as if coming from a great distance. They hovered before her in her mind's eye, gradually melding and merging into a single expansive vision in which she became entirely absorbed.

A vista of surpassing beauty lay outspread before her. There was a broad, fertile valley of green and yellow earth, and nearby wooded hills; in the south a chain of distant mountains, in the north a measureless sea that was like a floor of metal; and all of it lying under a brilliant roof of sun and blue sky. Where was this wondrous place? Certainly very far from foggy Pinewick and Crow's-end. Oh, most glorious of summer days — how very warm, how very sunny it was!

There in the fertile valley she saw Juga, or a monkey very much like him, clad in a red leather traveling-harness. He was gathering crocuses into a pot. Behind him lay an immense field bright with poppies. Butterflies quivered and danced upon a warm breeze redolent of coriander. She could taste honeyed wine on her tongue, and on tables round her she saw platters of olives, figs, pears, mint and sesame, pistachio nuts. There were fishes, too, and oysters, and starfish, and octopi. She wondered what cause there might be for such a feast, and where it was, and who had set it up.

In the valley, on a gradual eminence, stood an enormous, labyrinthine building of stone, timber and dried mud brick, several stories in height. Its interior walls were adorned with frescoes, its roof-tops and outer defenses with row upon row of bulls' horns, some real, some merely carved representations. Not a sign of life showed anywhere about its sprawling maze of courtyards and terraces and colorful colonnades; instead the entire edifice appeared to be falling into ruin. Beyond it, from the slopes of a tall mountain shaped like a volcanic cone, came the sound of a trumpet-call, or the call of something like a trumpet, directed toward the sea.

What did it mean? Why had this same vision been placed before her so often these past months, ever since the arrival of the wretched thing in the trunk? Why this beautiful picture, and others not so beautiful — pictures which she cared not to see ever again?

The scene passed in a flash to another — to the chain-bound trunk in the sitting-room and her own self standing before it, striving to overcome the brooding sense of oppression that radiated from it. "You shall trouble me no longer," she vowed, speaking aloud to the trunk as though it were a living, breathing thing. "Soon I shall be rid of you forever!"

The monkey stirred at the sound of her voice. Recovering all at once, she gathered her drowsy pet into her arms and returned it to its little basket-bedstead, which lay at the foot of her own bed, and shut the door of the room.

And like Mr. Arthur Liffey of Cargo, she locked the door and bolted it.

She went to her toilet-table and arranged some matters there. Then she struck a light and kindled a fresh taper and, as she had done ever since the coming of the dark cloud, left it to burn for the duration of the night; for she could no longer sleep in the company of darkness. Young Lucy had remarked upon this change of habit more than a few times, but had received no explanation save for a reminder that the night had ears, and eyes, too, and that it was, as usual, not to be spoken of more.

CHAPTER FIVE

As Tight a Ship as Ever Sailed

Came at last a break in the steady onslaught of fog, rain, and wave that had bedeviled the lugger since she had sailed. Heaving and rolling on the foamy brine, she had strayed a distance from shore on her run down the coast, partly to avoid the hidden shoals and treacherous reefs and other like hazards that marred her course, and which were rendered twice perilous by the weather; had strayed some dozen or so miles at least by the skipper's reckoning, for neither the skipper nor any of his men had had sight of land, or glimpse of sun or star, since they had fetched out from Cargo. Now the dreary fog mantle was beginning to rise, the rain abated, and lo! the shore put in an appearance to larboard. A dismal, cheerless, gloomy kind of shore it was — a rugged coast backed by range upon range of lonely, snow-packed mountains, sheeted giants whose upper reaches lay hidden in the clouds.

The improving weather held, the seas gentled, and for some hours they followed the coast due southerly. At mid-afternoon a lofty headland hove into view. With every forward surge of the vessel it grew upon their sight, a mighty towering monster of a headland with craggy cliffs rising straight up from the water. Clinging to its slopes and crown was a tumbling townscape of steep-pitched, narrow streets, winding thoroughfares, and precipitous boulevards, all of them crowded close with houses of flint and stone and rusty red brick; grave, sober houses with tall gables and jutting eaves, slate-tiled roofs and mullioned windows, and smoke upcurling from chimneys like the exhalations of a thousand infant volcanoes.

"Crow's-end ho! by St. Barbara," cried the look-out on the forward deck.

Round the foot of the lofty headland, along its protected south shore, lay the wharves and deep-water docks of the metropolis, with their attendant boat-yards and rigging-lofts, outfitting warehouses and provision-shops, sailors' inns, and other like establishments that flourish wherever ships and crews are found. The captain of the lugger issued his orders; responding to her helm, the ship stooped to the breeze and cleared the jetty, and with sails trimmed shaped her course for the forest of ships' masts and rigging dockside. In no long time she had gained a mooring and so was made all fast and shipshape.

The first mate of the lugger, a lanky, stiff-backed, soldierly sailorman with sidewhiskers and a nautical rolling limp, attended to the stores and cargo, while the skipper went below to what he liberally referred to as "the staterooms" — small, damp, chilly hutches abaft, very dingy and uninviting of aspect — to inform the group of unfortunates huddling there that they were "free to come 'bove deck, if so minded, and give run to their land-legs for a spell, while the ship lay at her tether and was made all a-tauto."

Miss Aspasia Veal, whose normal complexion was a pale shade of blanched, emerged from her burrow something green as to cheek and askew as to wig. She was aided by Mrs. Cargo, who was in not much better state herself, though she tried to disguise it by holding a pocket-handkerchief to her mouth. Her husband, although he hadn't the constitution of a tar, did have the perseverance of a sportsman, and seemed reasonably steady on his pins. Young John, however, was visibly suffering, but he kept a manservantly face on it.

As for Mr. Liffey, he was apparently the only member of the group possessed of genuine "sea-guts," as the skipper termed it. In the blossom of his youth the attorney had served, however briefly, on a vessel out of Chiddock, and had roamed the coastal seas, and dared the coastal fogs, and tempted the spirit of Davy Jones, before voluntarily running himself aground on the shoals of the law.

"I'm afraid I am not accustomed to such conditions," Miss Veal was heard to complain. She had been assisted off the ship by no less a personage than the captain himself, and was making with her companions now for some nearby tea rooms which the aforesaid skipper had recommended. "It is all rather — it is all rather *too* much —"

She had not cared to partake of anything substantial from the ship's galley during the run from Cargo, for fear that some unpleasantness might ensue; but now that her feet were planted on solid ground again — as solid ground as any wharf could be — her appetite was threatening to stir.

"It's beastly," said Susan, commiserating with her friend. "I should have thought that as Cargoes we could have secured something better in the way of accommodations for our passage-money. I should have thought we *deserved* something better. How very provoking!" As she spoke, she flashed a disapproving glance at her husband, whose job it had been to make the arrangements.

"As I've told you, dear," said Fred, a little defensively, "there was not a vessel with a single vacant stateroom to be had for a fortnight at least. They don't stop so often at Cargo, for you know the harborage there is not so good; and you know as well of the regular packet-boat from Salthead that last week was holed on the rocks. There was simply no alternative."

"Still, it's very provoking."

"But not to worry, dear. Mr. Liffey assures me this vessel of Captain Barnaby's is a most seaworthy craft, and the captain himself a most experienced sailorman. We have simply had a run of bad weather."

"We have had *nothing* but bad weather, Frederick," returned his wife.

"Bad weather is a blight!" declared Miss Veal, keeping a steady hand upon her wig as they went along.

"It surely must improve the farther south we go. In general the climate round Headcorn and Nantle tends to be rather warmer, if a trifle wet," said Mr. Liffey.

"Nantle is many hundreds of miles from here, sir. We have a long way to go," Susan pointed out.

"Which reminds me that I, for one, am famished!" Fred exclaimed, rubbing his hands in anticipation. "Seaworthy our good captain's vessel may be, tasteworthy his cook's victuals are not. Ship's biscuit, dried tongue, and a pickle do not a meal make. 'Belly-timber,' I believe he called it. Well, it's an ill cook who can't lick his own fingers, as the saying is. Now, where are these travelers' tea rooms? 'First street athwart the wharf-walk,' or so our captain said. Well, I should have looked out for a nice, smoky chop-house myself, or an oyster saloon. Ah, capital! A hot steak, some limpets and some oysters, some shrimps in tomata sauce, a pint of porter, a garnish of wine and I should be quite in heaven —"

Miss Veal uttered a little groan and suffered a relapse. She looked to be in danger of falling victim to one of the more unpleasant symptoms associated with a greenish countenance.

"It seems you're not a very good sailor, Miss Veal," Fred observed. "But not to worry, we'll get you a nice cup of tea, or perhaps some coffee and a macaroon or two, and a little sherry or raisin wine, or perhaps a caudle-cup. It's a shame your pastry-man isn't about, Mr. Liffey —"

"Thenk yaw," replied Miss Veal, in a faint voice, "but I don't know as

I should care for any kind of cup now. I don't know as I should care for anything at all just now . . ."

After some investigation they found their way at last to the tea rooms, which stood in Fishacre Lane.

"I didn't know that you yourself had been a sailorman," Fred said to Mr. Liffey, once the group had settled in a box and made their requests known to the hostess of the establishment.

"Well, yes, indeed, it's true," smiled the old gentleman, warming quickly to his subject. It was one that never failed to bring a glow to his face and a sparkle to his eyes. "Plying the waters from Salthead to Foghampton, and Foghampton to Nantle. Our family lived at Chiddock in those days. My father was in the nautical line — he owned a few ships — and rightly thought I should have some experience of the sea. Although it was not such a long apprenticeship, merely some nine or ten months, it was the sort of experience one never forgets. I must confess, however, I had not the instincts for the nautical life; once my term of service was completed, I was more than glad to take up my studies at Clive's Inn. Though for some months after I kept imagining the floor of my rooms to be in constant motion, always swaying from side to side, or plunging fore and aft, with clouds of white spray lashing the windows, so used had I become to the insistent rolling of the swell."

Miss Veal uttered a groan and pushed her plate aside, whereupon the attorney hastily apologized for his insensitivity.

Although their shipboard accommodations and galley-cook may not have been the finest, neither were they the worst. The lugger was merchant-class, employed chiefly for the transport of goods and only a sort of part-time passenger ship, with a small roster of cabins to complement her hold. It was only by serendipity that passage had been secured after the loss of the Salthead packet. The captain had found himself lying off Cargo with some vacant hutches, while the travelers had found themselves first out of luck, and then in it — or so it seemed at the time.

The fine town of Cargo, although situated on the coast, hadn't much in the way of coastal trade, owing to the inadequacies of its harbor. Most often travelers went overland to Crow's-end and entered aboard ship there. Miss Veal, however, was a little frightened of horses, and of carriages with more than two wheels. ("There are so many accidents, you know, so many upsets of the vehicles and the like, and attacks by wild beasts. The roads are not safe for the conveyance of respectable persons, and I'll not take them, thenk yaw!") As it turned out, then, even had an avalanche not blocked the coach-road, the party would have needed shipboard passage from Cargo. And now it seemed that Miss Veal was a little frightened of seas as well.

More than once Mr. Liffey had tried to dissuade his clients from making the long voyage, which he deemed an unnecessary hardship for them. Fred would have been perfectly happy to have remained at Tiptop Grange, for he had, in the time since the little conclave in the lawyer's chambers, undergone a gradual reversal of mind. He'd been hasty in volunteering his services, he said, as it became clear to him that his suspicion of danger at Nantle was little more than a fiction, planted in his brain by his wife and her theories regarding the mysterious Jerry Squailes. It seemed now that any likelihood of danger lay more in the sea voyage itself than in the hallowed precincts of an old cathedral city.

Having dispatched his meal, Mr. Liffey had a peep at his watch and, realizing that the night would soon be drawing in, thought they had best return to the lugger; and so off they went. As they arrived at the wharf, Fred called attention again to the name of their ship, as he had before when they had boarded her at Cargo.

"Rather a coincidence, don't you think, that it should be the *Salty Sue* carrying us to Nantle? Personally I think it a good omen for a fair and prosperous voyage, though Susan does not, for 'pon my life I believe she finds something to dislike in the name. To her it smacks of a certain impropriety."

"As it should to anyone," his wife answered. "I should never have consented to the accommodations but for the fact that we had no choice — we had no packet-boat. As the name of a ship it is hardly dignified."

"I am in complete agreement with you," said Miss Veal.

"Thank you, Aspasia. It's a great consolation to know I always can rely upon you."

"On the contrary," smiled Fred, "it's a capital name for a ship, don't you think, Mr. Liffey?"

"And as tight a ship as ever sailed this coast, or I'm a gooseneck barnacle," pronounced a voice from above.

Looking up, they beheld the captain of the vessel, rigged out in his wide blue coat and red jersey, and his blue dreadnought trousers, heavily patched, and his wide leather belt of many pockets, and his old sea-boots, and his shawls and mufflers slung round his neck like hawsers in a rope-yard. He was peering down at them from the bulwark of his ship, with his hands on the rail and a quid the size of a cow-pat lodged in his cheek. He was a typical strutting, stalwart, hatchet-faced old salt with forked brows, a bold beak of a nose, and a chin as long, narrow, and sharp-pointed as the prow of his vessel. He had a lion's head of silvery hair, which was struggling to escape from under the crush of his mariner's bonnet.

"Aye, she's stout and trim and true on a wind, and sweet to her helm," he went on, rhapsodizing from on high. "She's a right duck of a ship, sirs and madams, split me crosswise and sink me if she bean't."

"A staunch and seaworthy vessel, Captain Barnaby," smiled Mr. Liffey, as he and Fred helped the ladies across the gangway.

"And a *safe* vessel, too, we trust, Captain," said Mrs. Cargo.

"Safe!" exclaimed the skipper of the *Salty Sue*, a trifle offended. "Why, bleed me, madam, if she ain't. Scorch me, kick me endwise else! Ha'n't she cleaved her course through perilous seas, in fair weather and foul, with nary a drop o' bad fortune for all the years? Why, the answer's plain enough to see, bless yer dear eyes! Here she is in Crow's-end harbor, safe and sweet and all a-tauto. Prithee, madam, what's to fret as to safety? What's the worst as could happen to her, I ask ye? Why, the worst as could happen, sirs and madams, is she'd be dashed to pieces on the rocks, or broken up by seas running high, and sink fathoms deep like a stone!"

"It is reassuring," said Susan, looking hard at her husband as she spoke, "it is reassuring, Captain Barnaby, to know that that is the very worst that could happen."

The travelers spent a dull evening on shipboard, retiring at length to their cabins below decks. But as the ship's timbers *would* persist in cracking and groaning all night long, and the pintles in creaking and moaning as the rudder swung to the tide, they got little sleep, and so were arisen early in the morning. A small breakfast was had, after which they all went on deck to examine the gray dawn that was seeping through the clouds.

The captain was standing at the rail and greeted them with a mighty halloo. At about the same time the first mate rolled up and entered into some very loud and sailorly conversation with his skipper, of which none of the travelers could decipher more than a few words, not even Mr. Liffey, but which Captain Barnaby appeared to understand perfectly well. For answer he crunched brows and nodded his head, and gave a little tug at the lip of his bonnet, after which the first mate went rolling away.

"How goes it, Captain?" said Fred. "Is there something amiss?"

"Cherish my guts, sir, nary a thing. We've to stow aboard another passenger or twain, bearing down on us to leeward."

"More passengers?" returned Mrs. Cargo. "But I thought *we* were your passengers, Captain Barnaby."

"Aye, that ye be, dear madam, but there be room yet for more in such fair and capacious craft as the *Sue*."

"Room for more, Captain, when the five of us already are pent up be-low like common fowl in those cupboards you call staterooms?" Susan re-torted, a bit out-of-sorts after a wakeful night, and after hearing her name again so very ill-used. "My pillow feels as if it were stuffed with a litter of porcupines. It's beastly! I blame my husband for it."

"It really is too much," said Miss Veal.

The captain shrugged and rolled his quid from one cheek to the other, by way of ballast. "Split me, but it's got to be, madams and sirs, as there bean't so many runs down the coast this time o' year, and the Salthead packet has found her doom on the rocks. But stand by all, and look 'ee yonder — it's no more than a pair of 'em, a young lady and her maidservant. And a lady she be, too, by the cut of her canvas, or I'm a jack mackerel!"

Mrs. Cargo was about to remark that there was hardly any doubt, Cap-tain Barnaby, but that you *are* a jack mackerel, but was prevented from do-ing so by her husband, who knew only too well what was in her mind.

They watched as the luggage of the young lady was hauled aboard — some bags and band-boxes, a portmanteau, and a very large trunk weighted down with chains. Then the young lady herself made her appearance. She was clad all in dark furs, and her young maid in heavy woolens. In her arms she carried a tiny monkey, which was decked out in its own little coat and trouserings of wool and a fluffy fur cap.

"Douse me, but will ye clap yer eyes on *that*!" the captain exclaimed.

"The lady has herself a pet," said Fred.

"What a shocking thing to bring aboard ship with human people," Miss Veal snorted. "How very inconsiderate!"

"And which I believe makes *three* passengers more," said Mrs. Cargo, with a sharp glance at the captain, who affected not to hear her.

Her husband was of a more favorable turn of mind, however, for he raised his hat to the young woman as she passed by, and smiled at her and the maid, and at the tiny bundle in her arms, as the three were led by the skipper to their quarters below.

"You really shouldn't stare so, Frederick," said Susan, with a wifely cuff upon her husband's arm to reclaim his attention. "It doesn't become a gen-tleman and a Cargo."

"Yes, dear," Fred answered, still smiling, his thoughts transfixed by the lovely vision that had wafted past.

"All's right as a trivet and shipshape, Cap'n," announced the first mate, rolling up just as the skipper reappeared on deck. "She's ready for sea, and the wind serves, and the tide."

"All's right then, indeed, Bob Sly. Stand by to slip moorings."

"Aye, Cap'n."

"Stand by all to hoist sail!" the skipper bellowed to his minions.

"Aye! Aye!"

Rustle and scutter about the deck. The jib was loosed and the lug-sails stretched — foresail, main, and mizzen, and main- and mizzen-topsails — all filling with the breeze and bellying out. Slowly the ship gathered way. Passing round the jetty she glided from the harbor, and bore out and away for the open sea. In no long time the broad sweep of wharf and dock at Crow's-end, and the great metropolis itself rising above, were lost to view astern.

"Lay her on her old course, Bob Sly," the captain directed.

"Aye, Cap'n."

The captain settled his shawls and mufflers round his neck, and stowing his hands in his pockets commenced a skipperly pacing of the deck, as the lugger stood away southerly, her bows rising to the swell and the yellow gleam of her lights a-blink in the misty dawn.

The traveling-party meanwhile had returned to the dim realm below decks. After about an hour there came a brisk double-knock at Mr. Liffey's door. It was Fred Cargo, inviting the old gentleman for a turn around the ship, as the weather had slightly improved. It was an invitation Mr. Liffey readily accepted.

"You know, sir, it may have been a mistake for us to have entered upon this expedition," Fred admitted, once they had gained the open deck and made their way to the rail.

"It wasn't necessary for all of you to accompany me," said the attorney, looking out upon the water. "But of course you know my thoughts on that score."

"My wife believes she can break Grandfather's will. Well, perhaps not break it so much as *bend* it. She is most adamant that she can persuade this Squailes fellow to yield. Well, perhaps she can. She can be damned forceful at times, you know."

"Yes, I know."

"Though I fail to see what purchase she has. The money is certainly his. There can be little doubt of that, can there?"

"If Mr. Squailes can give evidence that he is who he claims to be, and if he wants the money. Your grandfather was most clear in the matter of the legacy."

"Well, it's in for a penny, in for a pound, as the saying is. Though I admit it intrigues me. Who the deuce can this Squailes fellow be? Why have we never heard of him?"

"I fear it is a secret your grandfather carried with him to his tomb," said Mr. Liffey. As he uttered the word *tomb*, a little shiver ran through him, at the recollection of a certain unholy disfigurement of his bedroom-door, and a ghoulish hand that had gripped him by the shoulder. "That is," he added hastily, "unless we can find Mr. Squailes."

"Well, at least there's one good thing," said Fred, rubbing his hands, and glancing round him with a cheery eye. "I've had a little chat with our captain and discovered that the young lady who came aboard at Crow's-end is bound for Nantle. For Nantle, sir! And so we shall all be traveling there together."

"I see," Mr. Liffey responded without any alteration of expression.

"She's a fine young woman, 'pon my life. Don't you think she's a fine woman, sir?"

"Oh, dear — I'm afraid I've been preoccupied, Fred. Please forgive me. What did you say, then?"

"Not to worry, sir, it's nothing very important. I was simply musing. Do you suppose there's any law against a husband's admiring a pretty face? Pretty face — a *capital* face! One, that is, that is not his wife's, and strictly from afar, of course. It would be a pity if there were."

"I shouldn't think so. But I'm afraid it's not in my sphere of experience."

"Oh, I'd forgotten, out of your own orbit, I suppose — never married! Though in some ways, sir, you must consider yourself rather fortunate. Compare your situation with mine, for instance. I've Susan and Miss Veal to contend with every day." He clapped Mr. Liffey upon the back very heartily, and said with a jolly laugh — "Enjoy thy liberty whilst thy may, sir. Bachelor days, Mr. Liffey, bachelor days!"

The weather having steadily ripened, and the seas calmed, and even a hint of sun breaking through the overcast, the gentlemen lingered upon deck, with Fred on the watch for a glimpse of the fine young woman with the pet monkey; but she declined to show herself. Together he and the attorney strolled the length and breadth of the ship, pausing every now and again to watch the seas spilling past them, wave after restless wave, and the distant line of coast playing at bo-peep behind stray patches of fog, and the lug-sails straining on their yards aloft.

Without warning a black tomcat with a huge head and jowls darted past them and bounced atop a locker, where it sat washing its paws for a moment before scooting underneath a tarpaulin.

"Well, there goes a nice fellow!" exclaimed Mr. Liffey.

"Aye, 'tis Melon-head, sir, the cappie's rat-catcher," said the first mate, rolling up.

"You have rats aboard this vessel?" Fred asked.

Mr. Sly nodded and smiled, and with his hands measured a space in the air before him no less than two feet across, to indicate the approximate size of these denizens of the bilge.

"Well, I am very fond of cats," said Mr. Liffey. "I suppose you know it's considered good luck for a ship to have a black cat among her company?"

"Cats? Hate 'em, beg yer pardon, sir," returned Mr. Sly, with a long shake of his head. "Hate 'em all, nor black, nor white, nor peacock blue. Right glad, howsomever, to have the precious devils about. Hate rats the more!"

"Though it's bad luck for a cat to cross a sailor's path, as I recollect from my own sailing days. Our captain was fond of scrutinizing every action of his ship's cat — its habits of grooming, its daily and nightly prowls about the deck, the quality of its appetite — for clues as to the weather that lay before us."

The first mate uttered a sound neither Fred nor Mr. Liffey thought very complimentary. Evidently Mr. Sly was not impressed, for bilge and bunkum, said he, the cappie and any thinking seaman had greater trust in the mercury in his weather-glass than in the habits of a gib-cat.

"And if a cat should be soused overboard, it foretold a storm on the horizon."

"Aye, sir, and the cappie's some mighty dairy-maid in sailor's breeches, by gum!" laughed Mr. Sly; at which point he rolled himself away on some errand or other that required his immediate attendance.

Fred and Mr. Liffey walked the length of the deck again, but still there was no sign of the pretty face from Crow's-end, much to Fred's disappointment. After a time Mr. Liffey offered to go below, to see if the others might care to come on deck now that conditions had bettered. To this Fred reluctantly agreed — reluctantly, because he had offered to go below himself, to spare the old gentleman the trouble (and to catch a glimpse perhaps of the pretty face), but Mr. Arthur Liffey of Cargo, mariner, had refused to hear of it.

As the attorney was making his way to the staterooms, a door swung open in the passage and a tiny monkey hopped onto his shoulder. The learned gentleman of the law pulled up in surprise, and rather sharply, too, from memory again of the ghoulish hand. An apology quickly followed from none other than the pretty young woman herself, who retrieved her pet and left it in the care of her maid before ascending to the deck. Mr. Liffey meanwhile proceeded with his mission; and so the traveling-party was shortly assembled at the rail.

Mrs. Cargo, seeing that the pretty face from Crow's-end was on deck as well, made straight for her husband, who had yet to notice the lady. And so Fred found himself with his wife on his arm just as he spotted the pretty face, and his crest fell a little. There would be scant opportunity now for him to chat with the fine young woman, what with his wife on one side of him and Miss Veal on the other, and Mr. Liffey and John nearby; and so he was trapped where he stood, peering out to sea and contemplating the infinity of waters.

Onward flew the lugger on the broad gray bosom of the deep, cleaving her southerly course miles out from the line of rocky shore, with the wind blowing steady and fair, and her bows alternately rising to the surge, and plunging forward in a white smother of foam; and over the days to come gliding down the long sea-road, past the narrow, misty entrance to the great bay of Foghampton and her fabled hilltop city, cloaked most all the year in fog; and so flying on with a joyous lift and roll, with straining sails and humming cordage, on and on towards Headcorn and Nantle and the southern islands, towards Jerry Squailes and Gilbert Thistlewood and what other mysteries none could say.

And all the while the captain of the vessel pursued his skipperly pacing, looking round him with contentment on trim decks and wide ocean, and feeling the salt wind blowing upon him sweet and fresh. But every now and then he could be seen crunching his brows, or tugging a little at his bonnet in puzzlement over his pretty-timbered passenger from Crow's-end, whom he had deemed something of a mystery herself; aye, a *mystery-lady* she was, sarten sure, as he was heard to remark more than once, or scuttle him for a spiny dogfish.

CHAPTER SIX

At the Sign of the Crozier

Morning, one week on. The *Salty Sue* lay mersed in fog and hove to, still a distance from Nantle but close enough inshore for a keen mariner to hear, albeit faintly, the barking of dogs and rattle of carriage traffic, and to smell, as the captain phrased it, "the odors o' the town."

At intervals the cry of a whistle-buoy came sighing through the mist. The weather, such as it was, nonetheless was an improvement over that of the day before, when a blusterous wind had come up and sent the ship plunging through heavy seas. Now the sea was smooth enough, and the breeze was light enough, but unfortunately the look-out could see no farther than his ship's length in any direction.

Mr. Liffey, too, was concerned about the fog, for he knew that there were hidden shoals and perilous reefs all throughout these channel waters. The threat of collision with one of these lurking assassins was among the greatest hazards of the coasting trade; indeed to proceed on their course for the harbor, given the circumstances, would have been not just imprudent but foolhardy. And so it was only natural that the attorney should inquire how long they might be detained while waiting for the fog to lift.

Captain Barnaby shrugged and filled his cheek with a quid. "It's a hazardous approach, sir, that's plain enough," he declared. "But somewheres to larboard yonder the reef gives way and opens into a fathomy trench, as broadens inside to safe and spacious harborage at the quay. It's a matter o' spying out that deep-water track and fitting yer keel to it. In fair weather it bean't difficult at all, sir, but a scurvy fog is a stopper; even yon buoy may not serve overmuch. Likely we'll be slacking sheets for some little while yet, sir, or I'm a starry flounder."

"Though as to the channel itself, it's rather broad here as I recollect," Mr. Liffey said, as much to the captain as to Fred and young John, who had joined them at the rail. "And it can be difficult to glimpse the islands, even in fine weather, from the salt mist that permeates the air."

The captain, whose heart had been gladdened to learn that one of his passengers was himself an old salt — if only for a slim nine or ten months, about a century ago — stroked his long chin and nodded.

"Windwhip, as is the furtherest island, she's too far out to do anybody any damage," he said. "But then comes Hove, closer in, and o' course Truro, closer in still. It's at Truro that the channel clinches down, 'twixt Span Rock and the mainland at Paignton Swidges. Afore the light was placed at Swidges, ages ago, there was many a duck of a ship killed on the reef as lies athwart the channel there. Even with the light, howsomever, it's a perilous passage."

"You'll not take on a pilot?" Mr. Liffey asked.

The captain chuckled and shook his silvery head with the bonnet on it, and champed his quid, and glancing aloft at mast and canvas, and away to windward with a sailorly eye, made answer —

"Love my limbs, sir, it's nowise necessary, for the *Sue* can find her way. Sink me, she can sniff out a bit o' reef as sure as my dog can sniff his supper. Look 'ee now, it's all a matter o' patience and watching. Aye, it's ever the way, sir, or if it bean't, I'm a spiced jurket, for fog be a great trampler of time to a sailorman. Howsomever, should matters go foul and a-wrack, the worst as could happen is she'd pile up on the rocks. Aye, one tide on the rocks would finish her; 'twould be a sure death and sarten. And so we'll bide awhile here, sir, with eyes and ears on the stretch, till she can be taken inshore all sweet and sailorly."

Revelations of such a kind were hardly balm to the ears of his listeners. The captain had a fine flow of language, but one hardly fashioned to provide landlubbers comfort of mind.

Within the hour the fog had given way a little, and so the captain nudged his ship closer in, using the voice of the buoy and the tint of the seas and the deadest of reckoning to guide his steersman. Yet still they stood off awhile more. Another hour lapsed, and another; all the while the skipper nodded and smiled and said it would not be long.

And then, miracle of miracles, the fog began to lift, and lift some more, until at long last the outlines of Nantle harbor appeared before them. There was a lengthy stone quay with some jutting piers, and a quantity of vessels lying at their moorings there, and others riding at anchor in the pool. Of the city of Nantle itself, however, there was little sign, most of it remaining hidden in the gloom back of the harbor.

The coast round Falaise had made a gradual easterly swing, the result being that the city of Nantle faced south, with the channel running east and west before it. Able now to get his bearings on the deep-water track to the quay, the captain hailed the steersman and issued his orders to the company. Now on deck was cheery stir and orderly bustle as the lugger hauled her wind and fetched into the harbor, leaving the perils of reef and shoal in the waters that rushed bubbling in her wake.

The harbor at Nantle was altogether different in appearance from that at Crow's-end. It was a very long, very low, very dreary sort of harbor, with no immense wall of rock rearing up behind it and no great metropolis looming overhead. Instead there was a flat, ramshackle spread of buildings along and back of the quay, warehouses mostly. A few merchant seamen and others of the sailorly craft could be seen going about their business, or lounging in doorways, or gathered in little knots under eaves, smoking and talking. There were cheap jacks in velveteen waistcoats, dock-laborers and ballast-heavers, and fish porters with their bizarre headgear. A couple of express-wagons, some drays, and a carriage or two were lumbering about the streets. Behind the quay the gray flint spire of a church rose up, piercing the gloom.

All of this Fred saw, and compared rather unfavorably to his own fine town of Cargo. Cargo was a far better style of town, he thought, and though small and not a power in shipping — her interests lay more in the way of timber, crops, and grazing-land — still she had, in his view, a certain quality of refinement about her. Why, the corn exchange at Cargo was a far better class of building than half the houses he saw now before him! His first impression of Nantle — bearing in mind that there were dreary, rain-washed streets all round, to color that impression — was of a rather lazy, shabby kind of place, an old channel port run to seed. It was nothing like Crow's-end, and nothing at all like the venerable cathedral town he had conjured up in his brain.

"Well," he said, "one person's swans are often another's geese, I suppose, or so the saying is. Though it doesn't seem so much warmer here."

"You'll observe there's not a trace of snow," Mr. Liffey said, glancing round him in proof that it was true. "Likewise you'll remember, I did predict the climate would be wet."

And indeed it was, for a cheerless drizzle had begun leaking from the clouds. Fred, who found the drizzle of little consolation, sighed and put his hands into his pockets, then stepped deftly aside as the gangway was placed. Immediately the black form of Melon-head went bounding over it onto the quay.

"My old captain thought it good luck for his ship's cat to cross the gangway before his men," said Mr. Liffey. "Perhaps this is a foretokening of our errand here."

"I'll not disagree with you, sir," smiled Fred.

Though Mr. Bob Sly evidently did, for he broke out in a laugh upon hearing such lubberly superstition, and went away shaking his head.

The first order of business was to collect the luggage and have it taken ashore. While this was in progress, Fred kept a watch upon the pretty young woman in furs, who was standing on the quay with her maid at her right hand and her curious little pet on her shoulder. Stepping forward, he gallantly offered — out of sight of his wife and Miss Veal, of course — to assist the young lady in obtaining a lodging, if she so required. The young lady did not; she had already engaged rooms, she told him, in the house of a person whose family was known to hers, but she thanked him for his kindness nonetheless.

The young woman spent no more time in idle chatter, but forthwith hired a carriage and went her way with trunk, luggage, maid, and monkey. In the pretty face under her umbrella — a capital face! — Fred thought he had detected more than a hint of anxiety, and a bit of impatience, and expectation, too. No one had come to meet her at the quay, and she had seemed in rather a hurry to be about her business.

What business could that be? he wondered; then straightway he chided himself for a fool, and an impudent one at that.

Not for the first time did Fred pause to wonder now about his own business in Nantle, about who this Jerry Squailes was and what right he had to insinuate himself into the will of Joseph Cargo. In the confinement of the voyage Fred had come again under the influence of his wife's sinister imaginings, and by now had devised all manner of explanations for his grandfather's willingness to hand over a chunk of his fortune to a nobody.

Mr. Joseph Cargo had been anything but a philanthropist. His reputation as a hard man, an unfeeling man, an uncharitable man, a ruthless pirate in quest of acres and more acres, income and more income, was well-known — and well-respected — throughout Cargo and the county. How else should a man have hoarded up such vast sums of wealth, so far above and beyond anything he'd inherited? It had been business, business, business. *Pelf for pelf's sake!* No room for philanthropy there; no room for a charitable legacy to a nobody called Squailes.

No, no, Fred thought now, his wife's suspicions simply had to be correct. For a moment he considered shouting the name of Jerry Squailes to the gray Nantle sky, imagining that the mysterious gentleman might hear him and step out of the crowd there at the quay; but of course this was nothing but a wild fancy.

It was a relief now to escape from the thraldom of the lugger and her tiny hutches that passed for cabins. But unlike the fine young woman from Crow's-end, the Cargo party had no lodgings in readiness at Nantle. Time had been short and the trip hastily arranged; there had been no opportunity for prior communication by the mails. During the course of the voyage, however, Captain Barnaby had made reference to a coaching-inn he thought might suit the travelers to a T. For the captain lived at Nantle, having been born and bred up there, and knew the city and its precincts well — "from the Compter to the sponging-house, aye," had been his exact words, "and from the quayside shambles to the smallpox hospital, and all 'twixt and atween."

As a result the travelers were preparing now to set off for the Crozier, the captain's worthy and respectable coaching-inn, which lay in the vicinity of the cathedral close.

There was one problem outstanding, however, and that was Miss Veal, who remained as fearful of horses and coaches as before the voyage. So a cozy four-wheeler was engaged for the Cargoes and Mr. Liffey and the luggage, and poor John dragooned into accompanying Miss Veal in a little, slow-moving pony-chaise. But Miss Veal, seeing the rain coming down harder now, and the proliferation of puddles in the street, and the sloppiness and sogginess of conditions generally — and of open pony-chaises in particular — at the last minute relented, and allowed herself to be conveyed in the four-wheeler with the others.

"It is the price I must pay," she sighed, steeling herself as she settled back on the cushion, "for looking after the interests of dear Susan and Fred, and Fred's parents before him."

Along the rainy streets clattered the four-wheeler, past the dockside shanties and sailors' haunts, then up a gently climbing hillside until the travelers had put some distance between themselves and the harbor. There they entered a quainter, quieter, and far more genteel neighborhood, one with houses finely built and well-apportioned. Half-timbered houses they were for the most part, with crossed oak beams richly carved and ornamented, graceful, pointed gables, red-tiled roofs, and chimneys in tall stacks. Now this was much more the Nantle that Fred had pictured! And as they went, he watched the road ahead, and through the mist descried the brooding pile of the great cathedral, or Minster, with its gray square towers, a little farther up the hill.

In a quiet by-street the carriage rolled beneath an old, weather-beaten signboard, which was swinging from a pair of rusty hooks, and rocking a little in the breeze, and dripping a little from the rain, and which had an image of a Bishop's crozier emblazoned on it. There the four-wheeler turned out of the road and passing under the arch came to a stop in the courtyard of the inn.

The party were quickly settled in their several chambers. Ancient, dark-looking, wainscoted sorts of chambers they were, with cumbrous furniture and heavy cloth hangings, and crucifixes on the walls, and old mural paintings of saints performing miracles, and massive stone-built chimney-pieces like castle keeps, and with the hush of cloisters pervading all. This grave and sober atmosphere appealed very much to Susan and Miss Veal, but to Fred and John and especially to Mr. Liffey, it was a trifle oppressive.

Young John, who was acting as valet to both gentlemen, saw to it now that their belongings were unshipped and stowed away in their rooms, while the gentlemen meanwhile went downstairs to inquire after dinner.

Dinner! What a lovely sound it had, and what a welcome change from the galley aboard the lugger; for despite Captain Barnaby's hospitality and personal good nature, his ship's victuals had been hardly fit for a cat, thenk yaw, or so said Miss Veal.

While arranging for dinner the gentlemen made some inquiries of the landlord in regard to Jerry Squailes, and whether he might be an inhabitant of the neighborhood roundabout. To their disappointment Mr. Squailes was quite unknown to the landlord, and the landlord's wife, and the porter, and the boots, and the ostler, and the one or two others in the house who were consulted.

"If the gentleman is a resident of *this* neighborhood, sir," the landlord said, with his portentious nose a little in the air, "he cannot be an important one, for I have never heard of him, and neither has anyone else. We know no more of him than the man in the moon. *Faugh*!"

Their host was a gentleman as sober of appearance as the establishment over which he held sway. In his habiliments of black cloth — black waistcoat, black knee-shorts, ditto stockings and neckcloth — his clean white sleeves, decorous shoes, and powdered head, he might have passed for a clergyman from the Minster hard by, for aught anyone knew.

"Then there is no one at all round here by the name of Squailes, no such family?" said Fred.

"If there be such a family, sir, I've never heard it spoken of on these premises or elsewhere. Of course, there *is* something more to Nantle than the Minster and the Crozier and the close."

This morsel of information the landlord surrendered reluctantly, as if admitting that, yes, there was indeed more to Nantle than the Minster and the Crozier and the close, but none of it worth anybody's time or bother.

"Yes, there is the quay, for instance," said Mr. Liffey.

"*Faugh!* Sailors, sir, and their ilk," the landlord said, making a face as though he had swallowed a large bug. "Entire city down there gorged with 'em. And we know what that means, don't we, sir? Loose and riotous ways. Wild, rumbustious, drunken fellows, ruffians and haymakers, rake-helly rough-and-toughs — bad eggs, the lot of 'em! We'll have none of that in *this* neighborhood, no, sir. *Faugh!*"

Fred was about to ask why anyone who didn't care for sailors and their ilk should be living in a town that was full of both, but was stopped by the arrival of a waiter, a thin, goggle-eyed young man with a shock of red hair, who announced that the travelers' table had been laid.

Dinner was a meal of loaves and fishes — nice fresh turbot and lobster sauce, cod and steelhead, fried soles, caraway-seed biscuits, and wholesome black bread — as befitted an establishment boasting of churchly associations. And of course there was plenty of wine — bumpers of mulled claret and bottles of old crusted Nantle port — to wash it all down.

During the feast some inquiries were made of the waiter, whom Fred and Mr. Liffey had not questioned before, as to the possible whereabouts of Mr. Squailes. Again the reply was in the negative, but the waiter, being of a less parochial and superior turn of mind than his employer, had at least one useful suggestion to make.

"Perhaps you might look in at Sprig's, sir."

"Sprig's?" returned Fred. "What might I ask is Sprig's?"

"It's a coffee-house, sir, about halfway between the Crozier and the quay. In Mock Alley, hard by the theaters. Most everybody who is anybody can be found at Sprig's, sir. Oh, indeed, it's quite the fashionable rendezvous. Chess rooms there, you know, sir. Many folk round Nantle mad about chess. Mayhap they'll know something of your gentleman there, sir. Mayhap you'll find the gentleman himself there."

"Capital idea, fellow!" Fred exclaimed, with a merry snap of his fingers. "We are tremendously obliged to you."

The waiter nodded crisply and withdrew.

"I believe," Fred concluded, looking round at the others, "that Sprig's it is, and Sprig's it shall be, for a start."

"I've never been in a coffee-house," said his wife. "Is it decent?"

"A coffee-house," volunteered Mr. Liffey, "is an eminent institution, a place of witty and pleasant discourse, where gentlemen of many interests gather to read the papers and discuss the latest news of the day, and transact affairs, and generally enjoy one another's conversation."

"Are there no women permitted?" Miss Veal asked. "Is it one of *those* places? For if women are not permitted, I'll have none of it, thenk yaw!"

"We shall have to ask our waiter what manner of coffee-house this Sprig's is, and whether its proprietor is amenable."

"He had better be," Susan warned, "for I'll not be hindered by anyone or anything, sir, including a coffee-house, till I can grasp our Mr. Squailes by the nose and shake him out, and make him confess what beastly power he had over Frederick's grandfather."

The partner of her cares smiled faintly at this, and looked askance, as though he were something familiar with the mode of discipline alluded to by his wife.

Mr. Liffey offered no comment on Mrs. Cargo's vow to inflict grievous bodily harm upon the person of Mr. Squailes, for Mr. Liffey was an attorney and well-versed in the concealment of his thoughts and feelings. Instead he dipped his biscuits and drank down his port, and joined in the conversation whenever it turned to a more genial topic, until he and his companions retired by and by to their several chambers.

And so the travelers' first night in the old cathedral city passed away, without a single creaking pintle or complaining timber to disturb their rest.

CHAPTER SEVEN

Boarders in Chamomile Street

There stands in Chamomile Street, in a shy, retiring neighborhood no more than ten minutes' walk from Nantle quay, a boarding-house.

This is not to say that it is the only boarding-house in the city of Nantle, or the only such house in Chamomile Street — a timid, tranquil, drowsy kind of street, like the neighborhood it inhabits — it is merely to say that there is one boarding-house in particular, and that it is of importance because of the roles certain of its inhabitants play in this history.

The boarding-house was situated at the end of a lengthy, many-chimneyed row of houses, surely as dull and monotonous a row as any to be found in the neighborhood. Like all the houses in the row, it had a little railed area with steps going down, and a street-door with steps going up. The door was of a navy-blue complexion — the sole splashes of color in such dull streets are often the doors — and it had a large knob in the middle of it, ripe for grasping, and a knocker, and above the lintel a fan-light in which a glow of candles shone out like a baby sunrise. Affixed to the door-post was a brass plate with the following inscription:

Mrs. D. Matchless
NICE ROOMS

This Mrs. Matchless was a pleasant, middle-aged lady, bright-templed and rosy-cheeked, whose condition, as her door-plate suggested, was that of a widow. The late Mr. Matchless having deserted these mortal precincts some few years since, she had by degrees become accustomed to her condition, had tried it on to see how it would fit, and having found it to her liking wore it now like a familiar suit of clothes. She had gotten over the loss of her "Mr. M." and resumed her superintendence of the house they had operated as husband and wife. It is doubtful however that her "Mr. M." had recovered as quickly from the loss of his dear Dottie, he being a gentleman who was in no position to recover from anything anymore.

Mrs. Matchless had under her roof a female servant, one Anne Feagle, who had been in her employ since she — that is, Feagle — was a young girl, and who had grown into something like a friend and companion to the older woman. In so doing she had attained that exalted position in domestic service which is commonly referred to as a confidential housemaid. Assisting them were a maid-of-all-work called Alice; a cook, one Mrs. Poundit, in the smoky kitchen below stairs; and a small boy in buttons called Pancras, first name William, who served in the combined capacity of page, boots, and embryo butler-in-training.

Also residing under Mrs. Matchless's roof were the boarders of the establishment, of whom there were four — or five, depending on how one viewed that fifth lodger, who was something of a special case.

There was a Miss Rivers, a young woman of character and refinement. She had russety locks, a creamy face given to blushing, and quenched-looking bashful eyes, like a Little Bo-Peep in a nursery-book. Miss Rivers was partial to all things tortoiseshell — tortoiseshell combs, tortoiseshell spectacles, tortoiseshell hair-brushes, tortoiseshell handbags, tortoiseshell cats. She could have been a walking testimonial to the tortoiseshell trade, but she hardly ever went out. She had a small independence worth £120 per annum, with which she devoted herself to the consumption of novels and exotic teas.

There was a Mr. Kix, a narrow, peevish, old-maidish sort of mustached bachelor. Mr. Kix was a man who looked always on the worst side of things, a grouch who thought the world a very dark place and the town little better. And there was his exact opposite, Mr. Lovibond, a plump, pink, full-bodied personage with a clean chin, a ready smile, and a bald head. Mr. Lovibond, too, was a bachelor — irretrievably single — but unlike the grouchy Kix he was always happy, hardly ever peevish, certainly never old-maidish, which annoyed Mr. Kix no end. Despite their differences the two were often in each other's company, the better to remind the other of his imperfections. Both subsisted on the income from annuities, which made them easy and spared them the trouble and inconvenience of engaging in the work-a-day world.

Mr. Frobisher was the fourth lodger in the house. He was a dark man of some attraction, in a rangy, cagey sort of way. His age was no more than five-and-twenty, and he passed most of his time out of doors, though as to the nature of his avocation no one had the least clue. Like Mr. Kix, he had a mustache, one which well suited his flowing hair, lustrous eyes, and lean good looks. The youthful Frobisher was a newcomer to the house, and had yet to accommodate his habits to that regimen of predictability which guided the lives of his fellow inmates.

The special case to which we have made mention was the fifth and final boarder. This was a Miss O'Guppy, who unlike the regular boarders resided in the attic rooms with the servants. She was rather a quaint young woman, very delicate of face and limb, with a nervous constitution that was — not to put too fine a point on it — rather delicate, too. In short, there were some who thought her a little unhinged.

Miss O'Guppy was an accomplished violinist, or fiddler as she liked to say. She was in great demand in the front-parlor, where she often accompanied Miss Rivers at the cottage piano. An habitual reader of the cards, she believed she could divine the future and predict the fortunes of those who consulted her in this capacity. More than this she saw and heard things only she could see and hear, and claimed to remember what she called a "morning time" before her own birth, a sort of earlier life unlinked to her present earthly existence — which was partly the basis for some persons' thinking her mad.

Miss O'Guppy helped out a little round the boarding-house, now and then, but mostly she did what she liked, having been supported for some time by her mother, who was a close friend to Mrs. Matchless. This Mrs. O'Guppy was employed in the house of Captain Jack Barnaby — that same salty mariner with whom we are acquainted — and paid for her daughter's board and attic lodging out of her own wages, although her daughter did not know this. Young Miss O'Guppy and old Mrs. O'Guppy had not spoken for more than a year on account of a disagreement that had arisen between them. Young Niamh was nothing if not a stubborn girl, and she it was who had broken off contact with her mother. She had the temperament of her late father, which, far from being an impediment, was simply further cause for her mother to love her so, apart from the fact that Niamh was her only surviving child.

Early one evening the regular boarders and Mrs. Matchless had taken their places in the dining-room, when a conversation something like the following broke out.

"Lovely walk to Mock Alley today — up to the theater — Royal Trident — *matinée* — Kix, too," said Mr. Lovibond, in the customary verbal shorthand which served him for speech. "Pass the pickled salmon, if you please."

"What, you and Kix together?" asked Mr. Frobisher, skeptically.

"Of course."

"What did you see there?"

"*Cuthbert and Phoebe* — finest thing in quite a spell — rapturous — pass the winkles, if you please."

"It was most certainly *not* the finest thing," grumbled Mr. Kix. "It was perfectly awful. No, I'll be plain: it was the most odious and deplorable thing imaginable. It was dross, sir, complete and utter dross."

"It was wonderful, sir, wonderful," countered Mr. Lovibond, ladling some giblet soup from a tureen. "Heart-rending tale — waterworks already by second act — pocket-handkerchiefs flying out — women weeping — girls fainting — men sighing — huge collective sob at the close — lovely thing, I can tell you — raptures —"

"An audience made of fishmongers' wives, idle mariners, superannuated apple-women, flower-girls, and disengaged hairdressers," returned Kix. "That's what you'll have at twopence for the gallery, and fivepence for the pit, and public boxes at less than a shilling. The theater's grown cheap in these times of ours, very cheap. All the wrong sorts attracted to *that*. I'd sooner play at skittles as attend there anymore — side-by-side, cheek-by-jowl with holland and canvas, fustian and corduroy! The odors are not to be believed."

"And what do you expect, sir, if you will attend a *matinée*?" said Mr. Frobisher.

"What I expect, sir, is stagecraft — not the vile, miserable example of egregious sentimentality that passed for a play today," said Mr. Kix, taking some wine. "Hack work, nothing but hack work. Why, the pantomime preceding it was far superior."

"Was it a romance, Mr. K.?" inquired their rosy landlady, from her place at the top of the table.

"The pantomime?"

"No, sir, the play."

"Naturally," interposed Mr. Lovibond, busily feeding. "Such things invariably are — plays, you know — theater — tales of love — tales of woe — Phoebe and Cuthbert, mighty woeful — pass the shrimps, if you please."

"But must it not end happily, sir, if it's a romance?" asked Miss Rivers, who was something of a gastronomical authority on the subject, from the many novels she had devoured.

"Dear Miss Rivers — afraid not — grieves me, truly — romantic tragedy, or tragi-comedy, or something or other — love lies a-bleeding — poor Cuthbert — affair of honor — transfixed by a smallsword — swoons —

heap on the ground — expires — Phoebe mourns the loss — drowns herself in a malmsey-butt — Duke of Clarence — pass the fennel, if you please."

"Though in not so brisk and artful a fashion as poor Clarence," said Mr. Kix, who, grouch though he was, knew his Shakespeare. "The credulity of some audiences is beyond belief. The entire thing was so odious, one's sole hope is that it was concocted as a jest, *and with poor Phoebe the butt of it.*"

Here his face relaxed into a flickery grin, which he endeavored to hide by keeping his head down and his eyes on his plate. His little fling at humor did not pass unnoticed, however, for Mr. Lovibond, staring at his fellow boarder in mock amazement, promptly rapped the table with a plump hand and exclaimed —

"You're a madcap, Kix — a madcap!"

"Well, I've not seen it," said Miss Rivers. "Perhaps I never shall. It has been so wet and gloomy these past days one hardly cares to go out."

"How lucky for you," said Mr. Kix, smugly, "for there's not a playwright worth his poundage to be found in the city of Nantle. Instead we are blessed with a proliferation of hacks, mere caterpillars on the leaf of literature. Hacks of every description, everywhere, so far as the eye can reach. Very sorry, Miss Rivers, but in my view we live in an age of hacks."

"True, very true — but try pulling a coach without one," quipped Mr. Lovibond.

"And how have you come by this view?" asked Mr. Frobisher, once the burst of merriment had subsided.

"From broad experience of the world, sir, and intimate knowledge of the human condition," answered Kix, gravely.

"Pass the decanter, if you please," said Mr. Lovibond.

While this discussion was in progress in the dining-room, young Mr. Pancras was downstairs in the kitchen attending to his own supper in the company of the cook, Mrs. Poundit, who herself was busy at her chopping-board.

This Mrs. Poundit was, appropriately enough, composed chiefly of stomach. She looked like an enormous cook-pot with an apron slung round it, perched on the shortest, thickest, squabbest pair of female legs in Nantle. The whole of her was surmounted by a queasy head, with a huge mob-cap bagging over the top of it like an overgrown *omelette soufflé.* She was a fubsy, frowzy, blowzy sort of old cook, in color and texture resembling a bad mushroom, though one smelling more of liquor than of mold. She was renowned throughout the neighborhood for the tales of bloodthirsty horror and excitement with which she regularly frightened any small children who happened by.

And as there was one such child within frightening range now — the kitchen being devoid of persons save herself and young William — a flash of bloodthirsty inspiration came shooting from the firmament, yea, and smote her where she stood.

"Have I ever told you, dearie, o' the sorry fate o' Squire Mulligrub o' Scalpen?" she asked with a roll of her good eye at William, while busily splitting and sculpting a piece of carcass on her chopping-board.

"No, Mrs. Poundit."

Young Mr. Pancras wasn't sure he cared to hear about this Squire Mulligrub or his fate, for Mrs. Poundit had scared him more than once with her stories, which for aught he knew might very well be true; she might be angling to scare him again now. More particularly he remembered her last tale, that of the hairy great goblin-spiders which were supposed to come in the night and suck his juices while he slept.

"Squire Jock Mulligrub, he was a fine hardened villain, and sharp as a weasel, that he were, dearie," smiled the cook, lopping chunks of flesh off the carcass with her mighty knife.

K-chop! sang the knife. *K-chop! k-chop! k-chop!*

Mrs. Poundit had one wandering eye, and the longer she spoke, and the greater the excitement with which she spoke, the more that eye tended to roam from its companion. In the hazy heat there in the kitchen, under the beams hung with sinister bunches of herbs and smoked meats on hooks like corpses a-swing from the gibbet, and with her bad eye turning round and round and the sweat oozing from her pocked face like a waxwork on a summer's day, she was a frightful spectacle.

"Years agone, dearie, Squire Mulligrub lived in a market town called Scalpen, in the Sawtooth Mountains away east o' Goforth. The squire was a-given to the butchering of the fowl for his table, acause he liked the moves of it, and the thrills of it, and acause he was too much the skinflint to pay his old cook for it. But there was more than pullets, dearie, as felt that squire's blade, I'll reckon, on many a day."

"More than pullets, Mrs. Poundit?" asked William, with an expression less than trusting.

"Even more, my precious. There was more than one fat hog from that town had gone missing since the day Squire Mulligrub took up his butchering. Why, his blade was like a living thing in his hand! That blade had thoughts and wills of its own, or so 'twas said. It was a blade what didn't

take to sitting in the block, calm as you please, but always must be working, working. So when Squire Jock left off his pulleting long enough, that
blade got to thinking, thinking, there in its block, what with all the hours
at its dispose."

While she spoke, Mrs. Poundit's own knife was busily working, working, illustrating by means of certain aggressive thrusts and postures the particulars of her story.

K-chop! sang the knife. *K-chop! k-chop! k-chop!*

"And what was that blade thinking of, Mrs. Poundit?"

"Butchering!" leered the cook, her ugly smile revealing a mouth something short of its full set of ivories. "One day a great hog's head draped
in tomata sauce was found stuck onto a stick and planted in the mayor's
garden. It were the head from one o' that mayor's very own hogs! The
pompous worshipful mayor o' Scalpen was never a favorite o' Squire Mulligrub's, no, sir, he weren't."

"What happened then?" asked William, growing uncomfortable.

"It was one afternoon, dearie, when Squire Mulligrub climbed over the
stile into the mayor's field — the mayor being out in the town then, to refresh the folk with his presence — so Squire Jock climbed into that mayor's
field, and took that mayor's prettiest cow from her pasture and led her
through the woods to his own stable-yard, where he meant to slaughter her."

The blood began to drain from the face of young William, as the chill
drained into it.

"The pretty cow he meant to murder, Mrs. Poundit?" he asked, squirming on his chair.

"Just so, dearie, with his busy blade — a blade very like this precious
knife o' me own here, as I'm told, so sleek it were and sharp and soft. For
he meant to tie that pretty cow to a stanchion, and drop her with his rope,
and slash her pretty throat with his blade, and watch the steamy ichor
come a-jetting out in a crimson fountain o' blood!"

K-chop! sang the cook's mighty knife. *K-chop! k-chop!*

"Oh! oh! oh! — you're frightening me, Mrs. Poundit!" cried the small
sufferer.

"Am I, dearie? And what's the matter with that, then, eh? Are you
afeard o' such things? Why, it's the way o' the world, it is, and you'd best
learn it sooner as late. But there was more as felt the touch o' that squire's
blade, so 'twas said, than pullets and hogs and cows, there in that town o'
Scalpen in the Sawtooth Mountains. For it were rumored that bright little
chappies like yourself now an' again went missing, too. It was told how the
younkers first was boiled in the squire's copper — one very like the big

brick copper out yonder there in the wash-house — and then arterward was cut to pieces and the fleshy parts of 'em salted down, and smoked, and slung up in the buttery like those big hams there. The rest, as was of littler use, was fed to the squire's cattle — or so 'twas said."

"Oh! oh! — oh, Mrs. Poundit, I hope I don't meet this horrid Squire Mulligrub!" cried William, clapping hands to his pained little cheeks.

"You've little danger o' that, my precious, for no sooner had Squire Jock gotten that pretty cow o' the mayor's to his stable-yard, than the cow let out the most awfullest bellow. The squire made to calm her, when he heard a noise like a stealthy wind aback of his shoulder; and as he swung round, what should he spy a-crouch there but a stripe-bodied scimitar-cat, with the slobber a-drip from its great heavy fangs!"

"Oh! oh! — a scimitar-cat, Mrs. Poundit? Is that not a most terrible kind of saber-cat?"

"The very prodigious worst kind, dearie — far, far the worst! So much the fleeter, so much the fiercer than Master Saber-cat in rending a little chappie's limbs from his body, and shearing the meat from his bones, and loosing the hot blood from his veins. Why, a mere babe o' the underwood is the tawny saber-cat aside Master Scimitar! And so it was, that Master Scimitar had planted his evil sights on one o' them two — either the juicy cow tied to the stanchion, or the juicy squire himself — and Squire Jock, he knew not which one it were. Ah, that set his murderous heart to thumping, dearie, I'm sure."

"What happened then, Mrs. Poundit?"

"Then, my precious, Squire Mulligrub flung his butchering blade aside, and stared that scimitar-cat down!"

"Stared him down?" asked William, looking puzzled.

"Just so, dearie — optic to optic, whisker to whisker, fang to fang. The squire stared deep into the soul o' the direful beast, through the bright windows of its eyes, and touched its essence. It were a mighty power that Squire Jock possessed — a gift, some said, as allowed him to hypnotize the pullets and hogs afore he slaughtered 'em. Just so, dearie! And so the squire had no use of his busy butchering knife that day in the stable-yard."

"And the cat bounded off, Mrs. Poundit, because of the squire's stare?"

"No, dearie," said the ogress, leering again. "For you see, Master Scimitar being a stranger to Scalpen and that part of the Sawtooth range, he cared little for Squire Mulligrub and his powerful stare. And so afore time enough had lapsed for a younker to cry 'Jack Truelove,' Master Scimitar had pounced on the squire and struck that gentleman's head from his shoulders, and torn open his carcass like a Christmas cracker!"

This cheerful tale she concluded with a fierce clawing of the air with her knife, to simulate the effect of the jaws of Master Scimitar upon the flesh of Squire Mulligrub.

"Oh! oh! oh! — gracious, Mrs. Poundit, you'll be giving me nightmares and perspirations, for I am hardly old enough to stand it!" cried William, trying first to shield his ears, then his eyes, from the slaughter of Squire Jock.

The cook then stepped away from her chopping-board, and brandishing her knife aloft proceeded to creep towards him with the most hideous contortions of visage. The terrified Pancras, thinking the ogress was about to murder him, bolted from the kitchen. Up the staircase he dashed like a squirrel in buttons. He scrambled past the gruff old giant of a clock on the landing — which seemed like a real giant now, intent upon dismembering him — and into the hall and on to the dining-room, where the supper-party was breaking up.

There the boarders and Mrs. Matchless were presented with the picture of young William in a state of shivers, his face as white as death, and heard from his trembling lips how he'd escaped a horrid fate at the hands of Mrs. Poundit. The gentlemen promptly broke out in laughter at the preposterous tale of Squire Mulligrub — for they knew a good cock-and-bull story when they heard one — before breaking out their pipes and cigars and adjourning to the front-parlor. And so it was left to the women, chiefly Anne and Mrs. Matchless, to comfort the lad, and to tell him not to set *too* much store by Mrs. Poundit's tales, which they assured him were little more than harmless gabble.

"Most extraordinary thing," remarked Mr. Lovibond, later that evening, as he sat with his newspaper in the parlor. He had been studying the columns for the past half-hour when he suddenly glanced up, reminded of something he had neglected to mention at supper.

"And what is so extraordinary?" said Mr. Frobisher. He was standing at the fire with his cigar in hand, idly examining the dried fish in a glass that hung above the mantel.

"Woman next door."

"Mrs. Juniper?"

"No — new woman, this afternoon — never seen her before — passing the area in front of Juniper's — after the theater — chattering monkey hops onto my coat-sleeve!"

"There's another bottle of port been nicked from the reserves, I see," came the voice of Mr. Kix, from behind the pages of the very large volume in which his nose was buried.

"Wine not a factor in it — tiny black monkey — odd sort of pet — chattering stuff and nonsense in my ear — extraordinary thing — new woman getting out of her vehicle, you see, carrying the beast — hops into my arms in the excitement — monkey, that is — gave me a fright, I can tell you."

"What do you mean, a new woman?" asked Mr. Frobisher, with an appearance of mild interest.

"Just arrived — lodging next door with Juniper."

"Has this woman a name, or are you bound over to secrecy?"

"Wastefield," said Mr. Lovibond, taking a whiff at his pipe. "Offered her my hand, when stepping from the carriage — the woman stepping, not myself — made introduction — exchange of compliments — wouldn't give me her name, though — odd — had to pry it out of Juniper."

This information seemed to pique the young Frobisher's curiosity.

"What is she like, this Miss Wastefield?" he asked.

"Decidedly attractive."

"Can't you be more specific?"

"Gorgeous face — lovely eyes — dimpled chin — beautiful hair — magnificent figure — oh, decidedly attractive!"

"It's little wonder then she wouldn't give *you* her name," smiled Kix behind his book.

There was a dead pause in the room, while the others took a moment to absorb this further example of the resident grouch's jocularity.

"Ha-*ha!*" Mr. Lovibond exclaimed, throwing up his hands in surprise. "You're a madcap, Kix — *simply a madcap!*"

CHAPTER EIGHT

What the Cards Said

The closest friend of Mrs. Matchless, aside from Anne Feagle, was a Mrs. Juniper, who dwelt in the next house in the row.

Mrs. Flora Juniper was a great admirer of flowers. She wore fresh flowers in her hair, irrespective of the season. She was partial to flowered hats and flowered shawls. She had flowered paper on her walls, flowered coverings on her furniture, and flower-patterned carpets on her floors. She had flowers everywhere. There was even a little parade of flower-pots marching round the railing in front of her house, and up the street-door steps, like a queue of new flower-boarders waiting to join the others inside.

Mrs. Juniper grew flowers in her tiny back-garden, and in boxes in the windows, and in pots on the roof, and in every way had proved herself a skilled and careful gardener. Mrs. Juniper loved her flowers, but even more she loved her very own precious flower, the one she'd raised from a seedling — namely her daughter Jilly. Miss Jilly Juniper was a lively, curious little slip of a little girl, with a face like a sunflower, pretty yellow hair, and eager eyes. And wonder of wonders little Jilly loved flowers, too! She wore them in her hair like her mother, and tended them in pots in her room, and wore pretty flowered dresses and pinafores that her mother had sewn for her.

It was a few days after the events of the last chapter, while Mrs. Juniper was having tea and sundries in the house of Dottie Matchless, that the subject of her new lodger was raised. The ladies were gathered in the lilac-colored front-parlor. Mrs. Matchless was relaxing in her favorite easy-chair, with her crochet-work in her lap and her confidential housemaid at her side. Miss Rivers was there, too, curled up on a sofa with a novel in her hand, and so was little Jilly, who was amusing herself at the cottage piano by describing semicircles on the music-stool.

"And she has traveled all that long distance?" Dottie asked, peering at Mrs. Juniper through her silver spectacles.

"That she has," said her neighbor. "Her family are the Wastefields of Pinewick, hard by Crow's-end. It was some years ago now, her dead dad and my late uncle Gerald, who had the old antiquary shop in Jacktar Lane, kept a professional correspondence. Oh, I'd not the pleasure of her acquaintance myself, for she's never been to Nantle, and I've never seen Crow's-end; indeed, I knew nothing of her till I received her line in the post. She wrote of her dad's demise, which I knew nothing of as well, and asked if I'd inquire into some lodgings for her at Nantle. Well, of course I must have her stay with us, I said to myself, what with the loss of her dad and all. He was a kind of scholar, I think — a very learned man."

"And she has an odd little pet with her? A little monkey?"

"That she has," said Mrs. Juniper, in rather a less generous tone. "She pays for the privilege, she does, for as you know, Mrs. Matchless, we rarely allow tenants to bring creatures into the house. I've no use for 'em — creatures, that is — for they'll eat the flowers, you know, or worse, and I'll not have 'em bothering Jilly there. But she pays the more for it, and so what is one to do? I've asked that she keep the little thing in her room, and not allow it to roam the house."

"It's not soiled the carpets?" asked Anne Feagle, ever the housemaid.

"Not as yet, and it had better not. She takes it with her when she and her maid step out to take the air."

"Do you like the lady's little pet?" Dottie asked, smiling at Jilly.

"I've hardly seen him," sighed the child. "She keeps him to herself there in her room, and I'm not allowed to go in. Miss Wastefield is not so friendly as our last lodger, I don't think. But I do like her. And she is very pretty!"

"She keeps to herself, she does," said her mother.

"A young lady such as that, traveling alone all that long distance!" Dottie mused.

"Oh, she's not alone, Mrs. Matchless. She has her maid with her, and Juga," Jilly said.

"Juga?"

"That's the monkey's name. I heard him chattering last night when I passed by her door. She talks to him a good deal, and he answers her back in his monkey way."

"Just why has she come to Nantle?" Miss Rivers asked, glancing up from her book.

Mrs. Juniper shook her head, and the flowers in her hair with it. "When she wrote me, she claimed she was making the voyage to recover from the death of her dad. But it's a number of months already since he pegged out! I suppose she must still be mourning. She seems a very troubled lady, for so young a lady. It must be from grief at her loss."

"And what of this maid of hers?" asked Anne.

"She keeps to herself, much like her mistress. Though I've a notion she'd very much like to talk to me, or to anyone, but is kept from doing so. She has a fearful, anxious look. And there's something, too, in the face of Miss Wastefield, as tells me she's had some distress in her life — more distress, I think, than just the loss of her dad."

"And she's got that enormous old trunk in her room!" exclaimed Jilly, her eyes opening wide. "It has great heavy chains and locks hanging from it. She hasn't opened it since she arrived, or so says our housemaid. Yesterday, when the lady's door was open, I saw it standing in a corner of her room, just where the porters had set it down. And it was still chained and locked."

"And there is another thing," said her mother. "A strange thing."

"What strange thing is that?" asked Miss Rivers. She had closed her book and put away her glasses, now that the conversation had taken so interesting a turn.

"She's kept a candle burning to all hours every night she's been with us. The first morning I stated to her very clearly that we can't have it, for danger of fire and all; but she assured me she's most careful with it. When I asked her why she must have a light to all hours, she seemed ill at ease, and mumbled how it was something left over from her childhood. A foolish thing, she said, but one which made it impossible for her to sleep in the dark.

"And then late last night as I was shutting up, I saw the door of her room open a crack, and the lady herself peep into the hall with a wary eye, as if watching for thieves and cut-throats in the passage. Thieves and cut-throats, Mrs. Matchless, in my own house — here in Chamomile Street! Then she closed the door and bolted it tight."

"I am certainly glad, Mrs. J., that it was you who had the second-floor furnished to let, and not I," said Dottie.

"Perhaps she's a smuggler!" exclaimed Miss Rivers. It was a colorful suggestion, brought to mind no doubt by the plot of one of her novels. "Perhaps she's smuggling port wine into Nantle, and has got bottles of it in that trunk of hers, and is kept awake to all hours for fear of being discovered by the excisemen."

Doubting looks from every quarter.

"Well, it is possible, is it not?" said Miss Rivers, blushing.

The colorful suggestion was quickly scotched by Mrs. Juniper. "I hardly think so, Miss Charlotte. The lady in question resembles no smuggler as I've ever laid sight on."

"There, you see? Exactly my point, Mrs. Juniper. Who would suspect her?" returned Miss Rivers.

It was at this juncture that young William Pancras entered the room, looking very scrubbed, very brushed, very buttoned, and also very small.

"If you please, Mrs. Matchless," he said, advancing on his little feet in shoes a-gleam with polish, "but Miss Niamh has come down from the attic, as her two scruffy friends have arrived to call on her."

In the same instant the sound of a violin reached them from below stairs. The tune it reeled off was a spirited one, well-known in town and country by the name "Molly McAlpin." The music was quickly joined by a rhythmic clapping of hands and stamping of feet on the tiled floor of the kitchen.

The widow laid aside her crochet-work. "I'll not have those two idlers in my house again," she said, with the nearest approximation to a frown her sprightly features were capable of mustering. "They're an unwholesome influence on Niamh. Who let them in?"

"If you please, ma'am," begged William, wringing his hands, "but they barged in at the street-door, the two of them, when I answered their knocking. I asked them what it was they wanted here, but they pushed me aside and told me to fetch Miss Niamh, which I did, ma'am, for they threatened to weazen me if I didn't. Please, ma'am, I've no desire to be weazened — whatever that may be!"

"Oh, Pancras, you've done it again," groaned little Jilly, with a pained expression that said, *Pancras, Pancras, how very young and helpless you are.* "It's Round-the-corner Jones and Planxty Moeran, is it not?"

"It is, dear," said Anne Feagle, already making for the staircase, "for I recognize the drum of the scoundrels' shoes. It's one thing for Niamh to associate with whom she likes when she's from home. It's her own life, after all, and she's of age, and free to come and go as she wills. But here in the house she'd best take care and attend to the wishes of Mrs. Matchless, or she must find other lodgings."

"Oh, I should not like that at all, Miss Feagle," protested William, following after, for the embryo butler-in-training was something fond of Miss O'Guppy.

The company proceeded down the two flights of stairs to the basement kitchen. There they found Mrs. Poundit seated on a crate, clapping hands and observing with her good eye the small, spare, delicate young girl who stood in the middle of the floor, a violin at her chin and her bow and fingers scampering over its strings.

Everything about this young girl was wonderful to behold — the uncommon skill and artistry of her playing, combined with a certain primitive abandon in its execution, the astonishing speed with which she played, not to mention the appearance of the girl herself, her face half-hidden in a rain of pretty dark hair, very long and curling, which flew about her with every nod and toss of her head. She played with a furious and self-absorbed concentration, her eyes tightly shut, her brows knit, as though she had been transported to another sphere and took no notice of what went on around her in this one. She had already done with the first tune and moved on to the next, one called "Blackberry Blossom," when the ladies and William arrived.

Holding company with Mrs. Poundit and the girl were two ragged, ill-shaven, out-of-pocket-looking street fellows, one lounging on a flour-barrel and the other on the high-backed settle, and both stamping feet in time to the music.

"Sarvice to yer landleedyship, Mrs. Matchless, jewel," exclaimed the fellow on the barrel, he of the lean, hollow cheeks, sneaking eyes, and crafty grin. His hair was thickly oiled and cemented under his muffin-cap, which he had doffed with a servile air in acknowledgment of Dottie, then thrown carelessly back onto his head. He wore a loose, shapeless coat some sizes too large, which lent him an attenuated appearance as though he had withered inside his clothes. He had a shirt but no collar, a waistcoat of snuff-colored cloth, and trousers of shepherd's-plaid. A little clay pipe of the *dudeen* variety completed his portrait.

"Round-the-corner Jones," said Mrs. Juniper, eyeing him with arms crossed and flowers cocked.

"Ah, me dear Mrs. Juniper! How passes the marning, jewel? And yer own darlin child there, too, dear Jilly, acuishla!"

"What cause brings you round today, Mr. J., you and Mr. M. there?" Mrs. Matchless inquired, with a bland smile.

"Ah, shure, 'tis come to see Niamh, we have," spoke up the gentleman on the settle, the aforementioned Moeran. He was a little fellow with a great wiry paintbrush of a mustache and the sort of face that belonged in a horse-collar. "Come from dear Mother O'Guppy we are, plase yer landleedyship, and by her command."

"Troth and faith, by her *hexpress* command it is, jewel," said Round-the-corner Jones.

"If Mrs. O'Guppy had wanted someone to look in on her daughter, she could hardly have chosen worse than the likes of you," said Mrs. Juniper. "Why she does it I'll never understand. Or has she, too, lost her wits?"

"Ah, shure, ye've wounded me heart now, and also me pride, jewel," returned Jones, with a look of injured virtue. "For as Mother O'Guppy is a dear cousin of mine by marriage-vow, d'ye see, 'tis only right and natural I should come round to see her daughter. Shure as Shrovetide, 'twas commanded for Moeran and meself to look in on the purty colleen."

"You're her dear cousin, and a sharper," Dottie said.

"A more useless pair of layabouts I've never seen treading on shoe-leather," sniffed Mrs. Juniper. "Make yourselves tidy! It's a miracle you've not been pitched into the Compter for debt, the pair of you. You're not fit companions for a delicate girl like Niamh."

Mr. Moeran uttered a loud exclamation. "Och! on the contrary, joy, it's to plase dear Mrs. O'Guppy we're come now, to give assurance the child be in the finest of health, d'ye see, as the two have not spaken for a twelve-month. And as to fit companions, joy, well, the colleen there knows her own mind."

"What remains of it. For you know as well as I do, Planxty Moeran, that poor Niamh is weak in the brain. It comes from her old dad, who wasn't much the better. He, too, heard voices in his head, and saw awful things as weren't there — and you know what it got *him*."

"An early trip to the bone-yard," nodded Moeran, his horsy features reflecting a sympathy that seemed perfectly genuine. He pushed back his round black hat from his brow and sighed. "'Tis said he went clean out of his skull — intirely cabbaged he was — God rest his sould!"

"True enough," affirmed his colleague. "Just as it wor wid Cadogan. Ye'll remember Colm Cadogan, then — Colm Cadogan, of Applemeads?"

"I do. Screwed up in the earth he is now — gethered into the church-yard mould, as true as ye're sittin' there."

"And so young Niamh has found harbor here in our house, where she can be looked after and due provision made for her," said Dottie. "It's the least I can do for my friend Mrs. O., though it's beyond me or any of us to watch the girl every minute. But here she has friends who care something for her."

"Ah, shure, jewel, and there's the truth of it, don't ye see," said Jones. "Savin' yer presence, yer landleedyship, but what better friends has she now than Moeran and meself? Shure, we've called on the colleen once a fortnight at the least, to spirit her up an' to plase her ould mother. And so there's no bad influence on her, as is claimed, as it's by Mother O'Guppy's due command. And if poor Dermot O'Kilcoyne wor alive today — he as was our friend and fellow, the best as ever lived, afore he fell dead on a sabbath marning — he'd be wid us here, too, to look in on the woman's child."

"Ah, true, true," agreed his colleague, sighing again. "Poor Dermot! He was a gintleman shure, and a Christian, too, for a fish porter."

The others had to admit that true it was indeed; that is, that some small portion, however minute, of what these two vagabonds had to say was not an outright lie.

Although Miss O'Guppy had been something wild when she first arrived, she had eased into life at the boarding-house remarkably well. The thing that troubled Mrs. Matchless most now was the girl's stubborn refusal to communicate with her mother. She had expressed not a jot of interest in the details of her mother's life, which caused Mrs. O'Guppy no end of pain. To be living so near her daughter — just a few streets away in Captain Barnaby's house — and yet never to see her or to speak to her! No one, it seemed, was bold enough to remind Niamh that in this she was, perhaps, not quite so charitable a daughter, or so forgiving a one. But there are strange chords in the human heart, and to mention her mother's name would send the girl into a rage, of just the sort that had precipitated the breach with her parent.

"And so how is Mrs. O.?" Dottie asked, having resigned herself to the fact that the vagabonds were to be her guests that morning. (Her attempts to dislodge the pair were always half-hearted at best.) Already Mrs. Poundit had begun laying on grub for them — some soda-bread and cheese, some pickled walnuts, a few oysters. "And a dhrink of some cheering kind wouldn't come amiss, if ye plase," the wily Jones instructed, with the result that a couple of pints of black stout were added to the board. All the while Miss O'Guppy kept up her music, for the special amusement of William and Jilly, who had been cutting capers and hopping about like peppercorns as the jigs and reels came flying from her violin.

"In the twiggest of health Mother O'Guppy is, troth and faith, and sthrike me crooked if she bain't," said Round-the-corner. He took a long draught of his stout, followed by two or three whiffs of his pipe. "Though sorra a minute of peace she has now, of course, sinst the captain's returned."

"And what of the captain's wife?"

"In the sevarest of tempers. Ye know how it is, jewel, when the two of 'em be flung togither in the same house. Och, like two cats they are — one's always got to be put out."

"Has Mrs. Barnaby still her music pupils?"

"Shure she do. That piano be tinkling a-night and a-day now wid the lessons. Though the quality of the playing be somethin' irriglar. Agh, shure it is, jewel, the little gossoon there could tinkle better than the lot of 'em!"

The "little gossoon," otherwise William Pancras, did not bat an eyelid at this reference to his small person, since he hardly knew the meaning of the term; and besides which he was too much entranced by Miss O'Guppy and her violin.

"But 'tis all the poor leedy can do to settle the house accounts," Jones went on, with a show of commiseration, "for ye know how fleetly the captain spinds what little he makes by his voyages. The sit'ation 'tisn't good at all, at all, as I've hard from the sarvints. The coastal trade 'tisn't what it was, what wid the evil weather of late an' the clearing of the coach-roads. And as for passingers, well — there be sich as would rather brave the dangers of the road than the lashin' of the seas."

Mr. Jones paused as the fiddle-playing abruptly came to an end. The kitchen seemed eerily quiet in its afterglow, so constant a presence had the music been till then. Miss O'Guppy laid aside her violin. Now that her eyes were open, it could be seen that they were very unusual eyes — strange, dark, expressive eyes, of a peculiar shade of green.

Her first words were addressed to the children.

"I've somethin' wid me here," she said, drawing a pack of cards from her dress. "I'll tell yez yer fortunes, childhers, that's what I'll do. I'll say truth, and dare the divil! Would yez care to know, darlins, what lies afore yez?"

"Oh, yes, indeed!" exclaimed Jilly, who was fascinated by anything in the magical way, anything in the mystical way, indeed anything out of the boring Chamomile Street way.

"I'd not care to, if you please, Miss Niamh," was the surprising response of William. Though fond of Miss O'Guppy, he had yet to recover from his fright at the hands of Mrs. Poundit; indeed, he was eyeing the cook distrustfully that very moment, and wasn't prepared for another fright now from the cards.

And so only two sat down at the table, the others gathering around with varying degrees of interest. Miss O'Guppy shuffled the cards, which were not ordinary playing-cards but had mysterious signs and symbols mingling with the usual pips and faces. She cut the deck, after first removing the Queen of Hearts and placing it face-up on the table. This card was meant to represent the person whose fortune was to be told — little Jilly. Eight cards she dealt from the stock, laying them face-down about the Queen in the shape of a square. One by one she turned the cards up, examining each with a scrutinizing eye. These cards, she said, represented the little girl's fortune.

"Hollo! D'ye see this first card, darlin? 'Tis a picture of the full moon, and as sich signifies ye shall have good and long luck in yer life. A fortunate card it is."

"It's a very good card!" applauded Jilly.

"Yes, darlin, a fair and fortunate card. And look here, now! Here be the card of the heart, all crimson and bloodied — a card as signifies joy. Ye will know happiness in yer life, child."

"But I'm already happy," Jilly pointed out.

"D'ye see then, darlin, how the cards know the truth! Look here, then. The moon, the heart, and now the third card — fire. The fire be another sign of good luck, for it quenches any evil as surrounds it. The fire watches over ye, darlin, and protects ye from harrum. Another fortunate card!"

"Why should *she* have so much good fortune?" grumbled William, craning for a look, his little head and eyes barely rising to the level of the table-top. "She has too much now as it is."

Which remark brought swift reprimands from Dottie and Anne, and an apology from the small offender to Jilly and her mother.

Miss O'Guppy pursued her reading. "Here be the home card, child. The home, as signifies pleasintness, happiness, prosperity. Another fortunate card, darlin! And here be the star card, as signifies earthly success. Upon me sould, ye're a lucky one, darlin, by sich of the cards as have spaken."

Little Jilly was eminently pleased, and her mother as well, not so much for what the cards had to say — for Mrs. Juniper put little faith in them — but for the fact that no evil had yet come from the reading. The remainder of the cards were turned up, with like results; it seemed that Miss Jilly Juniper was destined to be a most fortunate little girl indeed.

"She's a quick hand with her cards, that I'll give her," said Anne Feagle, "but what it all means is beyond my knowing. It's a game of guesses — a kind of charades."

"It's paganly superstition, is what it is," replied Mrs. Juniper, in low tones, "and I'm most happy there was nothing in it to frighten Jilly. For if there had been, I should have stopped it at once. It's not the most Christian of pursuits, or the most healthy, don't you agree, for a delicate girl? And you know, it's said that the devil rides on a fiddlestick."

"I see things, and I hear things, I do," said Miss O'Guppy, halting over the cards. An angry spot showed itself on her cheek, and there was that in her voice that caused Dottie and Anne to exchange concerned glances. "'Tis a gift, by the Holy, and naught to do wid payganly supersthition. And what I've seen now, this past day — and may the marciful Creator sthrike me dead if I lie — but what I've seen bodes little good for the house next door."

"Little good for our house?" said Jilly. "What do you mean, Miss Niamh?"

"Yes, what *do* you mean?" echoed Mrs. Juniper, leaning forward, afraid that the mad girl might be attempting to scare her precious flower.

Miss O'Guppy brushed back the hair from her shoulders, and peered round with a look of mysterious meaning. "A leedy, a monkey-crayture, and a secret," she whispered. "And a murtherin' bad secret it is, too, by the Holy!"

Which words only served to make Mrs. Juniper more uncomfortable. She was not at all certain she wanted Jilly to hear such stuff and nonsense.

"Do you mean our Miss Wastefield?" she asked. "Is that the lady? And what is the secret?"

"Shure, that's the leedy," said Niamh, her strange eyes growing dark with sorrow. "Poor, poor leedy!"

"Our Miss R. thinks she may be a smuggler," said Dottie. "Smuggling port wine into Nantle — imagine!"

"An' is it wine ye're thinkin' she's got in that trunk of hers, jewel?" asked Mr. Jones, as much as to say, *Ah, shure, woman, that's a ridiculous notion!*

"And just how do *you* know of her trunk, Mr. J.?" Dottie asked.

"By gannies, joy, 'tis the business of Jones to know things," said little Planxty Moeran, ruffling up the hair under his hat. "It's a trick of the trade, don't ye see."

"Ha! What 'trade' has such as he, and such as you, unless it be vagabond and underhand?" retorted Mrs. Juniper.

"If it's a smuggler she is, jewel, then shure she's the handsomest smuggler as I've spied in a twelvemonth," said Jones, conveniently deaf to the insinuations cast upon his character and that of his friend.

"The omins, they're murtherin' bad," warned Miss O'Guppy. "Twice it is I've seen her sinst she took up her lodgings, and each time the omins wor murtherin' bad."

"How have they been bad, Niamh?" asked Anne. "These omens, as you say?"

"There's no good for her here," replied the girl. "There's no good in store in these parts, though she has little choice about it. A secret, a powerful secret — an' so little she comprehinds of it! When I look on her leedy-like person, by the Holy, two faces I see there."

"Whatever does she mean by that?" asked Mrs. Juniper, glancing round.

"*I mane what I mane, an' that's what I mane — by Jasus!*" exclaimed Miss O'Guppy, blazing up. Again the angry spot on her cheek, again the exchange of glances between Dottie and Anne Feagle; but the girl's temper quickly cooled. "Then I took the cards, and shut me eyes and concentrayted me mind upon her, and dhrew three cards from the rest," she said, once the moment had passed. "Three cards I dhrew — the cutlass, the sarpint, an' the mountain."

She took the three cards from the stock and laid them face-up for all to see.

"The cutlass, as signifies peril," she explained, touching a dainty finger to each card as she described it. "The sarpint, as signifies treachery, or disaster. An' the mountain, as signifies the presence of a mighty enemy — a murtherin' mighty force ranged against her. For coming events cast their shadows afore — an' that's the truth av it!"

Further than this Miss O'Guppy declined to elaborate. Her face, like her eyes, had visibly darkened, and she rocked her head sadly. Then, in an effort perhaps to give vent to her feelings, she took up her fiddle and drew from it a plaintive song, the one known as "O'Carolan's Farewell." Nearly all in the kitchen knew the tune, if not all the name. So aching and heartfelt was the girl's performance of it, however — so magnificent the breadth and power of its melancholy grandeur — that even Round-the-corner Jones and Planxty Moeran were struck dumb. They could do nothing but watch and listen, marveling at the sight of Miss O'Guppy's tossing hair, her shut eyes, her rigid brow, her fingers leaping across the strings with such pliancy and vigor, such strength of attack and fierceness of purpose, as can hardly be described.

After the final notes had died away, the eyes of the girl opened again and her features reanimated. She shrugged up her shoulders and, as if to dispel the melancholy mood, launched at once into a wild, swirling, swaggering kind of hop-jig — in honor perhaps of Messrs. Jones and Moeran — which set the entire kitchen a-clapping. When it was over, she quietly retired her violin, shuffled her cards, and offered to tell the fortune of Mrs. Poundit. The cook promptly rubbed her mutton-fists and eased her heavy self onto a chair at the table — poor labored chair! — and with her bad eye rolling round in her head waited to learn what the eternal mighty powers had in mind for her.

Directly a loud *tap-tap-tap* was heard at the street-door of the neighboring house, accompanied by some lively whistling which drifted in through the area windows. Mrs. Juniper exclaimed that it was post-time and that Mr. Milo was come, and when she went upstairs in answer, her friend Dottie went with her. Going out at the door, they found a young man standing on the steps of Mrs. Juniper's house. He was a rather plain, unassuming, lazy-eyed young man, in the red jacket that marked him out for a general postman, and with his postman's bag hanging at his shoulder. He was whistling to himself and staring at his shoes while awaiting an answer to his knock.

"I'll have 'em, thank you, Mr. Milo," said Mrs. Juniper, briskly descending the steps of Dottie's house and ascending her own, and there taking possession of the letters.

"Have you anything for my house and my boarders today, Mr. M.?" Dottie called to him.

The postman threw up a forefinger to the brim of his hat. "That I have, Mrs. Matchless, that I have — though sorry I am it's no more than a few."

He presented Dottie with a small batch of letters, then raised his hat to both ladies and proceeded on his way, warbling like a songbird.

In glancing through her small packet, Mrs. Matchless found one letter addressed to herself. It was in a round and familiar hand, and had been sent from a place called Smithy Bank, Truro. Turning the rest of the mail over to Anne, the widow betook herself to the little back-parlor that served as her private sitting-room and sanctum. The sound of Niamh's violin reached her just as she was sitting down. Plainly the fortune of Mrs. Poundit as decreed by the cards was now common knowledge, and from the lilt of the music it seemed it was to be a jolly one.

For Dottie, however, the music faded quickly from her awareness as she immersed herself in the contents of the letter. An expression of delight filled her face, brightening up her temples, and rosying up her cheeks, and silvering up her spectacles. When she had finished the letter, she read it again, often looking up and smiling at nothing in particular, as one does when recalling some fond and far-off remembrance; and for once the gray skies of Nantle seemed not so dreary, nor the clouds so lowering.

CHAPTER NINE

An Honest Man and a Grocer

It was called Smithy Bank because there had once been an ancient forge on the site, though precious little evidence of it remained now apart from some charred bits of earth, and the occasional clump of iron turned up by plough or shovel. Nonetheless the association persisted in local memory, and when the manor and its great house were established on the spot, there on the island of Truro, they were christened Smithy Bank, and Smithy Bank they remained.

It was called a bank because it lay on the top of the country, above a rushing stream from which a line of bush-girt slopes tumbled down to the sea. At the foot of it was a white sand beach with a landing-place for boats, on a small cove that was as smooth and calm as an artificial pond. From the estate long views could be had in most directions where the sweep of forest did not intervene. Although subject to island weather — lots of rain, lots of wind, lots of fog — the situation of Smithy Bank was a pretty and an enviable one, at once sweet, fresh, and exhilarating.

The former master of Smithy Bank had been a Mr. Baxendale, a wealthy squire descended from the original builder of the house. He had yielded the ghost some years back and left all to his childless widow. In due course the widow was married again, to a short, thick, good-natured grocer from Nantle by the name of Threadneedle, who was a distant relation on her late mother's side. Mr. Threadneedle, who had been at the most a competent grocer, though a scrupulously upstanding and honest one, upon his marriage had relinquished his shop and taken up residence at Smithy Bank, or simply "the Smithy," as he called it. And almost at once the trouble began.

The chief servants of Smithy Bank were two — a tall, gaunt, humorless giant of a butler called Plush, and the housekeeper, a mouse-sized, gray-headed old woman named Kimber with steely eyes and a tongue like a rasp. Together the towering Mr. Plush and the tiny Mrs. Kimber had served the former Mrs. Baxendale for twenty faithful years, inclusive of the reign of the lordly Mr. Baxendale. No wonder, then, that at the time of the lady's second marriage — to a lowly *grocer* — an immediate coolness toward Mr. Threadneedle on the part of these two had set in.

Neither Mr. Plush nor Mrs. Kimber could abide the notion that an off-comer from the mainland, and a tradesman to boot, horror of horrors! — a person who actually had transacted *business* in the city of Nantle — should think himself the social equal of their mistress by marrying her. They suspected that he had snared his wife by stealth or cunning, or something worse; that perhaps he had bewitched her with some strange herb or exotic fruit from his shop, and clouded her judgment; and so from the outset they looked down upon him as an inferior, to be regarded with distrust and resentment.

In the case of Mr. Plush it was a very literal looking-down — that is, from the butler's high-placed head and down the length of his long nose to the ground-inhabiting Threadneedle. Mr. Plush viewed the good-natured husband of his mistress as little better than a costermonger — most certainly a pariah in the finer Truro circles — and beneath consideration. For tiny Mrs. Kimber it was more a matter of looking *up* at Mr. Threadneedle, and taking sight of him along the line of a bony forefinger, which she was in the habit of waving in his face whenever some breach of policy was brought to her notice — which was often, and for which he was usually responsible.

It was only through the good graces of his wife that Mr. Threadneedle had managed to survive the tyranny of these two. He had developed troubling nightmares in which Mrs. Kimber played a leading role — Mrs. Kimber in her long black dress, her menacing finger raised in reprimand, gliding toward him like a ghost along a haunted floor. *Lord save him from it!* So thoroughly had this dream infected his brain, that whenever he spied Mrs. Kimber making for him, he half-expected her to cover the ground without benefit of ambulation.

Shortly after her marriage, within a mere nine or ten months of it in fact, the wife of Mr. Threadneedle committed a most thoughtless act — she died. The upshot of it was that Mr. Threadneedle, having married a rich widow, abruptly found himself a rich widower. Thus Mr. Malachi Threadneedle, *quondam* grocer and person beneath consideration, in one fell moment was transformed into a lord of acres and sole master of Smithy Bank.

This catastrophe served only to stiffen the resolve of Plush and Kimber, for the death of their mistress meant that the two were now wholly subservient to a tradesman. Although it would have been quite within his prerogative as squire to have given them both the chop, and straightaway too, Mr. Threadneedle found he could not. No matter how thoroughly he gave his mind over to it, he could not. He felt unequal to the task; indeed, he couldn't muster the needed courage for it, for he thought something awful might ensue. He dreaded the idea of sacking the two old servants who had been so beloved by his late wife, fearing that she herself might come to him from the other world, in vengeful spirit, and terrorize him in his dreams after the manner of his housekeeper. It was not that he was averse to seeing his dear wife again; rather, it was simply that he couldn't bear the idea of seeing his dear, *dead* wife again. And so Mr. Plush and Mrs. Kimber retained their positions of power in the house, their chief function being, as it seemed to Mr. Threadneedle now, to put him in mind every day of his eternal unfitness for the squireship of Smithy Bank.

For their part Mr. Plush and Mrs. Kimber remained convinced that Mr. Threadneedle had been responsible for the death of their mistress, which had been attributed to an attack of "island fever." Try as they might, however, the pair could discover no cause to relate any action of Mr. Threadneedle's to his wife's fatal illness; although they were sure that if the late Mrs. Baxendale had *not* consented to marry him in the first place, she would never have died; and so it followed, that in the very act of asking for her hand in marriage, the grocer had pronounced himself GUILTY. For years upon years Mr. Plush and Mrs. Kimber had conceived of no finer glory in life than service to the Baxendales and Smithy Bank. Now the Baxendales were gone, but Smithy Bank remained; and so it was the estate itself which became, in their eyes, the sole rightful and worthy object of their servantly devotion.

That estate was comprised of a manor-house of tawny island sandstone, with mullioned windows, a slate roof, and cobblestone dressings; the stables and paddocks, barns, coach-house, kiln, dovecote and windmill, and a fleet of scattered outbuildings. The stables, barns, and paddocks were occupied by more than mere horses and cattle, for the late Mrs. Baxendale had had a liking for beasts of every description. Foremost among the menagerie were a tame gray fox called Foxy, a family of tapirs, a few bison, and an island dwarf mammoth. And there was a hulking, horse-like creature called a moropus — a magnificent rarity. It had been brought to the island by a trader named Hicklebeep, who called regularly with obscure and unusual merchandise to sell. And there were birds, too, of many sorts, all about the estate — brown pelicans, shags, murrelets, ospreys, sooty gulls, black oyster-catchers — many with nests high up on the slopes, or in the rocks and ledges down below at Cold Harbor, the quiet pool at the bottom of Smithy Bank.

Mr. Threadneedle was particularly fond of the dwarf mammoth, whose name was Mustard, owing to her thick coat of shaggy yellow hair. She, too, was something of a rarity. She rose barely five feet from the ground she stood on, had twin woolly knobs for a cranium, great floppy ears, an impish eye, an inquisitive trunk, and a liking for mischief. The little cat-like Foxy, too, was a delight. And like his late wife, Mr. Threadneedle was an admirer of birds. He loved to watch the gulls soaring across the sky, and the pelicans skimming the wave-tops in their search for fish. But for the hulking, horse-like moropus, however, Mr. Threadneedle had little use.

The chief occupation of this creature, which answered to the name of Ladycake — another legacy of his late wife's — was the munching of leaves and berries, and the grubbing-up of roots and tubers. Her feet were large and ungainly, and sported claws instead of hooves, like the feet of a megathere. Most of her time she spent alone in her vast paddock, munching and staring into space, for sadly, she smelled; indeed the odor that rose from her was not to be believed. She made the horses and other animals uncomfortable by her presence. Even Mustard found her a disagreeable thing (and Mustard found very little to dislike in anyone), while little Foxy wisely avoided her, for being a fox she knew a stupid creature when she smelled one. But the late Mrs. Baxendale had taken pity on Ladycake, and provided her with grazing-land and access to the stream and parts of the shrubberies and old fruit-gardens. And there the smelly moropus lived now, prospering mightily — another nuisance complicating the life of Mr. Threadneedle, though not so pressing a one as Plush and Kimber.

To escape the oppression of his chief tormentors, Mr. Threadneedle frequently sought shelter in the coach-house. He had rebuilt it virtually anew with his own skilled hands — it had lacked proper flooring and a chimney, and lattice windows, and certain other necessaries of a comfortable workplace — and made it into a kind of shop for his tinkering. From boyhood Mr. Threadneedle had loved to tinker, but as a man he'd found that the need to earn a living had gotten in the way; and so one of the more welcome benefits of his marriage to Mrs. Baxendale was the time and opportunity to tinker. The tyranny of Plush and Kimber had only fired his determination in this regard. Because the coach-house was out of view of the manor — being screened by a line of trees and a bosky hedge — it made his shop and sanctuary all the more personal, all the more private, and safe from the intrusions of his butler and housekeeper. *Here and here alone he was free of them!*

What would have particularly horrified his tormentors was the sight of Mr. Threadneedle decked out in his grocer's blue apron as he worked. This emblem of the trade he wore proudly and from long habit, from his many years of shopkeeping. It had always brought him good luck, and in view of his present circumstances had brought him something more besides — a feeling of triumph, however small, knowing as he did how sorely it would have vexed Plush and Kimber.

To assist him in his tinkering, Mr. Threadneedle had employed an apprentice of sorts, a youth from the nearby village of Plinth. Tim Christmas was the elder child of a woman who had worked as a laundress at Smithy Bank and other houses round Truro. This son of hers was an intelligent, well-mannered, cheerful lad, and like Mr. Threadneedle was gifted with his hands. Moreover he was keen to learn, and so Mr. Threadneedle had taken him in, at the suggestion of the local vicar. Side by side, master and apprentice tinkered away there in the coach-house, blissfully content, losing all count of time amid the happy sounds of hammering and sawing, and much pleasant conversation, and even the occasional bursting of Mr. Threadneedle into song, while little Foxy watched from the hearth-rug, and the impish eye of Mustard peered in at a door or window — all of this, of course, to the horrendous disapproval of Plush and Kimber, had they known of it.

"Mr. Plush," said Mr. Threadneedle one morning after breakfast, as the butler came creaking up in his suit of black broadcloth, and towered over him like the angel of death — "it has come to my notice, Mr. Plush, that Ladycake is being a bother again to the horses. You know that a part of her grazing-ground abuts the lower paddock of the bay roan and my favorite trotter. Might we have the groundskeeper shift the walling a little there, by the pepper tree, to keep Ladycake from getting too near them?"

Mr. Plush was unmoved. He shook his ponderous old head gravely, from an altitude so high above the landscape of the breakfast-room that a certain frostiness in the reply was inevitable. "I should not advise it, sir. Oh, no, no, no."

Mr. Threadneedle took the quizzing-glass from his eye, with which he had been perusing some letters, and regarded the butler attentively. "No? Whyever not, Mr. Plush?"

"Strongly not, sir. Oh, no, no. The present arrangements were made in the late mistress's time, by the late mistress herself. It was Mrs. Baxendale's wish that the paddocks and grounds of Smithy Bank be so delineated. It would be a terrible thing, indeed a *monstrous* thing, to disregard her intentions in the matter. It would be a violation of the highest order, a trampling upon her imperishable memory. No, no, sir, I should advise against it most strongly. Wouldn't you agree, sir?"

The butler always asked Mr. Threadneedle if he agreed or not, to maintain the pleasant fiction that servant was servant, and squire squire.

"Ah," said Mr. Threadneedle, wetting his lips, and making a little inward call on his courage — for although he had loved his wife, it was more than three years now since her death, and here he was still under the thumb of these two like a helpless schoolboy — "ah, but Mr. Plush, don't you think it's been long enough now? Surely my wife would not object to this very minor qualification of her design, and one with such a practical end in view. She loved the horses, too, as you'll remember, and I fear they've developed a positive dislike of Ladycake. It's their proximity to the moropus, the sharing of fences in that part of the grounds, that is upsetting them. A simple redirection of the boundaries would greatly alleviate —"

The butler cleared his voice and shook his head again on high, conveying such utter disapproval of the grocer's plan it was not worth dignifying by means of speech.

"I see," Mr. Threadneedle responded, only too conscious of his inferiority before the angel of death. And such a chicken-heart he was, too! The former grocer of Nantle was, as we have noted, on the short, thick, inoffensive side. His hair was of the pepper-and-salt kind, and for some years had been beating a hasty retreat from his forehead. He had twinkling gray eyes, a benevolent chin, and a meek little pair of curled-up mustaches. Not only did he feel inferior sitting there in his red flannel waistcoat, braces, and high-lows, he looked it.

He took a swallow of his coffee. "I see. Can't be done, Mr. Plush?"

"No, sir. Impossible. Never has been done. Never can be done. Oh, no, no, no."

"I see. Well, thank you so very much, Mr. Plush," said the grocer, acquiescing as he always did. *Yet another plan scuttled!* "I simply wished to inquire a little into the matter, and obtain your view of it, as it were, for you've lived at the Smithy so much longer than I and are more familiar with its traditions. I confess I've quite gone off the idea now, and shall rely on your judgment going forward in the matter of my late wife's endeavors."

Chicken-heart! Chicken-heart!

"Very good, sir." The butler peered down his long nose, bowed his head, and creaked slowly away. A parlormaid who had been busy at the sideboard paused in her duties, her face so full of sympathy for the squire that it made Mr. Threadneedle feel a little better. At least not everyone at Smithy Bank resented his presence.

He had gone to his study to fetch his hat, and was preparing to set off for the coach-house, when a rattle of keys reached his ear, betokening the approach of Mrs. Kimber. He saw her tiny black figure rushing toward him. Nightmare or not, the sight and sound of her caused his palms to water and his flesh to creep.

"Mr. Threadneedle," said the housekeeper, in a tone which implied that no words on earth could ever express the displeasure she felt, nor could anything Mr. Threadneedle say or do ameliorate it.

"Yes, Mrs. Kimber?" the grocer asked, wiping his brow.

"Mr. Threadneedle," said the housekeeper again, in her rasp of a voice which she used to grind her opponents into submission. She stopped within a breath of him and waved her finger under his chin. "Mr. Threadneedle, I fear that matters have gone quite beyond endurance."

"How do you mean, Mrs. Kimber? Which matters?"

"I refer to that boy of yours."

"Do you mean Tim Christmas?"

"The mean drab boy from the village, yes, sir. Do you know what he's done, Mr. Threadneedle? Do you know the liberties he has taken?"

Mr. Threadneedle was unaware that young Tim Christmas had taken any liberties whatsoever, certainly none that might warrant Mrs. Kimber's disapproval.

"Pray, what has he done, Mrs. Kimber?"

"He has had breakfast again in the kitchen without leave of either myself or Mr. Plush. He has taken food from this house, sir, freely and liberally, and in so doing has deprived those to whom it rightly belongs. We are not strictly opposed to charity here, Mr. Threadneedle; indeed, charity can be a fine thing, in its proper place and time, but we mustn't make it a habit. Your mean drab boy has had breakfast in the kitchen every morning this week — gorged himself there on eggs and ham, in the presence of Cook — *and every morning, sir!* The kitchen-maid has seen fit now to inform me of it; now I inform *you.* What do you propose to do about it, Mr. Threadneedle?"

"I admit, I've asked Cook to prepare something for the boy, and given him permission to have his breakfast here on the days he assists me in the coach-house."

Mrs. Kimber stared aghast on hearing such blasphemy. "*Your* permission, sir? May I beg to remind you, Mr. Threadneedle, that as housekeeper here for more years than I care to remember, it has ever lain within the sphere of my own duties to manage the domestic arrangements. These are matters that the master of a great house cannot and should not be troubled with, or we in service will have failed in our duty. Are you now removing the superintendence of the domestic arrangements from me? If so, sir, might I inquire into the reason for it? Am I no longer to be trusted with the responsibility? Are not my accounts always in order, my keys in their proper places? How have I given cause for my duties to be curtailed?"

"What would you suggest be done, Mrs. Kimber?" returned Mr. Threadneedle with some irritation. The "mean drab boy" from Plinth had been having his breakfast in the kitchen with Cook for quite a while now, and at a suitably early hour, long before Mrs. Kimber and Mr. Plush were disposed to rise from their separate coffins.

"We can't have orphans from the village applying to this house for *charity,*" declared Mrs. Kimber. "It will not do, sir. If one is allowed to do it, others will follow. Soon every last ragamuffin round here will be at our doorstep. Is that what you want, sir? Is that what the late mistress would have wanted, I ask you, Mr. Threadneedle, sir?"

"But my dear Mrs. Kimber," protested the grocer, his attention wavering, and understandably so, for he was busy formulating his plan of escape — "Mrs. Kimber, Tim is only one boy. And he is not an *orphan,* nor a ragamuffin, as you term it. He has a mother and a sister in the village. They may be poor in means, but I assure you they are rich in spirit. Perhaps you remember his mother, who was laundress here in the late Mr. Baxendale's time?"

"And a fine specimen of a mother and a washerwoman she must be, sir, if I may be so bold, to permit a son of hers to solicit charity in the house of another — in the house of her betters! I ask you, sir, am I to do nothing about it?"

"What I should do," said Mr. Threadneedle, tossing his hat on and edging his way past the menacing finger, "what I should do, Mrs. Kimber, were I in your place now — which I am not — is nothing. I should ignore the matter entirely. I myself shall continue to superintend the boy and his breakfasts, and you may apply yourself to the rest of your many duties. Good morning to you, Mrs. Kimber!"

Having delivered this little speech, the grocer made for the back-stairs, in something indecorously approaching a run; in short he cut his lucky and, before Mrs. Kimber could raise an objection, he had sped across the lawn and garden and into the trees and through the hedge, and so found himself at the door of the coach-house.

Where he heaved a great sigh of relief, and went in.

CHAPTER TEN

A Wizard Notion

"Good morning, young man, good morning!" Mr. Threadneedle exclaimed, striding in at the door with his shoulders back, like a man who has just rid himself of a heavy load — one called Plush and Kimber.

"Good morning, sir," replied the lad at the carpenter's bench. He was in age not above twelve or thirteen years, with clean-looking eyes, a thatch of crisp dark hair, and a sturdy face — hardly the picture of a "mean drab boy" in any sense whatsoever. He stood perhaps an inch or so taller than Mr. Threadneedle, but it was plain from his manner that he very much looked up to the gentleman grocer, and with considerably more reverence than Mrs. Kimber.

"And how is your mother today, Tim?" Mr. Threadneedle asked, doffing hat and coat, and making awful preparation for tinkering by girding on his grocer's blue apron.

"She is better, sir, though the cold weather is always a trial for her," answered the lad, who was dressed in a smock-frock. "It doesn't help her joints to be exposed to it, and it causes her hands to swell. She can get very low on occasion. But it's always the way, sir, at this time of year."

"Has the vicar been seeing to your needs? Have you enough there at your cottage?"

"We've enough, sir, thank you. Mr. Yorridge has been very kind."

"And your little sister? She is well?"

"Very well, sir. She helps our mother in the cottage, as you know, and takes in washing and sewing of her own. She has a talent for fancy-work."

"Well, that is all to the good, then. Now, let me see. We shall tinker till one o'clock today, I think, for I've ledger-books in my study that *must* be attended to or I shall hear about it. Once we've done, Cook will send some lunch out to us, and you'll have yours here, and will as well take something home to your family. Now, one thing more —"

He reached into his waistcoat-pocket and took out some yellow coins, which he placed into the hand of his assistant.

"There's for your diligence, Tim. You'll be so good as to give these to your mother."

"Five golden guineas! Oh, sir, we can't accept these," protested the lad, staring agape at the unexpected bounty.

"Can't accept them? Whyever not? You're my 'prentice of sorts, Tim. You've more than earned those guineas."

"Sir, you've already paid me most generously these last months, far more than is justified by the hours I've passed here. And I've not even my — my *articles,* as you call them."

"Tinkering is what sustains me, Tim. Without it I should be quite bereft, and you've proven yourself a most able assistant in every respect. Moreover I'm bound as your master of sorts — I regret we must maintain the informality of the relationship, for as a liveryman of the Grocers' Company I'm empowered to give instruction only in the trade of grocering — I'm bound to furnish you with sufficient food, clothes, and lodging. While I can't offer you *all* of these at the Smithy, I can at least provide you with some money and meals. Pray keep the coins — put them away and give them to your mother. Now, then, how have you been getting on this morning?"

"I've been at it solidly, sir," said the lad, indicating the assemblages, in various stages of completion, which lay upon the carpenter's bench. Mr. Threadneedle took out his quizzing-glass and proceeded to an examination of each, murmuring in steady monologue as he went along.

"Ah! Good, good. You've been to the kitchen at the usual stilly hour for your breakfast, I know, and a fortunate hour it's been, too, until today. It seems we've had a defection — somebody has peached! Well, well. Still it remains a fortunate hour, one where you've little danger of encountering the dreaded goblins that freeze my blood."

"Goblins, sir?"

"*Plush and Kimber,*" the grocer whispered, with a confidential wink.

"Of course, I've heard much of them from my mother, sir. They were in service since old Mr. Baxendale's time."

"And as little acquaintance with them, the better for you. Well, I see you've gotten on splendidly this morning. Do you know, I believe you love to tinker nearly as much as I! These refinements will do very well. I believe they should right the imbalance in the cage-coils, don't you think? A jolly fine idea of yours, Tim, for I confess it's been a total skull-cruncher for me. Now, where were we, then, when we left off yesterday?"

And so they plunged into a study of the latest problem, and discussed it in all its bearings, and turned it round and round until they'd looked at every side of it. There was still so much to be done before all was perfected! Little by little, however, they were closing in on their goal. And as it usually happened when master and apprentice were at their tinkering, time sped apace. Before either knew it, it was one o'clock; at which point lunch made its appearance in a hamper delivered by one of the servants. Indeed, they would have sailed right through the hour but for that, and for the bleating roar that erupted outside. A woolly head showed itself at one of the windows; a round and impish eye peered coyly through the latticed panes.

"Mustard's here!" said Tim.

"And is her usual punctual self, for she's always on the alert for hampers," Mr. Threadneedle noted. "The time has stolen on and we've nearly missed our lunch! Well, well — sufficient unto the day is the tinkering thereof, eh, young man? Though we've still this knotty problem remaining here, this new skull-cruncher. I admit I'm quite at a loss for a solution, but I am set upon finding one."

"I'll peg away at it tonight, sir, in my head," the boy promised. "Already I have a notion or two that may serve."

"Good lad! You are of invaluable assistance to me, Tim. It is squarely because of you that we are so far along. And you've no idea how much I value your company."

"It would seem that Mustard values *our* company, sir, for she's quite anxious for us to come out and join her."

"Do you know," said the grocer, removing his blue apron and taking the hamper in hand, "I'm really very grateful to my late wife for having adopted Mustard and little Foxy. As for Mr. Hicklebeep — well, I suppose I have yet to forgive him for inflicting Ladycake upon us. As regards the stones, however, I expect we must thank him for them, one day, and apprise him of our discoveries."

"And thank Captain Clipperton as well, in spirit," Tim added, "for were it not for him, we should have made no discoveries at all."

"Captain Wulf Clipperton — now there's a name to conjure with! One of the greatest of seafaring explorers in the time since the sundering. For it was he who found the stones and took them to the ore office at Goforth, before embarking on his last voyage — the one from which he failed to return. Or such is the tale Mr. Hicklebeep had from the auctioneer in Goforth when he acquired the stones. Well, so it may have happened, or so it may not; we'll never know. So many of the captain's exploits must of necessity remain speculation. So let us *go forth* ourselves now and have our lunch, and raise a toast to the memory of Captain Clipperton. For indeed it may be to him that we owe our success."

Suiting the action to the word, they stepped outside, where they found Mustard awaiting them. She was like a pocket edition of a mastodon, only far rarer: a dwarf mammoth, one of the few still remaining on the islands of Truro, Hove, and Windwhip.

"How are you, m'lady?" Mr. Threadneedle asked, patting her briskly on the shoulder. The mammoth curled her trunk about him and sniffed his face, his clothes, his pockets, his lunch hamper. He felt her heavy breath upon him like a stream of air from a bellows. Then she raised her trunk aloft and discharged another bleating roar, whereupon they all strolled round behind the coach-house, the honest grocer and his apprentice-of-sorts in the lead and the stout little pachyderm trotting behind.

An air of snug concealment pervaded the area. There was the bosky hedge running along one side, and a grove of trees on the other, and before them a view of the sea framed by the boles and lower branches of two clumber pines. Mr. Threadneedle and Tim settled themselves on an old stump in the midst of this grassy space, near a spreading fir. Not surprisingly there were a number of treats in the hamper for Mustard, and so the first few minutes were given over to feeding her. Her eyes, her lips, even her pink, blubbery tongue radiated happiness; but soon — too, too soon! — the treats were at an end. Though disappointed, Mustard accepted the situation as inevitable and, for want of something better, took to cropping the grass beside the hedge. With a tooting nest of gulls in a nearby tree supplying the music, grocer and apprentice tucked into their own lunch now with zest. In the course of it they offered the promised pledge to Captain Clipperton, who years ago had vanished with his ship in far southern seas.

The meal dispatched, Mr. Threadneedle drew a folding telescope from his coat and, stepping to the open space between the pines, trained it on the hillside below.

"Ah, there she is, unfortunately," he said, as the object of his search came in view. It was Ladycake.

What an immense, lumbering creature she was! As big as a Shire horse, she had a purplish hide the color of mulberries, and a black mane and markings. She looked something like a horse but something like a megathere too, what with her long, thick head, sleepy gaze, and ears slung far back. Her hind limbs were considerably shorter than her forelegs, producing a downward slope of the back from withers to rump. She was heavier than a horse and something lumpish, and in place of hooves she had her megathere-like claws with which she was digging for roots. Having found something of interest, she plucked it forth, and stood munching and staring — Ladycake was forever munching and staring — and managing to look even homelier than usual for a moropus.

Magnificently rare she might be; magnificent she was not.

"Can't be done, sir," the grocer muttered to himself, in a low, mocking tone, as he peered through the glass. "Impossible. Shouldn't advise it, sir. Never *has* been done, never *can* be done. Oh, no, no, no!"

"Did you say something, sir?" Tim asked.

"Ah! Nothing, Tim, nothing at all," said Mr. Threadneedle, recollecting himself. He ran a hand across his chin; his eyes sparkled again, a smile peeped from under his little curled-up mustaches. "Nothing but the remnant of an evil dream, I think. Not to worry."

He swung the telescope down toward Cold Harbor and the sea-bird rookeries to observe the progress of the tide, then upward and outward into the channel for a view of the mainland — or *offland,* as it was called by island folk. He spied the old light-tower on its craggy headland, across the channel at Paignton Swidges, then traced the long sweep of coast stretching north and west of it to Nantle, with its forest of ships lying at anchor in the harbor. At one ship in particular, a three-master, his glass came to a stop.

"Ah! I believe the *Salty Sue* is in port," he remarked.

"Captain Barnaby's ship?"

The grocer nodded. "Which makes it likely we'll receive a call from Mr. Hicklebeep."

"And then we may thank him for the stones."

"Well, now, Tim," said Mr. Threadneedle, gently but firmly, "you know, we needn't be quite so hasty as that. We shall need to keep our own counsel for a little while longer. This is a matter that should not be disclosed prematurely. We still have a good deal of ground to get over, you know, more improvements to be made; no detail must be overlooked. We must take care, otherwise we'll doom ourselves to failure in the eyes of the world. And we must have no more narrow squeaks! Not to worry, though — opportunity will serve soon enough."

His young charge readily grasped the wisdom of his argument. "Of course, sir. I had forgotten. All you say is very true."

"How was your lunch, then?"

"Excellent, sir."

"Mine as well."

"I thank you again for it, sir. And for breakfast, too."

"It's no more than you deserve, Tim. Let it never be said that Thread-needle the grocer was a pinchfist when it came to his 'prentices, or his customers. Now, you must take the rest of the food here home to your mother and sister."

There was a sudden bleat from Mustard — who had left off cropping the grass for lolling on it — as a bushy-tailed streak came flying round a corner of the coach-house.

"Foxy!" Tim exclaimed.

The fox bounded toward them, only to stop a few feet short as her senses caught wind of the hamper. Slowly she crept toward it along the grass, her huge fan-shaped ears erect, her whiskers a-quiver, her dainty nostrils tasting the air. Although island foxes survived chiefly on insects, eggs, and mice, they were not averse to seeking out other fare — Smithy Bank fare, in particular — and Foxy was no exception.

Mr. Threadneedle made a great show of objecting to her advances, before offering her a few tidbits from the hamper. She was about the size of a tabby cat and nearly as dear. Her coat was painted in shades of gray and rust, with whitish underparts. As she bolted down the food, she darted her quick, sly gaze this way and that — for though she had been tamed, in a sense, still she possessed that spark of the wild within her which she shared with many a common tabby.

"She has been a prize ever since my wife found her one day while riding," Mr. Threadneedle recalled. "The little creature had been abandoned — she was only a kit — and would likely have been pounced on by some predator. My wife's action rescued her from that fate." He scratched the little fox about the head and ears, which she graciously permitted him to do now that her belly was full. Mr. Threadneedle seemed to wax museful and retrospective. His gaze sought out a distant wooded knoll, just visible round the side of the coach-house. About a mile beyond it was the village of Plinth and the parish church of St. Brine's, in whose crypt lay the mortal remains of the former mistress of Smithy Bank.

Poor Mr. Threadneedle, Tim thought, for he knew that wistful, far-away look. *He misses the company of Mrs. Baxendale terribly.*

Almost at once he pulled himself up short, realizing he had called the lady by her prior name, the one by which she had been known for years and years to everybody on Truro. She and Mr. Threadneedle had been married for so brief a time that the name *Mrs. Threadneedle* had gained no currency whatsoever. It was as though Mr. Threadneedle had been joined in marriage to somebody else's wife, and never had a proper one of his own.

A knapsack was procured for Tim into which the leftover food was placed, and the boy, having thanked his benefactor again for his many kindnesses, took his leave and set off for Plinth and home. He went at a fast swing through the tranquil and sylvan solitudes, round the knoll and over the ancient clapper bridge and through the nooks and hollows of Smithy land, all of it richly wooded with venerable timber.

He arrived home in no long time, for home was not so very far, being situated on the outskirts of the village. It was a simple lime-washed cottage of two rooms, roofed with thatch. The floors were sunken and uneven, the ceiling blackened, the walls ungarnished. It was the smallest of small cottages, but it was a clean and a tidy one, well-kept and well-swept, with boxes of pretty flowers that Mrs. Juniper herself might have envied.

"Are you at home, Mother?" the boy called out, stepping in at the door.

"Here, Tim," answered a voice. His mother looked up from her sewing in her chair by the hearth. His little sister Kate stood beside her at the fire, stirring a pot of thin soup. The boy went immediately to his mother and embraced her, and Kate, too, and presented them with the remainders from lunch. Then he gave his mother the golden guineas he had received from Mr. Threadneedle.

"What are these?" she asked, drawing in her breath. Her eyes went wide; a look of fearful amazement came into her face, magnifying its pale and wintry aspects and traces of past affliction. "Where did you get this money, Tim?"

"Timothy, did you pinch them? Do tell!" cried his sister, managing to look appalled and overjoyed in the same instant.

"Of course I didn't pinch them, silly Kate! Don't be such a foolish thing. These are from Mr. Threadneedle," her brother explained.

"Oh, Tim, we can't accept his gifts," said their mother.

"They aren't gifts, Mother, they're wages for assisting Mr. Threadneedle in the coach-house. He said it is money I have earned, and as he can't make me a proper 'prentice, he'll not deny me proper wages. He was most insistent."

"But he's already given you small sums for the hours you have spent there. These are guineas, Tim, guineas! Why, this is more money than — than —"

She nearly said *more money than you are worth,* but checked herself in the nick of time.

She looked at the coins in her hand, and then at her only son. So bright, so cheerful, so genuine a boy he was — and worth ever so much more than five golden guineas! How could she have spoken, or very nearly spoken, so slightingly of him? Her heart smote her for it, and for the timidity and low esteem her station in life had bred in her. Why, the disproportion between shining guineas and shining Tim was vast beyond measure! *Of course* his labor was worth the money — how could she have thought otherwise? She bit her lip, hard, and from that moment felt her resolve oozing away.

"Mr. Threadneedle told me I am like a real 'prentice to him," Tim said. "He was a grocer and can't bind me by articles except to grocering, and grocering isn't tinkering. He looks forward to the company, too, for I think he must have very little at Smithy Bank but for Foxy and Mustard. He misses having a 'prentice round to help him. He seems to me one of the best-hearted men in existence — a very good man, but a lonely one."

"Mr. Plush and Mrs. Kimber," said his mother, sighing and nodding; then, after a little pause — "But guineas, Tim, guineas!"

"I think I should like to have some guineas," said Kate, "though I've never seen one before today. Oh, Mother, do let us keep them!"

"It's a great deal of money, Kate."

"Oh, yes, a monstrous deal!"

Tears were standing in the eyes of their mother, but she dashed them away. She put her bobbins and cushions aside and rose from her chair, and took the face of her son into her hands and kissed it.

"Five golden guineas!" Kate exclaimed. "Why, it's more than twenty silver crown-pieces — more than a hundred shillings — it's a ransom!"

"May the Almighty bless and keep him," said her mother. "May the Almighty bless Mr. Threadneedle. And what is the nature of this work, Tim, for which he's engaged you these months? What is this 'tinkering' of his?"

Her son hesitated a moment, shuffling his feet and squirming a little in his shoes. "It's — it's — it's still unfinished, Mother. Mr. Threadneedle has asked that I tell no one of his work for now. It requires more tinkering yet to reach that stage of perfection he desires. But, Mother, I tell you," he whispered, his face aglow at the secret thought of it — *"it's a wizard notion!"*

"Well," said his mother, looking again at the pretty coins, which to her were like ingots of gold, "who am I to press, or to pry? I'm a poor untutored washerwoman, one with a bright and shining boy for a son, who has taken his lessons at the chapel school to heart and now is a working-man with wages to show."

"And what of me, Mother?" asked Kate, twining her arms about her parent. "You'll not forget me?"

"You, too, are my joy and my life," said her mother, kissing her in turn.

"You keep our home tidy and can sew most excellent well. Your hands are young and strong, unlike these poor, tired, wretched things of mine. Already forty summers have passed over my head, Kate — forty summers!"

"Then please, please, Mother, may we keep the money? May we keep Mr. Threadneedle's golden guineas?"

Another minute's thought on the part of Mrs. Christmas; but it was all unnecessary — her resistance had quite drained away. She answered with a quick little nod, then turned to her son, her bright and shining boy. "We must thank Mr. Threadneedle for his generosity."

"That I have, Mother, several times already," said Tim.

"And we must thank Mr. Yorridge, too, for it was he who obtained your place for you at Smithy Bank. And of course we must offer a prayer to the Almighty, every day, for sending us Mr. Threadneedle and his wizard notion — whatever it may be!"

CHAPTER ELEVEN

In Mock Alley

This coffee-house of Sprig's was situated along a narrow, cramped passage called Mock Alley, one in which the upper floors of the houses on either side came jutting out over the heads of passers-by, murderously, like eaves. Mock Alley was so cramped and narrow a passage that a lowly pony-chaise, unladen, its driver bent forward with his head approximating the level of his knees, and his hat off, might just squeeze through it — on a good day. Why it was called Mock Alley no one exactly knew. Popular opinion held it was due to the fact that it *was* so very cramped and narrow, so much more like a dim corridor than an alley, and so was guilty of an imposture, enjoying the same relationship to other alleys as mock turtle has to turtle soup.

If one were going to Sprig's, one had to do it deliberately. One did not pass by in a carriage and decide on impulse to stop in, for one couldn't pass by Sprig's in a carriage at all; one had to be set down in an adjacent avenue of regular dimensions, like Bluefin Street or Great Codger Lane, and cover the remaining distance on foot. In truth most people walked to Sprig's, rather than rode or drove there, for its location was very convenient to clerical society (it was not so far from the Minster), and to Thespian society (it was a mere stone's chuck from the theaters), and to nautical society (it was just up the road from the quay), and to most every other society besides.

Sprig's was a cordial kind of place, and an ancient one, most of the existing neighborhood having sprung up around it long after its founding, like saplings round a hoary oak. Its public room served to fortify this notion, for it was positively stuffed with oak, in the shape of sturdy beams and pillars, burnished panels, and carved wainscoting. The floors were sanded, and the walls hung with prints of antique lineage, depicting fanciful woodland scenes or horses dashing over ground, the very kinds of prints for which coaching-inns are justly famed. But Sprig's wasn't a coaching-inn; indeed it wasn't any kind of inn at all, for it took no lodgers. Rather it was a place of resort for those with a liking for witty chat and pleasant discourse, and who relished fine coffees and cakes, scones, sandwiches, cherry wine, punch and negus, in an atmosphere of conviviality.

The noted chess rooms of Sprig's, which were gained through a door behind the bar, were scenes of high drama as fine as any in the town theaters. One could go to Sprig's to play chess, or to watch it played; to enjoy the company of others, or simply the company of one's self and a city paper; to learn new things, to scoop up fresh news from town, or the latest tidings from afar from those coming in off the ships. The coffee-house was a mint of information, and it was for this reason that Mr. Liffey, Fred and Susan Cargo, and Miss Veal made their way there one afternoon, a day or two after their arrival in the city.

Upon their approach a liveried youth standing by the door greeted them with a solemn leg, and collected the requisite penny-a-head for entry. He then rang the bell for a waiter, a thin, harried sort with a face like gruel, who ushered the visitors to a table.

As they were being ushered, they passed what looked to be a kind of shrine, set up on a dresser near the broad stone hearth. It consisted of a gilded cat's-head letter-box, approximately breast-high, which had its jaws spread wide and an opening in its mouth "for the receipt to all hours of such correspondence as shall be tossed into it." (This information was found on a plate affixed to the box.) Above the letter-box hung a miniature escutcheon and coat of arms depicting a golden lion rampant-guardant on a black field, its tongue and claws a glittering red. On a blanket beside the box, like some potentate at ease on his royal couch, lay a dozing cat.

The cat bore some faint resemblance to his gilded cousin on the letter-box, what with his fluffy jowls, his teeth, his serene and noble presence. A small brass plate before his couch was inscribed with the name SIR SHARP-NAIL in a regal hand, as though in designation of some Mighty Knight of the Realm. But it was only Sir Sharp-nail, a "cat of parts," as the landlord called him; Sir Sharp-nail, guardian of coffee-house correspondence and resident household deity. To have "fed the cat" at Sprig's was, in common parlance, to have left a message in the cat's-head letter-box, to be called for by the addressee at his convenience and discretion.

"I see you've made the acquaintance of Sir Sharp-nail," smiled Mr. Tozer, the landlord and one of the city's most noted coffee men, who came to greet the visitors as they settled into their chairs. "He is our ruling spirit of sorts, our talisman of the house and master of the post."

"It's a very *large* cat," said Miss Veal, eyeing it distrustfully. As we know, Miss Veal was frightened of horses, and she was none too fond of cats besides. For all she knew, the ruling spirit might arise from his torpor when her back was turned and fling himself at her wig.

"Which is in keeping with his very substantial duties and obligations," explained Mr. Tozer, a sort of scholarly lion of a landlord with a mass of white hair and whiskers, bookish spectacles, and a beaming countenance. "Sir Sharp-nail is our custodian of the mails, or so we fancy him."

"That is an actual post-box there?" said Mr. Liffey.

"It is, sir, in the sense that it is an actual *Sprig's* post-box, for the convenience of customers wishing to post letters here, or to call for them, in respect of certain private and particular business. There are those of our customers, sir, whose affairs are, shall we say, of a delicate or confidential nature, and who may desire that the whereabouts of their lodgings be kept private. We strive to accommodate them."

"I can understand how such a need might arise," said Fred, "but why not call for their mail at the General Post Office?"

"Ordinarily an eminent solution, sir, but as a practical matter an imperfect one," replied Mine Host. "For a gentleman must sign for certain letters, don't you see, at the general window, and present such proof of identity as he mayn't wish to disclose, or may not have about his person, or as may not exist. And if he is a box-holder there, well, he must be prepared to stand on record as one, which leaves him open to identification. And we're all aware of the garrulousness and scandal-mongering of general postmen! Well, we have no such trouble here at Sprig's, sir."

"Tell us, Mr. Tozer, who distributes these letters of a delicate and confidential nature? Who gives them out when they are called for? Certainly not your cat there!" said Susan.

"I confess, certain of the functions of postmaster do fall within the province of my own duties," Mr. Tozer admitted. "But we must take care and not reveal an iota of this to Sir Sharp-nail — it might affect him profoundly. He believes himself to be wholly in charge."

"As would any self-respecting cat," noted Mr. Liffey.

"Would one of these customers of yours, landlord, by chance be a person named Squailes?" Susan asked, getting briskly to the point.

Mr. Tozer paused for a moment to consider, then shook his head.

"It is an unfamiliar name. But perhaps you might inquire of the staff. They've a broad sphere of acquaintance in their own right."

The lion of a landlord hastening off upon an errand, his place was taken by the thin waiter with the face like gruel, who was similarly unhelpful with respect to the mysterious Mr. Squailes. He was, however, fully capable of imparting much useful knowledge as regards the bill of fare, which spurred the visitors to place their order for a round of coffee and *et ceteras*.

While waiting for the food to appear, the visitors had some leisure to look about them at the public room and those gathered there.

"I recollect hearing something of this house in my sailing days," said Mr. Liffey. "Our captain put in here at Nantle on a few occasions. What I remember most is talk of the vaunted chess rooms. You'll recall our waiter at the Crozier made reference to them."

"You didn't visit the coffee-house yourself then, sir?"

"No."

"I am happy to find that the company of women is welcomed here," said Miss Veal, stiffly, "for if women had not been welcome, I should not have come."

"And I've little doubt you should be welcome in the chess rooms, too, Miss Veal, should you find them to your taste," said the attorney. "Although it's been my experience that the grand and princely game of combat has drawn its adherents more usually from the ranks of men."

"We are not interested in chess rooms or games of combat, Mr. Liffey," Susan reminded him. "We have not traveled so far to watch a pair of tired drones nodding over a chess-board. We have come to find this beastly scoundrel of a person named Squailes and discover what hold he has on our family. If he was able to squeeze money out of Frederick's grandfather, he may attempt the same with us. We must learn who he is and what his game is. We are here on a matter of vital importance, sir, a matter of principle. Is that not so, Aspasia?"

"It is," said Miss Veal, with perfect indifference to any fool who might think otherwise.

"And I mean to put the matter right."

"If it can be put right, dear," said her husband.

"Now, Susan, I quite agree with you insofar as our purpose is to find Mr. Squailes," said Mr. Liffey, as the coffee and *et ceteras* were laid upon the board. "Once we've refreshed ourselves, Fred and I shall do some inquiring among the people here."

"Capital idea!" said Fred — likely he meant more the refreshing part than the inquiring part — and dove at once into the comestibles. "This coffee is very good. In fact, it's damned delightful! Don't you agree, sir?"

"The scones are excellent," said Mr. Liffey. "Please — indulge yourself, Miss Veal."

"Yes, have a scone, Miss Veal. It'll buck you up tremendously," Fred urged.

"Thenk yaw," replied the lady, with a gracious inclination of her wig.

"Nantle, Headcorn, Goforth — we paid call at most of the southern ports in my sailing days," said Mr. Liffey. "They were all of them interesting places to visit, especially for a young man like myself who'd seen little of the world beyond the gray streets of Chiddock. There is a world of wonder to be found in these old channel ports."

"Nantle, Headcorn, Goforth — hardly what I should call *the world*, sir," said a voice close at hand.

Startled, Mr. Liffey and his companions glanced up to behold a man standing in a doorway hard by. Evidently he had been giving ear to their conversation, an action which Mrs. Cargo and Miss Veal found highly impertinent. As to his age, it was impossible to determine, though he seemed rather younger than older, what with the mop of sooty-black hair that covered his brow. His eye was lean, his countenance swart, his mustache shabby, and as for his chin, he had left off shaving it days ago. He was attired in a blue frieze coat, much worn, and a striped waistcoat, ditto, drab trouserings, and boots much scuffed and begrimed. He had one hand propped against the door-post and a cup of cherry wine in the other. It was plain he was much enamored of the cherry wine; nonetheless his head seemed clear enough, and his demeanor friendly enough, despite his negligent appearance and his rudeness in listening at the door.

The stranger introduced himself in the simplest of terms ("The name's Devenham"), made a bow to the ladies as they were presented (the ladies still flushing at his impertinence), and touched an invisible hat-brim to Fred and Mr. Liffey.

"You were saying something about the world, sir?" Fred asked.

"And a dreadfully sorry state it's in, don't you think?" said the stranger. "What there is left of it, of course — just this long coast, from the frozen cities of the north to the southern wastes, and these islands in the channel. And there it is, that's the lot of it, man. So much for civilization. So much for mankind since the sundering! But it's all we've got, sir, all we've got, and it has become my life's object to visit every last corner of it."

This speech he concluded with an explosion of noise in his nostrils, like something between a laugh and a snort, and took a gulp of his wine.

"That's the sad history of things since the comet struck, or the volcano blew up, or whatever the deuce it was," Fred nodded.

"And what there is left of the world, sirs and ladies, *I* have seen," the stranger boasted.

"You are a traveler, Mr. Devenham?" inquired Mr. Liffey.

"I am, sir — a lonely wanderer over the face of nature," the other replied with a little flourish of his hand in the air, the one with the cup in it. "I have visited Saxbridge in the icy north. I have been to Salthead and toured its famed university and the halls of the Plaxtonian Museum. I have trod the streets of Richford, the sad, decayed city in the east, in the ancient county of Ruffolk. I have contended with disputatious ministers at Fishmouth, in the limewood corridors of governance there. I have seen Crow's-end, and Candlebury, and Newmarsh. I have journeyed overland into the provinces — into deepest Ayleshire, into Fenshire, Broadshire, Chestershire — with the mastodon men. I have been to Medlow town, and Winstermere, and have roamed the lonely peaks of Talbotshire. I have sailed upon the Bay of Foghampton and fished its waters, and dipped my boot into the oily tar-pools of Deeping St. Magma. I have sailed right round the islands in the channel, and far to the south of them, beyond the fringes of the cities. And I have seen what lies beyond."

"And what does lie beyond, sir?" asked Miss Veal.

"Wilderness, lady!" exclaimed Mr. Devenham, waving his cup again. (The wine being nearly gone, he was in little danger of spilling any.) "Nothing but a ceaseless, trackless wilderness, here waste, there forests graduating into rainy lagoons. A wilderness of ungainly camels, hulking megatheres, armor-backed glyptodonts, shovel-tuskers, and other beasts out of number. Saber-cats and panthers, lady. Dirk-tooths. Short-faced bears in the mountains. Teratorns prowling the skies, monstrous zeugs lurking in the seas. And more!"

"You are indeed a traveler of the first water, sir," admired Fred. "Is this by way of your occupation?"

Mr. Devenham laughed and snorted — a bit too loudly, perhaps, owing to the volume of wine he had consumed — and raised his cup.

"The world is my occupation, sir," he answered, majestically. "I live in it, I breathe it in, and it sustains me. In return I ask nothing of the world but to be allowed to roam in it, and contemplate its mysteries. All I ask of the world is that it *let me be.* I must have my freedom, sir. I must be free of the petty, puling cares of ordinary existence. Out of pocket, always out of pocket — and yet I don't care a fig for money! Money is a care, and so I must be free of it. What's money to me? Nothing. I must be free to contemplate the world, sir. Nothing so common as foul coin must bind or hinder me. It is my end in life, my appointed lot. It would be wrong to deny it.

Man, man, I can shrug it off no more than I can shrug off this skin of mine."

"Have you no family, Mr. Devenham?" asked Susan, after a little pause, during which the stranger seemed to lose himself in a restless fog of contemplation. This was another peculiarity of his, this drifting from mood to mood, from joy to gloom, from dark to light and back again; one moment looking very profound, as though he were busy calculating the weight of the world, the next grinning like the proverbial cat that has swallowed the mouse; or perhaps it was simply the cherry wine.

"Lady, you amuse me, truly you do," said Mr. Devenham, smiling at Susan as if he pitied her to the utmost extent of his being. "I have no need or use of family. Do not plague me with the thought of family! Families are such scurvy, vexatious, pestering things. The improvidence, the insolence, the atrocity of families! I'll have no truck with them. Oh, it's all very well, lady, when one is young like yourself" — (Susan secretly pleased) — "and knows next to nothing of the world" — (Susan not so pleased) — "but once one knows something of the world, one longs to be free of the tiresome monotony of *family*. The shackles, the curbs, the assaults upon liberty. The puling sentimentality of it, the dreariness, the sameness — and a sentence for life to boot! No, no — a family, lady, is an ugly business. I'll have none of it. Instead I long for spaciousness. I must have it; it is part and parcel of my being. I am for living in the moon, for chewing live bumblebees, for anything but *family*. Oh, no, no, lady — spare me the whining, confining prison-house of family!"

"But Mr. Devenham, have you no home? Have you no friends?" said Miss Veal.

"All life is but a wandering to find home, lady. And as for friends, they have little meaning for me. They are dross and disappointing things, every one, and I must be free of them. Even more I must be free of clergymen! I must have spaciousness. I am and must be mine own content. You seem shocked by this? Well, I am plain Dunstable, lady — I say what I feel."

As it happened, there was a balding, grizzle-cheeked clergyman sitting at the next table. He had been enjoying his paper and his dish of twist, but he looked up now as this latest speech came flying from the lips of Mr. Devenham. In the next instant, at the seeming pinnacle of his performance, the lonely wanderer noticed that his cup was in need of filling; and so he detached himself from the party and went off in search of cherry wine. This opportunity afforded Fred a chance to inquire of the clergyman, once the proper introductions had been gone through —

"Is he always so, sir? This Mr. Devenham?"

The clergyman patted his lips with a napkin, and looked over his blunt little stub of a nose at Fred and the others, with eyes peering from under thick dark brows. "Always," he replied, matter-of-factly.

"Is he a player? An actor in a theater?"

The reverend gentleman seemed to find humor in the question. "Hardly, sir. He is a noted idler, a picturesque vagrant of the dockyards, who never sees fit to come to church. He is impervious — wholly impervious — to the teachings of the Christian religion, and to all overtures of the clergy. He is, in the opinion of myself and most in this parish, a rank atheist. Though to his credit, Black Davy does possess some few scraps of learning."

"Black Davy? Who is Black Davy?"

"Mr. Devenham," said the clergyman. "Mr. David Devenham — though to most everyone he is Black Davy."

"Why is that, vicar?" asked Susan, in the polite voice she reserved for gentlemen of the cloth. "Is he some kind of criminal?"

"A criminal?" echoed Miss Veal, gripping her reticule. "This really is too much!"

"Perhaps," the clergyman replied, a trifle testily, as though hearing the word *vicar* used in connection with himself had stung him in his sensibilities — "though to my knowledge he has never been put to the bar at the quarter sessions. No, he is called Black Davy because of his general temper of mind, his solitariness, his prickly view of life. He is subject to the megrims — low spirits, you know — and is often out of sorts. And yet at other times he can be the boonest of companions. We in the church have tried to cure him of his affliction, but I fear our Mr. Devenham is proof against any such endeavor. He has such a belief in his own arguments, he will not be moved by Christian precepts; his recalcitrance is, I fear, a permanent condition. He is not so ungenial a fellow, however, despite his moods, and he does tend to rattle on a bit — chiefly about himself."

"His philosophy seems to me rather a self-interested one," said Mrs. Cargo. "He is a man somewhat too fond of his own way, I think."

"And what he would tell you in reply," said the clergyman, "is that all of life teaches one to be self-interested, that selfishness itself is no vice. That indeed nature herself is a selfish thing, and demands selfishness from her creatures if they are to survive. Isn't *that* a pretty doctrine to hang one's hat on?"

"Beastly!" Susan exclaimed, looking properly horrified. "He is like a great bladder swollen up with love of himself."

"Selfishness is a blight," sniffed Miss Veal.

"Ah, I fear he'll chop logic with you all day on that score. And there," said the clergyman, "you have Black Davy in a nutshell. I'm afraid there is nothing before him but ruin."

"Has he indeed traveled to all the places he boasts of?" Fred wanted to know. "For 'pon my life, I'm quite astounded by it."

The clergyman shrugged. "It may be, sir. He has been known to absent himself from town for long periods, and has served more than once aboardship. I suppose he could very well have visited the places he describes."

And so the reverend gentleman returned to his paper and his dish of twist, happy not to have heard the word *vicar* used again in reference to himself. A brief period of quiet ensued at the travelers' table, as the information about Mr. Devenham was digested, in concert with the coffee and *et ceteras*.

"Well, I myself should like to see the chess rooms," said Mr. Liffey, preparing to rise.

"I'll accompany you, sir," Fred offered.

"And leave Aspasia and myself alone here?" exclaimed his wife, in tones rather sterner than those she had bestowed upon the reverend gentleman of the cloth. "Frederick, where is your consideration of late? I am starting to believe you left it behind you at Tiptop Grange. Are you becoming as bladderish as Mr. Devenham?"

"But my dear Susan, it would not interest you," her husband protested, not unreasonably. "You told us so yourself."

"That is your justification?"

For this stopper Fred had no answer; indeed, we suspect few husbands would. In vain he glanced helplessly from his sharp-eyed wife to his kindly-eyed solicitor — from his fair enslaver to his special pleader, as it were — hoping against hope that Mr. Liffey might have some way out, some trick under his hat, some lawyer's dodge acquired from his years of experience.

He did.

"We shan't be long," the attorney said. "We shall inquire after Mr. Squailes there. If he is known to gentlemen of this city, they may very well be among the gentlemen frequenting the chess rooms. And such gentlemen may be more at their ease confiding their knowledge *in camera*, and in the presence of two gentlemen of like character, namely Fred and myself."

Having never been himself a *particeps criminis* — a partner in the crime of matrimony — Mr. Liffey found it a less troublesome matter to evade the snares and toils of a wife than did Fred, a poor ensnared husband. The grounds for their errand having been set forth, the gentlemen crossed the room and strode through the door back of the bar, to find themselves in one of two connecting chambers of middling size. A number of persons were assembled there, some in arm-chairs and some on their legs, gathered two and three deep round a central table. The attention of all was on the table and its loaded chess-board, and on the two haughty knights locked in battle there.

A fire was burning in a tiled fireplace. Before it a rough-coated dog lay on the hearth-rug, soaking in the warmth and atmosphere of the place, with, we assume, the generous leave of Sir Sharp-nail. On the mantel stood a bust of the immortal Philidor, the renowned French master of the game, who had amazed the London world with his blindfolded play — all of it many long, long years ago, of course, before the sundering.

Mr. Liffey edged forward a little, with Fred close behind, for a glimpse of the haughty knights and the state of the game. The combatants were, on the one side, a handsome young spark, neat, cravated, contemptuous, with a headful of hair, a screw of it oiled and curled over each temple in the ultra pitch of fashion; on the other, a gentleman of mature years, calm, assured, amused even, one eyebrow confidently arched, wearing a careless brown beard and a matching suit.

It was the young spark's move. He had been contemplating the arrangement of his forces for some ten minutes at least, hunched over the board with a terrible concentration. His opponent meanwhile had thrown himself back in his chair and was awaiting the result with an easy-going disdain.

"Turcott and Rainbow," murmured a voice.

Mr. Liffey turned to find the interesting Mr. Devenham inches from his right ear — Black Davy, vagrant of the dockyards and wanderer over the face of nature, his cup new-charged with cherry wine.

"Sorry?"

"The tidy fellow with the curls — that's Turcott," said Davy, taking care to point the gentleman out. "He's a play-actor with the company in Stinking Lane. The other is Rainbow — he's a theater critic. They've been contending for months now."

"Months?"

"They've knocked off six-and-fifty games so far, with thirty drawn and the rest evenly divided. It's a duel, sir, without the small-swords."

"How so?" asked Fred, intrigued.

"High words, man. Turcott called Rainbow out, demanding satisfaction, and as they're both crack players, they meant to settle it at chess. Turned out it was a drawn game. A second game was arranged — same result. Unsatisfied they made it into a match. That was eight months ago and they've been at it since, game after game — real cut-and-thrust stuff at times, up to the very hilts, with hammer-blows on both sides — whenever Turcott can wrest himself away from the theater, and Rainbow from his scribbling. They engage forces for as long as they're able, then resume their respective trades until they're free again to pursue the match. And so it's gone on and on, with no end in sight, and each wishing the other the fate of Cicero."

"Astonishing!"

"There's young Turcott, teeming with spite and spleen. A bitter apple, that one! And there's old Rainbow, not one to take sauce from a whelp like Turcott. Which one will go to the wall? Which one will shatter under the strain? It's what most everyone's waiting for."

"I've never seen the like."

"And all completely above-board and by the book. You'll note that each is attended by a second — the fellows sitting just behind them."

"Seconds? *Dueling* seconds?"

Mr. Devenham nodded and snorted. He downed some more wine and wiped his lips with a dirty coat-sleeve. "And each of *them* a crack player to boot. There's Cruft the surgeon seconding for Turcott, and Mainyard the pettifogging attorney for Rainbow. By the by, did you know old Canute was a chess-player? It's said his pieces were made from the tusk of a walrus."

"I was not aware of that," said Fred.

"Though it's nothing, for at Saxbridge I saw pieces carved from the tusk of an imperial mammoth. And King Charles the First, he was a player, too, before he lost track of his head — now there's checkmate for you! Isn't that so, Lanthorne?"

This last was directed toward a gentleman very tall and broad — a manful man in a black caped overcoat, buff-colored breeches, and boots with painted tops — who was following the game with a grave, observing stare. He offered Mr. Devenham no response apart from a barely perceptible nod. Unlike most of the spectators, he was smoking neither pipe nor cigar, and drinking no drink. He seemed wholly intent on the play, which he was viewing through a pair of large eyes very dark and shiny.

"What was the inciting offense? The insult that precipitated the match?" inquired Mr. Liffey.

"A scurrilous review in the papers by Rainbow, concerning Mr. Swuff Turcott's performance as Young Thorney in *The Witch of Edmonton*. 'Pointless gesturing,' I believe, was one of his more potent barbs — 'unrelieved awfulness,' 'much noise to little purpose,' and the like. It got Turcott's gorge up and he made answer in the same paper, informing the public that Mr. Edmund Rainbow was 'the lowest form of Anthropophaginian that ever tasted meat.' Rainbow denied it, of course, replying by way of counterstroke that Turcott was 'an unmitigated example to dunder-whelps everywhere.' Well, you know where that sort of thing will lead. First they pounded each other in the press, and now they've got themselves this little combat, to be played out on a small field of sixty-four squares. For you know, man, the game of chess is much more than a mere intellectual struggle."

"Rather so," agreed Fred, who had never in his life sat down to a small field of sixty-four squares, even at draughts, and wouldn't know a hostile King-side from a handsaw. He was fonder of blooded horses in the flesh than of mounted Knights carved from a mammoth's tooth. But he did find the game of some interest, and moreover he was fascinated by Black Davy, this idler and vagabond who seemed to know a good deal about a lot of things Fred himself knew little of.

"The two have vowed never to speak to one another till one has been utterly demolished in body and spirit. Only then will the match be over. For chess is a game of war, man — a King hunt! — a fight to the death played out on that small field of sixty-four squares."

"Ah. Indeed. 'Pon my life, who is that?" Fred asked, his gaze attracted now by a woman, one who looked to be the only representative of her sex among the spectators. "The thin, square-shouldered woman there, with the rusty face and sharp features. The woman smoking a pipe."

"You refer to Trickle?"

"I've never seen a woman smoke a pipe before."

"Miss Betty Trickle. She holds sway over the fruit shop and tea room in Stinking Lane, hard by the theater."

"Does she play?" asked Mr. Liffey, who unlike Fred was an avid follower of the game.

"Like a demon," snorted Davy. "She has a *bona fide* chess brain, she does, and superintends the wagering. Wagers nothing herself, mind you — just handles the coin and accounting. She's trustworthy. Upstanding as a kitchen-poker."

Having downed the rest of his wine, Black Davy observed that his cup was empty again and, without a word to either Fred or Mr. Liffey, vanished in the direction of the bar.

Minutes passed. At last the young Turcott roused himself and with scorn dripping from his every pore executed the long-delayed move. All watched in rapt suspense, looking for the expected counterstroke from Rainbow. A tide of comment flowed among the onlookers as they waited, regarding the quality of play, the placement of forces, and the strategy of the combatants, *viz.* —

FIRST GENTLEMAN: White is a Bishop down and his Rook is *en prise*. If he doesn't take care, he'll lose his head, and the game.

SECOND GENTLEMAN: Black's Pawn must queen now or later.

THIRD GENTLEMAN: I fear he may overreach himself. His forces are not so well-placed.

SECOND GENTLEMAN: I disagree. White's Queen-side is bound to come a cropper.

THIRD GENTLEMAN: I believe he can force a draw.

FIRST GENTLEMAN: Impossible. He simply has no play.

SECOND GENTLEMAN: It's but a matter of time, sir. His remaining Bishop has little scope, and his Queen's Knight is stalemated.

THIRD GENTLEMAN: Black's position is cramped and his Queen is out of play. His fate is very much in the balance. Another draw is the best to be hoped for.

FIRST GENTLEMAN: Are you blind, sir? Black has pressed his advantage admirably — he'll be threatening mate.

MISS TRICKLE: Too much wood-shifting, gentlemen, too much wood-shifting! Hardly an elegant game. In my view it's a botched job.

Fred's glance strayed again to the square-shouldered Miss Trickle and her pipe, then to the tall, broad gentleman standing close by, he of the caped overcoat and top-boots and shiny dark eyes. Although he felt oddly disturbed by the presence of this man — just why he had no idea, though perhaps it had something to do with the strange luster of those eyes — Fred felt he must persevere regardless. As he was about to inquire of the gentleman, whose name apparently was Lanthorne, if he knew a fellow called Squailes, Mr. Liffey touched him on the arm to remind him that they ought to rejoin the others, for he had assured Susan and Miss Veal that they wouldn't be long.

"What did you find?" demanded Mrs. Cargo, upon their return.

"There's a capital match going on in there," said her husband. "It's a duel. They've been at it for months."

"One of the men there is risking his King even at this moment," said Mr. Liffey.

"I was referring, sir, to Mr. Jerry Squailes," returned Susan, coolly. "Well, Frederick? What did you find?"

Her husband's face registered his embarrassment. He looked at Mr. Liffey, who was equally up a stump, although he concealed it well beneath his pink and kindly visage.

"No one to whom we spoke claimed an acquaintance with him," Fred stated. It was altogether the truth — a lawyerly sort of truth, the kind of which any respectable practitioner of the law would be justly proud. "I'm afraid we're still rather in the dark. But not to worry, dear, we shall ferret him out."

"I agree," said Mr. Liffey. "It's early days yet. We shall find him."

"We had better," said a determined Susan.

"What of that vicar?" Fred asked, glancing round.

"He has just this moment gone," his wife told him.

"Well, he should be a capital source of information. You asked him about Mr. Squailes, of course?"

Susan, caught for once in her own snare, traded glances with Miss Veal, and was obliged to admit that she had not. But she had *meant* to. The good clergyman had been so absorbed in his paper and his dish of twist, she had not wished to disturb him further. As for the clergyman himself, still smarting from the word *vicar* — for he was in truth a full-blown rector, and the holder of a prebend in Nantle Minster, and a Doctor of Divinity besides — he hadn't particularly wanted to be disturbed further, not by Susan at any rate, and had not encouraged her conversation.

Which was all something of a triumph and a relief for Fred, who for all his wife knew had been hard at it gathering information in the chess rooms, while she herself had failed to question a sitting gentleman of the cloth.

"Perhaps we may catch him up," Fred suggested. He strode to the house-door and stepped outside, but there was no sign of the clergyman. The liveried youth, however, identified him as a Dr. Pinches, from the church and rectory of St. Mary-le-Quay. This news Fred promptly relayed to the others, with a view to seeking out the gentleman at a more convenient time. He and Mr. Liffey then moved to the bar and subjected some of the customers there to the usual queries, from which they derived the usual responses. They searched for the interesting Mr. Devenham, but he had given them the slip; likely he had returned to the chess rooms. With little hope of success now, they were disposed to call it an afternoon. Nobody had heard of Mr. Squailes; certainly if he were a person of prominence in the neighborhood, somebody should have.

They paid the reckoning, took up their hats and umbrellas, and offered their parting devoirs to Sir Sharp-nail lazing on his throne. Emerging into Mock Alley, they bent their steps in the direction of comfort and cloisters, namely the Crozier. As they venture on their way, let us instead bend our own steps in the direction opposite, and follow in the track of the testy clergyman to the church and rectory of St. Mary-le-Quay.

CHAPTER TWELVE

A View from the Minster

The Rev. Giddeus Pinches, D.D., had held the living of St. Mary-le-Quay for more than a few years. He was considered by most in the parish to be an efficient, effective clergyman, and a fair sermonizer in the pulpit, one well-versed in all manner of the proper texts; a reverend gentleman of solemn perspicacity; a just man, a worthy priest, a credit to his cloth. What most in the parish did not know, however, was that he was also very bored.

After the many years of attendance on his flock the doctor had simply grown tired of it all. He was disappointed he had not advanced further in his sacred calling. Considering his education, he should have become a steady light in the clerical firmament; as it was he barely registered a single candle-power. True, he was the rector of a city parish, and he had a modest — a *very* modest — prebend in the Minster, with the sole stipulation that he give a sermon there once a year on a topic of his choice. This bit of preferment gave him regular admittance to the cathedral and its body corporate, to the homes of the minor canons and the other prebendaries — learned gentlemen all — and to dinners at the deanery; more important, it gave him admittance to the magnificent cathedral library and its reading-room.

Dr. Pinches was himself a learned man, a Doctor of Divinity, but this only added to his frustration. Why, why had he not risen further in the ranks of the ecclesiastical hierarchy? Why was he, the Rev. Giddeus Pinches, D.D., at the ripe age of sixty still ministering to common sailors and other dockyard folk in the humble parish of St. Mary-le-Quay? Why was he wearing away his life among the noisy denizens of the quay, when his true calling lay in the cloistered and reflective atmosphere of the glorious Minster on the hill?

The doctor much preferred dipping into the ancient books and manuscripts in the cathedral library to serving the poor and destitute, or even the well-to-do. He was, in short, fed up with his present situation, and this among other things made him testy. Vicar? *Vicar?* He was no vicar, no mere hired clergyman! Those meddlesome people at Sprig's might as well have called him *curate;* it would have stung him just the same.

For a lifetime he had administered to the temporal and spiritual wants of his parishioners. He had by now quite satisfied every requirement of his calling, and outlived his interest in it. In the process he had watched his opportunities, one by one, pass him by. Or perhaps he hadn't gone after them with so much zeal as he might have? Perhaps he had been too indolent, too reserved to promote himself. Perhaps he had expected opportunities to flow naturally to him, so self-evident were his talents. The patronage of the diocese lay in the Bishop's gift, but the Bishop knew him not from Adam. Were it not for his prebend and his visits to the library, he sighed, he should have nothing whatever to look forward to upon waking in the morning.

Which was not completely true, of course, for the doctor did have his sister Griselda, who lived with him at the rectory. Miss Pinches was about ten years younger than her brother and like him had never been married. She was a gentle, kind, peaceful creature, who attended to his every need and ran the household better than any housekeeper at a fat £60 per annum ever could. It was she who saw to it that all his comforts were assured. Truth to tell, the doctor really was quite snug there at the rectory, and in want of nothing. He had shelter, food, and leisure. He had no fear of debt; he had his income from the living and a handsome private supplement, and he had his dear sister, who acted also as his cook. She baked the doctor his cherished warden pies, superintended his wine-cellar, and saw that all was in order. He had a housemaid or two as well, and a gardener, and a servant called Cowle — a gloomy, bearded, bespectacled old quiz, even older and balder than the doctor himself — who said little but groaned a lot, and seemed always to be in danger of toppling over.

Still the doctor saw no future for himself at St. Mary-le-Quay or in the diocese of Nantle, despite passing as many hours as possible up at the Minster mixing with his fellow clergy, and often with the Dean himself. As for the Bishop and the Archdeacon, well, they were on quite another plane altogether. Dr. Pinches was only rarely invited to the palace to mingle with these higher powers, whose realm was too celestial for a mere dockside clergyman, and as far removed from the world of the Minster as the Minster was from St. Mary-le-Quay.

It was not that Dr. Pinches was unpopular with his congregation; quite the contrary, he was not. His parishioners tolerated him as much as parishioners will tolerate most any pastor. But of late his mind had exhibited a marked tendency to wander, his eyes a habit of fixing themselves on some distant, unseen prospect. More often than not the doctor appeared restless and dissatisfied, often nodding and musing to himself in public as if no one else was there. He was easily distracted, inclined to be short, and seemed at times not to listen — all of which his flock set down to impaired hearing, or incipient decay of the brain. But it was in truth nothing of either kind; it was simply the Rev. Giddeus Pinches, D.D., wishing he were someplace else.

In the blaze of youth he had hurled himself into his priestly duties with relish. He had preached his sermons and ministered to his flock, baptized their young, married them, visited their sick, mourned their dead. Over the course of years, however, his love of learning had blossomed, even as the hairs on his head withered and his cheeks turned gray. *Time fleets, aye, Time fleets,* so the poet says, and the doctor knew it, too. The older he got, the more he valued the scholarship he had so taken for granted in his youth, and the less he valued his tiresome, humdrum, parochial mode of living. It was like a sickness, this need of his for learning; the more he learned, the more he wanted to learn; more and more, the love of learning had taken command of his life.

But as his need for learning grew, so did his jealousy of his fellow clergymen. Why should they have progressed so far in their careers when their breadth of knowledge was so much less than his? How cruel the injustices of fate, how unsearchable the workings of Providence! Perhaps his own advancement was simply not to be. As a result, the doctor found himself retreating to his adored books and manuscripts in the cathedral library, to assuage his damaged pride and feed this great hunger of his to *know more.* And as his love of learning grew, so his interest in his flock waned.

Some little share of this jealousy of the doctor's was directed at no less a person than the Dean of Nantle Minster himself. It pained him to the quick that the Dean was several years his junior — his *junior,* and not even a D.D.! — and yet his career was leaps and bounds ahead of the doctor's. Even the Dean's very appearance annoyed him, with that face so fresh and scrubbed and that head still rampant with thick, youthful hair. But advancement in the Church comes at a price. At the urging of his physician, the Dean had taken of late to the drinking of cow's milk, to ease his bouts of ecclesiastical dyspepsia, and sworn off wine and coffee — all of which would have suited Dr. Pinches not in the least, for he was a man who enjoyed his glass or two and his dish of twist.

His sister greeted him upon his return from the coffee-house, while his servant Cowle took his coat and hat and tottered off with them somewhere, groaning. Miss Pinches directed him to the sitting-room, where the tea-urn was in readiness, but the doctor begged off his cuppa in exchange for a small glass of sherry. His sister then proceeded to regale him with an account of all that had transpired at the rectory since his absence, which was not very much. To the doctor it was simply further proof how wearisome and monotonous his life had become, and how the Minster was where he really belonged. He had, he felt, been made for higher things.

The next morning the doctor emerged from the rectory and set off on his walk to the cathedral. This was his most leisured day of the week and he was determined to make the most of it. Stepping forth into the crisp, cool air, with a leaden sky overhead but no rain as of yet, he strode through the grounds past the parish rooms, and past the church of St. Mary itself, with its tall flint spire and decorations of battlements and tracery. Ancient, gray, and moldering the church was, but impressive-looking all the same for a humble dockside parish; or so the doctor used to think before he was so enamored of the Minster.

As he went along, he raised his hat to those of his flock he encountered in the road. For the doctor was not always so disappointed a man, or so lofty a one, or so unapproachable a one — particularly not today when he was on his way to his beloved Minster. He didn't exhibit that arrogance and superiority towards his fellow man that so many of his brethren did. He truly valued his calling, and he valued his parishioners, or had valued them — which is not to say he was prepared to give them the coat off his back, but he was prepared to give them *somebody's* coat — it was simply that he valued the Minster and her library more. He felt that at his age his precious hours ought to be made over to learning, and the work of the ministry left to younger, stronger men than he. He had done his duty; it was the turn of others to do theirs.

Onward and upward he jogged, across the climbing hillside toward the cathedral. As he drew near the brooding pile, his admiration for the Minster swelled afresh. There were the two massive square towers, there the imposing west front and lancet work, there the south porch, the chapter house beside the ivied walls of the cloister, and there the library and reading-room, above the arcade adjacent to the deanery. It was a fine old monastic edifice of gray stone, one which didn't take the weather very well, however, for like St. Mary-le-Quay, its fabric was heavily mildewed and rain-dropped, as though the gods were forever weeping on it.

For a moment or two the doctor peered in at the south door, to inhale something of the hush and mystery of its interior. Not surprisingly it was cold and dark inside the cathedral. In the side-aisles of the nave, threatening shadows loomed. Dim and somber forms lurked in niches and around corners, behind tall columns and under frowning arches. The many monuments, the tomb-chests with their alabaster effigies gazing on eternity, the canopied choir-stalls, the gaunt, empty pews exuded an aura of ethereal gloom. Evidence of humanity there was none. The morning services were over, the servitors had temporarily dispersed, the worshipers had gone their way, and preparations for the afternoon had yet to begin. It was solemn, still, and meditative in the Minster — just the way the doctor liked it.

Amid the gloom the doctor's eye fell upon a long and narrow strip of gold in the cathedral floor. It lay in the area of the crossing, and was ornamented with astronomical symbols at various points along its length. At first blush it might have been taken for a simple, if odd, decoration; but Dr. Pinches knew better. The strip of gold was what in an earlier age had been called a meridian line, or *meridiana*. It was used for tracking an image of the summer sun, which, when projected through a hole in the cupola, was seen to cross the line around the time of the solstice. The Romish monks of yore who built the Minster had adopted this ecclesiastical *camera obscura* from their Italian masters, who had been placing such devices in churches all over Italy for centuries. The *meridiane* were useful for making certain astronomical observations: for measuring the diameter of the sun, for example, or detecting changes in the angle of the earth's axis. The *meridiana* of the Minster, like its vanished Italian cousins, was a relic of times past, of brighter days in Nantle and in the world in general, when the sun had shone more and it had rained and snowed less — a reminder of just how much the world had changed since the great sundering.

The doctor withdrew his head, quietly shut the door, and strode round to the library, which was gained by means of an exterior staircase. There was no one in the reading-room when he arrived, which greatly pleased him. He drew a handsome folio volume from the shelves and settled down with it for his day's feast of learning.

The book he had chosen was one of his favorites, an old and very well-regarded text, the *History of Aegean Civilizations, Their Myths and Heroes*, by the late Professor Greenshields, M.A. (Salthd.). His early education had instilled in the doctor a love of the ancient classical world, and over the years he had read widely and voraciously in the field. Some might have thought it curious that a reverend doctor of the Church, an avowed Christian and a true believer, should find so much to interest him in the annals of what many would term a pagan society, with its multiplicity of gods; but there it was. Dr. Pinches loved his Horace, his Vergil, his Homer. He could read Greek and Latin as well or better than any man, and no amount of immersion in the Bible of King James or Cranmer's Prayer Book could offer half the pleasure he derived from his library pursuits. When he was in the reading-room with his Greenshields, he was as good as lost in a vanished world. The years and miles would all melt away, and he would find himself adrift on a steel-blue sea under a burning sun, in ageless days of old — in glorious Aegean days — when the earth was warm, the sky was bright, and mankind was new.

And so the hours sped by, as they are wont to do, and before long it was time for the doctor to return home for his dinner, which Miss Pinches would have waiting for him. With a sigh he bade farewell to his glorious Aegean days for another week, restored his treasured Greenshields to its place on the shelf, and took his leave.

In the cloisters he encountered the Dean coming out at his deanery door. An exchange of the usual civilities ensued, which the reverend gentlemen ran through in so bland and mannered a fashion that both could recite the text by heart.

"Good afternoon, Mr. Dean."

"Good afternoon, Dr. Pinches." (The Dean smiling complacently.)

"A brisk day, Mr. Dean."

"Brisk indeed, Dr. Pinches."

"There looks to be rain in the offing."

"No doubt, no doubt." (The Dean inspecting his umbrella.)

"And how fares my lord the Bishop these days?"

"His lordship attends to his duties with his customary zeal."

"And Mr. Archdeacon?"

"My lord is flourishing as well." (The Dean, pulling out his watch, frowns.)

"I am heartily glad of it. Well, I am off home to the rectory now, Mr. Dean. Good afternoon to you."

"Good afternoon to *you*, Dr. Pinches."

As they chatted, the doctor had observed again how very young and hale the Dean looked, in comparison to the bald and grizzled image the doctor had viewed that morning in his shaving-glass, and it depressed him.

All his day's study in the reading-room had gone for naught. He had been up, and now he was down again; for just as Black Davy was subject at times to fits of melancholy, so, too, was Dr. Pinches.

The doctor was about to plunge homeward toward the rectory, toward his sister and his waiting dinner, when his glance strayed to the gray square towers of the Minster rising above his head. The bells had chimed the hour some few minutes before, and so he should have the time he needed. If he was down now, the doctor reasoned, perhaps he could spirit himself up if he *went* up, literally, and took in the airy prospect from above.

So up he did go — up the winding stair of the nearer tower, up to the ringers' loft with its shadowy lengths of rope dripping from the bells, up and up, until he came at last to the belfry and to the bells themselves there in the top of the tower.

With scarcely a breath left him, he stood awhile gazing out upon the scene. Most all of Nantle lay scattered about the hillside below the cathedral and its close; in essence the whole of the town rolled down and away from the Minster to the sea. The tower's height served to accentuate the effect, so that from the belfry much of the city looked very far down and away indeed. A sweet silence hung over it all, broken by the occasional cawing of a rook which, like the Almighty Himself, called the Minster and her towers home.

In the distance the doctor could make out the spire of St. Mary-le-Quay, and something of the various neighborhoods of the city. An ordinary person might have experienced some little tingle of fear standing before a balustrade at such an altitude, but not Dr. Pinches. Indeed, he would have been as comfortable had he been perched atop the mighty pharos at Alexandria, or the colossus at Rhodes. It always exhilarated him and lifted his spirits.

Looking up, he saw with pleasure that a rift had opened in the clouds almost directly overhead, and that a flood of sunlight had begun pouring through. Not only that, there was a glimpse of blue sky in the opening. Blue sky at Nantle! It was something to give thanks for in this dreary season of the year. Moments later something dropped through the hole in the clouds — dropped silently down, straight, straight down — and came to a stop in the air over the Minster. There it remained, motionless, like a chandelier hanging by invisible wires from the vault of heaven.

Now what, the doctor asked himself, *just what in the Devil's name is THAT?*

The doctor put a hand to his eyes and shook his head gently, to rid himself of this impossible vision. When he looked again, however, it was still there — which caused the doctor to open his eyes very wide indeed. He craned out a little over the parapet and stared in blank amaze.

It could be nothing real, he told himself; no, no, it must be a dream. What other answer could there be? How could a house be floating there in the middle of the sky — a house, with a gable and windows, a high-pitched roof, a brick chimney, and a weather-vane — a house riding motionless on the air, with a few stray wisps of fog streaming past it and the flood of sunlight above?

The doctor grabbed hold of the balustrade to steady himself. For minutes as he watched it, the house hung perfectly still; then without warning it pivoted swiftly round, like a knob turning in a socket. Straight up it went, back through the opening in the overcast, as though drawn up to heaven by the aforementioned invisible wires. When last glimpsed, the impossible object was moving in a southerly direction, a course that would take it out over the frigid waters of the channel.

What, what could it have been?

The doctor, shaken by whatever it was he had witnessed — and by the knowledge that he had imbibed absolutely nothing of a nature as might account for it — descended the steps with an uneasy mind and, not bothering to lift his hat to anyone he passed in the street, made his troubled and thoughtful way home.

CHAPTER THIRTEEN

Mr. Sly Effects a Rescue

Now that the *Salty Sue* had returned to port, the captain had returned to hearth and home in Jolly Jumper Yard. The Yard was not far from the drowsy confines of Chamomile Street, nor from the church and rectory of St. Mary-le-Quay. Captain Barnaby was something of a Christian and a church-goer, whenever he was in town, and had a passing acquaintance with Dr. Pinches; but as the captain was in town but seldom, his acquaintance and church-going went largely for naught. It wasn't so much that the captain avoided the doctor, exactly, but he didn't seek him out either. Salty, stalwart, hatchet-faced old warrior of the sea that he was, and an independent thinker, the captain was by nature suspicious of those who professed to be *fishers of men*.

In short the captain didn't particularly like Dr. Pinches or any of the black coats of Nantle. He had little use for their pretensions and moralizing, or their tales of fires in unhallowed regions, and of a Deity minded to smite His creations like a child swatting bugs. He didn't consider himself in need of being saved from anything but the attentions of meddling priests. He didn't much care for their views on just about everything, and he certainly didn't like having to sit and listen to them in a moldering pew in St. Mary-le-Quay's on a perfectly good Sunday. It was his wife who made him go.

Mrs. Barnaby was in rather fine trim for a sailing captain's wife. She still had a figure, and she was still pretty. She was a lively and a busy person, always fluttering about in a state of noisy disorder, always dashing here and dashing there like a horse at a point-to-point. She was always in a rush, always in a hurry. A greater contrast to the slow, steady, strutting figure of her husband could not have been imagined.

Mrs. Barnaby spent her hours introducing children to the mysteries of music and the pianoforte. She counted among her clients those from the highest echelons of Nantle society, for her skill as a teacher was well known, and she herself widely regarded as a person of authority and rectitude. She ruled her pupils with an iron glove. She rapped their fingers when they struck the wrong keys, and rapped their brains — metaphorically — when they failed to master their lessons. She was rigorous, she demanded perfection; she tolerated nothing that could be considered fractious or rebellious on the part of girl or boy. Her pupils were expected to mind their P's and Q's as closely as their B-flats and their F-sharps. She brooked no hooliganism.

Music and the pianoforte had come naturally to Mrs. Barnaby. She had learned to play at an early age, and had absorbed the principles of music with such ease and confidence that it vexed her when some other, less talented person — namely a pupil — failed to absorb them as quickly. She was a stern and dedicated teacher, and as a result had counted many successes among her pupils, but many failures, too. Nevertheless families from all over Nantle continued to send their offspring to her, the fees serving to contribute much needed cash to the coffers of the Barnaby household. But teaching fees will go only so far, and the coffers of the household were very lean indeed.

As she ruled her pupils, so did Mrs. Barnaby rule her husband. The captain always was filled with a mixture of emotions when returning home to the bosom of his family. He and his wife had no children, so that the bosom of his family was, quite literally, the bosom of Mrs. Barnaby; and it was not always so welcoming. The captain had sailed from Nantle on his recent voyage following another disputatious exchange with his wife — only a squall, really, when compared to the many storms the two had endured in their marriage — and had come back now, weeks later, to find the squall still gusting.

The stalwart old warrior of the sea was used to storms of the nautical variety, but he was less equipped to weather these peculiar tempests which were forever erupting in Jolly Jumper Yard. Aside from Mrs. O'Guppy only the captain's dog paid him much attention on his arrival home, and rendered no judgments of him. Often it happened, while his wife was having her supper at the dining-table, that the captain would be found sitting on the floor in the parlor, taking his own meal in the quiet company of his dog — for to have dined together in the same room with his wife would have been to invite a thunderstorm.

Such was the state of affairs in the captain's house on the day we describe. Mrs. Barnaby as usual was at the pianoforte, engaged in the instruction of a particularly troublesome child, one Miss Bright, who had been taking lessons for an enormous long time but with hardly anything to show for it. To be perfectly blunt, she had nothing to show for it. Her family was a good one and socially connected, and as a last resort they had sent her to Jolly Jumper Yard. But even the very considerable powers of Mrs. Louisa Barnaby were of little help in the face of such relentless inaptitude.

"No, no, no, Miss Bright. You must pass your thumb *smoothly* under the second finger, without turning your hand. Like so. It really is a very simple exercise; I fail to see why you can't grasp it."

"Yes, Mrs. Barnaby," said Miss Bright, so docile and patient there at the keyboard. She had an abundance of orange hair, all of it rolled up like a pumpkin on top of her head, and a white face as round and blank as a plate.

"And you must learn to cross the fourth finger of your left hand over your thumb — again, *smoothly*, Miss Bright. Like so. Do you see? I think you should have mastered this by now. Haven't I given you many exercises to sharpen your skills?"

"Yes, Mrs. Barnaby."

"And your finger legato in general — your arpeggios and your trills — your left-hand coordination — all leave a good deal to be desired."

"Yes, Mrs. Barnaby."

"Have you improved your wrist staccato? Ah, I see you have not. Well, if you can't develop your technical proficiency, Miss Bright, you will never play well."

"Yes, Mrs. Barnaby."

"What of your major and minor scales? Do you practice them faithfully every day?"

"Yes, Mrs. Barnaby."

"Then why is it you make no progress? Why is your technique so abysmal? I don't think there is much more I can do for you, Miss Bright, unless you practice, practice, practice — and *retain* what you practice. The music must become part of your being. Your scales, your finger legato, your arpeggios, all must become as smooth and easy as drawing breath. Really, Miss Bright, I've never in my life seen a pupil make so little progress after so much hard teaching, and so much practice as you lay claim to."

"Yes, Mrs. Barnaby."

"There — now stop a bit, Miss Bright. Didn't you see the line above that half-note? It signifies *sostenuto* — the note must be sustained, like so. And you must learn to relax your wrist. Really, it's like a crab with the tetanus."

"Yes, Mrs. Barnaby."

"And see that you review your tonic, your subdominant, and your dominant chords in all your major and minor keys, and your dominant sevenths, and your circle of fifths, by this same time next week. For you must not neglect your study of basic principles."

"Yes, Mrs. Barnaby."

"And more to the purpose, see that you retain what you study."

"Yes, Mrs. Barnaby."

So it went week after week with Miss Bright, who had never made any progress under anybody's tutelage and in all likelihood never would. But isn't every teacher of music blessed with such a pupil?

"Perhaps I should study the violin?" Miss Bright was heard to say — which remark brought a predictable answer from her teacher, frustrated as she was by her charge's unremitting lack of progress.

"If you can't master the pianoforte, Miss Bright, how on God's earth do you expect to master the violin? I ask you, miss, what are you thinking? Better you should take up the guitar or lute, for then at least you'll have your frets to save you. Besides which, Miss Bright, the violin is rather an unnatural choice. The violin is a gentleman's instrument. A woman's natural instrument is the pianoforte."

Overhearing this, Mrs. O'Guppy, who had been busy in the passage, stopped in the midst of her work to turn her head away and sigh — for these words of Mrs. Barnaby's had served to remind her of her daughter Niamh, and of the unnaturalness of the quarrel that had arisen between them.

In the next room the captain was sitting in front of the fire with a cold pigeon pie and a bottle of porter. Beside him at attention sat his dog, ears raised, eyes fixed yearningly on the pie. Every now and then the captain would fling a scrap of meat into the air; the dog would leap for it, gulp it down, and return to attention. This exercise was repeated several times until the pie was gone, at which point the skipper filled his cheek with a quid and, moving a little nearer the fire, sat with his hands clasped round his knees and his brows crunched in thought.

The housekeeper happening by, the captain broke off his meditations and, getting to his feet, sought to draw her out a bit, for he had noted she was something hove down of late.

"And how is yer daughter, then, Mrs. O'Guppy?" he inquired, all grins and salt and skipperly cordiality.

"As well as can be hexpected, sir."

"Be she lodged still in that boarding-house yonder?"

"Yes, sir, wid Mrs. Matchless and the sarvints in Chamomile Street."

The captain knitted brows and stroked his long chin. "Has she put herself on an even keel, then? Has she recovered something more of her wits?"

"No, sir. My cousin Jones looks in on the child for me, and brings riglar tidings as to her condhition. Though I'm afeared the tidings of late bain't so favorable. She hears her voices and convarses wid her invisible folk, just as did my poor husband her father, and has took up her cards agin for the telling of fortunes. Her sinses may be weak, sir, but her temper be as strong as ever. And there be the matter, too, of her fiddle-playing — she larned it from her father, ye know — and which it be an insthrument something unnatural for a woman, as the misthress says, and, I fear, a tool of the divil."

"Why, look 'ee now, Mrs. O'Guppy," the captain smiled, fixing his quid in his cheek and his thumbs in his wide belt of many pockets, "ye'll not be listening overmuch to all my wife says. Sarten sure it is her words do pain ye at times, that I see. But it bean't nowise the case, Mrs. O'Guppy, that a woman may not scrape a fiddle. Sink me and bleed me if I've not clapped eyes on more than a few lady-sawguts in ports up and down this coast, or I'm a shotten tomcod!"

His words elicited a thankful if weary nod from Mrs. O'Guppy. The resemblance to her daughter was evident in the spareness of her frame, in her dark, expressive eyes, and the general set of her countenance. But it was a resemblance marred by the ravages of time and toil. Her face was the face of Niamh as seen through a dirty window, one streaked and spotted by much ill-weather.

"That I know, sir, truly. I know the misthress manes not to be unkind when she speaks of sich things. But it saddens me it does at times, plase yer honor, to considher how our poor fambly has wasted away. Sorra a thing I have left on this earth but her, and she won't have the least to do wid me — won't even talk wid me! 'Tis enough to make a body lose heart, sir. But the Skeffingtons and the O'Guppys have alaways been a conthrary and a quarrelsome lot. I do hexpect it's no less'n our just desarts."

The captain was something moved by this speech. He paced the room a couple of times with large, skipperly strides. He shifted the quid in his cheek, and cleared his voice, and strutting up to Mrs. O'Guppy touched a comforting hand to her shoulder.

"Steady, Mrs. O'Guppy, steady. Ye must keep yer sails trimmed and yer bearings secure, and lay yer head to windward, and fight through it. It's not all fair weather on this troubled sea of life, but nor is it all foul neither. Ye've yer health and yer situation, and yer daughter, too, remains well in body, if not always so in brain. Ye must trust to yer own compass, Mrs.

O'Guppy; ye must lash yer helm and stand whatever comes yer way, though ye be kicked into the scuppers for it. For sarten sure this life of ours be a damnable coil and cursed pickle, and oft goes foul and a-wrack. But too much thinking on it, Mrs. O'Guppy — too much thinking on it and ye'll sink like a stone!"

The housekeeper sighed and nodded, knowing as she did that these words of the captain's were meant as consolation, the best he was capable of mustering. And so she thanked him for them and, taking up her mop again, resumed her duties.

Moments later came a loud, discordant rattling and growling from the music room — it could only be Miss Bright at the pianoforte — a clamor that was followed at once by a loud and discordant rebuke from Mrs. Barnaby. The skipper of the *Salty Sue,* hearing this latest example of youthful musicianship, felt the flesh of his neck creep. He shook his head in despair. Even his dog was troubled by it, and loped off to the kitchen, where the cook promptly put him to work on the spit-wheel at the big fieldstone hearth.

This interesting device was like a sort of water-wheel in miniature. It was raised several feet above the floor, and was connected by ropes and pulleys to a roasting-jack slung over the fire, on the spit of which a loin of mutton had been impaled. On the cook's signal the dog began to race over the paddles of the wheel, driving it round and round, and thereby revolving the spit and keeping the meat turning on the flame. Everything and everyone was made use of in the captain's household; and though the captain thought it demeaning that his dog should be transformed thus into a kind of kitchen-maid, he was sobered by the knowledge that it was cheaper than engaging one. And considering the state of the household coffers, the dog was a bargain.

Having finished his pie and porter, the captain had little to keep him at home. He went in search of his coat, only to run into another squall in the form of his wife, who, in light of the impending quarter-day, demanded to speak with him on the matter of the household finances. She asked him if he knew what a detainer was, or what insolvency meant, and if he'd seen the inside of Comport's lock-up lately? Had he perchance spied a bailiff's man skulking about the Yard? Did he know what distrained goods were, and what it meant to have brokers on the premises? Did he know there was no money to pay the tailor's bill, the butcher's bill, and half-a-dozen other bills? There would be no more kickshaws in Jolly Jumper Yard, she declared; no, no, it was to be ember days in the Barnaby household until the creditors were paid, every last one. It was either that, she said, or face the brokers, the bailiff's man, and the lock-up. Worse yet, she hinted, it was possible that the lugger herself might be seized there in the harbor, as security for their debts.

The captain, something taken back by this, strove to remind his wife of the vicissitudes of ocean voyages, and of the irregular income derived therefrom, and how heavy were the expenses in outfitting such a prime duck of a craft as the *Sue,* etc., etc.; but he failed miserably. To his great relief, however, footsteps were heard in the passage, and his first mate Bob Sly rolled through the door with a breezy hail.

"Ho there, Cap'n! How blows the wind? Can ye be persuaded to slip moorings and lay a course for Hinxton's?"

Smiling, Mr. Sly removed his cap and bobbed his head and sidewhiskers at Mrs. Barnaby, who returned the courtesy with a glare and then a scowl, before quitting the room in disgust.

The captain cocked an eye at his first mate. "Souse me for a grunion and stand by, Bob! Hearkee, we fetch out at once. I'll not be a minute more, shipmate. Ye've little notion how I've quested for a rag o' sail on *this* horizon."

"Aye, Cap'n — though I've something more than a notion," said Mr. Sly, clapping finger to nose and nodding towards the music room, where Mrs. Barnaby had retired in a huff. Considering that Miss Bright was in that room, abusing the keys of the pianoforte and the ears of everyone, her displeasure with Mr. Sly must have been very great indeed.

"Dear Louisa," said the captain, thrusting his chin and his bold beak of a nose in from the passage, "look 'ee, dear — I'm for Hinxton's now with Bob Sly."

"For Hinxton's, and drinking again, no doubt," his wife retorted. "Always drinking you are — always in liquor — always tippling — always tossing a pot, or twirling a glass, or draining a bumper. You, and that — that *scurvy* one!" (By this she meant Mr. Sly, whose identity was made plainer by a very ominous gesture of her thumb in his direction.)

"Dear Louisa, ye ha'n't be speaking such o' so prime a sailorman as Bob Sly," returned the captain, standing up to her a little. Though he knew it was futile, he was loath to yield.

"And here you are, Jack Barnaby, at sea for months at a stretch, and now you're home and what must you do with your time?" accused his wife, her voice and color rising as she spoke. "You must go skiving off, drinking and dicing — with *that* one!" (Another ominous jab at Mr. Sly.) "It's a fine life you have, Jack Barnaby, a fine life. I am so very happy for you."

The frown on the captain's face dissolved. "But dear Louisa — mouse — bless yer dear eyes —"

"I'll hear no more," said his wife, tossing up her chin and turning her back on him in favor of Miss Bright. "It is on your peril. And you may take your dog with you," she added over her shoulder, "if you are so minded, once his turn at the spit-wheel is done."

"Why, it bean't nowise necessary," said the captain, climbing into his coat. "Look 'ee now, dear Louisa — mouse — there bean't the time nor liberty to heave to for the dog. Moresomever I don't bleeve Hinxton much cares for dogs in his house."

"No dogs but *sea-dogs,* eh, Cap'n? *By gum!*" exclaimed Mr. Sly, with a hearty explosion of laughter.

"Soak me in bilge-water, Bob Sly," cried the captain, "if ye be not the wittiest sailorman for yarning with on all this long coast, and the primest, or I'm a gooseneck barnacle. Prepare to trip anchor!"

"Aye, Cap'n!" returned Mr. Sly, cackling so hard that the tears threatened to squirt from his eyes.

The captain unfolded his mariner's bonnet and drew it over his head, and before his wife could belay him further, he was out at the door with Mr. Sly and into the Yard. There the two sea-dogs quickly gathered way, sailing over the pack-horse bridge and down a smoky lane into Slopmonger Mews. In due course they emerged on the fair and spacious avenue known as Ship Street, quayside, where swung an ancient signboard announcing the Axe and Compasses, at which establishment captain and first mate found safe harborage.

CHAPTER FOURTEEN

Confidential

Mr. Arthur Liffey found himself early awake in the morning, in the faintest of faint Nantle light. For the first minute or two he lay quietly, trying to sort out in his mind where he was. Gradually it came back to him — this was his room at the Crozier, not his bedchamber at home, and he was in Nantle with his clients the Cargoes and Miss Veal. That puzzle solved, he turned himself round with a mind to go to sleep again, till such an hour as was more congenial to rising. At his age Mr. Liffey required more sleep than before, though hardly ever was it the lush, clean, untroubled sleep of his youth-time.

But he felt strangely restless and ill at ease, as though something were physically keeping him from sleeping, which of course was absurd. He rolled himself onto his side, so that he faced the large mirror that stood by his toilet-table. After a time he managed to lull himself into a kind of doze — into that drowsy, tenuous, twilight state between waking and slumber — when he was roused from it by the feel of a hand on his shoulder. Thinking it was his man John, or the good-humored boots of the inn, or perhaps Fred, come to wake him, he opened his eyes.

The first thing to greet his sight was the mirror. In it he saw a reflection of himself lying there in his bed. Something was leaning over him — something that was neither John, nor boots, nor Fred. It was something dark and ghoulish, and altogether monstrous to behold.

The hand on his shoulder began to force him down, firmly and insistently, as though to drive him into the mattress. He felt the pain of nailed fingers biting into his flesh, and a squeeze upon the pumping-chambers of his heart. He heard the pounding of blood in his ears, a coursing stream that had turned cold as a Cargo winter at sight of the thing in the mirror. A violent fit of trembling surged through his body. There was an angry snarl in his ear; then the hand pressing upon him suddenly gave way. Freed, he threw the bedclothes from him and staggered to his feet, coughing and trembling.

Staring wide-eyed round the apartment, he found that he was quite alone. No John, no boots, no Fred, and nothing in the mirror but his own frightened countenance. He rubbed a hand — his own this time — over his shoulder, the one the ghoul had seized. Then he got into his slippers and threw up the window, to let in as much air and light as possible.

It was a typical Nantle morning for the season — a dull gray haze in the streets, a misty rain dripping from the clouds, and the odor of wet earth everywhere. Mr. Liffey breathed it all in, deeply and pleasurably. Despite the chill he hesitated not a moment more. The atmosphere in his room had grown so thick and heavy he simply had to get clear of it. He was sure that what he had experienced there was no dream, but the very same evil that had visited him in the hansom cab and in his bedchamber at Cargo.

The ghoul had followed him to Nantle!

He didn't ring for John but instead forced himself to remain in the room, alone, long enough to douse his face and get into his clothes. Thank goodness for his beard, he thought, or he would have had to shave as well! His heart racing, his nerves straining, he snatched up his hat and umbrella and reached for the door. He was about to turn the handle when he felt it move in his grasp. Glancing down he beheld, where the handle had been, a gnarled and knotted human hand, tightly clutching his own.

Again the squeeze at his heart, again the blood shooting through his body. He nearly cried out as he struggled to free himself. He fought with the horrid thing, felt it crushing the bones of his hand, felt the nails digging into his wrist. In a panic he jerked his arm back, violently — and felt the door come with it. The grip upon his hand was relinquished. The door swung open with a creak and a groan, revealing the dim light of the passage without.

And the handle of the door was a handle once more.

Mopping his face with a handkerchief, Mr. Liffey collected himself for some few horrid minutes in the passage. Then he shut the door behind him, taking care not to touch any of the hardware, and fled down the staircase. At the desk he left a note for Fred, telling him that he'd gone out for an early walk and not to wait on him for breakfast. The clerk asked Mr. Liffey if he was ill, for, as he put it, the attorney looked as pale as a ghost. Mr. Liffey said he was not — was neither ill nor a ghost, though he might very well have seen one that morning — and putting up his umbrella escaped into the courtyard.

He wandered about for an hour or two, trudging through shiny, rain-washed streets he vaguely recollected from his sailing days of old. From the Crozier he made his way down the hill along one of the chief thoroughfares of the city. He passed the theaters, and Mock Alley, and Great Codger Lane — for some reason he didn't like the sound of that today — from which point he strayed into more nautical surroundings, and shortly thereafter found himself on Nantle quay.

He spent some minutes pacing its stony surface, gazing up at the ships as they strained at their moorings there, and looking out upon the larger vessels riding at anchor in the harbor. Walking on, he turned into Ship Street. Seeing that it was nearly half-past nine, and that it was still cold, dull, and drizzly, and likely to remain that way, and that he'd had no breakfast, it occurred to him that the inside of one of the sailors' inns that lined the street might be superior to the outside in such weather. So he strode in at the door of the first respectable-looking concern he happened on, one with a signboard depicting a boat-axe and a pair of navigator's compasses.

He entered feeling a trifle self-conscious, as it had been some years since he'd been in such a place. But it was early and the inn not yet at its bustling best, which made it easier to conquer his reluctance. He made his way to the common room and ordered some strong tea and anything else they might have to go with it. The anything else turned out to be a dish of brown toast and a petrified biscuit. He found a box near the fire and settled into it. And so there he sat, his back to the wall, sipping his tea and warming his bones.

He ran his eyes about the room, searching for something to engage his interest and take his mind off the horror of the morning. Like any sailors' inn, the Axe and Compasses was alive to all hours, although its pulse was rather low at present. A few people were shuffling in at the street-door to get out of the cold, a few others shuffling out to be about their labors. He observed a trio of sailormen amble up to the tap and order a round of whisky — whisky, at half-past nine in the A.M.! He shook his old head at the thought of it. Smoke from pipes and cigars, rolling sea-oaths, and snatches of song drifted on the air. He saw a bluff gentleman in a red-and-white checked shirt and a Welsh wig, with bushy half-whiskers and a withered arm, dispensing commands to the drawer, and reckoned him to be the landlord of the establishment.

After a time, when no one had come by to replenish his toast, the attorney got up to inquire into it. Just beyond the hearth he passed an open door, which led to one of the private rooms, and heard from inside it a colossal snore like a bagpipes. Curious, he peeped in, and discovered there two gentlemen, both soundly asleep. One was extended lengthwise on a sofa, the other draped across a cushioned chair like a human antimacassar. The silver-haired snoring one on the sofa he recognized as Captain Barnaby, master of the *Salty Sue,* the one in the chair as Bob Sly. An array of empty pint-pots and tankards, stale cheeseparings, bits of crackers, heads and tails of shrimps, oyster shells, and materials for smoking littered the table beside them.

No sooner had Mr. Liffey glimpsed these two drowsing beauties than a voice spoke into his ear. This action caused him to start violently and suffer another squeeze at his heart. Turning round he came face-to-face with no ghoul — at least not one of the supernatural kind — but with the lean, swart countenance of Black Davy.

"Man, man, the pair of 'em swaggered in yesterday to have a drain, and have yet to leave their bunk-hole there," said the picturesque vagrant of the dockyards. "The one hadn't the strength or inclination to toddle back to his house, the other to his lodgings. A dust-up with the lady of the house, I'll warrant, for the skipperish one. Dreadfully sorry thing it is in a sailoring man, don't you think, sir, to be petticoated? Now the sailorman and his galligaskins have made a bid for freedom from the torment of wifery! All he asks of the world is that it let him be, and I applaud him for it. He has no real home but his ship; he would be wise to stick to it."

"Do you mean Captain Barnaby?"

"There's no harmony in that household, sir, and perhaps never was any," said Davy. "But the world is full of terrors, man, and a wife is merely one of them. Ah, but what does Devenham know of such things? For I've no wife, sir, and no family, and never have had either. I'll have no part of 'em. Freedom and spaciousness are what I crave."

"And are you so completely free, Mr. Devenham?" Mr. Liffey asked as they made their way to the bar, the attorney to inquire about toast, Mr. Devenham most likely about a dram.

"Entirely free, man! And that is just as I require it. No apron-strings, no sentimental shackles to bind me and make me their prisoner. Nothing to keep me from my purpose. It's sheer bliss."

He approached the drawer and ordered some grog (no such nicety as cherry wine at the Axe and Compasses), but on delving into his coat, he found his pocket-book to be wholly and unexpectedly vacant of coin. A fine situation, though not so unusual a one for a man to whom money was a care. He glanced apologetically at Mr. Liffey and threw up his hands, to indicate he had nothing with which to pay the bill.

"If you'd be so kind, sir," he smiled, opening his pocket-book for the attorney's inspection, "for my purse is always short. Money means nothing to me and consequently I never have any. Man, man, I never can keep track of it."

Mr. Liffey was keen at the moment for any sort of friendly company, even Black Davy's, to avert his mind from certain ghoulish imaginings; and so he readily assented.

"My thanks to you, George Minty!" said Mr. Devenham, addressing the drawer, as that able-bodied minion handed him a foaming tankard of grog. "Good old glinty-eyed George! Always upstanding you are, George, always generous — as good a soul as ever tapped a barrel. Always the kindest of the kind to a lonely wanderer over the face of nature. Good old glinty Minty!"

The dismissive look in the eyes of Mr. Minty suggested he had little use for such compliments, particularly from one such as Black Davy.

"Have you many such friends here, Mr. Devenham?" the attorney inquired of his companion, as they settled themselves in the box wherein Mr. Liffey had established his camp.

"Friends? What need have I for friends?" snorted the lonely wanderer. "I wouldn't give you a straw for them. What are friends but disappointments in waiting? What are friends but blighted hopes, ever ready to let a man down? A plague of all friends, sir! Why should such a man as I — a man who looks after himself, quietly, and asks nothing of the world but to be allowed to roam in it — why should such a man burden himself with friends? For the truth is, sir, that nothing and no one can disappoint me. I am quite immune to sorrow — truly, I am! Should I hear of something dreadful befalling somebody somewhere, it pains me not, for he's no friend of mine and nothing to me. The world can't injure me. I exist in a state of perfect contentment, and a man must put distance between himself and others, as I've found, sir, to be content. That's why I've no need or want of friends or family. No, sir, no — I'll have no truck with them!"

Mr. Liffey's eyes lingered on his teacup as he digested these awful remarks. Awful remarks, true, but remarks which caused him now to reflect upon certain aspects of his own existence. With no living relations and no wife, and very few real friends, if any, was he so very different from Black Davy? Wasn't he himself little more than a lonely wanderer over the face of the law? He had devoted the long years of his life to the faithful service of his clients, whoever they happened to be at the time. He was a well-respected man in Cargo, but he loved no one and no one loved him. Of course there had been someone once, many years ago, but she was just a memory now — albeit a cherished one — a memory which every minute was receding fast into history, and would one day be forgotten.

Forgotten!

All of which put him in mind of a subject he'd very nearly lost track of, on account of ghouls and grips upon his shoulder.

"Mr. Devenham," he asked, with no expectation of success, "would you happen to know a gentleman answering to the name of Squailes? Jerry Squailes?"

The tankard of Black Davy was arrested in its passage to his lips. The eyebrows of the lonely wanderer flew up into his mop of sooty-black hair. He drew his coat-sleeve across his mouth, slowly and deliberately, his eyes fixed on Mr. Liffey.

"Squailes, you said? That's an unusual name for a gentleman, to be sure."

"Most unusual."

"And what might it mean to you, sir, if I *were* acquainted with him?"

Mr. Liffey felt a brief tremor of excitement, much more pleasing a tremor than those he had felt that morning in his room at the Crozier. His face and ears flushed pink under his white hair and beard, as he teetered on the tiptoe of expectation.

"I can tell you, Mr. Devenham, that it will be very much worth your while — considerably more worth your while than the cost of that drink there — if you were to inform me of the whereabouts of Mr. Squailes, if indeed you know him, or can tell me how I might communicate with him."

"Why should this fellow Squailes — assuming I know him — be of such importance to you, may I ask, sir?" returned Davy, with a few glances at his tankard, as though he were calculating the price of the grog and various multiples of it thereof.

"You may ask, but I fear I can't answer too particularly, for it is a private legal matter. It is most urgent that I speak to Mr. Squailes, in confidence, on a matter of vital interest to him."

Mr. Devenham found himself drifting in and out of a restless fog of indecision. He downed some grog to steady himself and threw his lean gaze across the table.

"The price of a drink is worth little to me, sir, for I've no need or use of foul coin. Coin is a care, and I must be free of care. I prefer the world, man. Have I mentioned, sir, that in my travels I have walked the streets of

Saxbridge, that I have seen Richford in the east, and the dreaming spires of Penhaligon —"

"You have, sir, and recently, too," Mr. Liffey interrupted him. "Don't you recall? It was at Sprig's coffee-house."

"Ha! Knew I'd seen you before, man — remember it now! Thought your ancient phiz was familiar. But as to the matter's being worth my while, sir, well — in the end money's of little importance in the grand scheme of things. Do you think money was important to Greekish Plato when he composed his dialogues? Do you think it was important to Emperor Claudius when he penned his history of the Etruscan peoples? Do you suppose money was important to Geoffrey of Chaucer when he wrote of the Tabard and the pilgrims? No, sir, money is important only to men like Hinxton there" — a flourish in the direction of the bluff landlord — "greedy men of business with little taste or inclination for learning. Money, sir, is a leveler; anyone can have it who can take it. But I will not be leveled. Far be it from Devenham to do anything for a ducat."

Here he drank down his grog until he found himself staring into an empty tankard. He reached for his pocket-book, then remembered that it was empty, too. Mr. Liffey, seeing this, waved to a rare passing waiter to fetch another drink. As the pint was laid on the table, two thin, ill-shaven, ragged-looking fellows entered the common room. One had sneaking eyes and a crafty grin, and wore a muffin-cap; the other was a horsy-faced little character with a wiry paintbrush of a mustache and a round black hat. Recognizing the lonely wanderer, the newcomers approached the box and offered him their salutations.

"Troth and faith, and if it bain't Black Davy, now," said Round-the-corner Jones, he of the muffin-cap. "How fare ye this fine marning, jewel?"

Mr. Devenham seemed not nearly so happy to see these two rogues as they were to see him.

"Man," said Davy, wringing his head, "it's been many a twelvemonth since I've spied *you*, sir, awake and conscious at such an hour."

Round-the-corner Jones answered with a smirk and tossed his cap back on his ears. "It's those of us as have business in hand, jewel, business in hand, as must be risen so early of a morning."

"And what business would that be, sir? For I've not known either of you to turn an honest hour's labor."

The newcomers registered their surprise.

"Ah, shure, and 'tis funnin' us ye are, Davy!" laughed little Planxty Moeran. "By gannies, joy, always funnin' us ye are!"

"I've no need for funning, sirs," returned Davy, "as I'm holding con-fabulation here with a distinguished visitor from the town of Cargo — a town I myself have seen, sirs, and have walked its bitter-cold streets. This is *real* business, man."

"Hollo!" Jones exclaimed, ducking at him with an air of servility. "Business of yer own did ye say, jewel? Pray, then, let us not incommode ye. Ah, shure, 'tis a fine thing, no doubt — and 'twas I as thought Davy Dev-enham had no need of business, and no need of tin! 'Give me air,' says he. 'Give me the world,' says he. 'Give me fraydom,' says he. 'Give me this an' give me that,' says he, and so much blarney else. So what need have ye of business this marning, jewel?"

"Whatever it is, it's none of *your* business," said Davy with an ugly scowl. "And what business are the pair of you about, might I ask? Small beer, no doubt, whatever it is. You're looking even more dilapidated than usual, I think. And you might get better traps, man!"

"And 'tis it not the frying-pan a-sayin' the kettle's black!" retorted Moeran, calling attention to Mr. Devenham's equally scruffy condition.

"What business?" repeated Davy, blithely dismissing this evidence of his own hypocrisy.

"Ah, shure, the ould trade's fallen off a bit, Davy, in partickler sinst our friend an' fellow Dermot O'Kilcoyne went off the hooks," said Round-the-corner. "He was a gintleman and a Christian, and as sober a man as ye'd find in a day's walk."

"True, true," agreed Moeran, sadly nodding in his horse-collar. "An' more's the pity. Poor Dermot! God rest his sould."

"But we've another trade to take the place. Wait a bit now. Agh! Look here, if ye plase."

From the bowels of his huge, shapeless coat Mr. Jones produced a busi-ness card, on which the following was inscribed in a florid hand —

Mr. Havergal Jones
Confidential Inquiries
DISCRETE — PROFESSIONAL

"And who is Havergal Jones?" frowned Davy.

"By the powers, 'tis he, dear joy!" exclaimed Moeran, pointing gleefully at Round-the-corner.

"Well, I'd not have recognized you, man. *Havergal,* is it? Dreadfully sorry to hear that. What do you inquire into?"

"Agh, everything and all, jewel," smiled Mr. Jones. "Frauds an' other sichlike deceitful schemes. Suspected defalcations. Fabrications an' farr-geries. Gintlemen as have gone missing, or gone to the wall. Harrumless flirtations, an' not so harrumless. Bigamanies. Blackmails an' briberies. Shure, jewel, there's little limit to the likes of it. I know 'twill stun ye to the quick, Davy, what wid the venality of it, but as Moeran here says, 'tis the way of the world, don't ye see."

"When were you last employed in this capacity?"

"Well, 'tis somethin' of a new thrade, as I've said, and so I've not spread about the word as of yet. But should ye know of any as needs inquiries of sich a sort at no fancy price, I'd of course be obliged to ye."

Mr. Liffey was about to strike in here, but Mr. Devenham forestalled him with a raised hand.

"That's well and good, sir, well and good," he told Jones, "but first you'd best learn to spell *discreet*."

The two vagabonds put their heads together and made a close exami-nation of the card, glancing distrustfully now and then at Black Davy, as if unsure whether to believe him or not. Unable to decide, they showed the card to Mr. Liffey, to whom they were finally introduced, and whose man-ner and appearance suggested to them a person of quality. To their disap-pointment, his opinion was the same as Davy's.

"Och, by the powers!" Jones complained with a sigh. "It's frusthrated I am, always frusthrated. Mayhap I should inspeckt the rest of 'em."

He took a number of cards of a similar kind from his pockets and laid them out on the table. Most bore the name HAVERGAL JONES, or H. JONES, or H.S. JONES, or some such variation, joined to such interesting occupa-tions as APOTHECARRY AND TOOTH-DRAWER, or MASTER OF ARTS, or CORN FACTOR, or VENDER OF SMALL WARES, or GENERAL ACCOUNTANT, or MEM-BER OF PARLIMENT — ("Ah, 'tis a back-bencher I was, jewel," smiled Round-the-corner, to which Davy responded, "I myself have been to Fish-mouth, sir, to the hallowed seat of governance, and never once have I seen *you* there!") — or SHOOING-SMITH AND VETERNARY SURJEON, or GENTLE-MEN'S HAIRDRESSER (which last caused Mr. Devenham to peer at Round-the-corner very hard).

"You are the publisher of the *Morning Chronicle*?" inquired Mr. Liffey, gazing in surprise at the card nearest him.

Mr. Jones responded with a sly grin and a chuckle.

"That I was, sir, that I was, for a day at least, by reason of a sickness as struck the gintleman as held that situation. The measles it wor, as I recol-leckt — or was it the distemper, now? I suppose I've kept the card for the sintiment of it, don't ye see."

Mr. Devenham took up another and read it aloud. "'SIGNOR JONESEPPI. PRACTITIONER OF THE NOBLE SCIENCE.'" He gazed doubtfully at Round-the-corner and snorted. "What say, man? Who would have guessed you were devoted to the fencing game?"

"By the Holy, 'tis a lie!" exclaimed Mr. Moeran, leaping at once to his colleague's defense, not to say his own. "Shure 'tis a ridiculous notion, for never once has Jones been received of stolen properties — leastwise none as could be proved by the magisthrate — nor has meself neither. And 'tis proud I am to say it!"

"I believe," interposed Mr. Liffey, "that the reference is to the noble art and science of swordsmanship."

"Ha," laughed Jones, in some little embarrassment at his friend's out-burst. "I ax yer pardon, sir. 'Twas only funnin' ye he was, don't ye see. He's a born eediot and will be the ruination of himself. Bedad, sir, where did ye leave yer inthelligence?" (This last addressed to little Planxty, the born id-iot, and not Mr. Liffey.)

Mr. Devenham picked up another card and read, to his considerable amazement, the single word OCULIST. To this he had no answer, not even a snort; he was speechless, and could only stare at Round-the-corner.

Mr. Jones was about to gather up his cards for stowage again in his pockets, when Mr. Liffey's glance fell upon one that drew his immediate interest. To wit —

H. Skeffington Jones
Solicitor
NO FANCY PRICES

"Oh dear, oh dear," the attorney frowned.

"I'll not mince words with you, sir," said Davy, addressing Mr. Jones, for he saw in the card the perfect device for getting rid of the troublesome pair. "Be advised that this gentleman seated here is himself a learned prac-titioner of the law, a noted legal man from Cargo, who's picked up more than a wrinkle or two in his career as concerns fraud and deception. Isn't that so, sir?"

"It is," Mr. Liffey replied.

"And as a legal man he knows what is to be done with swindlers and impostors. They're to be put to the bar and prosecuted. Isn't that so?"

"To the utmost rigor of law," stated the attorney.

"Now put that and that together, sirs — and avaunt yourselves!"

"Agh," said Round-the-corner, with a nervous scratching of his cheek.

He looked at Moeran; Moeran looked at him. In a flash he made the rest of his cards disappear, and seemed intent upon effecting the same trick with himself and his colleague. "And so we'll be leavin' now, yer honor, this instant minute," he said, while he and Moeran backed slowly away, grinning and ducking heads at Mr. Liffey. Their adieus thus bidden, they turned on their heels and scampered off.

"You'd best have no truck with weak-pated dolts and jolterheads, sir," advised Davy, more than happy to see them go. "Unfortunately such geese are thick on the ground in these parts. Not at all like your own city of Cargo. Don't recollect so many geese there; too cold for it. Well, I've saved you the trouble and put the knavish fellows off you for now. You were saying, then, sir, touching this Squailes as you've an interest in — ?"

Mr. Liffey folded his hands upon the table. "It is a most difficult but important business, sir. A fellow practitioner I engaged in the town has been unable to find Mr. Squailes, and so I have come myself to carry out the search. This is a duty which devolves upon me as the administrator of a late gentleman's estate; I have little choice in the matter. All I can tell you is that I have a very surprising bit of news for Mr. Squailes, which may alter the fabric of his life considerably."

"So that's how it stands," said Davy, throwing himself back in his chair. "And if I were to tell you where to look for this fellow Squailes?"

"It would be very worth your while, as I am given leave under the terms of the will to offer a degree of remuneration in exchange."

Mr. Devenham took this under advisement with various rufflings of his hair and brushings of his mustache, in concert with the usual snorts. He drank some more grog and endeavored to look very profound as he weighed the courses of action that were open to him.

"Naturally I shouldn't expect you to assist me for mere common advantage, for I know your feelings on that score," the attorney went on. "Money is a care, and you must have your freedom from care. However, it would be money very well laid out."

"You presume to know a good deal about me, sir," returned Davy. "It's true, I know nothing of money, nor do I wish to know anything of money. The foul chink of coin has no attraction for me. But the world presses; and as the world is my occupation, I've little choice in the matter, as you yourself might say. Nor have I any objection to aiding a fellow creature in that world, so long as it leaves me unfettered. You say you have something of importance to communicate to Squailes?"

"Yes."

"Then," said the lonely wanderer, after a reasonable show of hesitation,

"I believe I can help you, sir. Though it should pain me, I'll make an exception in your case, and accept whatever small token in return for services you see fit to offer. Mind you, sir, it's not for *me* — I don't need or want it. It is solely for the common necessaries of life, which the world presses upon me. So long as it is the charitable thing to do for a fellow creature, I am prepared to make the sacrifice."

"I understand you fully, Mr. Devenham, and am grateful to you. But there is one thing more. I must take you into my confidence, and inform you at the outset of a stipulation — a wholly minor stipulation — affecting our proposed agreement," said Mr. Liffey, hardly daring to believe his luck.

"Sir?"

"I am traveling in a party of several persons; you may remember, you met them the other afternoon at the coffee-house. I must ask one thing of you, sir — indeed, I must *insist* upon it — and that is this: that should you find yourself in conversation with any of my fellow travelers, whether in my presence or not, you will say nothing whatever of Mr. Squailes or of this agreement between us. Do you understand me, sir? As far as they are concerned, you and I have no agreement. It is imperative, Mr. Devenham, that you accept this condition and adhere to it."

"Tell 'em nothing," repeated Black Davy, lifting a negligent eyebrow. He put his head on one side and regarded the attorney through narrowed lids. "Tell 'em nothing. No Squailes. No agreement. Keep it dark."

"Yes."

The lonely wanderer snorted and leaned forward on the table. "Here, then, what's your game, man? What's your dodge?"

"I have no game, as you call it, sir, and no dodge. My duty is clear. This is a private matter of law between myself and Mr. Squailes."

"I see. It's in the confidential line, is it?"

"Very much so."

"And *discreet*?"

Mr. Liffey smiled gently.

"It's a rum thing," said Davy, frowning, "but what's clear to me is that Squailes has come into a sum of money. Now there's a stunner! And rather a tidy sum it must be, too, or you shouldn't have braved the journey from cold Cargo. That's no small feat for a man well-stricken in years like yourself. So much money, so much care! I feel for poor Squailes, I do."

Mr. Liffey apologized but he was not at liberty to say more.

Mr. Devenham considered the attorney's proposal for some few minutes before reaching a decision.

"Your argument has struck me most forcibly, sir. I trust we can be on comfortable terms together, for Devenham's never been a fellow to breach a confidence. The world is my occupation, sir, not other men's private affairs. What are other men's affairs to me?"

Mr. Liffey was both elated and relieved. And so the bargain was sealed.

While these two were talking, the pulse of the Axe and Compass had visibly quickened. The common room was alive now with stir and bustle. Among the patrons was a gray-bearded little man in a seal-skin cap. He'd been conversing for a while with those at the bar, during which time his voice had grown increasingly loud and argumentative, such that others round the room looked up now to see what was the matter.

"*I seen what I seen!*" declared Graybeard, quaffing off this statement with a vehement swallow of his grog.

His conversation had attracted a number of listeners, including Mr. Minty the drawer, and Stubbins the pot-boy, and even landlord Hinxton himself, who stood with his withered arm resting on the bar.

"So what is it you've seen this time, Hake?" the landlord inquired.

"Ah, shure, what now, dear joy?" said Planxty Moeran, for it was to the bar that he and Round-the-corner had scurried for refuge. "Is it a blue sky ye've seen? Or an ugly cloud, mayhap, as affrighted ye? Or a foul fiend a-howling in that lighthouse of yers? Is it cracked ye are, joy, or simply foxed? Mr. Hake Jobberley an' a pint o' grog — whood a bleeved, by gannies!"

"Ye'll not be laughing, sir," warned Mr. Jobberley — for it was he, the assistant keeper of Fairlight station — "ye'll not be laughing when it plunges down from heaven and crushes ye flat. Aye! Something awful it were I seen up there, something *wicked*. Even now the thing may be lurking in the clouds above all yer heads — may be about to drop from the sky this very instant, and land square atop the Compasses and smash her to atoms!"

This suggestion brought mingled cries of protest and indignation from the listeners, together with demands for an explanation.

"What have you seen?" asked Mr. Hinxton, stepping closer. "Tell us, Hake — give it mouth! Easy all, every one of you. Stint your gab now and let the wickie have his say."

"I ain't been drinking, if that's yer suspect," declared Mr. Jobberley — rather a brash statement, considering the loaded pint-pot he held in his hand. "I seen it from the lantern room. A prodigious large thing like a house it were, made of brick and timbers. It come flying out of the clouds and hung in air there aside the tower, as easy as ye please — and that's the truth of it!"

"A gull," nodded one of the listeners. "Hake Jobberley's seen a gull. Must be a spot-tail!"

"More likely we're the gulls to be believin' sich a story," groused another, a retired ship's-carpenter.

"Clear off, Job Sawyer!" retorted Mr. Jobberley, with sudden heat. "I ain't daft and I ain't drunk. I seen what I seen. A house it were, with a gable and a tall roof, and a brick chimbley, and windows with folk inside 'em a-starin' me in the face!"

"A flying house," smiled one fellow, shaking his head.

"Aye, sure the wickie's been drinkin' again — *sea-water!*" laughed another.

"And it's not just I that seen it, for the dog seen it, too, and knows the verity of it," Mr. Jobberley declared.

Not surprisingly, this statement generated no end of mirth and mockery all round.

"Ye'll not be sneering so when it drops from the sky and gives ye what-for by knocking ye flat. Then ye'll have the truth of it, all of ye!" cried Hake.

More jeers and laughter, which served only to aggravate the wickie further and solidify his position as a public scoff.

"See here, it's Jenny Mulks now," interrupted Mr. Hinxton, having spied the limber form of the lighthouse-keeper's niece enter at the door.

"An' a handsomer colleen I've not met in a week at least, by the Holy," sighed Round-the-corner Jones.

"True, true," nodded Planxty, in open admiration.

"Come along, Hake," said Jenny, her voice crisp and commanding. "The cart's laden and my uncle awaits us at the tower."

"I'll be along soon enough, missy," Mr. Jobberley snorted into his grog. "I knew none here would attend to the verity of it. All believe Hake Jobberley to be a fool drunkard, or touched in the cranium."

"Aye, his mizzen-yard be sprung, I rackon," nodded Mr. Sawyer.

"We have our stores and must be getting home," said the girl. "Beg pardon, Mr. Hinxton, for the botheration of him. He escaped my notice for a time, but I knew where to look for him."

"Not to worry, Miss Jenny," the landlord assured her. "My regards as always to your uncle Matthew. Tell him it's ever a — ever a pleasure, and an entertainment, too, to welcome Hake Jobberley to the Compasses."

"And a load o' bilge, plague and perish him!" someone laughed.

"A house as flies in air! What will he say next?" another asked.

"Aye, and he ain't had a nip in a fortnight, neither!" snickered a third.

"Ye'll learn! As I'm a Christian man, ye'll learn, the lot of ye!" cried Mr. Jobberley, grimly defiant.

In the end it required the assistance of a couple of stout tars to grapple the wickie fast and extract him from the house. He was slung into the back of the shay-cart with the stores Jenny had gathered, and off they started on the road to Paignton Swidges.

A gray tide was breaking upon the long sweep of shore, on the right-hand side of the road; on the left, cows in black and white were munching in rainy fields. Now and again as she drove, Jenny, skeptical girl though she was, was seen to steal a glance at the clouds, half-expecting perhaps to see something come dropping out of them; but of course nothing of the sort happened.

For extraordinary events occur mostly when we don't expect them to — and that, as little Planxty might have said, and as Dr. Pinches certainly would have agreed, is the way of the world.

CHAPTER FIFTEEN

Song of the Shell-horn

Mr. Kix and Mr. Lovibond, as we know, were patrons of the theater, and so it should come as no surprise to find them there of an afternoon at the *matinée* hour. There was another romantic tragi-comedy on the boards, one which pleased the jovial Lovibond no end, but which grouchy Mr. Kix found deplorable. At the conclusion of it Mr. Lovibond burst into applause, as did most of the common throng; Mr. Kix did not. Mr. Lovibond deemed the play rapturous, Mr. Kix thought it eighth-rate at best. While Mr. Lovibond was calling for an encore, Mr. Kix was calling for the author's head.

"Hack work," he proclaimed, throwing up his hands in disgust, "sheer hack work!"

The theaters being situated in Stinking Lane, near Mock Alley, the two old bachelors proceeded afterward to Sprig's coffee-house, where they were happily surprised — well, Mr. Lovibond at any rate was happily surprised — to find one of their fellow boarders very comfortably ensconced there.

"Hallo! What news, sir?" Mr. Lovibond exclaimed, as he eased his pink, full-bodied self onto a Windsor chair at the table of their friend.

"No news," replied Mr. Frobisher. He sent up a great blue haze of smoke from his cigar. "Where have the two of you dropped from?"

"Been to the theater — Royal Trident — *Lord Maurice*," said Mr. Lovibond. "Superlatives fail me — finest thing in a twelvemonth — heartrending — waterworks — far superior to *Cuthbert and Phoebe*."

"And I suppose you despised it," said Mr. Frobisher to the grumpy Kix.

"A miserable effort," nodded that gentleman. He, too, had planted himself on a chair, one as distant from Lovibond's as it was possible to be and still be sitting at the same table, in the same town and county. "Sad to report, I disliked it immensely. He calls it heart-rending; I call it fit for rendering."

"Why do you two insist on attending together? Either one likes the play and the other loathes it, or vice versa. Have you ever agreed on a point?"

"Never!" said Mr. Kix, staring indignantly, as though to have agreed on a point with Lovibond would have been tantamount to treason.

"How better to annoy the old stick-in-the-mire?" returned Mr. Lovibond. "And the *matinée* hour — small price very agreeable — only small funds available to me — barely manage to survive — but Kix there — has quite the cozy annuity — lavish — hardly ever speaks of it — so much the *skinflint* he chooses to live in a boarding-house — it's madcap!"

"It's prudent," countered Kix. "I'm not a man to be trusting servants, for you know they're always stealing from you. Besides which I can't abide the drafts in the large houses. And there's far too much money wasted on the likes of plumbers and chandlers, coal-merchants and chimney-sweeps. Moreover, dining alone does not agree with me."

"Ha-*ha!* Dining alone doesn't agree with him — bend your ear to *that,* Frobisher — prefers to be among people just to aggravate them — naturally disputatious — sent on purpose by the infernal gods to annoy us — cozy income — yet he lives in a boarding-house!"

"I dare say he's free to do with his money as he likes," opined Mr. Frobisher. "If he wants to save it, so much the better for him."

"Thank you, sir," said Mr. Kix, with something like gratitude. "I'm happy to find one sensible person who agrees with me."

Mr. Lovibond laughed very heartily at this, at which point a new object gained his attention, and the topic of Kix dropped as abruptly as a discarded card in piquet.

"Look, there's Hop!" he exclaimed.

The new object of his interest was in reality an old object — an antique gentleman of singular appearance, who had come bouncing through the door from the chess rooms. He was a little rosy pippin of an old fellow with a glossy cheek, a moist bright eye, and a puckish grin. He was dressed in the extreme of the prevailing fashion — unfortunately it was a fashion that had prevailed so many years ago it had gone quite out of fashion, *viz.,* a fancy broad-skirted coat and knee-shorts, both of a peculiar lime-green hue; a ruffled shirt of fine white linen; silk stockings; smart black shoes with gold buckles; and a jaunty wig, elaborately curled and powdered.

Despite his years the little gentleman was wonderfully spry and frisky. Mr. John Hop was forever enthusing over one thing or another, forever burning to know what was afoot in this quarter or that, forever leaping about and making merry like a new lamb. It was this lively interest of his in the world, he claimed, that kept his old age as green as his coat.

Mr. Lovibond waved a plump hand. "Hallo there, Hop!" he called out. "How goes the match?"

"They're at it, sir, they're at it," gushed the rosy pippin, trotting up. "They've been at it since the morning. Turcott's bearing down on him now — it'll be double-check any moment. I'm afraid Rainbow's King is done for. I've come out now because I simply must have a breather. The forces unleashed in there, sir — perfectly staggering! The atmosphere is so thick, one can carve entire loaves of it with a bread-knife. Even the two seconds are winded."

"Trickle at the wagering?"

"She is, sir."

"Have you ventured anything?"

"I've wagered a small sum, yes, sir — on Turcott. The gentleman can't lose; it's merely a question of time. He has Rainbow's Queen and nearly everything else."

"Shall we have a look?" invited Mr. Lovibond. His fellow boarders nodded agreement; and so the three of them made their way to the chess rooms.

They found the scornful Thespian and the confident critic very hard at it indeed, in the full blaze of scrutiny from the spectators gathered round, and the immortal Philidor on the mantel. Tension loaded the air. In the midst of the onlookers stood Miss Trickle, square of shoulder and rusty of countenance. She had her pipe in hand and her hair bagged in a net.

"Still taking wagers, Trickle?" Mr. Lovibond asked.

"You're rather *late,* sir, for the game's nearly won," she answered, something tartly. She stowed her pipe in her teeth and opened her tally-book. "Nonetheless we strive to accommodate. We shall make an exception, although we can't offer odds at this late juncture. Your wager, sir?"

Mr. Lovibond graciously declined. "Haven't the spare cash, I'm afraid — sorry, Trickle — never bet myself, but Kix here is loaded — I'll wager *he'll* wager something — Turcott's a sure winner."

"Game to Turcott?" asked Mr. Kix.

Miss Trickle bowed her head to indicate that yes, that was her informed opinion.

"Then I'll take Rainbow," he said, disinterring a solitary coin from the bottom of his purse. "Ever a champion of the underdog."

Miss Trickle, glancing at the coin, took note of its trifling denomination and choked back a laugh. "No blood to be gotten out of a turnip," she observed. She pocketed the wager and made a notation in her book — it was a very small one (the notation, as well as the book). "Tell me, sir," she asked, "do you follow the gees?"

"The gees?" said Kix, not understanding.

"Horses, sir. The races."

"The races? *Never!*"

"Pity," said Miss Trickle. "Though should you ever change your mind and care to wager, I'm *not* your man."

Their attention returned to the game. The scornful Turcott had made a move — and in rather dramatic form, too, in keeping with his profession — one that sent a hush through the crowd. As Mr. Hop had prophesied, it was double-check. But Rainbow, as calm and assured a player as ever we have seen, was not a man to panic; he was a critic and had gallons of self-confidence, some of which he poured into a glass now and swallowed. Then he smoothed down his beard, and surveyed with an easy-going disdain what was left of his forces on the board.

"He's done for," whispered Miss Trickle. "Hardly a thoroughbred game, gentlemen, but for once a just and decisive one. It'll be a pretty finish."

"Wicked play!" enthused a spectator. "White's been driven to the wall."

"He's bluffing," said Mr. Kix.

"Ridiculous! How can the man bluff?" retorted Mr. Lovibond. "It's there before your eyes, sir — precious few pieces on the board — no defense for Rainbow — Pawns massacred — Rooks gone — Bishops gone — Queen gone — *hope gone!*"

"He's bluffing," Kix insisted. "My money's on Rainbow. Ever for the underdog!"

"I admire your pluck, sir," said Miss Trickle, taking her pipe from her teeth, "but sooner or later you must come to your senses."

Mr. Frobisher had been observing all with a measure of interest, but in truth he was not so keen a devotee of the game as the others there. For him a game of chess was a game of chess — a few hours' pleasant exercise, a stimulus for the mind, a temporary diversion from weightier matters. Apart from this there was little in it to excite him. More to his taste would have been to see the two haughty knights locking swords like gentlemen in the meadow, rather than shifting bits of wood on a checkered board.

Observing how far his colleagues were absorbed in the play, Mr. Frobisher chose this moment to return to the public room. As he was going out, he passed Mr. Hop going in, the little rosy pippin having sufficiently restored himself as to be proof against the staggering forces unleashed by the combat. Mr. Frobisher had gained his seat and made acquaintance with a fresh cigar when his eyes were drawn to the street-door. A handsome young woman in a dark cloak and furs had just stepped through it. She had beautiful eyes and was marvelously well-formed. The hair spilling from her bonnet was splashed with gold, and there was a pretty dimple in the middle of her chin. Mr. Frobisher recognized her at once as Miss Wastefield, the new lodger at Mrs. Juniper's in Chamomile Street.

He watched her approach the scholarly lion of a landlord, Mr. Tozer, and engage him in conversation. The eyes of Mr. Tozer behind their spectacles flashed briefly to the cat's-head letter-box; then he shook his white hair and whiskers, an answer clearly disappointing to Miss Wastefield. He summoned one of his minions and put a question to him, but the answer was the same — which served to disappoint the lady more. She and the landlord then parted company. Visibly downhearted, she was on the point of going when Mr. Frobisher placed himself before her.

"By your leave, Miss Wastefield. My name is Frobisher — Allan Frobisher. I do hope you remember me? I am one of your neighbors in Chamomile Street. I am boarding in the house of Mrs. Matchless."

The lady started and fell back a pace. Recognition stirred in her eyes. "Mr. Frobisher," she said, a trifle unnerved by his sudden appearance.

"I happened to see you with Sir Sharp-nail's warden just now. You were rather dissatisfied by the outcome, I think. May I be of service to you?"

"I'm afraid not, Mr. Frobisher. I — I was in hopes that a message of some importance might have arrived for me, but unfortunately it was not the case."

"I see. You are expecting a letter here at Sprig's?"

"A message, yes, sir."

"In the letter-box?"

"Yes."

"A message from someone in the neighborhood?"

Miss Wastefield glanced away and wrung her hands. "I'm afraid I really can't discuss it with you, sir. It is a concern of rather a personal nature."

"Of course," said Mr. Frobisher, with a vaguely penitent air. "I apologize for intruding. I suppose you must think me a rude and impudent fellow; indeed, most people do. It's only that you seemed to me so — so — so in need of *something*, what with the look in your face after your talk with Mine Host. I simply couldn't help myself. I crave your pardon! I intended no disrespect, I assure you."

The lady weighed his apology for a second or two before replying — not because she was so keen to accept it, but because she was so keen to be gone.

"As you wish. Now I really must be leaving, Mr. Frobisher. Good day, sir."

"Please, a word, Miss Wastefield," said the young man, moving gently to detain her. "I shall pry no further, you may depend upon it. Would you care to have some coffee? It's very good here at Sprig's — the best in the town. It would be a joy and a privilege if you would join me, even for a few moments."

"Why is that, sir?"

"Why?" returned Mr. Frobisher, scrambling for an answer. "Well, Miss Wastefield, it is — it is so we may remain awhile, and talk."

"Indeed you *are* rather impudent, sir. What could you and I possibly have to talk about?"

More scrambling by Mr. Frobisher.

"Well, a great many things, Miss Wastefield — this and that — the weather in the town — how you find your rooms at Juniper's — how it is you've come to lodge there —"

"More impudence!" accused the young lady. "I am going now, sir."

"Please, Miss Wastefield — postpone your departure for a minute or two at least. I apologize, I had been intending for some days to speak to you — in Chamomile Street — I'm not a fellow of many words —"

"You've acquitted yourself rather nicely to this point, sir."

A little chuckle escaped the lips of Mr. Frobisher — a gentle, good-natured, self-effacing kind of chuckle, and so unaffected that Miss Wastefield, despite her misgivings, felt a twinge of sympathy for him. It was enough to soften her to compliance; and so she permitted herself to be led to his table, where a request for two coffees, one with chocolate for the lady, was given to one of the waiters.

"I'm much obliged to you, Miss Wastefield. Do you know, I was more than a little curious," said Mr. Frobisher. "I have never known anyone to keep an ape for a pet."

"Juga is not an *ape,* sir," Miss Wastefield said sharply. "He is a monkey, and so much more than a mere pet. I consider him a friend."

It was not the best of beginnings for Mr. Frobisher, but he persisted.

"I see. So that is the little creature's name? Juga?"

"Yes. And neither is he a *creature.*"

"I apologize again, Miss Wastefield."

"Apologies appear to be a habit with you, sir."

"You will admit, however, that it's most unusual. What does it mean?"

"Sorry?"

"Juga — the name of your little friend. What is the derivation of it?"

Miss Wastefield hesitated briefly. "I don't know the derivation of it. It seemed the perfect name for him when — when the thought came to me. But how it came to me I cannot say."

"Have you had him long?"

"For nearly twelve years now. Still, he remains very youthful. He is always full of his monkey tricks."

"How did you happen to acquire him?"

Just then their coffees arrived, which necessitated some few moments' employment of the sugar-basin and cream-ewer before their conversation was resumed. Mr. Frobisher looked often in the face of Miss Wastefield as they spoke — such a marvelously sculpted face, he thought, with such a pretty dimple, and such sweet hazel eyes, and such beautiful hair, and ears adorned with such odd little earrings. She was a remarkable picture indeed! Yet for all her loveliness there was a shadow clouding her brow, and a weight tugging at her shoulders — evidence of some deep and secret trouble that made her seem older than her years.

"Juga was given me by a friend of my father's at Strangeways," she said.

"Strangeways?"

"Now it's I who must apologize, for you wouldn't know. Juga came to me from Strangeways, the zoological gardens at Crow's-end."

"Ah, I see. You have come from that distant city?"

"Yes, sir. From Pinewick."

"And that is where you live?"

"Yes."

"I see. Crow's-end is a considerable distance from here. Have you visited Nantle before?"

"No, sir."

"And what cause brings you here?" Mr. Frobisher asked, eyeing her thoughtfully as he took a whiff at his cigar. "A family connection?"

The subject appeared to make the young woman uncomfortable. She averted her gaze and drank a little of her coffee with chocolate.

"Ah, I see," Mr. Frobisher smiled. "Impudent again?"

A nod from Miss Wastefield, but still no reply to his question.

"Again I crave pardon, Miss Wastefield —"

"You have craved pardon quite enough for one day, sir. Upon my word, Mr. Frobisher, you *are* a singularly bold and intrusive young man for a neighbor! It's not for me to explain myself to you, or my purpose in being here, which in any event would be quite an impossibility. And so we'll speak no more of it."

"Then we needn't — we musn't," urged the young man, fitly rebuffed.

"You must ignore me, Miss Wastefield. It's this curiosity of mine; it's always getting me into fixes. I must hurl it from me. There! Did you see that? It's gone — I've flung it away. Off you go, insolent pup! You need fear no more, Miss Wastefield. I shall never be rude or impudent again. You may depend upon it."

Miss Wastefield, taken something aback by his manner, was looking at him with a measure of curiosity now herself. Mr. Frobisher was encouraged by this — however faintly — and by way of making amends said nothing, asked her nothing, did nothing, except to allow a tranquil expression like a gentle rain to settle over his features.

"And for how long have you lived in the boarding-house?" Miss Wastefield asked him.

"Ah, I see. It's fair play, I suppose. Well, in answer to *your* query, Miss Wastefield, I must tell you — not long."

"I'm happy you are so precise. And your occupation, sir?"

"Well," said Mr. Frobisher, assuming an air of some reserve now himself, "let's say that I'm a fellow of semi-independent means and decent background who desires to see something of life."

"And that view you have found in Chamomile Street?"

"Well — no. The truth is, Miss Wastefield, that Chamomile Street is but one of many halting-places along the road. I've no settled habitation, I admit, and haven't had for some time. I suppose I'm rather like Devenham there."

"Who?"

"That fellow over there, the shabby one in blue frieze. He's a great traveler, or so he makes boast, for he's also a great talker. But one never knows quite how to take him. Myself, I think he's little more than a common vagrant. But I suppose we share one thing in common — we are both wanderers of a sort."

"And are you a vagrant, too, Mr. Frobisher?"

"No," he answered with a smile and a gentle shake of his head, "no, Miss Wastefield, that I most certainly am not. You really are the most charming young lady! You have the advantage of me, I'm afraid — you've taken me quite by surprise."

"Then I have returned the favor, sir," the young lady smiled in return.

The shadow still clung to her brow, but it seemed to Mr. Frobisher its grip might have loosened a little.

"Then I hereby acknowledge *touché*, Miss Wastefield. Now then, you made brief mention of your father a moment ago. You must tell me something of him."

The shadow fell heavily again. Miss Wastefield looked down at her spoon, and fidgeted with the handle of her coffee-cup, and seemed again on the verge of leaving. "There is no longer anything to tell," she said quietly. "My father passed from this life almost a year ago now."

"I'm indeed sorry, Miss Wastefield. I deplore your loss. And what's more, I seem to be prying again. So you have only your mother now?"

"My mother died when I was very small, sir. I scarcely remember her. So you see, Mr. Frobisher, both of my parents are dead, if that is what you wanted to know."

"Ah, I see. I'm very sorry for you."

"You've no need to be," said Miss Wastefield. She withdrew her gaze again, appearing content to remain within the bastion of her own thoughts.

Mr. Frobisher was in some doubt how to proceed, but his dilemma was rendered moot by a rise of activity in the room. A number of prosperous-looking town gentlemen had been arriving over the past minutes, as though on the clock, and taking their places at a long table which a trio of waiters had been garnishing for a feast.

"What is it? What is going on?" Miss Wastefield asked, emerging from her reverie.

"It's a Society meeting," said Mr. Frobisher, with a long draw on his cigar. "It must be three o'clock."

"Society meeting?"

"The 'Society for the Diffusion of Worthless Knowledge.' They assemble each week at the stroke of three for the edification and mortification of themselves and others."

"For what purpose?"

"To present to the members the most useless and insignificant bits of information they've managed to uncover since the previous meeting. Quite the thing, I'm told, among the well-to-do professional men of the neighborhood — a kind of spouting club for the trivial-minded. The member determined to have unearthed the most worthless piece of knowledge is amerced a fee, which is contributed toward the assistance of the poor in the neighborhood. In the course of voting, the members will find cause to impose any number of fines upon one another, for violations of protocol and rules of procedure, all of which money goes to the poor as well."

"And what knowledge might they be diffusing today?"

"Well, it could be most anything. Last week, for example, it was an exact count of the number of buttons on the leggings of the chief ostler at the Three Jolly Pigeons. Another time it was the name *and birthplace* of the fisherman who betrayed St. Brine to the Roman authorities. And then of course there was the startling disclosure of the hat-size of the Bishop of Nantle. On another occasion, as I recall, it was the median weight of the leather buckets hanging in the Ship Street fire office."

"So these are discussions of the deepest significance."

"Please to remember, Miss Wastefield, it's worthless knowledge they are presenting, but in a most worthy cause."

The young woman smiled briefly; then the shadow fell again as her glance lighted upon someone there in the public room.

"Please, Mr. Frobisher," she asked anxiously, "do you know that man there by the long table? The tall man in the black caped overcoat?"

"Where is that, Miss Wastefield?" said Mr. Frobisher, turning round. He had no trouble identifying the person of her description. He was standing by the fire watching the members of the learned Society assemble at table. He was a very tall man, indeed, and a broad one, wearing buff-colored breeches and boots with painted tops. In his hand he held a black chimney-pot hat. His eyes, which were unusually large, dark, and shiny, were focused in a grave, observing stare.

"I believe his name is Tom Lanthorne. I've seen him here on occasion. Why do you ask, Miss Wastefield?"

"There is something about him that disturbs me. I don't at all care for the strange set of his eyes, or the way they looked at me."

"But he's not looking at you now."

"But he *was* looking at me," insisted Miss Wastefield, with a shiver, "and I did not like it."

"I don't believe he's the sort of fellow to give trouble. I've had nothing but the most sober conversation from him the few times we've spoken. Admittedly his appearance is a trifle grim, but I shouldn't hold that against him. By all accounts he neither smokes nor drinks, which says something for him, though whether for good or evil is for each to judge. And he's a great follower of chess. I believe he was observing the match a while ago."

"The match?"

"Yes, in the chess rooms behind the bar. Messrs. Rainbow and Turcott are in the midst of another pitched battle. Would you care to see?"

"I'm afraid not. Really, Mr. Frobisher, I must go now — I must return to Chamomile Street." And she started up in preparation for leaving.

"Of course. You'll grant me the privilege of escorting you there?"

"I shouldn't care to take you out of your ordinary way. Perhaps you'd rather attend to your chess game?"

"Scant chance of that," Mr. Frobisher laughed, as he helped her with her cloak. "And my ordinary way is a rather dull and uninteresting one,

I'm afraid. Believe me, Miss Wastefield, I'm more than happy to abandon the field."

As they were making for the door, a thick-set gentleman with gold spectacles and no hair — a renowned haberdasher, who happened also to be chairman of the Society for the Diffusion of Worthless Knowledge — rose to convene the meeting. He gave a nod to another of his fraternity, who rose in his turn and took in hand a large and highly convoluted sea shell. It was a species of conch, turret-shaped, with a coarse, mottled surface and a flaring red lip. The gentleman marched to the top of the table, where he placed the conch to his own lip, and like a modern Triton drew from it a wild, deep-pitched, resonating sound. Hollow but tuneful, it was like a trumpet-call summoning some vast and unfathomable power from the sea's black abyss.

To the surprise and dismay of Mr. Frobisher, this action produced a most disastrous effect upon his pretty companion. Immediately she was stricken with a violent agitation of nerves. Her face became ghastly pale, her eyes wide, her breath short; her limbs trembled in a spasm of fear and sickness.

"Oh, that sound! Why is he making that sound? Please, sir, please make him stop!" she begged, clapping her hands to her ears.

"What is the matter, Miss Wastefield? Are you unwell?" said Mr. Frobisher.

"Oh, please, please, sir, if you are a friend and a gentleman — make him stop!"

Alarmed, the young man made haste to explain to her the innocent cause of the trumpet-call.

"It's how they begin their assemblies, Miss Wastefield. Each meeting is called to order by the sounding of the shell-horn, after which the chairman there addresses the members. It's nothing more than a —"

"Oh, sir, I can't endure it — I can't bear the sound of it! Stop him, stop him — *for pity's sake, it is killing me!*"

"But what on earth is wrong, Miss Wastefield?" asked Mr. Frobisher, yearning to help but not knowing how, for he hadn't a clue what the trouble was.

"I must leave, sir — I am ill — I must leave this place!" Miss Wastefield cried. On a sudden she clenched a fist, touched it to her brow, and held it there for some moments, as if in a kind of trance. Then she began to cough and gag. She gripped her throat, as though something had lodged in it. The color of her face changed from sickly pale to purple. She turned to Mr. Frobisher with an imploring, helpless kind of look.

"I can't breathe!" she gasped. "Help me, sir, help me — I am being slowly strangled!"

Before her eyes there flashed a picture of green hills and distant mountains, and an enormous, labyrinthine building of terraces, courtyards, and colorful colonnades. It was that same mysterious vision that over the last months had come to haunt her dreams. In her mouth again was the taste of honeyed wine, in her ears the horn-call, or the call of something like a horn, from the distant mountains. Attached to the vision was a nameless horror that filled her with dread. Then the honeyed wine soured on her tongue, the knot in her throat tightened down, and she felt herself falling, falling into a pit of darkness —

The sound of the shell had died away, mercifully, by the time Mr. Frobisher got her outside into the cool air. He held her gently by the arms to steady her, as she struggled to regain some measure of control. Slowly her breath and her color began to return. The youthful door-keeper in livery looked on with much concern, and asked if there was something as might be done for the young lady? Should he fetch Dr. Cruft from within, the medical gent who was seconding in the chess rooms?

But Miss Wastefield, in a voice very thin and ragged, declined his offer of assistance.

"I must return to Mrs. Juniper's," she said to Mr. Frobisher. "If only I can return to Mrs. Juniper's, I shall be better —"

The young man began searching for a carriage. Directly he spotted one at the end of the alley, in Great Codger Lane — a cab on the cab-stand. Signaling to the driver, he hurried Miss Wastefield toward it. Gently he helped her into the vehicle, which accommodated only a single passenger, the cabman occupying a little dickey beside the seat. He gave the driver the address of Mrs. Juniper's house and some coins with which to see the lady home.

"But Mr. Frobisher, I can't accept your kindness," Miss Wastefield protested. "And I must pay you for the chocolate —"

"No, no, my dear lady, you owe me nothing. The fault of it was entirely mine; I persuaded you to stay beyond your time. It was on account of my impudence! We shan't have you walking to Chamomile Street in your present state, and in this weather. The cab will take you there speedily and safely."

"But, Mr. Frobisher —"

"Please, Miss Wastefield, I insist."

Before she could object further, Mr. Frobisher nodded to the driver and stepped back from the cab. The driver flicked the horse with his whip and away the chariot whirled down the rain-drenched street, water spraying from its wheels.

Mr. Frobisher was left in a state of considerable perplexity there at the stand after the cab rolled away. When a few minutes' hard thinking on it brought no solution, he turned back, and beheld the grim figure of Mr. Lanthorne striding up the alley towards him.

They met at a point halfway between the stand and the coffee-house.

"The lady has been taken ill?" Mr. Lanthorne inquired.

"I trust she will improve once she's home," said Mr. Frobisher, looking up into the other's face, which hovered some many inches above his own. "A temporary faintness, due perhaps to want of proper rest. I'm sure she will recover herself."

The strange, dark eyes of Mr. Lanthorne glistened on high. "She appeared much disturbed. Did she seem frightened, perhaps?"

"Yes, sir, in fact she did."

"No cause?"

"No cause that I could discern. Although she claimed to find the sound of the shell distasteful."

"Did she? Well, that is something," said Mr. Lanthorne.

Mr. Frobisher did not grasp his meaning, nor did he care to at the moment; instead he nodded crisply to the gentleman — whose manner and appearance, he had to admit, did conform somewhat to Miss Wastefield's description — and went his way. He had gone only a few paces, however, when a new thought struck him, and he swung about to address Mr. Lanthorne again.

But the gentleman was nowhere to be seen. The cramped and narrow space of the alley was empty of his presence. Tall Tom Lanthorne and his chimney-pot hat had vanished.

Mr. Frobisher sought out the door-keeper and asked if he'd seen the gentleman depart. The liveried youth replied that he had not; more strange than this, he claimed not to have seen Mr. Lanthorne in the coffee-house at any time that day.

All of which left Mr. Frobisher with a very large question-mark stamped on his brain, and wondering if he ought not make a closer examination of this Mr. Lanthorne the next time he ran across him.

CHAPTER SIXTEEN

Night Without End

Somebody was whistling on the steps of Mrs. Juniper's house. It was a whistling both luscious and cheery, and very bright, like the voice of a lark in springtime. But of course it wasn't spring and that wasn't a lark there among the flowers on Mrs. Juniper's steps. It was only Mr. Milo the postman.

Having extracted some letters from his bag, he proceeded to hammer a brisk *tap-tap-tap* on the street-door. His knock was answered by a house-maid. As he handed her the letters, he slid a lazy eye past her and down the hall, as if searching for someone there. But there was only the housemaid, with whom he chatted briefly about the doings in Chamomile Street, before screwing up his nerve at last and asking her if Miss Wastefield was at home? He was told that she wasn't, but that her maid was there, and that if Mr. Milo had a letter for Miss Wastefield, he could safely entrust it to her. The postman replied that there was no letter and, raising his hat by way of adieu, descended the steps. Silently he trudged past the area-railing and the little parade of flower-pots to the next house, the one with the brass plate advertising the NICE ROOMS of Mrs. D. Matchless.

Again a tap-tap-tapping, though not so brisk as before. Mr. Frank Milo stood there at the blue door of the boarding-house in something like a blue condition himself, his whistle dead on his lips. He had entertained the hope of seeing Miss Wastefield today, and once again that hope had been dashed. Every day that week he'd entertained the hope, but apart from one brief glimpse — mere seconds, really, compared to the several minutes he'd passed with her one morning a week ago, when she and her maid and her little pet had been setting out for a walk, and he'd spoken to her there in the street — apart from that one brief glimpse there'd been no further sign of her.

Mr. Milo had hoped for another such conversation as he'd had on that morning, preferably without the maid standing by, but his stars had refused to shine on him. Mr. Milo was one of those young men who are readily swayed by a pretty eye, a pretty lip, or a pretty dimple; and as Miss Waste-field was possessed of all three, he was triply unhappy. But hope was one thing Mr. Milo had a full measure of, and each day he rallied by reminding himself that one day he was bound to see her again — it simply was not to be *this* day.

When the blue door was opened by none other than the good landlady herself, and she invited him in for some tea, as she often did, it was quite beyond the powers of Mr. Milo to resist. Mrs. Matchless, being a woman and a widow, was by nature sympathetic to his plight. But Dottie was al-ways being sympathetic to Mr. Milo, who was in the regular habit of con-fessing his infatuations to her — a habit as regular as the rounds he walked each day delivering the mails. Mr. Milo was always falling in love with some pretty someone, which was why he was always whistling. Mr. Milo, you see, was an optimist, despite having seen every one of his hopes knocked to smash before his eyes by a pretty frown, and ground underfoot by a pretty heel.

He had lots to tell Dottie today, and she did her best to buck him up. He'd not confided in Mrs. Juniper, he said, because she was too close to the object of his affection, and that made Mr. Milo nervous. He feared what Miss Wastefield might say or think if she discovered that a lowly postman, someone so far beneath her station, had enshrined her in his heart. And therein lay the gist of his predicament.

The heart of Mr. Milo had been spirited away by the pretty lodger, but how could he further his suit if she knew nothing of it? And yet in the same breath he feared the very disclosure of it! It was a plight familiar to many a shy young man and one for which we have no answer, except to observe that Mr. Milo was a victim of his own timidity — and deservedly so.

"What should I do, Mrs. Matchless, do you think, to gain her notice? Should I write her a letter? Should I speak to Mrs. Juniper? Should I speak to her maid?"

"You should perhaps speak to the lady herself," Dottie suggested.

"But that is just what I've *not* been able to do, for she is either from home, or indisposed, or otherwise engaged." The poor fellow sighed. His lazy eye drifted to the windows there in the lilac-colored front-parlor, the tall ones that looked out upon Chamomile Street. "Oh, sometimes I just don't know. Suppose I do write to her? Will she be displeased do you think, Mrs. Matchless, to see from whom the letter comes?"

"Only she can tell you that, Mr. M."

"I want so much to know, and yet I don't want to know!" groaned the miserable young man.

"It has been my experience," said Dottie, trying to be helpful, "that a smart costume is usually an attraction to a young lady. Indeed, in my own youth I looked upon a certain young man in a grocer's blue apron with considerable fondness. Why, it's better than a potion! How do you know your Miss W. might not find your own smart red coat there an enticement?"

"I've heard it said, Mrs. Matchless, that I have. But though it may apply as regards certain masterful fellows of the sea, whose lives are chock-full of adventures, it's of little use I think in the case of general postmen." Poor Mr. Milo sighed again. "Miss Wastefield has a most taking style of beauty. There is a radiance and a grace about her such as I've never encountered. And yet it seems to me she is laboring under some affliction. Do you know anything of it, ma'am? Is she in some kind of difficulty, from which I might free her and thereby gain her confidence and esteem?"

"I know nothing of any difficulty," said Dottie, "though I do know, from my friend Mrs. J., that she's an unusually reserved young person, one not given to an ardent show of spirits. And there is something more than a little odd about her, as I've myself observed."

"Her pet, do you mean?"

The widow nodded. "An unusual thing to have brought with her all that long way. But he seems to behave himself, and little Jilly finds him captivating. Of course it's the lady's own private business whatever her difficulty may be. I've learned from Mrs. J. that she's taken the second-floor furnished for only a month, after which she means to return to Crow's-end. Ordinarily, you know, Mrs. J. lets her rooms by the quarter and no less, but on account of an old family connection, she's exempted your Miss W. from that rule."

Mr. Milo's face wilted. Miss Wastefield in Nantle for so short a time! What chance, what chance had he now? What chance to persist, to persuade? He might never have another glimpse of her before she left, let alone an interview or anything more. The news put him quite out of heart.

"I've heard she has a large trunk in her keeping, and that it sits there in her rooms under strict lock and chain, and has not been opened," he said, though with not quite so much interest as before.

"Certainly it must contain something of importance. Though she is not averse to leaving it out of her sight, as Mrs. J. informs me. It's well-secured, as you say, and yet still —"

The landlady broke off, shaking her head, as though she hadn't the words to express herself.

Mr. Milo, conscious of the hour, rose to his feet and slung his bag across his shoulder. "I thank you, Mrs. Matchless, for your kindness. Sorry I am to have troubled you again with my poor complaints."

"Not to worry, Mr. M., you're always welcome to a cuppa here in the front-parlor. As for the matter of your Miss W., well — it's been my experience that whatever is most prized is hardest to find. I don't believe the lady is long for Nantle."

The postman, looking glumly at his shoes, offered a nodding acceptance of the fact.

"Do you know, I believe one of our gentlemen here in the house has conceived a liking for her," said Dottie, putting by her teacup. "Oh, he's not said anything to *me* about it, of course. But I sense there may be an attraction there."

"Who would that be, Mrs. Matchless?"

"Why, our Mr. F."

"Ah," said the postman, wilting again. "Your Mr. Frobisher. Of course it would be he. Hail fellow well met. He *would* find her of interest, he would, and she him, I expect."

"To my knowledge there's no more to it than what I've said. In fact, I'm not so sure of that either! It's only a feeling on my part."

The postman nodded again, all too convinced that it was established truth; and together he and the widow went downstairs to the hall.

"You must bear in mind as well, Mr. M., that your young lady may already be pledged to another — indeed, it seems only natural — and that our Mr. F.'s intentions, whatever they are, may be wholly in vain."

Mr. Milo agreed that it could well be so, though it hardly reassured him, considering that Mr. F.'s intentions were very likely the same as his own. And yet, in the final analysis what did all this unhappy news mean, really? Not a thing. It didn't change him. He was still the same Frank Milo, still the same whistling, red-jacketed postman of the general two-penny kind he'd been half an hour before. He was still Frank Milo, optimist. And though the advancement of his suit was about as likely now as the revival of that dried fish in glass in the parlor, there were always other fish waiting to be caught.

He was shown out by Anne Feagle, the confidential housemaid, and descending the steps resumed his rounds and his whistling. Anne and her mistress then retired to Dottie's little back-parlor for some talk about the pretty lodger next door and her proliferation of secret suitors.

"So you think our Mr. Frobisher has taken an interest in Miss Wastefield?" Anne asked, her eyes shining at the prospect.

"Well, as I told Mr. M., it's not for me to say, though I believe there *is* a chance. But as the lady is not stopping here long, I fail to see the future in it. Ah, I think I hear little Jilly in the hall. Come to visit our young William, I suppose."

It was indeed little Jilly Juniper there, but she had not come to see William Pancras (which eased that small young man's mind considerably). Instead she had brought a book and with it a request.

"Please, Miss Feagle, is Miss Rivers at home?" she inquired of Anne, who had come out to greet her.

"I believe she's in her room, dear. Our Miss Rivers is always at home! Would you like to see her?"

"Yes, ma'am. I wanted to ask her if she might help me with my reading-lesson. Miss Wastefield in our house had promised to read with me, for she's grown a little friendlier of late, but she's come home now in a most ill condition and is unable to see me."

These words drew a curious Dottie into the hall. "Your Miss W. is ill, did you say, Jilly? What is the matter with her?"

"We don't know, Mrs. Matchless. She was weak and trembling when she got out of the hackney-cab. When Lucy saw her, she rushed her up to their rooms and bolted the door, and we've seen neither of them since."

"When was this, dear?"

"About an hour ago, Mrs. Matchless."

"Has a doctor been sent for?"

"No, ma'am. She didn't ask for one."

"Well, Jilly, we will do what we can for you, of course. Anne, will you see if our Miss R. is disengaged?"

"Of course, ma'am."

While she was gone, young Mr. Pancras, who had been observing from a doorway out of sight of Jilly, accidentally coughed, which brought him instantly to the notice of both Jilly and Mrs. Matchless. But the embryo butler-in-training and his buttons were spared by the prompt return of Anne Feagle, with the report that Miss R. was available.

Shortly Miss Rivers herself appeared and took Jilly into the front-parlor for her lesson. Anne meanwhile called for the maid-of-all-work — tall, gangly, toothy Alice — to put some more fire on in the room. Young William heaved a great sigh of relief and crept off to the wash-house, where it was his job and questionable good fortune that afternoon to clean and polish the boarders' shoes.

The evening found Miss Wastefield still locked in her rooms in Mrs. Juniper's house. She had had nothing to eat since returning from the coffee-house, having absented herself from the dining-table. Since the sounding of the shell-horn she'd been alternately frightened, disturbed, fatigued, confused, sickened, not to say very nearly suffocated, and didn't know the reason for any of it.

She had had trouble sleeping ever since her father died, and since the awful truth of *how* he'd died and the resulting guilt had taken hold of her. And when she could sleep, she was beset by nightmares. Among the many images that haunted her dreaming brain was one of a beautiful dark girl, painted, coiffured, bejeweled, wearing a flounced skirt and a robe of sheepskin. She was standing at an altar on a rocky outcrop somewhere, blowing on a triton-shell. Certainly Sprig's was no outcrop and the long table no altar, and the gentleman who had played the shell-horn no skirted priestess! Whatever did it mean?

Why had the sound of the shell terrified her so? What transitory gleam of memory had it awakened in her? Why the taste of honeyed wine on her tongue, the knot in her throat? Had it all some relation to the dreams and visions that had been coming to her since her father's death — since, indeed, the wretched moment that the wretched thing itself had come to her, disguised as a gift, on her twenty-first birthday?

She prepared some more candles for the night — for as we know, she could no longer sleep in darkness — and checked the fastenings of the hall-door and windows. Having informed Lucy that she would be retiring, she shut the door of her maid's sleeping-closet, and placed Juga in his little basket-bedstead, where the monkey's tiny eyes, rather than closing, remained open and watchful of his mistress.

It was while she was readying herself for bed that Miss Wastefield felt her thoughts drawn to the trunk. All in an instant something came over her — something like a summons, something irresistible — which caused her to put her hair-brush aside. She rose and went to the trunk. Pausing before it, she ran her hands across its surface and along its edges and corners, as though to confirm the dreadful reality of it. From that moment forward she appeared to cede control of herself, as though she had come out of her body and was observing it from afar. She saw herself kneel before the trunk and insert keys into the padlocks. She saw the locks release. She saw herself lay the chains on the floor — gently, quietly, so as not to alert her maid. She saw herself hesitate for a moment and then undo the locks of the trunk itself and raise the lid, to reveal —

A second trunk, of smaller dimensions, resting inside the first. It, too, was locked, with fastenings set in the top of it. Another key quickly freed them. There came a burst of warning chirps from Juga, who had risen up in his bed and begun waving his arms at her and making wild faces. Her fingers trembled as she worked but she couldn't help herself. Deep inside her consciousness she recoiled in horror, even as she watched from afar; but there was nothing she could do to stay the image of herself.

Perhaps it's gone, she thought. *Oh, gracious God — please, please, it must be gone!*

The second trunk opened, she found inside it a third, still smaller trunk. This, too, she unlocked, and took from it a woman's dressing-case. It was a quaint, old-fashioned kind of case, of fine and intricate design, and all too familiar — it was in fact her own dressing-case.

She laid it on the table and, sinking down into a chair, proceeded to stare at it — thoughtfully, fearfully — for a very long time. Sat and stared at it, turning over and over in her mind what to do with it, what to think of it, how to proceed.

Dare she open it? Had she the courage? Might the foul, hateful thing inside it be gone at last?

The clock on the mantel ticked along, the fire burned down, and still she stared at the dressing-case. Little Juga had fled his basket and begun pacing restlessly at the foot of her chair. He hopped into her lap, then onto her shoulder, keeping one shiny bead of an eye on her and the other on the dressing-case. His fingers played with her hair, caressed her cheeks; his elfin voice chirped and cooed in her ear; but he was unable to move her.

At length Miss Wastefield rose and approached the dressing-case. As she had with the trunk, she spent a moment running her fingers over it — trembling fingers still — before producing the final key. *Did she dare?* Something was pulling her to the dressing-case, even as her other self was warning her off. But her other self was, like little Juga, watching from afar, and would be the loser this night.

She opened the case and from one of its compartments removed a lady's hand-mirror. The handle of it was sheathed in ivory and richly carved, with images of poppies and crocuses in bas-relief, and a line of scratch-marks that were almost certainly an inscription of some kind. The mirror itself was not of glass but of polished bronze, which reflected but poorly. It was so foreign and fragile a relic, and of such clear antiquity, it looked as if it belonged in a museum. She'd been praying that it might have vanished from the dressing-case, miraculously, magically; but of course it had not.

She turned the mirror over in her hands, examining every aspect of it with a mixture of fascination and dread. Her handling of it was something delicate, not so much because it was ancient and valuable and she feared damaging it, *but because it was the mirror itself she feared*. But nothing untoward happened, and after another minute or two she returned the relic to the dressing-case. She was about to close the lid when she heard it.

It was a noise like a hissing whisper, and it came from the mirror. A slithery, slippery thing it was, that whisper, dark and sinuous, like an evil vapor rising from a caldron.

"*Djhana,*" it said.

A cold breath of fear raced up her spine, chilling her to the marrow.

"*Djhana,*" said the voice again.

She stared, transfixed, into the mirror. And still she could do nothing! Her other self urged her to flee but her body refused. Little Juga was hopping excitedly round the carpet with his mouth open and his spidery arms in the air. But no amount of warning chirps and chutters and baring of teeth and clapping of tiny hands could help his mistress now.

"*Djhana of Kaftor,*" said the mirror.

"I do not hear you," she answered. "No, no, I do not hear you —"

"*Djhana of Kaftor,*" said the mirror again.

"No, no," said Miss Wastefield, her head turning slowly from side to side and her eyes shut tight. "No, no, no!"

"*Poteidan the earth-shaker commands you. Return, or beware the Triametes!*"

Several times these words were repeated; several times Miss Wastefield denied them. It was not the first time she had heard the hissing, whispered speech or felt its brooding air of menace, but she was determined it would be the last. Why else had she come to Nantle if not to rid herself of the hateful thing? She reached a quivering hand to the lid of the dressing-case. There followed a little chirp of encouragement from Juga, who had leaped onto the chair at her side. He reared up on his legs and with one tiny, human-like hand touched her arm, as though to aid it on its course to the dressing-case.

She looked deeply into the face of her friend, ordinarily so clownish and comical a face but now so full of worry. All in a moment she seemed to re-enter herself. She looked about her, saw Juga there, saw her hand over the dressing-case, saw his own tiny hand upon her arm, saw the opened trunks.

Hurry!

With the swiftness of terror she locked the case and returned it to the innermost trunk.

Hurry! Hurry, now!

She locked the trunk and sealed it inside the second trunk, then closed and locked the outer trunk and restored the chains and padlocks, as quickly and as quietly as she was able.

Exhausted, she threw herself onto the bed. Almost at once the ghastly, suffocating sickness that had stricken her at the coffee-house struck her again, sweeping over her in huge, rolling billows like the tumbling of a mighty sea. She felt as if she must drown. She sat up and grabbed hold of one of the bedposts to save herself. She must have cried out in the midst of her hallucination, or perhaps it was the wild chattering of Juga. The door of Lucy's closet turned on its hinges, and the frightened face of the maid, her nightcap on her head, came peering round its edge.

"If you please, miss, is all right with you?" she asked, in a small voice. "I was afeared, miss. I heard such awful sounds!"

"Oh, Lucy!" Miss Wastefield moaned, in despair; and clutching a hand to her brow, she fell back onto her pillow.

The sight of her mistress in such a state roused Lucy to action. In an instant she was at the lady's side. She raised her up, and cooled her face with a little lavender water, and chafed her wrists and held her near, assuring her that all would be well, miss, all would be well, for your Lucy would see to it!

How much more troubled might Lucy have been had she entered the room minutes earlier, and found the dressing-case open and the mirror in Miss Wastefield's hand? Fortunate Lucy — how close, how close you have come!

Little Juga hopped onto the bed and snuggled up to his mistress, twining his long arms around her and lavishing upon her the sweetest of monkey-looks.

"My dear, dear Juga," Miss Wastefield murmured softly. Tears glimmered under her lashes. "My dear old companion, my little one. You are always at my side. You, and my dear Lucy! You are the truest of friends. You must forgive my indisposition, Lucy. I — I have not been myself of late —"

"Are you better now, miss?" asked her maid. "If you please, miss, shall I stay with you tonight?"

"No, Lucy. Do not trouble yourself. It is this accursed illness of mine. Such feelings of dread — such terrible imaginings — such horrid fears and sorrows as I cannot express in words. Pray God I shall be myself again in the morning, and that all will be well. We've come to Nantle for a purpose, you remember, and when all's done shall return to Pinewick, God willing, with lightened hearts. *When all's done!* Oh, why, why has Mr. Thistlewood not answered? He knows I am here. Why does he not respond?"

"It's a long lane that has no turn, miss," Lucy said. "He'll write, surely."

"But it's late now, and so we'll think no more of it. I'm very tired. I've eaten scarcely a morsel today."

"Are you in want of something from the kitchen, miss? Shall I fetch you some tea and a scone?"

Miss Wastefield shook her head. "It's too late for that; it will disturb my sleep even more than it has been disturbed of late. Oh, Lucy, I have had such frightful dreams! Such beautiful, sunlit dreams they were at first — and now so odious! No, no food, for you must not venture outside the door tonight. The night has eyes and ears, and I was followed again today, I'm sure of it."

"Oh, miss!"

"You must return to your bed now, you must."

"But, miss, you must let me help you. I know more of your fears and sorrows than you think, for I've heard the slitherous whisperings from the mirror — Oh, yes! Oh, it's a foul, unholy thing — it's wickedness and perdition! Why, miss, why must you keep it always with you? Why do you not cast it away?"

"Because I can't!" cried Miss Wastefield, alarmed at this revelation of her maid's. "Why, Lucy, do you think we have come to Nantle? Why do you think I'm awaiting word from Mr. Thistlewood? He is the one person on earth who can rid me of the wretched thing. Don't you know I would have destroyed it if I could? I've tried by every means to cast it away. Don't you understand, Lucy, *that it always comes back to me?*"

A long silence followed, during which Miss Wastefield took time to collect her thoughts, and Lucy her frightened wits.

"Yes, miss," was all the maid could muster at the end of it.

"Go to sleep now, girl," her mistress urged her, in a softened tone. "I shall be all right here with Juga for company. I thank you for your selflessness, dear child."

"Yes, miss."

The maid dropped a little curtsy and returned to her bed. As she was leaving, she stole a glance from the corners of her eyes at the chain-bound trunk, and shuddered.

Despite her every intention to the contrary, Miss Wastefield did not sleep a single wink. Though she lay in a comfortable four-poster in the heart of deepest Chamomile Street, its drowsiness did not work upon her. Lost in the labyrinth of her thoughts, she waited for the dawn.

On and on went the night. With her quickened sense of hearing she was alert to the faintest sounds — a muffled voice, the rattle of a chain, the creak of a board on the stairs. Every now and again she got up to see that the trunk was still secure, and the bolt of the door firmly in its stanchion, and the windows latched. And still she was never easy, never sure of being completely safe.

Return, or beware the Triametes!

So the voice from the mirror had threatened. In her nightmares she had beheld them, these Triametes. They had come to her unmasked, in all their foul and hideous monstrosity of form and vileness of being, and she wanted never, never to see anything of their kind again.

She hoped very much she hadn't seen one today, in the shape of a tall, grim-faced man in a chimney-pot hat.

CHAPTER SEVENTEEN

More Colleens Than One

L ove, says the poet, is a fraud, and we are not inclined to disagree. Precisely which poet said this, you ask? A reasonable question, but one that we very reasonably decline to answer, for the truth of it is so clear, so far beyond dispute, that there is no need to be singling out dead poets.

What other direction-post upon the broad highway of life can so mislead as love? What other impulse can so exhilarate and so madden, all in the same moment? Can so defy rationality and good sense? What other glad emotion can burst out of thin air and vanish as quick? What else in life is so ethereal, so transient, while appearing so solid? What else is so deceptive in so endless a variety of ways? What else so treacherous? Nothing, we declare, nothing but love, that very same love our poet calls a fraud; and so we shall have none of it.

Having slogged through the mire of love in our formative years, we have outgrown all need or want of it. We are no longer susceptible to that "soft impeachment" which has proved so crushing for Mr. Milo. We've seen it, we've recognized it for what it is — a fraud — and have done with it. We have learned from our missteps and view with pity those who have not, poor wights like Milo and others of their kind. Of that kind unfortunately, there have been many in the lifetime of the world; and if we're not mistaken, here are two more of them approaching apace.

Mr. Havergal Skeffington Jones and his colleague, the horsy-faced Moeran, on their way to the Axe and Compasses, have come upon an oyster saloon in a smoky lane near Slopmonger Mews. Spying through its windows a shapely young dear whose acquaintance they had made on a previous occasion, the two pause before the shop to refresh their senses, and feast their eyes on the pretty damsel within.

ARIFAY'S is the name inscribed on the glass of the window, accompanied by the boast — OYSTERS IN EVERY STYLE.

"Moeran," says Round-the-corner, peeping at the young dear in her place behind the counter.

"What is it, Jones?"

"Would ye care, now, if we was to stop a bit at this fine esthablishment, and pay our compliments to the delightful Miss Conyers? For 'tis she there at the counther, I do bleeve, and it's in the mood for an oysther or twain and a dhrink I am."

"The colleen is it ye mane?" returns Planxty, in mock surprise. "By gannies, joy — I'd no notion ye'd sich a weakness!"

"Merely a call of Christian friendship on a fellow crayture," says Jones, pushing open the door. "And a good day to ye it is, me purty colleen! 'Tis plased I am to see ye."

The shapely young dear turns round, and affects a playful demeanor.

"Good day to you, sir."

At sight of her, Mr. Jones arrests his step, for though the shapely young dear has lines and lineaments very like those of the bewitching Miss Conyers, she is in point of fact *not* Miss Conyers. Not that Jones is entirely disappointed, however, for the lines and lineaments of this damsel are fully as charming as those of the absent one.

"And it's axing yer pardon I am, jewel," says he, doffing his muffin-cap, "but ye bain't that Miss Conyers as we've met afore."

"No, sir. Miss Conyers is no longer employed here, if by that you mean the young lady who preceded me in my situation. My name is Sisly Ingum, sir."

"And where be yer masthur this fine day, Miss Sisly Ingum?" inquires Jones, who, having already consigned Miss Conyers to history, darts a swift glance round the shop in search of the proprietor. But there appears to be no one else about the place. The boxes are vacant, the aisle empty, and the shadowy doorway behind the counter has the curtain drawn across it.

"I don't rightly know, sir," says Miss Ingum. Her bashful smile displays a nice little row of teeth to complement her lips, her blue eyes, and the ringlets of yellow hair that frame her lovely countenance.

"Ah. Well, if ye plase now, jewel, might ye open a dozen oysthers for me friend Moeran here and meself? I feel the weight of the day upon me, shure, and could do wid a taste of the natives to spirit me up."

"Dare say I can, sir," answers the girl, and with all diligence complies with his request, plucking the oysters from their watery reservoir and shelling them with her slim little hands.

"And a brace of ginger-beers, if ye plase."

Which bottles are obligingly procured, and their corks extracted, and the glasses filled, with a coquettishness that Mr. Jones deems wholly *charruming*.

"And how d'ye find yer sit'ation here, jewel?" he asks in a light conversational manner, once he and Planxty have had time to sample a few of the oysters and sip a little of the ginger-beer.

"It's a very nice situation, sir."

"Have ye been at it long?"

"No, sir; 'tis but my second week."

"Ah, yer second week is it? Shure, then, ye've earned a bit of a respite, I'll wager. Pray let me not incommode ye, jewel, but would ye care to join us at table? Plase to open yerself an oysther or twain, acuishla, and fetch yerself a ginger. Ye can lay the charge to Moeran here."

"Oh, no, sir, I couldn't do that. The master, Mr. Arifay, would never permit it."

"But yer masthur be nowheres about, now, bain't that so?" returns Jones, looking round again at the empty shop. "Troth and faith," he murmurs to himself, "is it every day they have so little custom in the place?"

"But I can't, sir, for he would reproach me severely," protests Miss Ingum, with a little shake of her ringlets. "Though I should be happy to talk with you till I'm needed again at the counter. But I can't take oysters or ginger-beer with you, sir, nor nothing else."

Mr. Jones, by nature a fellow of practicality and compromise, finds this compromise to his liking, as does Mr. Moeran; and so the *charruming* Miss Ingum sits her pretty self down to table with them. They were seated in one of the boxes ranged along the wall, and as no other customers had come in, or seemed to be in danger of coming in anytime soon, the two had the enchanting Miss Ingum pretty much to themselves.

"You are a gentleman of the law, are you, sir?" inquires the damsel (this directed to Round-the-corner, who just prior had been discussing with Moeran certain troublesome matters of a legal nature, affecting himself).

"Shure as Shrovetide, jewel, that I wor, and a smart enough one, bedad! But I've sinst given up the pracktice of the law, for the time at least," he replies, grandly dusting a bit of lint from his waistcoat.

"I'm sorry to hear it. And why *is* that, sir?"

"Agh, acuishla, there's no more the challenge in it," he sighs.

"No challenge, none," says Planxty. *Never was any*, is what he thinks.

"Me intherest in the law has waned, and so it's tired I am wid it. Agh, it's a perdickament common enough, jewel, to sich as have rose to the cusp of their perfession. Shure it's a sad fact, as many a mighty barristher, many a towering sarjent, many a lofthy lord has discovered. By the Holy, it's not all as takes kindly to the humdrum of murphies and buttermilk! And so 'tis new challenges, acuishla, 'tis fresh tinder as keeps me chimly smokin'."

Suiting the action to the word, Mr. Jones sets his pipe a-blazing, with leisurely care, then fishes up from his coat one of his business cards, which he presents to Miss Ingum as evidence of his newest challenge.

"'MEM-BER OF PAR-LI-MENT,'" she reads out, haltingly.

Mr. Jones smiles and inclines his head — humbly, wisely, graciously.

"You are indeed an ambitious man, sir," says the damsel, much impressed.

"Agh, that I am, jewel, that I am," says Jones, too honest a fellow not to admit it. "Shure, then, a few oysthers more now, acuishla, wouldn't come amiss. Half a dozen will do, if you plase. Thank ye. Bedad, 'tis hexcellent good ginger-beer, this is. Most revivin'!"

"Would you care for a little brandy-and-water, sir?"

Mr. Jones looks at Mr. Moeran, and vice versa. As if such a question was deserving of any other reply but one!

Miss Ingum takes a bottle from the shelves and pours it out for them, in a most beguiling fashion.

"Pay the colleen!" says Round-the-corner, with a brisk wave of his hand.

Mr. Moeran, visibly reluctant, counts the money from his pocket and lays it out.

"Thank you for your custom, sir," smiles Miss Ingum, sweeping up the coins.

"*That*," says Moeran, glancing at Jones and pointing to the spot where the money had been, "that, dear joy, was the very last of the tin as I have upon me parson at the moment. By the powers, Jones, we've spent all our brass an' copper boys, we have. Divil a penny have we now."

"But a right pleasint way to have spent 'em, and in sich charrumin' company," answers Jones. "Oysthers and ginger-beer, and brandy-and-water! And they've shrimps an' winkles too, as I've noticed, and red abalonies, and lobsthers, and pickled salmon. All of it at no fancy prices."

"Shure ye've a genius for outlay, Jones, by the Holy! And how much is it ye're owin' me now? The sum total of it I mane?"

"Agh, very pleasint it is, jewel, in partickler when her masthur's not about," Jones runs on, tossing the brandy down and motioning for the damsel to pour him another, while conveniently ignoring the protests of his colleague and banker Moeran.

"And how d'ye mane to pay for *that,* now?" his banker demands.

Again he is ignored.

"How do you know the master is not about, sir?" smiles Miss Ingum, leaning upon the counter in a pretty attitude.

Mr. Jones takes another look around the shop, though not with the steadiest or most scrutinous of gazes, for the brandy is already exerting its effect. On a sudden he rises from his chair and swaggers up to the counter, where he makes bold to tickle the chin of Miss Ingum.

"By the Holy, ye're a purty one, jewel!" he exclaims.

"You flatter me, sir," returns the damsel — not averse to being so tickled — and drops her eyes.

"Is she not a purty one, Moeran?"

"Shure she is," answers Planxty.

"And how ould might ye be, jewel?" asks Jones, nuzzling a pretty cheek.

"Eighteen years, sir," replies Miss Ingum, blushing.

"Ah, eighteen years, shure enough." He sighs, and rests his elbows on the counter and his chin in his hands, absorbing himself in the contemplation of her heavenly presence. "I remimber when I wor meself but eighteen years of age. D'ye reckollect it, Moeran?"

"Not a bit, for it's only years afther that I met ye, joy," says Planxty. "By the powers, Jones, don't ye know so yerself, or is it boozled in the brains ye are wid the liquor?"

Mr. Jones waves the question away, and with another swallow of his brandy boozles his brains even more. "And have ye no young gintleman in the town to spoon wid, acuishla?"

"None, sir," confesses Miss Ingum, sadly shaking her head. Mr. Jones in sympathy takes her slim little hands in his, and proceeds to a tender examination of each pretty thumb and each dainty finger, one by one, and the shiny nails of same, so neatly trimmed and polished.

"Agh, 'tis a shame, it is. No doubt 'tis the fault of that confounded masthur of yers. For I've seen him afore, acuishla, I have, in the delightful Miss Conyers's time. A big, gruff, ugly maggot of a spalpeen he is, that Arifay. A gargoyle, bedad! And as bald as a coot. The kind of masthur as would hold in tight leash a purty colleen of eighteen years. Bain't it so, Moeran?"

"'Tis the way of the world," nods his colleague.

"Ah, shure, and quick enough it wor he dismissed Miss Conyers from her sit'ation. The big, bald, ugly maggot — I recolleckt him well."

"A brawny one he is," says Moeran, "and a churlish."

"Wid an ugly mug."

"The ugliest, joy."

"And a scar, I seem to recolleckt, on the side of his bald head."

"A scar, by the Holy Mother — an ugly thing indeed."

"The scar or the head, Moeran?"

"Why, the pair of 'em, joy!"

"Shure and 'tis lucky the big ugly maggot bain't about the shop now, acuishla," smiles Jones, tickling Miss Ingum's pretty chin again, and thinking himself more than ordinarily amusing today.

"But sir — I never said my master was not here," laughs the damsel, with a pleasant little silvery cadence.

Comes the sound of a heavy, booted step from behind the curtain, the one drawn across the doorway back of the counter. Then the curtain is swept aside. Mr. Jones barely has time to turn around before an iron fist grips him by the coat-collar, and he is lifted into the air as easily as a kitten. Little Planxty, his eyes blown wide, gives a start of surprise and jumps to his feet.

"And is this here the big, bald, gruff, ugly maggot of a fellow, the spalpeen, the gargoyle as you say? And is this mug here the ugly mug, and this scar here the ugly scar, as you say?"

So growls a surly voice; and as Jones twists slowly round on the pivot of the iron fist, the big ugly maggot of his description swings into view — a gentleman very big and brawny indeed, with a pair of mighty arms, an evil slash of a mouth, and a ponderous brow. His head is tall and white like a boiled egg, and smooth too, except for the jagged scar trickling down its side. On the top of it is a fur cap thrown very far back, and on the bottom a black beard cut square at the end.

"Ah, shure, 'tis a fine thing to make yer acquaintance agin, yer worship," says Round-the-corner, dangling from the iron fist like a corpse from a gibbet. "Sarvice to yer masthurful parson! And so we'll be leavin' now, sir, if ye plase, this instant minute —"

"Has this villain been annoying you, child?" demands the proprietor.

"He's been tickling my chin, sir, and nuzzling my cheek, and squeezing my hands," replies Miss Ingum, with such chaste innocence of expression as beameth from the virgin moon. "Oh, sir, I could scarcely abear it."

"So! I see how it is. Tickling her chin and more, then, is it?"

"Just a — a harrumless bit of fun it wor, yer worship," protests Jones, in a squeaking voice. "It's tired I am wid it now, sir, and so we'll be leavin' ye —"

"Hold your din! Have they paid the reckoning, child?"

"Ah, shure, that we have, sir, every bit of it," Moeran interposes hastily, before the young dear has a chance to contradict him in the matter of Jones's final brandy.

"If they've paid their coin, then, and they've had their drink and their oysters, then it's high time the villains were about their business. Or is it a sprig o' the shillelagh they're waiting on?" the proprietor asks, with a dangerous glare.

No, Mr. Moeran assures him, they were waiting on no shillelagh, then follows after as his colleague is forcibly transported to the street-door and dropped in a sorry heap in the lane outside.

"Your coin is welcome," growls Mr. Arifay, a livid frown setting off the ugly scar on his head, "but your jolly fellowship is not. Villains, see that you do not forget. Good day to you."

The ogre vanishes, kicking the door of the saloon shut behind him. A moment later the door opens again, briefly, and the muffin-cap of Jones is flung into the lane.

The victim struggles for some minutes to climb back into his coat and cap, and thence into his dignity, for the treatment accorded him has quite wrenched him out of all three. His colleague then hands him his pipe, which Mr. Jones had lost track of during his precipitous exit.

"Moeran?"

"What is it, Jones? Are ye hurted? Shure it's a sevare conquassation ye've had."

"Divil take me if ever I patronize that bloody gargoyle's esthablishment agin," says Round-the-corner, waxing proud on his unsteady legs. "Ye'll curb me in me sthride if ever ye catch me a-walkin' this way, won't ye, Moeran — afore he provokes me to a breach of the peace?"

"Shure I will."

Mr. Jones draws his breath hard, and colors up to the very tip of his nose.

"'Twas lucky for him, Moeran, that the current of me temper runs so smooth, or I'd soon ha' sorted him out. The lily-livered weasel — let him go snick-up! We'll take our trade elsewhere."

"He'll not want to be gittin' into yer bad books, that's shure."

"What reason has he to be callin' me villain? Hang it, Moeran, I bain't afeared of the likes of *him* — the odious Jack-a-Lent! Bedad but he's a rough taskmasthur, as surly as a butcher's dog. It seems he's a new an' more splendid crayture in the shop every week. Don't it seem that way to ye, Moeran? Never satisfied wid their work, he must be, and so he gives 'em the chop. Well, the weasel's not worth a groat, nor she neither — the fair deceiver! 'Tis a great weakness of mine, I'll allow, Moeran, to fancy sich faymales. Well, they can both of 'em go snick-up for what I care! Troth and faith, jewel, there be an intire cityful of colleens in this world aside from *that* colleen."

"A cityful of 'em is true, Jones, to be chattin' up."

"What would our friend an' fellow Dermot O'Kilcoyne, rest his sould, ha' done in the same sit'ation, I ask ye?"

"Much the same I've no doubt at all, at all. A gintleman and a Christian he was, shure, one wid an eye for the leedies."

It will be rather evident by now that Mr. Havergal Skeffington Jones, unlike our postman Mr. Milo, was no sentimentalist. He was not a man to mope over a failed suit. Love for him was as easy as lying — and are they not often one and the same?

"Have ye seen the Axe and Compasses anywheres about?" Jones asks, as he and Moeran are passing a line of stables in the mews. Mr. Jones is still suffering the effects of the brandy-and-water, and already has mistaken more than one fat gelding for the bluff landlord, Mr. Hinxton, of the afore-mentioned inn.

"'Tis nowheres near, joy. Ye've to keep walkin' to the end of the lane there, then into the public road and so to Ship Street," Planxty informs him.

"Ah, shure, I recolleckt it now."

"The brandy it must be has addled yer concenthration."

"Ah, the brandy, jewel — most revivin' it was!"

Somehow, the pair of them manage to avoid being trampled by horses in the lane, and carriages in the street, long enough to make their way to the Axe and Compasses.

At a table there in the common room sat the stalwart captain of the *Salty Sue*, with his first mate at his side. They were deep in converse with a thin, sharp-beaked, pinch-lipped man wearing horn spectacles and a know-ing air. Their discussion was concerned with the spectacled man's need to cross the channel to the islands, and as the lugger was sailing for same two days hence, how it would be convenient for him now to book passage for himself and his very particular cargo. A general consideration of terms fol-lowed, all of it very cordial, after which the contract was sealed with a round of pipes and tankards.

The spectacled man was a trader named Hicklebeep, and was well-known to the captain and Bob Sly, for he and his very particular cargo were often aboard the *Sue*. As a result they had reached terms easily, and were making shift to enjoy the hospitality of the Compasses when noises of a dis-

turbance reached their ears. A shabby vagabond of a little fellow was observed being escorted from the premises by a stout coarse giant of a man,
who had taken hold of him by the shoulders and was propelling him
toward the street-door. A second shabby little character trailed behind
them making vigorous protest.

To Captain Barnaby and his companions, the stout coarse giant was a
familiar figure, and they knew all too well what this action of his signified.

"Sink me if it bean't Candy o' the sponging-house, or I'm a forked
radish!" the captain exclaimed.

"Aye, sir, it be Candy all right," said young Stubbins the pot-boy, who
was passing by with a few empty tankards in hand.

"Ha! And who be the scurvy rogue as he's grappled fast? I hadn't a peep
o' the lubber's face, the one in the muffin-cap. Sarten sure I'd not give a
louse for his fortunes now."

"Nor louse nor flea, by gum!" declared Mr. Sly.

"Rascally scoundrel by the name of Jones, sir," said the pot-boy.
"Taken for debt and on his way to Comport's lock-up, I'll be bound!"

CHAPTER EIGHTEEN

Of Glyptodonts and Moropi

It had been a difficult morning at the Smithy for Mr. Threadneedle.

There had been first the business of the books in his private study. As was usual for him, Mr. Threadneedle had arisen early and gone to his study to attend to some matters there. He was seated at his desk with his quizzing-glass in his eye and a batch of accounts in hand when he found his gaze straying to a certain bookcase across the room. It was a tall, handsome bookcase with windows of glass in its doors. Its inhabitants consisted of a number of volumes belonging to Mr. Threadneedle and his late wife. Well, to be frank the books had been chiefly hers; apart from a few texts of a scientific or practical bent Mr. Threadneedle had few books of his own, but his wife had been a prodigious collector.

Mr. Threadneedle was a tinkerer, not a reader, and so his wife had selected for him a few volumes she deemed instructive — certain tomes of a devotional nature, prayer-books, psalters, and the like; a biography of her father, published at that late gentleman's expense, with a sepia drawing of him for a frontispiece; a general history of Truro, in seven installments; a treatise on the husbandry of moropi; a manual of household potions; and an anthology or two — and had herself arranged them on the shelves, for his perusal in an idle hour. Sooth to say they had been little disturbed since then, for the subject matter in general did not appeal to the squire of Smithy Bank.

As his gaze strayed now to the bookcase, it occurred to Mr. Threadneedle that all might be better served if his wife's books were removed to the library, and the shelves let to other tenants — to his many ledgers, for example, and his accounts for the superintendence of the estate, and his notebooks recording the progress of his tinkering, all of which lay in heaped masses on his desk and side-table. Aware that if he didn't act now, he would inevitably delay and perhaps never act at all, the grocer began the task of ordering the contents of his bookcase there in the privacy of his study, his snuggery, his *sanctum sanctorum*.

He was in the midst of this act of vandalism when he was interrupted by a creaking of boots, followed by a startled gasp. Turning, he beheld his gaunt and normally impassive butler, Mr. Plush — a being nearly as tall as the bookcase, but not so handsome or so transparent of interior — standing at the door, his lofty features radiating shock and indignation.

"Might I inquire, sir, just what it is you are meaning to accomplish?" he asked, creaking up, and peering down his long nose at his employer, the former grocer and person beneath consideration. He asked it as a thing of course, for he knew already what his master had in mind, having caught him in the fact.

"I am shifting these books," said Mr. Threadneedle, innocently enough. There was a fair number of them, he explained, and he was hoping that the butler might assist him in the task. But Mr. Plush had another idea.

"I beg to observe, sir, that these are the late mistress's books," he said, in the tone of one defending the relics of some holy saint of yore.

"Indeed they are, Mr. Plush, most of them. I should like them taken now to the library. They're of little good to anyone here in my study, and I have other uses for these shelves. My wife certainly won't mind."

The butler was appalled. He shook his ponderous old head while looking at the floor, as if to say, *This fool is dog-mad!* What he actually said was this —

"I should not advise it, sir. Oh, no, no. Impossible."

"Impossible? How do you mean, Mr. Plush?" the squire asked. He was standing with his thumbs in the pockets of his red flannel waistcoat, and his fingers gripping the braces at his ample waist.

"It would be a violation of the first order, a trampling upon the imperishable memory of the late mistress. Wouldn't you agree, sir?"

"But I simply mean to take these books and —"

"But they were *her* books, sir. She placed them there with her own fair hands. We cannot violate the sanctity of her intent. We cannot transgress. Oh, no, no, no, sir!"

"But they are my books now, Mr. Plush. You seem to forget that my wife has been dead these three years and more. I know you were quite devoted to her, as was I, of course, and I mean no disrespect to her memory. I simply wish to remove these books to the library, where books belong after all, so that I might make better use of the shelves. Surely it is my own study to do with as I please, is it not, Mr. Plush, and my bookcase?"

Mr. Threadneedle seemed just a trifle uneasy questioning his butler in so pointed a fashion. Poor Mr. Threadneedle — so short, so thick, so little better than a costermonger, and an offlander from Nantle to boot!

The butler, gravely disapproving, shook his head again. "Never can be done, sir. Oh, no, no."

"Never?"

"No, sir, never."

The eyes of Mr. Threadneedle moved to the pile of books he had taken from the shelves — had torn from the shelves, wrested from the shelves, plundered from the shelves — and a feeling of guilt crept over him. It was as if he had violated a sacred trust, profaned a saintly shrine, defied a hallowed precept of Holy Writ. Sacrilege! Desecration! His meek little curled-up mustaches withered with the shame of it.

"In the late mistress's day," intoned the butler, the better to drive the point home, "such a thing would never have been countenanced."

"Of course not," said Mr. Threadneedle, mostly to himself, "because my wife would not have permitted it."

Why did he have to remind me of that? Why did I not give him the sack when I had the opportunity? Chicken-heart — I am such a chicken-heart!

"Please to remember, sir, that it was the late mistress's intention that the books be placed there, and we must honor that intention," said Mr. Plush, adding significantly — "we *all* must honor her intention."

"Ah," said Mr. Threadneedle, with a slow nod or two, as he felt the inevitable acquiescence stealing on — his own.

"It would be a monstrous thing, don't you agree, sir, to disturb her rest in such a manner?"

"Disturb her rest, Mr. Plush? Well, I — I suppose it would, or it might," the grocer said. He hadn't really thought about it. He certainly didn't care to have his wife's slumber disturbed by his vandalism; no, there was no need for her to come rushing back to him from the other world, absolutely none! But because he missed her — or more likely, because he missed the company she had provided — he found himself once more giving in.

"I take your point, Mr. Plush," he said, something chastened. "I've quite gone off the idea now. Of course I shall return these books to the shelves. If my wife intended for her books to remain here, then we must respect her intention. Well, thank you so very much, Mr. Plush."

The butler bowed his head with great solemnity, and with the faintest of faint smiles on his lips, and creaked away.

Directly the holy books resumed their places in the sacred shrine, and the doors of the sanctuary were closed upon them. And so the blissful slumber of Mrs. Baxendale was spared the hazard of disturbance.

The second difficult matter of the morning Mr. Threadneedle encountered in the breakfast-room, when he was accosted by his tiny housekeeper, who came gliding toward him with her menacing finger in the air.

"Mr. Threadneedle," said the voice like a rasp, "I fear it has gone quite beyond the bounds of endurance!"

"Pray, what has, Mrs. Kimber?"

"I refer to the limpet pie."

"Sorry?"

"The limpet pie," the housekeeper repeated, swishing her finger under his chin, "which Cook has informed me was prepared by *your* instruction."

"Ah, yes. A limpet pie, Mrs. Kimber, with raisins, marshberries, and an assortment of tasty herbs. It's rather a favorite of mine. I used to make it often in my bachelor days, when I had my shop in Chamomile Street."

Horrified, Mrs. Kimber recoiled on hearing the word *shop*. The next she knew he would be waxing expansive again upon his *blue apron* and his years in *the trade*. She shuddered at the thought.

"Cook informs me," she said, scraping her employer with her eyes, as though he were a kind of whetstone for the sharpening of them, "that a limpet pie was prepared in this house for the mean drab boy from the village. I ask you, sir, is this true?"

"For Tim Christmas, yes, Mrs. Kimber, and for his mother and sister. It's a gift, in consideration of the lad's fine work here at the Smithy."

"Charity again! And so what do you propose to do about it?"

"Do about it? Why, I propose that Tim take the pie home to his family."

Aghast, Mrs. Kimber sharpened her eyes again. "If I may be so bold, sir," she began.

"You may, for there is little I can do to prevent it," the grocer sighed, nerving himself for the onslaught.

"If I may be so bold, sir, this is not the parish workhouse. This is an ancient estate of noble lineage, and we must comport ourselves accordingly. In my own small capacity it has been my sovereign charge for above these twenty years to superintend the domestic arrangements here. How can I fulfill my responsibilities when persons are slipping round behind my back, dictating secret orders in the night expressly to escape my notice?"

"It was not in the night, Mrs. Kimber," the grocer assured her. "It was early yesterday morning. I simply asked Cook if she might prepare a little something for the Christmas family, and having offered her my suggestion of a limpet pie, with a recipe I'd worked out myself, she seized upon it gladly."

"I must have a talk with Cook, and sooner rather than later," said Mrs. Kimber. "She has been attending to others far too much of late. I beg to remind you, Mr. Threadneedle, that if you had wanted a limpet pie from the kitchen, you should have approached *me,* sir, and properly made known to me your request."

"But you are not Cook," said Mr. Threadneedle, sitting down to his breakfast, which a sympathetic parlormaid had laid upon the table. As she swept past Mrs. Kimber, the maid turned and made a face in her direction — though all out of her view — which nearly caused Mr. Threadneedle to disgorge the coffee he was on the point of swallowing.

"I see. I see how it is. You think it hilarious, then, sir?" said Mrs. Kimber, folding her arms. "Well, sir, it will *not* do. There has been a most serious breach of policy. Hitherto I've been most patient with you, sir, as patient as Grissel, with respect to your many quirks and eccentricities. But of late you have been positively straining the bounds of endurance. I fear I cannot disregard this latest lapse."

Either she or I must go to the wall, was the thought of Mr. Threadneedle. *But as I am an honest man and a true Christian grocer, I shall not yield.*

"You needn't regard it or disregard it," said the squire, bravely, "for the simple reason that it needn't concern you. It's a master's prerogative. But I thank you all the same for your devotion to policy. Good morning to you, Mrs. Kimber."

He shot her a glance as pleasant as it was firm and triumphant, to convey the idea that their discussion was at an end. The housekeeper, having loosed her arrows without apparent effect, was obliged to retreat. Turning on her heel, she glided from the room.

Fortunately for Mr. Threadneedle, the lowly coach-house was beyond the province of Plush and Kimber — quite outside the pale — as both considered it beneath their dignity to trouble themselves with matters there; and so to the coach-house he went as soon as his breakfast was done.

"Good morning, young man, good morning!" he exclaimed, his gray eyes twinkling like a pixie's.

Young Tim Christmas was already there, of course, busily at work at the carpenter's-bench. A pleasant bit of fire was burning in the grate. On the rug little Foxy raised her ears and sniffed, peering curiously at the newcomer. Her bushy tail fluttered, and having satisfied herself as to Mr. Threadneedle's identity, she laid her head down and resumed her former ease.

Tim thanked the grocer for the gift of the limpet pie, which lay on the bench, and expressed again his wonder at the many kindnesses that had been shown him and his family. As if his wages and his breakfasts and the five golden guineas were not kindness enough already, he exclaimed.

But Mr. Threadneedle would hear nothing of it.

"Tomorrow will be an important day for us, Tim," he said, warming his hands at the fire. "I believe you'll more than earn your share of that pie."

"Yes, sir. I'm very much looking forward to tomorrow."

The grocer hung his coat on a peg and girded on his blue apron. "We must pray for fog again in the morning. It's been steadily thickening each of these past few days, as I've noticed. Let's hope it continues. If so, then tomorrow should serve nicely for our next trial."

"I've further improved the pedal mechanism of the speed-coils, sir, as you directed. They should respond better now, I think, and prevent the sort of trouble we encountered in the first trial."

"Good, good. We'll not care for another narrow squeak, will we?"

"No, sir."

"Good lad!"

They were just getting down to some serious tinkering when the noise of carriage-wheels reached their ears, betokening the approach of a visitor. Mr. Threadneedle looked out to see not one visitor but two — a man and a young girl — in a pony-trap that was rolling up the gravel drive. Not far behind them trotted the shaggy figure of Mustard. The arrival of the trap had caught the attention of the stout little pachyderm, who was ambling over to see who had come for a visit so early in the day.

The driver of the trap was a middle-sized, middle-aged, middle-grade clergyman of the country variety. He had a heavy, hanging jaw, two deep, hollow eyes, and a pasty brow. The little girl beside him resembled nothing less than a female edition of Tim Christmas, if a somewhat younger, smaller, and prettier one.

"Who is it, sir?" Tim asked, as he joined his benefactor at the door.

"Well, now. It appears to be your sister Kate and the vicar."

The grocer and his apprentice-of-sorts traded glances. They looked round them at the unusual appurtenances and apparatus that filled the coach-house, and then at the two alighting from the trap, and then again at each other.

"I don't think we want visitors strolling about the shop just yet," Mr. Threadneedle suggested.

"No, sir," Tim said, emphatically echoing that opinion.

"Not even your sister, I'm afraid. It would be premature to say the least."

"I agree, sir."

Hurriedly Mr. Threadneedle exchanged his apron for his coat, and Tim his smock-frock for his old jacket, and they went outside. M'lady Mustard had arrived at the carriage and, recognizing the clergyman, offered him a bleating roar of welcome. As for Kate Christmas, well, she was a stranger. Ordinarily it required a little time for Mustard to become acquainted with anyone. On this occasion, however, she was greatly aided by Tim, who encouraged the woolly pachyderm and his sister to be friends. The similarity between brother and sister no doubt speeded the effort. Soon Kate was on such good terms with the little mammoth as to be permitted to caress her trunk and tickle her big floppy ears.

The clergyman, looking on with a virtuous expression, strode round the trap and placed himself at Mr. Threadneedle's side. It was well known that the Rev. Mr. Yorridge, on these little country visits of his, was apt to be touting donations for the parish fund. "Unto whomsoever much is given, of him shall be much required, to relieve the wants of the needy," was his stock appeal, delivered with a particular view to Smithy Bank. In consequence Mr. Threadneedle, as chief squire and churchwarden of St. Brine's parish, Plinth, had become conditioned to reach for his pocket-book whenever he saw the vicar approaching. It was a sort of reflex with him. Exercising that reflex now, he realized that his pocket-book was up at the manor.

As it turned out, however, money was not the reason for the vicar's call; he merely wished to see how Tim Christmas was getting on in his apprenticeship-of-sorts. On the drive from Plinth the vicar had passed the family's cottage, and there had had conversation with Mrs. Christmas and her daughter. Because little Kate was eager to learn what this "tinkering" was that her brother and Mr. Threadneedle were engaged in, the vicar had invited her along.

This presented something of a dilemma now for the tinkerers, one which was solved by the quick-thinking Tim, who fetched the limpet pie from the coach-house and presented it to Kate. She expressed more astonishment even than her brother had; and so the conversation was temporarily diverted from the topic of tinkering.

Knowing more than a little about the tyranny of Plush and Kimber, the vicar marveled that Mr. Threadneedle had been able to slip the pie past the wary housekeeper. How had he managed such a feat in the face of such opposition, he wondered? To which Mr. Threadneedle simply smiled, and assured the clergyman that as squire of Smithy Bank he brooked no insubordination in the matter of his help.

The heavy jaw of the vicar fell, and his eyes widened. "Miraculous!" he exclaimed. "I never would have believed it."

The grocer smiled again and nodded.

"Well, well. Incredible! It seems we have miracles round us every day. And so how are you keeping, then, Tim?" the clergyman asked, turning his attention now to the sturdy youth and object of his visit.

"Most excellent well, sir."

"And what is it exactly that you do here? What duties has Mr. Threadneedle given you?"

"Ah, well," said the grocer, adroitly stepping in, "it's some of this, vicar, and, ah, some of that. He's an able lad with his hands, as you know. Jolly fine with blades and hammers, and chisels, and the carpenter's square, and mastering his skills now at the forge."

"Ah! So he's learning something of the smith's craft, then? The shoeing of horses and mending of harness, the fashioning of wrought iron? Good gracious, that's excellent!"

"Just so. For you know, vicar, this is the *Smithy.*"

"Well, well! It's a very large estate, and no doubt there's much mending to be done. It was a fine idea of mine to send him to you, that I can see, and very squirely and charitable of you, Mr. Threadneedle, to take him in. Perhaps Kate and I might have a peep inside the coach-house now, and see how you go about your work?"

"I don't think it would be advisable, vicar," said Mr. Threadneedle, insinuating himself between his visitors and the coach-house door, which Tim had shut behind him after fetching the limpet pie.

"Why not? I assure you, Mr. Threadneedle, we're very much interested."

"Ah, well, vicar, because — because — because it's all in rather a jumble at present. Yes! A jumble. That's it! A dreadful state. We've not had the chance to tidy up from our tinkering of yesterday. Isn't that so, Tim?"

"It is, sir," stated the lad — honestly, for it was in fact the truth.

"We weren't expecting callers, you know, particularly not so early. Indeed, vicar, I fear you could make very little out of the shop this morning."

"It really is quite a mess," Tim agreed.

"Oh, Timothy, don't be such a fussy-wussy!" his sister exclaimed. She was longing for that peep inside the mysterious coach-house. "We shan't tell anyone it's a mess, especially not Mother. We shan't give you away."

"Perhaps we can have a look in at the windows?" the vicar suggested.

"Yes, you *must* show us what you get up to here, Timothy. Mother wants to know, for 'tinkering' as you call it is hardly informative. And what is this 'wizard notion' you spoke of?"

Before anyone could stop them, she and the vicar had flattened their noses against the latticed panes and were peering in.

"God bless my soul!" Mr. Yorridge exclaimed, as his eyes swept the dimly seen interior. "It looks very cluttered and complicated in there."

"It is," the grocer assured him. "In point of fact we're in the midst of re-furbishing the entire shop."

"To provide greater comfort," Tim explained.

"It's been used for housing carriages, you know, not tinkerers. There are a thousand and one jobs that need doing to make it a proper workshop."

"It doesn't seem such a wizard notion to me," grumbled Kate, a trifle disappointed by what she saw. "I can't make anything out."

Mr. Yorridge admitted that it *did* seem rather a jumble in there. It was this moment that m'lady Mustard chose to lumber forward a little, and stopping back of him, she raised her trunk and vented a cloud of steamy breath in his ear. The vicar jumped in alarm and nearly lost his hat; but finding that it was only Mustard, he recovered fast. A hearty laugh on his part sealed the job of dislodging him and Kate from the window.

"She has a way of surprising one," said Mr. Threadneedle, patting the mammoth's shoulder. "But she's a dear old thing. Aren't you, m'lady?"

Mustard blinked a round and mischievous eye, and dipped her woolly head, and flapped her ears, as though she agreed completely with his assessment. Then she swung round and transferred her attention to the pony-trap, and to the limpet pie with raisins, marshberries, and herbs reposing therein. Her curious trunk reached out again, her jaws opened, her pink, blubbery tongue appeared, and —

"No, no, Mustard!" cried Mr. Threadneedle, rushing to stop her. "That pie is for the Christmas family. You've already had your breakfast. Off you go, then."

The mammoth responded with a little bleating roar of protest, then bounded off across the turf to resume her gorging amongst the shrubberies.

"Oh, she is as cute as a pin!" Kate exclaimed. Her heart was fast melting with love for the little mammoth, and she had half a mind to follow her. "Timothy, why didn't you tell me she was as cute as a pin?"

"And as mischievous as an imp," said her brother. "Only yesterday she made off with a hoard of Cook's best biffins, which were sitting in a basket at the wicket-gate of the garden. The basket was tracked down, eventually, but no biffins."

"She's always eating — as hungry as a stable full of horses," said Mr. Threadneedle. "Your pie would have disappeared in a trice, my dear, if m'lady Mustard had had her way."

The vicar was about to chime in with an observation of his own, concerning the peculiar discomfort of steamy breath in one's ear, when a voice reached them from beyond the hedge. It was the gamekeeper, alerting Mr. Threadneedle to the fact that a ship had arrived in Cold Harbor. The fog had broken a little down there, said the man, and the vessel had fetched in smartly and dropped her hook.

"Do we know her, Henry?" the grocer called aloud.

"'Tis the *Salty Sue*," the man replied from a distance, his hands cupped round his mouth like a speaking-trumpet. "She's put off her surf-boat, and the captain and Bob Sly and the trader Hicklebeep be aboard."

"Mr. Hicklebeep is here!" said Tim. "It's as you predicted, sir."

"Yes, unfortunately," the grocer said.

"But we're *not* to tell him of the stones just yet?"

"Which stones are those?" Tim's keen-eared sister asked.

"Merely some old rocks, my dear," Mr. Threadneedle spoke up hastily. "Some trifling oddities I acquired from Mr. Hicklebeep, quite some time ago now. I've thanked him for them already; anything more would be superfluous."

"Just some stones, Kate, as Mr. Threadneedle says," Tim agreed. "They've made excellent fine doorstops up at the manor-house."

And so there was an end to it — for the moment.

It was decided that all should walk down to Cold Harbor to see what Mr. Hicklebeep had on offer today. Having hidden the limpet pie in the back of the trap, to prevent further mischief by a certain pachyderm, they set off along the winding path that led to the beach.

At a point about midway down, their senses were assailed by a vile odor. It was an odor something like a boar's stall and something like bilge, compounded by the smell of rotting orchids — only far worse. It was an odor of nauseating foulness and pungency. It was the rankest and most villainous smell that ever offended nostril, a truly ghastly stench. It was the smell of Ladycake.

The moropus looked up from her grazing and stared at them through dim, sleepy eyes. Munching and staring, munching and staring — such were the chief concerns of Ladycake there in her pasture, which commanded nothing less than the cream of the view. Like any moropus worth her salt, Ladycake was innately suspicious of anyone or anything that infringed on her domain. As a consequence she left off her grazing now and made strides toward the dry-stone wall to see about the intruders. The walling round her pasture was rather higher than most and topped with a row of iron spikes, which moropi found hindersome and so were less likely to be getting over.

As she drew near, the nauseating stench intensified. It became apparent, too, that she was a formidable beast in more than just aroma. At the withers she stood some twenty hands; posterior to this her back sloped downward to immense loins and hocks and a short, brush-like tail. Her chest was deep and wide, her limbs robust and heavily muscled. On her padded feet were the claws she used for rooting in the ground. Her coat was of that odd purplish hue like mulberries, her mane and markings jet-black. Cross-tempered, homely, sleepy-faced, useless, out-of-sorts, evil-smelling, magnificently rare — all terms that have been used to describe moropi, and all with equal currency.

Sidling up to the wall, Ladycake craned her head and long neck out over it, sentry-like, and scrutinized the intruders. Her ears were lifted half in curiosity, half in threat. The smell of her was quite overpowering; it was like a great solid wall of stink, as dense as the wall that penned her in. Everyone fell back a step or three and grimaced.

"She *is* rather strong today," Mr. Threadneedle admitted.

"Oh, she's a monstrous, smelly thing!" exclaimed Kate, who had never before seen a moropus, let alone caught scent of one.

"She's a proper stinkpot," acknowledged her brother.

"She is a blessed creature of the Lord, one of the Almighty's sacred Creation," intoned the vicar, raising a pious hand. "We must not judge her. 'Judge not, that ye be not judged.' We must be charitable toward all God's creatures regardless of their station. We must remember that all the creatures of the Lord possess equal beauty in His eyes."

So the simple country clergyman reminded them, with just a hint of pomposity. Having expressed this wise and moral sentiment, however, he was promptly overcome by the stench and, turning aside, buried his nose in his pocket-handkerchief.

Ladycake — mute, inscrutable, unswayed by any such trivial concerns as sentiment or morality — looked from one to another of the intruders, her eyes surveying them from under heavy lids. Her ears twitched, her jaws champed, her teeth like grindstones crunched.

The vicar of Plinth, so eloquent in his defense of her, took his handkerchief from his nose for a moment — but a moment was quite long enough. The moropus saw her opportunity and, puffing out her cheeks, sent a green wad of spittle flying in his direction. The reverend gentleman leaped back, surprised. Fortunately the missile landed wide of its mark, striking the ground beside him with an ugly *plop!*

This interesting development, coming as it did on the heels of the stench, was motivation enough for the intruders to beat a hasty retreat. They resumed their journey down the bush-girt slopes, at rather a livelier pace than before, however, and with many apologies from Mr. Threadneedle.

They crossed the graceful old bridge of brick and stone over the stream, and skirted another tract of hillside, a breezy expanse dotted with red cows, tapirs, and bison grazing in well-hedged fields. In due course they arrived at the bottom of the hill, to find the sand beach and the quiet waters of Cold Harbor spread before them.

The fog had largely abated there, as the man Henry had reported, well enough to allow Captain Barnaby to guide his vessel into the shelter of the cove. Her surf-boat lay drawn upon the strand, having borne ashore the salty warrior of the sea and his first mate, and a couple of prime sailormen to ply the oars. In their company was the sharp-beaked trader Hicklebeep, pinched of lip and horned of spectacle. A smartish tweed cap and neck-shawl, Norfolk jacket, and drab trousers tucked into boots of the water-proof kind comprised his wardrobe, knowingness his air.

Riding in the stern sheets of the boat was Melon-head, the captain's black tomcat, who hissed at Mr. Threadneedle before bounding off in pursuit of some sandpipers at the water's edge. He was an independent cat and a loyal one, and took seriously his charge to patrol all grounds upon which the captain, his master, set foot.

Mr. Hicklebeep had brought with him a diverse cargo of baskets, crates, and boxes, the contents of which he and the sailormen were laying out on a tarpaulin before the boat. Included among the merchandise was a small box of wood-and-wire construction in which a creature of some type was stirring.

"A fair morning to you, Mr. Baxendale, my good friend!" the trader exclaimed, lunging at Mr. Threadneedle with arms outstretched. He seized the grocer's hand and wrung it with both fists like the handle of an old pump.

Mr. Threadneedle immediately took exception to the trader on a point — not that it was not a fair morning (which it wasn't), but that his name was *not* Baxendale but Threadneedle, Malachi Threadneedle, and that it was his late wife who had been a Baxendale — that is, before she'd married him and become Mrs. Threadneedle. But of course, to all who had known her, Mr. Hicklebeep included, she would forever be Mrs. Baxendale of the Baxendales of Smithy Bank. And if she had been Mrs. Baxendale, then logic prescribed that the inoffensive-looking fellow who had been her husband ought to be Mr. Baxendale. To his credit, however, the trader made swift reparation once his error was made known to him — it was the same error he perpetrated on his every visit to the Smithy — and assured his good friend Threadneedle that he would not be caught out again.

"Now then, sir," he went on, "I have here today a number of rare and particular items for your consideration," and so proceeded to expound upon the merits of the varied treasures he had on offer. Among them were some sparkling gems, some coins, and some gold and silver thimbles; a silver porringer; a musical box in a quaint, old-fashioned case; some pouches of shag tobacco and a box of rappee, both of the Richford variety, and very hard to come by; a vizard mask of dirk-tooth hide, ideal for fancy-dress parties; an unsigned portrait of a lady who had flourished in a bygone century, by an artist who had never flourished at all; a handsome dispatch-case for letters; some mithridatum and dragon's water, impossibly rare, and said to be proof against the plague; a sheaf of quill-pens made of teratorn feathers; the dried foot of a mummy, wrapped in linen and smelling of spices; some turreted marine shells, very strange and beautiful; some daggers made from saber-cat teeth — slim, wicked canines with serrated edges, harvested from safely defunct cats; and other like items for those of particular and discerning tastes.

"Split me crosswise and sink me!" Captain Barnaby exclaimed, strutting to and fro, scratching his head and assuming odd postures as he stooped to examine the trader's latest curiosities. Despite his show of admiration, he seemed faintly disappointed not to have found one rare item in particular among the treasures.

"Teeth of saber-cat? A right wicked monster, sarten sure, but let me perish, sir, have ye no fangs o' the zeug among this lot?" he asked, with a crunch of his forked brows.

Ever accommodating, the trader took from one of the crates a broad, sharp, cone-like object considerably larger than his fist, and held it out for all to observe.

"From a zeug, sir, at your request," he announced. "A tooth, my good friends, from the ravenous maw of one of the mightiest serpent-behemoths ever to roam the chilly dark waters of the sea."

The captain's brows relaxed, and his eyes lighted up with satisfaction as this rarity was placed into his hands.

"Smite me dumb and roast me!" he exclaimed.

"Have you seen a zeug, Captain Barnaby?" asked Tim. "I have heard they're something frightful to behold. Monstrous toothed whales!"

"Aye," the captain answered, turning a grim sailorly eye on the young 'prentice. "Aye, sink me and bleed me, years agone in southern waters, when I were a seaman on Clipperton's ship. Hurled beyond the horizon we were by a roaring great tempest — blown clean off the shelf and into the deepest of cold fathomy waters, which abyss be the kingdom of Lord Zeug.

Howsomever they do come inshore, on occasion, when seas are high. But for sarten, boy, a fang sich as this beauty be as near as most care to come to the serpent-behemoth. Ship-killers — swampers o' boats — leviathans — hugeous gliding demons of the deep — sink me, that's plain enough!"

"Man-eaters, by gum," averred Mr. Sly.

"A seaman on Clipperton's ship? Do you mean, captain, that you once served under Wulf Clipperton?" Tim asked, with rising excitement.

"So-ho! Why, souse me for a grunion, boy! Be there any seafaring Clipperton but he, now? Though he's gone to bunk with Davy Jones, sarten sure, these long years agone. Lost! Lost he was in the fathomy trenches." And the captain paused to shake his silvery head at the tragedy of it.

"Aye, Cap'n," mourned Mr. Sly, sharing in the atmosphere of reverence, for indeed the name of Wulf Clipperton was one of the grandest and most storied of names in the pantheon of their sailing brethren.

"Well, what think you, Mr. Baxendale, sir?" said Mr. Hicklebeep, once the moment had passed. He rubbed his hands briskly in anticipation of a sale. "What has taken your fancy today, my friend?"

"Threadneedle," corrected the grocer. "My name is Threadneedle. You forget, Mr. Hicklebeep, that my wife Mrs. Baxendale — by that I mean Mrs. *Threadneedle,* of course — is no longer among us."

"Ah, true, no more she is," the trader nodded, with a sympathetic heave of his shoulders. "It always gives one pause when a customer has made the dread exit, and journeyed on to the great darkness. It's a pity there's no longer a Mrs. Baxendale at Smithy Bank. She was a lady who knew a goose from a capon, sir. A very regular customer, she was, very particular, and a dear friend and person to boot."

"A very dear lady indeed, and most active in the parish," said the vicar, who, like the others, had been looking over the trader's cargo with great interest.

"What is this, sir?" Kate asked. She had come upon the box of wood-and-wire, and was peering through the open-work at the odd little animal inside.

It looked to be a kind of turtle, but one unlike any turtle she had ever seen. It was about the size and shape of a large gourd. It had the furry cheeks and muzzle and velvet ears of a beaver, but the rest of it was encased in a shell of bony armor. Two timid little eyes squinted at her from under a bony head-shield. From beneath the shell four clawed feet protruded, on legs very broad and squat.

"What is it?" Tim asked, joining his sister in her examination.

"A *she* it is, actually," said Mr. Hicklebeep, delighted to see young people taking an interest in his merchandise. The younger he snared them, he reasoned, the longer he could rely on them for their custom. Here he was now at Cold Harbor, the gateway to Smithy Bank; for all he knew, these youthful customers might be heirs to great estates. How little he comprehended of their true circumstances!

"My youthful friends, I see you are intrigued by my glyptodont," he smiled, rubbing hands again.

"Ah, I've heard of these creatures," said Mr. Threadneedle, showing interest despite his better judgment.

"The glypts are native to those rainy southern lagoons lying far beyond Goforth and the Flinders range. I believe Captain Barnaby has run across them now and again on his voyages — have you not, my good friend?"

"Scorch me and burn me," the captain nodded. "One of the peculiarest o' creatures 'twixt this bit o' shore and that. Though look 'ee now, never have I clapped eyes on a glypt of sich midgetosity. How say ye, Bob Sly?"

"Aye, a mighty minikin of a glypt, by gum," his first mate agreed.

"Is it a baby?" Kate asked.

"An infant of the glyptodont species, indeed," the trader informed her.

Her eyes brightened at the information. "Hoo, hoo! I see you in there, baby glyptodont!"

"And, being an infant, may be readily tamed. One needs to acquire them when they are young, like most creatures, if one is to train them properly. Mr. Baxendale, my good friend — perhaps this small creature has taken your fancy? For these glyptodonts are among the most convenient of pets for keeping. They do not move about much and so cannot stray far. They do not bark or otherwise cry out, and will not disturb one's rest or that of neighbors. They are tidy in their habits, and easily cared for. They are plant-eaters — some grass, some lettuce and some kale, a little celery, some turnips, some carrots, a sweet potato now and again are all they require. They are friendly and even-tempered, when raised from an infant, and make for pleasant company. A glyptodont serves excellent well for an ottoman on a lazy evening, for as I've said they don't move much. One need only lay a blanket over the carapace, for comfort, as the bony plates may be a trifle hard on the heels."

"What is an ottoman?" Kate asked.

"A sort of cushioned footstool," said the vicar.

"She *is* rather like a piece of furniture, a very small one, with a head and tail poking out," Tim observed.

"The glyptodont is protected by these bony plates, which we in the trade call *scutes,*" Mr. Hicklebeep went on. He knelt beside the box, the better to point out the finer aspects of the odd small creature to the children. "Very like a turtle or tortoise she is, or the rare armadillo, in her externals. There is, too, as you can see, a smaller plate covering the roof of the cranium; this we call the *casque,* or head-shield. The tail is wound round with overlapping rings of armor in a sort of sheath. Ah, yes, a glypt makes for excellent company! Placid, unobtrusive, compliant creatures they are, having few demands of their owners. They must have their water, of course, and need merely be turned out on pasture having a pond or watermeads. Watermeads, very fond of watermeads they are."

The trader rose to his feet. "What say you then, Mr. Baxendale, sir? One infant glypt for Smithy Bank? Very nice for the children here. I assure you, my good friend, it is money well spent. Shall we consider it a sale?" Already he had his sales-book in hand and was preparing to make the entry.

"We shall not," said Mr. Threadneedle, who proceeded instead to inquire about the armored tail of the glyptodont, as to how far the creature could swing this weapon and with what result? For a weapon it most certainly was. Mr. Hicklebeep with big-hearted benevolence assured him that he needn't worry, that the chance of injury was vanishingly small. Farther to the south, he said, there were species of giant glyptodonts with a knot of bony spikes like a mace at the end of the tail — now there, sir, he declared, chuckling, *there* was a weapon that could inflict real damage! Captain Barnaby, soak him and bleed him, confirmed this account of Mr. Hicklebeep's, for he had seen such creatures with his own eyes on the shores of an unnamed lagoon far south of the Flinders range.

In spite of its small size and timid aspect, Mr. Threadneedle had his reservations about the infant glypt. Of course the question of its adult appearance was a matter of some interest to a prospective buyer, or should be. It was a question which he now pursued.

"This animal being an infant, there is good reason to believe it will grow?" he asked.

"Of course, sir," the trader smiled confidently.

"And what size might it be expected to attain at maturity?"

Mr. Hicklebeep assured him that some eight or ten feet in length would not be at all unusual, sir.

The grocer frowned. "That's a fair-sized ottoman."

"Well, naturally, sir, as the creature ages, other uses may apply."

"And how long before this one attains a length of eight or ten feet?"

"Ah, not before the next year is out, certainly, sir — perhaps two years at most."

Despite the less-than-subtle appeals of Tim and Kate, Mr. Threadneedle

would not be persuaded. He had more than a few ottomans up at the house
already, he explained, and no more were needed. Certainly he had little use
for a footstool some eight or ten feet long and who knew how tall. In this he
remained firm; no doubt the example of Ladycake was weighing on his mind.

"What else have you got today?" he asked, changing the subject.

The trader replied that he'd gotten a line on another moropus, a fine
specimen that could be paired with Ladycake. Ah, yes, a brace of moropi
was infinitely better than one, he claimed, as they would provide company
for one another and trouble their owner less. They were rather *roguish* creatures when left to their devices, he hinted, with which admission Mr.
Threadneedle readily agreed. Mr. Hicklebeep had discussed the outlines of
just such a scheme with Mrs. Baxendale, at the time Ladycake had been
brought to Truro, but a second sale had never been consummated.

"What say you, then, Mr. Baxendale? Have we an agreement, my good
friend?" he asked. "For I'll not have another such bargain till after Can-
dlemas at the earliest."

But "Mr. Baxendale" graciously declined the invitation, saying that one
moropus was quite enough, thank you, and that a brace of them would be
nothing if not a surfeit of riches. And for good measure he reiterated his
decision regarding the baby glypt, saying that not one of the ottomans up
at the manor-house was expected to grow appreciably for the next year at
least, or require any maintenance apart from the occasional dusting; nor
would they walk off in the midst of his nap, and send his heels crashing to
the floor; and not one of them had an armored tail with which to pum-
mel him.

Here was a stopper! Not a single item of the trader's rare and particular
cargo appeared to interest the squire of Smithy Bank. Shutting his eyes, Mr.
Hicklebeep pulled off his cap and spectacles and massaged his head, as if to
wring the disappointment from it. But he was nothing if not resilient; as a
merchant-trader in the diligent pursuit of custom, he had to be. *I shan't be
offended*, he said to himself, as he always did when an offer was rebuffed,
for you can't offend me. Then he returned his cap to his head, and his spectacles to his eyes, and was restored to his usual appearance.

To humor him, Mr. Threadneedle agreed in the end to the purchase of a
few small items from among the treasures, to wit: some cave-bear claws
(these he presented to Tim and Kate), a pouch of shag tobacco, and a couple of book ends in wolf's-leather — these last to prove useful as regards
the ledgers and notebooks in his study, now that his late wife's collection
would not be moving to the library.

Something mollified, Mr. Hicklebeep happened to make mention of the stones he'd sold Mr. Baxendale a while past — the odd stones that had been found by Wulf Clipperton, that illustrious mariner who had vanished on a voyage of discovery to southern seas, and under whom, as it turned out, Captain Barnaby had once served.

"It was said they had rained down from the sky at the time of the great sundering," the trader recalled. "Although none could state positively that it was so, Captain Clipperton's views on the matter were greatly respected. Beyond question they were unlike any stones ever before seen. He deposited them in the ore office at Goforth in the event they should prove of value, intending to return for them. But of course he never did."

"What kind of stones were these?" asked the vicar, who was always interested in whatever Mr. Hicklebeep and others had to tell of the wider world. The Rev. Mr. Yorridge had traveled little beyond the islands on which he'd been raised — to Nantle, briefly, for some clerical training, and to lonely Paignton Swidges, equally briefly, as curate of the parish there — so that most anything offlanders brought with them to Truro, whether cargo or information, was to him a potential wonder.

"Odd stones, reverend sir, of an unusual weight and texture," the trader informed him. "They were believed to be remnants of the mighty comet or shooting star that precipitated the sundering."

"Cherish my guts, sir, I do recollect 'em among the cargo," said Captain Barnaby. "Above a year ago or more."

"I should like to see these stones, these relics of the cataclysm that visited such devastation upon the world," said the vicar.

Mr. Threadneedle shot a quick glance at his apprentice-of-sorts, which was instantly returned. A brief pause followed, and then he smiled and turning to the vicar declared that yes, indeed, you ought to pop round and see the stones someday, vicar — but not to-day — and that they had been put to excellent use up at the manor-house.

"Jolly fine doorstops," he nodded.

Mr. Hicklebeep was all delight. He was always pleased, of course, when a customer was happy with a purchase, for it meant that the customer was likely to purchase again, as indeed the grocer had that day. As for the vicar he made it clear he planned to examine these celestial doorstops the very next time his duties brought him to Smithy Bank.

The captain, seeking to fulfill a duty of another sort, now presented Mr. Threadneedle with a letter, a personal missive from an address in Chamomile Street, Nantle. The captain knew very well from whom it came. He recalled the many times the *Salty Sue* had carried Mr. Threadneedle out to Truro to visit Mrs. Baxendale when the two had been courting. He knew that there had been several of these letters from Chamomile Street, and had taken to wondering whether a new attachment might have been formed with a certain rosy-cheeked landlady? But the captain was far too circumspect a man, too much a man of the world, to give voice to his suspicion.

Mr. Threadneedle, pocketing the letter, happened then to inquire as to the general well-being of the captain's wife. It was an unfortunate choice of topics, one which set the normally chatty captain to hemming and hawing, and caused his first mate to execute several violent contortions of visage. From this, Mr. Threadneedle surmised that the weather in Jolly Jumper Yard was as squallish and tempestuous as ever.

Later, while the captain was occupied with other matters, Mr. Sly took the grocer aside and in primest confidence told him that the wind had been blowing particular bad in the cappie's house of late, and that there looked to be money troubles there, but that it was anybody's guess how to work it out and nothing else to be done about it nohow, by gum. Some further discussion then ensued concerning news of Nantle and what was afoot there. There was a team of shovel-tuskers in town, said Mr. Sly, mighty creatures that had been brought in from Falaise for the purpose of clearing roads. And there was Mr. John Jarvey, the mastodon man, who had arrived from Goforth with his sons and his shaggy red thunder-beasts to receive cargo from the ships for overland transport. Mr. Hicklebeep, overhearing, saw fit to interject that it was this same Mr. Jarvey who had delivered the infant glypt to him, having come upon it on the journey north to Nantle.

"By the by, Mr. Baxendale, sir," the trader said, now that most of his merchandise had been stowed away in the surf-boat, "as we are on the subject, would you yourself have need perhaps of a shovel-tusker or two? Beyond the simple clearing of roads, these cousins of the mighty mastodon have proved themselves eminently serviceable for plowing fields and digging trenches, which no doubt are important and practical concerns of yours here at Smithy Bank. I have a line now on a pair which I could obtain for you, my good friend, at a just and reasonable cost. What say you, sir?"

But it was not to be. No, Mr. Hicklebeep, the grocer told him a trifle brusquely, we do *not* have need of a shovel-tusker or two at this time, but we shall be certain to send word should that rare and particular need ever arise in future, thank you very much, sir.

Meanwhile the vicar, who was an admirer of sailing-ships, had engaged Captain Barnaby in a few words of discussion regarding the *Salty Sue*. The reverend gentleman spoke glowingly of her qualities, and flattered her immensely, and pronounced her a beautiful ship. "A prime duck of a craft, sir," her skipper boasted, scanning her from waterline to lofty mastheads with a sailorly eye, "so stout and trim, and sweet to her helm. Aye, sir, the tightest ship as ever sailed!" The two then proceeded to exchange views on the relative merits of lug-sails versus a square rig for the coastal trade, the captain pointing out the superior weatherliness of the lug-sail and its advantages when working the tides.

"Love my limbs, sir," said he, filling his cheek with a quid, "but ye've a discerning eye and a loving heart for a clergyman, that's plain enough. A fisher of men ye may be, but I'll not gainsay ye. Any man what cannot love such fair and capacious craft bean't nowise capable of love in his heart, or I'm a jack mackerel. Good luck t'ye."

The vicar was as taken by these sentiments as the captain himself, and so the two warriors — the one of the sea, the other of God — shook hands and parted. The captain strutted up to the surf-boat and, giving a hitch to his dreadnoughts, announced that the *Salty Sue* must trip anchor now and away, for there were ports to be called at in Plinth and Whitchurch and on the other islands, before her return three days hence to Nantle.

Mr. Hicklebeep expressed his regret that the squire of Smithy Bank had no need of a baby glyptodont — or a shovel-tusker or two, or another moropus ("for a brace of moropi are splendid garnish for a well-tended pasture," he rhapsodized) — but he was confident he could persuade someone at Plinth to take the infant in. On impulse he approached the vicar, but the reverend clergyman informed him that he, like Mr. Threadneedle, already had an ottoman. The vicar recommended him, however, to a Mr. Parsloe of the Greens, in nearby Feltram. This gentleman, he said, was an elderly bachelor and a connoisseur of curiosities. Mr. Hicklebeep immediately pricked up his ears and, nodding, said that he remembered the old hunks, and that he would make bold to call upon him as soon as they arrived at Plinth.

Then the surf-boat was thrust off. The sailormen pulled briskly for the *Salty Sue,* with the captain and Bob Sly and Mr. Hicklebeep waving to those on shore, and the adventuresome Melon-head directing all from the stern sheets. Once they were aboard the lugger, the ship's anchor was raised, and her sails hoisted, and bending to the light breeze, she fetched out into the channel and was gone.

Mr. Threadneedle and the others retraced their steps along the path, an uphill exercise which, for the two adult members of the party at least, required significantly more exertion than the journey down. In due course they arrived at the coach-house. As the vicar was about to hand little Kate into the trap, to convey her and the limpet pie home, something in the corner of his eye drew his attention.

"Weren't those trees there on the left a bit farther from the coach-house?" he asked. "And the hedge — wasn't the hedge there on the right a little *closer* to it?"

Mr. Threadneedle, trading glances again with Tim, assured the reverend gentleman that he was almost certainly mistaken. After all, how could it be? How could the trees and the hedge have been grubbed up without somebody's noticing, and without leaving any trace?

The vicar was standing on the gravel drive with his arms crossed, gazing in perplexity at the coach-house, at its walls and lattice windows, its steep-pitched roof, brick chimney, and weather-vane.

"Perhaps it's the coach-house itself that has moved?" he wondered.

"Nonsense, vicar!" Mr. Threadneedle laughed. "How can a coach-house move?"

The vicar frowned and shook his head, and was forced to admit he knew not how; and so off he went in the pony-trap with Kate and the limpet pie.

Greatly relieved, Mr. Threadneedle went inside and sat down in one of the well-stuffed chairs by the fire to read his letter from Chamomile Street. His eyes twinkled as they lighted upon a flood of cheery words concerning, among other things, the general attractiveness of a grocer's blue apron. His course was clear — he must prepare a cheery letter of his own in return. This he did at the little writing-desk by the side-casement. Then, informing Tim that he would be back soon, he made his way up to the manor-house. He approached it cautiously, alert for any sign of Plush or Kimber, until he ran across the gamekeeper Henry. To this trusty gentleman he gave the letter he'd written, asking that he ride at once to the docks at Plinth and hand it to Captain Barnaby for delivery at Nantle.

"We shall hope for fog again in the morning, Tim," the grocer reminded his apprentice-of-sorts later that afternoon, when their tinkering for the day was done. "With the fog we'll have a clear field before us — in a manner of speaking."

Young Tim agreed and shortly after departed for home, fired with enthusiasm for what the morning would bring. Reluctantly Mr. Threadneedle had to turn little Foxy out; then he closed the shutters and locked the coach-house door behind him. Arriving at the manor, he managed to evade both Plush and Kimber by a furtive climb of the back-stairs to his study. Once there he charged a pipe with his new tobacco and smoked it for a while in thought.

Rousing himself after a time, he went to the window to examine what was left of the day.

A rolling sea of fog was fast approaching from the northwest, swallowing all before it like a hungry giant. Standing there with his hands in his pockets and his pipe in his teeth, Mr. Threadneedle smiled, and his meek little mustaches smiled too. Unlike most of us, he seemed to view a nasty fog as a jolly fine thing, and a propitious omen for the important day to come.

CHAPTER NINETEEN

Conquerors of the Cloud-tops

In the morning Mr. Threadneedle awoke to find he'd been granted his wish. The whole of Smithy Bank lay buried under a thick mantle of fog. The hungry giant had done its job; it had swallowed the sky, the sea, the bush-girt slopes, the pastures, the brow of the hill, the manor-house, the stables and paddocks, the grand sweep of forest. It had swallowed most everything, in fact, and left nothing behind but its own self, a chilly gray monster busy gobbling up the world.

It required a little effort for Mr. Threadneedle to find his way to the coach-house through the gloom, but find it he eventually did. There he came upon Tim Christmas waiting for him at the door. His apprentice-of-sorts had followed the well-marked carriage-road from Plinth and arrived only a few minutes before. Punctual to a fault, with his hair neatly combed under his cap and his clean-looking eager eyes a-shine, Tim was more than ready for the important trial ahead.

Mr. Threadneedle came not alone to the coach-house, for he had with him the day's hamper of food from the kitchen, victuals to be feasted on at a more convenient hour. There would be no dallying for breakfast today.

"Good morning, Tim, good morning! Lovely fog, isn't it?" he exclaimed, with that especial good humor that marked him on days such as this.

"Yes, sir!"

"We are prepared for it, then?" he smiled, unlocking the door.

"Yes, sir."

"Ah, good, good!" Mr. Threadneedle laid the hamper by and together he and his apprentice undid the shutters, to coax some murky light into the coach-house. While Tim set about kindling a fire in the grate, the grocer lighted the swing-lamps that hung from the oak beams of the ceiling.

"The mechanisms look to be in fine order, sir. I examined every one of them yesterday before leaving," said Tim.

And many mechanisms there were, too. In each corner of the coach-house, for example, stood a narrow, cage-like structure extending from floor to ceiling, with a threaded shaft or screw running down through it. At the bottom of each cage was a large, flat stone of singular appearance. It was a lush, creamy kind of stone, generally white in color, and crossed by a number of regularly spaced, parallel veins of green and blue, all very fine and straight. These were intersected at intervals by cross-striations of a crimson hue, forming a complex, grid-like pattern. The surface of the stones showed signs of weathering, as though some process generating heat had burned away small portions of it. Each stone was set into the base of its cage and held there by a rigid frame of iron that extended under the floor.

Threaded onto each shaft at its upper end was a coil-like structure, or *cage-coil*, composed of several thin metallic disks, stacked one above the other. Atop each cage the shafts were fitted to sprocket-wheels, which were linked by chain-belts to a meshwork of wheels, cables, and pulleys strung about the ceiling. Most of the meshwork converged on a spot near the front bay window, where two belts running down made connection to a pair of roller-like devices — common household mangles, each with a large crank-handle. The mangles were positioned one across from the other, with sufficient space between for a person to stand and work both simultaneously while looking through the window. Like most of the apparatus in the coach-house, the purpose of this mechanism was not immediately clear.

In the center of the house stood a low platform of oak boards with steps leading up to it. On the platform was a large spoked wheel mounted vertically on a post like a ship's steering-wheel. It looked suspiciously like a wheel from one of Mr. Threadneedle's old gigs. The platform and wheel were situated behind the two mangles, and like them faced the front bay window.

Above the platform was another mechanism, one connecting the gig-wheel to a horizontal screw-shaft that ran across the ceiling. There was a coil on the shaft at approximately its midmost point, and a white stone positioned at each end of it. There was another wheel within easy grasp, a small one — it had been taken from an old garden barrow — and was attached to a rod that extended to the weather-vane on the roof. An old ship's-compass, or *bittacle*, stood beside the gig-wheel, and round the front and sides of the platform was a balustrade of varnished wood, which looked to have been scavenged from some rustic wagonette. Running fore and aft on either side of the house — that is, on one's right and left as one faced the bay window — was another threaded shaft, each mounted horizontally and with a single white stone positioned abaft.

These, together with other, smaller mechanisms placed here and there about the interior, and some storage-lockers, the carpenter's bench, and the like, comprised the chief appurtenances and apparatus of the coach-house — the end-result of the many hours of tinkering by Mr. Threadneedle and Tim Christmas. No one gazing on the mechanisms for the first time could easily discern how they worked, or what they did. Nonetheless their concealment had been of sufficient importance as to have foiled the plans of the vicar and Kate for a leisurely stroll about the coach-house.

Mr. Threadneedle stepped to the door for a last check of the fog. There was no one about but Mustard, whom he could hear cropping grass somewhere close by. Satisfied he shut the door and double-latched it, and examined the windows to be certain they were secure. Then he and Tim turned down the swing-lamps and extinguished the fire in the grate. The fire had made it comfortably warm inside, what with the door and windows being shut; that warmth would have to last now for a while.

Mr. Threadneedle straightened his coat and settled his necktie, and drew his gloves on tight, and fixed his hat on his head with great precision, as though preparing himself for a ceremony of some kind. Tim, following his example, bundled himself up tight. Master and apprentice-of-sorts then glanced at one another, the one with a brash twinkle in his eye, the other with excitement showing on his cheek.

"Ready, Tim?"

"Ready, sir."

"You may take your station, then — Mr. First Mate Christmas, sir!"

"Aye, sir — Captain Threadneedle, sir — *by gum!*" exclaimed the youth, after the manner of Mr. Bob Sly. Both apprentice and master grinned a trifle mischievously at this, before exchanging sailorly salutes.

As Tim assumed his post between the mangles, Mr. Threadneedle stepped onto the platform, like a sailing captain mounting to the helm of his vessel. He touched his gloved hands to the gig-wheel and ran his fingers lightly along its rim. The top of the wheel reached all the way to his chin, where it threatened to graze his mustaches.

"Clear field, Tim?"

"Clear field, sir," nodded the youth, despite the gloom standing in the bay window. It was evident, even amid the clutter of the appurtenances and apparatus, that this window occupied the space where a door had stood for the passage of vehicles in and out, in the days when the coach-house had been a coach-house. Now that door had been replaced by a wall and a wide window of diamond-pane lattices.

"The steering-coil is under command," Mr. Threadneedle announced, taking hold of the gig-wheel.

"Yes, sir."

"Stand by to slip moorings."

"Yes, sir, standing by."

"Slip moorings, Tim!"

"Aye, sir."

The first-mate-of-sorts spun a wheel that stood before him, and pulled a couple of levers. There followed a weird, hollow sound, as of bolts unbolting, or clamps unclamping, somewhere under the floor. For just a moment the house quivered, faintly.

"Mooring-bolts released, sir."

"Stand by to go aloft. Stand by your cage-coils."

"Yes, sir, standing by."

"Down coils, then, Tim, and easy aloft. Take us to one-quarter and heave to."

"One-quarter, aye, sir."

The first mate proceeded to crank the mangles on either side of him in synchrony. This action was aided by a pair of reciprocating springs, very cunningly placed, which reduced the friction and made the cranking easy. Immediately belts and cables started to roll, pulleys and wheels revolved in the creaking meshwork overhead. The threaded shafts in the four corners of the house began turning round. As a result the cage-coils started to move down the shafts toward the white stones below. As they did so, something strange and mysterious and wonderful began to happen.

Came first a scattered chorus of squeaks and groans from all about the house. Then the shutters began to rattle a little, and the swing-lamps began to sway. At the same time Mr. Threadneedle started to feel a bit heavy in his shoes. It seemed as if he were gaining weight — as if his short, thick form hadn't weight enough already! — and that he could feel the added pounds pushing him down toward the floor. But it was all an illusion, of course; instead it was the floor that was pushing *up* against his shoes.

The fog was curling and writhing in the windows like a murky haze on the move. But it was not just the fog that was moving. The mangles continued to spin in the capable hands of Tim; the cage-coils continued moving down the threaded shafts, until they arrived at the one-quarter position, which was marked in bold lettering on the cages. Several other positions —

one-third, one-half, two-thirds, three-quarters — were marked as well, in descending order, down the length of each cage.

"One-quarter and heaving to," Tim announced, and left off his turning of the mangles. At once all the mechanisms stopped their rolling and creaking and revolving; the threaded shafts stopped turning round, the cage-coils stood motionless. As he locked each mangle in place with a strap, he felt an odd "popping" noise in his ears.

"Excellent!" Mr. Threadneedle called out from the helm. "The recent improvements, Tim, have succeeded to a T. She rides marvelously well now, thanks to your fine efforts. The cage-coils seem to be nicely balanced. At last we've achieved the harmony of the hoverstones! Jolly fine work, lad."

Apart from some residual groaning from the timbers and rattling from the shutters, there was little else to be heard inside the coach-house. It was an eerie sort of quiet, what with the obscuring fog in the windows, and the slight movement of the swing-lamps, and the odd sensation of buoyancy underfoot.

"Down coils to one-half, Tim, then heave to," was the next instruction of Mr. Threadneedle.

"Down coils to one-half, aye, sir."

The mangles spun again; the coils resumed their downward course on the shafts. Suddenly a brilliant light came streaming through the windows. The oppressive fog all melted and vanished away, to reveal a vast, far-spreading ocean of cloud rolling beneath the coach-house. Here and there surging billows of foam gathered themselves into mountainous waves that rose above the broader surface. Violet shadows lurked in and about the cloud-stuff, round swelling banks a-blush with the ruddy tints of dawn. Over everything lay a cobalt heaven so deep and liquid it was like a dome of crystal, its farther edge ablaze where the sun was peeping, flooding sky and coach-house with golden bars of light. It was magnificent, it was magical; it was like some fantastic picture in a dream.

"Coils to one-half, sir, and heaving to," said Tim. Again the mechanisms stopped, again there was nearly complete silence in the coach-house, as captain and first mate gazed in wonder upon the dazzling vistas that surrounded them on every side.

"Steering-coil to starboard," Mr. Threadneedle announced at length. As he swung the gig-wheel to the right, the horizontal shaft above him started to turn, sending its coil moving toward the white stone on the left. The view in the windows shifted as the coach-house pivoted to starboard.

"Coming to larboard now."

He swung the wheel to the left; the steering-coil moved in the opposite direction, the house pivoted to larboard. (It was all *larboard, starboard* in the coach-house, for Mr. Threadneedle had picked up certain fine points of sailorly speech on his trips cross-channel in the *Salty Sue*). Each time the house swung round, the floor stayed perfectly level, and so it would remain as long as the cage-coils were in balance.

"It's very smooth, sir," Tim observed.

The eyes of Mr. Threadneedle fairly beamed. "Very much improved, Tim. We have been amply rewarded for the long hours of skull-crunching. What we have here, lad, is one flying coach of a coach-house!"

He took hold of the small wheel above him, the one connecting to the weather-vane, which served as a kind of rudder for maintaining flight in a steady direction.

"We'll lay a course due south," he said, making an adjustment to the wheel and another to the helm, while keeping his eyes on the compass-needle. "Just so. You may come to speed now."

"Aye, sir, coming to speed," Tim nodded. He pressed a foot against one of two pedals on the floor. Springs sprang into action, and he felt something begin to turn under the floor-boards. The speed-coils — the ones running fore and aft on each side of the house — began creeping toward their hoverstones; as they did so, captain and first mate experienced a feeling of slow, gradual acceleration. The ocean of cloud began to slide under the front window.

With Mr. Threadneedle keeping a steady hand on the gig-wheel, and a twinkling eye on the compass and the way ahead, Tim pressed the pedal again. As the speed-coils advanced toward their hoverstones, the coach-house gained velocity. In no little time it was skimming briskly over the cloud-tops — an insignificant speck cleaving a trackless course through a sea of blue sky, with the clouds sailing past it on every side like a fleet of ghostly galleons.

The eerie quiet returned, for once they were at speed there was little noise inside the coach-house, except when some adjustment of the mechanism was needed. Their altitude was fixed, their heading was fixed, their speed was fixed, and so the house simply flew on. There was little else but the sound of the wind whistling round eaves and corners, and a slight rattling of the shutters, and the creaking of the swing-lamps.

Little else, that is, until Mr. Threadneedle voiced a sudden and enthusiastic *huzza!*

"That's done it, Tim!" he exulted. "Level flight — effortless control — no pitching, no swaying — all smooth and even — and all at altitude!"

The first mate answered with a joyful cry of his own, as he watched the ocean of cloud flowing beneath him.

"'Keep your shop, and your shop will keep you,'" the grocer smiled, glancing round in triumph at his own shop which was the coach-house. "It was a maxim we had in the trade, you know. 'Look after your business, and your business will look after you.' I learned it from one Miss Betty Trickle, who had a shop in Stinking Lane — fruit and gilt gingerbread, toffee, penny toys, and such — with a tea room above. She's the only woman I ever heard of who smoked a pipe. What's more she's a jolly shrewd one at a chess-board." (Mr. Threadneedle himself was never very fond of chess; he was always for tinkering with the rules, which his opponents for some reason objected to.) "Well, now we may apply the same maxim to ourselves — 'Keep your coach-house, and your coach-house will keep you.' The hours of tinkering have repaid us tenfold — twentyfold — a hundredfold!"

Soaring over the cloud-tops like one of the grocer's beloved pelicans above the waves, the flying coach of a coach-house flew on. They could ram the spurs in and ride slap-dash at a gallop, or they could rein the speed-coils down to a canter, or a trot, or pull up altogether and come to a standstill there in the sky, motionless but for the lunging of the wind at the coach-house walls. It was everything a lover of birds like Mr. Threadneedle could have hoped for, and the most glorious of apprenticeships that a young apprentice-of-sorts could have imagined.

"There's a break fast approaching, sir," Tim announced, scanning the way forward. "A long rift in the cloud bank directly ahead."

"We'll make for it, Tim, and determine our position," the grocer directed. "We've been running southerly for two hours now. It's nearly time to come about."

Tim drew aside a panel no more than a foot square in the deck at his feet. Immediately light came pouring through the aperture, which consisted of a window with back-to-back panes of glass in it — double glazing — and beneath it very little else; indeed nothing else, apart from the vast canyon of air that lay between the coach-house and the clouds far below. With this porthole of a sort the first mate was able to observe the lay of the land beneath the house and thereby guide their descent.

"Steady on our heading, and prepare to go alow," said Mr. Threadneedle.

"Ready to go alow, aye, sir."

By degrees their pace slackened, until the coach-house came gliding to a stop over the break in the clouds, which Tim had been watching closely while turning down the speed-coils with his foot. He then took up the mangles and began turning them in the reverse direction. The cage-coils started to rise, drawing away from the hoverstones. Both captain and first mate began to feel a little light-footed, and their ears popped again. They were descending at a goodly pace. With a careful eye on the porthole, Tim guided the house down toward the long rift in the clouds, Mr. Threadneedle holding the gig-wheel steady at the helm.

Mist and fog came rushing up to the windows, obscuring the crystal sky and the spacious views as the house plunged through the cloud-stuff. As soon as they emerged underneath it, Tim left off his mangling and brought their descent to a halt. And there they remained, floating in the air with the cloud ceiling riding just above them, and a misty spread of gray ocean-surface below — a *real* ocean this time, one with a tangle of white-caps washing across it.

"Ah! This is as nice a place as any, Tim, as few can spy us here," said Mr. Threadneedle, lashing the helm. "On the strength of the trial thus far, I believe we're approaching perfection of the mechanism."

The grocer stressed again the advantage of conducting these trials under cover of fog, so that no one round Smithy Bank might observe the coach-house's departure or arrival, or notice that it had gone missing in the interval. It was necessary that they proceed in this manner until all had been perfected. Keeping above the clouds for much of the flight allowed them to remain hidden from view of the populace below. Mr. Threadneedle was concerned that they not frighten anybody, or endanger anybody — themselves included — by straying too near the ground.

"We nearly dealt the lantern at Fairlight a severe blow on that first trial," he reminded his apprentice. "Poor Matthew Mulks — not to say the lighthouse authority — would never have forgiven me. But henceforth we'll have no more narrow squeaks, I think, what with these new improvements."

"No, sir," Tim agreed.

"And now where are we today, do you suppose?"

Mr. Threadneedle stepped down from the helm and came alongside Tim, and together they examined the scene in the front bay window. There was much less of the obscuring mist and fog here, so that their vision reached considerably farther than it had in the murky channel. An irregular line of coast was visible curving away some miles to leeward. They were a goodly distance out to sea, as expected — two hours' run due south of Truro, by clock and compass, and by the look of things rather south of Goforth as well.

"I think there's a harbor afar off there, sir," Tim said.

"Very likely."

"Is it Goforth?"

"Rather too small, I think. Squidleigh, perhaps, or Kelpförd, or Sourbury-on-sea. It appears we've come a fair way indeed. We've yet to devise a velocity gauge for our craft, you know — an instrument to measure how fast and far we've traveled. The placement and shielding of the compass were difficult enough. Ah, another knotty problem, another skull-cruncher to be worked out! Until then we must rely on reckoning and inference."

"It will be a hard thing to fashion, sir, though I'll peg away at it once we've returned."

"As will I. That said, I believe we may declare today's trial a success. Now we'll lay a course due easterly and take her over land for a bit. Then we can swing about and work our way back to the Smithy, and be home and dry in time for supper. We'll give her a galloping run of exercise today, eh, young man?"

What a wonder she is, how mighty staunch and skyworthy! the grocer thought. Mounting again to the helm, he looked round him with pride and admiration on this latest and best jewel of his fancy. His sanctuary, his refuge, his place of glorious retreat from Plush and Kimber. How his years of tinkering had blossomed! How much more exhilarating than a ride on horseback, or a drive round Truro in the jaunting-car!

Freedom! Freedom! Freedom up here in the clouds, far from the tyranny of Plush and Kimber!

At that moment a family of gulls went sailing past. A couple of the birds floated up to the windows and dipped their wings before veering off. Mr. Threadneedle watched them go, not a little envious of their gift of natural flight. Unfortunately the sight of them recalled to mind a certain troubling nightmare of his, that vision of Mrs. Kimber floating towards him without benefit of ambulation. Then he thought again of the triumph of the limpet pie, and was glad.

"Coming to larboard," he announced. As he turned the gig-wheel, Tim brought the coils slowly to speed. The house swung round to the east and gathered way, tickling the misty underbelly of the clouds as she sped off towards the mainland south of Goforth.

"It's little thought Mr. Hicklebeep has of the prize he had in hand," Tim remarked.

"True," said Mr. Threadneedle, nodding. "But as you know, Tim, it was the merest chance on my part to have discovered it — the *gravitite*, as I call it. As you remember, I happened one day to be tinkering with one of the hoverstones outside the coach-house. They're such wondrous, mysterious things — so very light for their size, and so oddly marked, and I was attempting to discover the reason for it. By chance I happened to bring a small piece of magnetic ore — a loadstone — in close proximity to the stone. You can imagine my shock and surprise when the hoverstone jumped off the table and went sailing into the forest! It took me some little time to find it. It was the magnetic principle in the ore, of course, acting on the gravitite in the hoverstone. Or is it vice versa?"

"And still we have no idea how the gravitite works."

"Nor do we understand how a loadstone works."

Indeed, how could they hope to solve the mystery of the hoverstones if they could not solve the mystery of a magnet? It was only Mr. Threadneedle's chance discovery that had made the impossible possible, and made a flying coach of the coach-house. By bringing the coils of magnetic ore on their threaded shafts and the hoverstones together, under precise, balanced conditions, he had unleashed the power of flight.

"We're coming over land, sir," Tim announced from his station.

"Is there any sign of habitation below?"

"None, sir."

"Ah, good. Well, let's maintain our course for a while then. We must be mindful, however, of the Sawtooth Mountains, which lie a distance ahead. They are very tall mountains, you know, and I should not care to make their acquaintance at speed. Yes, we must be some miles south and east of Goforth now . . ."

"Have you been to Goforth, sir?"

"No, never. I've heard from Captain Barnaby that it is a place something like Nantle, though not so large."

"And what lies to the south of it? Aside from Squidleigh, Kelpford, and Sourbury-on-sea?"

The grocer shook his head. "Not so much, I'm afraid, Tim. In general the towns grow smaller and lonelier past Goforth, more sparsely situated, as one nears the rainy lagoons. And beyond the lagoons — well, there one approaches the zone of the sundering."

"Is that where Captain Clipperton found the hoverstones?"

"So it's believed. What little I know of such remote country I've learned from Captain Barnaby and Bob Sly, who have visited there in the *Salty Sue*."

Looking out, they found that a dull screen of cloud had insinuated itself between the coach-house and the earth, to all effects veiling them from spying eyes. There were no Sawtooth Mountains rearing up as of yet. Having missed breakfast, both Tim and Mr. Threadneedle were feeling some pangs of hunger, and so they brought the coach-house to a stop and secured the mechanisms. They lit a fire to warm some tea and settled down in the chairs by the hearth. There they feasted on the good things in the hamper — some sandwiches, some wedges of cheese, a little sponge-cake, a couple of biffins. All the while the house remained suspended there in the sky, with the full blaze of daylight around her and the dull screen of cloud drifting underneath.

"We'll take her down now and have a peep round," the grocer said, once their lunch had been concluded. Hunger is the best sauce, it is said, and the meal had been a particularly satisfying one. They had eaten well, and sung a nautical air or two, as the mood took them, in honor of the occasion. They had even had time for a clattering game of backgammon. Now both food and hunger were gone and it was time to be getting on with the important business at hand.

Mr. Threadneedle mounted to the wheel and took command again of his vessel — like the mighty Captain Clipperton himself, perhaps, except that the vessel of Captain Threadneedle was a coach-house and his sea the sky. And what a notable good sky-boat of a vessel she was, too!

"Coils up!" the captain directed.

"Coils up, aye, sir!"

The mangles spun round again, the wheels and pulleys revolved, the cage-coils rose on their screw-shafts. The house began dropping toward the screen of cloud. Soon the windows were filled again with an obscuring haze. The wind seemed to have gained a measure of strength, judging by the sound of it as it sped round the walls.

Without warning the house began to sway a little from side to side.

Mr. Threadneedle shot a quick glance at his first mate. "What's wrong, Tim?" he called out.

There looked to be trouble with one of the springs, Tim replied, affecting the belt and sprocket-wheel controlling one of the cage-coils. Gingerly he advanced the crank-handles. There came an ominous squeal, followed by a sudden roar as wheels and pulleys spun wildly, then came to a wrenching stop. The troubled shaft had ceased revolving, its cage-coil standing idle while the others continued to move. The house swung loosely underfoot, then one side of it abruptly lurched upward in the direction of the affected coil.

Tools and tackle, notebooks, writing implements, backgammon board, lunch hamper, everything that was not safely stowed went flying from table-edges and sliding across the deck. Interestingly, none of the furnishings in the house went with them. Unlike the movables, every item of furniture, from the clock on the wall to the well-stuffed chairs to the little writing-desk and the carpenter's-bench, was fixed solidly in place. A useful safeguard as it turned out!

As for Mr. Threadneedle, he was very movable, and had seized the rail of the balustrade to keep himself from tumbling over it.

"The chain-belt is free on its wheel there, sir!" Tim reported, quickly spotting the difficulty. "There was too much energy released from the spring — it unwound too fast and trapped the belt. Several of the eyelets have torn loose. They were pulled out by the teeth of the wheel while the belt was locked up. Oh, I thought we'd solved that problem! Now the cage-coil is free on the shaft."

One of the belts was no longer drawing, it seemed, which affected its associated pulleys, links, and wheels, and of course its cage-coil; as a result the hoverstones had gone out of balance.

"I shall try revolving it by hand," Mr. Threadneedle said. "Down coils on the other shafts, Tim, and bring us level again. We'll work conjointly."

The mangles spun in reverse. Belts and chains rolled but only three of the shafts went round. The house gradually righted itself, not completely but well enough to suffice. Meanwhile Mr. Threadneedle had made his way to the affected coil. Reaching into the cage-like structure, he slid a bar through a hole in the shaft. Then he gripped the bar and bore upon it hard, first one end and then the other, to make the shaft turn round. Without the help of the springs, it was a tedious job. With one eye on the grocer's movements, Tim revolved the mangles in close accord, to preserve a level deck. In such manner did the coach-house pursue her journey earthward, though at a cautious snail's pace in comparison with her earlier rate of descent.

"We'll set her down and tend at once to the mechanism," said Mr. Threadneedle, panting a little from his exertion.

The dull screen of cloud fled from the windows as the coach-house dropped under it. Raindrops began splashing against the latticed panes.

"Any Sawtooth Mountains, Tim?" the grocer called over his shoulder.

"No, sir. It looks to be lowland, from what I can make out through the drizzle."

"Inhabited?"

"Impossible to tell, sir."

"It will have to serve."

In order for the coach-house to descend smoothly, all four cage-coils had to act in concert, had to pull away from their hoverstones by slow and equal

degrees. With Tim closely matching his actions to those of Mr. Threadneedle, the two were able to accomplish this, but it was not an easy task.

"We're very nearly there, sir," Tim said.

"Let us stop for a moment," said Mr. Threadneedle, taking advantage
of the pause to catch his breath. He took his telescope from his coat-pocket
and swept the windows with it.

"Some broad fields there," he reported. "A wild moorland tract, backed
by a range of hills — foothills of the Sawtooth Mountains, I think. Some
detached groups of trees, some hedgerows, and some inky patches I can't
identify. Ah, and a village or two, it would appear. Well, we've little choice
now, these fields will have to do. But we must be wary of marshland. I
shouldn't care to settle her on watery ground."

They resumed their cautious descent. Slowly they drifted down and
down, the coach-house still sagging a bit but not so precariously as before.

All at once the earth came rushing up to meet them.

"Gently, sir, gently!" Tim warned.

The cage-coils rose nearly to the tops of the threaded shafts. Mr.
Threadneedle looked round from the cage and offered Tim a nod of encouragement. There followed a considerable jolt that rattled everything
and everyone in the house; and so they were down.

Almost at once the coach-house sank a little on one side.

"Are you damaged, lad?" said Mr. Threadneedle, scrambling across to
see about the condition of his young charge.

"Not a bit, sir. And you?"

"Not dashed to pieces as I feared, nor the coach-house either. Well done,
Tim."

Together the two moved to the front window. What they saw in it
caused them to look at one another in mute astonishment. Disbelieving,
Mr. Threadneedle opened one of the side-casements. He winced as a strong
smell of tar invaded his nostrils. A pungent smell, he thought, very pungent, though not half so pungent as Ladycake.

Before them lay a miry townscape of ruin and decay. Gaunt, gabled cottages of stone with disheveled fronts were tilted crazily this way and that,
like boats on a choppy sea. They looked to be sinking into their founda-
tions, indeed into the very ground they were built on — the same sort of
ground on which the coach-house had come to rest. With their crumbling
walls and eaves, tottering chimneys, and windows vacant and staring, they
had obviously been long-abandoned. Looming high above them was an ancient parish church, gray, towered, pinnacled. It, too, was foundering,

though not so dangerously as the cottages. In its lorn condition it seemed to be brooding over its shattered flock, in sorrow perhaps at its failure to save them. Nearby lay the town cross, which had fallen completely over like a drunken clergyman.

Everywhere about, a substance black and oily could be seen oozing from the ground, forming broad, irregular pools that lay smoking in the rain. The pools glistened like springs of pitchy slime, and bubbled in places where a steamy vapor was rising out of them. Very likely they were the unknown inky patches Mr. Threadneedle had spied from above.

There was no sign of anyone about, no evidence of habitation either human or animal. There was only a mournful hush, broken by the soft patter of raindrops on the coach-house roof.

Tim turned to Mr. Threadneedle with a bewildered expression.

"What kind of place is this, sir?"

"I haven't the least idea," the grocer replied, in awe himself of the desolate scene.

"It appears we've run ourselves into a scrape."

"Perhaps. Not to worry though, Tim," Mr. Threadneedle reassured him, "for I dare say we'll not stay long."

Came then the roar of a mighty beast, from somewhere amid the steaming ruin.

CHAPTER TWENTY

Miss Trickle Recommends

"I am most deeply disappointed, Frederick, in your Mr. Liffey. Here it is nearly a fortnight now we've been at Nantle, and not hide nor hair of this Squailes person has he unearthed. It's beastly!"

"He's not *my* Mr. Liffey, dear, he's *our* Mr. Liffey — yours, mine, and Miss Veal's. I'm sure he's doing his utmost to ferret out Mr. Squailes. 'Pon my life, he must be; we've scarcely had sight of him these past days. But you've no cause to complain, Susan, really you haven't, for it was your idea to accompany us to Nantle."

"Accompany *us*? By that do you mean yourself, Frederick, and your Mr. Liffey? Why, what has he involved you in of late? Has he sought either your counsel or your company on these investigations of his? No. And so you go sallying abroad every day, you and that servant of his, on your rambles upon town, leaving Aspasia and myself to our resources. All the while your Mr. Liffey seems to be acting entirely on his own. When we do see him, he claims to be making progress, but then he's gone again and we hear no more. He is forever out and about somewhere, 'attending to the case,' as he says. For all we know he may be attending to the case-bottles in the nearest wine-vaults. I tell you, Frederick, it is very *odd* of him."

To bolster his argument, Mr. Fred Cargo handed his wife the morning's newspaper. "Look there, Susan, where he's placed a fresh advertisement in the columns. He's been making inquiries throughout the town, in consultation with the legal man with whom he's corresponded over these last months. He has been tireless in his exertions, as it seems to me. He's working on the behalf of all of us, Susan, to see that the provisions of Grandfather's will are satisfied. How can you speak of him so?"

"He is never here," his wife returned, flashing her eyes, "and I am simply wondering what he has been getting up to, and why it's taking him so long. Nearly a fortnight in Nantle and still he hasn't found this interloper!"

"I'm sure he's doing his best," Fred smiled, with that geniality of spirit that was so characteristic of him. He stuffed his hands into his pockets and paced up and down a little before the fire, jingling as he went. "Young John, his valet, and I speak of the matter often on our rambles. He says that Mr. Liffey is constantly puzzling his mind over the business. At the very least he seems much troubled by it."

"So we are taking the word of servants now, are we?" returned his quick-spoken little wife. "Have you learned nothing, Frederick, from your grandfather's example? You are far too much among common people for your own good."

"But, my dear, I hardly ever saw him until his last illness. And more to the point, you seem to have forgotten that Grandfather remembered his own servants in his will."

"A few trifling bequests — not a quarter of the cash residue, as he would have us squander on Mr. Squailes!"

"And as regards the common people, there, too, I'm afraid I must differ with you. People are people, dear, everywhere, regardless of their station."

"Yes, you and your ostlers and your hunt servants and your whippers-in, all of you just alike! How very dignified of you, how very *beau monde*. Why you persist in associating with such persons is beyond understanding."

"Indeed," nodded Miss Veal. Her pale, drab oblong of a face was looking more than usually stiff and solid today, like the wig perched atop her head.

"Tiptop Grange simply couldn't function without these people you so easily disparage," Fred responded. "It should fall to the ground without them. These servants of ours deserve some little measure of respect, don't you think? Without them to care for the Grange and for ourselves, we could hardly advance our social position."

"Yes, that will certainly advance your social position, associating with horse-dealers and ostlers and whippers-in," retorted Susan, with a brisk, dismissive little laugh, the kind that wives customarily reserve for husbands.

It was a dispute of long standing between them. Despite his outward show, his manners, his smart and spiffish appearance, his love of fancy waistcoats, Mr. Fred Cargo was more at ease in the company of hunt servants and gamekeepers, grooms and stablemen, cob-riding farmers and veterinaries, more comfortable in a horse's saddle following the hounds, than he was among the set of people his wife and Miss Veal preferred.

"It is true, he has been acting very peculiar," remarked the latter lady.

"Who is that, Miss Veal?" Fred asked.

"Why, Mr. Liffey of course."

"As for instance," said Susan, "why has he changed his rooms again? *Twice* now since we've been here, he has changed his rooms. I fail to understand it."

"Perhaps he found the mattress uncomfortable, or the flue a trifle drafty, or perhaps there was too much noise in the stables outside his window," Fred suggested. Nonetheless the mystery was puzzling to him as well. Why had their attorney become so dissatisfied with his accommodations? He'd never known Mr. Liffey to be so particular. He had been too polite to inquire into the cause of it himself, nor had John any real insight to provide.

"And he is out so much of the day, and tells us so little, one wonders what he does with his hours," said Miss Veal, who was standing at the mirror touching fingers to her wig, here and there, in admiration of her appearance. She had joined the Cargoes in their private sitting-room at the Crozier in advance of a proposed excursion into the city.

"You'll remember what the landlord, Mr. Blackshaw, told us," said Susan. "Your Mr. Liffey appeared visibly troubled when he asked to change his rooms. Both times he requested a room with a sturdy door, one with a heavy bolt and stanchion, and ditto fastenings on the windows. One would think he was afraid of burglars."

"Burglars!" exclaimed Miss Veal, making such a face in the glass that she inadvertently startled herself. "Burglars here by the Minster, when we are hedged in on every side by reverend clergymen? This really is too much, thenk yaw!"

"I question, Frederick, whether your Mr. Liffey is making a sincere effort to find our man, if he expends time worrying over burglars and locks in such a respectable establishment as this. A fortnight in Nantle and no result! But no matter; I shall look forward all the more to getting the nose of Mr. Interloper Squailes between my thumb and finger, and squeezing the truth from him. I shall shake him out until he confesses, and unburdens himself of the designs he has on Grandfather's money — on *our* money, Frederick!"

"Dear, we have been over this ground before," her husband sighed. He ceased his pacing long enough to take his watch from its pocket, and glancing at it, saw that it was nearly time they were off.

"I'll tell you what ground we've *not* been over, Frederick," said Susan, drawing on her bonnet.

"What ground is that?"

"That ground which obliges us to consider engaging another attorney."

A second time Fred left off his pacing and jingling. "That's a capital idea, Susan!" he exclaimed, with a snap of his fingers. "Another local man to provide Mr. Liffey and his colleague with assistance. Yes, capital!"

The partner of his cares shook her prim little head with the bonnet on it. "You misunderstand me, Frederick. I propose engaging an attorney *in lieu* of your Mr. Liffey. A forthright, Nantle-bred gentleman who knows the city well, and who can find this Squailes person double-quick."

"Are you suggesting, Susan, that we dispense with Mr. Liffey's counsel? That we dismiss him out of hand like one of his own office clerks? My dear, we have no legal standing in the matter. Mr. Liffey is the duly-appointed executor of Grandfather's will. Sack Mr. Liffey? My dear, we dare not — we *cannot*!"

"I am not suggesting, Frederick, that we sack your beloved Mr. Liffey. I am suggesting that we engage another attorney *independent of* your Mr. Liffey — a man of our choosing who can make separate inquiries on our behalf. We may do this entirely on our own; Mr. Liffey need know nothing of it."

"But Mr. Liffey already has a Nantle man."

"But who is he?"

"Well, I can't give you his name —"

"Aspasia, do you know his name?"

"I do not," stated Miss Veal.

"Exactly! Nor do I. None of us knows his name. For all we know, he may be a complete humbug. *He may not even exist.* And for all the assistance he has rendered, he might as well not."

Fred was rather taken aback by this. He made a few crisp tugs at his waistcoat, and straightened his neat, trim figure, and smoothed down his ditto hair a little, and stroked his mustaches, to gain time while he thought up a response.

"Are you intimating that Mr. Liffey has been less than truthful with us? 'Pon my life, dear, how can you doubt his allegiance? I'm quite astounded to hear it. Mr. Liffey is far too kind a man to do us any ill office."

"Perhaps not his allegiance, then, but instead his judgment, or his competence," said Mrs. Cargo, softening just a touch. "Perhaps this Nantle man of his is of an inferior mold — a rank neophyte, perhaps, or an ignoramus, or as ancient as Mr. Liffey himself and no longer clear in his thinking. And therein lies my point: that we should hunt up a new adviser, a local man with a fresh view of things who can conduct the search more effectively. We shouldn't hang all our bells on one horse, or even two, as you yourself are fond of remarking."

But her husband would not stir an inch.

"Again I must disagree with you, Susan. I'll not go skulking round behind the coat-tails of Mr. Liffey. He is a devoted friend of our family, and has been as true to us as the dial to the sun. Why, I have known him since I was little higher than a nutmeg-grater! I can in no way doubt Mr. Liffey, nor should you. So you would have us hire ourselves a stranger here in Nantle, some rascally knave to make crushing costs of us? No, Susan, it simply isn't on. We can't do it. We should be monsters of ingratitude."

"We've had scant cause to be grateful to your Mr. Liffey heretofore."

"No, no," Fred insisted, shaking his head vigorously.

"Have it your way then, Frederick, for what I care," returned his wife, with a little shrug of feigned indifference. "But when another fortnight has come and gone with still no Jerry Squailes, perhaps you'll be persuaded of your folly. For my part I am content to wait. It will be reward enough to behold the look of pained consternation in your face."

"No Jerry Squailes is a blight!" said Miss Veal.

"To think that you, Frederick — the one person in this world left to carry on a noble name, as Grandfather Cargo's sole surviving blood relation — to think that you of all persons should —"

All at once the words died on her lips, and she whisked round to stare at her husband, her eyes brimming with thought.

"What is it, dear?" Fred asked.

"His sole surviving blood relation," she repeated, half to herself. "Suppose it were the case, Frederick, that you are *not* the last of the line? Suppose there is another family heir? Suppose — however beastly and unthinkable — that this Squailes person is a *relative* of some kind, and that Mr. Liffey has kept the news of it to himself? For as you'll remember, he wanted none of us to come with him to Nantle. He wanted to come *alone*."

Fred's response was one of incredulity. The idea of an unknown relation of the family — it was patently nonsensical!

Or was it?

The Cargo family tree, although well-delineated, had been a slender enough one to start with. Surely there was no hidden branch, no derived or collateral descendant of the parental stock — none that remained alive, that is. But his grandfather had been a secretive and unsociable old rascal, as Fred himself had so often declared. Perhaps before his death he had bound Mr. Liffey to secrecy in the matter of Mr. Squailes. But if so, why? Why keep the existence of another heir secret, unless —

Steady on, Fred! Surely it wasn't possible — ?

As these and other unhappy ideas were stirring within him, Fred realized, no matter how strongly he might have denied it, that the first few seeds of doubt had been successfully planted in his mind regarding the trusted family solicitor.

"I sincerely hope, dear, that you are wrong," represented the summation of his thoughts on the matter — for now.

Owing to Miss Veal's aversion to carriages, the party were obliged to go a-walking into the town; but as rain seemed not a danger today, and since Fred already had a comfortable route worked out from his rambles with young John, the problem was easily solved. From the Crozier they made their leisurely way down the hill, through the quaint, quiet, genteel neighborhood and into the theater and market districts, which comprised that portion of the city lying between Bluefin Street and Stinking Lane.

Everywhere about them shopkeepers in white neckerchiefs and spruce coats were busy conducting the day's business. Aproned muffin-men were ringing their bells and loudly extolling their wares, which they carried about in trays on their heads. Fishmongers and news-vendors, too, knife-grinders, umbrella-menders, and sandwich-boys all were in full cry.

Having arrived in Stinking Lane, the party amused themselves for a time by peeping in at the windows of the different shops — in particular at the windows of a certain bun-house (it was at Fred's urging, for it was a shop he'd grown fond of on his rambles) and at the variety of items temptingly displayed there. FRAGRANT AS HONEY, read a bill wafered on the wall; FLAKY AND LIGHT, said another; SURPASSINGLY SCRUMPTIOUS, boasted a third. Unfortunately, Miss Veal had developed an aversion to buttered buns, and to buns in general, which was nearly as severe as her aversion to coach travel; and so they had to pass the bun-house by.

It was not long before they stopped again, this time under a signboard of inlaid-work heralding an establishment known as BETTY'S FRUIT SHOP AND TEA ROOM. The fruit shop was below and the tea room above, as was the usual custom. As Miss Veal had no discernible aversion to either fruit or tea — or to shops, or to rooms, or to persons answering to the name of Betty — they went inside.

The place was packed out with agreeable young mammas buying fruit and biscuits and other like necessaries for their families, and with servants of a domestic stripe gathering provisions for the houses they served. To attend to their needs several pretty shop-girls in lace caps and purple ribbons were at work behind the counters. While Miss Veal and Susan spent a little time taking stock of the goods on offer, Fred spent a little time taking stock of the shop-girls. Susan, as soon as she observed this, promptly abandoned the goods in favor of her husband and led him upstairs to the tea room.

It was a tall, light-filled, wainscoted little parlor of a tea room, very neat and orderly, with shiny floors, and papered walls hung round with colored prints, and windows with blue valance curtains and the blinds drawn all the way up. They were ushered to a table beside one of the windows, which commanded a view of Stinking Lane and the theater over the way. Mrs. Cargo pronounced the tea room not so grand a one as that in Crow's-end, but declared that it would suffice, with which assessment Miss Veal confidently agreed.

They were not long sitting before their attention was drawn to a chess game that was in progress in the chimney-corner. The rivals in the game were, on the one side, a plump, pink, bald-headed gentleman of a jovial aspect, and on the other a sharp-featured, rusty-faced woman with a pipe in her teeth. From the appearance of the board it was clear that the end-game was on, and that the rusty-faced woman would be checkmating soon. Despite this the plump gentleman spent most of his time smiling and shaking his head in wonderment at his adversary's every move, watching as piece after piece of his was plucked from the field by her marauding forces.

The general appearance of the marauder occasioned some remark among the Cargo party.

"Do you see that, Frederick?" Susan asked, raising her nose a little.

"See what, dear?"

"That woman there with the pipe. I don't believe it. Is it considered decent here at Nantle for a woman to be smoking? Such behavior would never be tolerated in Cargo."

"Shocking creature!" exclaimed Miss Veal. "She looks like a barber."

"I've seen her before," said Fred, thinking for a moment. He snapped his fingers. "In the chess rooms at the coffee-house! Miss Trickle, I believe, is her name?" he inquired of the waitress, as she approached on a light foot to recite the bill of fare.

"Yes, sir, that's our Miss Trickle," smiled the damsel, who was of the same pleasant pattern as the shop-girls. "She's our missus, sir."

"She is the proprietor of this establishment?"

"Yes, sir. Miss Betty Trickle — she is the 'Betty' in Betty's Fruit Shop and Tea Room."

"Of course! So I was informed by Black Davy — by Mr. Devenham, that is. She has a *bona fide* chess brain, as he termed it, and superintends the wagering at Sprig's. You remember Mr. Devenham, don't you, dear?"

"That bladderish person," sniffed Susan.

"A damned interesting sort of fellow, 'pon my life."

"But Frederick — the woman is smoking a pipe!"

"Yes, marm," said the waitress. "She has a great many of 'em. You ought to see her churchwarden!"

"In Cargo, where we reside, a woman never would be seen smoking. It wouldn't be considered proper."

"I'm sure not, marm," commiserated the waitress, with an understanding face. Clearly she had been well-schooled by the proprietor.

"I have myself been known to favor a pipe now and then," Fred remarked. "What's sauce for the gander is sauce for the goose, or so the saying is, or something like it. Well, I for one am famished! I could eat a cabbage-stalk."

"Yes, sir. Will it be tea all round, then, sir? Tea and cakes?"

It would indeed be tea and cakes, and once they had made their appearance, it was discovered, to the joy of the party, that the cakes were very good cakes indeed, and the tea very good tea. What was more, the peppermints and jam and marchpane proved to be of like quality. Even the chinaware and silver were superlative. And so the party fell to with an appetite. And despite the spectacle of Miss Trickle smoking like a chimney in the chimney-corner, it was resolved by everyone, even Fred, that they had chosen well in forsaking the bun-shop for Betty's.

It was not long before the bald-headed gentleman gave up the chess ghost and, clapping his hands in admiration of his opponent's skill, smilingly proclaimed it a "lovely finish, Trickle, lovely!" Such equanimity in the face of abject defeat could be the signature of no other person than Mr. Lovibond, he of the boarding-house of Mrs. Matchless in Chamomile Street. Miss Trickle in her turn consoled him with a nod and a wave of her pipe-hand. "Very game, sir," she congratulated him, before taking off on her rounds of the establishment, to see that all was in order and that her damsels were being sufficiently pleasant and accommodating.

It was inevitable that she should pass the Cargoes' table in the course of her circuit, and so she did.

"Ah, Miss Trickle," said Fred, to gain her attention.

"Sir," nodded the hostess, pipe in hand.

"The name's Cargo. This is my wife, and this is our good friend Miss Veal. I happened to make your acquaintance at Sprig's coffee-house not so long ago. In the chess rooms. Turcott and Rainbow. How goes the wagering?"

Glances of disapproval from both his wife and Miss Veal; but Fred seemed hardly to notice.

"The wagering goes," said Miss Trickle, squaring her shoulders a little, "but the match does not."

"How so?"

"Turcott has been on the boards these past days."

"On the boards?"

"On the stage, sir, at the theater over the way."

"Ah. So the match is on holiday for a time?"

"That is so, sir."

"I'll confess to knowing little about chess myself. Who has had the advantage of late?"

"The match so far belongs to Turcott, but by only the slenderest of margins. There have been many drawn games. The two gentlemen are remarkably evenly matched, given their dissimilarities of age and temperament."

"It's a kind of duel, isn't it? A combat played out on a chess-board, without resort to the drawing of swords?"

"The gentlemen are deciding the matter in a civilized fashion," Miss Trickle replied, "and a far better fashion, too, in my opinion, than playing stick-the-pig at sunrise on Stiffun's Acre."

"Astonishing."

"Beastly!" cried Mrs. Cargo, shrinking at the mention of swords and combats and — Heaven forfend! — pig-sticking, and a place of such sinister connotation as *Stiffun's Acre.*

Not insensible of the effect she was having on the prim little wife and her matronly friend, Miss Trickle threw back her head and sent up a great cloud of smoke from her lips. "And further to that, if it's wagering you want, sir," said she, squaring shoulders, "I'm your man."

"Shocking!" cried Miss Veal, closing her eyes in horror.

"Though mind, sir — I never wager myself."

"So Mr. Devenham told me," said Fred. "Apparently you're considered a most trustworthy person in this neighborhood."

The hostess acknowledged the fact with a brusque but cordial nod.

"And so the match will go on, then, once Mr. Turcott returns from the stage?"

"Yes, sir. And on and on, one might suppose."

"Like this search of ours for Mr. Interloper Squailes," remarked Susan, half aloud to Miss Veal. "On and on."

"Who is Mr. Interloper Squailes?" inquired Miss Trickle.

In answer Fred felt obliged to tell their hostess something of the errand that had brought him and the others to Nantle from far-away Cargo. Miss Trickle, listening with an air of professional interest, regretted to inform them that she knew no one named Jerry Squailes, and never had. She'd known a person called *Wales,* she said, and another called *Thierry;* but as for Squailes, no, sir, sorry, sir, she wasn't your man. And because they knew nothing of his appearance or occupation, or anything else about him at all, there really was little she could offer in the way of help.

"You couldn't recommend an attorney, could you?" Susan asked, struggling mightily to get past her disapproval of the woman, for the better good of the family. "A respectable man who knows the town well, one with the diligence to unearth the person we seek?"

"I never recommend," said Miss Trickle, blowing smoke. It was simply policy, she explained, for she'd become acquainted over the years with so many solicitors and physicians and other suchlike professional men, from their wagering in the chess rooms, she couldn't play favorites. Nevertheless she did consent to rattle off the names of one or two useful people, without prejudice as she said, in the event they might prove of service.

There were Dodger and Fleece, of course, the oldest and most respectable firm in Nantle, with chambers in the Commercial Road. Then there was Mr. Chuckster, although he was in danger of retirement now and rather selective about his cases. And of course there was Mr. Lyall, and old Mr. Skalatar, and young Mr. Youlgreave. Then there were Maule, Pick, and Slaughter, of Great Codger Lane; however, their palms required a sizable amount of greasing. There was Mr. J. Joshua Fettiplace, of Fettiplace and Bungle, but he was kept so busy so much of the time he was unlikely to have any to spare. And there was another practitioner, one of whom she'd heard much but seen little, a man named Hook, with chambers on Gull's Wharf. A *very* professional counselor, or so it was worded about, very zealous and innovative in his methods — perhaps the very best man in the city. If one needed sharp lawyering, it was said, then Hook was your man. It was more than a dead certainty he could hunt up anybody in the town, high or low, if said person was there in the town to be hunted up. There were other men, too, of whom she knew something, but the foregoing roster, as she called it, ought to serve for a start; though mind, she never recommended.

"Awfully civil of you, Miss Trickle," said Fred.

"We're not from this city of yours, as you know," his wife explained. "We are from the fine town of Cargo."

"Indeed?" returned Miss Trickle. She cocked an eyebrow and smiled — a touch slyly, perhaps — behind her pipe; then drawing up her thin figure of many corners, she took her leave to resume her superintendence of the staff.

For just an instant Fred entertained the wild idea that if this fellow Hook could find anybody who was to be found in Nantle, then perhaps he could find that deuced fine woman from Crow's-end who'd been aboard the *Salty Sue;* then just as fast he abandoned the idea, with a little inward sigh, after hearing the lady of his heart deliver a stern command to pay the reckoning, Frederick.

As the party was getting up to leave, having enjoyed a largely harmonic interlude there in the tea room, a ragged, ill-shaven, horsy-faced little character could be seen watching them from a door nearby. He had overheard something of the matter of Mr. Squailes, and it had occasioned in him a deal of thought. This in itself was not so unusual, but for the fact that the little character was Mr. Planxty Moeran — a fellow not known for his cogitative gifts. Once the Cargoes had gone, he proceeded to chat up the waitress who had served them, and learned they were strangers from far away north and were stopping at the Crozier. Armed with this information, Mr. Moeran betook himself downstairs and, after tendering several smiling ducks of his head and hat to the shop-girls, departed the premises.

Once in Stinking Lane, he hurried off in the direction of Jekyl Street, rubbing his hands and chuckling to himself as he went.

CHAPTER TWENTY-ONE

Toads' Eyes and Spiders' Knees

Mr. Lovibond, having returned to Chamomile Street after his defeat at the hands of Miss Trickle, and encountering in the hall his nemesis, as it were, namely Mr. Kix, lost no time in describing for him all that had transpired in the chimney-corner in Stinking Lane. Mr. Lovibond's admiration for Miss Trickle knew no bounds. Never before, he said, had he witnessed such dashing play, not even at Sprig's. He went so far as to wonder whether it shouldn't have been Miss Trickle herself rather than Rainbow who'd answered the challenge of Turcott the Thespian. For if such had been the case, he declared, the match would have been decided long ago.

"You should have seen it, Kix — crushing gambit — King-side attack, masterful — Queen-side attack, extraordinary — murderous offensive — snatching pieces right and left — King driven to the wall — glorious finishing stroke — smothered mate — superlatives fail me —"

"She smashed you up," grunted Kix, stating the obvious. "It's little wonder *you'd* be impressed. How many times now has she smashed you up?"

"Five," said Mr. Lovibond, proudly extending a fat hand with the thumb and fingers spread wide. "Five games — utterly demolished on every score — glorious play — Trickle a genius — true poet of the chess-board."

Mr. Kix received the news with smug satisfaction. "How lucky for you. But as it was not she but Rainbow who slighted Turcott in the public papers, it hardly seems reasonable that she should take up the gauntlet."

"Nonetheless she's a lovely player."

"But plays only when she's not at her wagering. I suppose I'll be expected now to wager good money on *you*. Ever the champion of the underdog I've been, but you are without question the underest of dogs. Sorry, sir, but I'll forgo the pleasure for now, as you're in little danger of winning. I gather Turcott's obligations have put off the match?"

"Mr. Swuff Turcott — lovely performance — *The Boor of Venice* — high romance — waterworks — pocket-handkerchiefs — fainting in the boxes, fainting in the aisles — delightful melodrama — our Miss Rivers would have loved it — better than any novel —"

"Hack work, sir, that I can tell without even seeing it. But Rivers wouldn't attend. She never stirs from home. Despises the weather."

"We'll ask her — invite her ourselves — can't hurt — the fog is lovely this time of year —"

"And how do you propose to finance this expedition? You'll not have her lay out fivepence of her own for a seat in the pit, certainly? Or will it be twopence for the gallery?"

"We'll divide it — small price — shillings — public box, of course — cozy annuity you've got — lavish — you can afford it — plenty of spare cash — I'll put in my poor share —"

"Damned kind of you to be spending my own money for me. Is there anything else of mine you'd care to appropriate? Speak up, sir!" demanded Mr. Kix, with an indignant crossing of his arms.

"I'll float the cost of her, if you're disinclined — sacrifice — our dear Miss Rivers — less than half a shilling, sir, half a shilling — moldy purse — tight old devil — old stick-in-the-mire!"

"I am not a stick-in-the-mire, sir, nor am I 'tight,' as you say. I am a man who leads a well-governed life and is prudent with his money — which is vastly more than can be said for another man in this house."

"Hallo! Not a stick-in-the-mire? Not tight? Absurd fellow — you're a madcap, Kix, a madcap — if a prudent one!"

So they marched upstairs to the front-parlor — Mr. Lovibond laughing very heartily, as he usually did, and Mr. Kix looking grumpy and out-of-sorts, as *he* usually did — where their rosy-cheeked landlady and her friends were keeping company with tea and sundries. As usual Mrs. Matchless was busy with her crochet-work, with her confidential housemaid on the one side of her and Mrs. Juniper on the other side. Mrs. Juniper was draped in one of her flowery shawls and there was a large bouquet sprouting from her hair. The women had gathered near the fire for some gossipy chat, to which the stuffed fish in glass over the mantel was listening in open-mouthed surprise. In attendance on them was the small boy in buttons — Mr. William Pancras — looking very scrubbed and brushed, and ready at any moment to dash off like lightning to replenish the tea and sundries.

Sitting a little apart from them, so as not to be distracted by their conversation, was Miss Rivers. She was absorbed in the pages of her novel, which her quenched-looking little bashful eyes were squinting at through her tortoiseshells. At her right hand was a cup of hyssop tea, well-spiced, a strengthening tonic brewed specially for her by Mrs. Poundit.

The gentlemen begged pardon for the intrusion and hastened to the side of Miss Rivers, where Mr. Lovibond propounded his case for the theater. Miss Rivers, with all due courtesy and decorum, closed her book and heard him out, whereupon she blushed up to her eyes and down to her chin and shook her head. She didn't care to go out, she said ("What did I tell you?" cried the look in Kix's face), for the weather was so very damp and gloomy, and as she was so very comfortable there in the parlor with her book and her tea, it really would be too much for her to venture out-of-doors. Besides, she added, the theater was always so crowded, and she didn't like crowds, and there was always so much noise, and she didn't like noise. Mr. Lovibond was at pains to acquaint her with the many advantages of a play over a novel, and expressly of the play in question, but it availed him nothing; no, no, Miss Rivers would not go.

And so it was the gentlemen instead who went, but each his separate way — Mr. Lovibond, still his jovial self despite Miss Rivers's refusal, mounting like a mastodon to his room upstairs; and Mr. Kix, with much triumphal nodding and smirking, descending to the street-door, where he intended to go out for a walk. The grouchy Kix had so little to occupy his time that a walk seemed like a miraculous deliverance. Even better, it meant forgoing *The Boor of Venice* and so would spare him any expense of his purse.

As he stood there in the hall donning hat, coat, and gloves — gravely, methodically, like a knight-errant making awful preparation to confront the dark world beyond the door — he spied young Pancras, tray in hand, creeping downstairs from the parlor with hardly the alacrity one associates with lightning. As it happened, an unlikely rapport had sprung up between these two inhabitants of the house, the grumpy bachelor so misunderstood by everyone (or so he thought) and the embryo butler-in-training. Perhaps in the small boy in buttons Mr. Kix recognized something of his own frail, creeping self from days long past — so little appreciated, so little respected, so little regarded by all.

"To Poundit?" he inquired, fixing the boy with a sardonic eye.

"Yes, sir," William admitted, looking none too thrilled.

"How lucky for you," smiled the Misunderstood One, and coming on guard he proceeded to attack the air in the hall with the point of his umbrella — quarte! octave! sixte! septime! — as though the umbrella were a cutlass and he a dashing swordsman. It was meant as an exercise in encouragement, to nerve young Pancras for his bearding of the dreaded cook in her lair. After this little display of feints and lunges, Mr. Kix sheathed his weapon (that is, he tucked it under his arm in readiness for going out) and declared that the boy had his full sympathy.

"Thank you, sir," said William, to all appearances unmoved, and resumed his slow, snail-like way down the stairs. He would have preferred to be boiling linen in the wash-house with Miss O'Guppy and Alice, or polishing the boarders' shoes, or most anything else than descending alone to the infernal regions to face Mrs. Poundit.

Too soon he came to the kitchen and stepped into the presence of the ogress, who at the moment was busy elaborating on the contents of the "spicery" — a fragrant clutter of spice-boxes, tins, jars, cruets, sifters, graters, and pepper-mills, which occupied the interior of a dark cupboard — to an audience of one, namely Miss Jilly Juniper.

Oh, double the torment! Not only Mrs. Poundit but Jilly Juniper as well, that other bane of William's existence. She had come calling with her mother, but in the course of his labors he'd lost track of where she had gotten to. Where she'd gotten to was the kitchen, where she was sitting on a flour-barrel and listening to the blowzy, mob-capped, mutton-fisted old cook wax fiendish on the subject of spices.

There was another voice, too, that of Miss O'Guppy in the wash-house adjacent, where she and Alice were busy with the laundry. She was humming one of her tuneful airs — it was rather hard to scrape a fiddle while boiling linens in a copper — and every now and again would interrupt herself to remark aloud on something Mrs. Poundit had said, or to answer some transgression of the gangly Alice's with a burst of ill-humor.

Mrs. Poundit, taking note of young William's arrival, carried on with her disquisition, which she delivered in that banter she found so pleasant to inflict on neighborhood "younkers" of every sort.

"And here be garlic," she chuckled, with a hideous roll of her eye at Pancras, "which be just the thing for improving the disposition of a precious little chappie! And here be capsicum for sneezing, as sneezing be fine for flushing the sweetness from younkers. And here be dill seed, dearie, as will put any younker in a pickle, and a sour one. And here be vanilla, for the whipping o' creams — and a whipping's a fine thing for the discipline o' younkers! And here be capers now, for caper sauce, very hot — hot enough to set most any younker a-capering. And here be cinnamon and cloves for a plum pudding, with suet squeezed and drained from the hair of a precious little chappie as I knows of. And cinnamon and cloves be fine, too, for a mince pie, for a pie o' minced younker be a rare delicacy o' sorts — and a dainty younker like yourself, dearie, would make a fine filling! And here be ginger and treacle, for gingerbread —"

"I'm not a dainty younker," said Jilly, "and I think you're making this all up."

"Making it up? And what reason would you have to doubt me, dearie? Why, look here," said the cook, taking a brown jar from the spicery and waving it before the eyes of the children, "look here, younkers, here be something! What think you, now? Conjure-dust? No! Crow's gizzard? No! 'Tis neither — 'tis toads' eyes and spiders' knees."

"I've never heard of toads' eyes or spider's knees," returned Jilly, skeptically.

"What! Do you doubt me again, my precious?"

"You're just making up stories. There are no such things as toads' eyes and spiders' knees, not in a kitchen anyway. *Our* cook doesn't need to be making up stories. Our cook is a very good one; she doesn't need to be frightening anybody, or bullying anybody. You might frighten Pancras there but you don't frighten me."

"Ah! So your cook be a fine one, eh, dearie? So much finer than Mrs. Poundit?"

"Yes, she is. And very much nicer, too."

The good eye of Mrs. Poundit stared very hard at Jilly. Then a wicked smile split the cook's lips, and she threw back her head and made a noise like gargling in her throat.

"Why are you laughing?" Jilly demanded.

Mrs. Poundit sank a fist into the jar and took from it a small, dark, oval object, as shiny as a toad's eye and about as large. Suddenly she flicked it into the air, which action caused Jilly to jump and William to cry out. The object bounced from the chopping-board to the floor, and rolled a little across the flags, before coming to a stop and resolving itself into — an olive.

The reactions of the children provided the cook much additional cause for hilarity.

"You do such things to scare people. You did that to scare Pancras. He's young and helpless and easily frightened, but I am not," Jilly declared.

"Ah! And are you not afeared o' things, dearie? Are you not afeared o' the darkness, then?"

"No. It's all so childish. Everybody must grow up sometime, even Pancras."

"Ah! Well, we'll see as to that, dearie. But first a younker must *live* long enough to grow up, eh? Have you never wondered, my precious, why it is there are no parsons in heaven?"

"What does that have to do with anything?"

The mistress of ceremonies of the kitchen had it in mind to recount another of her tales, it seemed, and Jilly for one was determined not to be frightened by it. As for young William, he wanted only to be about his errand, but instead found himself riveted to the spot.

"Why do you think it is, younkers, that there be no parsons in heaven?" the cook asked again. "Why, 'tis acause every last man of 'em hides a sinful secret, and death and damnation be the penalty for sin ever since Eve ate an apple. There is as example the Reverend Mr. Juggins of Falaise, one such parson with a secret. 'Twas a dainty younker very like Miss Jilly Juniper, I think, as discovered the Reverend Mr. Juggins in his parish crypt one day, lunching on a corpse. Well, that parson he were very cross. What to do, what to do? If only the dainty younker had a-come to Mrs. Poundit aforehand! For 'tis Mrs. Poundit as has in her trove o' treasures a potion to guard against corpse-eaters.

"Once upon a time 'twas common for the younkers to wear round their little necks an amulet. In the amulet was toads' eyes and spiders' knees, to perserve the younkers from demons and save 'em from being taken off to Fairyland. But the dainty one as discovered the corpse-eater had no amulet, and so was eaten herself — swallowed entire like a juicy dumpling, and the bone and gristle of her picked clean. And what do you think became o' the wicked Juggins? Why, he lived a long life and a merry one there at Falaise, o' course. And then he died and took form of painted stone in his church, as he was a very rich parson, and a memorial was put up as fine as that for a wealthy squire. What took him off, you ask, my precious ones? 'Died by visitation o' God,' 'twas ruled. Visitation o' God — visitation o' the Foul Fiend! His wicked secret the Reverend Mr. Juggins carried with him to his damnation. But the dainty younker might've lived had she 'pon her person an amulet o' toads' eyes and spiders' knees.

"Do you know now o' the celestial-hounds, as can be heard a-barking in the dark sky over Hound Tor? Or of the hairy great goblin-spiders as creep into beds of younkers arter midnight? Or the candles as be made from the fat of a murderer? For it's by the light o' such candles that younkers may be stolen from their beds by the fairies, if they haven't their toads' eyes and spiders' knees. You'll not want to be stolen by fairies now, will you, my precious ones, in the burning fat-light of a murderer?"

The telling of such tales seemed to give the cook no end of pleasure, and set her chuckling and gargling again as she commenced her operations at the chopping-board.

K-chop! k-chop! sang her busy blade. *K-chop! k-chop!*

"Oh! oh! if you please, Mrs. Poundit, may I have more sundries for Mrs. Matchless?" William asked, having screwed up his courage sufficiently to approach her.

Mrs. Poundit turned her crazy eye on him, and with it her face like a bad mushroom, its pocked surface glistening in the hazy glow. "Sundries?" she cried. "Is it sundries you'd like now, little chappie?"

K-chop! k-chop!

"Yes, ma'am — if you please!" answered William, wringing his hands.

"Well, dearie, I'll give you sundry to think on," the cook whispered, with an ogle of particular meaning.

K-chop! k-chop!

She took a menacing step toward him. All at once her blade leaped into the air. In deathly silence she brandished it aloft — this way, that way, this way — in readiness for the carving-up of someone. The small boy in buttons, sure that he was that someone, cowered beneath her, all thought of Mr. Kix and courage long forgotten.

"Who's afeared o' the leaves must not go to the wood," said Mrs. Poundit, grinning horribly.

"Oh! oh!" cried William, going as pale as his face could manage.

"Oh, Pancras, don't be tiresome," Jilly sighed. "She's not about to harm you. She's fooling you. Have you learned nothing yet? She won't eat you. She's not a cannibal!"

Here Jilly laughed, although strangely Mrs. Poundit did not.

"A cannibal! Why, what would a dainty younker like yourself know o' cannibals? What of corpse-eaters?" said the cook, turning her attention from William to the little slip of a girl with the golden tresses. "Tell me, my precious — you've tasted meat from Mrs. Poundit's kitchen of late, have you not? And a good tuck-in it were, too! Cold venison was it, then? Cold *venison* indeed!"

Jilly felt a sudden chill. She combed her memory to recall the last food she'd had in the Matchless kitchen. She hoped — she prayed — it had not been venison, but sadly it had. She remembered how the venison had tasted, what with the spices and all, and how it had felt on her tongue. Her eyes were drawn to the smoked meats on hooks that hung above her there in the hazy light of the kitchen. What dark, ungainly, sinister things they were! All at once an awful suggestion flashed upon her. *No,* she thought, *oh, no, surely it could not have been —*

Whereupon Mrs. Poundit exploded again into a laugh, and Jilly realized that she, the very grown-up little slip of a little girl so critical of young William, had just been gulled by the sly cook. This opportune moment Pancras chose to snatch the tea-tray (which Mrs. Poundit had magically replenished) and cut his lucky. It was as if he'd been crouching on a spring, so fast did he go shooting from the kitchen and up the stairs to the front-parlor, where the tray was safely delivered, its contents shaken a bit perhaps, like William himself, but none the worse for the adventure.

A moment later Miss O'Guppy put her head in round the wash-house door and wagged a finger at Mrs. Poundit.

"Shure, and 'tis a fine picture of a woman y'are, auld banshee," she snickered. "A fine one y'are for a taste of the whisky, enough to sthiffen a tinker! So she affrighted ye, did she, darlin?" (This last addressed to Jilly, who denied the charge.) "'Tis murtherin' bad y'are, auld Poundit, when ye're half-sozzled — murtherin' bad!"

Her words prompted another burst of hilarity from the cook, who retaliated in kind by inquiring which younker it was Miss O'Guppy was a-boiling there in the wash-room? "For he's bound to come a cropper, who's popped in a copper!" she exclaimed, in allusion to the well-known Squire Mulligrub o' Scalpen, who had long been rumored to be boiling up juicy younkers in a copper of his own.

Such foolery notwithstanding, talk of fright had brought to Jilly's mind a matter that had been troubling her a lot these past days. It was the matter of Miss Wastefield, of course — the pretty lady from Crow's-end who was staying in her mother's house, and who seemed to be very frightened of something. It was to Miss O'Guppy that Jilly turned now for aid, for it was Niamh who had glimpsed the future of Miss Wastefield in her cards. And a dismal future it was, too, crossed as it was by the shadow of a mighty enemy.

"I know her maid believes something is very wrong," Jilly said. "She has allowed me a little time with Juga, the lady's pet monkey, and has told me things in private. Miss Wastefield's illness has something to do with the trunk she keeps in her room. You said, Miss Niamh, that the lady had a secret, and that when you look at her, you see two people. What did you mean?"

Miss O'Guppy answered with a sigh and a mournful rocking of her head. There was nothing to be done for the poor leedy, she said; it was all there in the cards. "She has little choice about it. For I see things, and I know things, I do. 'Tis a gift left over from the marning time."

"What is the morning time?" Jilly asked.

The green eyes of Miss O'Guppy — such strange, dark, expressive eyes — swelled full large at the thought of it. "Ah, darlin, the marning time! 'Tis the time afore our own birth — 'tis a fresh, dewy time, in a place of warrumth and light unlike any place on this earth, as comforts us and keeps us safe from harrum. But at our birth we are parted from it, and sent here to this place of sorrow to live our lives, to suffer, and to die. Answer true now, darlin — have ye yerself no remimbrance of the marning time? For the childhers often keep the memory of it for some years, d'ye see, afore it fades from recollecktion."

Jilly shook her head; then just as quickly she unshook it, as a scattering of images, little more than fragments most of them, began passing before her mind's eye.

"Sometimes," she said, slowly and thoughtfully, "I have a dream in which I'm laughing and playing with my sister. We're very happy together, in my dream. We play and we play, and the day seems to go on forever. But Miss Niamh — I have no sister! And it seems, too, that I have a different mother in my dream. Can it be possible that I had a sister once, and a different mother?"

"There! 'Tis yer own memory, darlin, of the marning time. 'Tis an enchanted place, where all are gifted wid wondhrous powers. There be no clocks there, nor days nor nights, nor past nor future. That is why the childhers on earth have sich little sense of time — 'tis left over from the marning world."

"And is that how it is with you, Miss Niamh? Do you think of such things when you think of your own mother?"

An angry spot flared on the cheek of Miss O'Guppy. "Never do I think of me own mother," she replied, in a changed tone, "for no mother have I on this earth!"

"What do you mean?"

"I mane what I mane! She called me daft for seein' things, she said, and for telling lies, she said. She told the same to me father, too, her own husband, that he wor daft for seein' things. But I *do* see things, I do, just as me father did — and may the marciful Creator sthrike me dead if I lie! But she cursed us for it, and called us daft and insthrumints of the divil. And so I'll have none of her, d'ye mind? I dono' her. I'll have no mother in this place of suffering."

K-chop! k-chop!

It was Mrs. Poundit again, busying herself at her chopping-board. Jilly began to feel a trifle uneasy, but strove to conquer it for the sake of her mother's pretty lodger.

"Can you help her, Miss Niamh? Can you speak to Miss Wastefield?"

"Speak to her I can," said Miss O'Guppy, the angry spot subsiding, "but help her I cannot. There bain't none on earth can help *her*, darlin, nor priest nor holy waters, by reason of the mighty force ranged against her. 'Tis all there in the cards!" And humming to herself a sad little tune, she returned to the wash-house, having forgotten, it seemed, all about the mother who thought her daft.

Jilly, not caring to pass many more minutes with Mrs. Poundit — who already was eyeing her with another tale in readiness — tripped up the stairs to the front-parlor, where her mother and friends were still chatting round the fire. Miss Rivers had dispensed with her book now, for she'd overheard a word or two of the ladies' cozy talk that intrigued her, and found the draw of their conversation irresistible.

It emerged that Dottie, having lately exchanged letters with an old friend, one Mr. Malachi Threadneedle, formerly of Chamomile Street, and a widower, had been invited to visit him at his splendid manor-house across the channel. More to the point, she had accepted the invitation. Although she had not yet received a reply to confirm her visit, the landlady assured her audience that it was as good as done. It was through the agency of Mrs. O'Guppy in Jolly Jumper Yard that the letters had been conveyed, and by which same means her passage would be booked on the *Salty Sue*. Her old friend Mr. T., of whose grocery she had been a client for many years, had written her of the ferocious housekeeper and overbearing butler he'd inherited there at Smithy Bank. In her turn Mrs. Matchless had expressed a desire to meet these ungrateful people, for if they had been mistreating him, she said, she'd quickly sort them out — which threatening declaration she had made while smiling through her spectacles, as only she could do.

Jilly, still seeking help for Miss Wastefield, addressed her plea now to Dottie and the others. An animated discussion followed, led by Mrs. Juniper, with many bobs of her flowery head, but in the end nothing much came of it. Miss Rivers apparently had abandoned her idea that the lady was a smuggler, in favor of a theory that she had jilted some gentleman of consequence, who had dispatched his agents in pursuit of her. Not a smuggler, then, but a fugitive lover!

"Just so she don't set our house a-fire while she's here, what with her lights all night," sniffed Mrs. Juniper.

Speculation, supposition, conjecture, but little more. Jilly found it all quite discouraging.

"If only it were true," she sighed, "that toads' eyes and spiders' knees could help Miss Wastefield."

"What did you say, dear?" Dottie asked.

"What kind of foolish talk is that, Jilly?" said her mother. "For you know we'll not be having foolish talk in Mrs. Matchless's house."

"Oh, just plain foolish talk, I suppose," said Jilly. Disappointed, she turned and went slow-footed down the stairs to the hall. There she ran into the handsome Mr. Frobisher coming in at the street-door. On seeing Jilly his face immediately brightened and a gleam of amusement came into his eyes.

"Well, hallo there, moppet! What brings you to the Matchless domain?" he said as he hung up his coat and hat.

"My mother brought me."

"Ah, I see. Why, Jilly, are you unwell?" he asked, kneeling beside her. "You seem rather down."

Indeed, for the long face of Jilly beneath her curls was like rain in sunshine.

As Jilly knew something of Mr. Frobisher's unspoken affection for Miss Wastefield — for most everyone knew of it by now — she decided to ask him then and there if he could help the lady. Of course, Mr. Frobisher already was suspicious of something very odd afoot respecting the pretty young lodger. His thoughts turned at once to Tom Lanthorne, to Miss Wastefield's evident fear of the man and to his mysterious vanishing in Mock Alley. Unfortunately Mr. Frobisher had not chanced upon him again since that day, and had no new knowledge of the fellow.

"Her trouble has something to do with the trunk in her room," Jilly said. "It's something she carries about with her, something *unholy,* or so Lucy told me. She can't get rid of it — the trunk, or whatever is locked inside it. Even Juga knows that something is very wrong. Miss Niamh thinks the lady is doomed and that no one can help her. Oh, but Allan — is there nothing you can do?"

Hearing all this, Mr. Frobisher grew strangely silent and thoughtful, and remained so for more than a minute, before rousing himself with a brisk clearing of his voice.

"Chin up, Jilly," he said, patting her little shoulder affectionately. He rose to his feet and drew a long, deep breath, like a man resolved at last upon some unspecified course of action. "Do you know, I believe there *is* something I can do. And it's well past time it were done, too!"

CHAPTER TWENTY-TWO

Shadows in the Road

Whatever it was Mr. Frobisher meant to do, he didn't do it at once; and so Jilly returned home less than satisfied. Another day came and still no Frobisher. The afternoon of that day was a brisk one, with a frigid wind. A rare sun had shone since the morning, driving blades of cold light through the shadows in Chamomile Street, like strokes from Mrs. Poundit's knife. Jilly, having not much to do, was looking through the drawing-room windows at the meager traffic in the road, when she heard the sound of footsteps. Turning, she beheld Miss Wastefield and Lucy descending the stairs. They were accompanied by little Juga, who was decked out in his coat and trouserings of wool and his tiny fur cap. Like Juga, the women were dressed for taking the air, although in rather more fashionable and la-dylike garb.

"Hallo, Miss Wastefield," Jilly said as the three passed the drawing-room door. "Are you feeling better today?"

"Indeed, yes, Jilly," the lady replied, with rather more energy than she had shown of late. Even Juga seemed to be in good spirits, chirping and cooing and making faces as he played round her feet.

To Jilly it was clear that Miss Wastefield was much attached to her odd little pet. From Lucy she'd learned that Miss Wastefield had been given the monkey many years ago as a present, and that the two were inseparable. It seemed almost as if they could speak to one another, could understand each other's thoughts, so close was the bond between them.

"I'm happy you're better, Miss Wastefield," Jilly said. She thought Miss Wastefield looked even prettier than usual in her bonnet and her furs, with her curious earrings like coiled shells, and her lovely eyes and the dimple in her chin. She was a very beautiful lady indeed, Jilly realized, and evidently Mr. Frobisher thought so, too.

"Has Mr. Frobisher called upon you?" she blurted out, hoping it were so.

Miss Wastefield seemed puzzled. "Mr. Frobisher? Why, no, Jilly. Should I have been expecting him to call?"

It was difficult for the child to hide her disappointment. "No, ma'am," she answered. "I suppose not."

As there was little more to be said on the subject, Miss Wastefield tucked up her gloves and smiled her good afternoon to Jilly. The street-door was opened by Lucy and her mistress swept through it onto the landing. Almost at once Miss Wastefield uttered a little gasp and put a hand to her mouth.

"What is it, miss?" Lucy asked, startled.

"Shut the door, Lucy!" Miss Wastefield commanded, retreating into the hall. "Shut the door and bolt it — quickly, quickly!"

In a panic of uncertainty the maid obeyed, alarmed to see her mistress gone so pale, as though all the blood had drained from her face.

"Stand clear of the door, both of you!" Miss Wastefield said, meaning Lucy and Jilly.

"If you please, miss, what is the matter?" Lucy exclaimed, casting frightened glances from her mistress to Jilly and back again. "What did you see on the doorstep?"

For answer Miss Wastefield rushed into the flowery drawing-room and, placing herself beside the nearest window, stole a look round it into Chamomile Street. It was the same window through which Jilly had been peering not many minutes before.

"He's there!" she whispered, with a hushed intake of breath.

"Who is, miss? Who is there?" cried Lucy.

"Whom do you mean, Miss Wastefield?" Jilly asked.

"That man there, over the way," said the lady, drawing back from the window. "Do you see him? The man standing under the overhang of the house opposite — the house to let, the one with the green shutters. He is watching *this* house. He is waiting for me to come out."

Trembling, Lucy peeped round the curtain and through the latticed panes and across the road.

"Asking pardon, miss," she said, hesitatingly, "but I don't see as there's anybody there."

"Nonsense, Lucy. Look again."

The maid did so, then shook her head in timid apology.

"He can't have gone so quickly," said Miss Wastefield, stealing another look. "What do you mean you see no one? Are you blind, girl? Can't you see him there, lurking in the shadow of the overhang? A man very tall and grim, with a black chimney-pot hat, standing with his hands thrust in his coat-pockets. He is watching this house!"

Bewilderment flooded the countenance of Lucy. She looked again, this time in concert with Jilly. They saw the occasional foot-traveler trudging by in the street, and some listless carriage traffic, and a lone rider or two — for it was Chamomile Street, after all, as drowsy a street as any in the neighborhood — but try as they might, they could see no one standing in the shadows over the way.

"I don't see him, Miss Wastefield," Jilly said, speaking both for herself and for Lucy. (The maid, despite the testimony of her eyes, seemed unwilling to contradict her mistress again.)

Irritation mingled with disbelief blazed up in Miss Wastefield.

"What do you mean you can't see him, Jilly? Upon my word he is standing there — *there!* — just across the way. He's dressed in a caped overcoat and breeches and painted tops. Do you see him now?"

"No, ma'am," Jilly answered, with such earnest innocence of voice it was impossible anyone could doubt her. Like Jilly, Lucy, too, was trying desperately hard to see something there, *anything,* in particular a man adhering to the description her mistress had given.

"What nonsense is this? What are you two playing at?" Miss Wastefield demanded. She stole another look round the curtain. "There! There he is, as plain as daylight. *And he is staring at this very window!*"

But there was nothing to be seen, as the blank looks on the faces of Lucy and Jilly testified. Frustrated and apprehensive, Miss Wastefield gave vent to a little groan and, with Juga at her heels, fled upstairs to her room.

Lucy and Jilly remained at the window trading mystified glances. By degrees their puzzlement gave way to uneasiness, and then to discomfort, and finally to a state of shivers, at least for Lucy. Was it possible, she wondered, that there really was someone standing there, some invisible being with his cold gaze even now fastened upon her?

"Miss Niamh!" Jilly suddenly exclaimed. "I shall fetch Miss Niamh. Oh, I hope she's at home! She reads people's fortunes in cards, you know, and can see things others can't. Perhaps *she* can see the man across the road."

Lucy undid the bolt of the door and out Jilly went, skipping past the flowers round the area-railing and hurrying up the steps of Mrs. Matchless's house. Her knock was answered by Alice, who responded with a toothy grin that Miss O'Guppy was indeed at home, and promptly summoned her. In the fewest words possible Jilly explained what had happened.

"Can you see him, Miss Niamh?" she asked, eagerly. They were standing just inside the open street-door, under the lamp in the hall, and were peeping round the door's edge. "Can you see a man in a tall hat and top-boots over the way?"

The strange eyes of Miss O'Guppy reached across the road and touched something there. At once there was an odd stirring in them, and like Miss Wastefield before her, she uttered a startled gasp.

"By Jasus!" she exclaimed.

"What is it, Miss Niamh? Do you see him?"

"I do!"

"But how can that be?"

Miss O'Guppy ignored the question. "Keep where ye be, darlin," she said, sternly. "Ye'll not want to be venturing out. Look here — where be the unfortunate leedy now?"

"She's gone up to her room."

"I will go to her this instant minute," said Niamh. She stepped outside and closed the street-door after her, leaving Jilly to the company of Alice, then dashed round the area to Mrs. Juniper's house. Together she and Lucy ascended to the chambers occupied by Miss Wastefield.

It required some coaxing on the part of Lucy to admit Miss O'Guppy, for in truth the young woman and Miss Wastefield were scarcely acquainted. As Lucy explained it, Miss O'Guppy lived in the house next door and was a dear friend of Jilly's; moreover she knew something of the trouble Miss Wastefield was facing and had come to help.

"How can she know of my trouble?" said a voice through the door. "What help can she possibly be?"

For answer Miss O'Guppy proceeded to describe, at some length, the features, dress, and manner of the person in the shadows over the way. There was a brief silence; then footsteps were heard approaching the door, the door was opened a space, and the figure of Miss Wastefield appeared in that space.

"You see him?" she asked. Her eyes examined with some curiosity the spare, delicate form of Miss O'Guppy with her curling dark hair and her eyes so green and strange.

"I see him, leedy," said Niamh.

"How is it you can see him when Lucy and Jilly cannot?"

"I see things, and I know things, leedy. 'Tis a gift, by the Holy. A leedy, a monkey-crayture, and a secret — and a murtherin' bad secret it looks to be! 'Tis in the cards I've seen the lines of it, and in yer own sweet faytures. 'Tis a mighty force be ranged against ye. That it is which ails ye, leedy."

It was more than enough for Miss O'Guppy to be admitted. Miss Wastefield then shut the door and placed the key in the lock.

"His name, I am told, is Lanthorne," she said, sinking into a chair with Juga in her lap. "I have seen him before at Sprig's coffee-house. It was most uncomfortable the way he stared at me — so cool, so brazen, so scrutinizing. Since then I've returned to the coffee-house on three occasions, and each time I've sensed his presence, or the presence of *someone,* following me. Whether walking in the street or riding in a carriage, I have felt the weight of someone's gaze upon me. Now he's there in the shadows watching me again, daring me to come out. Who is he, Miss O'Guppy? What does he want of me?"

"I dono' the man," stated Niamh.

"How is it that you can see him?"

"I see things, leedy, as my father did afore me. 'Tis a gift left over from the marning time afore birth, the time atwixt these earthly lives of ours. Most cannot remimber the time afther a sarten age, but I can recolleckt it marvelous well. And sarten of the powers an' senses as are manifest there remain wid me in this life."

Both the lady and Lucy cast doubting glances at Miss O'Guppy — neither unkind glances, nor unfriendly glances, but nonetheless with a particular suspicion writ large on their faces.

"For the love of Christ, I bain't mad, if that's what ye bleeve," returned Niamh, crossly, for she knew only too well what was in their minds. "'Tis true I bain't like others, but a Christian I am, shure, and not a madwoman. May God sthrike me dead at yer feet if I lie!"

"Pray, Miss O'Guppy, I do not think you are mad," said Miss Wastefield. "On the contrary, you are the only other person to have seen Mr. Lanthorne over the way."

The conversation then took an even more interesting turn.

"What I see others cannot, or choose not," said Niamh. "I can see the fading glow of the marning time as invests the little childhers. I can see craytures walking the earth — unseen visitors sich as yer Mr. Lanthorne there — as most others in this life have no knowledge of. Many sich craytures have I seen, beings of a shadowy sort as glides about us in this world every day, and not all of which be human."

"Not human?"

"Not human, or human no more. And I can sense something of the other lives of a person, as may still be manifest in this life afther the marning time."

"Other lives? Morning time? Forgive me, Miss O'Guppy, but I fear I don't understand you."

Indeed, neither Miss Wastefield nor Lucy understood much of what Niamh had told them, or necessarily accepted what they did understand; but they were not the first to be baffled by the puzzle that was Miss O'Guppy. In recognition of this she took something from a pocket of her dress — it was her fortune-telling cards, which she carried with her always. From them she selected three cards and laid them face-up on the table.

"A mighty secret it is ye're keepin', leedy, though 'tis all unknownst to ye," she said, in a careful tone. "For ye have in thruth *forgotten it*. 'Tis a secret as cuts very deep. Look here! These be the cards I drew wid me mind an' sould concentrayted upon ye. These be the cards of yer fortune, leedy, past an' presint. The cutlass here, it signifies danger. And the sarpint here, it signifies treachery, or disaster. And last the mountain here — 'tis the sign of a mighty enemy. Agh, 'tis beyant the reach of question!"

"A mighty enemy," echoed Miss Wastefield, touching a hand to her brow. "But why should I have an enemy of any kind, Miss O'Guppy? What harm have I done to warrant such an enemy as Mr. Lanthorne, or anyone else?"

"Oh, miss, I'm certain you've done no harm at all," smiled Lucy.

"How little yez comprehind of it, both of yez," said Niamh. "Answer me this, then. If ye have no sich enemy, leedy, who gave ye that which ye keep mewed up in that trunk there?"

The question caused Miss Wastefield to gaze at the speaker in some amazement. Even Juga raised his little head and peered at Niamh.

"How do you know of this?" Miss Wastefield demanded. For a second her eyes touched Lucy's, but the poor girl shook her head vigorously to deny the charge. No, miss, she protested, she hadn't popped it all out. She had revealed nothing to Miss O'Guppy, to whom she had hardly before spoken.

"Yer maid there has naught to do wid it at all, at all," said Niamh, to relieve Lucy of suspicion. "Don't be afeared, leedy; 'tis a thing I've sensed. For the troubles of people, often they themselves can't see the causes of 'em. But I can sense the causes, I can. 'Tis the gift. And 'tis a mighty load of trouble ye've got for yerself, bedad!"

Miss Wastefield sat and thought over her words for a time, while Lucy chafed her hands in silent worry, and prayed that Miss O'Guppy might be able to help her mistress and free her of the burden that haunted her.

"It follows me everywhere," Miss Wastefield sighed, gazing wearily upon the trunk and its harness of shackles. "Just as Mr. Lanthorne follows me in the street. It is the shadow I can't get clear of, the black cloud that hangs over our house."

"'Tis the secret," said Niamh. She studied the face of Miss Wastefield with a slow and thoughtful scrutiny. "Shure, now, I see it again. The other one there — 'tis the faded light of another life afore. 'Tis an auld life, it is; 'tis ancient as dust. Poor child — poor leedy! 'Tis a jealous and a selfish power as threatens ye."

"Oh, can't you tell me something of it, Miss O'Guppy — something of this power — and of myself?" implored Miss Wastefield. "For of late I've had the awful feeling that I don't know myself. I feel as if I am someone other than who I am."

"I'll say the truth, leedy, and dar' the divil. When I see yer leedylike person, I see two people. Shure one of 'em is yer own purty self, but t'other is younger — one of the childhers! And I see, afar off an' long ago, on a mountain, a kind of altar of dull, dead stones, and poppy-juice and wine to be dhrunk, and olives, and figs, and a black monkey very like yer own darlin pet there — which be a remarkable crayture himself, too." She shut her eyes and cocked her head a little to one side, with her brows tightly knit, as though she were straining to catch something faint and distant on the air. "I hear a voice askin' ye — nay, commanding ye — to sleep, and I hear the call of a trumpet-shell on the mountain." Then her remarkable eyes, opening, grew extraordinarily large and peculiar. "I sense a death there. 'Tis an ancient death. Och, by the Holy — 'twas murther!"

Miss Wastefield scarcely knew what to say. "But what has it to do with me, Miss O'Guppy? What sin have I committed that I should be tortured so? And what do you mean that you see two people?"

"Ye are in this life," said Niamh, mysteriously, "something still of what ye once were in another. 'Tis so, bedad! For ye've not lost all memory of it — ye've kept something of yer life afore, an' though it be weak as yet, 'tis gaining sthrength. Agh! Poor leedy. Ye've yerself had no marning time for sich a long time. But 'tis not yer doing — 'tis the doing of the jealous lord as commands ye, and seeks to have ye once more under his hoof."

Miss Wastefield, upon reflection, began to wonder if the images in her dreams and visions, the sound of the shell-horn and the illness it had engendered, might not indeed have their origin in memories of past events. Oh, if only she could remember the where and the when and the wherefore of them!

And what did her gift tell her, she asked Miss O'Guppy, of the grim and sinister figure lurking over the way?

"An ancient crayture," Niamh replied, "and a powerful one himself, too. One of the unseen visitors as can be glimpsed by sich as I, on occasion, and by sich as they themselves choose to be glimpsed by. A higher sould, by the Holy, than ye or I may hope to become in a hundred lifetimes!"

"A creature? Do you mean that Mr. Lanthorne is not a man — that he is *not human*?"

"That is what I mane."

"But what of his intentions? Why should he wish me harm?"

"Sich an ancient soul as he has his reasons to be watchin' ye. He's come for a purpose, pleasint or otherwise, that ye may be shure of! Whither to fear him or no, leedy, I've not the least notion. But mind ye — he bain't the mighty enemy of which I spake."

Having delivered this rather ambiguous judgment, Miss O'Guppy rose to leave. "There be little more I can do for ye, leedy, for 'tis all I see now. I wisht it were otherwise, I do. But if ye like, I'll come wid ye wherever ye be goin' now, to give warning in case of danger, so ye'll be easier in yer mind."

"If you please, miss," Lucy urged her mistress — "to be on the safe side!"

"Yes," Miss Wastefield said after a moment's thought, "yes, I should like that. I must attend at the coffee-house this afternoon. I'm expecting a letter there, which I hope will lead to a resolution of this odious business. But first Lucy and I must get ourselves a cab. Perhaps, Miss O'Guppy, you could accompany us as far as the stand?"

Niamh answered with a quick little nod; and so they returned downstairs to the hall. Miss O'Guppy herself opened the street-door and, slipping out onto the landing, made a careful survey of the area round.

"Is he still hanging about?" Lucy asked. "The grim gentleman?"

"'Tis gone he is," Niamh announced.

With sighs of relief Miss Wastefield and Lucy issued forth into the open air. At once the door of the next house flew open and Jilly came rushing down the steps.

"Are you better now, Miss Wastefield?" she asked, and in a low voice added — "Is the tall man still there?"

"Gone he is, darlin," Niamh answered in the lady's place. "Which is to say he's no more makin' himself known to me senses, which be his choice."

"I should like to speak privately with your mother, Jilly," said Miss Wastefield. "Will you inform her of this when she returns? Perhaps she can spare me an hour this evening."

"Yes, Miss Wastefield. But what of Mr. Frobisher?" Jilly asked.

"Mr. Frobisher?"

"Mr. Frobisher told me there was something he could do to help you, and that he was going to do it, too."

"How can Mr. Frobisher help me?"

To this, Jilly admittedly had no answer; and so while Mrs. Juniper's precious flower returned to her home, Miss Wastefield, flanked by Lucy and Miss O'Guppy, set off at a brisk pace for the cab-stand. A shiversome wind blowing along the street helped propel the three on their way. Long slanting shadows thrown down by the houses fell across them as they went. The eyes of Miss Wastefield examined each and every shadow, but no evidence of Mr. Lanthorne did they find, nor was any alarm raised by Niamh.

On reaching the stand, Miss O'Guppy saw her companions safely into a hansom, having received their grateful thanks, and watched after the cab as it rattled away. Retracing her steps to the boarding-house, she paused for a moment on the landing before going in.

"Poor leedy," she murmured, with a long, sad shake of her head. "'Tis a murtherin' mighty foe she faces, and an unmarciful one. He'll stick at nothing to take back what's his, that's shure. There's not a soul in Christendom can help that leedy, no, sir, and sartenly not a schemin' spalpeen like Masthur Allan Frobisher. May the holy saints keep ye and guard ye, leedy — if they dare!"

CHAPTER TWENTY-THREE

The Stirrings of Remembrance

She opens her eyes, and gazes upon the lonely, frost-hardened road that stretches before her, and the new-risen moon overhead, and the threatening loom of forest all around. She knows instinctively that she is dreaming. She knows, too, who she is and where she is, though in truth she couldn't swear to either. The lonely, frost-hardened road could be Chamomile Street, and the threatening loom of forest the tall rows of houses along it; but perhaps not. Remarkably she seems to be floating above the road rather than standing on it. Looking down, she can see the points of her shoes hovering a few inches above its surface. This defiance of gravity, she recalls, is a common occurrence in the wild land of dreams.

Her attention is drawn from this phenomenon by the tread of footsteps rapidly approaching along the road. In one direction the road vanishes into the looming forest; in the other it disappears round a turn. It is from beyond the turn that the footsteps are coming on.

She doesn't stop to reflect or consider. Someone is running fast along the road to capture her. She has been followed for so many days now and felt so many invisible eyes upon her — spies and listeners all around! All that is left to her is to run now herself and try to outrace her pursuer.

But how? She is floating like mist in the moonlight above the road. With all her strength, physical and mental, concentrated on the task, she struggles against this obstinate buoyancy of hers. She tries to push the points of her shoes down to the surface of the road, to gain a foothold so she can escape. But it is labor lost; all she manages to do is to run in place, like a frantic skater slipping on the ice, while getting not an inch closer to the road.

She looks over her shoulder at the turn round which her pursuer will appear. At last a figure emerges into the moonlight. As it does, it is revealed to her disbelieving senses as nothing but a pair of legs and feet — no head, no arms, no torso — running, running, running along the road.

She turns to flee these horrid running legs, but has lost the contest even before it's begun. Already she is out of breath from slipping and sliding on air and gaining no ground. The exertion of it is depleting her resources. She watches helplessly as the horrid running legs draw nearer and nearer. It's no use; exhausted, she goes limp and surrenders to the inevitable. The horrid running legs close in fast. Afloat there in the moonlight above the road, she summons the energy for one last look across her shoulder, and sees —

Her own self.

She gives a sharp cry and is jolted into wakefulness. Instantly the dream-landscape is refashioned into her chambers in Chamomile Street, where she has been dozing on her bed for the past hour. She'd been intending to go downstairs and speak again with Mrs. Juniper, but had grown tired and fallen asleep, and so another dream had come to her. Little Juga is peering at her from his basket-bedstead, unsure whether to disturb her or not. Her cry has alarmed him, but he understands that she has been napping.

Miss Wastefield is certain now that she has been followed by the man called Lanthorne, but why he should be following her she can't begin to know. The words of Miss O'Guppy, while bringing some new light to bear on her troubles, had also brought new shadows. But relief was still no nearer, for having gone to the coffee-house she'd once again found nothing there — no, miss, sorry, miss, the scholarly lion of a landlord had informed her, there was no letter for you today.

That day had been yesterday. Then, on returning to Chamomile Street, she'd found that in her absence a gentleman had called for her at Mrs. Juniper's door. The housemaid didn't know who he was, having never before seen him in the neighborhood. Neither could she furnish a proper description of him, save to say that he was a young gentleman, and a good-looking one she thought, from what she saw of him, and not so tall — points which straightway disqualified Mr. Lanthorne. A large hat with a drooping leaf, a neck-shawl, and a heavy greatcoat had served to conceal much of his appearance. He had asked the maid, in a pleasant enough voice, if there was a Miss Jane Wastefield lodging in the house? And she had replied that yes, there was indeed, sir, but that she was from home at present. The housemaid didn't know when or if the gentleman would call again, however, for he had left no card and no message, but had turned round and walked swiftly away.

Miss Wastefield contemplates this latest puzzle which has left her nerves in an even more jangled state. Who could this stranger have been if he were not Lanthorne? Who else but the mighty enemy of whom Miss O'Guppy had spoken? But if he were her enemy, why should he have called at her lodgings like a gentleman, and in a "pleasant enough voice" inquired as to her presence there? For surely he knew already she was living in Mrs. Juniper's house!

Like most of her other puzzles, it made no sense.

And so her eyes stray as they so often did to the trunk standing in the corner. With every tick of the clock she is getting nearer the point of desperation. It is the point where her fear will begin to fuel her courage, the point where she must get to the bottom of the problem no matter the cost. She had spoken with Mrs. Juniper the night before, and their conversation had identified a source of aid she hoped to make use of. But here she sat now, alone, and there was the trunk with the answers to all her questions lying inside it, if only she dared ask them; and so perhaps the direct approach might be the better expedient.

She looks first into her maid's closet, to see if Lucy might have come in, but the room is empty. She'd given the girl the morning to herself, saying she wished to be alone for a time. And so, it seemed, she was.

In haste almost she frees the trunk from its shackles, and unfastens the locks of the smaller trunks inside it, and places the dressing-case on the table. Barely hesitating, she opens the case and, removing the hand-mirror from its compartment, settles down with it in a chair. Juga, alarmed, attempts to dissuade her with a host of warning growls and chutters, and many windmill-like motions of his arms and wild contortions of visage; but for all his efforts Miss Wastefield chooses to ignore him.

I will get to the bottom of it, she repeats to herself, with a new grimness of will her fear has forged within her. *I will get to the bottom of it!*

For a time not much of anything occurs. There is no evil, hissing whisper from the mirror; there is, indeed, nothing but her reflection, imperfect as it is, in the ancient polished bronze. Another few moments pass by, during which her eyes drift about the handle of the mirror with its carved poppies and crocuses in bas-relief and its inscription in a mysterious, unknown tongue. Then, as her attention returns to the mirror itself, the realization strikes her that a face other than her own is looking at her from the bronze.

Instead of her own pretty features she sees there the image of a solemn, dark-haired woman she does not know. The face remains perfectly still as she watches it — large painted eyes, smooth cheeks, lush red lips, a mass of hair thick and dark like spun coal. Some of the hair is piled atop the woman's head, while the rest flows down in braids and long wavy ringlets before and behind her ears.

It is not the first time Miss Wastefield has seen this face, or other faces, in the mirror. Still the sight of it startles her, although she manages to restrain an urge to cast the mirror from her, for she is as fascinated by the unholy image as she is repelled.

Who is this woman? What has she to do with me?

Gradually, imperceptibly almost, the image undergoes a change, transforming itself into the face of a man who presents to her the same fixed, expressionless gaze. A commanding face it is, clean-shaven, with firm, steady features. The man, like the woman before him, wears his hair in long streaming braids and curls. There is something about him, however, that Miss Wastefield finds oddly familiar, but what it is or why it should be so, she cannot say. Thinking on it now, she believes that her impression of the woman may have been in error, that indeed she may know her, too. It was all so very deep, so very hard to dig out. If only she could pierce the veil that separated herself from remembering!

As she ponders this mystery, the face in the bronze undergoes a second transformation, melting and merging into the image of a little girl round ten years of age. Her eyes are dark and painted like the woman's, and she, too, has waves of black hair trickling down her head. Miss Wastefield peers closely at this new image; then abruptly she reels back as if struck by a blow.

"I know you," she whispers. "But how can that be?"

Like the others before her, the child responds with a frozen stare.

"Who are you, little one? Where have I known you? *When* did I know you?"

It was at this moment that Fate bade Lucy return. Thinking that her mistress might have gone out — she'd been tapping gently at the door for the past half-minute and received no answer — the maid had brought Jilly round to spend a little time with Juga. Both are surprised to discover that Miss Wastefield is not out, but in; and so there they stand, as speechless as the strangers in the mirror.

Miss Wastefield hasn't heard the tapping, has neither seen nor heard the door open, as her attention is absorbed elsewhere. Lucy gapes in horror to see the dread mirror in her mistress's hand, and her mistress speaking into its ancient polished bronze. She is too shocked to do anything but beg Jilly to go downstairs, for she is afraid of what may happen next. But of course, Jilly would not leave the room for worlds!

Then a change comes over Miss Wastefield. She goes pale and, with a gasp, turns the mirror face-down on the table. She drops her head into her hand, and swallows hard several times, and darts her eyes about the table-top, struggling to collect her thoughts. That child, that child — so familiar! Could it be possible — ?

A slight noise causes her to look up, at which point she becomes aware of Lucy and Jilly at the door.

Flushed with anger, she breaks out of her chair and orders them away. It is for their own good, of course, so they'll not come to harm, and not because she thinks they are spying on her. She is angry, too, at herself for having left the door unfastened. The vehemence of her response, however, surprises even Miss Wastefield, not to say Lucy and Jilly. She had never before been so cross with Lucy, never treated her in so summary a fashion. And poor Jilly! She will apologize to the both of them later, she vows; at present she is too overwhelmed by what she has seen in the bronze.

As Lucy and Jilly flee downstairs, Miss Wastefield bolts the door after them and eagerly takes up the mirror again. She is set upon solving the mystery here and now. Answers, answers, she will have answers! The faces in the mirror *will* speak, they *will* tell her what she wants to know — she is determined to make them.

Instead of faces, however, it is something quite different that confronts her in the mirror. It is the vast panorama she has so often seen in her dreams and visions. In the foreground stands the enormous, labyrinthine building with its maze of terraces and courtyards and colorful colonnades. She can see people moving in and around the building, which she understands now is a kind of temple, and can discern many details within it — walls adorned with vivid, spring-like frescoes, shields of cattle-hide, ceremonial leopard-axes, daggers and swords; countless pairs of sacral bulls' horns, or "horns of consecration," ornamenting its façades and roof-tops; priestesses and their attendants going about the central court and the sanctuaries, small chambers graced with votive statuettes in stone, clay, and bronze; smiths and potters laboring in workshops; women spinning sea-purple wool into garments, workers pressing grapes and olives into sacred wine and oil; guards keeping watch over storerooms replete with tribute and provisions; small troops of monkeys, some in leather harness and looking very much like Juga, playing about the courtyards under the watchful eye of temple servants.

Beyond the temple and its adjoining cluster of town dwellings, on the side of a mountain commanding far views of the countryside, she sees an altar and on it some honeyed wine standing in a cup. On tables beside the altar are some dishes of figs and olives, some oysters, starfish, and octopi, some olive oil perfumed with sage, and a coiled triton-shell. She sees poppies from the fields being made into juice, which then is mixed with the honeyed wine in the cup. At the altar the beautiful dark priestess in the flounced skirt and robe of sheepskin beckons to her, and offers her the cup of wine to drink, all the while telling her to sleep, Djhana, sleep.

These pictures — so enigmatic, so exotic, so remote from anything she had ever known at Pinewick. *And yet so familiar!*

"I lived here," she murmurs to herself, with rather more certainty than she cared to admit. "I lived in this place once — a place as different from Pinewick as chalk from cheese —"

Lived there? How absurd! She'd been born at Pinewick; she'd been raised at Pinewick; she'd never lived anywhere else in her life.

Ah, but which life was that?

Was she going mad now, or was there indeed some truth in the claims of Miss O'Guppy?

Before she has time to speculate further, the picture vanishes, its place taken by the images of the people she had looked on before. No longer fixed and expressionless, the images have consented at last to speak.

"Djhana," says the woman with the painted eyes. "Dear Djhana — how changed you are!"

"Come back to us," says the man.

His name! What was his name? She feels she can spell it out, almost. But how did she know him? For with his flowing locks he resembles no gentleman the streets of Pinewick or Crow's-end has ever seen.

"Come back," the woman calls to her softly. "Come back, dear Djhana!"

"You have displeased our great and mighty lord," the man says. "Why have you done this? Were you not happy here?"

"Better you were never born," warns the child, "unless you return to us. Our lord Poteidan the earth-shaker demands it."

At mention of the name Poteidan, Miss Wastefield reflexly plants a fist to her brow and holds it there, in an attitude of worship — that is, she knows somehow that it *is* an attitude of worship, but what has impelled her to it, she has no idea. She can taste the honeyed wine again, and the laudanum, even as her ears fill with the wild sound of the triton-shell. Then a wave of nausea engulfs her. She feels something twine itself about her throat and slowly tighten down, as though to strangle her.

"Pray God — *no!*" she manages to stammer out in a fit of coughing and choking. "I defy you — this is the blackest treachery — confess it — you're tricksters, all of you — you are the murderers of my father!"

The voice of the little girl speaks again from the polished bronze. "You should never have disobeyed. Remember, Djhana, and take heed."

Chilled to the heart, she sees something reach out to her from the ancient polished bronze, and feels a tugging sensation in the middle of her forehead. It is the people in the mirror, the owners of the stern faces whom she does not know and yet somehow knows she does, trying to pry the soul from her body and draw it into the mirror-world.

Then the ground underneath begins to tremble — that is to say, the ground in the mirror. The scene has returned in a flash to the temple building, which, it can be seen, is shaking underfoot. She watches in awe as its terraces and courtyards are cracked asunder. One by one the timbered colonnades start to fall. Its stairways crumble, its walls with their graceful, glowing frescoes quiver and come crashing down. Dislodged boulders come rolling off the nearby hills as the earth suffers a furious convulsion. Terrified, the inhabitants of the building scatter in a panic. Many are crushed beneath the shower of bricks and falling blocks of stone, their cries going unheeded amid the thunderous roar of the cataclysm.

And all the while Miss Wastefield can feel herself slowly being pulled into the mirror, can feel her spirit being sucked out of her and plunged headlong into the upheaval.

At the last moment comes the touch of tiny hands on her arm. It is little Juga, frantically chattering and barking in his shrill monkey-voice, pleading with her to resist.

It is enough; it is her own dear Juga. With every bit of strength remaining to her, she tears herself free of the mirror's grasp. Pulling back from the mirror-world, she drops the ancient polished bronze onto the table and sinks exhausted into her chair.

"Oh, Juga!" she whispers, folding the little monkey into her arms. "My own dear Juga — my old friend — my little one — thank God for you!"

Only seconds pass before she remembers she must return the mirror to her dressing-case and lock it in the trunk. Barely recovered, she takes hold again of the unholy object. She tries very hard not to look at it, but finds that she must, for lo! there is something stirring again in the bronze.

It is another face, and a ghastly face it is indeed. It is a sinister and a shocking face, and one which she knows unfortunately only too well. It is a monstrous face — a tall, crested head with huge furred brows, two hungry, glaring eyes of crimson, a goatish beard, a mouthful of finely chiseled teeth and broad nostrils exhaling fumes of burning acid. Worst of all are the two tusks or horns that can be seen protruding from behind the jaws, and curving round in front of the teeth, like two pincers for the grasping of prey.

A fouler, more hideous, more terrifying face could hardly have been envisioned on even the darkest of All Hallows Eve. It is the face of a Triamete.

The denizen of her nightmares leers at her, then swivels its head about to reveal another orb gleaming redly wicked in the nape of its neck — a third eye, observing her from behind.

"Djhana of Kaftor," says this gargoyle, in the horrid, hissing whisper she has heard so often. "We are watching you, my brothers and I. In the name of our father Poteidan, we have inscribed your soul upon the imperishable slate of memory. Djhana of Kaftor, your time has passed. Beware the sons of Poteidan — *beware the Triametes!*"

CHAPTER TWENTY-FOUR

Hallo My Turkey Chicken

After Mr. Planxty Moeran departed the fruit shop and tea room of Miss Trickle, he went straight to a certain house in Jekyl Street. It was a gaunt, morbid, gloomy species of house, a dilapidated stone mansion with bars on its windows and a heavy door faced with vertical strips of iron, on the portcullis model. To this cheery haven Mr. Moeran was granted quick admittance and, in an upstairs apartment, made known to his friend and colleague Jones what he had learned in the tea room. What he had learned was that there were strangers in town who stood in want of Mr. Jones's singular expertise, and who, from their appearance — especially that of the "toff gintleman" and his wife — were likely to pay handsome for it.

Eager nods and gleeful looks were exchanged between the two cronies, and a plan concerted, following which Mr. Moeran took his leave of the gloomy prison of a house — for a prison of sorts it was, a sponging-house for the temporary confinement of debtors — and trotted up the hill to the Crozier. There, upon the return of the Cargoes and Miss Veal, he made bold to introduce himself to them and to wax effusive upon the talents of his friend Jones. Mr. Moeran spoke, the strangers listened; and so it transpired on the day following, that Mr. Moeran rejoined his colleague in the lock-up to await the arrival of the toff gentleman and his party.

It was a close, cramped, ill-lighted apartment in which Mr. Jones had passed his time while a guest of Mr. Jacob Comport, whose lock-up it was. This apartment was called the coffee-room, though why it should have been so designated no one knew, as coffee was hardly ever served there. It had only a single window, one which, like the other windows in the house, was so heavily barred as to afford little useful light. As well the apartment had only a single door — a stout coarse giant of a door, plainly a near relative of the outer street-door — which was under the superintendence of a person named Imbercand.

This Mr. Imbercand was, like the door he guarded, a stout coarse giant, whose job it was to keep debtors in and busybodies out. In his wider capacity as bailiff's man, he was called on to apprehend defaulters and other like miscreants for his master Comport; to act as overseer of those who came to view the inmates, and who sometimes brought them the funds they needed to go out; and to bid said inmates a sweet adieu when they did go out, or if they didn't, to hand them over to the men from the dreaded Compter, the debtors' prison from which moldering pile few were likely ever to emerge.

The apartment was partitioned off into a number of boxes, each with a table and deep, low seats. On the floor was a ragged carpet for stepping on — from its looks it had been stepped on mightily, and much, in its day — and overhead a ceiling turned black by the smoke from generations of wax-lights. There was a fireplace at one end with a small fire in it, one nearly as dim and seedy as the light in the room. The air smelled of old cigars, mustard, oysters, stale leavings, and spiritous liquors, scattered evidence of which could be found in and around the boxes. There was little in the way of furnishings — a broom here, an oak stool there, a pair of bellows, a kettle on the hob, a paper fly-cage dangling from the ceiling, a wash-hand stand and shaving-glass, some newspapers, a prayer-book for the uneasy-minded, an old harp from which a few strings were missing — all of them languishing there since time out of mind.

About half of the boxes were occupied, by small numbers of generally bleary-eyed men and women, some alone and some in pairs, and looking for all the world like departed souls who, having awakened in this purgatory, had little recourse but to await further news — some with assurance, some with hope, some with despair — as to the disposition of their cases. Most of them were going out again directly, of course, or harbored some such illusion that their affairs would be quickly settled; for the door of Mr. Comport's palace had never closed on a debtor who wasn't going out again directly!

Mr. Havergal Skeffington Jones was one of the more assured of these lost souls, sitting fist-to-unshaven-cheek in his box with a smile on his lips and his cap set at a rakish angle. He was puffing with vigor at his little pipe, and although there was no clock in the room, and no useful light in the window, and so no passage of time — which well-suited this purgatory — he was making count in his head of the hours, minutes, and seconds until the arrival of his rescuers. His truest friend in life, Mr. Moeran, sat opposite him, and was smoking and counting, too.

The stout coarse giant Imbercand was the servant and general factotum of Mr. Comport, the ostensible host of the establishment. Mr. Comport, however, enjoyed the curious distinction of having never been seen by most of his servants or any of his guests. He dwelt in mysterious splendor somewhere in the upper reaches of the house — like a deity abiding in the firmament, oft imagined but never glimpsed by his creation — while allowing such of his minions as Imbercand to guide the daily affairs of the lock-up. Mr. Jacob Comport was not a creditor of anyone, but an agent of creditors and the Court in the matter of distraints and arrests. He was, in short, a city bailiff and, like any bailiff, was entitled to his costs — those expenses incurred by his guests while lodging under his roof, and which were borne by none other than the guests themselves.

Most of those in Mr. Comport's care were waiting to be bailed out by relations, friends, acquaintances, lawyers, wives even; others, too far dipped for bailing, and having no relations, friends, acquaintances, etc., who would admit to knowing them, let alone stump up, had no prospect but the dreaded Compter to look forward to. Such souls as these were simply marking time — an odd pursuit in a timeless purgatory — until such hour as they were conveyed to Turtle Street, where the gates of the dreary prison would close on them forever.

Mr. Jones was one of those who was going out again directly, once his debts, which amounted to the trivial sum of £38 5s. 7d. and costs, had been discharged by his rescuers. The landlords of certain public houses had become restive for payment, and in frustration had appealed to the city sheriff, who in his turn had appealed to Mr. Comport, who in *his* turn had dispatched the giant Imbercand to nab Mr. Jones. Mr. Jones had one day more left to him in the lock-up; if his debts were not settled in the next four-and-twenty hours, he would himself be shipped to Turtle Street. But a measure so extreme was all unnecessary, of course, as Mr. Jones was going out again directly.

The stout coarse giant having come in at the door, he glanced searchingly about and, locating Messrs. Jones and Moeran in their box near the fire, directed his steps thereward. As he swaggered up, a great bullying grin broke like caustic sunshine from his curly red beard. Raking the two vagabonds with his eyes, he inquired in mocking tones as to the condition of the poor imprisoned one, and how he was keeping today, and what his chances were of going out again, if any, or would he be bound over to the men from Turtle Street and taken to rot in the Compter?

Such prattle was the meat of everyday conversation for Mr. Imbercand, and pleasant music to his ears. Both Moeran and Jones, like many a swell upon town, found him a daunting figure, but as Round-the-corner was going out again directly, it hardly mattered.

"Hearkee, my pigeon," said the giant, in a very loud key, "how d'you like your chances now, eh? Bailed out of Comport's today, is it? Ducats produced, debts discharged? Not likely, my cabbages! Driven to the wall is more probable. What chance the pigeon be bailed afore the van from Turtle Street draws up at the door? Dreadful slim, thinks Candy, dreadful slim!"

This pronouncement he capped with a vicious wink, and a smiling wag of his head overgrown with fiery red locks.

"Och! on the conthrary, joy, a near sarten chance it is, near sarten," said Mr. Moeran, with a confident air. "Shure, now — and 'tis proud I am to say it — this very minute persons of honor and quality, friends of meself and me friend Jones here, be rushing on towards this fine esthablishment, plase yer masthurship, to see he's made free of it."

"Oh-hoh, my bold partridge!" exclaimed Mr. Imbercand, crossing his mighty arms on his chest and raining frowns onto little Planxty. "By cock and pie, is it so, my biscuit?"

"'Tis so, by gannies!"

"Do you mean it?"

"I mane it, joy."

"And such would be a fine trick, to be sure, for to borrow one of your own dear phrases — you lie like the devil, sir! D'you know how many it is gets clear o' Comport's scot-free? Not many, my bully beeves, not many! 'Tis a sad tale, a man as cannot govern his finances. 'Tis the saddest tale in the world. But there's no help for it, and so what's to be done — eh, my cabbages?"

And placing hands on hips, he threw back his head and laughed — a mighty, roaring, thunderous kind of sarcastic bellow of a laugh — as if the rigors of insolvency were, apart from Jones and Moeran themselves, the funniest thing in creation.

"What ye fail to perceive, dear joy," returned Planxty, "is the plain truth that me friend Jones here bain't one of these Compter soarts. The black darkness of the prison-house bain't for him, for he'll not thrive there, no, sir. The crowded, sthinking chambers, the dismal paving-sthones, the narrow yard, the dreary walls wid spikes atop — no, no, joy, 'tis not for Jones at all, at all."

"Oh-hoh, my plumcake!" cried Candy. "'Tis another sad tale, to be sure. 'He'll not thrive there, no sir, he has not the constitution for it.' Well, who is it as *does* thrive in the stone jug, eh, my partridge? Nobody. *The stone jug ain't for thriving!* All you see round this room here raise the same sorry cry, every man jack of 'em. 'No, sir, please, sir, do not send me to the Compter, sir, for I'll not thrive there.' Why, my pretty capons, the entire sit'ation would be comical if it wasn't so hilarious."

Saying which the giant exploded again with laughter, and sauntered off to spread similar joy among the others in the room.

"*He's* a happy one, by the powers," commented Planxty. "Ye'd think he'd a goose-feather in those breeches of his, to be ticklin' him so."

"A man sich as that," said Mr. Jones, following the doorkeeper with his eyes, "a man sich as that, Moeran, bain't worth throublin' about. Where did he leave his manners, bedad? Troth and faith, jewel, that weasel's not worth the blood in a blood pudding. Bain't it so?"

"Ah, shure, and 'tis right enough ye are, Jones," nodded his friend and champion.

"A man sich as that be little more than an ignorant spalpeen, wid no more brains than a tack."

"True enough."

"And he don't behave the least like a Christian."

"He bain't a man of delicate feeling, joy."

"I'd weazen him if I'd a mind to. I'd give him sich a conquassation! But hang it, Moeran, a man sich as that bain't worth the time of thinkin' on him. Sorra a friend he has in this world, I'd hexpect, wid a temperament sich as that, and a mug as ugly."

"There bain't uglier at mop fair, that's shure."

"Well, the fool can go snick-up for what I care. He's as odious a weasel and as knot-pated as that oysther-masthur Arifay — divil burn him!"

Then Mr. Jones abruptly grew very quiet and museful, and a swainish expression came into his face, as he thought of the pretty, blue-eyed damsel who served the oyster-master — conveniently forgetting how the damsel had so cruelly misled him, and toyed with his heart-strings, and in the end rejected him. But sich was Round-the-corner, as Mr. Moeran often said, so very forgivin' of the leedies.

"What is it ye're thinkin' on now, joy, as has ye throwin' the sheep's eye like that?" Planxty asked.

"I be reflecktin' in me mind agin, Moeran, on the charrums of the delightful Miss Ingum."

"Agh! Miss Ingum is it, now? Shure and have ye intirely forgot, joy, how that faymale misused ye? Have ye forgot the tratement accorded ye by that brawny masthur of hers, that Arifay? I ax ye, d'ye not recolleckt that speech of yers aftherwards as regards the fair deceiver?"

"Hot words, Moeran, hot words! For a gintleman could not long remain displased wid a colleen of eighteen year as handsome as Miss Sisly Ingum."

Hearing which Mr. Moeran threw up his hands in disgust, for he was not a fellow to be besotted of anything in lace — or so he liked to believe.

Shortly after, a visitor arrived in the shape of Miss O'Guppy. She was admitted to the coffee-room by a youth, another of the vassals of the unseen Comport, the merry minion Imbercand having gone out for a spell to refresh himself. (Mr. Imbercand, of all those in the coffee-room on any day of the week, was the most likely to be going out directly.) Miss O'Guppy had in her possession an offering — a flask of brandy — which she had brought to rouse the courage of her cousin by marriage-vow, and which said cousin and his friend were most gratified to accept.

It fell to Moeran to apprise Miss O'Guppy of the glad tidings that strangers from far-away north were expected at any time who would deliver Mr. Jones from his captivity. Miss O'Guppy responded by inquiring into the motive for perfect strangers from far-away north to be bailing out her cousin? To which Planxty in turn replied that he'd acquainted them with the sorry case of Mr. Havergal Skeffington Jones (a description the said Jones found not so much to his liking), a gentleman of substance and character (he liked this better) who had been clapped in the sponging-house due to a temporary embarrassment of funds in the amount of some £38 owing. And inasmuch as these strangers were in urgent need of the expertise of Mr. Jones, it presupposed that he should be bailed out of the lock-up before they could avail themselves of it.

Her curiosity satisfied, Miss O'Guppy took up her violin, which she had brought along for the purpose of entertaining her cousin, and setting it to her chin began to tune the strings. The derelict harp meanwhile was taken up by Planxty with a view to accompanying her. Mr. Moeran was in truth a fine harpist, having studied the instrument at the knee of his father, but having no harp of his own, he had few opportunities for exhibiting his talent.

And so they plunged into it.

The first song from the fiddle of Miss O'Guppy was a relic of olden times, the one known to most as "Down Among the Dead Men." Mr. Jones smiled at his cousin in wry acknowledgment of the tune, and of the ironical fact that he and his fellow inmates were not dead yet — merely dead broke.

The next song, "The Week Before Easter," was rather more to the taste

of Mr. Jones; it was in point of fact a great favorite of his. His friend
Moeran provided a most spirited accompaniment to Niamh's violin, given
the limitations of his wounded harp; and after several more numbers —
including such delights as "The Flowers in May," "Sellenger's Round," "The
Wearing o' the Green," and "The Lingonshire Poacher" — the lively recital
was brought to a close, to the general acclaim of most everyone present.

No sooner had the concert ended than the door of the coffee-room
opened to admit three newcomers — the Cargoes and Miss Veal. They
crept into the apartment rather than came in, their faces radiating distrust
of most everything they saw there, from the shabby carpet to the melancholy walls to the ditto inmates. It was as if they feared some unseen menace was about to spring at them from this corner or that, so dark, cramped,
and dingy an apartment it was, so cave-like and so smelly. This was particularly true as regards the ladies, both of whom were vastly experienced in
turning up their noses at things, and who found ample cause for same in
the palace of Mr. Comport.

"Frederick!" said Susan, giving a sharp tug at her husband's coat-sleeve.
"Frederick, are you quite certain this is the proper address? I can't believe
it. You must've misunderstood that beastly little man, his speech was so
odd. This can't be the place. What think you, Aspasia?"

"Shocking!" exclaimed Miss Veal, who had gone even paler than her
normal shade of blanched, although it was hard to see given the dimness of
the light. Her reaction was similar on glimpsing the small form of Niamh,
she of the wild dark hair and unladylike fiddle. To her dismay Miss Veal
discovered that this creature was attached to the persons she and the Cargoes sought — namely Messrs. Jones and Moeran, both of whom had
doffed their hats and were grinning and ducking at the newcomers with a
servile air.

It was Mr. Moeran who supplied the necessary introductions, identifying Fred to Round-the-corner as the "toff gintleman" of whom he'd spoken
so highly. Mr. Jones obligingly proffered his card, the one announcing MR.
HAVERGAL JONES. CONFIDENTIAL INQUIRIES. *Discrete — Professional.* Mr.
Moeran then recounted, for the amazement of the newcomers, certain exploits of his colleague in finding those who didn't care to be found —
swindlers and impostors, for example, gentlemen who'd become entangled
in flirtations, or had sunk to bribery, blackmail, fraudulent conversion, and
other like pursuits. But of course, there was not an atom of truth in any of it.

"Ah, shure, and if there's a gintleman yez have as needs sniffing out, 'tis
me friend Jones here can help yez," he boasted. "There's none knows the
town like Jones, for he's thriven in it all his life an' more, d'ye see, an' has

rose to the cusp of his perfession. Shure he knows the way of the world, does Jones, and 'tis no blarney!"

Such praise notwithstanding, the disheveled appearance of Mr. Havergal Skeffington Jones was hardly one to inspire confidence in prospective clients. Even Fred, so generous and good-natured at heart, was more than a little doubtful as to the qualifications of this attenuated, untidy, out-of-pocket-looking street fellow.

Was this really the man to find Jerry Squailes for them?

He began to wonder if this idea of his was such a capital one after all; that he ought not to have been swayed so by Mr. Moeran, and that indeed it was too good an idea to prosper, as his wife had informed him. Beyond this there was still the matter of the debt that had landed Mr. Jones in the lock-up, and which would retard his prosecution of the search — the peevish matter of some £38 odd owing, plus Mr. Comport's costs, which brought the total to an even £50.

To encourage his benefactor a little, Mr. Jones offered to discount his fee once the debt had been paid. This sounded logical and sensible — to Fred at least, if not to his wife and Miss Veal.

"For the world is me hoccupation, sir," said Round-the-corner in his own defense, "and 'tis only in the world I thrive. But always needy I am, sir — ach, 'tis the curse of a poor Christian! Savin' yer gintlemanship's pardon, but I must have me libertee. I must be free, sir! Though 'tis not foul tin as moves me, but sarvice. For sarvice I do mane to render ye, sir — if only I may get clear of this odious dark castle of a prison-house!"

"'Pon my life, that sounds rather like Mr. Devenham," Fred remarked.

"Mr. Devenham?" echoed Planxty, shooting a glance at Jones. "Mr. *Davy* Devenham, is it, joy?"

"Black Davy, of course — capital fellow! Do you know him?"

"Ah, shure, do we know him? Of course we know him, joy — our ould friend and fellow Davy is, and himself a varitable Christian, too, and as sober a man as ye'll find in a day's trot."

"Mr. Devenham — that bladderish person — sober, and a Christian?" returned a disbelieving Susan.

"Indeed so, leedy."

It emerged that Messrs. Jones and Moeran were rather well-acquainted with the lonely wanderer over the face of nature — a worthy Christian in the eyes of Mr. Moeran, a rank atheist in those of Dr. Pinches and most others. As for Fred, he had found the well-traveled Davy a damned interesting sort of chap, and one to be envied in a small way — in that way that hopelessly petticoated husbands know only too well. This connection to Mr.

Devenham, freedom-loving excursionist and bachelor, succeeded in raising Mr. Jones a notch in Fred's estimation, but had quite the reverse effect on Susan and Miss Veal.

"Mr. Devenham!" exclaimed the latter lady, wincing at the mere thought of him.

"Dhrink?" said Planxty, pouring her a little brandy-and-water, with a view to moderating her opinion.

"No, thenk yaw."

"'Tis most revivin' it is."

"No, thenk yaw!" repeated Miss Veal, firmly.

It made little difference, Planxty would drink it himself if she refused it.

At this juncture the Cargo party detached themselves a little from the others as they debated what they should do. They spoke in low tones, to discourage eavesdropping on the part of the two vagabonds (both of whom were craning their necks most shamelessly to hear). For the most part they were intensely skeptical, especially the ladies. Even Fred had to admit he didn't much care for the look of Mr. Jones or his champion (though he was perhaps more than a little impressed by the delicate and fascinating Miss O'Guppy). The sneaking eyes and crafty grin of Jones, his evident liking for spirits, his unctuous servility, and the nagging suspicion that he was secretly laughing up his ragged sleeve at the visitors, were not at all encouraging. Still Fred put forward his case, and wondered aloud what loss they stood to incur by employing Mr. Jones and testing him out? To which Susan replied fifty pounds for a start, Frederick, fifty pounds!

Well, Fred went on to say, here they'd undertaken the long and arduous voyage from Cargo, hadn't they decided now that *something* must be done in view of Mr. Liffey's lack of progress? And as Fred couldn't yet bring himself to engage another attorney — he still thought it a betrayal of an old friend — might not Mr. Jones serve as a legitimate compromise?

"We shan't be contravening Mr. Liffey's lawyerly prerogative as executor. We shall simply be helping him along, by engaging an assistant he doesn't know he has," or so he explained it.

But the women remained firm. They wanted another *professional* on the case, they said — perhaps that Mr. Hook of Gull's Wharf whom they had heard such good things of — and not a bedraggled tramp who was likely to bolt as soon as his debts were paid. This opinion Mrs. Cargo communicated to her husband with some vigor, together with a stamp of her foot and a flash of her eye.

Fred, under threat of mutiny, reluctantly agreed; and so it was decided that they should look elsewhere for an assistant. Who knows, Fred thought, perhaps there would be good news from Mr. Liffey waiting for them at the Crozier — thereby betraying a degree of optimism which both his wife and Mrs. Veal considered farcical.

As the ladies could not be quit of the palace of Mr. Comport too soon, they made a rush now for the exit, while Fred lingered behind. As they reached the heavy door, it swung open, magically, to reveal its giant keeper with the fiery hair and vast spread of shoulder poised on the threshold. Mr. Imbercand was busily wiping his lips and beard with a greasy fist, having just refreshed himself in an ale-house opposite. When his glance met the ladies', he let fly an oath and tossed them a wicked leer. Thus were Miss Veal and Mrs. Cargo presented with a sight for which they were scarcely prepared.

"Well, hallo, my sugarplums!" he exclaimed in a great thunder of surprise. "And what matter is it brings such sweetmeat to Comport's, eh? How much are you in for? What's the amount of the debt? How many pounds? 'Ods-bobs, you must tell Candy now." (Mr. Imbercand eyeing them all over.) "Oh-hoh! 'Tis likely more than a few pounds for *you*, my butter-boat, to be sure!" (This addressed to the stoutish Miss Veal.) "And you, my dumpling — my turkey chicken — a monstrous pretty one y'are!" (This, delivered with a saucy wink, to Mrs. Cargo.)

"Oh, beastly!" Susan cried, indignant and aghast.

"Shocking creature!" exclaimed Miss Veal, clutching at her wig.

Mr. Imbercand laughed and, following some more banter at the women's expense, consented to give ear to their demands. The ladies informed him with all due severity that they were not *in* for anything, but were going *out* directly — which of course was the refrain of every inmate — and that they should prefer to stand in the deepest mud and mire till the Last Judgment rather than endure another second of Mr. Comport's hospitality. Fortunately, the youthful minion who'd been guarding the door in his absence confirmed their story for Mr. Imbercand, and so the women were permitted to leave.

"*Au revoir* then, my tartlets, my bona-robas," said Candy, ogling them, and blowing each a kiss as they passed — which actions sent the women scurrying from the apartment, Miss Veal protesting that "it really is too much!" as she fumbled for her smelling-bottle.

Fred, seeing that the ladies were safely gone, took out his pocket-book. The friendship of Mr. Jones and Black Davy had much impressed him, and feeling sorry now that he couldn't employ the vagabond, he decided to offer him the £50 that he needed, so long as he and his champion promised to treat Davy to a round of drinks when next they saw him. (To this stipulation the two cronies readily assented.) Miss O'Guppy was pleased that her cousin would be going out directly, and thought Mr. Cargo a worthy gentleman, and offered to tell him his fortune. Fred politely declined the privilege, and informed her cousin and his friend that they were under no other obligation to him. He didn't require the services of Mr. Jones after all, he said, and so they were free to go their different ways.

"By gannies but ye're the toffest of gintlemen, sir, and a mighty Christian shure, and may the marciful Jasus reward ye," gushed Moeran, with all imaginable humility.

"Me sarvice to ye, sir," said Round-the-corner, making repeated bows through his pipe-smoke while shaking Fred's hand. "And the longest of lives to ye, for by the Holy 'tis plased I am, bedad, to honor yer gintlemanship wid all me heart an' the marrow of me bones. Pray let me incommode yer vartuous person no longer, sir, but if it plase yer worship to haccept me t'anks now and those of me predecessors afther me."

Then they called for Mr. Imbercand, so that the debt and costs could be paid and the inmate released from his confinement.

"Oh, hoh! my bully beef, so you'll be deserting your Candy, eh?" sneered the giant. "Ducats produced and debt discharged. Well, well! Going out — who'd have believed it? But 'twas a comfortable three days you've passed at Comport's, to be sure, and no doubt you'll not be forgetting Candy anytime soon. Hearkee, my cabbage — mayhap next time it'll be the van to Turtle Street!" And he broke out in another explosion of laughter, such that his guts shook and the coffee-room with them.

Thinking the atmosphere in the apartment more than a little noxious, Fred made for the door to rejoin his wife and Miss Veal. He was not far behind Miss O'Guppy when he saw her way barred by the towering Candy.

"Well, hallo, my turkey chicken!" the doorkeeper exclaimed, rubbing his hands and grinning. "Candy's not seen the like of *you* in the house afore. Going out are you, eh? Will you not stay for a time and humor Candy, my pretty tartlet?"

The face of Niamh underwent a sudden and profound alteration. Her mouth opened, her brow contracted, her strange eyes grew very large and dark as they gazed upon the giant.

"Oh-hoh, and aren't we the pert and pretty one, my precious duck! You'll not be leaving Candy so soon now, will you? Why, what is it as ails you? Will you not reconsider, my bon-bon, and strike up your fiddle there and make fine music for Candy?"

"She will not, sir!" Fred answered. Ever the gallant, he hesitated not a moment before placing himself between Niamh and the doorkeeper. "This young woman owes no debts here. She is free to go, and she is going. Have the goodness to step aside, fellow. Who the devil are you to be hindering her?"

"By cock and pie, are we not the bold one, my little strutting bantam of a cockerel!" thundered Candy through his beard. "And have you not a crown-piece for Candy now, eh? Surely a crown-piece, my partridge?"

Fred, who already had surrendered £50 to liberate Mr. Jones, was reluctant to surrender one farthing more; and yet he did — one silver crown-piece, to satisfy the doorkeeper for his trouble. On receiving the coin in his greasy fist, the giant threw back his head and laughed and, turning aside, allowed the two to pass.

"Ye'll keep a sharp watch on that one, sir, for I cannot read him at all, at all," Niamh said in confidence as she and Fred emerged onto the street. "I'd not trust that blustherin' spalpeen for a single instant minute, and by the Holy Mother that's the truth of it!"

CHAPTER TWENTY-FIVE

In the Ossuary

"I don't like the sound of that."

It was Mr. Threadneedle, and the thing he didn't like the sound of was the roar of a mighty beast, the echo of which could still be heard amid the steaming ruins. It appeared that he and his apprentice-of-sorts had company of some kind in the crazy devastated village.

"What was it, do you think, sir?" asked Tim Christmas. "It sounded rather fierce, and not so far off."

The grocer hesitated a little before answering. "There have been no reports of saber-cats or other forms of wild cat on Truro, thankfully, for quite a few years — since long before I came to the Smithy, in fact. But I *have* heard the voices of such cats in the foothills back of Nantle, when I had my shop in Chamomile Street. Every now and then one of the monsters would find its way into town." He cleared his throat uncomfortably. "I believe that may have been the voice of a saber-cat we heard just now."

"Did you ever see one of them, sir?"

"I did."

"Are they every bit as fearsome as people say?"

"They are. And I confess, I shouldn't care to see one again."

"We shouldn't go outside, then?"

"No, no. Nor shall we need to, I expect. Now, then, we must tend to the mechanism at once. We shan't want to dally, with that beast at large."

"No, sir!"

The disagreeable odor of the tar was abated some by the closing of the side-casement, through which small aperture the two had been observing the desolate scene. A little curtain of raindrops was dripping from the eaves; beyond it, clouds of steam could be seen rising from the oily black pools. With the voice of the beast still in his ears, Mr. Threadneedle checked to see that the coach-house door was securely fastened — it was — and the windows, too, in the event the shock of landing had jarred something loose. It hadn't; and so he and Tim set to work inspecting the mechanism and seeing how it might be repaired.

It was clear that for now their marvelous flying craft was *hors de combat,* for in its present state it would be hard to maintain level flight. Several of the eyelets in the troubled chain-belt had torn free of their bindings, and this had caused the belt to come off the sprocket-wheel that drove the cage-coil. Moreover, the metal frames that comprised the eyelets would themselves require mending, for in tearing loose they had been wrenched into odd configurations. They would need to be hammered straight and sewn again into the material of the belt. Then the mechanism would need to be greased and balanced, and the reciprocating springs re-wound. All in all, it would be a time-consuming operation.

Looking to waste none of that time, Mr. Threadneedle and his apprentice began diving into lockers in search of the needed implements and supplies. The hours passed as if they were minutes, as they always did when the two were at their tinkering. But this was tinkering with a brisker purpose, spurred on by a desire to get clear of the gloomy ruin and its threat of saber-cats lurking nearby. The windows of the coach-house were merely glass, after all, and would stand no chance against the force of a saber-cat's plunge. Neither would the shutters provide much of an obstacle.

The two paused in their work only once, and that briefly, for a bit of lunch from the hamper. At least one favorable event transpired in the interval: the dull bank of cloud that had brought the rain began to move off, leaving behind it columns of amber sunshine streaming through fissures in the overcast. Unfortunately this served only to highlight, with rising clarity, the weirdness and strangeness of the scene around them. But even as the amber beams were making it brighter, the sun was dropping in the sky, and so it was getting darker, too.

And still the tinkerers had not finished their work.

Mr. Threadneedle was hunting again in one of the lockers when an unexpected sound reached his ears — a rapping at one of the windows of the coach-house. He glanced up and spied a dark shadow at the side-casement.

Someone or something was looking in through the glass!

Mr. Threadneedle took up the first thing that came to hand — it happened to be a carpenter's foot-rule — and Tim an iron crow, in anticipation of trouble.

"Who's there?" the grocer demanded, stepping warily toward the casement with a very determined-looking Tim at his elbow.

More rapping.

As they neared the window, they saw what looked to be a human head outlined in its tiny latticed panes.

"Who is it?" Mr. Threadneedle asked.

"Moldwort," said a voice outside.

The grocer undid the latch and opened the casement. A man's head with a thick woolen cap on it peered curiously in. The man stared speechlessly at Mr. Threadneedle, then turned up his eyes and flung them round the inside of the coach-house.

"How did this get hyar?" he asked, in tones of the deepest puzzlement.

"How do you mean?" said the grocer.

"This house. How did it get hyar? How did *you* get hyar?"

"We landed here," Mr. Threadneedle told him, matter-of-factly, as if setting down a flying house in the middle of a dismal ruined village choked with tar was an event of regular occurrence.

"What do you mean you landed hyar?"

"We brought her down here, in this spot — and on rather unsteady ground as it turns out. We brought her down from the clouds."

"Do you mean this house *flew* hyar?" returned the man, staring in openmouthed amaze.

The grocer smiled and nodded, the little glint in his eye and curl of his mustaches betraying his pride in the achievement.

Some momentary skepticism crossed the face at the window, then swiftly evaporated.

"Well," concluded the owner of the face, "I suppose I must believe you, inasmuch as I've no other explanation for how *this* got *hyar*. I've no other explanation for how a house happens to be standing aside a blackpool where no house was yesterday."

"Do you live here, sir? Is this place your home?" Tim asked. He had lowered his iron crow, and Mr. Threadneedle, his suspicions less excited now, followed suit with the foot-rule.

"In a word, yes."

"And your name again?" said the grocer.

"Name is Moldwort," the man replied.

"Ah, I see. Pray, would that be your surname, sir, or your Christian name?"

"Surname. None round hyar with a Christian name like Moldwort!" the other exclaimed with a chuckle, and a good-natured wag of his head.

"I see. I asked only because it's so unusual a name."

"Never seen a house standing hyar afore today — certainly not a house such as this one. And by the look of things it won't be hyar much longer, neither, for 'twill be sinking slow into that muck of asphaltum and bitumen unless something be done."

"Where exactly have we landed?"

"At the edge of a blackpool, as some calls tar-pools."

"And where is that? This place here, this village. What is it called?"

"Why, this be the town of Deeping St. Magma, in Gloamshire."

"Who lives here?"

"None but myself lives hyar now. All the others be gone away. All but Moldwort."

Mr. Threadneedle and his apprentice, though still a trifle wary of the stranger in the woolen cap — for that was all they could see of him, a head and cap framed in the side-casement — by degrees relaxed their guard further and, being convinced of the man's essential good nature, allowed him entry at the door.

His appearance was a remarkable one. He was constructed almost entirely of leg, and that very long and lean, like a stork, with feet cased in enormous, tar-stained boots that had furred tops and reached to the knees. But where he was long and straight below the waist, he was short and bent above it, with a crook in his back and another in his neck, so that the upper part of him was hunched forward and down, like a man searching for pins in the street. In profile he resembled nothing so much as a human question-mark.

His face was mustached and half-bearded, and his complexion oily and dark, as if the tar had seeped into his skin. His eyes were bulging and fish-like, his hair black and clipped evenly round, with the ends peeping from beneath his cap (which garment all too plainly had served as his guide for cutting them). He wore an old pilot-coat and neck-shawl, and thick cord trousers stuffed into his huge boots with the furred tops. A human question-mark indeed was Mr. Moldwort, and in more ways than one.

He proceeded now to relate, in a leisurely and amiable fashion, a brief history of the town of Deeping St. Magma in Gloamshire, and how it had come to ruin — how it had come to be sinking, in short, after a series of land tremors had brought the asphaltum and bitumen bubbling to the surface, gradually drowning the village in ooze and suffocating it with gaseous emanations. Their geographic situation? They were many miles to the south of Goforth, the county town, and a good distance inland as well, in a district that was only sparsely peopled. The town lay not far from the Sawtooth Mountains, in fact, which, with the passing of the rain, could be seen clearly now in the east — a lofty chain of jagged peaks and storm-battered pinnacles rearing up just behind the town, very grim and somber in their majesty.

So the coach-house had set down almost at the very foot of the mountains. If there hadn't been trouble with the mechanism — if the spring and chain-belt had *not* malfunctioned, and the house instead had raced on at speed through the drizzly weather — it might have run smack into them!

The horridness of the fate they had cheated, and the sheer blind luck of their escape — the utter and perfect capriciousness of it, and the miracle of it, and the mystery of it — how the misfortune of their being grounded had turned itself into the great good fortune of not having flown on — all impressed themselves on the minds of Mr. Threadneedle and his young assistant, and left them appropriately chastened.

Meanwhile their new acquaintance had been examining, with much curiosity and bewilderment, the appurtenances and apparatus of the coach-house — the meshwork of chains and belts and wheels sprouting from bulkheads and ceiling, the mangles, the speed-coils running fore and aft, the helm of oak boards with its old gig-wheel and bittacle, the cage-coils standing in the corners. He seemed most taken by the appearance of the odd white stones, which, unbeknownst to him, were the source of the house's power and the key to its secret of flight.

"We were disturbed earlier today, Tim and I, by a noise from somewhere about — a mighty roaring, like the voice of some large animal," said Mr. Threadneedle. "Would you happen to know, sir, what it might have been?"

"Ah," Mr. Moldwort nodded absently, as he strolled here and there with his queer, stork-like gait, his shoulders stooped and his hands clasped at his back. He didn't seem disposed to answer Mr. Threadneedle — or perhaps the "Ah" *was* his answer — so absorbed was he in scrutinizing the unfamiliar objects that everywhere presented themselves to view.

The grocer, abandoning his inquiry after a third failed attempt, informed Mr. Moldwort that several more hours of tinkering would be needed to complete the repairs to the mechanism, after which they would take their leave and not impose on him further. Mr. Moldwort, breaking at last from his trance, replied that he was at their complete dispose — for, as he put it, he had nowt much in the way of visitor folk round hyar anymore — and that they were free to avail themselves of anything he had that might speed them in their work. There were, he told them, some spare stores of great sort and variety in the church, where he had formerly acted as verger and where he was now living, as there existed no other habitable abode in the town. Having concluded his exploration of the wonders about him, Mr. Moldwort invited the grocer and Tim to accompany him there.

"'Tisn't far," said he, "for you can see the tower of St. Magma above the cottages thar. And 'twould be not so much danger thar as hyar."

"Danger?" echoed Mr. Threadneedle. "Do you mean the roaring we heard?"

"Ah," said Mr. Moldwort again, inscrutably.

Mr. Threadneedle was loath at first to accept his offer. But it already was late afternoon; it was scarcely possible to finish the necessary repairs in the hour or two of daylight that remained, and even if they could, they certainly were not about to be flying off in the dark. It appeared they had little choice; they were doomed to remain in deepest Gloamshire until tomorrow. As for their host, whom they judged to be rather a harmless sort — he had, after all, been a verger once — it was clear he was fascinated by the coach-house and how it had come to be there. Despite his peculiarities he was not an ignorant person, nor did he seem threatening in any way, merely curious. And judging by his appearance, which was nothing if not unusual —

But whose appearance wouldn't be unusual who was the last human inhabitant of an isolated ruin like Deeping St. Magma?

And so they were persuaded to go with him to the church, for there were some clamps among the stores there that they thought might be useful in mending the chain-belt. Once outside, however, they stopped first to make an inspection of the coach-house and its situation.

The house lay perched on the edge of a tar-pool, just as Mr. Moldwort had said, with its farther wall dipping into the ooze. Mr. Moldwort explained that the topmost portion of the pools was composed chiefly of water, several feet of which overlay the asphaltum and bitumen. It looked to him now that the submerged foot of the house lay within that column of water above the tar. It hadn't yet been gripped by the sticky asphalt, which was a good thing, he told them, but which was unlikely to last.

"For it'll slip, sure enough, into the asphaltum and bitumen, if nowt's done about it," he predicted.

"But certainly she'll not slip in the short time we're away?" said Mr. Threadneedle, gravely concerned lest the beloved jewel of his and Tim's many months of tinkering should fall victim to the tar's oily clutches. Of equal concern, perhaps, was his realization that he and his apprentice had spent most of the afternoon teetering on the brink.

Mr. Moldwort strode stork-legged round one side of the tar-pool and then the other, viewing with a grim and fishy eye the angle of lean of the house, and testing the stability of the ground; then he turned to Mr. Threadneedle and said —

"No, sir, I don't believe she will. But of course, that means little round hyar. Howsoever, it does appear to me so long as you've not been caught by the asphaltum and bitumen, you've some time to avoid being drawn into it. But something needs doing soon."

"This then is what we must do," the grocer told his young assistant. "Once we've returned, we'll float her on her three good coils as best we can, some thirty feet or so above ground. Not only will that free her from the pool, it will provide sufficient safety, I should think, for the night hours."

"And before we leave for the church, we can attach her mooring-cable to that large tree there," Tim said. "That ought to keep her from slipping in the interval."

"Good lad! That's a jolly fine idea. A wise precaution. So we'll complete the repairs in the morning, in comfort and safety, and then it will be coils down and easy aloft!"

Once the cable had been secured, they locked the coach-house door and fell in behind Mr. Moldwort. They kept close together, the three of them, and proceeded in haste and with a grim kind of watchfulness, particularly on the part of Mr. Moldwort — which led the grocer to believe that their host was only too cognizant of the beastly roar of the morning.

"Now mind how you go, for the way be treacherous round hyar." Mr. Moldwort was an expert at minding how he went, but then of course he would be. He dodged the doubtful spots in the earth with practiced ease, hurrying along on his storkish limbs in their huge boots with the furred tops, his head and shoulders bent forward like the curl in the question-mark.

"You'll not want to step *thar*!" he warned, indicating an especially bad patch as they passed it.

Everywhere the odor of tar assailed their nostrils, the steamy vapors rising from the pools like unholy exhalations from the underworld. On every side were rows of abandoned cottages, all of them listing dangerously on the sea of asphaltum and bitumen, their doors and windows ajar, their roofs fallen in, their chimneys sundered brick by shattered brick. In some places the ground had opened up completely and swallowed whatever had been there, leaving vacant spots like gaps in a line of teeth.

Came then the sound of a fearsome roar, identical to that which Mr. Threadneedle and Tim had heard earlier in the day, although it seemed much closer now. Perhaps it was because they were outside the coach-house rather than in it; or perhaps not.

"There it is again! That noise, that roaring. What is it?" the grocer demanded of their host, who finally consented to give them an answer.

"Ah," said Mr. Moldwort, with a glance over his shoulder. "Cat, sir, hyarabouts."

"As I feared — a saber-cat!"

"Not saber-cat — scimitar. *Gladiodon,* sir. We've the stripe-bodied sort round hyar. They'll be abroad soon, as they don't care so much for the rain — it's kept 'em down today. These cats, they're pouncers, you know. They like a bit o' cover and a clear view of their prey."

"Isn't it dangerous then to be abroad now?" returned Mr. Threadneedle. "The rain has stopped. And what's more, we haven't any weapons!"

"And there's none would aid you if you had, sir, save cunning. Might be better to lodge in the church tonight, and safer, too, since you've not time to mend that remarkable house of yours afore dark. Ordinarily you'd not want to be out thar in the night, sir, working by fire and taper, for you'd attract the cats soon enough. But thirty feet above ground!" he exclaimed, wringing his head in amazement. "How does it work, by the by, this remarkable house of yours? Astonishing thing, it must be. I'd like to see it fly someday."

"I dare say you'll see it soon enough," Mr. Threadneedle assured him.

He was confident about this, was Mr. Threadneedle, but he was worried, too, not only about the coach-house but about Tim, whose safety was in his care. He was worried about Tim's mother and sister and what they would think when he didn't return home today. And he was worried, too, about matters at the Smithy. He prayed that the fog was holding there; otherwise there would be reprisals from Plush and Kimber, and the secret revealed before the coach-house had attained its final state of perfection.

But he must think of such things no more; he must think instead of the church that was their objective, and of a swift check of the stores and an equally swift return to the coach-house.

Before he knew it, they were upon it — the ancient parish church of St. Magma. It was the travelers' first clear view of the edifice, and rather a picturesque pile it was, too, and a large one, finely built of sandstone and well-appointed in its day. Now, however, it looked as though it belonged in the casualty ward of some heavenly hospital. Like the cottages, it was leaning dangerously to one side. Its tower in particular had sustained much damage, having been shorn of the lofty spire and cross that crowned it in times gone by, as their host informed them.

Viewing the church's condition now at close range, Mr. Threadneedle and Tim exchanged dubious glances. It didn't look to be a particularly safe place to be standing near, let alone a place to enter or abide in. Its very fabric seemed to be trembling in the air above their heads, as if debating whether to collapse on them or not. Mr. Moldwort had no such reservations, however, for the church was his home. He motioned to them from the south porch; reluctantly, they followed him in.

Most everything inside the church was as jumbled and awry as everything outside. The stone flags were cracked and shattered, and piled up into heaps here and there. The wooden stalls, pews, screens, and pulpit lay strewn about as if some monster-child had taken them up, played with them awhile, and cast them away. The whole interior — nave and chancel, aisles, pillars, arches, with choir and triforium above — was sagging in places, and drooping in places, and tilted sideways, as though the church were a ship, and the ocean beneath it had frozen at an inconvenient angle. To his tinkerer's mind, it looked to Mr. Threadneedle as if the cage-coils of the structure had gone permanently out of balance. But of course, there were no cage-coils, only a mortal coil, which the church seemed to be in imminent peril of shuffling off.

Mr. Moldwort gave his guests a brief tour of the dilapidations, and indicated where certain supplies of materials could be found, in the vestry, for example, and the old rector's quarters. Then he led them through a doorway to the tower at the west end, where a newel staircase wound upward to the triforium — the long gallery running along one side of the church, above the aisle, where the tall windows were and where his own quarters now lay. There were additional storerooms up there, he said, which held the clamps and quantities of leather and cord and other items that might be of use to them.

Mr. Threadneedle was none too keen to mount the stairs of the tottering structure. He looked at Tim, and Tim looked at him; but by the time they looked back at Mr. Moldwort, his storkish figure had vanished into the shadowy dimness, where his boots could be heard ascending the staircase.

"I'm not sure we ought to go up there," the grocer said with a frown. "The way doesn't appear at all safe. For all we know, this building will come crashing down about our ears at any moment."

Mr. Moldwort, thrusting his face over the rail above, inquired whether the two of them were coming or weren't they?

Mr. Threadneedle pondered for another moment. Looking up, he noted not only that their host had survived the climb, but that the church itself had survived without complaint the addition of his weight to the triforium. Both of these were favorable signs. Mr. Moldwort exhorted them again to follow, with mysterious promises of rich reward; and so they found themselves persuaded once again.

They climbed the winding staircase — a rather solid and stony staircase, as it turned out — and emerged on the next level. As they trailed their host along the gallery, which was an unusually spacious one for a parish church, they came to a place that had been made into a kind of workroom, complete with a bench, chair, and table. There were a number of basins, too, with some brushes, cloths, jugs, some pots and vats, a horn lantern, and a spirit-lamp, all very neatly and comfortably arranged.

More remarkable, however, was the collection of objects laid out on some open shelving by the clerestory windows — the shelves had been taken from the old rector's library, their host informed them — a collection that was, in short, nothing if not startling to behold.

Mr. Threadneedle stuck his quizzing-glass in his eye and advanced for a closer look.

"My very word!" he exclaimed.

Ranged in an orderly fashion on the shelves like jars of jam in a village shop, their hollow sockets and grinning jaws capturing the grocer's astonished gaze, lay row upon tidy row of polished skulls.

To his great relief, no human skulls appeared to number among the specimens, and Mr. Moldwort was quick to assure him he had none. *These* skulls, he said, had been taken by his own hand from creatures trapped in the blackpools, those beasts unfortunate enough to have perished in the sticky grip of the asphaltum and bitumen. He had over the years become adept at recovering carcasses from the pools, those whose water levels had receded sufficiently to allow the remains entombed there to emerge. He first took the skulls from the bodies; then, employing methods of his own devising, he cleansed the bones of their accumulated tar, coated them with varnish (this, too, was of his own invention), and placed them on display there in what he termed the ossuary. It was a kind of hobby of his, he said — for really, what else was there to do in a place like Deeping St. Magma? As a youth he'd been apprenticed to a taxidermist, and received training in the art and science of anatomy. He was plainly an artist of a kind himself, judging by the fine appearance of the specimens and the obvious pride and pleasure he took in them.

Originally he'd housed the skulls in the church crypt, like a proper ossuary, but the asphaltum and bitumen had seeped in and flooded the lower chambers. As it turned out, that wasn't such a bad thing, for it had been rather dark down there and required wax-lights to see by — not the best conditions for displaying his work. So he'd removed the specimens upstairs to the brightness and security of the triforium. The skulls were of all manner of shapes and sizes; some were of common creatures like the pronghorn and wild boar, while others were of such bizarre appearance it seemed they must descend from some dim and distant time long before the Age of Man.

Mr. Threadneedle, once he'd recovered from his surprise, found himself curiously intrigued, as did Tim, for it was after all a kind of workshop Mr. Moldwort had there in the church, after the manner of the grocer's own workshop in the coach-house. As a result, he and his apprentice began to see in their host something of a fellow-tinkerer.

The skulls, unlike ordinary bones, were stained a muddy shade of brown like Mr. Moldwort himself — a product of the asphaltum and bitumen that had soaked into them and never could be gotten out. Once he'd scoured the tar from their surfaces, he said, he varnished and polished them until they were as presentable as any museum specimen. But as no one ever came to Deeping St. Magma, there was no one to show them to; and so he was especially thankful for the coming of Mr. Threadneedle and Tim and the opportunity it afforded.

He took certain of the skulls in hand now, one by one, some of them of impressive size, and enlarged upon their features of interest.

"This chap hyar I call *Magmatherium pigrum moldworti* — 'lazy St. Magma beast of Moldwort.' He's a sort of smaller cousin to this other chap hyar, the one I call *Megatherium pigrum moldworti* — 'big lazy beast of Moldwort.' They're the both of 'em ground sloths, o' course — or 'megatheres' as some like to say. Have a peep at those grinders thar!"

"Monstrous fine, sir," said Tim, clearly impressed.

"And this big chap, this one as looks something like a horse but is no horse at all, him I call *Moropus moldworti* —"

"It's very much like our Ladycake. These moropi — proper stinkpots!"

"Ah, I see you are familiar with the species," returned Mr. Moldwort, with an appreciative glance.

"Only too," Mr. Threadneedle nodded glumly.

"Now, this chap hyar I call *Canis dirus moldworti* — 'dire wolf of Moldwort.' Very common in the pools this one is, and for good reason. See that? Not much brain-space thar, nohow."

"I tend to agree."

"And this chap hyar — this long and narrow skull-case hyar. What do you think of it, now? Do you think it mammal?"

"Why, of course not — it's a bird!" the grocer exclaimed. "And a very large one it is indeed. I don't think we've anything like it round Truro. That's where we've come from, by the by. Is it a vulture of some kind?"

Mr. Moldwort shook his head. "Too big, sir, for a vulture."

"A condor?" Tim suggested.

"In a word, no."

"An eagle, then?"

"In another word, no."

Their host seemed to revel in this little game of guesses for which only he had the answers. Smilingly he extended the skull toward them for a closer view. "I call this chap *Teratornis horribilis moldworti* — 'horrible teratorn of Moldwort.'"

"A teratorn!" Tim cried, staring in admiration at the gaping orbits and wicked sharp beak. "I've never seen the like. I've never seen a teratorn, in fact."

"We have no teratorns on Truro," Mr. Threadneedle explained. "They abhor the coastal fogs. I'm happy it's only a skull, for if this fellow were here in flesh and feathers, we should all be diving for cover. Do teratorns roam these skies of Gloamshire?"

"In a word, sir, yes," replied Mr. Moldwort. "And mind you take heed of that once you've mended that remarkable house of yours. Now, have a peep at this chap hyar — one of my best. Not many of 'em in the pools for they're not so common roundabout, and, too, they're wondrous intelligent. This one I call *Ursus simus moldworti* — 'flat-nosed bear of Moldwort.' Or as some will say, your giant short-faced bear. Lovely, is it not?"

Next Mr. Moldwort produced what he considered his rarest and most valued treasure — the skull of a saber-cat, its jaws and huge bladelike canines fastened tight round the hip-bone of a mastodon calf. The specimens were just as he'd taken them from the asphaltum and bitumen, Mr. Moldwort said, the teeth of the cat still plunged deep into its prey, and gripping there, even as both had sunk struggling to their deaths in the ooze.

"Not much brain in this chap with the sabers, but a nice specimen nonetheless. I call him *Megadon moldworti* — 'big-tooth of Moldwort.' Very common in the pools he is."

"Have you named every one of these creatures after yourself?" Mr. Threadneedle asked.

"And how else will I be naming 'em, sir? It's myself as finds 'em and preserves 'em, after all; and besides, there's none else lives round these parts to be naming 'em after. Now, have a look at this chap hyar."

Mr. Moldwort offered for their inspection another saber-cat cranium, one much larger than the first and with canines even more savage.

"*Megamegadon moldworti,*" he announced, proudly observing it in his hand. "The 'big big-tooth of Moldwort.'"

"A very fine specimen, sir," Tim agreed.

"And now have a peep at this chap hyar!"

Triumphantly he produced a third skull, this one even larger than the others — so large in fact that it was nearly twice the size of *Megadon*, with sabers to match.

"*Megamegamegadon?*" Mr. Threadneedle ventured.

"*Ultramegadon,*" smiled the keeper of the bones — "*moldworti.*"

"Jolly fine," said the grocer.

"And as for this one, sir —"

Strangely Mr. Moldwort broke off his presentation here. He laid the final skull by and, cautioning his guests to silence, cocked his head aside to listen.

"Beg your parding, but which of us hyar shut the porch door?" he asked, in a hushed voice.

Mr. Threadneedle replied that he hadn't, nor had Tim; and neither had Mr. Moldwort. Apparently no one had shut the porch door.

Without explanation their host crept stealthily along the gallery to the newel staircase and shut the door there, and latched it, and drew a sturdy bar across it. Then he folded his long legs under him like a human penknife and dropped into a crouch, his knees on the ground. Leaning forward, he placed his hands on the gallery-rail and slowly and carefully slid the tip of his nose over its edge, just enough to give his eyes room to scan the scene below.

Mr. Threadneedle and Tim went quickly and quietly to his side.

"Look, sirs — look there!" Tim whispered.

What they saw froze them in their shoes. A huge cat in a striped suit was gliding through the nave of the church. The creature was easily the size of a large horse. Every couple of feet it would stop to sniff at a discarded pew, or brush its cheek against a pillar, or turn over a heap of flags with a massive paw. Looking for all the world like some heathen beast-god sprung to life, it was prowling the spaces where once parishioners had gathered to worship a God of quite another sort. The waning sun in the high windows spread its beams across the monster's hide, which was a tawny shade of yellow overlaid with bands of umber. The head of the cat was carried high on a very long neck, and with its tall forelegs and its back sloping to shorter hindquarters, it resembled a sort of feline version of Ladycake, only much sleeker and fiercer. The sunlight added luster to its green phosphoric eyes, and threw into relief its razor-sharp fangs, which were thick and powerful and dripping with menace.

Mr. Threadneedle saw the monster and swallowed hard. He was praying it had not detected them yet; but he was too late, for the creature already was sniffing the air and glancing curiously round. It must have gotten wind of their human scent but knew not whence it came.

"*Gladiodon perfidus moldworti,*" whispered Mr. Moldwort.

"What does that mean?" the grocer asked.

"'Treacherous sword-tooth of Moldwort.' Thar be your stripe-bodied scimitar-cat, sir! Very common type round hyar, though not so often found in the pools. Your *Gladiodon* be a smarter beast on the whole, I believe, than your *Megadon* or your *Megamegadon*. Very common in the Sawtooth Mountains, and in the coffee-lands in the east."

"That's not very encouraging."

"Female of the species, this one. In *Gladiodon* it's the lady of the house mostly as does the shopping. I've nowt but a handful o' the specimens from the pools — too wise for it!"

"I see. And how are we to escape from here?" said Mr. Threadneedle, of the opinion now that sufficient unto the day were the natural-history lessons thereof.

"South porch," said Mr. Moldwort.

"Impossible!"

"That's likely the way by which the animal entered," Tim whispered. "It must have followed us in."

"I fear so, as the porch door be the one door in the church as was not blocked up for safety's sake," their host informed them. "As for the north door and vestry entrance, the both of 'em were closed up tight yar upon yar ago."

"Not to worry, Tim," said Mr. Threadneedle. "More than likely Mr. Moldwort has a plan for just such an emergency. He lives here in the church, after all, with these cats constantly about. I'm sure he has an alternative."

The two looked at Mr. Moldwort, who seemed genuinely embarrassed.

"Well, you see, sir," he explained, averting his fishy eyes, "'twas an oversight on my part — in my excitement at receiving visitor folk — not so common round hyar — for sir, in all these yars I've never *not* shut the porch door."

This didn't sound promising.

"But certainly there's another way out of the church, Mr. Moldwort? A postern door? A sally-port?" said Mr. Threadneedle.

The human question-mark shook his head and tossed up his hands.

"In a word, sir, no," he replied, with a sheepish grin. "No sally-port hyar!"

CHAPTER TWENTY-SIX

Ageless Isle of Olives

Midday, one day, found the balding, grizzle-cheeked Doctor of Divinity, the Rev. Giddeus Pinches, poring over his Greenshields in the reading-room of the cathedral library. He had been there for some hours, enveloped in a studious fog and only dimly conscious of the world without. Now and then a fellow cleric would stroll past him, and the doctor would offer up his usual nod — the depth of the nod being in general proportional to the eminence of his brother clergyman — before resuming his researches, his thick dark brows drawn up like ruffled curtains on a rod, and his blunt little stub of a nose deep-plunged in his book.

The reverend doctor had gone to the reading-room in search of inspiration for that one sermon he was to give every year at the Minster, the date of which was fast approaching. It had to be so much finer a sermon than those he cobbled together each week at St. Mary-le-Quay, for this was the Minster after all. And so he had struggled, valiantly, to turn his mind to it; but alas, as always happened when he was in the reading-room, his mind would not be turned, except to that particular interest which his resurgent love of learning so delighted in — his Greenshields, his Vergil and his Homer, his Hesiod, his Thucydides and his Herodotus, his ancient classical world, his glorious Aegean days.

The doctor was looking forward to the time when he could spend all his free hours in the library, and not be bothered by troublesome things like parishioners. Time, time — there never would be, never could be, enough of this thing called Time! At which point he took out his watch and saw to his disappointment that his own precious time in the reading-room had been exhausted. Although he had no sermon to show for his hours there, he *had* received his weekly dose of Greenshields, and this satisfied him for the moment, and nerved him to face again the hardened sinners of his dockside parish and his tiresome, humdrum mode of living.

Before departing for hearth and home, he stopped for a few minutes in the cathedral, as was his custom. On this particular day he found himself in the choir loft. Glancing down, his eyes took note of the long, narrow strip of gold, the meridian line, where it crossed the cathedral floor; glancing up, they sought out the cupola, through which dazzling summer suns once had peeped to light up that line. But there was no sun today, of course, not so much as a hint of one. So little use for a *meridiana* in this land of endless Cimmerian gloom!

Thought of the cupola brought with it thought of the cathedral towers and the doctor's last visit to the belfry, and of the inexplicable *something* he had seen there in the sky. A house floating on air! He remained convinced that it had been no illusion. He'd taken no wine that might have accounted for it; of that he was certain. It was, he'd been forced to conclude, but another of those things in this life, like dogma and men's wives, for which there was no explaining.

He left the Minster through the west door and bent his steps homeward to St. Mary-le-Quay. Along the route he lifted his hat in greeting to a postman in a red jacket, who was hammering his way down the street with a cheery whistle on his lips. Young Mr. Milo was a good-hearted chap who attended services like clockwork and gave the doctor no trouble, having never once approached him for counsel in regard to his many infatuations — so varied and numerous they were, and all so futile! — and thank goodness, too, the doctor sighed, for that was what Dottie Matchless was for.

He arrived home, and pausing briefly for a glance inside his own house of worship — so much less imposing a shrine than Nantle Minster — he was surprised to find someone sitting in one of the pews at the back. It was a man, and he appeared to be doing little more than gazing round him at the walls and roof of the church, in admiration perhaps of their humble adornments and subtle harmony of proportions. Not only was it rather dim inside the church of St. Mary-le-Quay, it was rather quiet, too, for like the sun, the rumble of the traffic and the noise from the quay hardly penetrated there.

"Mr. Porter?" said the doctor, approaching the man from the aisle.

The worshipper rose out of respect and offered the doctor an apologetic smile. "Very sorry, your reverend, I'm sure," he said. He was a short, strong, sturdy man with an unshaven chin. His hair was thick and untidy and peppered with gray, and he reeked of fish. In his hands was an odd-shaped leathery hat, which he was rolling absently round and round by its brim.

"We've not seen you here for some little time, Mr. Porter. However, it's always a pleasure to welcome stray lambs home to the fold. May I be of service to you?" the doctor asked.

"Beg indulgence, reverend, but I don't means to be a bother. I've been away, you see."

The speaker having moved a little into the light, it was observed that his coat glittered here and there with some small flecks of silver that clung to it; these proved to be fish-scales. His odd-shaped hat, too, was sprinkled with them — a hat that was generally round in shape and ridged and padded at the crown, as though to support a weight of some kind. The brim was deeply guttered and had a scoop-like extension at the back that resembled a spout.

"You're rarely if ever in attendance on a Sunday, Mr. Porter. And yet you are sometimes in the church, I know, by your solitary self, on days like today. Have you some personal bereavement that brings you here?"

"No b'reavement, your reverend, if by that you mean sorrow; I merely likes the quiet o' the place. It's such a change from the noise and stir o' the market. Why, from peep o' day there's naught at Musselgate but bustling and shouting, and mad hallooing from the costers, and auctioneers calling for bids and crying for porters. At Musselgate Market, you see, your reverend, I'm naught but Porter the fish porter to be shouted at, just another poor jack with crates and baskets o' fish to be nutting. But here in the peace o' St. Mary's there's no such distractions, and I can rest my mind."

The doctor's own mind was something altered by this. He'd never before exchanged so many words at one time with Mr. Porter the fish porter. Here was a being of whom he heartily disapproved, one of those sinners of the kind who hardly ever came to church; yet the fellow was wise and sensitive enough to appreciate the reflective atmosphere of a house of prayer. The doctor could identify with such a feeling — on a far grander scale, of course — in connection with his beloved Minster.

"I bean't much of a Sunday church-goer, your reverend," Mr. Porter confessed, still rolling his hat round in his hands. Despite his placid demeanor, he had a hard, weather-beaten look to him. His face was a strong, pugnacious face, with a contracted eye, like a man forever looking into a wind. "And I've a need to get away from the city now and again. Why, it's for some little time now I've been down to Paignton Swidges, to bide awhile with a mate o' mine — Hake Jobberley, him as helps the keeper o' Fairlight there, Mr. Mulks. We're old acquaintances."

"If you enjoy the atmosphere of the church so much, Mr. Porter, then why do you not attend on the Sabbath?"

"Too noisy, your reverend, for my taste, what with the chanting and singing, and the reading o' the lessons, and the speechifying. Oh, beg indulgence, your reverend — I don't means to offend. But I likes the quiet o' the place at times like this now. It soothes the spirit, it does."

The doctor accepted his explanation without complaint, despite feeling a trifle put out that the man disliked his services and his pulpit eloquence. Didn't the fellow know how much time the doctor spent cobbling together — pardon, composing — his sermons? The example of Mr. Porter was just another reminder of how tiresome and unrewarding his life had become — chatting with a smelly, fish-scale-littered denizen of the quay as to the value of Sunday services! — and how much he yearned for the Minster and the hallowed close. How long, he asked himself again, how long now before that looked-for retirement?

Taking his leave of the man, the doctor made his way to the rectory. In the hall he was met by his sister Griselda. She had that morning baked him a warden pie, his favorite, and it was awaiting him at the conclusion of his dinner. But before that, she informed him, there was something else awaiting him — a caller, and that of an unusual sort, in the drawing-room.

A caller? The doctor had not been expecting a caller. Doubtless some member of his grisly flock, whom he dreaded receiving now in his present self-pitying frame of mind. More than that, it would delay his dinner and his warden pie! As a man of the cloth and a parish pastor, the doctor had loads of compassion, but most of it of late had been expended on himself.

"Who is it?" he demanded testily.

"A young lady, though not a member of the parish," his sister told him. "She is from Crow's-end and is staying with Mrs. Juniper. She seems much troubled, and has come seeking counsel on a matter of importance."

Oh, what is it with this one? the doctor grumbled. Was it doubts as to Christian belief, an overbearing husband, or womanly pangs of guilt? It usually was one of these. Just then the clock at the stairhead began sounding the hour. "Three o'clock!" it cried — the usual hour of dining at the rectory. The doctor groaned. But he was reconciled to his lot; and so he strode into the drawing-room to meet his dinner-delaying caller.

"You are Miss Jane Wastefield?" he said, mustering what priestly cheer he could, given the circumstances. It was *Miss* Wastefield — well, the doctor observed, that at least let the overbearing husband off the hook.

The pretty woman in furs acknowledged that Jane Wastefield was her name, and that she was from Pinewick, near Crow's-end.

The doctor was not an ungenial man for a clergyman, nor an insensitive one, and on such occasions he usually managed to put a well-meaning face on. He was at heart a well-meaning man, but his chronic dissatisfaction had taken a toll. He saw now that his caller was indeed an unusual one, as his sister had reported — a young person of quality, and a beautiful one at that — and this spurred him to rally.

He'd been recommended to her, she said, by the landlady of the house where she was lodging, a Mrs. Flora Juniper, whose family was known to hers. Yes, the doctor replied, he knew Mrs. Juniper well: an admirable woman. Miss Wastefield then told him she knew not how to broach the subject of her visit, exactly; knew not how to explain to him the trouble under which she labored. The easiest way it seemed to her, however, was the most straightforward one, which was simply to speak it out. And so she did, informing the doctor of her growing suspicion that she was in all likelihood — *possessed*.

Dr. Pinches was a little taken aback at first. Then, as the relative rarity of the complaint fixed itself in his brain, he became rather interested, for here was something out of his ordinary course — here was something *different*.

Anything, anything that would be a departure from boredom! Anything, anything but the everyday tusslings of his noisy flock! It was some time now since there'd been a possession in the parish; more usually it was the other way round, with persons being *dis*possessed, in a congregation like St. Mary-le-Quay's.

"And what has led you to this view, Miss Wastefield?" the doctor asked.

They were seated by the doctor's snug and comfortable fire, with the doctor observing his guest over a little church steeple he had constructed by placing the tips of his opposing thumbs and fingers together.

Miss Wastefield proceeded to explain to him, with a deal of nervous hesitation, the entire state of the case. She started with her twenty-first birthday, which evil day had come and gone many months ago now, and the odious gift she'd received from an unknown somebody.

"It was clearly a very ancient thing. My father, Dr. James Wastefield, was a noted scholar and recognized it at once as a valuable artifact. Although he couldn't identify it with certainty, he believed it to be Greek, or something very similar."

The doctor's eyebrows rose. "And the person who gave it to you? He didn't identify himself?"

"No. Like the other gifts, it came wrapped up in paper, but with a note unsigned and in a hand neither I nor my father recognized. My father, who knew something about the trade in artifacts, suspected from the anonymous nature of the gift that the mirror had been stolen."

The doctor was even more interested now, particularly since the word *Greek* had escaped his caller's lips. Interested? He was positively fascinated!

"Likely it came from some private collection. Yes, I would agree, it may very well have been stolen — otherwise why conceal the identity of the giver? There is a good deal of trafficking in such items, I regret to say. But why should the mirror have been given to *you*, do you think, Miss Wastefield? And how had it come into your house?"

But Miss Wastefield had no answers for his questions. Then, in tones of a graver sort, she recounted the events that led to the death of her father not long after this accursed birthday. She described, with understandable emotion, how she'd been shocked to hear a voice speak to her from the mirror, and to see a face other than her own in the ancient polished bronze; how this had happened more times than once; how she'd dropped the mirror on the table in her sitting-room one day, and left in a fright; and how her dear father, coming by in search of her, had picked it up to examine it; how she'd summoned her courage and returned with her maid to the sitting-room, to discover her father staring into the mirror with an expression of the most dreadful horror; whereupon his eyes had rolled up and he'd fallen down onto the sofa, stricken to death by a fit of apoplexy.

"So you see, Doctor," said Miss Wastefield, after a brief silence, "had I not quitted the room and left the mirror unguarded, my father wouldn't have come upon it and instead would be alive today. I must forever live with the knowledge of that."

Thus did Miss Wastefield pronounce herself guilty of the death of her father, a judgment whose harshness the doctor attempted to convince her of; but she would not be moved. She went on to give a further account of the voices from the mirror and of the mysterious images in its polished surface. Then had come the letter to her father, many months after his burial, from one Gilbert Thistlewood of Nantle, offering to relieve him of the burden of a certain precious antiquity.

The doctor disassembled the church steeple and folded his hands together. "It seems clear to me this man Thistlewood is a receiver of stolen goods, which would confirm your father's suspicion as regards the mirror. Oh, yes, one becomes rather too familiar with such things in a dockside parish like St. Mary-le-Quay. What was the man's price?"

"He named no price. He said that an arrangement would be negotiated here at Nantle. I was so anxious to be rid of the hateful thing I didn't care to quibble. I would freely have given it to Mr. Thistlewood. I would freely have given it to anyone who would accept it, and who could keep it."

And so she had responded to Mr. Thistlewood's offer, and agreed to his terms. Even before she'd left Pinewick, however, the voices in the mirror had intensified their assaults, such that she'd had no recourse but to lock the foul object inside her trunk of trunks. She went on to describe for the doctor all that had transpired thereafter, and her present certainty that she was under observation by a stranger who had been following her.

Such and more, then, comprised the foundation for her belief that she had been possessed by some supernatural agency, acting through the medium of the mirror and the dreams that nightly came to disturb her sleep.

The doctor was much struck by all he heard. He had hoped for something out of the ordinary, true — but *this!*

"How can you be certain you are being observed?" he asked. "Is it the same man always?"

Miss Wastefield described the grim figure very tall and broad who had been tracking her movements as one Mr. Tom Lanthorne, whom she'd first glimpsed at Sprig's coffee-house. The doctor, himself something of a regular at that establishment, didn't know the man, which was hardly surprising, Miss Wastefield remarked, for apparently he was seen only by those whom he wished to see him. The doctor frowned and said he didn't understand, but Miss Wastefield did not see fit at the moment to enlighten him.

She had gone to the coffee-house, she said, to see about a letter of instruction from Mr. Thistlewood, for he'd written that it would arrive for her there and that they should not meet until then. (This was something the doctor *could* understand, and furthered his conviction that the elusive Mr. Thistlewood was a receiver of stolen properties.) She had been inquiring at Sprig's nearly every day and still there'd been no line from him. Already she'd been in Nantle for almost a fortnight. Why had he not communicated with her?

Then had come her mysterious visitor, the young man who'd inquired after her at Mrs. Juniper's door one day when she was out, and left neither his card nor a message.

"Perhaps he was your Mr. Thistlewood?" the doctor suggested. "Perhaps he'd taken it upon himself to call at your lodgings to secure the mirror?"

"No, it could not be, for I hadn't said in my reply where I would be lodging. He could have discovered it only by the merest chance, and as he knew nothing of my appearance, he couldn't have followed me. He knows nothing of Mrs. Juniper or her late uncle, Mr. Delancey, or of Mr. Delancey's professional connection with my father."

"Ah, but we can't be certain of all that, Miss Wastefield. There are several doubtful points. He may have known of the connection, for example, but said nothing of it in his letter; indeed, he may have been a friend or colleague of Mr. Delancey's. How did he know that the mirror was in your possession? Perhaps he knows who gave it to you. But why did he write to your father rather than to you, and only many months after your father's death?"

The doctor remembered Mr. Delancey, who had been in the antiquarian line with a shop in Jacktar Lane. An upright, honest citizen he'd been, another of those rare sorts who'd given the doctor no trouble. But the doctor declared he didn't at all like this practice of receiving letters at Sprig's, which Mr. Tozer had instituted for the convenience of his guests. He told Miss Wastefield that it was, in his view, a shady sort of business, one that people in embarrassed circumstances or with criminal purpose often made use of. Her Mr. Thistlewood likely was one of these latter types, his aim being to separate her from her valuable artifact.

"But Dr. Pinches, that is just what I want him to do," Miss Wastefield explained in some frustration. She wanted *anyone* to separate her from it, she didn't care who, so long as the vile thing was gone from her forever; and not so much as a penny-piece would she take for it in return.

How to explain a mirror that spoke to her? How to explain the unknown but strangely familiar faces and vistas in its polished bronze? How to explain the dreams that plagued her? She described for the doctor in greater detail her vision of the enormous temple-building, and the high mountain altar, and the dark priestess and the shell-horn and the call to drink the honeyed wine laced with poppy juice. She told of being slowly strangled, and of seeing the temple destroyed by an earthquake, and of being drawn into the mirror-world by a force of almost irresistible power. Last of all, she described for him that most ghastly and terrifying of her visions — the crested, three-eyed, giant pincered fiend of a Triamete.

"Good heavens!" the doctor exclaimed, more astonished even than before. He began to wonder if outright mental derangement, rather than possession, might not be a sounder diagnosis for Miss Wastefield — that is, until she repeated for him certain words that had been spoken by the people in the mirror.

"Kaftor, did you say?" he asked, leaning forward in his chair. "Hmmm. Kaftor. Yes — yes! Might that not be *Caphtor*? The island of Caphtor, home to the Caphtorim. Are you not familiar with the names, Miss Wastefield? Ah, I see you've been neglecting your Genesis, your Amos, your Jeremiah."

Miss Wastefield blushed before the reverend doctor of the Church, and admitted she was no Scripture student and likely had forgotten much.

"The Caphtorim, Miss Wastefield — the reputed children of Ham, son of Noah. They dwelt on their ageless isle of olives in the midst of the Great

Green Sea, which later generations knew as the Mediterranean. The Philistines are believed to have been descended from these Caphtorim, for as the Lord said — 'Have not I brought up Israel out of the land of Egypt, and the Philistines from Caphtor?'"

"But what was it, Dr. Pinches, this Caphtor?"

"Long, long ago," the doctor explained, waxing historical, "in the dark centuries before Homer — in the distant, dim-remembered Age of Heroes — even then this island of Caphtor was renowned as a land of plenty. Not only the Greeks but the Egyptians, too, knew of it, referring to it and its people as *Kefti* or *Keftiu*, or so we think. Much later, in medieval times, it came to be known as Candia, and still later as Crete. 'A hundred cities strong,' that is what Homer says of it at its peak of glory. Ancient Greek tradition and the historian Thucydides tell us of a legendary King Minos who commanded a great empire of the sea from his palace-temple there. Under this temple, in a labyrinth constructed by Daedalus, was imprisoned the hideous offspring of Pasiphaë, wife of Minos, and a white bull sent by the god Poseidon, whose displeasure the King had evoked. That hideous offspring, half human and half bull, was the creature known as the Minotaur."

Miss Wastefield recalled the legend of the labyrinth from her mythology, and thought at once of the sprawling temple with its broad central court, its terraces and colonnades, its adornments of frescoes and ceremonial bulls' horns.

"Poteidan, you say," the doctor remarked. "The name as such is not a familiar one. It occurs to me, however, that it could be another form of *Poseidon*. An early Greek form, perhaps, or even a Cretan form, for many of the Hellenic deities were derived from earlier Aegean models. But it's only a guess in the dark. To the ancients, Poseidon was the bull god, and the many-rayed sun god, and the foamy sea god, and the god of earthquakes. He was venerated and rightly feared for his dread powers right across the ancient Mediterranean world."

Miss Wastefield recalled some of this, too, from her mythology, and for the first time related it to her vision of the temple lying in ruins after the earth beneath it shook.

Of course, of course — Poseidon, the god of earthquakes — *our lord Poteidan, the earth-shaker!*

"But then, I suppose it's all rather hypothetical, isn't it?" the doctor said.

"How do you mean, sir?"

"Well, there is no actual evidence, you know, that this magnificent sea-empire of Minos ever existed. It was but one of many legends promulgated by Homer and other ancient authors. It's rather like the Trojan War in that respect. Oh, yes, I know, for I have just this week been reading of it in my Greenshields! Even before the sundering destroyed any possible remains, nothing had been found on Crete to indicate that a mighty civilization had once been headquartered there. The writings of the ancient Egyptians are perhaps the nearest we have come to it, but even there we can't make a *positive* connection between Kefti or Keftiu and Crete. There is, to put it simply, no proof."

Seeking proof of anything was not the usual province of a man of faith, but the doctor as we know was more than capable of a little contradiction, especially when it came to his glorious Aegean days.

"What is this 'Greenshields' of which you speak, sir?" Miss Wastefield asked.

"An authoritative text by an eminent professor in the university at Salthead, now deceased. It's generally accounted the most thorough and knowledgeable work concerning the ancient Aegean world, which happens to be a subject of some interest to me."

"But I myself know nothing of this island of Kaftor or of an empire of Minos. If this empire did exist — if it is indeed more than a legend — what has it to do with me? 'Return to Kaftor.' How am I to return to a place which, even if it once existed, no longer does?"

The doctor shook his head; he didn't know.

"What crime am I guilty of? How have I disobeyed? I've never harmed anyone that they should treat me so. And who would send me so horrid a gift for my birthday?"

Again the doctor didn't know.

"There are times, Miss Wastefield," he said, trying to calm her, "when the mind simply plays tricks. A vivid imagination may take strange flights. Sometimes it is one's own self, or one's memories, that may be the cause of a 'possession,' rather than demonic agency."

"Oh, I don't know what it is," Miss Wastefield sighed, with a weary heave of her breast. "I had come to Nantle in hopes of finding a solution. Now Mr. Thistlewood seems to have failed me. What shall I do, Dr. Pinches? Have you any guidance for me?"

She looked him earnestly in the face, entreating him with her eyes, hungry for even the slenderest and most worn-out scrap of hope from the learned divine.

"Have you consulted a physician, Miss Wastefield?" was what she got in return.

Miss Wastefield indicated that she had not.

"I ask only because there are certain ailments known to inflict trouble-some fancies on the intellect. However, you seem perfectly healthy to me — outwardly at least — but of course I am another sort of doctor! Perhaps I should make an examination of this mirror of yours? I confess, I'm rather curious to see it. From your description it may be very ancient indeed, and very important — a relic from a vanished world. Do you know what that could mean, Miss Wastefield? If the mirror were shown to be of *Cretan* ori-gin — if it could be proved to have come from the land of Minos — it would be a very valuable relic indeed. It could well explain your Mr. Thistlewood's interest in relieving your father of his 'burden.' Ha! Burden indeed!" he sniffed.

It seemed that the doctor's love of scholarship and his enthusiasm for his Aegean days had gotten the whip hand of him, for he seemed not to no-tice the little fall Miss Wastefield's face took on hearing this speech.

"But, Dr. Pinches," she said, realizing that he still did not comprehend her plight, "that is the very reason I have come to Nantle — to be relieved of it! I have no means of ridding myself of this unholy thing which you deem so blessed a discovery. Mr. Thistlewood by his own admission has the means; from his letter he makes it clear he knows the evil it harbors. And what is more important, he knows how to free me of it!"

"As I've said, I know of no family in the parish called Thistlewood, or in Nantle for that matter, and so can't advise you on the trustworthiness of the man. But, Miss Wastefield — why do you say you can't rid yourself of the mirror? I fail to understand you."

Here, indeed, was the very crux of the matter, the singular point which the clergyman had yet to grasp.

"That is just what I mean, Dr. Pinches," she replied, struggling to pre-serve her composure. "The awful thing will not leave me — it *never* leaves me! I have ridden out in my carriage, at Pinewick, and thrown the mirror into the underbrush beyond the roadside. I've cast it into the trees, the bog, the river. I have traveled to Crow's-end, to the cliff road, and flung it into the harbor waters. I have sent it away a dozen times, but to no purpose. *Each time it has come back to me.* The very next day, or the day after, there it will be again — on a chair, on a sofa, on my toilet-table, in my dressing-case. It is as if by some wicked and secret art that it does this! I have had the bronze smashed by our farrier. I have tried burning it in the fire. I have buried it, I've sent it to distant cities by post, I've had it thrown overboard at sea — and always in a day or two it is back again, magically restored while I sleep. On one occasion I stayed awake the entire night and it did not appear; then I dozed for but seconds in the morning, and there it was on the counterpane! The ceaseless worry and the nightmares I have endured have reduced me to a state of nervous dread. *And still the foul thing dares to come back to me!*"

The doctor looked closely at Miss Wastefield and at the shadow that lay across her brow, and frowned. He was perplexed by the contrast between her exceptional beauty and the tale she had to tell. Even her curious, coiled earrings drew his attention — very unusual they were, like the lady herself. Her tale was evidence, like the earrings, of something decidedly odd, but just what to do about it, the doctor couldn't decide.

Was she possessed by some supernatural agency, as she would have him believe, or had she imagined most of which she spoke? Or was she perhaps on the edge of madness? She seemed to him like a most proper and well-bred young woman, the very picture of the daughter of a learned man, which gave her claims a certain credence. Possessed — mistaken — or mad? Or was she perhaps in another kind of peril? For if she was being followed, it implied that she was subject to a very real danger from *this* world rather than another.

Which was it? *And how to explain her father's death?*

The doctor, simply put, couldn't make up his mind; he really didn't know. What he *did* know was that all this talk of a marvelous mirror of ancient polished bronze had fired his curiosity.

"I think it doubly important, Miss Wastefield, that I examine this mirror of yours," he told her.

Miss Wastefield at first did not concur in this opinion, for she knew only too well what had happened to her father. She reminded the doctor why she'd confined the unholy thing in her trunk of trunks — it was not only from her fear of it, but to prevent others from being harmed by it as her father had been. It would be dangerous, she declared, for him to examine it.

In the end, however, the doctor managed to persuade her of the reasonableness of his suggestion; at any rate it was a place to start, he said. The doctor seemed to know something about the possible origin of the mirror, and of these visions of hers; he was, by his own admission, a specialist; and so she relented, and an hour was settled on for him to come round the next day to Chamomile Street.

"Do not despair, Miss Wastefield, we shall get to the bottom of it," he assured her as he conducted her from the drawing-room. His sister offered Miss Wastefield some tea from the tea-urn, but she politely declined; and so the doctor's beautiful caller in furs took her leave of them.

Dr. Pinches seemed nearly as pleased as he was mystified, as he stood at the window with his sister and watched Miss Wastefield mount into a cab at the foot of the rectory steps. Then he turned aside, rubbing his grizzled cheeks in pensive rumination, his mind struggling to digest its latest food for thought — and quite a meal it had been, too!

Which thought itself suddenly brought to mind his long-delayed dinner and his helping of warden pie; and so off to the dining-room the doctor went.

What neither he nor Miss Pinches could have seen from the window, however, was a figure standing under the trees in the churchyard adjacent. It was the figure of a man very tall and broad, wearing a black caped over-coat and a chimney-pot hat. His eyes — large, dark, and strangely lustrous eyes — were on Miss Wastefield, and they remained on her as her cab rattled off down the street.

By the time the cab disappeared from view, so, too, had the grim figure under the trees. To some the man was known by the name of Lanthorne; although we have it on authority that to others he was known by more names than that.

But more of this later.

CHAPTER TWENTY-SEVEN

Word of Jerry Squailes

"Jerry! Jerry! Ho, Jerry! Jerry Porter!"

The fish porter, bending under the weight of his load, glances round him with a puzzled stare. Balanced on his head is a crate of codfish he is toting along the wharf, from one of several fishing-smacks that are moored there, for conveyance to the stalls at the market. Mr. Porter the fish porter is but one of many porters who can be seen treading the gangways of the wharf, some marching upward toward the quay with their crates and baskets filled to bursting, the rest returning to the boats for fresh supplies.

Tramping from boats to market and back again for several hours each morning is the porters' monotonous task and lot. Their faces lie crushed and buried under their odd-shaped headgear, their scooped "bobbing" hats which when applied to the cranium look something like a medieval bow-man's leather helmet. Gutter-brimmed with a spout at the back for run-off, the hats are thickly padded for cushioning the heavy loads of fish that weigh on the bearers' heads and necks.

"Jerry! Ho, Jerry!" comes another shout from above.

"Who calls?" Mr. Porter cries out in a loud voice. "Who calls for Jerry Porter?"

Having traversed the wharf, he is on the point of ascending the gang-way when he stops to peer upward. Returning his gaze is a tall, lean, iron-haired man — Mr. Lamert, a dealer in marine stores, whose shop lies nearby. He is standing at the edge of the quay and looking down at the wharf, which floats some ten or twelve feet below him, its height varying with the rise and fall of the tide.

"There's a cove on the spy for ye, Jerry, as has come along with Black

Davy," says Mr. Lamert. "They're both of 'em at Slinger's now. The cove says it's more than worth your time to yarn with him for a spell."

"Black Davy I knows, this cove I don't. D'you know him yourself, Lammy?"

"Stranger to these parts — don't know him from the man in the moon. Ancient gent, respectable. A lawyer he is, says Davy, come all the way from Cargo."

"What's a lawyer to do with me?"

A careless shrug from Mr. Lamert, followed by a jerk of his thumb over one thin rail of a shoulder. "They're a-waiting for ye at t'other end o' the market, by Slinger's throne. What's yer answer?"

"Tell 'em I'll see him, once Mason's catch here be loaded out. It's my last o' the morning."

Mr. Lamert instructs the small boy who brought the message to communicate the porter's reply to Mr. Devenham and the stranger. Mr. Porter then proceeds to tote several more crates of cod and steelhead from boat to market-stall, where the auctioneer to whom they had been consigned is engaged in some spirited bidding with the purchasers round his table. His table is one of several tables there, each heaped high with fish and superintended by a salesman. The tables lie under the covered portion of the market, which occupies one stretch of the long quay.

Mr. Porter, once his final load has been delivered, scrapes the scales from his canvas apron, and mops his face with a gaudy handkerchief, and with his bobbing hat still on his head hastens along the quay toward the farther end of Musselgate Market.

The fishing-smacks and other vessels being moored at a level below that of the quay, all he sees of them as he passes are their masts rising stiff and straight out of the morning fog, which has spread its customary gloom over market, quay, and harbor. The bell-clock in the central square had just struck the hour of nine. There is not quite so much bustle and animation as earlier, but still it remains a lively scene. The day is growing advanced for the wholesale market, however. By ten o'clock there will be fewer buyers, and as a result the late-arriving cargoes will not demand so much at auction. Then it will be time for the bargain-hunters, the hawkers, fishmongers, and other retailers to descend on the tables. Until then, however, it is the salesmen and auctioneers who reign supreme, their voices ringing out in loud and boastful praise of their goods.

"Five bob! Five bob, sirs, and ye may take 'em away!"

"'Andsome cod! 'Andsomest in market! Cowcod, lingcod, tomcod, gen'l'm'n — best in market!"

"Tur-bot! All a-live, oh! Tur-bot!"

"Freshest skates in market, ten bob! Ten bob for skates!"

"Beeee-u-ti-ful butter soles! Gorrrr-ge-ous lemon soles! 'Ere they be!"

"Mussels! Abalones! O-ho! Mussels, precious cheap, cheap, cheap! Delicious abalones, cheap, cheap, cheap!"

"Steelhead, steelhead! What'll I 'ave for steelhead, gen'l'm'n?"

"Shrimps an' winkles! So-ho! This way for shrimps an' winkles!"

"Yo! Yo! Lookit these 'ere! Starry flounders — can't be topped!"

Mr. Porter hurries on past the stalls, past the covered area and some low booths and sheds quay-side. Beyond them, behind the low and rather lorn and ramshackle spread of warehouses, the spire of Mr. Porter's beloved St. Mary-le-Quay, his Church of the Blessed Quietude, can be seen rising like another ship's mast into the fog.

At the edge of the market the porter's eyes are greeted by the sight of four monumental forms, so massive and ponderous they could be mistaken for galleons drawn upon the shore. Galleons they are not, however, but four shaggy red mastodons in full harness, resting on their knees with their bellies on the ground. They are patiently waiting as the cargo from a merchantman at anchor is loaded aboard the freight compartments that line their backs and flanks. These thunder-beasts have rightly been compared to majestic ships of the road, and the four at the quay are no exception, being seen to dwarf most of the small craft lying stranded in the boat-yard adjacent.

A crisp-haired, stiff-faced, timber-looking man in loud plaid trousers and a pork-pie hat is supervising the proceedings. Three younger, haler editions of this gentleman are the workers being supervised, and we may hazard a guess they are the sons of the mastodon man, so like him are they in every respect. They can be seen moving up and down the cord-ladders, hauling aboard the smaller items and stowing them away, while the weightier cargo is taken up by means of rope and pulley.

A couple of gamboling dogs take notice of Mr. Porter as he approaches and tips his heavy hat to the leader of the mastodon train.

"Hallo, John Jarvey! And how goes it with you?"

"Proper fine, Mr. Porter, proper fine. We're back for another run, as you can see, our second this month. Surprised I am to find you at Nantle, though, for I'd heard it over a tankard at the Goat and Porpoise in Paignton Swidges as you'd been observed in that vicinity of late. Calling on Mr. Jobberley of Fairlight, no doubt?"

"Hake Jobberley, sure, an old friend o' mine the wickie is," Mr. Porter acknowledges.

"As are my boys, and these beasts of ours, too, and our dogs, as well you know. It's been some while now, ha'n't it, since you've seen my boys and the train? And proper fine they all are, Mr. Porter, proper fine!" With his arms akimbo and his pork-pie thrown back on his head, Mr. Jarvey gazes with satisfaction at the shaggy titans on the quay and the three nimble images of himself working busily about them.

Mr. Porter is himself rather fond of mastodons and, despite the press of his summons, takes a moment to greet each of the thunder-beasts in turn. The lead bull, a noble specimen with a wrinkled ear and two flaring tusks, is called Silvertop, owing to the peculiar blaze that marks his huge head and brow. The bull observes Mr. Porter beside him there on the quay and, pondering his minute figure, commences an investigation of him with his trunk. Once the identity of Mr. Porter has been confirmed, the trunk is lifted high, and a joyous roar of welcome shatters the air.

Behind Silvertop is his younger brother Acorn, nearly as large now as himself. The brothers are accompanied by two shy, doe-eyed, but no less imposing female cousins, who answer to the names of Chloë and Mavis. It is usually the case that the trains are operated by blood relations, and that the thunder-beasts within a train are themselves kin to one another, as the driving of mastodons has ever been and largely remains a family concern.

"Have you had rest sufficient, then, Mr. Porter, on your excursion to Paignton Swidges?" inquires Mr. Jarvey.

"Rest sufficient, I'm sure," nods the fish porter, "but now Lammy tells me as there's a cove wants to see me, and I b'lieves that's him just yonder — the old one there with Sawyer and the captain and Black Davy. It's Black Davy as brought him."

"Black Davy it is, sure enough. An avowed champion of the beasts Davy is, though I shouldn't care to trust him *too* far, Mr. Porter. He's traveled some few times with the train, last about a twelvemonth back, through the hills and salt marshes round Foghampton and the bay. He is, as we call it in the business, a great trumpeter of his own interests."

"Davy knows his own mind, that's sure, and makes no bones of it. He has a fine flow o' speech, has Davy, with that philosophy of his — jaw-tackle it is, more like — for at close o' day it's less to do with philosophy and more to do with Davy himself. A bag o' wind most times he is, and a mannerless rogue, who knows not when to stint his gab."

"No doubt you'll take proper care, Mr. Porter, in any dealings with him — though of the gaffer there I've no knowledge."

"He's a lawyer, and come from Cargo as I hear."

"Cargo! Well, he's more than a hop and a skip from home, then, as are we. You'll need to make up your own mind, Mr. Porter, as regards the gaffer, for lawyers be all of 'em great trumpeters of their own interests. Good luck with it now, and don't be forgetful of us. We'll not be going out till morning at the earliest." So Mr. Jarvey informs him, and throwing up a finger to the brim of his hat returns his attention to his sons and his thunder-beasts and his own kind of cargo.

Not a stone's throw from the spectacle of the thunder-beasts, beside the sea-wall, stands a spectacle of another sort. There are four persons in the *tableau,* grouped round a device of unusual appearance, the center-piece of which is a levitating elbow-chair — or more precisely, the body of a chair with the legs sawn off, hanging by its arms from a large spring balance with a circular dial. The balance in its turn is strung by chain and hook from the apex of a tripod some ten feet tall. The cushioned seat of the chair is suspended at just the proper height for sitting on.

Beside this device, in a chair of a more conventional type, sits a nautical gentleman in a dark blue coat and a peaked cap. With his smoking chimney of a pipe and his crinkly eyes and his white beard and hair, he beams good cheer and benevolence upon all who happen by. A former merchant sea-captain, now retired, he has passed the better part of his twilight years at his station on the quay, collecting small fees from persons wishing to learn their weight. Needless to say there were few if any persons on the quay needing or wanting such information, nor was that of much concern to Captain Slinger. His weighing-chair was merely a pretext for him to linger at the quay and yarn with his mates old and new, and cast a sailorly eye on the ships coming and going with the tide, while serving some useful (if rarely needed) purpose.

With him there beside his levitating throne is Mr. Job Sawyer, a wizened little ship's-carpenter, also retired, who once served aboard Captain Slinger's vessel, and whom we met briefly at the Axe and Compasses. Next to Mr. Sawyer stands a person lean of eye and negligent of manner, with an unwashed face and a mop of sooty-black hair. He has been holding forth with animation for some time, punctuating his words with an occasional explosion of noise through his nostrils. He is, of course, Mr. David Devenham, otherwise Black Davy.

"Man, man, and where have you gotten to?" he exclaims, rushing to greet Mr. Porter as he heaves into view. "I'll not mince words with you, sir — we've been playing at 'hunt the hare' for above a week now, and not a sign of you round ship or quay in this harbor! It's flat gone you've been, man, and with a noted legal light from Cargo searching for you in every nook and corner. Never let it be said that Devenham was one for inquiring into other men's affairs, but where have you been, sir?"

Mr. Porter, accustomed to such effusions from Black Davy, shrugs this latest off like the others.

"Paignton Swidges," he grudgingly replies, then adds as an after-thought — "on holiday."

"And what need have fish porters of holidays, I wonder?"

"The same need as you, sir."

"The same as I? Need I remind you, sir, that I am no fish porter? It is the *world* that is my occupation, man! I am for roaming in it and contemplat-ing its mysteries, not for fish porting. I am for eating Sourbury cheese, or rank mutton, or living in the moon; I am for anything but fish porting. I'll make hob-nails first, or pick oakum, or mend old kettles in a pest-house. I didn't ask to be thrust into this sundered world, but now that I'm here, all I ask of it is that it let me be."

"Aye, I rackon ye're always on holiday, Davy Devenham," cackles Mr. Sawyer. "Bone-idle it is ye are, and always have been."

"Nor has he changed, nor ever will change, will Davy," nods the genial Captain Slinger.

"What I'll tell you, my skipperish friend," returns Davy, drawing a dirty coat-sleeve across a ditto cheek, "is that the world is for living in, not fish porting. Do you see, sirs, the evil that money has led this man to? You're a prisoner, Porter, a captive of foul coin! You are in the stone jug of filthy lu-cre. Why do you fish-port, sir? I'll tell you in one word, man — *ducats*. It's your greedy lust for coin that confines you; it has deprived you of your free-dom. You are in quod, sir!"

"I works for the fishermen, sir, and the auctioneers," returns Mr. Porter, a trifle restive now and wishing to be about the matter at hand. "And what's more, I works when I likes to work. I'm an independent sort, sir, much like yourself, but I've a need from time to time for the *ducats*, as you say, as keeps the likes o' Jacob Comport from my door."

"Comport! Man, man — I'll have no truck with Jacob Comport."

"Nor will I, sir, nor hope to."

"A plague of all Comports! Knavish fellows who care for nothing but the pounds, shillings, and pence that may be wrested from poor squits like yourself. What will scurvy coin avail you? Only misery, man. Don't plague me with talk of coin! It's life, sir, and freedom that matter to me. Our lives already are half-spent before we know it; it's a bitter truth, man, but there it is."

This last pronouncement Mr. Devenham follows up by clapping his fin-ger to his nose and nodding, in sign of the remarkable truth of his obser-vation.

The remaining member of the little *tableau,* who has been attending to the wayward currents and eddies of the discussion, is an elderly gentleman with a beard as white as the captain's, but short and neatly trimmed, and hung upon a pink face and ears. He sports a dark city suit and carries a blue bag of that sort generally favored by attorneys. He is, of course, Mr. Liffey. He requests now that he and Mr. Porter detach themselves from the others so that they might speak privately. Black Davy — in words that would occupy several pages in the telling, and from a consideration of the reader's patience will not be quoted here — assures Mr. Porter that the gentleman is a legal eminento, an ornament of his profession, one who "knows meal from bran," and with a bow and a flourish relinquishes Mr. Porter to his keeping.

So the two of them, the one a bearer of news and the other of fish, step a ways farther down the quay, by the sea-wall, where their conversation is unlikely to be intruded upon.

"You are Mr. Jerry Porter, as I am informed?" the attorney begins, with a gaze something thoughtful and scrutinous, but kindly, too.

"Yes, sir, Jerry Porter's my name," returns the other, frowning a little. He can't in his wildest imaginings conceive what a learned practitioner of the law from far-away Cargo might have to say to him.

"In point of fact, isn't it true that Porter is not your given name?"

The contracted eyes of Mr. Porter undergo a further narrowing, as though the wind blowing into them had gained new force. "How do you mean, sir?"

For reply Mr. Liffey opens his blue bag and takes from it a small picture painted in oils. It is the portrait of a young woman with a laughing face — almond-haired, smooth-cheeked, cherry-lipped. It is the same gilt-framed portrait that has resided for so many years in his cabinet sanctuary at Cargo, and which he had brought with him expressly for one purpose.

"Do you know this young lady?" Mr. Liffey asks.

Mr. Porter gives a start of recognition, which shakes some of the scales from his apron and bobbing hat. "By the Lord, sir, where did you get this?"

"Porter is a name you have appropriated, is it not?"

"I've not 'appropriated' it, sir, for Porter *is* my name — or rather it was my mother's name, and this be her picture. This dear face I've not looked on for full many a year! I'll ask you again, sir, where did you get this?"

"Porter was your late mother's maiden name?"

"Yes, sir. Rose Porter was my mother, God bless her immortal soul. But damme, sir, will you not tell me where you found her picture?"

"Why did I not think of it?" Mr. Liffey is heard asking himself. "But as soon as Mr. Devenham mentioned the name *Porter,* I *did* think of it. Of course, I told myself, of course — confound it all, I should have known it would be *Porter*!"

"It's Porter I am, sir, and a porter I be, but I'm damned if I know who you are or what you want. Beg indulgence, but would you be so good as to tell me, sir?"

"Forgive me, Mr. Porter — I fear I've not been so straightforward as I might, but be assured there is very good cause. It's a difficult business after so many years. However, my duty is clear. Tell me, now — does the name *Drownder* have any significance for you?"

Mr. Porter falls back a step, greatly surprised. "Drownder was the name o' my father, sir — or so my mother told me, for I never knew him. My *true* father he was, the one as absconded with the squire's coin and shamed my mother so, and later died o' grog and a fever. Fred Drownder was his name — a name I never thought to speak again, or think again, for the disgrace he brought on my mother."

"And your stepfather, Mr. Porter? What was his name?"

"Squailes, sir, him as married my mother soon afterward. That gentleman I *did* know, sad to relate, for he brought me up. Rodger Squailes — him as treated my mother murderous bad and ended his days worse than Drownder, stabbed through the heart in a row over a pot-house bill. 'I'll make your head sing like a church bell,' is what he often told her, and how he used her, and myself, too. It was enough to drive any man's heart into his boots to see it. No, sir, I never could live with that monster's name, and it's a fine justice he was slain, I'm sure. Nor Squailes nor Drownder could I be, after a time, only Porter, after my mother as was so wrongly served in this life. So kind she was, sir, and so pretty, too, as can be seen from her picture — the daintiest thing under a bonnet, and dead so young! It was to honor the memory of her, sir, that I took her name."

Mr. Liffey appears much affected by these words. But why should that be? Why should his pink face and ears be flushing red? Why should the hand holding the picture be trembling, and why should there be moisture standing in his gentle blue eyes?

"Oh dear, oh dear," he murmurs, in a barely audible voice. "I never knew —"

"Sir?"

There follows a brief pause, during which Mr. Liffey tries to recover something of his lawyerly self-possession. Then he turns again to the fish porter and says —

"Jerry Squailes was your name at the time, those many years ago, when the news of your mother's death reached me. I knew so little of her circumstances then, or of her fall in life, or indeed of you. I would have helped her if I could, but she would never have taken charity from one such as I, or from anyone. The last word I had of her was at Falaise, and of you here in Nantle."

"She died at Falaise," says Mr. Porter. His contracted gaze hardens suddenly upon the enigmatic old gentleman. "Just who are you, sir, as knows so much of me, and what's your intent? Is this a put-up job? Is it Black Davy as concocted it? For sure it's no more than two or three round Nantle knows I was once Squailes, and one o' them be dead."

"I can assure you, Mr. Porter, it's no put-up job, for I am in utmost earnest. I have known your name for a goodly while — both your names, in fact, and the third as well, if I'd been intelligent enough to think of Porter! I lost all track of you some years ago. I knew nothing of your condition, your trade, your fortunes; I knew only that you were last at Nantle. It was your change of name that confounded my search."

The wind comes up again; the eyes of Mr. Porter narrow down again. "Lost track o' me? News o' my mother's death? Smite me dumb, sir, but I'll ask it again — who are you, and what business have you to be keeping track o' folk?"

"My name is Liffey, Mr. Porter, and I have come from Cargo on a private legal matter which devolves upon me as the administrator of a late gentleman's estate. More particularly I've come to make identification of one Mr. Jerry Squailes, son of Rosemary Drownder, *née* Porter, later Rosemary Squailes, deceased. For months now a colleague of mine here in Nantle has been making extensive inquiries after you, and placing advertisements in the newspapers, all with no result. It will be necessary for you to demonstrate, to the satisfaction of myself and the Court, that you are this Mr. Squailes, for I've some news regarding the late gentleman's estate that may alter your life considerably — very good news, Mr. Porter, be assured. Moreover I have some information respecting your late father, Frederick Drownder, that may well surprise you. I'll ask you now, Mr. Porter — are you prepared to swear an oath under God and offer evidence that you are this man Jerry Squailes, son of Rosemary Squailes, late of Falaise?"

A further pause ensues while Mr. Porter gives thought to a response. He takes his bobbing hat from his head and turns it round and round in his hands a time or three, to aid his thinking; flicks a couple of scales from the crown of it; looks off toward the fog in the harbor, then back again; peers curiously into the eyes of Mr. Liffey; and finding there nothing but kindness and good will, makes up his mind and replies —

"I am, sir, that man, as Black Davy himself knows, too. I served aboard ship with him once, under command o' Captain Slinger there. A great talker is Davy; he'll swear an oath a minute for you, I'm sure. But if it's evidence as you require, sir, well, you may ask me what you please and I'll give you the honest truth as best I knows it. And there be some letters o' my mother's, sir, as I've kept these long years, as may stand for proof. As for the newspapers, well, I'm very sorry to have been a bother, sir, but I don't reads 'em, and neither, I think, does Davy."

Scratching a little at his head of untidy hair flecked with gray, he places his odd-shaped hat back on it, and awaits whatever else Mr. Liffey may have to tell him.

The attorney for his part has heard nearly all he needs to hear, and seen all he needs to see; the rest, to his way of thinking, is mere formality of law.

"Yes, there's little doubt you are Jerry Squailes. Seeing you closely now, and observing your general manner and countenance, has well-nigh set the question at rest. The likeness was not so immediate — there is far more of Drownder there than of Porter, I fear — but round the periphery, round the arch of the brows and edges of the eyes — the line of the mouth, the chin — yes, yes, I see it particularly round the chin — it is *her* chin —"

"Did you know my mother, sir?" the fish porter asks, in a tone of the profoundest respect.

Mr. Liffey didn't realize he'd been speaking his thoughts aloud.

"Forgive me, Mr. Porter," he says, flushing again. His eyes stray for a moment and assume a wistful look, as thoughts old and sad come welling up inside his heart. He grows silent as if in the spell of a distant remembrance; then, abruptly recollecting himself, he shakes off his reverie.

"Yes, Mr. Porter, I did know your mother, many years ago in Cargo."

"Cargo is where she was born, sir, as was I. That's as she told me — that her family came from the place called Cargo, which be not so far from Crow's-end."

"Yes, that is so, although the Porters are long vanished now. Apart from yourself the entire family is, I believe, quite extinct. That is, unless you have children of your own?"

Mr. Porter replies that no, sir, there be no children, nor be there thought of any. "But who was this late gentleman whose lawyer you are," he asks now, "and what had he to do with me?"

"Tell me, Mr. Porter," the attorney says, "what do you know of a place called Tiptop Grange?"

For several minutes more the two continue their discussion there at the sea-wall, while the icy water splashes against the quay, and the fog drifts in wave after ghostly wave through the harbor. Once they part, however, Mr.

Devenham moves quickly to join Mr. Liffey, while the fish porter trots off toward Musselgate with instructions in hand for another interview with the attorney.

There follows the transfer of a sum of cash from Mr. Liffey to Black Davy for the finding of Jerry Squailes, as per their agreement of the week before. In the process Mr. Devenham takes care to remind the attorney that he would have performed the service for no cash at all — "for I don't need or want it, but the world, sir, it presses" — but so long as it was the charitable thing to do for a fellow creature, he was happy to make the sacrifice. Mr. Devenham looks at the money in his hand and smiles, and dreams of cherry wine at Sprig's and tankards of grog from glinty Minty of the Axe and Compasses. His cup of satisfaction is full.

"Such a sad case," he overhears Mr. Liffey remarking to himself. "Her child, her only child — a fish porter toiling on Nantle quay! Things should never have come to this. But I mean to put the matter right, and give him a chance to begin the world again — poor fellow!"

"Poor fellow? *Rich* fellow now, I'll warrant," Davy laughs, with a particularly violent snort. "Poor Squailes — poor Porter! But I feel for him, really I do, sir, for a poor fellow he remains. The cares of coin will weigh heavily on him now."

"He has the look of one who has endured much in his life."

"Hardly the pleasantest sort to gaze on, true, and miserable traps to boot. But there are worse faces have looked out of black bags, man!"

"He has absolutely no family, none," sighs Mr. Liffey, as he prepares to take his leave. It was a statement that could well have described Mr. Arthur Liffey himself.

"Tush, man! A family is a scurvy thing. He should consider himself lucky to be spared," snorts Davy. "As for myself, sir, I'll not brook the tyranny of family. I must be free of petty, puling cares. I must have spaciousness! Family and the foul chink of coin will never hinder me." Happily he counts the bank-bills in his hand, to see that he has not been cheated, and stuffs them one by one into his battered pocket-book. "No family, no confinement, no cares! Better by far to be one's own master. All who demand freedom must of necessity be alone. But you know," he adds, his face suddenly darkening, "in the end, sir, we're all of us alone — totally alone, every man jack of us, from birth-day to death-day. The greatest joy is never to be born, and the sooner we accept that, the easier it is."

"Yes," says Mr. Liffey, with a poignancy that was all but lost on his companion, "yes, Mr. Devenham, we are all of us quite alone."

CHAPTER TWENTY-EIGHT

Five at Table

It is a little short of eleven when Mr. Liffey returns to the Crozier. He is feeling hungry, for his early rendezvous on Nantle quay had deprived him of his breakfast, but it is still some time yet before the luncheon hour. So he decides to lie down for a spell, in part to recover from the morning's exertions — for he was after all, in the touching words of Messrs. Lamert and Jarvey, an "ancient gent" and a "gaffer," and needed his rest.

He had changed his rooms since the haunting, twice now in fact, and had experienced no trouble since the second move. Still he is feeling a little tired as he drops his head on the pillow and closes his eyes, seeking a bit of sleep before his lunch with Fred and the others.

His thoughts go drifting off, lightly and gently. His eyelids are like two pebble-stones, his breathing grows long and deep, and in a short time he is blissfully a-slumber. But such bliss was not meant to last. A door opens and closes somewhere, waking him. Raising his head, he looks about him but sees no one. He calls out for his man John and receives no answer. He is on the verge of falling back to sleep when the door intervenes again.

And still there was no one there!

Mr. Liffey rubs his eyes, and rubs all the sleep out of them in the process. It seems clear he will have no further bliss today.

He gets to his feet and walks across to the sitting area. There he rakes up the fire a little with the poker, then sinks down into a chair to contemplate the victory he has achieved after so many months of striving.

He has found Jerry Squailes! He has learned enough to convince him and the Prerogative Court at Cargo that Mr. Jerry Porter and Mr. Jerry Squailes are one and the same being. And so how to proceed now? When and how to break the news of the victory to Fred and Susan and Miss Veal? How to break the news that the late Joseph Cargo, that eminent and well-respected grandee of the town of Cargo, and its most voracious — how to break the news that such a man has left a quarter of his money to a fish porter on Nantle quay? More ticklish still, how to explain the reason for his doing so?

"Oh dear, oh dear," the attorney murmurs, growing more uncomfortable the more he thinks of it. "I hadn't supposed it would come to this. I hadn't anticipated a fish porter!"

As he sits there alone, immersed in thought before the fire burning inside its huge castle-keep of a fireplace, he feels the absence of his Cargo *Coast Intelligencer,* which it was his habit to peruse at home while taking his ease. True, there is a city paper on the table, the local *Channel Chronicle,* but it's not so good a paper as the *Intelligencer,* nor so interesting or relevant a one. Nonetheless it serves to divert his attention for a while. At length his interest wanes and he lays the paper by. He reaches for his blue bag and takes from it the picture of the young Rosemary, twice wedded in this life and once dead, and gazes on her remembered features in silent meditation. He marvels again and gives thanks, as he often has through the years, for the miracle of brush and oils and painterly skill, that has preserved unspoiled the image of she who had long since turned to dust.

"Amends shall be made," he vows. "It is my bounden duty. If I have done but one right and proper thing in this life, let it be this."

He lays the picture on the table and eases back in his chair. With half-closed eyes, he turns his attention to the fire and, folding his hands, seems content to wait out the time until lunch.

As he sits there watching the smoke and flicker, contemplating his good luck at uncovering Mr. Squailes, and thinking on her of many years past, he becomes aware of a noise in the room. He sits up and listens, but as with the closing door finds nothing to merit alarm. He is about to settle back again when the noise repeats — more of a rustling or a scuttling sound now, and with it a vague sense of motion, as of something crawling along the floor.

He peers distrustfully round. Abruptly the hairs on his neck rear up and he freezes in place, as he spies a shadowy form creeping towards him on the carpet. The moment his eyes light on it, it stops; then it creeps forward again, and stops again; and so again; and all the while nearer and nearer it comes, making directly for his chair by the fire.

Mr. Liffey wants very much to call out for John, or Fred, or anyone, but his lawyer's voice fails him. He can feel his body quaking in its seat, stricken with dread at the sight of the thing on the carpet.

It is at the foot of his chair now, and he can hear it scratching at the fabric as it works to reach him — a human hand, black and rotted from time in the grave, clawing itself up the side of the chair by its fingers and thumb.

It turns him cold; it turns him sick. Paralyzed, he can do nothing but watch in horror as it gains the arm of the chair; then, before he knows it, the thing is upon him, scuttling up his own arm like a tarantula, and planting itself on his shoulder and pressing him with dreadful force against the cushion. He feels the bite of the nailed fingers, and hears again the rush of angry words in his ear —

"Foul traitor! Foul *trusted* traitor!"

The heart of Mr. Liffey leaps inside his chest. Terrified he struggles against the grip of the hand, which is thrusting against him with all the tenacity of a vise, pinning him to the back of the chair like an insect to a specimen-board.

"It is my duty!" he gasps, regaining some measure of command over his voice. "None but mine!"

His struggle is a valiant but a hopeless one, and he is on the point of giving up and surrendering himself to whatever may follow, when the grip on him is suddenly relaxed. The black and rotted thing at his shoulder vanishes, and he finds himself released from the prison of the chair.

Diving into his coat and shoes, he flees downstairs, some hour or more in advance, as it turns out, of the luncheon hour. It troubles Mr. Liffey not a whit, however, to be so early; indeed, it will be glad comfort to pass the time there in the dining-room amid the bustle of the servants to-ing and fro-ing, with no sinister hand creeping about the floor to waylay him. Happily will he endure the hour or more that must intervene, for it will give him time to recover his shattered wits.

Presiding over the operations in the dining-room is the sober figure of the landlord, Mr. Blackshaw. He carries himself among his servants just as he does among his guests, with his plump and portentious nose a little in the air, as though challenging all and sundry to deny the fact that this coaching-inn of the Crozier was the finest and most respectable of all the coaching-inns of Nantle.

The time wears on. At last the hour of dining arrives, and the other members of the party assemble themselves at table. The meal is laid on under the careful watch of Mr. Blackshaw, and superintended by the same goggle-eyed waiter with a shock of red hair who had introduced the travelers to Sprig's coffee-house.

Fred, noting Mr. Liffey's face as he sits himself down, is struck at once by what he sees in it. Even the hour or more intervening has not been enough to erase the scars of his latest fright from the attorney's countenance.

"Mr. Liffey — 'pon my life, sir, are you ill?" Fred asks. "You do look as though you'd seen a ghost, as the saying is." (He very nearly said, "You are almost as pale as Miss Veal there," but checked himself in time.)

Mr. Liffey denies that there is anything the matter. He fell asleep, he claims, and had only just awoken and come down a moment before, and is still a trifle drowsy. (Mr. Blackshaw, overhearing, cocks an eyebrow in surprise at such perjury from a respectable gentleman of the law.) The attorney assures one and all that he will recover directly, but his appearance belies his words. To Fred and the others, he looks ashy and drawn; his thin hair is disordered, his clothes hastily arranged, and his hands are trembling.

Observing this, Mrs. Cargo flings a triumphal look at her husband, who tries not to notice — a look that acts to reinforce, by a kind of ocular telepathy, her view that Mr. Liffey is too old and frail a man for the task that brought them to Nantle. She turns to Miss Veal, and the both of them direct critical glances at Mr. Liffey where he sits munching his bread.

"You were not at breakfast this morning, sir," Susan remarks. "Didn't you sleep well last night? Are your quarters becoming uninhabitable again?"

Mr. Liffey overlooks this allusion to his changes of rooms, and replies, in the steadiest voice he can manage, that he'd an early errand in relation to the case, another inquiry which, unfortunately, produced no outcome.

"A common enough result these days," says Susan, with another glance at her husband. "It is abundantly clear we are getting nowhere. Here we've been at Nantle for a fortnight and still no Mr. Interloper Squailes!"

At mention of the name, Mr. Liffey raises his head and seems about to speak, when his eyes are drawn to a figure sitting there at the table. It is occupying the empty chair beside Fred and, rather than partaking of the meal, is staring at Mr. Liffey with a ghastly expression. The attorney identifies the cadaverous thing immediately — it is the fiend he saw in his glass, the ghoul that had followed him from Cargo.

As if to drive the point home, the phantom raises a black and rotted hand and dangles it a little in the air, while throwing Mr. Liffey a host of smiling nods and winks. Then to make matters worse — oh, infinitely worse! — the thing unhinges its jaw and drops it onto its chest, then rolls back its head and eyes — the perfect picture of a corpse, silent, spectral, chapfallen.

Mr. Liffey's heart nearly ceases its pumping with the shock of this atrocity. A faint inarticulate exclamation, half gasp, half choke, escapes his lips.

"This entire matter has been a blight," he hears Miss Veal saying somewhere. "So much time and effort expended on a nobody! Were it not for you, my dear Susan and Fred, and the honor of the family Cargo, I should never have come. I wanted no part of tracking down a nobody, and a nobody he appears to be, for he doesn't seem to exist."

"Mr. Liffey," says Susan, "what is the name of that colleague of yours here at Nantle? For you know, we've never once heard it mentioned."

"How's that?" returns the poor shocked man, his attention still riveted on the fiend.

"This lawyer — this fellow practitioner of yours who has been inquiring after Mr. Interloper Squailes for so many months. What is his name?"

There is more than a hint of skepticism in her voice, as though she suspects that the legal man, like Mr. Squailes himself, doesn't exist.

"Ah, his name — indeed — his name is Wringham — George Wringham," is the halting response of Mr. Liffey.

"That is not one of the attorneys recommended by Miss Trickle, is it, Aspasia?"

"It is not," says Miss Veal, unable to suppress a wince at mention of the mistress of teas and wagering.

"I should hope he is a trustworthy and a competent person, this Mr. Wringham. A trustworthy and a competent person is what is needed if one is to ferret out a blackmailer. Yes, Frederick, a blackmailer, for that is what I believe lies behind this beastly disposition of the will. Surely it was blackmail that forced Grandfather Cargo to name this Squailes a beneficiary! Perhaps it had something to do with your grandfather's land dealings, some impropriety he dared not see come to light — as much as that may stagger belief."

"I can't agree with you, Susan," her husband replies, shaking his head.

"Can't you? How then would you explain it, Frederick? Leaving his money — *your* money — to a nobody?"

"I can't explain it. That's why we are here."

"Once we have this Jerry Squailes in hand — if he exists — I mean to take him by the nose, and to —"

"Fred," says Mr. Liffey, interrupting them.

"Yes, sir?"

"Fred, who is that in the chair beside you?"

Mystified looks from the others at table.

"Why, it's my wife, Mr. Liffey. It's Susan."

"No, no, I mean in the other chair — the chair on your right."

Fred, seeing no chair on his right but an empty chair, makes no reply at first. In Mr. Liffey's poor tortured eyes the ghoul can be seen twisting its distended lips into a smirk, accompanied by an indecent flaunting of its brows.

"'Pon my word, there's no one in the chair, sir."

Fred is more than a little troubled now, and gives his mustaches a thoughtful swipe or two, and his fancy waistcoat a tug.

"You see no one there?" the attorney asks.

"No, sir."

"Do *you* see someone there, Mr. Liffey?" Susan asks.

The phantom, having hooked up its jaw again, wags its head and its dangling dead hand at Mr. Liffey in mocking reproach.

"Do I see someone? Well — well — of course not," Mr. Liffey answers, turning quickly from the sight. "No, most decidedly not. There is no one there. *Oh dear, oh dear!*"

"I am heartily glad of that, sir. Are we not glad of that, Aspasia?"

"Very glad, indeed," nods Miss Veal, "for if there *was* to be some person sitting in a chair, where no person was seen to be sitting, it would be a blight."

"What is it you saw?" Fred asks, hoping for some reasonable, if not lawyerly, explanation from his old and valued family friend.

"Nothing," says Mr. Liffey, clearing his voice. "Nothing whatever, Fred. I must be more tired than I imagined."

At which point the ghoul summons up a monstrous frown and, in a cold perspiration of anger, levels its accusing hand at Mr. Liffey, crying out to no ears but the attorney's own —

"Foul, dissembling traitor! You ungrateful old wretch — old fool — let this be but a taste of things to come!"

The pink face of Mr. Liffey turns whiter than his beard.

"No! No!" he stammers, addressing the empty chair. "It is you who are the dissembler. My duty is clear — *and honorable!*"

Blurting out an apology, he pushes back his own chair and hastens from the room — hastens from the entire coaching-inn, in fact, going straight out of the Crozier and into the yard. The others can do little but stare after him at the air he has vacated, not only the Cargoes and Miss Veal but the portentious landlord as well, who, given his publican sensibilities, no doubt takes Mr. Liffey's exit as a vicious slap against his establishment.

Astonishment gives way to concern on the part of the three remaining at table (the fiend, having played its little sport to a conclusion, has obligingly relinquished the chair in which it never was sitting). Fred is visibly disappointed; his faith in Mr. Liffey's competence has been dealt a hammer-blow. No longer can he disregard the opinion of his wife and Miss Veal in the matter of the family solicitor — indeed, he feels himself beginning to come round now to their view. Yes, yes, perhaps it *was* time to engage another attorney, perhaps this Hook fellow they'd heard something of, this very zealous and innovative practitioner on Gull's Wharf. It was clear that Mr. Liffey and his Mr. Wringham had accomplished nothing, and that the travelers' long sea-voyage and fortnight's stay at Nantle had been time misspent.

Meanwhile Mr. Liffey, on emerging from the inn-yard into the quiet by-street, realizes he has neither his hat nor his umbrella, both of which he left in his room; but there is nothing under heaven that can induce him to return for them now. Luckily it isn't raining at the moment, nor is it threatening rain; and so he makes his way to the nearest avenue, where he selects a cab from the rank — a one-seater rather than a hansom, to exclude any invisible companions — and in short order is rattling through the gray streets with Mock Alley on his mind.

It is to Sprig's, of course, that he is going. He wants to get away from his haunted chambers and from his sense of being alone. He wants to go someplace altogether pleasant and convivial, where he can be diverted for a while by the talk of those around him and scrub his mind of the fiend.

Having paid his devoirs to Sir Sharp-nail, he is ushered to a table and asks the waiter to bring him a particular drink, an unusually stiffening concoction for one of Mr. Liffey's temperate habits, and by this means gets down to the business of scrubbing his mind.

His conviction of purpose had thus far seen him through, though not without exacting a toll. It was a most difficult business, perhaps the most difficult of Mr. Liffey's long and dutiful career. His moral direction-post had taken the severest of buffetings. But he had achieved his aim and he would not have it taken from him now.

He remained undecided, however, how best to make the announcement to Fred and the others that he'd found Jerry Squailes. Meanwhile there was another interview to be held with the fish porter, to explain some further particulars of his surprising turn of fortune — some few items to be sorted out, and confidences to be exchanged, before the identity of Mr. Porter was made known to the other heirs of Joseph Cargo.

He is in the midst of these and other reflections when a little rosy pippin of an old fellow, decked out in antique clothes of a peculiar lime-green hue, comes bouncing up to his table, unannounced, and favors him with a puckish grin. It is such a shockingly warm and good-humored grin, after the malignant smirking of the fiend, that it quite startles Mr. Liffey into a better humor himself.

"A drawn game, sir, another drawn game!" are the first words from the mouth of the rosy pippin.

"Have we met, sir?" returns Mr. Liffey, searching his memory.

Mr. John Hop tenders his respects and, inclining his head with the jaunty wig on it, introduces himself. "We have not met," says he, "although I've seen you once before, sir, in the chess rooms."

Here Mr. Liffey acknowledges a like recollection of the bright-eyed Mr. Hop from those chambers.

"I'm afraid they've thrown it in, sir," says the little old gentleman.

"Thrown what in?"

"Why, the match, of course — Turcott and Rainbow, sir. You've not forgotten?"

"No, no, of course not, Mr. Hop — although I fear it's escaped my notice for a time. The grand and princely game of combat! Another drawn game, you say?"

A brisk little nod from Mr. Hop. Another fierce struggle in the chess rooms, he says, and another drawn result — so unsatisfactory! Miss Trickle was sorely disappointed. And so Mr. Turcott, upstart Thespian, had returned again to the boards, and Mr. Rainbow to his scurrilous pen, until the next game in the drawn-out affair of honor could be concerted.

"Do you know, I hadn't seen you here before that single time, sir, in the chess rooms," notes Mr. Hop.

Mr. Liffey replies that he has been in Nantle for only a couple of weeks, although he had visited the town before, years and years ago.

"I've been a regular here for so long, sir, it's likely I saw you then as well," says Mr. Hop. "Ninety years spry I am, but the coffee-house is older still. And how old might you be, sir, if I may be so bold? You're a young chap, I think, and I'm an ancient one, so I've the privilege. Fifty winters, perhaps?"

Given the recent events, Mr. Liffey can't help but be feeling twice that age; nonetheless he accepts the compliment with grace, knowing it to be excessive, and that Mr. Hop knows it, too.

"Have you ever noticed, sir, how time can pass like a flash between the thinking on some bygone day and the present?" asks the rosy pippin.

"How do you mean, Mr. Hop?"

"It's a singular thing. As for instance, I may think of some small incident from my youth — something from my schoolboy days, perhaps — after which I turn my mind back to the present, and in so doing the past event seems no further removed than an instant of time, the mere snapping of a finger. The one event years since, the other in the here and now; and yet in the eye of my mind they're very nearly the same. Have you never experienced the phenomenon, sir?"

Mr. Liffey acknowledges, after some reflection, that perhaps he has.

"The memory from my boyhood long ago, and the sight of you here today — and yet the two seem separated by no more than a moment. It's as though in my mind's eye I'm able to bridge the span of years at a single jump. Ah, so you *have* known the like, sir, this little trick of memory! Sometimes it's my old dad and mum I'll remember, as they were in those days, and both gone so long now; and yet from the remembering of them, followed by the flash to the present, it seems they were here no more than a second ago."

Mr. Liffey, to his surprise, finds himself listening with much interest to the little rosy pippin.

"And yet the life I lived in those days — those dear days long gone by! — it seems to me now a wholly different life. I suppose it's because we are altered so much by the years; my former self seems not like myself at all. Have you known the like, sir? I'll confess, at times such thoughts lead me into heretical quarters. For example, do you believe, sir, as most do, that we pass this way but once? Or is it possible, do you think, that some of us — all of us perhaps — have lived other lives on this earth?"

Such heresy indeed went against the teachings of Mr. Liffey's creed, as he freely admits — and in the same breath confesses that he'd more than once entertained the possibility.

"Perhaps my old dad and mum are here now, in this very room," says Mr. Hop, glancing round him, not in a melancholy way, but joyful at the thought that such a wonder might be. "And my brother and my sister, too, and my dear wife who died young. Perhaps they're here as well, in other shapes. If so, then I am happy for them. For alas, there's not so much left of our family now. It's what comes, sir, of being ninety years spry!"

Mr. Liffey is greatly moved by these words, just as he was by the revelations of Mr. Porter that morning. He thinks again of the pictures in his cabinet sanctuary in far-away Cargo, and of the little gilt-edged oval one in his room at the Crozier, and of the ocean of self-doubt through which he'd lately been swimming, and it nerves him anew.

"Thank you, Mr. Hop," he says, putting by the stiffening drink, which he no longer has any use for. He squares himself with an air of dignified resolve, and looks out upon the world with refreshed eyes. "Thank you for your counsel. The past is always with us, and it is left to those of us who live to keep its memory green. And thank you, too, for your encouragement. It is just what I needed today."

CHAPTER TWENTY-NINE

Which Is a Chapter of Surprises

To the great relief of Miss Wastefield, and to her great excitement, the longed-for communication from Mr. Thistlewood had at last arrived. It was on the morning following her talk with Dr. Pinches, and it was her neighbor, Mr. Frobisher, who brought it.

Mr. Frobisher knew from their prior conversation at Sprig's that Miss Wastefield had been eagerly awaiting the letter, and he hoped she didn't think it rude or presumptuous of him now to have brought it round to her. He'd overheard the scholarly Mr. Tozer, he said, remarking to one of the waiters that a message for the lady from Crow's-end had been dropped into the cat's-head letter-box. Mr. Frobisher had gallantly offered to deliver it, seeing that he was her neighbor and was on the point of returning home after his morning's draft of buttered ale. And he was glad now he had, as he read in her face how much the letter meant to her.

Miss Wastefield was full of gratitude; but then, inexplicably, there crept into her consciousness a vague whisper of suspicion. She informed her neighbor that she intended to read the letter at once, and in private. And yet she hesitated. She looked questioningly from the letter to Mr. Frobisher and back again, and frowned. No, no, there was something amiss here — she knew it, she felt it, but what it was she couldn't put into words.

They were in the drawing-room of Mrs. Juniper's, and Mr. Frobisher was about to depart, having performed his good office, when he found himself delayed by the appearance of Lucy and little Jilly Juniper. Jilly was eager to know if Miss Wastefield was feeling better today? The lady replied that yes, she was, and thanked the child for her concern, but now she meant to go upstairs to read a most important letter that had arrived for her.

Again Mr. Frobisher was on the brink of leaving, and again he found reason to delay, when Miss Wastefield unexpectedly halted in her steps just as she was breaking the seal of the letter.

A cloud had darkened her brow, cousin to the shadow that had so often lain across it, and stayed her hand. Mr. Tozer, she remembered, had assured her that *no one* apart from herself would be told of the letter's arrival. He'd been quite emphatic, saying that it was a matter of gentlemanly principle, and that everything transmitted by means of the cat's-head letter-box was done so in perfect confidence; indeed, that was the very point of it.

And so how was it possible that this letter was here today?

Certainly Mr. Tozer wouldn't have given it to someone to deliver — especially not to someone like Mr. Frobisher, whom he hardly knew. It would have been a rank violation of his duties as custodian of the mails. Either Mr. Tozer and his postal system were a fraud, she reasoned, or Mr. Allan Frobisher was lying.

It seemed to her that her neighbor could read the thoughts that were crossing her brain at that moment, but no, it was her countenance that betrayed her; anyone might have read her thoughts there. No sooner had Mr. Frobisher perceived them than he rang for the housemaid to bring him pen, ink, and paper. Miss Wastefield was mystified, as were Lucy and Jilly. When the materials arrived, the young man quickly dashed something off on a single sheet and handed it across.

It was not much, Miss Wastefield saw, just her name and the address of the coffee-house as they appeared on the letter. But the writing, however, was positively and unmistakably in the hand of Gilbert Thistlewood, being very nearly a perfect copy of the cover of that letter.

"What does this mean, Mr. Frobisher?" Miss Wastefield asked, in some confusion.

For answer her neighbor laid by his wide-awake, and turned for a moment to her maid and little Jilly.

"I say, moppet," he smiled, "would you mind very much if Miss Wastefield and I have a moment to ourselves?"

"Are you going to help her now, Allan?" Jilly asked, her face brightening. "For indeed you said you could, and that you would."

He patted her shoulder and nodded. So Jilly went happily out at the door and round to Mrs. Matchless's house to torment young Pancras, while Lucy, dropping a curtsy to her mistress and Mr. Frobisher, climbed the staircase to her room. As it happened, though, it was Jilly alone who heeded the young man's request; for Lucy, so protective of her mistress, stole back down the stairs and remained there, out of sight, determined to hear what went on in the drawing-room.

"This writing," said Miss Wastefield, meaning the paper to which Mr. Frobisher had touched pen, "is without doubt Mr. Thistlewood's. It was familiar to me at once, for I've read his letter through a hundred times. But I don't understand."

She delved into a pocket for that very document, that precious communication that had been received at Pinewick, the one whose words guaranteeing deliverance she had committed to memory.

"This letter, Mr. Frobisher, which was posted to my father months after his death. It came from Nantle, from someone calling himself Gilbert Thistlewood. Do you know the man, sir?" she asked.

"I should," replied her neighbor, without hesitation, "for I posted the letter myself."

Miss Wastefield stared.

"You, sir? You are Mr. Thistlewood?"

Mr. Frobisher dipped his head in acknowledgment of the fact. "Gilbert Thistlewood at your command, Miss Wastefield."

"But your name is Frobisher."

"Ah, and a very real name it is, indeed. It's the elusive Mr. Thistlewood, I'm afraid, who is a creature of the imagination — mine."

"It was you who wrote to my father?"

"I did. I admit it. Once again, Miss Wastefield, I crave your pardon for my impudence."

Still disbelieving, Miss Wastefield unfolded that earlier letter — her salvation, as she'd termed it, and which she kept always about her person — and read aloud from it a few key lines, with a view to testing Mr. Frobisher's claim.

"You are the author of these words, sir? 'For I can assure you, Dr. Wastefield, of the sincerity of my intentions, in offering to relieve you of the burden you have so needlessly assumed.' And what of these lines here — 'I have the means to dispose of *that particular object,* discreetly and effectively, so that no taint will be attaching to you or your family from its possession thereof —'"

"'— and further to which, be assured, Dr. Wastefield, you shall never again have cause to be troubled by it, that you may depend on,'" said Mr. Frobisher, completing the sentence for her.

And so the proof was sealed.

"There was no exact address specified for return of post — merely instructions that the reply be sent in care of Sprig's coffee-house, to be called for. That is how my letter reached you? At the coffee-house, where you called as Gilbert Thistlewood?" said Miss Wastefield, her voice rising a little.

"Yes, for as Frobisher they know me not there. And it was that reply of yours that caused me something of a turn, I'll admit, and induced me to alter my plan."

"Your plan? And what plan was that, sir?"

"To receive the mirror from you, of course — or rather from your father, or your father's agent, as was intended. To put it in plainer terms, Miss Wastefield, I have a special facility for negotiating, in confidence, the sale or trade of such rare and precious objects as your mirror, through certain knowledgeable connections I've had the good fortune to develop. It's but one of several lines of business with which I concern myself."

Miss Wastefield, unable to grasp it all, sank down in Mrs. Juniper's favorite chair, with expressions of hope, dismay, happiness, bewilderment, and finally distrust vying for dominance in her lovely face.

"I still don't understand, Mr. Frobisher. How did you come to learn of the mirror? Why did you write of it to my father, who was then many months dead? And why did you call yourself Thistlewood? It was I who'd been given the mirror, nearly a year ago now, and I who answered your letter. I adhered to your instructions on my arrival in Nantle and awaited word from you at the coffee-house. Here I've been in the town these two weeks and gotten no line from you, not a hint of one — and all the while you've been lodging in the house of Mrs. Matchless next door! I think you had better explain yourself, sir."

The look she gave the handsome young Frobisher, despite her confusion, was a stern one, although it altered not a jot the glory of her features, nor the young man's admiration of them.

What followed was an account of how he had learned of a certain mirror of ancient polished bronze, which resided in the house of a noted scholar in far-away Pinewick, Crow's-end. It was through an acquaintance and occasional confederate of Mr. Frobisher's, who'd been employed in the antiquarian shop of Mr. Gerald Delancey, the late uncle of Mrs. Juniper. All unbeknownst to his daughter, Dr. James Wastefield had some time ago dispatched a letter of inquiry to Mr. Delancey, with whom he'd exchanged professional correspondence for many years, describing his daughter's receipt of the anonymous gift, and asking Mr. Delancey if he had any knowledge of the relic's origin. For it troubled Dr. Wastefield greatly just how the mirror had come into his house, and by whom it had been sent, and for what purpose. He'd suspected from the start that it had been taken from some valuable collection, but why it should have been given to his daughter, and in such a fashion, was a mystery. Like inquiries had been sent to other trusted colleagues, one at the Plaxtonian Museum of Salthead University, and another at the great rival institution at Penhaligon. The contents of Dr. Wastefield's letter to Mr. Delancey, who alas had died shortly after receiving it, had become known to Mr. Frobisher's friend there in the shop, and thence to Mr. Frobisher himself, who had investigated the matter for some little while before deciding to proceed.

Mr. Frobisher had dispatched a letter of his own to Dr. Wastefield — that same letter now in the possession of the scholar's daughter — offering to relieve him of his burden. For, like her father, Mr. Frobisher suspected that the mirror was, as he termed it, "hot property." There seemed no other answer, no other rationale for a birthday gift of such value from an anonymous giver. But as to *why* it should have been disposed of in such a way, or how it had entered the household, he admitted he had no knowledge.

Dr. Wastefield, being a man of virtuous and upright reputation — a scholar of unassailable integrity, as Mr. Delancey called him — had grown uneasy sheltering in his house an article of such questionable provenance. Indeed, he'd gone so far as to wonder if an enemy might not have placed it there to do him mischief, with a view to accusing him of thievery and blackening his character. But what to do? Should he openly acknowledge its presence and proclaim his innocence, or should he seek another way?

It was while he was exploring that other way that he met his untimely demise. He had thought to dispose of the mirror quietly, by returning it to those same shadowy channels whence it had come, through means known to him and Mr. Delancey and all professional men of an antiquarian bent. Mr. Frobisher, many miles distant, independently had formed the same opinion, and might have become that shadowy channel had the doctor lived. In his letter, Mr. Frobisher had offered the doctor a way out of his thicket, which Miss Wastefield, in her eagerness to be rid of the mirror, had caught at.

As for his use of another's name, well, it was accepted practice in the trade when brokering rare and precious items of doubtful ownership. Mr. Frobisher had the acquaintance of certain persons in Nantle and elsewhere, who likely could direct the mirror to its rightful home (or to a higher bidder perhaps, and at a handsome profit, a part of which Mr. Frobisher would realize — but of this he said nothing to Miss Wastefield). Unfortunately, by the time the young man had written off to Dr. Wastefield, the doctor was several months dead, which Mr. Frobisher didn't know, for Mr.

Delancey, too, had died. And that was how the daughter of Dr. Wastefield had come to open the letter meant for her father.

All this, Miss Wastefield realized to her amazement, and never once had her father confessed to her his own misgivings as regards the mirror!

It had been to Mr. Frobisher's considerable surprise to find that a Miss Jane Wastefield had responded to his letter. He'd never intended for Dr. Wastefield himself to make the long voyage, of course; rather, he had expected that a trusted agent would be sent to manage the transaction. It was the usual way such matters were handled. Never could he have dreamed, however, that that agent would be the doctor's own daughter, and that the doctor himself would be dead.

To Mr. Frobisher's further surprise, he'd discovered the agent lodging next door to him in Mrs. Juniper's house. Upon reflection, however, he ought to have expected it, he said, knowing as he did of the late Mr. Delancey's kinship with Mrs. Juniper. He'd made excuse to meet the new lodger, and was instantly in her thrall — this he rather boldly and unashamedly declared, to Miss Wastefield's own considerable surprise, not to say discomfort, and to the astonishment of Lucy on the stairs. As a result he'd found himself continually putting off Mr. Thistlewood's appearance, and instead taking every opportunity to speak with Miss Wastefield and to learn what he could about her.

He apologized again for intruding, at Mrs. Juniper's and Sprig's and elsewhere; it was that innate curiosity of his, he said; it was always getting him into fixes! She must have put him down for the most rude and impertinent fellow on the face of creation. But he wanted nothing more than to be of service to her, as Frobisher or Thistlewood or whoever; for he knew that once her errand had been accomplished, she would return to Pinewick, and that there was scant chance he would see her ever again.

"Be assured, Miss Wastefield," he told her, "you may depend on me to discharge my office as pledged, and relieve you of the burden of the bronze mirror exactly as I described. Nothing whatever has changed; you are to all effects your father's representative, and so Mr. Thistlewood shall be mustered post-haste. The mirror shall be restored to its proper sphere and none shall be the wiser for it."

Mr. Frobisher rubbed his hands and was prepared to apologize again for his impudence, as often as necessary in fact, so confident was he that success was in the offing.

With a sickening qualm the unhappy truth fell cruel and hard upon Miss Wastefield. Her heart sank within her. Her eyes dimmed, so bitter was her disappointment. Her single hope of rescue from her plight — that hope that had seen her through since the receipt of Mr. Thistlewood's letter — had been dashed to pieces there in the drawing-room of Mrs. Juniper.

Oh, God, God — so it all had come to nothing!

"You have no idea, do you, sir?" she said, meeting his eyes. "You have no idea what this mirror is, or of the evil it contains?"

"Evil?" echoed Mr. Frobisher. "My dear Miss Wastefield, I know nothing of evil, and hope I never shall. I know only that this mirror of yours is a prized memento from some vanished race — indeed, your father suspected it to be pre-Hellenic — which has been thieved no doubt from someone's private collection, for the museums deny any knowledge of it."

It was clear to Miss Wastefield that Mr. Allan Frobisher knew absolutely nothing of her burden. She had assumed too freely, had read too much into the simple words of his letter. He understood nothing of the evil dwelling in the mirror because he knew nothing of it, viewing the relic simply as one more rare and precious object to be brokered. Cognizant now of the full extent of her predicament, and of the hopelessness of it, and of the fact that there would be no help from Mr. Gilbert Thistlewood this or any other day — that she was doomed to be plagued forever by the vile, unholy thing that was the mirror — she rose to her feet.

"You are an impostor, sir," she declared, her cheeks flaming. "You are a swindler and a fraud, and most certainly no gentleman. You are a trafficker in stolen properties, just the sort of man Dr. Pinches warned me against. Well, sir, you have toyed with my hopes for long enough. You and your underhanded scheming have made a waste of my time. And you have tormented me as well, you and that Lanthorne creature, by following me about in the streets. Do you need money so very badly, Mr. Frobisher? You say you want the mirror, but beware of getting what you want! Well, you'll not have it now. You'll never have it, for our negotiations are at an end. You will be good enough to leave me, sir."

"But my dear young lady —" protested Mr. Frobisher.

"Please, sir! And you will not address me in such familiar terms."

"Miss Wastefield, by your leave —"

"Sir, it is *you* who will be leaving, and on the instant, too, or I shall call Mrs. Juniper!"

Mr. Frobisher was bewildered by her response; nonetheless he hastened off the treacherous ground. Miss Wastefield was in frightful earnest, and on the verge of losing her self-command, so much so that Lucy, hearing everything from the staircase, came rushing to her side.

For his part Mr. Frobisher was reluctant to yield, and as usual he delayed again. For several moments he stood in thought; then, consigning to eternal perdition his letter and the mirror and however many guineas that relic of ancient bronze might have brought him, asked to know what was the matter with Miss Wastefield? What cause had she to detest him so, when he'd offered her the means to achieve what she sought? Had she not agreed to his terms in her letter? Why else had she come to Nantle? He could understand her response to his delaying, that was natural enough, and to the necessary fiction of Gilbert Thistlewood. But hadn't he justified himself as best he could, and assured her of his good intentions?

But most of all what was this evil she spoke of, and of which she was so frightened?

As before, when they'd talked at Sprig's and she had suffered her bout of illness and gone home in a cab, his manner — so disarmingly generous for an impostor and a fraud — began to win her over.

"But I have most definitely *not* been following you about the streets," he assured her. "On my word of honor, Miss Wastefield, you must believe me. What cause would I have? As for Lanthorne — well, I know no more of the man than I've told you already. I have, in fact, not seen him since that afternoon at the coffee-house. But I'll admit I've developed some very grave doubts in his regard."

Miss Wastefield, observing him closely, seemed to know somehow that what Mr. Frobisher was telling her was the truth.

"Believe me," he went on, "I knew nothing of your father's death the day I wrote off to him, and it grieved me much to learn of it in your reply. It was a complete surprise to me when *you* answered my letter! Craving your pardon, Miss Wastefield, but won't you tell me something of this trouble that afflicts you? For I assured Jilly that I would help you."

"Oh, miss, I feel you may trust Mr. Frobisher," said Lucy. Despite her shortcomings she was on the whole a fair judge of character, as her mistress well knew. "If you please, miss, won't you confide in him? Perhaps he can help you. Asking pardon, miss, but we have come such a long way to be disappointed!"

"It would be an honor, Miss Wastefield, to be of service," said Mr. Frobisher.

"No one can help me now," said Miss Wastefield, sinking down again into Mrs. Juniper's chair. "You see, Mr. Frobisher, you are not what I thought you were. Quite the contrary."

"For that I'm sorry, and again crave pardon. But perhaps if you explained your trouble, I might be of help in a way you hadn't foreseen. I am not uninformed about the world and its ways, and have experienced more than a little something of life. Please consider, Miss Wastefield."

A pause followed while the lady in fact did consider, glancing at the earnest and ever-faithful Lucy, and then at the disappointing and ungentlemanly Mr. Frobisher, whom, whatever her opinion of him at the moment, she could not find it in her heart to dislike.

Yet there remained one great fear, one gnawing suspicion, that must first be eased.

"Before I begin, sir, there is a request I must make of you."

"Anything, Miss Wastefield."

"Will you show me the back of your head, please, Mr. Frobisher?"

A curious request indeed! Nonetheless the young man complied and, at Miss Wastefield's direction, sat himself down on the sofa by the window, where the light was a little stronger. Miss Wastefield, after a hesitant and frankly self-conscious start, spent a minute examining the long hair that covered the back of his head and neck, parting it carefully with her fingers and looking underneath it, as though searching for something there. More than once Mr. Frobisher glanced at Lucy for an explanation, but the poor girl hadn't a clue what her mistress was doing, or why.

Satisfied at length that all was well, Miss Wastefield resumed her seat.

"You will not think my request so odd once you have heard my story, Mr. Frobisher," she said.

What followed was the narrative she had related to Dr. Pinches the afternoon before. She described her wild dreams and visions, and the voices demanding she return to a place that did not exist, to atone for a transgression she knew nothing of. She described the faces in the mirror — the people whom she didn't recognize and yet strangely felt she knew. It was as if there was another part of her that belonged with them there, in the place called Kaftor.

"Who would give this mirror to me, Mr. Frobisher, knowing the horror it contained? And why?"

Sadly, like the doctor before him, Mr. Frobisher had no answers for her. He was by turns fascinated and appalled by each new detail of her story, and began to understand that far more lay behind this relic of ancient polished bronze than he could have imagined.

"What are these Triametes you speak of?" he asked. "I am not unschooled in the subject of mythology — for it is part and parcel of the trade — but I must admit I've never heard of them."

The brow of Miss Wastefield went dark as the shadow fell across it. At the same time she was gripped by an icy chill which Mr. Frobisher and Lucy could almost feel themselves.

"Then I'll beg leave to acquaint you with them," Miss Wastefield replied. "They came to me first in my dreams, and then in the mirror. They are here in this sundered world of ours — here indeed in Nantle — and can assume a human-like form when it suits them. They are everywhere about us, these agents of the lord Poteidan on earth. They are cruel, cunning giants, whose natural form is quite hideous to behold. They have a goatish beard, and nostrils jetting acid fumes, and teeth filed sharp, and a tall crest atop the head, and a pair of claws like pincers with which they seize their victims. They have two crimson eyes facing forward, and a third in the back of the head which they use to see behind them, so as not to be taken unawares. When in human form it is this third eye that betrays them."

While poor Lucy looked aghast and recoiled in horror, Mr. Frobisher leaned forward on the sofa with mounting interest. Admittedly he was a trifle suspicious at first. Cruel, cunning giants with crested heads and pincers and three burning eyes — preposterous! Like the doctor, he wondered, briefly, if Miss Wastefield's mind was disturbed, or if she was addicted to something in the narcotic or *aqua vitae* line. But he didn't think either was the case.

"Oh, surely such monsters as these Triametes can't exist!" Lucy begged. "Certain sure there are saber-cats and short-faced bears and teratorns — they're monsters enough for this world — but not three-eyed giants, miss!"

"What is worse than their appearance," said Miss Wastefield, continuing with her story — "what is *infinitely* worse, and even more odious, are their habits related to diet."

"How do you mean?" Mr. Frobisher asked. Lucy, wanting to hear and yet not wanting to, resisted an impulse to stop up her ears.

"These giants — these Triametes — these agents of Poteidan — they survive by eating the flesh of the human beings among whom they live. We — all of us, Mr. Frobisher — are their prey. If I do not return to this Kaftor, this place that no longer *is*, and of my own accord, they will come for me. Even now they are watching me — watching and waiting — I can feel it! It is for this reason that I am never easy for a second."

"*Oh, no, miss!*" Lucy cried out, her own flesh in a vivid crawl.

"I have been followed several times since coming to Nantle. It is these Triametes, of that I'm sure. Indeed, it had crossed my mind that — that perhaps you, Mr. Frobisher, were one of them."

"I see. Well, I am much obliged to you, Miss Wastefield, for absolving me of so heinous a connection," returned Allan, not without a trace of irony. "I gather then that you suspect Lanthorne of being one of them?"

She nodded slowly.

The young man reflected for a moment, then shook his head. "By your leave, I can't agree with you there. He's an odd fellow, true, and a bit grim, and not so talkative, but Lanthorne a — a three-eyed giant of a cannibal — well, it simply beggars belief."

Still he had to admit that it troubled him, his memory of that day in Mock Alley, when Mr. Tom Lanthorne had vanished as cleanly and completely as if he'd never been there.

"What I've told you I entrust to your confidence, Mr. Frobisher. I must rely on you — and you as well, Lucy — to repeat nothing of what you have heard to anyone. And so what am I to do now? You were my one hope, Mr. Frobisher. How am I to free myself of this curse of the mirror?"

Poor lady — how bleak was her prospect now, how thorny the thicket that surrounded her!

"Begging pardon, miss, but perhaps Dr. Pinches will be able to help you," reminded Lucy.

"What has the old rector to do with it?" Mr. Frobisher asked.

"He is to call today to view the mirror and advise me further," answered Miss Wastefield. "He is the only other to whom I have entrusted my confidence. But I'm not so sure now of the usefulness of his visit. I fear there is a power here that laughs at clergymen."

"He is a doctor of the Church, miss, and will know how to rid you of devils," said Lucy, so naïve in her beliefs, so trusting in her faith, her prayers, her holy men of the cloth.

Silly fool! What proof are your holy men against an unholy evil? What is your faith but a sham, perpetrated for their own gain by these same holy men? How little you know of truth in this world. Silly fool — how little you know of *anything!*

"Will you allow me to view the mirror as well, Miss Wastefield?" asked Mr. Frobisher. "For I have rather a personal interest in this relic of yours. Ah! I know what you're thinking, and what you think of me, but you need have no fear. I wish only to see the object for myself, this one time, to satisfy that curiosity of mine."

"Oh, it is a wicked, unholy thing, sir!" cried Lucy, for once knowing of what she blabbed. "Please, miss, you'll not be taking it from the trunk — not until the reverend doctor is here to safeguard you!"

Miss Wastefield gathered herself and, rising from her chair, turned to her young neighbor.

"You will please go now, Mr. Frobisher," she directed him. "It is for your own good. I can't subject you to forces and dangers none of us here can comprehend. I'll not see you come to harm, and risk suffering a fate similar to my father's. Dr. Pinches is, as Lucy says, a man of the Church, and may perhaps provide some shield against this thing. But you yourself must go, sir, and at once. Our bargain is canceled, as there is nothing either you or your friend Mr. Thistlewood can offer in the way of help now."

"But Miss Wastefield —"

"Go, Mr. Frobisher — please! For pity's sake. Now, we'll speak no more of it."

He cast her a look of entreaty, but saw there in her face, in the midst of her trouble, a determination that would not be overridden. He saw that there was indeed little more that a trafficker in stolen properties could do.

"It grieves me to have disappointed you, Miss Wastefield. Believe me, it was never my intention. I could hardly have known these secrets of yours, which on my word of honor I shall guard with my life. My only wish, dear lady, is to be of service to you."

He paused, as if debating with himself on the wisdom of going; but his decision had been made for him. So he took up his hat and with a regretful bow turned and went his way, leaving Miss Wastefield to her thoughts and fears and the attendance of her maid.

And what of the letter from Mr. Thistlewood? What of the letter Miss Wastefield had so longed to receive, and which that very day had been placed into her hand? What of the letter that was to have been her salvation, the answer to her prayers, the letter that was to have relieved her of her burden?

That letter — her longed-for hope, her dream, her way out of the thicket — she tossed into the drawing-room fire, unread.

CHAPTER THIRTY

No Sally-port

Escape was all but impossible, or so it appeared to Mr. Threadneedle. While the stripe-bodied scimitar-cat prowled the nave of the crooked ruined church of Deeping St. Magma, the grocer and young Tim Christmas and the ossuary-keeper, Mr. Moldwort, kept a watch on it from the triforium above. The creature had detected their scent but not their position, and was actively sniffing the air to remedy that deficiency.

"Might such a monster climb stairs?" the grocer inquired of Mr. Moldwort, in a low voice, as he and Tim huddled with their host behind the gallery-rail.

"Stairs? In a word, sir, yes, for sure enough your *Gladiodon* would climb a tree as soon as a stair," returned the human question-mark, he of the hunched shoulders, lean shanks, and enormous tar-stained boots.

"That door there," Mr. Threadneedle said, meaning the door to the newel staircase which Mr. Moldwort had latched and barred. "Will it stand fast, do you think, if the cat should make bold to assault it?"

"I believe it should, sir," said Mr. Moldwort, scratching his beard and thinking. "But that one down thar — she's a monstrous large specimen for a treacherous sword-tooth. I don't believe I've seen her round hyar afore."

"It's for certain a female?"

"Ah, female of the species, yes, sir. She has no mane, and as I've said, it's the lady of the house as does the shopping. Wondrous intelligent they are! And she looks to be an especially hungry one. You'll note the leanness about the flanks, sir."

"That's comforting!" was Mr. Threadneedle's response, which for Tim's sake he kept to himself.

"And short-tempered, too, by the look of her."

"Is she, just?"

"She's not found us yet," said Tim, in a hopeful whisper.

"Not as yet, my young friend," Mr. Moldwort agreed, "but she'll spare no pains in the attempt."

There followed more whispered discussion among the three of them, to devise some strategy to get clear of the monster. But with no sally-port available to them — no postern door, no vestry entrance, not even so much as an open window — there was quite literally no way out except that by which they'd come: the door of the south porch. And standing between them and that door was Mistress Scimitar.

All at once the cat paused in her tracks and looked up, her ears erect. Something of their whispers must have reached her hearing. Her eyes fixed themselves on the gallery-rail. She uttered a low growl, and came gliding stealthily toward the triforium for a closer look at what she saw up there.

"It appears she's spotted us," Tim whispered, ducking down.

"I fear so," Mr. Moldwort agreed.

"My word!" gasped Mr. Threadneedle.

"Have a peep at those canines thar," nodded the keeper of the bones, appreciative even in so dire a situation of the fine qualities of his treacherous sword-tooth of Moldwort.

The cat began pacing the floor beneath them, head upraised and jaws gaping, throwing look after hungry look at the gallery-rail.

"And an extra-super-large specimen she is!" enthused Mr. Moldwort.

The ossuary-keeper had spent his life among these creatures in this tarry, sinking ruin of an ancient town. Surely, Mr. Threadneedle reasoned, he knew what he was doing? Surely the three of them were safe up there in the triforium? After all, Mr. Moldwort had established his workroom there. Surely he wouldn't have done so if it were not impervious to monsters?

But of course, Mr. Moldwort had never *not* shut the porch door.

"No, sir, never seen this lady afore," murmured their host, confirming his earlier suspicion. "She's a stranger hyarabouts. What do you think of her, sir? What a specimen she is, even with the hunger in her flanks. Not so many of her sort in the pools — too wise for that! My friends, I'd like to have her skull-case."

"Let us pray she doesn't have ours first," retorted the grocer, a trifle upset by Mr. Moldwort's veneration of a horse-sized brute of a saber-toothed monster that could with the swipe of a single paw annihilate them all.

"Little fear of it, sir," Mr. Moldwort assured him, glancing round in mild satisfaction. He slid his hands comfortably into the pockets of his coat. "We're safe enough hyar in the workroom, I believe."

No sooner had he made this announcement than the cat, collecting herself for a spring, sprang — that is, she bounded from the floor of the nave straight up the side of a carved pillar and onto the arch, as easily as a house cat might leap a fence, and throwing her long forearms above her, reached out for the gallery-rail. They could hear the sound of claws scraping viciously at the moldings just below the rail, before the pull of gravity dislodged the beast and sent her crashing back to the floor. Roars of anger and disappointment followed, as the cat bemoaned her failure to seize the dainties she knew were up there — so near her grasp, and yet so far!

Mr. Threadneedle could scarce believe his eyes. He turned on Mr. Moldwort. "Did you know, sir, that that creature could leap to such a height?" he demanded.

"Ah, in a word, sir — yes. She can leap, sir, for as I've said, *Gladiodon* will climb a tree as ready as a flight of stairs. But I've never known one yet to reach the workroom. Howsoever, the truth of the matter is, sir," their host confessed, after a pause and a rub of his woollen cap, "as I've never known *Gladiodon* to find her way into the church at all, for yars at least, for as you know I've always kept shut the porch door."

The conscience of Mr. Threadneedle smote him for the danger he'd placed his young charge in. "I shouldn't have let you come along here," he told Tim. "I should have left you at the coach-house and floated it above the tar-pool. We should never have come seeking those clamps. I blame myself." For the first time in their adventures in tinkering together Mr. Threadneedle was gravely concerned, and he showed it. "The clamps may speed repairs but we could have managed without them. I fear we've run ourselves into a very serious scrape —"

"Not to worry, sir," Tim said, his eyes shining with all the eager-eyed confidence of youth. For once it was the apprentice whose job it was to encourage the learned master. "We'll find a way out, I'm sure of it, and make our way home to the Smithy."

Mr. Threadneedle, heartened by the lad's resolve, answered with a smile that lifted the wings of his meek little curled-up mustaches. For an instant his gray eyes twinkled again as of old.

"Ah! Well, sufficient unto the day is the worry thereof, I suppose — eh, young man?"

Meanwhile the scimitar-cat had resumed her pacing, her restless roars and growls echoing throughout the church. Without warning she made another leap and succeeded in burying her claws in the wood moldings of the gallery-wall. For several seconds she clung there, her body swaying in space, her hind limbs flailing about under the arch. The three above retreated to the barred door, and watched helplessly as the forepaws of the monster planted themselves, first the one and then the other, atop the gallery-rail. Slowly two tawny ears and a massive head began rising up behind them.

"She's coming over, sir!" Tim warned.

"We'll not want to stand round *hyar*!" said Mr. Moldwort, exclaiming the obvious.

But the cat's enormous weight, and the sustained effort of hanging by her forelegs as she strove to haul herself up, had exacted a price. Just as she seemed poised to clamber over the rail, her muscles failed her. Paws, head, and ears slowly sank from view. There came a dull crash and another outburst of growling as she plunged to the floor. More pacing ensued, more snarling, more glaring at the triforium.

Then, as if struck by a new idea, the cat began nosing about the foot of the newel staircase.

Mr. Threadneedle's attention turned to the shut door beside him, which was the only material object intervening between beast and prey should the animal choose to climb the stairs.

"You're certain, Mr. Moldwort, that this door is sturdy enough?" he asked. "For if it isn't, I fear we'll be very seriously menaced."

"Ah, 'tis sturdy enough, sir, or so I've every reason to believe," answered their host.

Cautiously they peered over the rail. The cat was sniffing about inside the arch that opened onto the staircase. Only her powerful haunches and her short brush of a tail were visible.

"Sir, what if we ourselves were to climb up into the tower?" Tim proposed. "Is there another door up there at least as strong as this one?"

Mr. Moldwort nodded. "Two there be, one in the ringers' loft and another in the belfry. Though there be no heavy bells now, for they were taken down yars ago to stay the tower from lurching over."

"In the tower the cat will have no rail to leap. And if we place two doors between ourselves and her, she may lose interest in our scent, and in us. But the doors *must* be sturdy enough, sir."

"That they are!" declared Mr. Moldwort. Thanks to young Tim, he could see a way out now, and that way was *up*.

But Mr. Threadneedle was not so confident. He saw only too plainly how the church was listing to one side, bells or no bells, like a ship on a heaving sea. He recalled his view of the tower from without, when he had stood in its shadow and observed its distressing deviation from the perpendicular. He was, he admitted, not so keen to go up in such a crazy, crooked structure.

"For it's rather a risk," he explained, "and while we're on the stairs, the cat will be gaining on our heels."

"Ah, beg your parding, sir," said Mr. Moldwort, politely but firmly, "but having this remarkable specimen down thar in the nave, we'll not want to be passing the night hyar in the workroom, I don't believe. What other choice have we now?"

"Passing the night!" cried Mr. Threadneedle, who, although he recognized the grimness of their situation, had hardly foreseen the need for a night's stay in the tottering church of Deeping St. Magma.

"Well, sir, by the look o' things, so long as *Gladiodon* scents us hyar, she'll await us in the nave, or worse, make even more brazen efforts to reach us. In the tower, howsoever, as your young friend says, she'll not scent us so well and may venture abroad in the night, which after all be the best time for shopping."

"I see. So she's likely to ramble off in search of other — ah — sport?"

"In a word, sir, yes."

"But first we must draw her away from the stairs," Tim pointed out.

"Then we must open this door hyar and make for the belfry, and be quick about it, too," said Mr. Moldwort.

But Mr. Threadneedle's aversion to the church tower remained strong. "I don't think we should chance it," he said, "for the tower appears to me none too steady a —"

His objections were silenced by a loud and hideous growling near at hand. The huge, padded feet had reappeared at the rail, their claws like butchers' blades digging into the soft wood. Behind them the two ears and massive yellow head had risen up like the demon in some hellish nightmare. One glimpse of blazing green eyes fastened on him was all the grocer needed to be convinced. For an awful instant his heart stood still in his chest.

"*Good — God!*" was all he managed to blurt out.

"Quickly, sir, quickly!" Tim urged, as he and Mr. Moldwort lifted the bar from the door. "We must get to the tower!"

The door was thrown open and the three sped through it, just as the cat came bounding over the rail into the workroom.

The triforium shook from the force of her monstrous bulk's striking it. With her nostrils blown wide, saliva dripping from her fangs and evil from her eyes, she was a fearsome spectacle. She was so much muscle and sinew and rippling hide, an entire horse-sized mountain of it in fact, with her tall head, craggy shoulders, and long sloping ridge of a backbone. And how much of her, too, was blazing eyes and a gleaming mouthful of teeth — oh, how very much of her was a gleaming mouthful of teeth!

Mr. Threadneedle shuddered. He could feel the cat's eyes burrow into him, just as its teeth and claws meant to do any second now.

And then the monster jumped.

She covered the ground in a single leap, just as Mr. Moldwort pulled the door shut. There came a rending crash as the body of the cat slammed against it. A thunderous outburst of snarling erupted; claws tore at the oak panels in a frenzy of rage. Mr. Moldwort clung to the handle for dear life, to prevent the door from opening, for there was no other means of securing it from that side. But the hinges were such that the door normally swung inward onto the triforium, and so there remained a scrap of hope. The cat would need to pull the door toward itself to reach them; perhaps by the time it had worked that out in its brain, Mr. Threadneedle said, they could be down the stairs and out at the porch door.

"*Down*, sir?" questioned Tim. "But I thought —"

"Into the tower!" Mr. Moldwort exclaimed, flinging his eyes tharward while continuing to battle the door-handle.

"No! Not the tower — the porch, the porch!" the grocer exhorted them.

It was, he saw, their opportunity not only to escape from the church of Deeping St. Magma, but to imprison the creature within it as well; Mr. Moldwort could then release it at his leisure. There was more than a little justice in this, the grocer thought — for wasn't it their host, the oily, tar-stained, bucket-booted keeper of the bones, who had gotten them into this pickle?

Down and round the stairs he went, with Tim close behind him. They heard a shout from Mr. Moldwort as he let go the handle, heard his boots crunching on the stone steps as he hurried after them. They would have to cross the nave on a long diagonal to reach the south porch, where they could fasten shut the outer door and gates and be safe at last from the monster. Let Mr. Moldwort deal with it then!

As they reached the foot of the stairs and cleared the arch, however, their luck changed — for what should they spy but *Gladiodon*, looking down at them from the rail and snarling as she prepared to hurl herself upon them.

Canny scimitar! No wonder there were so few specimens of your kind in the pits of asphaltum and bitumen!

There was no chance now of crossing the nave before the cat would be upon them. Indeed, even before the calculation had registered, the beast had sprung from the rail and plunged to ground no more than fifteen paces off. She whirled to face them, her head lowered, her ears flattened, a hideous growl rumbling in her throat. Her whiskers quivered as she opened her mouth wide for a full display of her cutlery. Eyes flaming, jowls slavering, the devil-faced monster coiled herself on her haunches, ready for another spring —

"*Back!*" cried Mr. Threadneedle, abruptly changing course. "Back, now! Quickly, quickly!"

No urging was needed. Spinning round on their heels, the three dashed under the arch in full retreat.

"Desperate-minded *Gladiodon*!" exclaimed Mr. Moldwort, bounding onto the staircase.

"Into the tower, sirs, into the tower!" Tim urged.

With their breaths, their thoughts, their very lives, and seemingly Time itself momentarily suspended, they fled up the stairs. Indeed it was the tower now or nothing. But because of the awkward lean of the church, what followed was, for Tim and Mr. Threadneedle at least, a considerable challenge, for they weren't used to negotiating a winding-stair at such an angle. It was like being on board ship: one was first pulled in one direction by an invisible force, and then had to strive against that same force in the other, as one went round and round on the stair. The pitch of the tower gave the staircase an illusion of rolling from side to side, putting unwary climbers at risk of seasickness.

But thought of the savage creature that was moving rapidly to overhaul them kept their legs working and their minds clear.

Close behind they could hear the ominous *pad! pad! pad!* of clawed feet, and the bloodthirsty roars of the cat as she lunged after them. Given her tremendous bulk, however, her progress was hindered some by the walls of the staircase, and by that same challenge inherent in a crooked tower faced by her fleeing prey.

Up and up Mr. Threadneedle and the others went, and round and round. Two stages they climbed before coming to a landing where the stone steps ended. They passed through a door and into a room of moderate dimensions, save for its height: its ceiling was formed by the roof of the tower, which lay still a goodly distance above their heads. They had arrived at the ringers' loft, which had housed the ropes by which the bells were sounded to call the faithful to service — when there still were faithful in Deeping St. Magma to be called, that is, and bells in her tower to be rung.

Once the grocer and Mr. Moldwort had scrambled through the door, Tim closed it after them and secured the bar. Not waiting to gauge the effectiveness of this measure, they hurried up the narrow stairs that skirted the tall chamber. They didn't slacken their pace until they reached the belfry, where there was another stout door to be latched and barred behind them.

Only then did they stop to retrieve what was left of their breath, and to wait and to listen, and perhaps to pray, their fate *vis-à-vis* the scimitar-cat still very much in the balance.

They peered into the ringers' loft with its sheer drop to the floor beneath. Given the lean of the tower, there was a certain dizziness attaching to this maneuver. From below came a host of muted roars accompanied by a forceful crashing. It was Mistress Scimitar, throwing herself against the door of the loft. The three waited with a tense, fearful expectancy for any sign that door, bar, or latch was giving way, that stout oak panels were being splintered by raking claws. The door shook, the bar rattled in its stanchions, but ultimately they held. After a time the roaring and crashing ceased; then, and only then, after a further period of silence and no shocks, did those in the belfry begin to relax their guard.

"A narrow squeak," said Mr. Threadneedle, still breathing hard.

"Ah, that'll shake up your liver, sir!" nodded Mr. Moldwort.

Never in all his years in Chamomile Street — even taking into account the times a saber-cat had crept into town from the foothills back of Nantle — never had Mr. Threadneedle endured so wild and heart-pounding an escapade, and so needless a one, as he had that day in Deeping St. Magma. He seemed genuinely surprised to find himself still drawing breath, surprised to find that his knees had not turned to water, that his body was not racked by fits of trembling, that his voice and lips were still capable of forming the elements of speech.

Mr. Threadneedle's was a short, thick, inoffensive little figure, one not exactly in trim for such exertion. His apprentice and Mr. Moldwort looked to have fared better than he in this regard, Tim because of his youth, and Mr. Moldwort because he lived here in Deeping St. Magma among his treacherous stinking blackpools and his skull-cases and his perambulating marauders of the sword-toothed variety.

Their escape from horrid fangs and ripping claws had been little short of miraculous. Still they were not out of the wood yet, or the tower.

The orange ball of the sun was going down in the west, bringing night to Gloamshire and to the ruined parish church and to the three pent up in its belfry. Mr. Threadneedle remained uncomfortable with the thought of a crooked tower, let alone the reality of it. It was disturbing how the room leaned to one side, and how insistently one was drawn to that side by gravity and threatened to be chucked out o' window. All they needed now was an earthquake and it would all be over.

And this from the noted captain of a flying coach-house, its mechanism so disabled it had been listing just as badly, and in the middle of the sky! Ah, but there was the difference — for a flying coach-house could *fly*, couldn't it, while a church tower, however heavenly and holy, never ever would.

Looking out at one of the aforementioned windows, which were tall and deeply recessed and open to the elements, the grocer and his companions examined the fast-vanishing scene. Little remained of the sun now but a pale glow along the horizon. Overhead a vertiginous swath of stars was blinking and staring in the eternal darkness. In the midst of it the tail of a shooting-star was briefly glimpsed, which caused young Tim to wonder aloud if it were such a thing as that as had brought about the sundering of the world.

The night proved to be a chilly one, as nights in Gloamshire usually are, but the three in the tower were dressed to withstand it. Gradually the anxiety and excitement of their escapade began to wane, like the sunset glow. There was little to do now but to wait, and to give thanks to Providence for such things as latches and bars and stout oak doors, and to talk over such things as the sundering, and Mr. Moldwort's own escapades among the stripe-bodied clan, and the state of the mechanism that powered the coach-house. Mr. Moldwort for his part was fascinated by this last topic, and wanted to know more about these remarkable hoverstones of Captain Clipperton's. As for Mr. Threadneedle and Tim, they were curious to know more about Deeping St. Magma, and what sort of place it had been before it had run so spectacularly to seed.

"Deeping St. Magma, 'twas a pottery town," Mr. Moldwort explained in his leisurely way. "Are you not familiar with it, sir? 'Twas all the rage a hundred yar ago, afore the tremors commenced, o' course. For shaking ground can be a bothersome thing for delicates like pottery, as asphaltum and bitumen is for houses of stone. But there's nowt to be done about it now."

"Of course — Magma ware!" said the grocer. "My late wife was quite taken with it. We have a number of fine pieces at the Smithy."

The town of Deeping St. Magma had been built by the potters of Gloamshire, and this church had been a "pottery church" endowed by the rich local merchants, which accounted for its spaciousness and the former splendor of its adornments.

"If you look closely at the columns in the nave, sir, you'll see the figures of the wealthy potters carved on 'em, and their names inscribed on all the plaques and monuments and such. And the chantry chapel, too, 'twas their gift, from the profits o' the pottery trade, which be all but extinct hyar-abouts. Ah, there's none left at Magma now but Moldwort."

Saying which their host uttered a little reflective sigh there in the starry light, and was quiet for a time.

Reflection being good for the spirit, Mr. Moldwort at length confessed that he'd refrained from telling his guests of the dangers roundabout so as not to frighten them away, in hopes they would come to the ossuary and view his skulls. He hadn't expected the rain to subside, he claimed, and so hadn't anticipated trouble. And he certainly hadn't meant to detain them so long, or under such circumstances.

Round midnight the moon came out, and in its cold light a shadowy form of great size could be seen moving about the grounds below. Mr. Threadneedle, who was on watch at the time, was uncertain as to its identity but he thought it was the cat. As for the moon, it didn't stay out, for clouds soon began moving in to replace those of the afternoon. It was the usual case, their host had informed them, that the rain didn't abate for long; but it was a blessing, too, for it was the rain that kept the cats down.

By morning the sky had grown as thick and lumpy as a bad porridge, and there was a cheerless drizzle leaking from it. Cheerless, but a cause for cheer as well, Mr. Moldwort pointed out, because it meant his visitors could return to their remarkable house with little fear of attack. But first they needed to learn if Mistress Scimitar was still hanging about the church.

They crept downstairs to the ringers' loft and approached the door there. They listened intently, and held their collective breaths as Mr. Moldwort removed the bar and swung the door aside. Nothing charged at them from the darkness beyond; there were no heavy fangs or ripping claws to contend with, only the newel staircase winding down and down.

On the lower landing they peered into the triforium and workroom, which seemed little damaged but for the splintered door. Carefully they eased their eyes over the gallery-rail and saw what appeared to be an empty church. To test this hypothesis Mr. Moldwort picked up a stray flagstone and hurled it over the rail. It made a loud sound as it struck the floor and broke into pieces. But it was the only sound to disturb the quiet; no others followed, no savage roars, no snarls, no growls. Nothing rushed out from the shadows to investigate. From this, Mr. Moldwort deduced that all was safe below.

A few minutes' searching among the keeper's stores brought to light the clamps Mr. Moldwort had offered his guests. Looking at them now in his hands, Mr. Threadneedle reflected, they seemed such needless and inconse-quential objects — certainly nothing to have braved so much to acquire, or endured what they had, merely to spare a few hours' labor. It was these clamps that Mr. Moldwort had used to lure his visitors to the ossuary to admire his tidy rows of polished skulls.

Their senses still very much on the alert, the three descended now to the floor of the church. Quickly and quietly they crossed the nave and slipped out at the porch door. There, in the moist ground beyond the gates, the impressions of four huge clawed and padded feet were discovered leading away from the church. Here then was the final proof that Mistress Scimitar had slunk off in the night.

Despite the security of the rain, it was a grim and vigilant march back to the coach-house. On this occasion Mr. Moldwort took with him a beadle's large-headed staff, for the reassurance of his guests — although a lot of good a beadle's staff would have done them had they run into Mistress Scimitar. Fortunately neither she nor any other wild beast of Gloamshire intruded upon their course.

When they reached the coach-house, they found it just as they had left it, thanks to the mooring-cable which had prevented it from slipping. Inside, the repairs were gotten to with relish, the clamps being put to use at once to mend the damaged chain-belt. They spoke little as they worked, for both master and apprentice were acutely mindful of the urgency of their task. Mr. Moldwort, having conveyed his visitors safely from the church, went off about his daily business, returning from time to time to observe the progress of the tinkerers and to bring them food and drink from his larder. Mr. Moldwort had never seen a house float in the air, and he was looking forward very much to having that pleasure today.

By afternoon the trouble had largely been rectified. Further repairs would be needed at the Smithy, of course, to improve the mechanism, but enough had been accomplished to get them there. The mended belt had been aligned again on its wheels, the cage-coils greased, and the springs that eased the action of the mangles carefully wound into position. Only then did Mr. Threadneedle take a moment to describe for their host, in the briefest terms, the principles of coach-house flight, and the varied functions of the appurtenances and apparatus.

He explained the action of the magnetic ore on the hoverstones, which gave the cage-coils the power to lift the house, and how that power was conducted through the ironwork running under the floorboards. He opened a compartment in a bulkhead and showed him how the walls and floor had been reinforced by lengths of ship's-cable, which were wrapped about the house to form a kind of internal sling, to ease the strain on the timbers and masonry. He then described the workings of the other coils, and the reciprocating springs, and the weather-vane on the roof and the mooring-bolts under the floor.

At the conclusion of it their host could do little but shake his head in wonder.

"It's a mystery to me, sir," he admitted, rubbing his head, "for I've never seen nor heard of the like round hyar, ever. An amazing thing it is!"

"I dare say that's understandable, for if one isn't familiar with the principles, it may seem a perfect skull-cruncher," the grocer smiled. Naturally he was rather proud of his achievement — his and Tim's — and like Mr. Moldwort and his skulls, was not above crowing a little.

As for the keeper of the bones, he was a trifle offended by the grocer's remark until he realized that "skull-cruncher" was just a figure of speech and not meant to be taken literally. As a parting gift he presented his guests with one of his specimens — one of his rare *Gladiodons,* as it turned out, and a handsome specimen it was, too — to remember him by. The grocer thanked him for this dubious honor, which young Tim at any rate was thrilled to receive. Their host then seized the hand of each of them in turn and wrung it heartily, and apologized again for detaining them, and assured them that should they ever return to Deeping St. Magma, he was always at their dispose.

And so it was time to go. The mooring-cable was loosed from the tree and returned to its storage locker. Mr. Threadneedle mounted to the helm and, taking the gig-wheel in hand, addressed his first mate at the mangles.

"Ready, Tim?"

"Ready, sir."

"Down coils, then, lad, and easy aloft!"

Round went the crank-handles. Belts and pulleys and wheels sprang into action, cage-coils revolved. All in a moment the coach-house seemed to take a breath and come alive. Mr. Threadneedle felt once more that welcome pressure under his shoes. The submerged foot of the house rose from the tar-pool. Then, with the swing-lamps rocking gently to and fro, the sad, sinking world of Deeping St. Magma dropped from sight in the windows.

Mr. Moldwort, bent forward on his long legs, craned his neck to the limit as he followed the house with his eyes. He managed a little wave of his cap in farewell to his rare visitor folk; then the house swung round in the air above his head, and before the human question-mark had time to gasp, it had sailed out over the fields in the west and was gone.

Left alone in the dreary expanse, the figure of Mr. Moldwort remained standing by the tar-pool for some few minutes after. With his beadle's staff planted beside him on the ground like a scepter, he looked like the last king of his shattered kingdom, marking the spot where the magical coach-house had stood. Then he shook his head again and ambled off, more stork-like than king-like, and returned to his crazy ruined town and his skulls and the solitary existence to which Fortune had doomed him.

Captain and first mate wasted no time in making for Truro and Smithy Bank. The obscuring clouds were everywhere about them as they sped out over the water and turned their marvelous flying craft gracefully round to the northwest. Given the conditions, it seemed wiser today to brave the rain and keep the mainland in view by following the sweeping line of coast. Instead of soaring above the cloud-tops, they would skim the misty under-belly of the cloud blanket, which ordinarily they didn't do so close to land.

With her lamps creaking, her shutters rattling, and her timbers groan-ing, with the weather beating at her walls and roof and water jetting from her eaves, the coach-house raced headlong into the wind. The prevailing westerlies were driving the storm right across her bow; yet on she flew. What a gem and a jewel she was, Mr. Threadneedle exulted, how staunch and skyworthy!

An hour passed, two hours, three, and still the coach-house pursued her rolling, swaying, windward course, tracking the coastline and the gray tide that was breaking upon it. The day by now was far advanced. Night would be falling soon, and still the wind droned on and the rain lashed at the walls and windows. How much farther yet, wondered captain and first mate, how much farther?

Then Tim, his eyes straining ahead, voiced a shout as he spied a blink of light in the gloom, a familiar beacon that grew swiftly upon his sight as he watched it. It was their clearest signpost on the long road home.

"It's Fairlight station, sir!" he called out.

"At last!" the grocer exclaimed, jubilantly. With a close eye on the com-pass, he swung the gig-wheel to larboard. "Prepare to reduce speed. All we need do now is adhere to our heading due west and follow our land-marks — first Fairlight and the channel crossing, then Span Rock, then Ri-dler's Tor, and finally Cold Harbor and the Smithy, like so many skittles in a row. Let's hope no one's noticed the coach-house has gone missing!"

"I must think of something to tell my mother and Kate, sir."

"Ah," said Mr. Threadneedle, recognizing the rub. "Well, you must tell them the truth, Tim."

"How may I do that, sir, without telling them all?"

"We shall have to work that out at the Smithy."

"Perhaps I'll say there were repairs to be made, and that they took longer than anticipated. For isn't that the truth, sir?"

The grocer frowned but, after a little consideration, had to admit that it was indeed the very truth.

It was at about this time that Mr. Hake Jobberley, tending to the light in the tower, happened to glance out of the windows of the lantern room. What he saw caused him to utter a startled exclamation and make a dash for the platform outside. Miss Jenny Mulks, about to descend to the lodge with her dog Christian, demanded to know what the matter was.

"There!" cried the wickie, pointing excitedly at an impossible something that was speeding across the sky. "There, missy, *there!*"

The pretty dark girl stepped onto the platform. There indeed, standing out plainly against the overcast, was a squarish something very like a house, half-timbered and lattice-windowed, with a pitched roof, chimney, and weather-vane. It went streaking past the light-tower, and on out over channel waters, where it was quickly lost to view in the fog that shrouded the islands.

Mr. Jobberley was in high glee, rejoicing and clapping hands. "What did I tell ye, missy? What did ye see, now, I ask ye? Are ye daft? Are ye drunk? Well, neither be Hake! Aye, ye know the verity of it now, don't ye? So ye'll please to tell yer uncle Matthew I ain't a tosspot and I ain't mad-dish. I've said it were something awful — something fantastic — a house where no house has business to be — and ye yerself know it now, too!"

The girl for her part said nothing. She could have said that it didn't matter, but that would've been a lie. She was in fact too amazed at the moment to say anything, too shocked to admit that her nemesis, the grizzled, mole-like Mr. Jobberley, he of the seal-skin headgear and flying bottle of gin, had triumphed.

"Aye, I told ye so, Miss Goody Two-Shoes!" said Hake, dancing a little jig on the platform. "They'll not be laughing at Hake Jobberley now. They'll be a-learning from him instead. Even the old dog there knows the verity of it! Don't ye, dog?"

"Woof!" said Christian.

CHAPTER THIRTY-ONE

Oysters in Every Style

The harsh, discordant rattling and growling of a pianoforte streamed unchecked from an open window of Captain Barnaby's house, like a noxious vapor from the grounds of Deeping St. Magma, and cast an audible pall over Jolly Jumper Yard.

"Bedad, sir, and will ye listen to that?" said Round-the-corner Jones, as he trotted into the Yard with his friend and associate, Mr. Moeran. "Divil take me if it bain't a breach of the peace."

"A caterwaul an' a thunderwup it is, joy, and a cacophony, too," nodded Moeran, "and murther it is to hear it."

"'Tis Miss Bright, 'tis what it is," Jones declared.

"Agh, the small pumpkin-head of a unmusical colleen is it ye mane?" returned Planxty, with a twist of the wiry paintbrush he called a mustache. "Jasus be marciful to us all!"

"True enough. Troth and faith, jewel, how Mother O'Guppy endures it in that house I'll not understhand. 'Tis enough to make a sthurgeon weep."

Mr. Havergal Skeffington Jones, freshly sprung from the lock-up, had come to Jolly Jumper Yard for the purpose of informing his cousin Mrs. O'Guppy of his surprising change of fortune, and to offer tidings of her daughter Niamh. As there was always the threat of discipline in the air at the captain's house, owing to the presence of the captain's wife, Mr. Jones and his colleague sought entrance by the most unobtrusive means possible — through the servants' door in the kitchen — so as not to draw the ire of the mistress of the house and dedicated teacher of music.

The first thing they came on in the kitchen was the captain's dog, who was busily at work on the spit-wheel. The dog recognized the two the moment he saw them, and so he stopped his racing and with eager tail and dripping tongue gave every sign of yearning for their company.

"Hero!" barked the cook, sternly.

At once the dog's tail was stilled, and after giving up a few brief, plaintive whines, he hopped back on the wheel — not only from obedience to the cook, but because his ears had caught the horrid rattling and growling from the music-room, which din the noisy wheel was particularly effective in drowning out.

Mrs. O'Guppy the housekeeper entered the kitchen then and, letting fall her mop, rushed to greet the visitors, begging to know how her cousin had come to be liberated from the grip of the evil unseen Comport. Being so plied for an explanation, Mr. Jones gladly offered one: that three virtuous strangers from far away north, being impressed with his many admirable talents and qualities, had taken pity on him and settled his debts out of the goodness of their hearts, his predicament having quite mollified the marrow of their bones and moved the bowels of their commiseration.

He went on to inform his cousin that young Niamh had visited him there at the sponging-house, and had played a host of delightful airs for him on her violin, and had seemed in the twiggest of health. Mrs. O'Guppy, grateful for even such spare news of her child, could scarce restrain a watering at the eyes, despite her conviction that the violin was an instrument something unnatural for a woman and a tool of the devil.

"For sorra a thing I have left on this earth now but my darlin Niamh, the child of our fambly, and still she'll not have the least to do wid me. 'Tis enough, sometimes, to make a body lose heart."

In this she was consoled some by her cousin, and by Moeran, too, before they were disturbed by the arrival of the captain's busy wife and overseer of his household.

Mrs. Barnaby, the newcomers had been advised, was in a bit of a temper today and inclined to be snappish. She had come now from the music-room, and she looked it. She was all grimness and frustration, all irritation, exasperation, if not outright aggravation. The cause of her displeasure was the same as it always was on this day of the week — Miss Bright, whose relentless inaptitude had made a mockery and a laughingstock of the sublime glory of music. No amount of hard teaching, no amount of rapping of fingers or of brains, had injected so much as an atom of proficiency into the child, or ever would. It was hopeless; one might as well have stitched the ear of Mendelssohn to her head and expected it to be musical.

Such noise may have been enough to make a sturgeon weep, but it was certainly sufficient to cause Mrs. Barnaby to flee the music-room for the refuge of the kitchen. But though she was quick to complain about her pupil, she couldn't deny that Miss Bright paid well — or rather, her parents paid well. With the improvident captain of the *Salty Sue* for a husband, Mrs. Barnaby needed all the money she could lay her hands on, and music fees were money. The finances of the household were in a precarious condition, and so she was left with little choice but to endure Miss Bright, to the considerable peril of her nerves and the dismay of her neighbors in the Yard.

Round-the-corner Jones, no stranger himself to pecuniary embarrassment, could well appreciate such a state of affairs, and made bold to say so.

"And what would you know of it?" Mrs. Barnaby retorted at once.

"Me sarvice to yer misthress-ship," he fawned, ducking his head and smiling, "but axing yer pardon, 'tis not so long sinst I wor meself in circumsthances of a like nature, true enough."

Mrs. Barnaby suddenly crossed her arms and fixed him with a very sharp glare. "What the dickens are you doing here?" she asked. "I thought you were in the Compter."

"Rumors, yer misthress-ship — rumors cruel and parjured! Shure, and 'twas not the Compter but *Comport's,* and glad I am now to be clear of it. Me friend an' fellow Moeran here and meself, we've come to yer charruming abode to pass time wid Mother O'Guppy — as happens to be me dear cousin by marriage-vow, don't ye know — on purpose to spirit her up wid word of young Niamh."

"Well, you've had your time for spiriting with my housekeeper, I think. Now you may go your way, and take that scurvy one there with you."

By this last she meant Planxty, who answered with a look of injured surprise, like a horse that has taken a knock on the muzzle.

"Och! on the conthrary, dear joy —" he began.

"Are the two of you in league with my husband?" said Mrs. Barnaby, interrupting him. "For you seem very likely companions of his. Drinkers and dicers! Spiriting up my housekeeper, were you? It's little wonder we never have money in this house. Well, there's nothing to detain you here — no tumblers or tankards, no sugarplums, and no gaming. We're a meager household and of scant interest to tosspots. Now, off with you — and step lively!"

These words she uttered just as some particularly frightful-sounding chords from the music-room set her and the others to gagging. If her husband the captain had been present, it would have crawled his flesh and stood his silvery hair on end. And it would have stood the hair of Jones on end, too, were it not so thickly oiled and cemented to the crown of his head.

The dedicated teacher of music took in hand a strong cup of tea that had been brewed for her by the cook and drank it down. So fortified, she glared again at Jones and Moeran, then whisked round and returned to the music-room, girded for battle with the unrelenting Miss Bright.

Following Mrs. Barnaby's suggestion, the vagabonds smartly took their leave now of Mother O'Guppy. As Mr. Moeran had gotten himself a little cash, and Mr. Jones a few gold boys from Fred Cargo with which to set himself right, both gentlemen were feeling rather flushed as they swaggered off into town.

They managed to make their way without incident to the Axe and Compasses, where for some hour or more they regaled the patrons with the tale of the rescue of Jones, much enlivened by *aqua vitae,* and much enhanced besides, with many an added twist and exaggerated detail that Mrs. O'Guppy had not been privy to. The liquor, however, like the money, soon went to their heads, and eventually they found themselves obliged to remove their persons from the premises, at the very strong urging of the landlord. Tumbling out into Ship Street, they staggered along that broad avenue for a while until, after a number of false starts and unproductive sallies, they found themselves in the neighborhood of Slopmonger Mews.

"By the by, joy — d'ye know the reason that sthranger from Cargo had for callin' on ye? D'ye know what information it was he desired?" asked Planxty, yawning, and scratching at his horsy chin, as he and his colleague wended their way through the lines of stables.

"He was lookin' to find some person or other, as ye told me, Moeran — so fargetful y'are! But he never spoke of it. Why that was I can't meself think, and a dhreadful shame it wor, too, for I'm lookin' to make a raputation in that trade, and at no fancy price neither."

"Shure y'are!"

"I'd av been much obliged to him if he'd engaged me sarvices, for 'tis fresh tinder alaways as keeps me chimly smokin'."

"Changed his mind he did, I suppose. Mayhap it was the goodness of his heart afther all as saved ye."

"What was the name of the one he wanted found?"

"Never heard of him meself. Cove called Squailes."

Even in his present condition, Mr. Jones started at the name. He turned to his companion and gripped him by the shoulders and stared him in the face.

"Squailes? Bedad, Moeran — is it *Jerry* Squailes ye mane?"

Little Planxty, alarmed at being so accosted, answered with a nod; whereupon his friend released him, and then dealt him a reproving thump.

"By the powers, Moeran, ye ignorant spalpeen! D'ye not know Jerry Squailes?"

"That I do not," said Moeran, pushing back his hat from his brow, as though hoping to improve his memory by better illuminating his brain.

"Ach, 'tis Porter, jewel — *Jerry Porter!* The friend of our ould and late fellow O'Kilcoyne, God rest his sould. D'ye not remimber how once he told us of his fellow fish porter Squailes, him as had took to callin' himself Porter?"

Mr. Moeran shook his head, for which he was rewarded with another thump.

"Troth and faith! Well, ye *should* remimber, Moeran, for it'll not be requirin' a genius to do so. Porter the fish porter be Squailes! Have ye no recollecktion of it, sir? Musselgate Fish Market! Augh, bedad — sorra a minute more I have to waste upon ye, Moeran, for our mansion-house awaits. Sthrike me crooked if we bain't soon in the everlasting tin!"

"How d'ye mane, joy?"

"What d'ye suppose the trusting cove'id give now for sich inthelligence?"

"The trusting cove?"

"The vartuous gintleman wid the fancy waistcoat and gold watch-chain. The jingling sthranger from Cargo."

"D'ye mane the toff gintleman, Jones? Him as bailed ye out of Comport's for no sane reason, and spared ye from Turtle Sthreet? Is that the one ye mane, joy?"

"Shure as Shrovetide, the very same. What d'ye suppose he'll give to learn where Squailes be found? What d'ye suppose I'll have now for me pains? Put that and that togither, sir, and think on't."

The eyes of Planxty blossomed in their sockets. "Och! and what then of yer no fancy prices? By gannies, the gintleman's already paid yer debts for ye and gi'en ye coin asides, and still ye'll be axin' more of him?"

For this he received another thump.

"Moeran, ye fool! Where is it he's lodging? The toff gintleman, and his prim little colleen of a wife, and the fat old custard?" Jones demanded.

"By gannies, 'tis a schemin' scoundrel y'are, joy! Will ye ne'er be shamed like a decent Christian?"

"And ye're a born eediot if ye'll not grasp yer hopporthunities. Now where be their abode, if ye plase, sir, as I've quite forgot — which house?"

"It's at the Crozier they are."

"Then it's to the Crozier we're goin', jewel, to call on the toff gintleman and offer our sarvices in regard of Squailes — then 'tis in the clover we'll be, in regard of tin!"

The two vagabonds exchanged a few sly winks and grins and, with gladdened hearts and exalted expectations, staggered off through the mews and into the smoky lane hard by.

They had not gone far before Planxty, recalling his friend's prior injunction, touched him on the arm and advised him to proceed no farther, for ahead lay the oyster saloon of that ugly maggot of a master Arifay, and Moeran was to "curb him in his sthride" if ever he caught his friend tending that way. But Mr. Jones, in his newly emboldened frame of mind, waved this objection aside. If the lily-livered weasel be there, he declared, the odious Jack-a-Lent, the great bald gargoyle of an oyster-masthur, well, too bad it was for him! Besides which Mr. Jones remained flush with coin, and was in a mood to cast his eyes again on the delightful Miss Ingum ("a splendid crayture!") and pay her his compliments.

Entering the shop, they found it to all appearances void of company. The little circular basins on the counter were laden with oysters and others of their brethren, just as before, and the shelves behind crowded thick with bottles of port and brandy and ginger-beer, also as before. But the counter itself was unattended, and the aisle and boxes vacant. No shapely damsel of a Miss Ingum, all pretty blue eyes and yellow curls of her, awaited their pleasure; indeed no one, it seemed, was about the place.

"It's disappointed I am," said Round-the-corner, "as there be no sign of the fair deceiver, and so no hopporthunity of her to make amends to me pride."

"Och! by the Holy, joy, she's cut up about that, I'm shure," said Moeran.

Grasping his opportunity now, Mr. Jones prepared for himself a nice little dish of oysters and, pulling down a ginger-beer from the shelf, invited Planxty to follow his example. His friend and associate declined, however, being too much engaged in casting glances about the shop and out of window for the gargoyle Arifay.

But no one, least of all the proprietor, came to interrupt Round-the-corner in his feast. Having finished off the oysters, he stood up and, with ginger-beer in hand, coolly peeped behind the curtain back of the counter. At the same time, his friend Moeran urged him not to venture there, and not to chance too much, for shure 'twas a mistake an' a trespass. It was clear that Miss Ingum was nowheres about, and so should they themselves be, in view of the horrid Arifay and his inevitable return, likely sooner rather than later.

The room behind the curtain was something of a jumble, its light deriving from a few greasy candles and a low fire where a caldron slung from a chimney-hook was quietly venting steam. There was a sanded floor, and a clutter of rude furnishings, and a spittoon that had seen much recent use. A staircase on the right led to an upper level of the house, from which no sounds were heard. Another curtain, one of faded damask, had been drawn across one side of the apartment. An odd arrangement, thought Jones, and being by nature a curious sort, he pulled the curtain back. Behind it he found a long, narrow table with a row of hairdresser's head-blocks on it, and ladies' wigs displayed on the blocks.

"Hollo! I'd no idea there was a Misthress Arifay," said he, staring at the sight. Then he shrugged his shoulders and thought no more of it. If there was indeed a wife, then he pitied her. Sipping some of his ginger-beer, he trotted over to the caldron and raised the lid.

"By the powers, joy, we must leave the place!" Moeran urged. "It's plain the crayture Arifay be somewheres near — his dinner that must be there in the pot. The gargoyle, he'll not take kindly to yer rummaging about his house. Ye'll recolleckt all he told ye that last time, how he reprimanded ye most sevarely and threatened the sprig of shillelagh."

"Och, Moeran, don't be frettin' so! Mayhap ye should sprinkle a dust of the holy water over yerself, to ease yer fears. Bedad, it smells delicious," said Jones, inhaling deeply from the caldron.

"What say?"

"The weasel's grub here. Looks to be stew, it does — or is it soup?"

"Is it sheep's-head? For it smells a bit like."

"Bain't sheep's-head," said Jones. "Cock-a-leekie, mayhap, or a carbonado, wid onions, potato roots, an' greens. Agh, 'tis for shure a stew o' some greasy kind —"

He stirred the pot with a ladle and examined its contents in more detail. Some peculiar triumph of the culinary art it must be, he thought, the work perhaps of the mysterious Mrs. Arifay. He transferred a sample of the liquid to his tongue. Immediately his eyebrows rose.

"Delightful!" was his approving verdict.

He plucked some bits of meat from the caldron. They, too, were delightful, although the taste was unfamiliar to him. He ate another piece, and another, both equally delightful; but still the nature of the meat eluded him. He pondered it for a time, observing the various ingredients of the stew afloat on its oily surface, until the thought crossed his mind that something was *not quite right*.

All at once he shivered and, glancing round, stared very hard at the wigs on the blocks.

"Wait a bit, now. Wait a bit! Tell me, Moeran — what color be that last headpiece there? That one upon the end?" he asked.

"Yallow. Yallow and curlied, like the hair of Miss Ingum. By gannies, joy, d'ye think what I think? I'd not the least notion 'twas a wig she wore. Shure, it seemed her own hair to me. Bewigged, bedad — and so young an' well-thriven a colleen!"

"Bain't what I'm thinkin', Moeran," said Jones, with mounting anxiety. "Bain't what I'm thinkin' at all, at all. What color be the piece next of it?"

"Yallow, too, but lighter an' sthraighter — like the hair of Miss Conyers as was here afore Miss Ingum. For ye know, joy, he's had a sthring of the leedies to attend in the shop — bedad, a new one it seems every week!"

"Like the hair of Miss Conyers," Jones repeated to himself, struggling to clear his brain of the *aqua vitae* and ginger-beer. "And the one next of that?"

"Black and curlied like Miss Grime, as purceded Miss Conyers."

"And the next?"

"A purty soart of red, like a sthrawberry roan."

"Sich as might discribe Miss Chennery?"

"That's it, joy — Miss Chennery, she as came afore Miss Grime."

There followed a queasy silence on the part of Jones. A strange, cold, ugly, icksome feeling stole over him, chilling him to the bone. Beads of moisture popped out on his forehead.

"What ails ye, joy?" Planxty wanted to know. "For ye look a bit peculiar. Bain't the vittles so fine?"

"Moeran," said Jones, in a voice as sick as his stomach, "come here, if ye plase, this instant minute, and tell me what ye think o' this."

His friend obediently joined him at the caldron, and peeped into it.

"Cast yer eyes over the grub there," said Jones. He stirred the contents a little, and as he did so, some more chunks of meat appeared, one or two of which looked rather like human fingers — looked so much like fingers, in fact, that there was a dainty nail at the end of each.

A round, creamy object like a cue-ball floated to the surface and drifted onto the ladle. The object was observed to have a small round spot on it. Then a second globe emerged and came to rest beside the first. Together they seemed to be peering at the vagabonds like a couple of eyeballs.

Like his friend before him, little Planxty turned to stare at the wigs on the head-blocks.

"Ah, shure, it's a ridiculous notion," said Moeran, in a faintly scoffing voice, but succeeded in convincing neither himself nor Jones.

The two gentlemen swallowed deeply and uncomfortably. A tide of perspiration was oozing from both their foreheads, as wave after wave of heaving seas washed over their brains, plunging them down and down in a noxious smother of foam, then up and up on a vast tumbling spume of waters. No, no, it was not so ridiculous a notion after all —

"Holy Mother of God!" gasped a horrified Planxty.

His friend Jones proceeded to turn as green as a leek — as green indeed as any of the leeks that were swimming there among the fingers and eyeballs of Miss Ingum. His stomach rebelled against it. Dropping the ladle, he clamped hands to mouth to suppress a violent impulse that was welling up from his nether regions.

"I really think me senses are leavin' me," he moaned.

"'Tis murther, it is!" cried his colleague. "Divil take us, joy, if we don't get clear o' this hell!"

"Too late, bedad, Moeran — for there be the very divil himself now!"

It was true. There came a rush of heavy feet on the stairs, and lo! standing at the bottom of them was the figure of the oyster-master Arifay. The combined light of the flames and candles played across him eerily, like the fires of Hades leaping and dancing round Beelzebub. The figure itself remained perfectly still but for the tall white head like a boiled egg, which was turning slowly from side to side in its collar as its eyes searched the dimness of the apartment.

Mr. Jones and his colleague scarcely dared to breathe, for fear those eyes should spy them where they cowered behind a brewing-tub.

Then the oyster-master swatted the fur cap from his head, and glided stealthily and crouching into the room. With his back to them and his cap off, they could see the ragged scar running down the side of his head, and something else, too — something that looked very much like another eye glowing crimson in the back of that head. This third eye like the others was scanning the apartment, but in the opposite direction, as the tall head swiveled this way and that.

The shock of it caused Moeran to utter a muffled cry.

Instantly the head of the ogre spun round.

"Villains!" he growled, fixing them with the two orbs under his livid brow. "Did I not tell you your jolly fellowship was not welcome here?"

"Where — where — where be Miss Ingum?" demanded Jones, in a display of bravado which he quickly regretted.

The proprietor put hands to hips and laughed derisively. "Why, villains, it's oysters in every style, is it not? Have you not worked it out for yourselves, then?" He gave a jerk of his head toward the caldron. Then his lips curled themselves into a sneer; he bared his teeth and took a menacing step in their direction.

"And now, villains, it's time you were diving into the pot with her," he threatened.

"And so we'll be leavin' now, yer worship," said Jones, raising his muffin-cap and grinning. He and Moeran started to back themselves towards the door. "Pray let us not incommode yer masthurful self —"

"You'll be going nowhere," said the oyster-master, in a voice that portended nothing pleasant. Suddenly he dropped his arms to his sides and seemed to freeze in place. As he stood thus, his face began to twitch and squirm. Then his shoulders followed suit, and his great muscular arms, the flesh pulsing and throbbing in a hundred places, as though something inside of him was struggling to get out.

All at once the scar on the side of his head parted, like a seal coming undone. The head proceeded to divide itself in half along the scar, then collapsed in sagging folds like the hood of a cloak, as another head extruded itself from the first. It was a supremely vile, dark, and ugly head, and entirely unhuman, with a thin-shelled, bony crest rising from it like a sail. This second head had three eyes in it as well, a pair before and one behind, all glowing redly wicked, and sported a goatish beard in place of the square black one of Arifay. Two huge, curving pincers extended from the angles of the jaw, their tips meeting some foot or two in front of the mouth. It was a mouth lined with rows of sharply filed teeth, and above it broad nostrils belched forth acid fumes.

While this unspeakable transformation was taking place, the body of the oyster-master was undergoing other changes as well, increasing rapidly in height and breadth before the terrified gaze of Jones and Moeran. As it swelled full large, its old skin and its clothing, unable to keep pace, were blown off it and tossed aside. Out of this emerged the creature that had been Arifay, all monstrous shoulders and giant, hairy limbs of it, riding on two hoofed feet — a creature of horror and nightmare, and one that was growing ever larger with each passing second, as though inflating itself like a balloon.

The air in the room was quickly becoming poisonous from the exhaled acid, which stung the eyes and lungs of the vagabonds. Then there came a *thump!* as the expanding torso of the monster collided with the ceiling. The creature that had been Arifay was growing too big for the room. It had gotten itself wedged between two ceiling-beams, and was threatening to fill the entire apartment with its hideous bulk.

With a *snap-snap* of its pincers, the creature made a lunge for the puny invaders of its realm. But their very puniness turned out to be the salvation of Jones and Moeran, for they were quick and agile things by comparison to the giant, which was so large now it had scant room to maneuver. Squatting low with its back and shoulders and hideous head pressed against the ceiling, for the moment it was trapped where it crouched, unable to reach them.

This served only to enrage the monster more, and caused it to give vent to a bloodcurdling bellow, which, being amplified by the hollow passages in the crest atop its head, threatened to shatter the very fabric of the house —

"V-I-L-L-A-I-N-S-S-S-S-S-S!"

"Holy jumping Jasus!" cried Planxty, gaping in stupefied amaze at this glimpse of perdition.

Faster even than Jesus did they jump then. Mr. Jones nearly chased himself out of his coat as he and Moeran fled through the curtained doorway and out the shop-door and into the smoky lane. Toward Slopmonger Mews they scampered on flying feet, and not once did they stop to look behind them. Like bolts of lightning they flew, dashing pell-mell through narrow alleyways and lines of stables which the giant would have difficulty traversing, and executing many sharp and unexpected changes of course designed to make their tracks harder to follow.

And so on and on they ran for their literal lives, while giving not another thought to the delightful Miss Ingum, or Miss Conyers, or Miss Grime, or any of the other shapely young dears of a flirtatious bent who had tended the counter at the oyster saloon, and paid the price for it.

CHAPTER THIRTY-TWO

They Cometh from Afar

It was afternoon, and Dr. Pinches was walking with a hurried step along the road in the vicinity of Chamomile Street. As he went, he was seen to glance impatiently now and then at the face of a very old pocket-watch, which dwelt at the bottom of a very old waistcoat-pocket. The learned doctor, it seemed, was late. He'd been detained at the rectory by a particularly troublesome parishioner, and was making as speedily as he could for his appointed meeting with Miss Wastefield to examine the marvelous mirror of ancient polished bronze.

Caphtor! Could the mirror really have come from that mysterious, shadowy land of vaunted legend? An artifact of ivory and bronze surviving from the days of Minos, Sarpedon, Rhadamanthys — what a magnificent treasure, if treasure it was, proof that legend had been bronze-solid reality! The implications of it staggered him. His love of learning would at last be rewarded, his talents acknowledged by his peers and the hierarchs of the diocese — even by the Dean himself! No mere dockside clergyman now, his humdrum mode of living would be transformed into a glorious retirement. Why, with such a discovery in hand, he mused, he, the Rev. Giddeus Pinches, D.D., could re-write his famous Greenshields!

Once in Chamomile Street he closed swiftly upon the abode of Mrs. Juniper. Ahead of him he spied Mr. Milo the postman, and heard him, too, whistling and hammering his way down the street. As the doctor hurried on toward the lazy-eyed man of letters, and Mr. Milo came whistling and hammering toward *him,* it was clear they were bound to meet — which they did, on the flower-pot-garnished steps of Mrs. Juniper's house.

Young Mr. Milo wasn't surprised to find Dr. Pinches calling there, but he *was* surprised to find that the doctor was calling on Miss Wastefield rather than Mrs. Juniper. In this the poor stricken young man couldn't help but be interested. Of course, after his recent talk with Mrs. Matchless he'd resolved to cure himself of his infatuation with the beautiful young lady from Crow's-end — and indeed, he thought he had. Still, it was difficult for him to hear news of her without pausing in his rounds, difficult to resist lingering on the step to gather whatever stray words of conversation might drop into his ear *vis-à-vis* the object of his recent affection.

Then it was the doctor's turn to receive a surprise when the housemaid informed him that Miss Wastefield was not there. A letter had arrived no more than an hour before, by private messenger, which appeared to have upset the lady very much. So said Lucy, who had come downstairs and, having heard the doctor's inquiry, confirmed that her mistress had indeed gone out, and that the doctor's visit evidently had slipped her mind.

Mrs. Juniper then made a flowery entrance in the hall, and apologized to Dr. Pinches for her lodger's absence. On further questioning it was learned that Miss Wastefield had murmured something about Jekyl Street before going out; but what there might be in Jekyl Street to interest her, no one knew.

The doctor was puzzled, and Mr. Milo was puzzled, and so was Mr. Frobisher — for he happened to be passing by the steps just then, on his way home, and had overheard some of the conversation. Mr. Frobisher was not only puzzled but concerned as well. He remembered what he'd been told of Miss Wastefield's mysterious caller — that caller who had failed to identify himself — and of her belief that she was under a constant watch. And so he suspected that what awaited her in Jekyl Street was trouble.

What else could it be? What else was in Jekyl Street? There was a pawnbroker's, and the livery stables, and an old-clothes shop, and the sponging-house, and the cheesemonger's, and any of several inns and ale-houses. Whose request could have drawn her to that neighborhood, he wondered, but that of her mysterious unknown caller? At this, Mrs. Juniper turned to Dr. Pinches and, with an emphatic motion of her head and the flowers in her hair, demanded what was to be done to save her lodger?

It was decided that they would set out at once to find Miss Wastefield, the doctor and Mr. Frobisher, for it was possible she was in the way of danger. The doctor, mindful of the unsettling particulars of his talk with her, could do no less. And so for the moment all thought of glory and Green-shields and the mirror of ancient polished bronze was dismissed from his mind — it was big of him, but it was good of him, too — as he and Mr. Frobisher set off at a rapid pace for Jekyl Street.

As for Mr. Milo, he was left there on the steps, sorely wishing he could go with them but knowing he could not, for he was chained to his letter-bag and his rounds.

Mrs. Juniper gave a long shake of her head and hair with the flowers in it. "Such a troubled lady," she sighed, "for so young a lady. Thieves and cut-throats and their messengers here in Chamomile Street — and at our house! Where is Jilly? Jilly, where are you?" she called up the staircase in the hall. "Jilly, are you there? Are you safe?"

"Safe, Mother!" returned a small voice from the rooms above.

There had indeed been a letter delivered that day to Miss Wastefield. The handwriting she knew well, like Mr. Thistlewood's, and so she didn't need to read the name there to know that the writer was — *Martin Somerset*. But the sight of it produced a strange response in her. A mixture of wonder and relief, affection, joy, hope, fear, anger — all were there to one degree or another, in shifting combinations, like clouds and sun roving across the turbulent landscape of her heart.

The writer had asked if Miss Wastefield might grant him leave to see her, and was she angry to learn he had followed her to Nantle? He had gone himself one day, he admitted, to the house in Chamomile Street to confirm that she was lodging there. He hadn't left his card chiefly from un-certainty, for he remained bewildered by the enigma of her flight from Pinewick. He wasn't sure how his presence would be received. And so he'd requested an interview now, but as Miss Wastefield had no great store of time at her disposal, or patience for that matter, she had taken it upon her-self to call at once, unannounced, at the inn where he was stopping. That inn was the Bunch of Grapes, and it was in Jekyl Street.

It was a startled Mr. Somerset who opened the door of his room to find a young woman in cloak and furs standing in the passage, with a lively lit-tle monkey on her shoulder.

"My word — *Jane!*" the young man blurted out.

It was, as novelists like to say, an awkward moment. Mr. Somerset fell back a step in surprise; as for Miss Wastefield, her reaction was more diffi-cult to gauge.

"Martin! How? How?" she demanded. "How did you find me?"

Little Juga seemed nearly as interested in his reply as Miss Wastefield, chirping and chattering there on her shoulder, his expression so clownish and comical, and so changeable from one second to the next.

With alacrity the young man showed his guests to a chair, where Miss Wastefield settled herself on its generous cushion, and Juga on one arm of it.

"Mellors," said Mr. Somerset, in answer to her question, as he sat himself down opposite.

At this mention of her coachman — he who had driven her and Lucy and Juga from Pinewick to Crow's-end harbor — Miss Wastefield exhaled softly.

"Of course!" she sighed, mentally chiding herself for her blindness. "But I had pledged him to secrecy."

"You mustn't blame the poor fellow," said the young man, "for I threatened him with the direst and guiltiest of consciences, and held him liable to account if he didn't tell me where you'd gone. I explained to him that there was no knowing what dangers or accidents of fortune might await, and that it would be all on his head. In the end he relented and told me of a ship bound for Nantle, and of a Mrs. Juniper in Chamomile Street whose family had been known to your father."

"But you had my letter?"

"It was delivered by a servant two days after your departure, as per your instruction. But of course —"

"And so you chose to disregard my wishes and followed me here?" said Miss Wastefield, completing the sentence for him.

"But, Jane, you left me no alternative," he protested. He was a brisk, trim young man, sandy-haired, aquiline, mustached, with fine eyes and hands and an agreeable manner. He sat now with those hands flung wide, and those fine eyes gazing with an imploring emphasis into her own.

He had been lucky, he told her, in securing accommodation on a packet-boat, but the voyage had been a difficult one as they'd had nothing but bad weather down the long coast. Yes, he'd gotten her letter, but after due reflection it had served only to persuade him that he *must* follow her and see that she came to no harm, whatever the cause of her trouble might be. And it was on this latter point that he pressed her now.

"What is it, Jane? What lies behind this mad adventure of yours? Of all persons, why must I be excluded from your confidence? What is this dark cloud over Pinewick, this trouble that has so oppressed you these past months? Has it to do with your father's death?"

These and other like questions he sought answers for, as he took her letter from his coat and, unfolding it, held it out before her.

"If you had read a little more, you would have seen that I asked you to have faith in me. Have you so little of that commodity, Martin, that you would disregard my wishes?" said Miss Wastefield, with a heightened flush in her cheek.

"And have you so little faith in me, Jane, that you'll not tell me why you must hasten off in secret to this unknown place so far from home? What has come over you, dear?"

"I promised to tell you all upon my return, did I not?"

"Yes, but in the meanwhile —"

"Pray, Martin, I don't care to hear anything more. I regret that you've deemed it necessary to follow me here. You have caused me so much added fear and distress, in wondering who it was who was inquiring after me and what his purpose was. Do you imagine it was a pleasure for me to endure such uncertainty?"

The young man admitted, in retrospect, it may not have been the most gentlemanly or considerate of actions on his part. But in his defense he explained he'd had no means to judge her response to his sudden appearance in Nantle. Then he begged her again to unburden her heart and tell him of that which afflicted her.

"Are you unhappy in our engagement?" he asked. It was a subject that required some effort on his part to broach. "I hope — I hope I have not been ungenerous to you, Jane, or unkind, for I haven't intended it. If so, I beg your pardon for it; you are of age, and mistress of your own future. Have you reservations now with regard to the understanding between us?"

"Believe me, Martin, it is all unrelated to our engagement. But as to its exact nature, that I cannot and I will not divulge," she replied, with a calmness he found not altogether persuasive. She was putting a brave face on, he thought; she didn't mean all she said. Moreover she was looking at the carpet rather than at him as she said it, in fear of what might happen if their eyes should meet. Something indeed was radically amiss, for this was not the Jane Wastefield the young man had come to know and love.

"Why will you not confide in me?" he asked.

"I *must* not," she answered, softening just a little, "for I'll not see you harmed, or possibly worse. I'll not bear the responsibility, Martin! The less you know of my trouble, the better it is for you."

She refused to hear more, but her pained expression betrayed her. It hurt her deeply to speak so to the young man of her heart. In truth that heart of hers was very full, but its contents she refused to bare on account of her love for him. And yet at the same time that very heart smote her for it! As for Mr. Somerset, his own heart was heavy because he saw the woman he loved in distress and there was nothing he could do to help her.

Little Juga, being less reserved than his mistress, was overjoyed to see Mr. Somerset again, and would have hopped onto his shoulder had he not been prevented by the hand of Miss Wastefield. Indeed, he seemed happier to see young Martin than she did herself; but of course, he had only a monkey's brain and a monkey's understanding, and was not privy to the peculiar self-tortures of humankind.

Although the interview was at an end, the central issue of it remained unresolved. Not only was her flight still a mystery to Mr. Somerset, his aid had been refused and he rebuffed. And although he had lots yet to say, Miss Wastefield was not in a mood to hear it. It was clear from her voice and manner that a struggle of great magnitude was going on within herself. Out of nowhere two small tears broke from her eyes and stole down her cheeks; hurriedly she dashed them away.

"I hope you'll not judge me harshly," was her only remark, delivered in a faint, gentle, regretful tone.

"And I don't care if I'm knocked to smash," was his unspoken vow in reply, "I'll understand this trouble of yours, Jane, and I'll free you of it."

Mr. Somerset was not the type of young man to be yielding until the mystery had been explained to his satisfaction. At the moment, however, nothing had been explained and nothing decided. For the present they were at an impasse, and Miss Wastefield desiring now to take her leave, he escorted her from the inn. She had noted the time and suddenly remembered her appointment with Dr. Pinches, and so had an urgent need to return to Chamomile Street. She was in a positive rush to return, in fact, and with Martin's assistance began searching for a cab in the street.

They walked a little up the road, passing on their way a gaunt, morbid, gloomy kind of house that had bars on its few windows and an outer door like a portcullis. It was the gritty pile of Comport's lock-up, which stood next door but one to the venerable Bunch of Grapes. There they stopped, and there Miss Wastefield happened to glance across the road, and a little ways down it, where she beheld a grim-faced man in a black caped overcoat and a chimney-pot hat — a man whose strange, dark eyes at that same moment were watching *her*.

She gasped in horror and drew Martin close.

"What is it, dear? What's wrong?" he asked.

She didn't answer at first, not knowing what to tell him, owing to a caution that had become habitual. In truth she wanted very much *not* to tell him, for fear of what he would think of a *fiancée* who'd taken to seeing ghosts and monsters in the street. Yet below the surface of her thoughts she was crying out to tell someone that there, there was the odious Triamete!

"There is a man over the way," she whispered.

"What of him?"

She turned to Martin in surprise. "Do you mean to say that you see him? The creature in the tall hat and painted tops?"

"I see a gentleman standing there, one of respectable appearance. But what of him? Is he known to you?"

"That 'gentleman,' as you call him, has been shadowing me since I arrived in Nantle. His name is Lanthorne, and his habits I fear are anything but respectable. He is an enemy. He is in fact a — a —"

She very nearly said *Triamete,* or *cannibal,* or *son of Poteidan,* but in the end said none of them.

"What I wish," she said instead, "is for that creature to stop following me!"

At once she regretted having spoken, for now she had placed the young man of her heart in mortal jeopardy.

"By God, I'll soon sort him out," he vowed, with a manly brushing of his sleeves.

"No, Martin, no — I beg of you!"

But it was too late. Suiting his action to his word, young Mr. Somerset marched off to confront the creature over the way.

As it happened, the rector of St. Mary-le-Quay and Mr. Frobisher had turned into Jekyl Street only moments before, and could hardly fail to note the scene. They halted in their tracks. The eyes of Mr. Frobisher lighted first on Miss Wastefield, and then on the man in the chimney-pot hat.

"Lanthorne!" he exclaimed, and broke into a trot. It was young Martin, however, who reached the point of convergence first.

"Who are you, sir, and what do you mean by persecuting my *fiancée*?" he demanded of the grim-faced man.

This query pulled Mr. Frobisher up short as he arrived, and rather than challenging Mr. Lanthorne, he turned instead to the sandy-haired stranger.

"And who the devil are *you,* sir, and where have you dropped from?" he asked. He stared the young man up and down and eyed him all over, from the crown of his broad-leafed hat to the very bottom of his boots.

"My name is Somerset, sir, of the Somersets of Wakely, Crow's-end. Who is it who inquires, and what business is it of yours besides?" retorted Martin, bridling up.

"Ah, I see how it is. Well, my name is Frobisher, sir, of the Frobishers of Common Report. And what have you to do with Miss Wastefield?"

"She is the lady who is to be my wife, if that's any concern of yours," returned Martin, with that sense of proprietary right that comes from being engaged.

"Wife! Look here, I'll have you know —"

"Just who are you, sir, to be speaking so to me? And what are you to Miss Wastefield?"

"It was my tender of assistance that brought her here."

"Then you are the one to blame for this mad adventure of hers! And what assistance? I'll ask you again, sir, what are you to Miss Wastefield?"

"No more than you, sir, or so it would appear," Mr. Frobisher snapped.

"By God, you are over the mark, sir, over the mark — have a care!" warned young Martin in his fierce short way.

And there they stood, toe to toe, eye to eye, mustache to mustache, glaring at one another like the rivals they were, fists tightly clenched at their sides, until a voice from on high broke in and said —

"Leave off your tiresome posturing, gentlemen."

It was the voice of Mr. Lanthorne, and so unexpected it caused the two young blades to stare at him in wonder.

"Look here, Lanthorne —" said Mr. Frobisher.

"Who are *you*, sir, and what's your game?" Martin demanded, returning his attention to its original object. "Why have you been watching my *fiancée*?"

"Because the lady needs watching," said Mr. Lanthorne. "She is at the mercy of a mighty and a vengeful power."

"Power? What power?"

It was at about this time that a stout coarse giant of a man with fiery hair emerged from the house over the way — the house of Jacob Comport — and descending its steps, approached Miss Wastefield at the roadside. As he sidled up to her, a lurid grin broke from his curly red forest of beard. Miss Wastefield, intent upon the activity across the road, paid him no heed until he turned around and, parting the hair behind his head, revealed there a third eye glowing crimson in the middle of it.

"Hallo, my turkey chicken!" said Candy, fixing her with the eye.

Miss Wastefield shrank under the scrutiny of the awful orb. She was too overcome to offer more than a brief exclamation; and so it was left to Juga to answer for the both of them. Immediately he rose up on her shoulder and began to jabber excitedly, making wild faces and hurling a torrent of threats at Mr. Imbercand. He showed his teeth and challenged the air with his spidery limbs, making clear his intention to protect his mistress to the very last inch of his tiny life.

But the doorkeeper and general factotum of the lock-up calmly ignored his antics.

"Djhana of Kaftor," said the towering Candy.

A colder or a more cunning voice Miss Wastefield had never heard, except from the trunk — the slitherous whisperings from the mirror of ancient polished bronze. With one huge hand the doorkeeper seized her cruelly by the arm; the other, balled into a fist, he touched to his brow in that attitude of worship that was so inexplicably familiar to her.

"Djhana of Kaftor, I claim you for my lord and father Poteidan the earth-shaker. Make orisons to many-rayed Poteidan, lord of earth and wave, and none but he!"

She resisted, struggling against the power of his grip. Juga, meanwhile, had launched himself on the giant and was assailing him high and low with a furious campaign of biting and clawing. But for all its violence, it caused the ponderous Imbercand not an ounce of discomfort.

Unable to free herself, Miss Wastefield cried out for help.

"Oh-hoh! and aren't we the plucky one, my pretty tartlet, my sweet bon-bon, my precious bona roba," laughed the doorkeeper, his eyes — all three of them — ablaze with a cruel, sarcastic glitter. "By cock and pie, you'll be coming with Candy now. Father Poteidan demands it!"

The cry of Miss Wastefield having alerted those over the way, both young men promptly wheeled round and dashed into the street.

"Halt! Halt, you dirty blackguard!" Martin shouted, dodging all manner of wheels and hooves as he fought his way through the traffic.

Dr. Pinches had by now reached the side of Mr. Lanthorne, and was looking on in open-mouthed disbelief.

"Good — heavens!" he exclaimed, too shocked and out of breath to say much else.

A closed carriage drawn by a pair of fast trotters rattled to a stop before the lock-up, obstructing the view of the young men hasting to the aid of Miss Wastefield. The lady's struggles having proved ineffective, she was flung by Candy into the vehicle. With little Juga still battling him like a hairy gamecock, the doorkeeper sprang inside the carriage with Miss Wastefield, calling out to the bald-headed driver on the box —

"Fly, my brother!"

"All glory to Father Poteidan!" cried the coachman Arifay — for it was he, restored now to his human shape and stature. He lashed the horses with his whip and away the carriage rolled at a lively pace.

Young Martin set off after them on foot, but of course he was hopelessly outmatched. Mr. Frobisher, however, was not to be thwarted so easily. Clamping his wide-awake down tight on his head, he made for the nearest conveyance — it happened to be a hackney cab — and leaping astride the horse like any good postilion, exhorted the nag, Candy-like, to *fly, fly!*

The astonished driver in the little dickey at the side, finding himself driven off in his own cab, had no choice but to go along. He spent the first minute beating time with his whip on the hat and coat of Mr. Frobisher, urging him to desist, even as Mr. Frobisher was calling to him over one shoulder and urging *him* to desist, and assuring him he'd receive full fare for the use of his cab.

All the while Mr. Lanthorne stared after them with his strange, dark gaze, and an expression as grim and unsearchable as Time itself.

Such a frenzy of activity had not gone unnoticed by others. Among them was Mr. Fred Cargo, who moments before had strolled into Jekyl Street with young John on one of their rambles about town. It had all happened so quickly — the brazen assault on a young lady, the young lady being forced into a carriage and driven off, one rescuer sprinting after her while another commandeered a cab — but it was long enough for Fred to have recognized the victim as the fine young woman from Crow's-end, 'pon my life, and about whom he'd been musing and pondering for a fortnight.

"Well, I'm hanged, as the saying is!" Fred exclaimed.

Without another thought, he gave his hat to John and proceeded to accost a rider in the street, though in an altogether more genteel fashion than Mr. Frobisher, what with his fancy waistcoat and his jingling gold watch-chain, and the little shower of coins with which he greased the rider's palm. His manner was so very persuasive, in fact, that he had the obliging horseman vacating the stirrups even as he stepped into them. Daring rider that he was and follower of the hounds at Tiptop Grange, he'd gone far too long without a good, stiff, smoking, rolling, grinding, pounding slap-dash of a gallop; and so he took the reins in hand and, spinning his horse about, rode off in furious pursuit.

The result of all this was that the rector of St. Mary-le-Quay was left behind in the company of Mr. Lanthorne, and young John in the company of Fred's hat.

"God bless my soul!" Dr. Pinches exclaimed, quite appalled by what he'd witnessed.

Beside him, Mr. Lanthorne laughed gently, and inquired of the learned doctor of the Church —

"And what might your fanciful God have to do with it, sir?"

When the doctor turned to offer a response, however, he found that the grim-faced stranger had vanished from his sight, and from that of John as well.

CHAPTER THIRTY-THREE

His Name Is Lanthorne

The ogre Arifay on the box, as he drove the carriage through the streets, burst into laughter at the easy success of his brother Triamete and himself in the capture of the woman; and as he laughed, the evil scar on the side of his head flared, and his third eye glowed redly wicked, and the mouth behind his beard opened to reveal two rows of knife-like teeth, very finely chiseled. Then he cracked his whip and sent the horses dashing ahead at an even faster rate, and the people in the road scattering. Mr. Arifay enjoyed seeing people scatter, for he was by nature contemptuous of the human villains among whom he lived, and on whom he fed. His was a life lived in service to an ancient lord whose existence a sundered world had long forgotten. But the servants of these ancient lords are everywhere about us, even today, working the will of their exalted masters, although it is largely beyond humanity's power to recognize them.

It was while he was laughing and pluming himself on his success that he spied something out of the corners of his three eyes and, turning his head, discovered a stranger seated beside him on the box.

The oyster-master stared at the man in fierce surprise. "Who are you, and how came you here?" he demanded.

"I am your lord and father Poteidan. Don't you know me, sir? Well, that's interesting."

"What mischief is this? You are not Poteidan. You are a villain!"

"And you," said Mr. Lanthorne, with a cold smile stealing across his lips, "are a blunder-head."

"Ha! What?"

"And a halter-sack. A gallows-bird. A jolly ass."

"You shall smart for this, villain!" warned the short-tempered offspring of Poteidan.

"A bee has more brains than you, and not nearly so thick a cranium."

It was too much for the oyster-master. He dropped the reins so as to lay hands on Mr. Lanthorne and pitch him from his seat. But when he lunged for the villain, he found no villain there — found nothing, indeed, but empty space. His momentum, however, carried him through the empty space and clear over the side of the box. Headfirst he went, and at an accelerated velocity, as if an invisible someone had hastened his exit by means of a forceful thrust. It was the same invisible someone who deftly picked his pocket as he went over — that is, removed a key from a pocket of his coat — before taking command of the reins.

As he plunged into the street, the oyster-master was set upon at once by a pair of large and formidable dogs, which had been squabbling at the roadside, and were quick to welcome this new diversion. As we know, dogs are unusually keen judges of character, and two of them united in their hostility can be a potent match for anything, even a gargoyle.

The horses drawing the carriage scarcely noticed the exchange of drivers, so easily did Mr. Lanthorne assume the role of coachman. With practiced skill and not a little daring, he guided them along the busy avenue — for a busy avenue it was now, no less a one than Ship Street — threading his way through a maze of slow-moving carts and drays, milk floats, and delivery vans, and like Arifay before him, sending the foot-passengers scattering. But there was a kind of order in Mr. Lanthorne's threading and scattering, with the traffic giving way before the horses as if under some weird influence of the driver, thereby allowing the carriage to pass freely and at the top of its speed.

Farther down the street Mr. Lanthorne swung the horses to the left and sent the carriage rattling down an alley, and then clattering down a by-street, and bumping along a smoky lane. Several moments later the appropriated cab of Allan Frobisher — with Mr. Frobisher bouncing bareback, having no stirrups to stand in — and the horse bearing the more genteel Fred Cargo in its generous saddle, went galloping past the alley entrance. But the noise of their pursuit fell off quickly, as neither gentleman had seen the carriage turn out of Ship Street.

Bumping along the smoky lane, the carriage and its steaming horses pulled up before a shop in whose window the boast OYSTERS IN EVERY STYLE was prominently displayed.

Mr. Imbercand, unaware of the violent departure of his brother Triamete from the box, backed out of the carriage with one arm of Miss Wastefield clutched in a greasy fist.

"A brisk ride, my brother," he called out to the driver. "Make ready your caldron now, and we'll return this pretty tartlet of a renegade to her place. Hearkee now, ain't that so, my bona roba?" he chuckled, with a hungry leer that left Miss Wastefield in no doubt as to his intentions regarding the caldron, or her. "We mean to send the pretty sugarplum home to our great father Poteidan, her lord and master, and to whom she was pledged on the altar of Juktas long ago in the quaking-time."

Miss Wastefield, helpless in his powerful grip, cried out for assistance. But her voice, a thin sound weakened by fright and exhaustion, barely registered in the smoky air, which moved Candy to further laughter. In response, little Juga hurled himself at the giant's throat. This action sent Mr. Imbercand into a rage — for the irksome, irritating, annoying little mosquito of a hairy gamecock hadn't once paused in his attacks during the carriage-ride — and taking the monkey in hand, he flung him away, sending him crashing against a water-butt.

"Juga!" Miss Wastefield cried, rushing to the monkey's aid; for the giant in shaking off the hairy nuisance had been forced to release his hold on her.

Tenderly she took her pet into her arms, and to her relief found him wounded more in spirit than in body. Then she rose, and as she turned round to face the giant again, she caught her breath, for there was the figure of Mr. Lanthorne, so tall and broad as to frame and darkly lustrous as to eyes, standing between herself and Mr. Imbercand.

"Oh-hoh! And who might you be, my bully beef?" sneered Candy, with an easy arrogance. "Well, well! Where did you arise from? By cock and pie, you're not my brother. Where is my brother?"

"My name is Lanthorne," replied the stranger, "and no, sir, I'm no brother of yours, and heartily glad of it."

"'Ods-bobs, where is he now, eh?" said Candy, glancing round, and putting his head inside the carriage and then under it, and between the horses, as though he suspected his brother of a prank and would find him lurking somewhere about the vehicle.

"Gone to the dogs, probably," suggested Mr. Lanthorne, "which is far better than he deserves, no doubt — or you."

Candy, finding no trace of his brother, and with the thought growing on him that the stranger was responsible for that, made to seize the grim-faced man; but as his brother had discovered before him, Mr. Lanthorne was not a man easily snared. The greasy fists of Candy closed upon nothing, for the stranger had magically transported himself to the other side of the carriage, and there was observing Candy over the backs of the horses.

"You're rather bungling and unskillful for a servant of Poteidan," Mr. Lanthorne declared.

Such talk was tinder to our friend Candy of the lock-up.

"By cock and pie!" he thundered angrily. His hands went through the action of twisting the top off something — we suspect it was the head of the cheeky stranger — as he marched himself round the horses, only to find once again that Mr. Lanthorne was not there. Instead, the grim-faced man was peering at him from inside the oyster saloon.

"Oh-hoh, my nimble pigeon! Now Candy has you in the toils of his net. Escape Candy this time, think you? Not likely, my cutlet, not likely. *You're dead as mutton!*"

With a pouncing eagerness the giant threw himself at the shop-door. It gave way readily, but once inside he found himself alone. As if that weren't humiliation enough, he saw that the door had been closed behind him and that the stranger was on the step outside, turning the key in the lock.

"Please to board the carriage, Miss Wastefield," said Mr. Lanthorne, suddenly appearing at the door of the vehicle. "You and your small friend there. He is unhurt?"

Miss Wastefield drew a startled breath, still in a state of considerable shivers, and of wonder, from all she'd seen and experienced.

"Your pet — your old friend. He is not injured?"

"No," she answered slowly. "No, he is unharmed."

Little Juga had hopped onto her shoulder now, from which spare perch he was observing Mr. Lanthorne with a curious expression. Despite the gentleman's actions seemingly on her behalf, Miss Wastefield did not trust him. And yet there was no denying what she'd witnessed. There was no denying that Mr. Lanthorne was no ordinary person — if person he was — and that he had rescued her from the Triametes. But was it simply to further his own purposes, and might she now by entering the coach be gliding into another trap?

But there was no denying either the sight of the scowling Imbercand in the shop-window, making ready to smash his way through the glass.

Her heart and pulse were throbbing, her mind racing. *What to do, dear God, what to do?*

"Quickly, quickly, Miss Wastefield!" Mr. Lanthorne urged, flinging the carriage-door wide.

It was the ugly sight in the shop-window that decided it. Throwing caution to the winds, she accepted Mr. Lanthorne's proffered hand. He then shut the door with a clang and leaped onto the box.

"Where are you taking us?" she called out to him, just as a vengeful Candy came bursting through the shop-window.

"To safety for now!"

The whip cracked, the horses snorted, and away the carriage sped down the smoky lane.

"With no explanation, Mr. Lanthorne?"

"That, too!" he called back to her.

Through a warren of grimy streets in the area of Slopmonger Mews they went, bumping and rattling. Before long they came to a halt near a cab-stand, where Mr. Lanthorne jumped off the box and helped Miss Wastefield from the carriage.

At the stand they engaged a comfortable chaise. As they were boarding it, Mr. Lanthorne instructed the driver to take them out along the northwest road, toward distant Falaise. Hearing this, the driver stopped and seemed about to make some objection, before taking the whip and reins reluctantly in hand.

"Get along, then!" he said to the horses; and along they got.

Miss Wastefield was puzzled by her companion's choice of destination.

"We must get well away from Nantle for a time," he explained.

"But what of my *fiancé*?"

"I shall see that a message is conveyed to him. Not to worry, Miss Wastefield — the lord Poteidan hasn't everyone in his thrall."

She had been looking closely at Mr. Lanthorne. There was nothing else to do now, she realized, but to summon up her courage — which had been sorely tested already — and place some very crucial questions before the grim-faced man.

"Are you, sir, another of these Triametes?" she asked, hesitantly.

"Most decidedly not."

"What are you, then? Miss O'Guppy called you a creature, an ancient one and a powerful one. A higher soul, she said. I myself have seen you when others around me could not. And today I've seen you vanish and appear again in front of my eyes! What else can you be but another of those horrid Triametes?"

"No Triamete," Mr. Lanthorne assured her. "What I am I shall explain later. Fear not, Miss Wastefield, I mean you no harm. But we must remove ourselves from the city for a time. We shall be going on to Falaise."

Miss Wastefield had observed the curious way Juga had been looking at him. By no means was he distrustful of Mr. Lanthorne, or frightened; and he plainly had no inclination to be assaulting him about the body as he had the Triamete. He seemed more relieved than anything, welcoming almost, as if grateful for the gentleman's presence. He had calmed down now and was resting quietly in her arms. It struck Miss Wastefield as odd and improbable, but it seemed almost as if Juga *knew* Mr. Lanthorne.

"What are we to do at Falaise?" she asked, after a little pause.

"It is more a question of what you choose to do."

"I? Forgive me, sir, but I don't understand —"

"Don't trouble yourself at present, Miss Wastefield. You don't understand because you don't remember, or remember only imperfectly. The well of forgetfulness must first be drained. The 'waters of Lethe' some have called it — which, as the rector Pinches might say, you'll recollect from your mythology — otherwise known as the waters of oblivion, from which spirits must drink before they return to the world."

"But I am no spirit." Then a shadow crossed her visibly. "Yes," she murmured, after a little reflection, "yes, that is just what it is, a kind of forgetting. Upon my word I do remember it now — or, rather, I remember *something*! Indeed, I've remembered many things this past year, or half-remembered them — strange and vaguely familiar things, lying just beyond the reach of my mind. It was Miss O'Guppy who told me of a mighty secret I'd forgotten, and of a mighty enemy. I thought that enemy was you, but she said it was not."

"And when she looked at you, she saw two people?"

"Yes! Yes! I didn't understand her, and I still don't. But how do you know these things?"

"Later, Miss Wastefield," he said, gravely but gently, "when there is more time for private conversation. Time! It is so troublesome a construction. There is a choice you must make, and it is only just that you have the full reach of memory at your disposal to make it. We mustn't allow the waters of Lethe or the threat of Triametes to deprive you of that."

They had passed beyond the limits of the city and were driving hard through seaside country toward the distant port-town of Falaise. On their left lay a wide strip of beach bordering the restless sea; on their right the crowding underwood and beyond it the foothills of the mountains, gradually sloping to the higher ranges. They had not gone many miles, however, before the driver brought the chaise to an unexpected halt, and proceeded to inform Mr. Lanthorne that he didn't care to venture much farther from town.

"For I'm only a city driver, don't ye see, sir," he explained, with a troubled face, "and there's been misfortune on this road here of late. Saber-cats, sir, come down from the mountains! The horses won't stand for it, nor the driver neither."

As he spoke, he cast many an anxious glance around him, as if watching for hidden monsters in the brush.

"We shall have no trouble with saber-cats," Mr. Lanthorne told him.

By some means marvelous or otherwise, the driver accepted this without objection. He knew it to be the truth, so confidently had his passenger spoken, and with such assurance. How indeed could it be otherwise? Of course there would be no cats! And not only the driver but Miss Wastefield, too, believed it.

"A little farther, driver, if you please," Mr. Lanthorne said then. "You needn't take us all the way to Falaise, of course. You may set us down at the first posting-house you come to. It is the Sea Horse, I believe."

The chaise-driver, nodding his thanks to Mr. Lanthorne with many quick touches of his hat, took up the reins again; and so they continued on their way.

Before long they came to a solitary inn. It lay on a broad sweep of ground on the seaward side of the road, above the beach. Quaint of gable and tall of chimney, it was a comfortable-looking house of cinnamon-colored stone. A mantle of ivy covered much of it in pendent masses. A painted sign depicting a stallion with webbed feet, a scalloped fin, and a fish's tail, bounding over a crested wave, swung above the house-door — confirmation that this was indeed the inn of the Sea Horse.

The driver, having deposited his passengers in the yard, was in a visible hurry to turn chaise and horses round and return to town. To Mr. Lanthorne he said little, apart from thanking him for the fare and wishing him and his lady the best of luck in reaching Falaise; then he and his carriage rumbled out under the arch and were gone.

On the generous ground beside the inn stood four shaggy red mastodons, their bridles, tug-lines, surcingles, blanket cushions, and related equipage all very trimly and smartly arranged. It was a train of thunder-beasts in full harness, with passenger cabs and freight platforms riding atop their backs and shoulders. The creatures were gathered round a large water-trough from which they were drinking. Three hale young fellows in plaid and corduroy were lounging in the vicinity, keeping a watch on the beasts. Likely they were members of the team of drivers.

No sooner had Mr. Lanthorne and his party entered the travelers' room of the inn than they were accosted by a person lean of eye and swart of countenance, who had a cup in one hand and a cigar in the other and was applying himself freely to both.

"Lanthorne, man! What say? Haven't clapped these optics on you of late. Step up to the engine and have a drink, man! They're as good souls here as ever tapped a barrel. This grog of theirs is a stunner, enough to burst your brain from its stanchions. A little of it goes a long way."

Mr. Lanthorne politely declined the offer. Undaunted, Black Davy took another pull at his drink and a whiff at his cigar.

"No? Well, I've never recalled your draining a glass at Sprig's, now I think of it — never seen you down a pint or fill a pipe. A damned teetotaler, eh? Man, man, a plague of all teetotalers. Untrusty fellows! You'll bear with me, sir, for I'm plain Dunstable in this — I say what I feel. Come, man, let's not mince words. I've had no sight of you at Sprig's for a time. Where in the world have you been keeping yourself?"

"Elsewhere," said Mr. Lanthorne.

"Well, that's as good an answer as any, I'll warrant. Spare me the tyranny of answers — spare me the tyranny of *questions*! But the truth, man! What brings you here?"

Mr. Lanthorne gave no answer, or made answer in only a trifling way. Black Davy couldn't say which, for he'd just clapped his optics on Miss Wastefield. Immediately he offered her a deep and courteous bow. In so doing, some of the grog spilled from his cup, and his cigar very nearly ignited his coat of blue frieze; but he noticed neither.

"Lady!" he said, impressed by her very considerable beauty. "Lady, I am wholly yours."

Little Juga chirped and made a host of silly faces, reflective perhaps of his opinion of Mr. Devenham. Black Davy looked askance at the monkey, unsure how to respond to such behavior from such a creature, and so chose to ignore it.

"And what brings *you* here?" Mr. Lanthorne asked the lonely wanderer.

"Why, man, it's Jarvey brings me here," said Davy, indicating a timber-looking man in plaid trousers and pork-pie hat who stood nearby, and whose resemblance to the three fellows minding the thunder-beasts was self-evident.

"You are with the train?"

Mr. Lanthorne seemed displeased, not because Black Davy represented some kind of threat to him or Miss Wastefield, but something more like a bother.

"Bound for Falaise!" snorted Mr. Devenham, with a little flourish of his grog. "For Falaise today, sir and lady, but afterwards, who can say? For I must wander — I must have my freedom — and I was no longer free at Nantle. Spare me the tyranny of everyday existence; I find Nantle as dull as ditch-water. I've been there for long enough, and must be out and about in the world again. I must roam! I'll go where the road and the sea take me. We're all but wayward droppers-by in this sorry inn of life; we are all of us so much brittle dust. Man, man, the years are numbered and there are only so many of them accorded us for roaming. It's a bitter pill, but there it is."

Davy's flow of words was great, but his flow of *aqua vitae* was greater. From his coat he plucked his battered pocket-book, and searching through his store of ready cash — which represented in chief part the largesse of Mr. Liffey — counted out a few coins, then toddled off to the bar for a fresh supply of grog.

Mr. Lanthorne took advantage of his absence to approach Mr. Jarvey, the mastodon man, and held a brief discussion with him. The discussion bearing fruit, instructions were conveyed to the sons of Mr. Jarvey by way of the good-natured boots of the inn, while Mr. Lanthorne returned to Miss Wastefield and Juga.

"I have secured two places with the train. They are going out soon, and will be stopping the night at a well-provided house farther on. It will serve to muddle our Triametes for a while and allow us some needed time. We should reach Falaise in a couple of days. At the harbor we shall take passage aboard a vessel there, a merchant lugger under the command of one Jack Barnaby."

"That is the ship that brought us to Nantle — Lucy, Juga, and I," said Miss Wastefield.

"There is an old mastodon trail a little ways on that we shall be following into higher country. Few saber-cats of judicious mind will venture to attack a train of thunder-beasts, as any driver of mastodons can tell you. You shall be quite safe, Miss Wastefield, as we work our way to Falaise."

"And what then, Mr. Lanthorne, after we go aboard ship? For where is the captain bound?"

"He will first return to Nantle, where your maid may join us, after which he will be sailing for Truro. By that time, however, you likely will have made your choice. It will be perhaps the most difficult and important decision of your life. But it is better than the alternative, and the very least that you deserve."

"It is all such a mystery," said Miss Wastefield, shaking her pretty head, "but as Juga appears to trust you, I'll not question his judgment. There have been many things about which he seems to know far more than I."

Shortly thereafter Mr. Jarvey and his sons and the train went out, and when they did, Mr. Lanthorne and his party went out with them.

With a trumpet-roar splitting the air like a mail-guard's key-bugle, and many rumblings and shakings of the Sea Horse and the ground on which it stood, the thunder-beasts swung out into the road. In the lead was Silvertop, the noble bull, with Mr. Jarvey riding in the cab on his shoulders. One of the Jarvey offspring held sway over each of the remaining beasts. Miss Wastefield and Mr. Lanthorne had received places in the cab on top of Acorn, Silvertop's younger brother, in the rear of the train. Between the brothers marched their two doe-eyed cousins, Mavis and Chloë.

With their massive limbs like pillars plunging and pounding, their hot breath rising in clouds of steam, and the jingle of their harness making merry music, the train rumbled on. It wasn't long before the coach-road was left behind in favor of one of those ancient trackways blazed by mastodons of ages past. Through misty and forest-darkened glens and summit woods they went, in general following the coast but passing through upland towns and villages that the coach-roads, for the safety and convenience of carriage-travelers, had largely forsaken.

More than once Miss Wastefield found her glance straying to the grim profile of Mr. Lanthorne, silhouetted in the windows against the rolling landscape beyond. So far above that landscape were they there, on the shoulders of a full-grown thunder-beast, that it seemed it was the landscape that was moving rather than they. It was an illusion, of course; but it led Miss Wastefield to wonder whether Mr. Lanthorne himself might not be an illusion, too. She was far from sure that she wasn't in a dream at the moment, or had not in fact been in a dream the entire day. For his part Mr. Lanthorne had lapsed into a stony silence, his eyes with their strange, dark luster fixed on the passing vistas. As her own eyes watched him now, searching his face for the slightest clue, she found herself wondering again just who or what he was.

He had shown her nothing but kindness this day. Grim he certainly was, though not unfriendly, and what she'd witnessed in his handling of the Triametes had made a profound impression on her. He was an enigma, and a little frightening — but at least he was no three-eyed crested giant of a cannibal. If Mr. Frobisher in his guise as Gilbert Thistlewood had proved a disappointment, perhaps Mr. Lanthorne would prove otherwise; for one never knew from what quarter a way out might chance to open. And since little Juga seemed to be comfortable in the gentleman's presence, Miss Wastefield put her worries to bed for a time, and turned her attention instead to the flow of scenery in the windows.

And so on they plodded in the direction of Falaise towards an unknown future, and an unknown choice that would shortly be hers to make.

CHAPTER THIRTY-FOUR

Thus in Ancient Days

At Falaise, in a private sitting-room in a quaint old house overlooking the harbor, on the afternoon of their arrival there, Miss Wastefield sat deep in conversation with Mr. Lanthorne.

Little Juga was there, too, clinging to his mistress's arm or perching on her chair. He was watching Mr. Lanthorne, and as he watched him, he would cock his tiny head now and then in his monkey way, but so human-like too, as if he understood all that the gentleman was saying.

Mr. Lanthorne had begun by explaining to Miss Wastefield that he could not forestall the actions of the lord Poteidan, although he could mitigate the danger. He could protect her against such earthly threats as the Triametes for as long as she wished; he could guard her against these and the other minions of Poteidan, but against Poteidan himself, however — well, there was little that one such as he could do.

"But who are you, sir? *What* are you?" she said in reply, looking again for the answers to those questions that so mystified her.

"It may be difficult for you to understand, Miss Wastefield. Perhaps it would be simpler if I showed you."

He stepped to the window and drew the curtain across. Almost at once Miss Wastefield saw that there was a kind of glow surrounding his body that had not been visible in the daylight. It was as though someone had traced his outline in luminous paint. The light appeared to come from within Mr. Lanthorne himself, and as she watched, its strength increased rapidly. Brighter and brighter it grew, gaining force and brilliance and clarity until its glare became so powerful she had to shield her eyes from it. And when it seemed it had grown to be as bright a thing as any thing could possibly be, it grew even brighter, and brighter, and brighter still, as though burning with the heat of a thousand suns, and flooded the chamber with a radiance so dazzling that the figure of Mr. Lanthorne was entirely consumed by it.

Juga, meanwhile, had hopped onto her shoulder and, keeping his eyes averted, thrust a tiny hand toward the blazing wall of light. He chirped and cooed in Miss Wastefield's ear, and jabbered something in his wild monkey tongue, as if he knew what the light signified and was eagerly expounding on it to his mistress.

Before a minute had passed, however, the light began to wane — gradually, steadily — until the figure of Mr. Lanthorne became visible again. The light contracted, swallowed itself, and retreated to the margins of his body, and in the end was restored to that faint glow Miss Wastefield had first espied.

Mr. Lanthorne stepped to the window and pulled the curtain back, so that the light of Falaise harbor and its forest of mast and canvas looked again into the room.

Miss Wastefield was much affected by what she had seen.

"Pray God, is it possible? Are you — an *angel*?" she asked, hesitatingly. For an instant the thought ran through her mind that she had died, and this was her judgment. "Are you one of the seraphim? One of the thrones or dominations? Surely one of the archangels —"

The being of light that was Mr. Lanthorne, having resumed his all-too-earthly seat, shook his head.

"But you are a kind of attendant spirit?"

"Of a sort, I suppose."

Strangely, his lips did not move when making his reply; instead Miss Wastefield found that she could hear his words in her mind. It seemed that Mr. Lanthorne had the power to convey his thoughts to her without the intervention of speech.

"You are certainly no human, but no shadow either. Certainly you are nothing the like of which I have any knowledge," she said.

Here little Juga chirped in her ear again, and pointed excitedly at Mr. Lanthorne.

"What you've seen was but a glimpse of my true form," the gentleman told her. "I am indeed a kind of spirit, one inhabiting a realm of existence quite outside your own. But I assure you, Miss Wastefield, it's nothing to be feared. Your own spirit, body-bound as it is now, and that of your small friend there, differ from mine and others in little but degree."

"There are more like yourself, then? More unseen visitors?"

"Countless more, with no longer any need of physical bodies."

Miss Wastefield's eyes were filled with thought. "Yes," she said slowly, "yes, I recall it now. I recall Miss O'Guppy's speaking of other spirits she'd sensed — others like yourself whom few else could see, gliding about the world every day."

"Although I'll confess to being rather a solitary sort, ordinarily, and not given much to mingling. But it doesn't mean that I'm unsociable."

"But if you are a spirit, sir, how is it you are sitting in that chair?"

"Ah! But I am not sitting in this chair, Miss Wastefield. You may think you see me here, but in truth it is only an image I have placed in your mind, the easier for us to talk together. The light you observed represents my true self; but of course it's a hard thing for the brain to compass, and so I have assumed an appearance of human form. But it's not altogether illusory, for I, too, was bodied once — many times, in fact, on many worlds. I have lived an entire string of lives, all of them long before this present age of yours was born. Long before the sundering ruptured the ties of these cities to England — indeed long, long before there was an England — a thousand thousand years before — I already had lived and died, and lived again, many scores of times."

"But our faith, sir, it expressly denies that such a thing is possible —"

Mr. Lanthorne offered her a skeptical smile. "Has your faith room within its narrow strictures for a being such as myself? And yet here I am. As for your angels — your seraphim and dominations — I've never in my travels encountered a single one, although I have encountered many others like myself, most of them busy about their own quests and seeking fulfillment."

So he said and, further to it, told her of many things there in the room by the harbor, this ancient and powerful being called Lanthorne. He told her of the years out of number he had spent exploring the great starry heavens. He was a tireless observer of things, he said, and was driven by his very nature to travel from world to world, observing things. There were many worlds in this great garden of the universe that were inhabited by beings of thought and reason. Indeed, this earth of hers that swung its way about its sun was just one of many swinging their way about many suns, those countless glittering jewels that adorned the night sky. The enormity of the void in which those jewels were hung, the sheer scale of it, the vast distances, were beyond all human comprehension; but to a being like Mr. Lanthorne they were as nothing. By means of the extraordinary power available to him, he had traversed the heavens and peered into their many mysteries, forever fascinated, forever curious. He was, he admitted, compelled always to be learning, to be growing, to be seeking wisdom from his experiences, and by such means gain ascension to still higher realms of existence.

Not very long ago, he told her, he had returned to this earth, which he'd visited often in the past, to see how it was faring after the great catastrophe that had shattered it.

"Your wisest minds believe it to have been caused by a meteor or comet that struck the ground, or perhaps by a volcanic eruption. What if I were to tell you, Miss Wastefield, that it was in fact none of these?"

"It was said that a fireball — a comet perhaps — appeared in the southern skies before the sundering. That is what I was told by my father."

"And he was partly correct. There was something observed in the southern skies, but it was no comet. Just as this ship we are about to take passage on sails the seas of earth, so there are other kinds of ships — vessels which in your wildest fancy you couldn't imagine — that sail the seas of the universe, navigating the great empty spaces between the stars, and carrying within them bodied beings like yourself. Having bodies, they cannot themselves safely cross those empty spaces; they must travel in ships to protect their delicate anatomies from the perishing heat and cold, the want of air, the poison of unshielded starlight. But spirits have no such restrictions, and no need of ships to carry them; their force of will propels them wherever they care to go without regard to distance or time.

"It was upwards of two hundred of your years ago that one of these ships — a prodigious large craft the size of a small moon, a floating city, carrying an entire population of beings intent upon settling new worlds — struck the earth. It had suffered a fatal collapse of its life-giving machinery, and all aboard had been lost. For thousands of years this ship drifted among the stars, until it was captured by your sun and sent hurtling toward the earth, where it plunged into a southern sea. Although most of the territory up and down this long coast was spared, by an accident of geography, there's little else I'm afraid that was. First the skies grew dark from smoke and soot, then the earth cooled and much of it became locked up with ice. And so it remains today."

The very thought of it caused Miss Wastefield's blood to run as cold as that ice; the very enormity of it, the wonder of it, the impossibility of it, set her mind to spinning.

"There are many like myself who roam the heavens seeking knowledge and understanding," Mr. Lanthorne went on. "Indeed, I've quite lost count of the number of worlds I have visited; and always there is more to discover, more to learn, more wisdom to be gained."

"And are there so many like you here on earth? Do we live surrounded by these spirits, these phantoms, these beings of light? Pray, sir, don't answer — for already I know it must be so!"

"They are everywhere about. Indeed, your poet Milton, despite his own physical blindness, recognized it — 'Millions of spiritual creatures walk the earth unseen, both when we wake and when we sleep.' Does the notion unsettle you? Not to worry. Tell me, Miss Wastefield — have you never had a sudden change of feeling come over you, as inexplicably as if it had dropped from the sky? Perhaps one of us was near. Have you never sensed company in a room with you, somewhere close at hand, although you saw no one? Perhaps one of us was there. Consider the experience of your friends in Chamomile Street, those whose eyes were blind to my presence. Have you never been struck with an idea or flash of inspiration that seemed to come from nowhere? Perhaps it came from one of us, standing there at your side."

"But what has this to do with me?" Miss Wastefield asked, visibly uncomfortable in spite of Mr. Lanthorne's assurances. "What have the Triametes and this lord Poteidan and returning to Kaftor to do with me? How am I to return to a place that no longer exists, and why? And who is this Poteidan? Is he, too, one of these ascended spirits?"

"He is, but a far older and mightier one than I. It is the case with some of these ancient souls, that their great knowledge and experience gives rise not to wisdom but to vulgar pride and arrogance. They come to feel that a degree of worship is owed them by the lesser spirits, and by bodied beings such as yourself. Some have called these most ancient of souls gods, but they are not gods — they merely believe themselves to be and act accordingly. Some of them, to their credit, are at heart kindly beings, and seek only good for those they hold in thrall. Others, however, are possessed of a hardened cruelty quite astonishing to behold. To this latter class, unfortunately, I must assign the lord and master Poteidan.

"There exists among the spirits a hierarchy of sorts, which has its basis in the power and experience each has amassed. We are most of us striving to improve our stores of both, so as to gain admittance to still higher realms of awareness and achieve a deeper understanding of things. Most bodied beings like yourself, I regret to say, occupy rather humble positions in this hierarchy, as your spiritual faculties are but poorly developed. Of course there are always exceptions, such as your Miss O'Guppy, whose acquaintances, interestingly, seem convinced she is not in her right wits."

"But if you and these other ancient souls are not angels, then what of Almighty God? What of Providence? What of all we have been taught? What of our *faith*?" Miss Wastefield demanded.

"I know nothing of this 'almighty' god, for I've never encountered it and know of no one who has. As for the lord Poteidan — well, to be plain about it, he is a bully, and unfortunately a powerful one. Throughout time he has assumed many forms, and made his presence felt on many worlds. Some have called him Neptune, some Amon, some Tarbalis, Kemfer, Zival, Anawanax — all of them names to conjure with. He has been worshipped as a god, but he is no more a god than you or I; however, his subject spirits and bodied beings believe him to be. Many such mighty ones have their adherents on the different worlds over which they claim dominion. It is this that sustains them, for like Poteidan they are excessively proud and selfish, having little but contempt for those they view as their inferiors. This lord Poteidan, he, too, is such a mighty one. How else to describe a being that demands to be worshipped? How else to describe a being that demands unthinking submission and punishes transgressors accordingly?

"He has been called the earth-shaker, and the many-rayed sun god, the god of the sea, the bull god; but he is none of these. He is, in fact, most unlike any sun, for his is a dark and sinister spirit bent on dominion and self-glory. He inhabits a realm of awareness that suits him, and cares not to further his understanding of existence. Cruel and selfish spirits such as he have their agents everywhere, even in a sundered world, ready to do their bidding. Among the hidden spies of Poteidan on earth is the race of Triametes, those whom he calls his 'sons.' It was one of their kind that sent you a relic from vanished Kaftor — the hand-mirror of polished bronze."

"But why give this unholy object to me?"

"It was meant to awaken your buried memories, to remind you of your earlier life and of days long past and of how you had transgressed. Before each bodily rebirth the soul must be washed clean, the memories dissolved in the waters of oblivion. But the washing often is incomplete. The mirror was intended to encourage remembering."

It required some minutes for Miss Wastefield to absorb all she'd heard. Once more the words of Miss O'Guppy came back to her, and when she spoke again, her voice was tense with a fearful expectancy. She knew she was closing in on the mighty secret that had been struggling for release ever since the ancient polished bronze had entered her life.

"Do I understand you rightly, sir? Do you mean to say I've lived another life before this one?"

"One other, and only one."

"Indeed," she murmured, and to her surprise found herself accepting the fact almost at once. Her eyes grew wide, as if she were staring down the very throat of Time itself; back, back, still farther back she gazed, across the many long centuries that intervened. "Indeed, I'm sure of it now. It explains the familiarity of the pictures in the mirror — the people there, the sunny fields, the shimmering sea, the temple-labyrinth. The temple-labyrinth!

Of course — it was my home once. *My home!*" she gasped, and turned her face again to Mr. Lanthorne. "It would seem my heart has remembered a thing my mind did not."

"And it is only fair that you do remember it, thoroughly and completely, and all that happened there in that time."

Little Juga chirped again at her side — a chirp of encouragement, it seemed to Miss Wastefield — and gently touched her arm.

"What then is this choice I must make, Mr. Lanthorne?" she asked, prepared at last to confront the mystery of her own existence.

For answer, the grim-faced man offered her his hand. The moment she touched it, she felt it grow warm in her grasp; then in a burst of rain the dirty window that had clouded her mind's eye was rinsed clean, and the light of memory came shining through. Before her lay the familiar valley with its hills and mountains and temple-labyrinth, and beyond it the sea like a floor of metal, all of which she remembered — not from one of her dreams or visions, but from life. It was the ageless isle of olives in the middle of the Great Green Sea. It was Kaftor.

She was home.

Then followed the cataclysm, the horrific scene of dust and rubble and death, the toppled labyrinth, its terraces and courtyards once so full of life, its colorful frescoes and colonnades, its walls and roof-tops studded with sacred bulls' horns — horns of consecration, and the symbol she remembered now of Poteidan himself, who in his displeasure smote the land of Kaftor and its people in the quaking-time — all of it lying in a heap.

Her vision shifted to a place some few miles off, across the valley and beyond the hills, where a lone mountain climbed into the sunburnt sky. This mountain, thrusting itself straight up from the earth like some sinister god's head emerging from the underworld, was called Juktas, and on a rocky outcrop on its northern slope was a sanctuary dedicated to Poteidan. There were several low altars there within the sanctuary enclosure, each constructed of stone and surmounted by a pair of bulls' horns. Spread round one of the altars on tables of clay was a feast of offerings — olives and figs, pears, pistachio nuts, coriander, mint and sage, oil, grain, milk and honey, oysters, starfish, octopi.

On the altar itself was a small bundle — a little girl, barely more than a child. Her eyes were dark and expressive, her face painted, her black hair elaborately coiffured. Finely dressed and bejewelled she was as she lay there on her back, quietly, although perhaps not so willingly, for her hands and feet were bound with thongs of ox-hide. She was shivering, not from the cold but from fear. But ritual dictated she could not show her fear; she *must* not show her fear. Watching from nearby was a tiny black monkey in a leather harness — a very Juga-looking monkey he was, and one whom Miss Wastefield knew and remembered.

Came then the call of a shell-horn — a triton-shell — and the sound of it chilled Miss Wastefield to the marrow. At the altar stood the beautiful dark priestess, her face and hair as lushly adorned as the child's. It was she who had blown upon the shell to summon the lord Poteidan. Next, honeyed wine laced with poppy juice was poured into a cup; this the priestess gave to the child on the altar to dull her senses.

Seeing this, remembering this, Miss Wastefield turned deathly pale. Instinctively she touched a finger to one of her odd small earrings — baubles, she recognized now, that were very much like those worn by the little girl. She watched in silent agony as the child began to drift away, her eyes closed, her shivers gradually diminishing. She was as composed now as anyone might have been under the circumstances, trussed like an ox upon the altar of Juktas.

While an attendant played on a sacred pipe and the tiny monkey watched, fearful and sad, a cord was drawn round the child's neck by the priestess of Poteidan, and slowly tightened down. A brief struggle ensued — for the child was not fully asleep — until both breath and life had been extinguished. With the strangling complete and the small body lying perfectly still — as still now as if it had been carved from the same stone as the altar itself — a dagger in the priestess's hand severed a vessel in the child's throat. As the blood flowed out, warm and steaming, it was drained into a pottery jar bearing the image of a red-spotted bull — a sacred receptacle for the life-blood of sacrifices to Poteidan.

"The child. You know her, don't you?" Mr. Lanthorne asked.

"Yes," said Miss Wastefield. Her heart had turned to lead in her breast; tears were pouring down her cheeks. She gazed mournfully on the pathetic little bundle. She was transfixed by the horror of it — by the *memory* of it. "Her name is Djhana. She is my prior self, not yet ten years of age, lying on the sacrificial table — the sacred stone —"

"Thirty-five of your centuries have passed since she was given in sacrifice to the earth-shaker. It was done to spare Kaftor from destruction, to prevent this bully Poteidan from leveling its towns and temples. You were offered to him by your parents. Do you remember your parents? Your father was himself a high priest of Poteidan, and your mother a lesser priestess, and you their last remaining child."

Yes, she told him, she remembered them now; she remembered it all now. At last she understood the cause of the mysterious illness that had afflicted her — the suffocating constriction in her throat, the nameless fear, the nausea, the taste of honeyed wine on her tongue.

"You were a gift to Poteidan from the people of Kaftor," said Mr. Lanthorne, "and so had no leave to be reborn without his consent. You are Poteidan's to do with as he pleases, for you exist within that realm he has claimed as his own and are subject to him. But yours is a youthful, inexperienced soul — a mere codling, having been bodied but twice. You have scarcely lived."

Miss Wastefield made no response, so shaken was she by the knowledge she had regained. Unconsciously she made a fist and touched it to her forehead, in that ritual pose she remembered now was a gesture of worship and submission by the Kaftorites to their deities. Yes, she remembered it all now, and so vividly, too. She had been ritually slaughtered on the altar of Juktas, and at so innocent an age, to appease the earth-shaker and avert the destruction of Kaftor, and then been reborn without his consent.

Such had been her transgression!

"I have never lived," she heard herself say, although no words formed on her lips. "I, who had not yet seen ten summers, had never lived. Oh, Mr. Lanthorne — I have wanted so much to *live*!"

Launched into eternity with so few years to her name, given in thrall to Poteidan to do with as he pleased — such had been the sad lot ordained for her. How uncaring of Fortune! How unjust! Yes, she wanted so very much to live, but was prohibited from being bodied again; otherwise it would be a renunciation of the offering her parents and the people of Kaftor had made in the quaking-time.

It was these so-called gods, she understood now, these ancient souls of Mr. Lanthorne's, who had devised the laws and principles by which whole worlds revolved. Bodied beings had no choice but to obey these laws, for good or evil; and so all good, and therefore all evil, was the product — or the fault — of these same governing spirits. It was they who were to blame for the misery that plagued humankind, because it was they who had devised the rules of the game. Any good that humans did, and therefore any evil, flowed ultimately from these beings. The venerated doctrine of free will, she saw now, was just so much humbug.

"First the mirror was sent to you, in hopes it would stir your soul to remembrance," said Mr. Lanthorne. "But your soul refused to be stirred; it had drunk too freely of the waters of Lethe. Rather than heeding the mirror, you put it away. You were so very young in Kaftor, and remain so very young and inexperienced a spirit, having been denied your rebirths."

"And the choice I must make? It is whether to return to Kaftor as I have been commanded — or to resist?"

"As I've said, the power of the earth-shaker far exceeds my own. I am, however, able to fend off his earthly servants, and will do so for as long as you wish. But I cannot fend off Poteidan himself, should he choose to intervene and push matters to their final issue. Of course he may never intervene, or he may do so tomorrow. One can never know."

For a long time they sat in silence. Little Juga, hanging onto his mistress's shoulder, twined his long arms round her neck and peered into her eyes with an expression of the deepest sympathy. Poor Juga! His tiny heart wrung for her.

"Your small friend is a good friend," Mr. Lanthorne observed, "and an old one."

"But why should you wish to help me, sir?" Miss Wastefield asked him, having debated this point with herself for nearly the whole of the past day, indeed since the very moment Mr. Lanthorne had come between her and the Triamete in the smoky lane. "What am I to you? Have you followed me my entire life?"

Mr. Lanthorne hesitated a little before answering. His grim features reflected, for perhaps the first time, something like dissatisfaction — or was it regret? "I have encountered this Poteidan more than once in my travels, and have observed his actions which have been all of a piece. On every occasion I have allowed them to pass unchallenged, with lamentable results. I suppose it's from a sense of obligation that I resolved to aid you as best I could. I could not stand by and see him treat another as he has treated so many before."

"Oh, it is a foul, evil thing," cried Miss Wastefield, meaning the mirror of ancient polished bronze. "It will never let me rest. A foul thing it is that threatens me in hissing whispers, and shows me the odious faces of Triametes, and kills my dear father!"

"In that it *is* a foul thing," Mr. Lanthorne agreed. "I should have intervened sooner, that I recognize now. I hadn't anticipated the consequences as regards your father. For that, Miss Wastefield, I am truly sorry."

"And for what purpose does it do this? So that I might appease a bully — a heartless, merciless fiend at whose altar I was *murdered*!"

They were words addressed as much to the air as to Mr. Lanthorne. Tears came again into her eyes. She had endured so much — so much uncertainty, so many wakeful nights, so much nervous dread. So many dashed hopes! She thought of Martin and his love for her, and of a future that in all likelihood never would be theirs. Oh, that this horror would simply vanish away, like one of her nightmares upon waking!

"Must we always be trodden underfoot by these cruel, unseen beings, these Poteidans? Must we remain forever in the grip of their slavery?" she asked.

"Alas, Miss Wastefield, it is too often the way," said Mr. Lanthorne. "I fear there is little help for it. Even I in my travels often am hindered by spirits like Poteidan. But it is part and parcel of existence, and one must accept it as such and be ever on the alert. To flail at the universe serves no purpose."

There followed another pause, and rather an uncomfortable one it was for Miss Wastefield. By degrees, however, the tenor and direction of her thoughts changed, and raising her eyes to Mr. Lanthorne's, she asked —

"And what of you, sir? What of your fate? Must you always be wandering?"

"Always."

"There is no end to it, then?"

"That I can't say, Miss Wastefield, although one hopes there is no end of knowledge," the gentleman replied. "For if there is an end to it, what would be the point of going on? There would be no mystery left; one would simply wink out of existence from boredom. That is why I believe it all must extend forever, it absolutely must. How very tiresome it would be if one knew everything there was to know!"

It was such an answer as conveyed to Miss Wastefield, bluntly and succinctly, how vast was the gulf that lay between a being of light and her own poor infant candle of a self. It crossed her mind that perhaps Mr. Lanthorne had some ulterior motive in wanting to aid her, but it was an idea she quickly discarded. The boldness of his knight-errantry in saving her from the Triametes, his straightforwardness and sensitivity in the recovery of her past, were proof against any such suspicion. If ever she was to get over her difficulty, it would only be with his help.

"One thing I do know for certain," said Mr. Lanthorne, speaking aloud now, "is that our ship sails in the morning. You must consider, Miss Wastefield, the courses of action that are open to you. I shall remain with you for as long as you wish, should that be your choice. Though you may not see me, I shall ever be close at hand."

Saying which, her grim-faced guardian escorted her from the sitting-room. Upon the misty morrow they removed themselves from the inn and, making their way to Falaise harbor, joined Captain Barnaby aboard the *Salty Sue* for the voyage to Nantle.

CHAPTER THIRTY-FIVE

A Puzzling Revelation

In the little back-parlor of the boarding-house in Chamomile Street, Mrs. Matchless had gathered with her staff to instruct them in the matter of their duties and conduct during her coming absence. The arrangements for her holiday at Smithy Bank had at last been made, and she was set to depart next morning for her visit with a certain old and valued friend who once had kept a grocery in Chamomile Street.

Closeted there with her in her private sanctum were Anne Feagle, and young Mr. William Pancras, and Miss O'Guppy, and gangly Alice the maid-of-all-work. Miss Feagle, as befitted her rank, had received the keys of the house and been invested with her employer's power of authority as regards the bills and accounts. To Pancras had been entrusted the bearing of messages to and from boarders, staff, and tradesmen in the neighborhood. Impressed on him also was the need to keep himself tidy, and to pay heed to the state of the boarders' coats and shoes. To Niamh had been given the task of helping with the meals, and running errands to and from the market, and an injunction applied to exercise restraint in practicing her violin at odd hours of the night. And to tall and toothy Alice — well, to a maid-of-all-work is ever entrusted all that work no one else is maid enough to do.

Mrs. Poundit was the sole member of the staff absent from the discussion. Knowing that the cook and her carving-knife would be otherwise engaged below stairs, Dottie had discussed with her separately such matters as related to the kitchen. For this young William was thankful. The bloated cook he had long suspected of being a cannibal, but of course he never could prove it. It had been the particular pleasure of Miss Jilly Juniper to chide him for this, and for being so young, helpless, and impressionable.

But it did no good; whenever Mrs. Poundit would fix him with her eye and go through a piece of fiendish pantomime with her knife, or *k-chop-k-chop* her way through a joint of meat on her chopping-board, or regale him with gore-drenched tales of stripe-bodied scimitar-cats and hairy great goblin-spiders, it never failed to rattle his bright buttons and send chills racing up his spine.

The invitation to visit Smithy Bank had been extended by Mr. Thread-needle, of course — a gentleman who had been the subject of much recent discussion in the house — and having in hand now his reply to Dottie's ac-ceptance, a booking had been secured for her on the *Salty Sue*. This latter had been accomplished through the agency of Mrs. O'Guppy in the cap-tain's household. The captain and his prime duck of a craft were bound down-channel from Falaise, and were expected to arrive that afternoon. As for Mr. Threadneedle, he was looking to receive Mrs. Matchless on the day following when the lugger was to call at Cold Harbor.

Once these matters had been discussed to everyone's satisfaction, the subject turned naturally to that of Miss Wastefield, the pretty lodger of Mrs. Juniper's who had disappeared.

What had happened to her? Mr. Frobisher and the rector had dashed off to Jekyl Street out of concern for her safety. Sadly, Mr. Frobisher's intuition had proved only too true. The poor leedy, as Niamh called her, had been forcibly thrust into a carriage and driven off. Since then there had been no news of her. Mr. Frobisher and two others had given chase but had lost her track. Later the carriage had been found abandoned near a cab-stand, with no sign of Miss Wastefield or of her abductors either. Such had been the train of events as related in fitful bursts by Mr. Frobisher, who, ordinarily so quick-spoken and plain of speech, and untroubled of manner, had seemed much altered upon his return.

It was deplorable what had happened to Miss Wastefield, everyone agreed, and something had to be done. But it was a matter for the sheriff's men, not the inhabitants of Chamomile Street. Meanwhile it shouldn't de-ter Mrs. Matchless from taking her long-anticipated holiday, especially now that the details had been settled.

"Still, I am much afraid for Miss W.," Dottie admitted, feeling a trifle guilty now about that holiday.

"Can it be she was a smuggler after all?" asked Anne. "Smuggling port wine into Nantle in that trunk of hers — and now the excisemen have got her!"

"I don't believe the excisemen have taken to abducting young women in coaches," the widow said.

"Or a fugitive from love, fleeing some gentleman suitor?"

"Oh, it's so romantic!" exclaimed Alice, her hands clutched in a transport of longing.

"Pull yourself together, girl," said Dottie. "No, I don't think either explanation is at all likely. But of course one can't be certain with young people these days."

As for Mr. Frobisher, he had remained in his dark mood since the loss of Miss Wastefield. Anne had seen him in the front-parlor not long before, slumped in a chair by the fireplace with a cigar in his teeth and his boots on the fender. Mr. Kix and Mr. Lovibond and Miss Rivers had been there as well, but their conversation had done little to spirit him up. Every now and again he would dash his heel against the floor, or plunge a fist into his hand, or mumble some words about how it was his own fault, how he could have prevented it, how he *ought* to have prevented it; but no one knew just why or how this should be. Then he would get up and get down, and stare at the fire or out of the window, and curse himself under his breath for having no more brains than the dried fish in glass over the mantel.

Miss Wastefield's mysterious caller at Mrs. Juniper's had turned out to be none other than her *fiancé*. He had only recently arrived from Crow's-end, and was one of those who'd given chase and found the abandoned carriage. After lodging a complaint with the sheriff, he had returned to the Bunch of Grapes in a similar state, if not a worse one, than Mr. Frobisher's, considering it was the promised lady of his heart who had been stolen away.

"Indeed, I thought it likely she'd been pledged to another, and told him so. Poor Mr. M.!" said Dottie — meaning M. as in poor Milo the postman. "It was only natural that a young person of her years and quality should be engaged. Mr. M. was most grievously smitten. I do hope he has managed to temper his fondness for her."

"It's very possible, ma'am," Anne declared, "for he's been spoony on so many in the neighborhood that I've lost all count. He is too easily swayed, though it does seem he has a strong drive to recover. How else to survive so many infatuations?"

"I should think that with his smart red jacket would come a measure of self-confidence. I myself have ever been fond of a gentleman in a smart costume. Have I told you how Mr. T., years agone there in his shop, in his grocer's blue apron —?"

"Yes, ma'am," hinted Anne, "and certain of us here remember him, too."

"I forget it hasn't been so long since he left Chamomile Street for the Smithy, as he terms it," smiled the widow. "Do you recall the time he faced down the saber-cat in the street — the cat that had wandered down from the hills? Imagine! He was very brave, I thought, in seeing everyone else safely into their homes before thinking of his own self. I have myself thought of him often since those days. For Mr. M. — that is, my *own* Mr. M. — has been gone for these few years, and one does take to thinking now and again. Whatever is most prized, you know, is hardest to find."

It was the first time Anne or anyone could recall hearing Dottie, who to all appearances had survived the loss of her Mr. M. rather well, say anything to counter that impression.

"Are you going to marry the groceryman, Mrs. Matchless?" inquired a worried Pancras. "For if you are, I shall lose my situation, I think."

"Oh, William!" exclaimed Anne. "Mrs. Matchless would never desert you. She has your training to think of. Nor you, Alice — you needn't goggle so!"

"Not to worry," Dottie assured them, with a sprightly face. "If I were to marry Mr. T. — and mind, that remains a very substantial if — but if I were, I should of course take all of you with me. That ferocious housekeeper he has written on about, the one with the menacing finger, and that butler with the very elevated opinion of himself —"

"Mrs. Kimber and Mr. Plush?"

"Indeed! I shudder to think of what he has endured out there at the hands of those ungrateful people. Well, it's beyond question — they simply will have to go."

"And what of Niamh?" asked Anne. "Will she come with us?"

"Ah, shure, an' bain't *that* a ridiculous notion!" exclaimed Miss O'Guppy, with a dismissive fling of her hand. "'Tis nonsinse it is, by the Holy. Like the little gossoon there, I should look out for another place first. A cross-day 'twill be when *I* cross the water! Yez all may put off for that island, I'll not care to folly — I'll not care to be tossed about on open waters and *dhrownded*. Death by dhrownding bain't a fit end for a Christian. I'll not care to be leavin' Nantle, if yez plase, for the cards ha' spaken agin it."

"There may be more to things than can be read in your cards, perhaps, Niamh," said Dottie — gently, diplomatically, so as not to rouse the temper of the young woman, whose novel opinions frequently met with resistance in the household, and in Chamomile Street in general.

"That I dono'," returned Miss O'Guppy, "but I'll not care to take the chance. Ye may call me daft — there's many as do. I'd rather say truth an' dar' the divil. The cards mane what they mane, an' that's what they mane, by Jasus!"

"And then of course there is our Mr. F.," said Dottie, briskly changing the topic, for she had observed an angry spot starting to form on the girl's cheek. "He, too, has a liking for the young lady who's gone missing — the young *engaged* lady. It appears he had words with her young man there in the road, just at the moment she was spirited away."

"Poor leedy," sighed Niamh, shaking her head.

"And poor Mr. Frobisher," said Anne. "He really is very low, and berates himself something fiercely."

They were interrupted at this point by activity of some kind in the hall. Someone had arrived to see Mr. Frobisher. The knock had been answered by of all persons Mrs. Poundit, who had emerged from the smoke of the kitchen long enough to open the door, greet the visitor with a menacing stare, and then return chuckling to her den. That visitor being Jilly Juniper, she wasn't one to be awed by the queasy cook and, being familiar with the house, had conducted herself upstairs to the front-parlor.

"I say, moppet!" exclaimed Mr. Frobisher, with a show of animation that quite surprised the others.

"Hallo! If it isn't our dear Miss Juniper," said Mr. Lovibond, breaking out of his chair, pipe in hand. His jovial countenance fairly beamed. He motioned to Mr. Kix, who alone had refused to stir from his seat. "Give a hallo, Kix — old misery-guts — don't be a grump — Jilly Juniper — house next door — lovely child —"

Arms crossed on his chest, Mr. Kix reluctantly disgorged a salutation. Mr. Kix didn't care much for children and, despite his seeming rapport with young William Pancras, viewed them much the same way he viewed the world, which was the same way that Pancras viewed Mrs. Poundit — darkly, and with suspicion.

"Hello, Jilly," said Miss Rivers. "May we help you? How are you getting on with your studies? Have you need of another reading lesson?"

"Please, Miss Rivers," said Jilly, "but I should like to speak with Mr. Frobisher for a moment, if I might — in private."

Looks of surprise and amusement were exchanged by all but Allan Frobisher, whose quickened senses told him that something of importance had brought the child there. The manner of Jilly was so very earnest; he saw it in her eyes. He knew the likelihood was great that whatever she had to tell him bore upon Miss Wastefield, about whom she had been much concerned.

"You may use the library, Jilly, you and Mr. F.," said Mrs. Matchless from the doorway.

"Thank you, ma'am."

"And how is your mother today?"

"She is very well, Mrs. Matchless."

"Have you any news of your missing lodger?"

Jilly's response was equivocal enough, and elusive enough, to pique the interest of everyone; and so all followed the two with their eyes, if not their ears, as Jilly and Mr. Frobisher retired to the little back-study beside the stairs. It was called the library because it was too small for a boarder's bedroom, but too large for a cupboard, and home to a shelf of moldy books that no one had read or ever was likely to.

Of course, there were one or two curious persons who *did* follow the pair with their ears, by straining very hard to listen at the keyhole of the library-door — persons whose names shall be unrecorded here so as not to embarrass them — and it was there in the room too small for a bedroom but too large for a cupboard that the something of importance was made known to Mr. Frobisher.

It turned out to be a very mysterious and important thing indeed. Jilly told him how she had that morning spied the man in the chimney-pot hat — she'd recognized him from Miss Wastefield's description of him, for he had been invisible on that earlier occasion — holding conversation with Lucy in the lady's rooms. No one had seen or heard him enter; no one had let him in at either door, and all the windows had been securely fastened; no one knew how he had gotten into the house. *That alone was mystery enough!*

The man had informed Lucy that Miss Wastefield was in health and aboard the *Salty Sue,* which was to anchor soon at the quay, and that she must collect her mistress's belongings — everything, that is, but the chain-bound trunk — and join her there. They were to depart next day on a voyage of some length that was intended to guarantee the safety of Miss Wastefield. Lucy's relief was unmeasured. She cried like a watering-pot, so thankful was she to receive word at last from her mistress, albeit by rather surprising means.

Mr. Frobisher was at once suspicious of the means, however. Tom Lanthorne! Why should this adversary of Miss Wastefield's, this three-eyed pincered giant in human guise, be telling Lucy this if it were not a trap? But why should he want to trap Lucy? And how came Miss Wastefield on a ship from distant Falaise? And what of the mirror locked in her trunk, which Mr. Lanthorne had directed be left behind?

Mr. Lanthorne had commanded Lucy to tell no one of her plans. But Jilly was under no such obligation; on the contrary, she could scarcely wait to tell Mr. Frobisher.

"Please, Allan," she begged him, "will you go to the harbor and meet the captain's ship there? Will you see that no harm comes to Miss Wastefield?"

The look on the face of the young man prophesied his answer.

"Chin up, Jilly," he smiled. "To the harbor it is — *that* you may depend on!"

Despite the privacy of the library, the news was soon all over the house. The missing lady was aboard the very same ship that was to carry Mrs. Matchless to Truro! When the news came to Dottie's attention — we are glad to say she had not been one of those with her ear to the keyhole — a decision was made to inform the rector; and so Pancras was dispatched to St. Mary-le-Quay. Miss O'Guppy and Alice meanwhile went down to the kitchen, where Mrs. Poundit found much to wag and noddle at in the information.

Mr. Milo the postman, having mounted the steps of the house, was on the point of applying knocker to door when the door unexpectedly swung open. There stood Mr. Frobisher with his floppy wide-awake on his head and Jilly Juniper at his side. In one voice they offered the postman their hallos and hurried down the steps. Little Jilly proceeded only so far as the door of her own house, however, while Mr. Frobisher continued on at a rapid pace down the street.

Mr. Milo was quickly apprised of the situation by Dottie and her staff. His response was immediate: he was prepared to fling his letter-bag from his shoulder and set off for the quay, until Dottie reminded him that the rector and Mr. F. already were hasting to the young woman's aid, and what was more, that it was the job of a postman to deliver the mails, not ladies in distress.

"Your Mr. Frobisher — ah, yes, well, of course he would be hasting to her assistance, wouldn't he?" said Mr. Milo, wilting a little inside his smart red jacket. His hopes, his dreams, all knocked to smash again, and so quickly, too — and the lady herself not even there to do it!

As a result of the postman's being apprised, however, everyone round about soon knew of Miss Wastefield and the *Salty Sue* and of Lucy's visitor who came and went at will. For secrets are secrets only so long as they can be kept; and in such a neighborhood as Chamomile Street secrets may travel very fast indeed, at something like the rate of a postman's brisk *tap-tap-tap* along its otherwise dull and drowsy streets.

CHAPTER THIRTY-SIX

The Two Miss Wastefields

A clear morning dawned at Nantle. That alone was such a surprise that not just its inhabitants but the ancient city itself sat up and took notice. Spires of parish churches, bastions of city gates, points of gables, climbing turrets, tall stacks of chimneys, windmills on hills, the square-towered pile of the Minster, all rose as one like eager hounds at attention and looked about them. A sun as rosy as the cheeks of Mrs. Matchless filled the streets with its darting rays and threw down long shadows. The light flushed pink and glittered in the glass eyes of the houses, which winked and nodded in reply, as much startled by the absence of fog as by the unfamiliar sight of one another, and saying for the first time in a long time — *"I see you!"*

In Nantle harbor the masts of the ships stood out in bold relief, having for once no channel fog to obscure them. Mr. Bob Sly, first mate of the *Salty Sue,* was watching them from the quay, having witnessed the peep o' day with Captain Slinger at that venerable skipper's post beside his weighing-chair. In their company were Mr. Sawyer, the wizened little ship's-carpenter, retired, and Mr. David Devenham.

While at Falaise, Mr. Devenham had been obliged to alter his plans. Having parted ways with Mr. Jarvey on account of some trifling dispute between them, he had taken passage aboard the lugger. And so he found himself back in Nantle, the city he had lately abandoned after pronouncing it as dull as ditch-water. But for once the swart and gloom-ridden Davy had resolved to look on the sunny side of the wall: for Nantle was where Sprig's was, and the Axe and Compasses, too, and many another favored haunt, and some small portion of Mr. Liffey's cash remained to be disbursed in such places.

Man, man, he snorted, why squander ducats on a boorish knave like Jarvey, one who failed to appreciate the value of a noted traveler's patronizing his services? It was so very selfish of him to have treated a passenger so, and to have chucked him from the train. But it wasn't so unexpected, either.

"For it's life itself that teaches us to be selfish," said Davy, waxing philosophical on this, one of his favorite topics, to the amusement of his companions. "Man, man, you've only to look around you! See those briny waters and the creatures out of number lurking there. Are they not selfish, every one of 'em, and weren't they made so by nature? Is it not self-interest that drives the steelhead, the shark, the leviathan zeug? It's food that drives them; but in man it is more than food, it is the foul chink of coin. A plague of such a world that presses its creatures so for a penny-piece! This entire sphere, sundered or not, has all the marks of a botched job. So there you have the bitter truth, sirs, as regards the nature of nature."

"And what o' love, eh, Davy?" inquired Mr. Sawyer, knowing this to be a subject that would get the lonely wanderer's goat. "Bean't there room in sich a world for the soft impeachment? For there be self-interest in love, too, I rackon."

"Aye, 'tis bilge and bunkum be love, by gum!" cackled Bob Sly, looking forward like Mr. Sawyer to the wanderer's response.

"Love, sir? And of what use is *love*?" answered Davy, with a snort of such indignance it threw his mop of sooty-black hair over his face. "A pox on love! For love leads to wooing, and wooing leads to a wife, and a wife leads to a family, and a family is a scurvy, vexatious, pestering thing. Spare me the tyranny of family! Who has need of love? Does a steelhead love? Does a zeug love? Man, man, it's self-interest that guides every impulse, it's *self-love* — it is the pressing command of nature. That, sirs, is what my study of the world has taught me. When the world presses, we must obey. We can't do otherwise or be pressed into oblivion."

Captain Slinger took a whiff of his pipe and nodded into his white beard, and traded smiling glances with Mr. Sawyer.

"Pressed like a grape ye are by nature, is that it, Davy?" said the ship's-carpenter, who had been long convinced that Mr. Devenham was suffering from an excess of bees in his cockpit. "For if it's like a grape, then so much *whining* by sich individuals as yerself be more than understandable."

"Ho, ho!" chortled Mr. Sly, slapping his leg and shaking his head at such waggery. "Ho, ho, *ho*!"

Mr. Devenham was about to deliver a riposte when his attention was attracted to the figure of a man very tall and broad, and wearing a chimney-pot hat, who was making for the gangway of the *Salty Sue*.

"Lanthorne!" he exclaimed, insinuating himself into the man's path such that it was impossible for the other to avoid him. "Man, you've been scarce with your company of late. Where have you kept yourself aboard ship? Not once did we glimpse your sternish phiz in the galley. Look here — I'm in some disagreement with these sailorly types as regards a matter of principle. I feel for them, truly I do, they are so very disappointing. Tell me, sir, have you traveled much?"

He asked this in a semi-distracted way, for at the same time he was scraping through his pocket-book for what remained of Mr. Liffey's cash. "Well, sir? Have you seen much of the world, man, what there's left of it to see?"

"A little of it," Mr. Lanthorne admitted.

"Well, I myself have traveled much, sir, and observed more than a few things, and I'd advise you to do the same. It's my occupation, and though the world is a botched job devised by a fiend and a madman, I demand the freedom to see it all and prove it so. That fellow Jarvey would take my liberty from me with his irksome, petty restrictions. A plague of all mastodon men! I'll not be mewed up for hour upon hour in a prison of a passenger cab bound to the withers of a thunder-beast. I must be free to go where I will. What, no opinion? You always have so little to say. You appear to me like a man something in want of worldly experience."

"I shan't contradict you, sir," replied Mr. Lanthorne, and stepping neatly round the obstruction, he marched over the gangway to the lugger.

Captain Barnaby, all rust and salt, nodded his grim-faced passenger aboard — he was a friend of the mystery-lady's, he knew — and crossing the gangway in the other direction informed Mr. Sly that they would be putting off at once. He then took his first mate aside and confided to him that he'd received a dire warning from Jolly Jumper Yard that there were bailiff's men on the premises — his wife's prediction had come true — and that it might be wise if the lugger were to slip quietly from port now, to prevent its being seized.

"Nuthooks, by gum!" said Mr. Sly, growling and spitting. "Damn and blast their deadlights!"

It made perfect sense. The captain had only one ship, but many bills afloat; and as he'd never yet actually dishonored a bill, if he were not in port to be apprehended then he could not, in fair conscience, be said to have dishonored one now. It was but a temporary ebb of fortune, he assured himself; in time the winds would be more favorable. For now, he must be prepared to lash his helm and stand whatever came his way.

"Soak me in bilge-water, Bob Sly, and scuttle me," he vowed, with a determined jut of his chin, "if ever a bailiff's man sets toe to plank o' the *Sue* while Jack Barnaby lives to skipper her. Mark me! Now stand by drackly to slip moorings and hoist sail."

"Love yer limbs, Cap'n, sir, aye — by gum!" cried Bob, snapping to.

In light of the emergency, the captain was happy to have taken on a few passengers, for it meant additional income; but it would be of little consequence if the ship were seized by the bailiff's officers. So he urged Mr. Sly to keep his blinkers peeled and his ears on the stretch, even as he did the same. The captain was exceedingly anxious to heave anchor, as he stood there at the rail with his brows crunched and his gaze sweeping the quay. He was on the watch not just for nuthooks but for the last of his passengers, one who had yet to arrive, and whom he should hate to leave behind in case the nuthooks arrived first.

"Cherish my guts but she's as tight a ship as ever sailed, and 'tis love I have for her that no man knows," he muttered. "I'd rather she sink fathoms deep like a stone and be lost to Davy Jones — aye, 'twould be right sailorly — than be laid hold of by so scurvy a thing as a broker's man!"

It was then he heaved not an anchor but a sigh of thanks, as he spied his final passenger alighting from a cab. Relieved, he strutted briskly across the gangway and, pulling off his bonnet, offered Mrs. Matchless a wide blue arm. He escorted her and her luggage aboard with every grace and courtesy, and so much skipperly cordiality, as if every minute that had lapsed since the creation of time were at his disposal. He would not allow bailiff's men to defeat him; he was determined to keep a bold heart and to be of cheery fellowship, come what may.

As Dottie had arrived in the company of Dr. Pinches, it was only natural that the clergyman should come aboard to see her settled in her tiny hutch of a stateroom. In the process he and Captain Barnaby were observed to exchange wary glances. The stalwart warrior of the sea and the fisher of men had little in common. Each knew the other's leanings, but in deference to Dottie they chose to keep their opinions to themselves; instead, it was the bold heart and cheery fellowship of the captain's that prevailed.

It was at this juncture that Black Davy, having watched the proceedings from the comfort of Slinger's throne — he had eased himself onto it, with its owner's blessing — exploded in a snort as a pair of ragged-looking street fellows came trotting by.

"Well, if it's not for funning, sirs," said Davy, hailing them, "what business might a pair of jolterheads have in these fishy precincts? Man, man, we've not had geese on this ground since Bartholomew Fair!"

"Troth and faith, and if it bain't Davy, now," smiled Round-the-corner Jones. "May the Almighty keep ye an' guard ye! Bain't it so, Moeran?"

"Shure it is," nodded Planxty, grinning through his horse-collar. "By the powers, joy, 'tis Davy indeed! Whood a bleeved? I'd no notion he'd sich consarn for his weight, now, he as was always so skin-and-bony a crayture. Eighteen stone it is! Is sich how ye read it, joy?"

"Hardly a stone less, jewel," said his colleague, peering at the dial of the balance from which the chair was slung, "for Davy's ever been a solid fellow, bedad. Me sarvice to ye, Davy, and a long life t'ye."

Such banter and spirits were intended as commentary on Mr. Devenham's appropriation of the weighing-chair. But despite their chatter the two vagabonds seemed not quite themselves, or so Davy imagined. They kept glancing about them to distant corners of the quay, their eyes shaded against the unfamiliar dawn, as though on the look-out for someone. He suspected it was Comport's men they sought — or feared — and declared as much, loudly and boldly; which caused Mr. Sly, who had been eavesdropping from the gangway of the ship, to redouble his watch.

"Man, man," said Davy, wringing his head as he swung in the chair, "you drones would be advised to keep your distance from Jekyl Street and avoid a dust-up with Jacob Comport. You'd best have no truck with Comport, and that's flat."

"Shure, and 'tis most kind of ye, Davy," returned Jones, "and much obliged we are, but we've no need of the reminder. It bain't Comport as consarns us; 'tis Porter. I'll ax it of the noble captain here, a gintleman and a Christian, and Mr. Carpenther Sawyer, and ye, too, Davy, if ye plase, if ye've seen Jerry Porter anywheres of late? 'Tis that Jerry Porter as lays claim to the perfession of fish porter, and was known to our late friend an' fellow Dermot O'Kilcoyne, God rest his sould. For at Musselgate we've had no sign of him at all, at all."

At mention of the name of Porter a shadow crossed the face of Mr. Devenham. He brought the levitating chair to a standstill and, rising slowly to his feet, fixed his lean and greedy gaze on the vagabonds. Was it Jerry Porter they sought, he wondered — or Jerry Squailes?

"And what business might knavish riff-raff have with Porter?" he asked, with nothing of his usual negligent air, but more like a dog's surly defense of a buried bone. His eyes were hard and cold, like marble, and there was the faint gleam of an unpleasant sneer showing through his mus-

taches. It was a rather changed Davy Devenham that confronted them, one
the vagabonds had rarely glimpsed before.

"Agh, by the gannies, joy, 'tis but a favor for the widow of auld O'Kilcoyne," spoke up Planxty. "'Tis a private matter, don't ye see, Davy, as consarns only the widow and friends of poor Dermot. And may the marciful
Creator sthrike me crooked if it bain't!"

It was an answer that didn't completely satisfy Mr. Devenham. For a
long moment he scowled at the pair. He touched a hand to his coat, to ascertain that his pocket-book and the cash it housed remained secure; but
aside from this, and the scowl, and a very ugly curling of his lip, no other
response was forthcoming.

Mr. Sawyer and Captain Slinger volunteered that it had been some days
now since they'd clapped eyes on the man Porter. It was the day the old attorney from Crow's-end had come seeking him — the old attorney who
had been brought to the quay by none other than Black Davy himself.

Hearing such, the vagabonds proceeded to put this and that together
rather quickly. They looked again at the surly dog, and then at each other.
They thought of the toff gentleman from Cargo, and saw their hopes for
easy money fade. The jig was up; and so, grinning and ducking heads and
hats at Davy and his companions, they scurried off.

Meanwhile Lucy had gone aboard the lugger the day before, at Mr. Lanthorne's behest, and been reunited with her mistress and Juga. Miss Wastefield was unwilling to leave the ship, having had her meals brought to her
from the galley, and refusing to go on deck for fear of being seen by the
brother Triametes or other agents of the lord Poteidan. She had had a few
visitors, however, one of them being Dr. Pinches. Having been alerted by
young Pancras, he had gone to see her soon after the ship docked. In carefully chosen words she had described for him and Lucy much — but not
all — of what had happened to her. The most surprising thing was the
transformation of Mr. Lanthorne from a foe into a kind of friend, or at the
very least an ally. But it remained a puzzle to her listeners how her guardian
and shipmate could have visited Lucy in Chamomile Street at the same time
he was sailing down-channel from Falaise in the lugger.

One visitor to whom Miss Wastefield had *not* granted an interview was
Allan Frobisher. He had craved her pardon, and importuned her repeatedly
in the name of friendship, forgiveness, and the late Mr. Delancey, and even
Jilly Juniper, but to no avail. Apparently there was no service he could render, however admirable and well-intentioned, that could atone for his deception. In the end he left without seeing her and, returning to Chamomile
Street, had relapsed into his black mood.

There had been another knock at Miss Wastefield's door, and another caller announced, one who had been admitted — it was Mr. Somerset. He, too, had received a visit from Mr. Lanthorne while the *Salty Sue* was running down-channel. Miss Wastefield declined to explain how this could possibly be. She in fact refused to enlighten him to any appreciable extent, something it pained her to do; but she would not have him involved on account of the danger. He'd been most anxious to see her, naturally, and to learn who the blackguards were who had abducted her, and why they had abducted her, and how she had come to escape. All she chose to tell him, however, was that it was Mr. Lanthorne who had rescued her and that he was a person she had gravely misjudged.

And so the puzzle came round again to who this man Lanthorne was, and what he was, and how he had contrived to be in two places at one time.

Miss Wastefield had then informed her *fiancé* of her plan to remain aboard the *Salty Sue* for an extended period. While at Falaise, Captain Barnaby had been much pleased to see his pretty-timbered passenger from Crow's-end, the mystery-lady, and to receive her again on board; but he was even more pleased, now that the bailiff's men were threatening, to have received her passage-money. And he was pleased, too, with Mr. Somerset, who at dawn had gone aboard ship as a passenger now himself.

Miss Wastefield was greatly dismayed. She had sought all along to prevent Martin's coming in the way of harm, from the moment she'd written off to him at Pinewick asking him not to inquire after her. But who were these men who were chasing her, and why, he wanted to know? Indeed, he *demanded* to know! But she held firm — she would not involve him. Perhaps it hadn't occurred to her that being her *fiancé* and embarked aboard ship, he already was very much involved.

Just as Martin arrived at her stateroom that morning, to press his case again, came fresh news. It came by way of a sturdy sailorman, one of the ship's company, who informed Miss Wastefield that her trunk had been safely stowed away in the hold below decks.

But Lucy had not brought the trunk with her, and Miss Wastefield had not ordered it brought; it had been left at Mrs. Juniper's at the request of Mr. Lanthorne. Miss Wastefield's heart sank, for she knew only too well what it meant.

Of course there had been no need to bring the trunk, as Mr. Lanthorne well knew — *it would bring itself.*

As she had so many times before, she felt herself strangely drawn to it even as she was repulsed by it. She was struck with an irrational desire to view the chain-bound monster in the hold and remove all doubt. She in-

sisted on going alone, but Martin insisted on going with her. Indeed he insisted on it as a right and would not be deterred, even though he knew
nothing about the trunk or why she wished to see it. At first she thought she
must put it off, but she saw rather quickly that it was useless, that Martin
for good or ill *was* involved and that she had no choice.

So they set off together for the hold. On their way they encountered Mr.
Frobisher, who had returned to the ship and was keen to speak with Miss
Wastefield (though Martin, recognizing the impudent Allan, was not so
keen that Miss Wastefield should speak to *him*). She had refused to see him
the day before in her cabin; she could not refuse him now that she was out
of it — or so ran his argument. Again, he craved her pardon; again, her
protests were in vain, and she found herself joined by both young men on
her trip to the hold.

"I can never be rid of the awful thing — it follows me wherever I go,"
she sighed, giving in.

"Do you mean this fellow?" returned Martin, meaning Frobisher.

"I mean to see this trunk," said Allan, briskly canceling him. Of course
he knew something already about the trunk and its contents, which served
only to trouble young Martin further. Here he was Miss Wastefield's *fiancé*
and yet he knew less of the danger that threatened her than did this presumptuous sort of a rangy, cagey, mustached whelp of a character in the
wide-awake hat.

"Won't you tell me what it all means, Jane?" he demanded, reaching for
her arm to detain her. "This trunk? Your leaving Pinewick? The purpose
for this mad adventure of yours?"

"I shall," said Miss Wastefield, pausing briefly in her stride. "I promise
you, Martin, I shall — in due course."

It was then that a third addition to the party made his appearance in the
shape of Dr. Pinches. He had assured Miss Wastefield he would look in on
her again before the ship sailed, and had come now to honor that pledge.
To Martin's chagrin, even the grizzled old clergyman seemed to know more
about the mystery enveloping his lady than did he — he, the scion of the
Somersets of Wakely, Crow's-end! — which frustrated him all the more.

They arrived at the narrow companion-way that descended to the hold,
and clambered down it. A shaft of light pouring through a hatchway amid-
ships provided the only illumination below decks. And lo! there in the dim
recesses, in a chamber piled high with stowage of every kind and reeking of
bilge, lay the foul cargo — chains, locks, and all.

Ah! So therein lies the marvelous mirror, thought the doctor, and so
thought Mr. Frobisher, too. Both were anxious to examine the treasure, for

differing reasons perhaps; but to their credit neither gave voice to their desires out of concern for Miss Wastefield.

Although no sound was heard from the trunk, no hissing whispers, no threats of menace, and nothing to break the silence but the creak and groan of the ship as she swayed at her moorings — still, to Miss Wastefield the trunk seemed to crouch before her like some awful beast of portent, readying itself for a spring.

And still she was drawn to it!

For several moments they stood in thought, Mr. Frobisher and the doctor a little aside of the others, contemplating the trunk, and Miss Wastefield painting upon it every sort of phantom that had haunted her since her accursed birthday.

"It doesn't seem so evil an object," said Mr. Frobisher.

"What do you mean evil?" returned Martin at once. "What can be evil about a young lady's trunk?"

"It does seem harmless," said Dr. Pinches, advancing a step or two closer.

"It is not harmless," Miss Wastefield assured him, with dreadful conviction — "oh, no, Doctor, it is not harmless!"

As if to drive her point home, the cargo chose that moment to speak.

"You'll not escape us again, my pretty tartlet," said a voice from the trunk.

All stopped and stared, especially Martin. The surprise that flashed across the faces of the men, the disbelieving looks, the sudden upsurge of horror in the eyes of Miss Wastefield — all this we leave to your imagination.

They quickly discovered that the voice had come not from the trunk, however, but from the darkness behind it. Up rose the brother gargoyles Arifay and Imbercand — awful beasts of portent that had indeed been crouching there, all out of view. Their eyes gleamed in the close, noxious atmosphere of the hold; the muscles of their broad arms and shoulders rippled; their teeth glistened.

The doctor fell back a step. Miss Wastefield gasped and turned pale. Mr. Frobisher, had he chosen to speak, knew not what he would have said. It was left to Martin, unschooled in the mysteries of portents and cannibals and ancient polished bronze, to brush up his sleeves and place himself before his lady.

"Behold yon villains," said the oyster-master Arifay, he of the tall white head like a boiled egg.

"Oh-hoh, my turkey chicken!" chimed in his fiery-haired brother. "We'll have you flushed out in no time, and plucked, and dressed, and dipped in the caldron — eh, my brother? 'Ods-bobs! We'll have a feast, by cock and pie, and it's the pretty bon-bon shall be served up first."

"A ravishing beauty — a damosella — a sweetmeat, one well worthy to mind the counter at Arifay's."

"That's for certain sure, brother!"

"And what o' the other villains?" demanded Arifay, his lips back-drawn and the scar on his head flaring. "What of their chances?"

"Dreadful slim, thinks Candy, dreadful slim; but 'tis the pretty bon-bon that interests the earth-shaker. We've a warrant for her apprehension, a *mittimus* from the lord Poteidan! And so how's it to be served, brother? Shall we boil her? Shall we roast her? Shall we sprinkle her with nutmeg and dip her in negus? Howsoever it's *au revoir,* for we'll have a good tuck-in, that's sure, and send our pretty sugarplum off home to the lord of earth and wave!"

"*Odious!*" cried Miss Wastefield, flinging the word at him like it was a dagger.

In return, the doorkeeper of Comport's shot the lady a fleering smile that showed his teeth, to which he applied an imaginary toothpick; and so his intentions and those of his unholy brother were plain to all. As for Martin, the sight of it raised the hairs on his neck, and though he understood little of the menace that threatened his *fiancée,* he understood enough.

"Run, Jane!" he commanded her, and stepping boldly forward began to revolve his clenched fists in the air, in a martial display meant to warn the gargoyles of the tremendous blows he intended to deal them. Mr. Somerset had had some experience of the gentleman's sport of pugilism, or the *fancy,* and knew well how to use those fists in polite combat. Unfortunately, he had yet to match them against anything quite so formidable — or so impolite — as a Triamete.

"Oh-hoh, my bully-beef — my little bantam of a cockerel!" exclaimed Candy, and throwing back his head, roared with laughter.

"Little more than squits, the lot of 'em," sneered his brother. "The puniest of villains."

"Run, Jane!" Martin called to her again, as he advanced with mechanized fists upon the gargoyles. "Run, I say!"

Oh, pray God, where was her all-seeing guardian? Miss Wastefield wanted to know. *Where was Mr. Lanthorne?*

It was then that the giants came for her, one round either side of the trunk; it was then that their third eyes glowing behind their heads were glimpsed by one and all.

"Good heavens!" cried Dr. Pinches, reeling back.

"Take charge of the lady, Doctor," Mr. Frobisher barked over his shoulder. "Get her well away from this ship — and yourself as well!"

So saying, he flung his hat from his head and, brushing up his own sleeves, took up a position at the side of his rival.

"And be lively about it!" Martin added, still sparring away like clockwork.

The chief aim of the brothers being to recapture Miss Wastefield, the focus of their attention was on her; and so the two young men made a valiant charge at them in her defense.

"Villains, your cause is lost," warned the oyster-master.

"Stow the gammon, Triamete!" retorted Allan.

And so the battle was joined. It did not last long. One result of it was dreary and predictable enough — the charge was repulsed and the gentlemen sent bouncing, their frail human persons tossed aside like the children's dolls they were, mere trifling, insignificant nothings in comparison to the warrior sons of Poteidan. The second result, however, was more encouraging, for the charge had given Dr. Pinches time to bundle Miss Wastefield up the companion-way, with his own self close behind.

In trembling haste they burst forth on deck. Darting round a corner, they sped past Captain Barnaby, who was at the moment preparing to raise sail, trip anchor, and away. The tide served and the bailiff's men were not far off, and they were likely very keen to serve *him*. Mrs. Matchless happening to be in his company at the time, the two watched what followed in mutual amazement.

"Smite me dumb and split me!" the captain exclaimed, as the brothers Arifay and Imbercand came hurtling after the mystery-lady and the fisher of men, with the bruised but otherwise unhampered Martin and Mr. Frobisher speeding in their wake.

"Why, it's Miss W. — and our Mr. F.!" cried Dottie, as they galloped past her like horses at a point-to-point.

The captain scratched his silvery head, and crunched his brows, and looked concerned — not so much because there seemed to be a cross-country of some sort taking place aboard his vessel, but because he'd recognized one of the participants as the hulking Candy of the sponging-house, and concluded that the bailiff's men had stolen aboard to seize his ship.

Here be damnable coil and cursed pickle! But why they should be making to seize his pretty-timbered passenger the captain had not a clue, split him and burn him; it merely added more mystery to the mystery-lady. Regardless, the skipper was prepared to defend his vessel, his men, and his passengers against any and all perceived enemies, and calling for Bob Sly, he joined in the chase.

As for the mystery-lady, she had pulled well ahead of the old doctor, and having fled round a corner aft, where she sent the captain's cat scampering, to her immense relief she ran smack into Mr. Lanthorne.

"Into the skiff, Miss Wastefield!" said he, handing her fast into the lugger's surf-boat, where she concealed herself under cover of tarpauling.

In such wise did the lady vanish, if only for a moment; for when Mr. Lanthorne turned round again, his figure, very tall and broad, had disappeared, and in its place stood a woman who was the very spit and image of Miss Wastefield.

Immediately the woman made a dash for the gangway.

The brother Triametes came round the corner and, fast overhauling both Dr. Pinches and the surf-boat, gave chase after the fleeing figure, believing her to be Miss Wastefield. Over the gangway and onto the quay they thundered and away in the direction of Musselgate Market.

It was at this moment that Messrs. Jones and Moeran, loitering round the stalls of the auctioneers, happened to glance up, their attention drawn by a sudden commotion. They saw a woman who was being chased hurry past and, to their unutterable horror, recognized the oyster-master as one of the two men pursuing her.

"*Holy Mother of Jasus!*" yelped Planxty, his eyes nearly leaping out of his head.

"No Jerry Porter hereabouts, Moeran!" said Jones, in rapid conclusion; on which note he and his colleague turned tail and scattered themselves among the tables and carts of the market.

Captain Barnaby, rushing toward the gangway, was startled to look round him and find Miss Wastefield standing there — Miss Wastefield, newly risen from the surf-boat like another Venus from her shell, although with considerably more in the way of wardrobe. Both he and Dottie were in fact quite bewildered, not to say elated, as were Martin and Mr. Frobisher and Dr. Pinches — for hadn't Miss Wastefield just been seen fleeing the ship with the bailiff's men in hot pursuit?

In the final analysis, however, it signified little; Miss Wastefield plainly was aboard and the bailiff's men were not, and that was good enough for the captain, split him cross-wise and sink him.

Straightway he bellowed to his minions, giving orders to loose sails and slip moorings, and be sharpish about it, too. Then was noise and stir enough on deck as the *Salty Sue* got under way, a trifle ahead of sailing time and with more in the way of passengers than expected — for both the doctor and Mr. Frobisher remained aboard — and with the deepening mystery of the mystery-lady and her trunk, and the bailiff's men, and the man Lanthorne, and the mirror of ancient polished bronze.

Right smartly and sailorly the lugger fetched out of the harbor and, with her sails bellying and her pennants flying, plunged full-joyous into the heaving waters of the channel.

CHAPTER THIRTY-SEVEN

Her Last Refuge

Where the gnawing sea broke ashore round the foot of Smithy Bank, just east of Cold Harbor, it had hollowed out a line of caves at the water's edge, and running in a distance of some twenty or thirty yards. Over time the shallow tide-pools within the caves had combined to form a maze of interconnecting chambers or grottoes. With their arches and groin-like ceilings rearing above the sea surface, their shelving niches, their pillars riven and etched by the endless slapping waters, these caves of Truro resembled nothing so much as a kind of crazy catacomb, a briny temple for sea-minded troglodytes, a Minster for the doughty mariners of the islands in the channel.

In their small oar-boat, Mr. Threadneedle and Tim Christmas, having glided in through one of the cave openings, were looking less like doughty mariners now, than like doughy babes rocking in a cradle. The ocean swell was particularly lively today, and the breakers curling something smart, and the pitching of the oar-boat something brisk; but given the rare glory of sunshine in the channel, the tinkerers could not be kept away. More than a few times they had laid by their work to explore the shoreline caves round the north coast, and on every occasion the wonder of these mysterious fissures in the earth had delighted them beyond expectation.

Ordinarily torches were needed to light the deeper confines, but in the outermost chambers the sun was more than sufficient. Here the bright morning served well to illuminate the rocky walls and pillars, which through the ages had been dyed by sea-salts to create a shimmering rain of colors, fleeting as ghost-light. Each wave splashing against the rocks bathed them in a weird, phosphorescent drapery, which poured down the walls in gleaming rivulets of ever-varying design. There were beautiful marine gardens thronged with corals, seaweeds, anemones, abalones pink, red, and blue, and a good store of other shells; while all around was much hissing of air and spouting of foam, much growling and spraying, and booming, and gurgling, as the seas ran in and then ran out again — a veritable thunder of waters produced by the surge of the swell as it rolled through the cave entrances.

Having feasted their eyes for long enough on the magic of the grottoes, the tinkerers made now for the opening through which they had entered. They bent to their oars and strove against the swell — it was no easy task — until they had left the caves behind and, working their way round one of the sheltering arms of stone, returned to the calm of Cold Harbor. There they pulled leisurely for the shore and beached their boat.

Almost at once a trumpet-roar broke upon their ears, and lo! there was Mustard bounding toward them with her ears flapping and her tail a-swing. She had accompanied them on their excursion as far as the strand, and while they had idled away their hour in the caves, she had passed hers amid the plantage back of the beach, exploring for dainties. Upon the reappearance of the tinkerers, she had come forward now to join them, her spirits as always lifted by the pleasure of their company.

After their return from Deeping St. Magma, Mr. Threadneedle and his apprentice-of-sorts had undertaken certain needed repairs and improvements in the coach-house, operations which were still ongoing. All had not as yet been perfected to Mr. Threadneedle's satisfaction, but considerable headway had been made. No one, it seemed, had observed that the coach-house had gone missing for a time; the channel fogs had been exceedingly dense and persistent in the interval. As for Mr. Plush and Mrs. Kimber, they had hardly noticed the squire's absence. Only Henry the gamekeeper, and Cook in the kitchen, and the sympathetic parlormaid had remarked on it.

Mr. Threadneedle had made excuse to the household that he had gone to Plinth, to attend to various matters regarding the estate. The squire was not above prevaricating when it came to Plush and Kimber, for in his view it was better than they deserved; but as for Henry and Cook and the maid, and more especially the family of Tim Christmas — well, they were another thing entirely. On his return Tim had told his mother and sister exactly what he'd intended to tell them: that the day's work had been more extensive than first thought, and had taken longer than either he or Mr. Threadneedle had anticipated. And because Mrs. Christmas and Kate both had confidence in the squire and knew Tim to be in safe hands while in his employ, they had not been as anxious as they might have been.

In some ways their acceptance of things troubled Mr. Threadneedle all the more, because he knew this excuse of Tim's had been a stretching of the truth; even more troubling, however, was the danger to which he had subjected the boy. It stung his conscience, for the well-being and safety of her only son had been entrusted to him by Mrs. Christmas. He was resolved that from hereon his duty to the lad should rank uppermost, and that he would not place him in the way of such danger again. But how to keep from danger, he wondered, when one's tinkering involved a flying coach-house?

His reflections were interrupted at this point by another trumpet-roar from Mustard.

"What is it, m'lady?" he asked as the mammoth, striding forward a little, butted her woolly head at him, inviting it to be brushed and patted. Her glassy eyes, like chocolate saucers, gazed into his own twinkling gray dittoes. "What is it, Mustard? Are we boring you?"

"I hear she plundered Cook's biffins again while we were away," Tim said.

"Ah! I see. Well, I believe we must do something about that."

"But what can we do, sir? She's rather persistent, and Cook tells me that not only were the biffins snatched but the basket as well —"

The air was rent by another trumpet-roar, and rather a loud one, too; this time, however, the little mammoth had turned away before giving utterance to it. It was then that they saw Henry, the trusty gamekeeper of Smithy Bank, approaching at a fast clip. Evidently it was he to whom Mustard had directed her greeting.

"Offcomers, sir!" the gamekeeper called, motioning toward the water. "'Tis Captain Barnaby and the *Salty Sue*."

"My word," said Mr. Threadneedle. He pulled out his watch, looked at it, and frowned. Then he glanced up at the clock of the sun hanging in the sky, and it promptly squelched any doubts he might have had.

"The captain's early, is he not, sir?" said Tim.

"Indeed. He was not expected until later. And Mrs. Matchless aboard! Well, it's a good thing we brought the jaunting-car."

By this he meant the light, two-wheeled chaise something like a gig, with a single horse between the shafts, which was standing at the foot of the hillside.

In due course the *Salty Sue* dropped anchor and put off her surf-boat. To the surprise of the tinkerers, the boat was filled nearly to capacity, and not just with Mrs. Matchless and her luggage and a couple of sailormen to ply the oars. There were five others aboard as well — *five!* — including a pretty young woman in furs, with a girl beside her who looked to be her maid; two young gentlemen, one dark and one light, and strangers both; and a balding, grizzle-cheeked clergyman whom the grocer recognized as the shepherd of his former parish of St. Mary-le-Quay.

Hardly had the boat touched shore than it was drawn upon the strand, and its passengers disembarked with the aid of the sailormen and Tim.

Mr. Threadneedle moved at once to welcome his lady visitor, his old friend and frequent confidante from his shop-days in Chamomile Street.

"My dear Mrs. Matchless," he smiled, making a stiff little bow, which was as much as his girth allowed. "It's jolly good to see you again. Welcome to the Smithy!"

"Thank you, Mr. T," said Dottie. "Why, you have changed not a jot that I can make out, although your sailorly togs seem a distant cry from your grocer's blue apron. You have been boating?"

"And you, Mrs. Matchless, are yourself just the same — and so very cheery! Boating we have been indeed, for we hadn't expected your ship so soon. And how are things in Chamomile Street? You must acquaint me with the latest. Ah! Here is my young 'prentice, Tim Christmas, whom you shall see something of during your stay. Tim, here is Mrs. Matchless, the fine lady from Nantle of whom I've told you . . ."

As for Dr. Pinches, Mr. Threadneedle had not seen him in a few years — not since he'd last seen Dottie, in fact — and was rather surprised to see him now. The doctor had accompanied Mrs. Matchless on the channel crossing, as it turned out, and the young woman in furs as well, although such had not been his original intention. It was, as he and Dottie explained it, rather a tangled story.

The passengers had been removed from the ship as a precaution. During the crossing Captain Barnaby had observed that a small seam had opened in her planking and she had begun taking on water. Though a notable good sea-boat and prime duck of a craft, he explained, the *Salty Sue* was not immune to minor breaches of her hull and other like hazards of the trade. A more extended anchorage in the harbor thus was called for so his men might set the pumps a-going and plug the seam with oakum. But all would be right and tight and shipshape again directly, he assured them, after which they would be bearing away for Plinth — all to bear away but Mrs. Matchless, of course, for she was stopping at Smithy Bank.

To fill in the time, Mr. Threadneedle invited them up to the house for a brief refreshment. It was evident that the young woman in furs, however, who had a tiny monkey riding on her shoulder, could not be away soon enough. She was exceedingly nervous, and anxious for the captain and his men to be about their work; nevertheless, she accepted the squire's invitation with grace.

Mr. Threadneedle had not anticipated so many callers or he would have brought the basket phaeton. As it was, he placed Dottie, Miss Wastefield, and Lucy in the jaunting-car, while he himself led the horse by the bridle; and so they began the winding ascent to the house and grounds above, with the others marching afoot on either side and Mustard trotting behind.

When they came to Ladycake's domain, Mr. Threadneedle gave the horse a signal to quicken its pace, and his guests the necessary warning to stop their noses. All obediently held their breath — all but Juga, of course, who was reduced to making sour faces as the awful odor came drifting across the road. Still a distance off, the moropus raised her purple head and squinted at the intruders, then began to lumber across. By the time she arrived at the wall, however, and poked her head through its line of spikes, the intruders had moved safely on.

When they gained the summit and came round the drive to the coach-house, they found that the vicar was there. He had just rolled up in his pony-trap with little Kate Christmas. From habit, Mr. Threadneedle reached into his pocket for a donation, but discovered he hadn't a crown-piece on him. But with so many introductions to be gone through, he was able to stall the vicar for a time, and with some help, ironically enough, from Dr. Pinches.

The doctor and Mr. Yorridge made their salutations to one another in proper priestly fashion — a brisk nodding of heads, a clearing of voices, a hunching-up of black coats, like a couple of rooks meeting on a church-tower. Then the heavy jaw of the vicar fell and his eyes widened as he learned just who this snub-nosed, dark-browed, grizzle-cheeked old clergy-man was. In no time the offlander had swollen full large to become, in the eyes of Mr. Yorridge, nothing short of a visiting dignitary. Not only did Dr. Pinches come from the wondrous outer world of Nantle, but he was a full-blown city rector and a learned divine of the Church, and a prebendary in the mighty Minster to boot. To the vicar, who was fascinated by anything from beyond the pale of his humble parish sphere of St. Brine's, anything from the wider universe, the figure of the Rev. Giddeus Pinches, D.D., was akin to a marvel.

As for Dr. Pinches, he was unaccustomed to serving as an object of respect to others in his profession. Resigned to his life of ministering to the noisy denizens of the quay, to his reputation as a parochial drudge, a mere dockside clergyman and a testy one at that, he was pleased by the vicar's compliments; what was more, he found he rather enjoyed being pleased by them. Here was a fellow cleric who genuinely looked up to him! His breast inside his black coat swelled up with pride. No sooner had he waxed lofty, however, than a shadow came across him, and glancing at the vicar, another thought struck him in a flash — *there but for the mercy of God go I.*

But for the mercy of God he could have been this humble country parson he saw before him, eking out his living on a lonely, dismal, fog-drenched island with little or nothing in the way of city comforts. No warm and cozy rectory with a wine-cellar, a sister, and warden pies to cheer him. No Sprig's and no newspaper and no dish of twist. No serene and glorious Minster to resort to. No cathedral library in which to reflect and peruse, no Greenshields to revel in. When viewed in such a light, neither his present circumstances nor his dockside parish with its comfortable church and garden seemed nearly so tiresome, or so humdrum. He was forced to admit it; he lived in clerical clover. He knitted his brows and thought some more on the subject, even as the vicar was talking at him, and vowed to think on it again very soon. Once back in Nantle, he would make a fresh appraisal of his life, he decided, considering how much more badly matters could have turned out!

The visitors were set to accompany Mr. Threadneedle to the manor-house when there was a shout from Tim Christmas. He had gone round behind the coach-house, to the grassy area with its small open space that offered a view of the harbor below. He was standing now at that space and calling for Mr. Threadneedle and his pocket-telescope. The grocer, unsure what the trouble was, hurried across and produced the instrument from his coat.

"What is it, young man?"

"There, sir, there — *monsters*!" Tim said, pointing.

Mr. Threadneedle put telescope to eye and swung the barrel down toward Cold Harbor and the *Salty Sue*. What he saw there defied description. The look in his face said as much to Mr. Frobisher, who along with Martin Somerset had followed him across; though precisely what the look meant, and the details of it, were a mystery.

"My very word!" the grocer exclaimed.

"Do you see them, sir?" Tim asked.

"I certainly do — but I can hardly believe it!"

He passed the telescope to his apprentice-of-sorts for confirmation.

"What is it? What are they?" Mr. Frobisher asked, having observed with his naked eyes that something odd was going on in the harbor.

Tim handed him the glass. What he saw astonished him just as it had the others. The sight chilled his bones and, in a single instant, verified all that Miss Wastefield had told him.

"It's true — every word of it!" he breathed.

"What's true?" Martin demanded. "What do you see there, sir?"

He accepted the telescope from Mr. Frobisher. He gazed — he stared — he gaped — his skin crawled, the blood in his veins froze —

"What in God's name are they?"

"Triametes!" said Allan.

From the streaming channel without, two creatures of remarkable size and appearance had swum into the harbor. At present only their heads, shoulders, and parts of their hairy, muscular arms were visible as they cleaved a path through the dark water. They weren't fish, these creatures, they weren't sharks, they weren't whales or zeugs even, as Mr. Threadneedle instantly recognized; in fact, he didn't recognize them at all. Whatever they were, they were giants — monsters, as Tim had declared. They had glowing red eyes, and pincers reaching round in front of their jaws, and a bony crest rising from their skulls. Like visions from some horrific dream they were, a nightmare become flesh — here, at Smithy Bank!

Whatever the creatures were, Mr. Threadneedle observed with alarm, they were closing swiftly on the *Salty Sue.*

Scutter and confusion reigned aboard ship. Captain Barnaby and Bob Sly appeared to be making haste to get under way, leak or no leak, so as to put distance between themselves and the monsters. But it was of little use. Mr. Threadneedle and his companions watched helplessly as the Triametes swam up to the vessel, one on either side, and taking hold of her bows, proceeded to hoist themselves aboard. The ship rocked precariously as they swung their heavy bodies over the rails, and landed with a crash of their hoofed feet upon deck. There the creatures towered over the deck-house and the ship's company, standing fully three times taller than the tallest of her prime sailormen. They shook the water from their limbs and from their crested heads, which rose to half the height of the lugger's masts.

"Good heavens!"

It was Dr. Pinches. He had joined the others at the open space and just taken a disbelieving peer through the telescope.

"The Triametes have found us," said Mr. Frobisher. "They must have been trailing in the wake of the ship."

"But what are these Triametes?" Martin wanted to know.

"Monsters of legend, creatures of ancient Caphtor — that is, ancient Crete," Dr. Pinches informed him, "and the purported sons and earthly servants of Poteidan."

"Who is Poteidan?"

But the doctor and Mr. Frobisher hadn't time to go into that now.

The *Salty Sue* swayed and rolled as the Triametes stalked about her deck. Every member of her company had drawn sword and cutlass, poniard and falchion, bodkin and boat-hook, and were swarming round their unspeakable foes to drive them from the ship. Chief among the defenders were the captain and Bob Sly, both of whom had sprung at once to the head of the men. Slash upon slash, thrust upon thrust, and yet scarcely a drop of blood did they raise. The monsters for the most part ignored their puny opponents, as they went about the task of searching the ship and its cargo — peering in at portholes and sniffing at scuttles, inserting hairy arms through hatchways and down companions, hunting under canvas and tackle. It shortly became clear, however, that what they sought was not aboard; and so the creatures turned away and, lowering themselves over the rails — and nearly swamping the ship in the process — slid back into the frigid water.

And struck out for shore. Along the way they nearly overturned the two sailormen in the surf-boat, who had been rowing fast to the aid of their captain and shipmates. As they drew in to the beach, the creatures reared up onto their hoofed hind limbs, which, like their beards, were of a vaguely goat-like appearance. Like Gog and Magog they stood there, their ugly heads turning slowly from side to side as their eyes scanned the beach and its environs. With their nostrils they sniffed the air to windward, between steamy exhalations of acid fumes, hunting for the scent of their quarry.

There came a muffled cry from Dottie Matchless. "Oh, my stars! What in heaven are they?"

She, together with the rest of the group, their curiosity aroused, had strode round to the space between the pines. And there they all were gathered now in a little knot, united by their fascination, horror, and revulsion of the ungodly creatures prowling the sands below.

"I confess, Mrs. Matchless, I've no idea what they are," said Mr. Threadneedle, scratching his head, "but this gentleman here — Mr. Frobisher, was it? — and the doctor seem to know something about them."

"The monsters have smelled something," said Tim. "Perhaps it's Ladycake they're after!"

"What should they want with Ladycake?" Mr. Threadneedle wondered.

"It is I they are looking for," spoke up Miss Wastefield, she who knew the horrid truth of it only too well.

"You?" returned Martin with a start. "Jane, what are you saying? What have these creatures to do with you?"

"It was they who abducted this lady from Jekyl Street," Mr. Frobisher explained, "and it is they whom we battled in the hold of the ship at Nantle. They are one and the same. Isn't that so, Miss Wastefield?"

"The same," she answered. "They can assume a human-like form when needed, but *that* — what you see there below — is their true appearance."

Dr. Pinches could scarce believe his senses. Mythical monsters of ancient Caphtor! He had beheld them in their human-like shape aboard the lugger, their three eyes glowing redly wicked in the dimness of the hold. But now he saw them as they truly were, in the bright of day and the full horror of their nakedness.

Oh, how he longed to rewrite his Greenshields now!

"This is your doing, sir," said Martin, turning sharply on Mr. Frobisher. "What do you mean?"

"By your own confession it was you who lured my *fiancée* to Nantle — it is because of you she is here — from a motive that remains past my understanding, but it surely can't be an honorable one. It is you who are to blame if her safety is compromised. Your conduct in this regard has been worse than reprehensible. You are no gentleman. You are a scoundrel, sir!"

"And you're daft, sir," retorted Allan, coolly. "I offered this lady every assistance in ridding her of the mirror. It was she who responded to my offer of help. It was she who chose to come to Nantle, of her own accord, and evidently without going to the trouble of informing *you.*"

Toe to toe, eyeball to eyeball, mustache to mustache they stood again, and glowered at one another.

"Mirror?" said Martin, wavering after a moment. Again — maddeningly — he found himself lost in the black dark of ignorance. Mirror? What mirror? "What the devil is this all about? Now Jane, you *will* tell me —"

"No time!" warned Mr. Frobisher.

No time had they indeed, for the Triametes, having sought their quarry round the beach and found her not, were peering up now at the brow of the hill. One of them motioned in that direction — indeed it seemed to be pointing out to its brother the very spot where Mr. Frobisher and the rest were hidden — and straightway the two of them flung themselves onto the hillside and began to climb it.

"Good Lord, they're coming up here!" said Martin.

They were more than coming; they were bounding fast up the bush-girt slopes. No need had they for any road, horse-track, or common footpath. The speed and agility of these Triametes were as remarkable, given their size, as their appearance was hideous. Like the goats they dimly resembled, they used their hoofed feet and powerful hind limbs to spring from point to point. Already they had leaped the rushing stream and were approaching the domain of Ladycake.

"My word!" cried Mr. Threadneedle.

"What are we to do, sir?" Tim asked, starting to look very worried, as were the others. "We can't let them have Miss Wastefield."

"They'll not have her," Mr. Somerset vowed, brushing up his sleeves again. "I'll not permit it!"

"Don't be more of a fool than you already are, sir," Mr. Frobisher advised him. "Have you no memory of our grappling with these creatures in the hold? The outcome was not so favorable, and they were of something like human stature then. By your leave, sir, we've not a chance against them. They're giants — titans — *cannibals!*"

"Cannibals!" echoed the vicar, inexpressibly shocked, and looking to his esteemed fellow, the D.D. and Nantle prebendary, for an explanation.

"Oh, miss!" Lucy whimpered, shrinking against the side of her mistress. Meanwhile little Juga was spinning himself round and round like a top, in a frenzy of alarm.

"Mr. T., have you any suggestion?" Dottie asked anxiously.

Even as she spoke, the Triametes were bounding nearer and nearer. Already the thunder of their hooves could be heard on the slopes immediately below. How swiftly the monsters could cover ground — and all uphill!

Although Dottie remembered Mr. Threadneedle's bravery as regards the saber-cat in Chamomile Street, she knew that in the present circumstance bravery did not apply; there seemed to be quite literally nothing the grocer or anyone else could do. There was no time to take refuge in the manor-house, and even if there had been, what protection could it afford against these fast-advancing creatures of nightmare?

But Mrs. Matchless had underestimated the resourcefulness of her old friend and former neighbor. Though all had not been perfected yet, Mr. Threadneedle saw that one means of escape reamined open to them. He shot a glance at Tim, and Tim returned it in kind. Came then a trumpet-roar of warning from Mustard, which set the seal on their decision.

"We must take shelter in the coach-house," said Mr. Threadneedle, hurrying to open the door.

Hardly anyone other than Tim moved to follow him.

"That's no security against these Triametes," objected Mr. Frobisher. "Look at it! They'll knock it to pieces in no time. All those windows! Are you as daft, sir, as this other fellow here?"

"You must trust me, sir, for I know what I'm talking about," the grocer insisted. "Everyone now, please — come inside! Mrs. Matchless, vicar, Kate, Miss Wastefield, Dr. Pinches —"

"Come along, Kate, come along!" Tim cried, with a frantic wave of his hand. "Come along, *everyone!*"

It was while the tinkerers were struggling to rally the rest that Miss Wastefield happened to glance away, and there, standing by the ancient stump in the middle of the grassy space, she saw Tom Lanthorne. No one else took any notice of him, and so she knew he was invisible to all but her. Turning to her companions, he trained his strange, dark eyes on them, and she heard him say, not in her ears but in her head —

"You would be well advised to heed this gentleman."

By *this gentleman* he meant of course Mr. Threadneedle; and almost as soon as he had conveyed the words — dropped them, as it were, into their minds — the conversation began to assume a more favorable tone.

MR. SOMERSET: It all quite staggers me, but nonetheless I think we should listen to this gentleman.

DOTTIE: We should all hearken to Mr. T. He is the squire of this place and knows better than we what to do.

MR. FROBISHER (reluctantly): We're all of us daft now, but I suppose we've little choice.

MISS WASTEFIELD: We must go inside, and hurry. Lucy — come, girl!

DOTTIE: Doctor? You are in agreement as well?

DR. PINCHES: I wholly concur in your opinion, Mrs. Matchless.

MR. SOMERSET: Absolutely.

DOTTIE: I am very glad you agree.

Hearing all this, Mr. Lanthorne smiled grimly; but when Miss Wastefield looked again at the ancient stump, he was gone.

"Kate, you must come with us!" Tim called to his sister, as the rest hurried past him into the coach-house.

But the vicar, who alone seemed to resist the influence of Mr. Lanthorne, perhaps because he had stood a little apart from the others, had glimpsed what was climbing fast up the hillside and was not about to be waiting around for them. He was bewildered by the actions of Mr. Threadneedle; to him they seemed almost mad. Quickly he lifted Tim's sister into the trap — despite her evident desire to join her brother — and was about to whip the horse into a gallop when something over his shoulder caught his eye. That eye and the one beside it promptly turned to goose-eggs; and though his heavy jaw fell so far it sprained his foot, still he managed to utter, in a kind of strangled gasp —

"God — bless — my — soul!"

The Triametes had gained the brow of the hill, where the two huge, gliding shadows that were their bodies could be seen moving stealthily behind the trees next to the grassy space. All at once the higher branches in one spot were parted, and an ugly head with a tall crest, curving pincers, and nostrils jetting acid fumes appeared in the opening. Its lips were turned back in a wicked leer, revealing row upon row of knife-like teeth. Glowing eyes of evil fixed themselves on the vicar.

Mustard, beholding this frightful apparition, let out a squeal and bolted for the nearest spinney.

The vicar lashed the horse with his whip and away he and Kate went on the road to Plinth. Mr. Yorridge was not so sure now that he cared for anything from beyond the pale of his humble parish sphere. In one fell moment, with one single horrific sight, his illusions had been shattered as certainly as the coach-house soon must be. Poor Tim Christmas! Poor Mr. Threadneedle! Such a calamity never would have happened in Mrs. Baxendale's time.

Offlanders! Offlanders be damned! he thought, a trifle uncharitably.

Meanwhile Mr. Plush and Mrs. Kimber had stepped forth from the manor-house to receive their visitor from Nantle. From the windows they had seen the lugger arrive in the harbor, but they had not seen what followed. Their chief purpose in the coming days, they had resolved, was to chagrin and mortify their visitor — respectfully, of course — in every and any way possible: to provoke her, to vex her, to irritate her, to discompose her so, as to scrub from the mind of Mrs. Matchless any thought of calling at Smithy Bank again. A lowly boarding-house-keeper come to visit their master the squire, himself a former tradesman, a grocer, a wallower in the common slop of business — it really was too much!

Such was the state of their thoughts as they watched from the back lawn, and waited for Mr. Threadneedle and Dottie to emerge from the tall screen of trees and the bosky hedge.

And waited.

Unbeknownst to them, the door of the coach-house had just been shut with a bang, with Mr. Threadneedle and Mrs. Matchless and several more inside.

"Hold fast, everyone!" the grocer commanded, mounting briskly to the helm. "Tim! Release the mooring-bolts, double-quick!"

"Aye, sir!"

Came the sound of the bolts unbolting somewhere under the floor. The house quivered faintly, as the natural buoyancy of the cage-coils exerted itself. Mrs. Matchless and the other visitors exchanged puzzled glances, wondering what it meant, and whether there had been a small earthquake — or was it the footfall of one of the monsters lurking outside? How long now, they worried, before the creatures sniffed them out?

"What do you mean by enticing us into this house, sir?" Martin demanded. "Now we are in a fine mess!"

"Do you think these walls will hold against Triametes?" chimed in Mr. Frobisher. "You've shut us up in here like cattle for the slaughter!"

"I don't believe this idea was such a good one after all. I don't know why we agreed to it. Jane, we must leave at once. We shall all be crushed!"

"Or eaten," Allan reminded him.

The influence of Mr. Lanthorne appeared to be waning in his absence.

"Should we not hide ourselves somewhere?" Dottie said.

"Mr. Threadneedle, are you unwell?" asked Dr. Pinches. "Perhaps the strain of managing so grand an estate has unsettled your — your —"

"Not unwell, Doctor," Mr. Threadneedle assured him, "and certainly not daft, as some of you may suppose. Ready, Tim?"

"But what do you mean to do?" the doctor persisted, glancing round him in confusion. "What sort of coach-house is this? Where are the carriages? What is all this apparatus? Why have you a gig-wheel mounted on that platform? Should we not at the very least close the shutters? Don't you understand the danger that threatens?"

"I understand something of it, Doctor. But she's a staunch and skyworthy coach of a coach-house and will serve us well. Everyone make fast now and prepare yourselves. Stand by to go aloft, Tim!"

"Skyworthy? Go aloft?" returned Dr. Pinches, with a blank expression.

"Prepare ourselves for what, Mr. T.?" asked the widow. A note of doubt had found its way even into her voice now.

No answer came, however, for at that moment something monstrous and awful loomed in the front bay window.

"Now, Tim!" the grocer cried. "Down coils! Down coils and full speed aloft!"

To the astonishment of Dottie and the others, the floor of the coach-house suddenly lunged up against their shoes. In the same instant, to their horror, the Triamete right aboard of them made a charge at the window. It was all pincers, teeth, and fumes of acid there in the latticed panes, and raging eyes of crimson, and a monstrous hand outthrust to smash the glass —

Then the ghastly vision dropped from sight, as completely as if it had fallen off the earth.

Straight up into the air shot the coach-house, up and up, soaring high above the startled Triametes. Exclamations of fear, wonder, perplexity; queasiness of stomachs, fluttering of hearts, lightness of heads — such were some of the responses of the visitors, who were as startled as the giants by the turnabout. All around the coach-house timbers were creaking and groaning, shutters were rattling, swing-lamps were swaying. In those initial moments Time seemed to stand still, even if the house did not.

The first to regain useful command of his voice was Allan Frobisher.

"Well, I'm jiggered!" was his single remark.

On the back lawn Mr. Plush and Mrs. Kimber looked on with disbelieving stares. The butler uttered a wordless gasp; Mrs. Kimber screamed, or tried to, but no sound came. Their hands trembled; their knees shook. But it was no less than they deserved — not just the sight of the coach-house leaping into the air, but the spectacle of a pair of three-eyed, pincered giants with crested heads bursting through the screen of trees.

Butler and housekeeper turned and made a dash for the manor, together with Henry, who was in search of a cutlass with which to defend Smithy Bank. They fled inside and shut the doors behind them, and latched them, and locked them, and locked them again, and peeped with frightened eyes round windows and window-curtains, awaiting whatever was to come.

On the road to Plinth, in the furiously driving trap, Kate and the vicar saw a shadow come across their path. They glanced up into the blue heaven and saw something there that greatly surprised them. Just as surprising, however, was the reaction of little Kate, who answered not with fear but with a wave of her hand, and a glad shout of triumph —

"Oh, brother Timothy — so *that* is your wizard notion!"

The vicar, too, had seen the coach-house glide overhead, but unlike Kate he neither waved nor shouted, but drove on as hard as he could go. Then, just as they were about to enter the woods, the two of them saw the house swing round, pick up speed, and disappear over the tops of the trees.

CHAPTER THIRTY-EIGHT

Gulls on the Wharf

"Squailes," frowned the gentleman behind the desk, placing the tips of his bony fingers together and addressing the dark ceiling above him. "Mr. Jerry Squailes. Mr. Jerrold Squailes. Mr. J. Squailes. No, the name is not known to me. But fear not, Mrs. Frederick Cargo — it *shall* be known to me directly."

"You're certain, sir, you have it in your power to find this man, be he at Nantle or elsewhere?" said Susan. "For we have ourselves been in the town for weeks and have had no news of him."

"No news," intoned Miss Veal, with a shake of her head and the black wig on it, "is a blight."

"We must find this man Squailes and learn what his game is. We mean to prize it out of him."

"This acquaintance of yours who is assisting you — he is a competent person?" inquired the gentleman at the desk. He dashed away a spot of drool that had trickled from a corner of his mouth. The face in which that mouth was planted was a hard one, and a taut one, the skin of it dry and parchment-like, as was the skin of his hands, the palms of which he was rubbing together with a slow, steady motion.

"We *presumed* the gentleman to be competent," Mrs. Cargo replied, with a sidelong glance at her husband.

Mr. Fred Cargo could not allow such a slander to pass. "He is an elderly gentleman, sir, and a professional man," he said, "if perhaps not so spry or efficient as he once was."

"The gentleman is past it," Susan explained.

"I regret to say that Mr. Liffey's efforts hitherto have gained no appreciable result, nor have our own small attempts," Fred admitted. "But we can't fault Mr. Liffey for that, for we've found no one in the world who has heard of this Mr. Squailes. It's a rum thing."

"It's a beastly thing," said his wife.

"I see," nodded the gentleman at the desk, gravely and consequentially. He was an attorney, as evidenced by the black legal livery in which he was encased, head to foot, like a bad mummy. His face, as we've said, was a hard one, his jaw narrow, his eyes sharp, his hair sleek, dark, receding. Most unusual was that skin of his — the peculiar, bloodless sort of skin one might find investing a dead pharaoh. But this particular pharaoh was very much alive, and making a cold, steady scrutiny of his visitors.

"We would never have engaged this gentleman, sir, but for the fact that he is an acquaintance of long standing of the family," Susan went on. "He was in fact an associate of Frederick's grandfather, whose lunatic will and testament lies at the root of our difficulties."

"Ah. And so you fail to understand, Mrs. Frederick Cargo, why such a man as Mr. Joseph Cargo should have numbered among his heirs an unknown person? That is, a person who is unknown to *you*?"

"A nobody," corrected Miss Veal, touching up her wig.

"An interloper," said Susan. "A person unknown to anyone in the family, and so he cannot be *of* the family. Moreover he has steadfastly refused to make himself known. It's very provoking."

"My grandfather made it clear in his will that efforts were to be made to find this man Squailes, if he didn't volunteer himself," Fred explained. "If after seven years he hasn't laid claim to his inheritance, then it shall revert to the surviving heirs. That is how my grandfather wished it, and that is how he willed it, and how our good friend Mr. Liffey drew it up for him."

"Ah!" exclaimed the attorney, leaning forward with interest. "This Mr. Liffey of yours — he is a fellow practitioner of the law? It is your own solicitor, then, who has failed you?"

There followed a chagrined silence on the part of the visitors. They had not wanted it revealed that the "acquaintance" of whom they had spoken was a fellow legal man. They had not wanted the man behind the desk to know it was a brother attorney whose counsel they were endeavoring to circumvent; they had not wanted to prejudice their case. But it had all come out now, owing to Fred's slip of the tongue.

"And you ask me to interject myself into that sanctuary of trust that stands between solicitor and client?" inquired Mr. Hook — for so it was he, Hieronymus Hook, solicitor, sitting behind the desk in his high-backed leather chair, and these dark, tomb-like quarters were his legal chambers, and these chambers but one of many sequestered nooks comprising the warren of apartments and passageways that was Gull's Wharf. The atmosphere in the room was stale, the air faint, the ceiling low, the light dim, as one would expect in the tomb of Pharaoh. "You ask me," Mr. Hook went on, "to slip round behind the back of a fellow practitioner in the discharge of my duty? Is that what you ask of me, Mrs. Frederick Cargo?"

"Well, I — I shouldn't have expressed it in quite those terms, Mr. Hook," Susan replied, in a voice of conciliation. "It is simply that we've grown rather impatient with our man's efforts to this point. They seem to us so very limp, so very feeble, and we are in hopes that somebody else — somebody with a bit more *steam* at his disposal, as it were, might put a little of it on now and make progress toward finding Mr. Squailes."

"Your solicitor is unaware you have consulted me?"

"He is unaware."

"I see." Mr. Hook rubbed his hands again. "I see how it is, Mrs. Frederick Cargo. And what's more" — here his eyes grew suddenly sharper and colder, and a thin smile stole across his lips like a creeping sunrise — "and what's more, Mrs. Frederick Cargo, *I like it!* I approve of it. Oh, indeed. I am entirely at your service."

"You approve of it, Mr. Hook?"

"But of course," said the attorney, with a gracious bow of his head. "All is fair in the practice of the law, and all are equal in the eyes of the law. We solicitors, we like to be discreet, but to practice discretion one oft must practice deception. We'll play a little prank on this old friend of yours, eh? Truth be told, Mrs. Frederick Cargo, there's little I like more than slipping round behind the back of a fellow. For you know, practitioners will be practitioners!"

Saying which Mr. Hook chuckled quietly to himself, shaking a little as he did so, and looking so much the mummy that one could see the dust and spices rising from him as he shook, like a visible gas. Then he drew himself up in his chair and, leaning forward with his elbows on the desk-top, twined the bony fingers of his hands together to form a little bridge and, peering over that bridge at the Cargoes and Miss Veal, inquired, slowly, deliberately, and with a particularly heavy drool —

"And so what are we to do about it, eh?"

"We must find Mr. Squailes," answered Susan.

"And how do you propose we go about that, Mrs. Frederick Cargo?"

"That is what we mean to engage your services for, sir."

"I see. And how do you propose I accomplish the feat, assuming I agree to take the case up?"

"That is for you to answer, I should think. You are the professional man here, Mr. Hook, and have been well-recommended to us. Certainly you must have your resources in the city, your informants, persons known to you who may scour the town for Squailes. Our own rather feeble Mr. Liffey —"

"The gentleman who is without steam?"

"As you say. Our Mr. Liffey is a stranger here, as are we. To the best of anybody's knowledge this Squailes is a cipher, but we are compelled by the lunatic stipulations of the will to find him. Such is the beastly state Frederick's grandfather has left us in."

"Lunatic wills are a blight!" sniffed Miss Veal, speaking from infinite knowledge of the subject.

"Ah. You have told me all you know of Mr. Squailes, which I am afraid is nothing, and so that is where I am obliged to begin — with nothing. It is a challenge, eh? But there are ways and there are ways, Mrs. Frederick Cargo, to make something from nothing. *Ex nihilo nihil fit* is no impediment for a skilled practitioner."

The attorney leaned back a little in his chair, then stood up and took a thoughtful turn or two round his desk, nodding to himself and drooling. Mr. Hook was a tall, thin man with a slight stoop, and was possessed of that inward shrewdness of expression which is so common among members of the legal fraternity. After a few minutes he resumed his seat, giving off more dust and spices, and rubbing his hands looked his visitors calmly in their faces.

"We shall," said he, raising a forefinger so long and bony it was like a chicken-neck, "we shall commence an action in the Court. Blinkin!" he exclaimed, calling for his clerk. "We shall undertake a suit — a private prosecution — and at once. *Blinkin!*"

"A prosecution? Against whom, Mr. Hook?" Fred asked.

"Against your Mr. Liffey, of course. Now, then — surname, Liffey. And the Christian name of the gentleman, if you please, and an address where papers may be served?" the attorney directed, while his clerk — a little, cadaverous man in knee-breeches, with a squeezed-up face, a patch on one eye, and a handkerchief tied round his head, which lent him some semblance to a pirate — stood by with pen and ink at the ready.

The Cargoes, husband and wife, looked at one another in mute surprise. This was not the sort of "action" on the part of Mr. Hook they had foreseen.

"A suit, Mr. Hook? For what cause?" Fred wanted to know. He had allowed himself to be persuaded by his wife and Miss Veal that consulting Mr. Hook was a good thing, after so much time in Nantle and still no satisfaction from Mr. Liffey. Now he was not so certain it was such a good thing after all.

"Neglect of duty. Failure in the proper execution of his office. Incompetence. Misfeasance. Nonfeasance. *Magna culpa.* Failure to protect the interests of beneficiaries, namely yourselves. Whatever you like, Mr. Frederick Cargo. As your solicitor, as your professional adviser, as your *provider of steam,* I shall be ever at your service and attending to your interests. A haven of hospitality and benevolent counsel is what you shall find here, Mr. Frederick Cargo, not to say cleverness, not to say skill, which are ever the instruments of the artful practitioner."

Mr. Hook sat back with his arms folded upon his chest, impassive, immovable, like the dead image of Pharaoh gazing across the centuries — or the desk-top — and took quiet measure of the effect of his oration on his visitors.

"I'm afraid I'm still rather in the dark, as the saying is," was Fred's reply — literally and figuratively, considering the murky light in the room.

"May I presume upon you, Mr. Frederick Cargo, to clarify a point of professional interest?"

"How so, Mr. Hook?"

"What is it you have come to Nantle to accomplish?"

"We have come to ferret out Mr. Squailes, who is to share in the estate of my grandfather."

"I think not, Mr. Frederick Cargo," said Pharaoh, with a smiling shake of his head. "Quite the contrary. You have come to Nantle to see that Mr. Squailes, whoever he may be, is *denied* his lunatic share in the estate of Mr. Joseph Cargo. Is that not the case, sir?"

The attorney was venturing uncomfortably near the truth here, like a surgeon probing a wound, or a dentist a painful bicuspid.

"I'll not disagree with you, sir," Fred replied, with a few quick strokes of his mustaches — "in that there may be something of the like in the case."

"And what of it, sir?" spoke up Susan, flashing her eyes. "Why should this man Squailes receive so much as a groat? He is nothing to us or our family. Grandfather Cargo is dead and my husband is his sole remaining blood relation. Why should we be denied our proper share in favor of a nobody who refuses to surface? Why should we be constrained for seven years — seven years, sir! — while waiting for Mr. Squailes to show himself? What a brute was Grandfather Cargo to treat his grandson so!"

"Ah, I see your point, Mrs. Frederick Cargo," said Mr. Hook, rising in his chair and fixing Susan with a gimlet eye. "Let us grasp the nub of the matter, then. Let us put it in even plainer terms. Let us put the case that your Mr. Liffey's inaction in finding Mr. Squailes is not what troubles you. In truth you do not care to find Squailes any more than I do — you must admit it — because you fear that if you do find him, he will produce evidence he is deserving of the legacy. Is that not the long and the short of it, Mrs. Frederick Cargo?"

Susan was obliged to admit that something of the long and the short of it had indeed crossed their minds, but it was not the chief consideration.

"We fear there may be something sinister afoot," she explained. "We fail to see any cause for Grandfather Cargo to have made such a settlement unless this man Squailes held some power over him. There is something decidedly *fishy* here, and it's on this account that the interloper must be found and brought to book."

"Ah! You allege undue influence? You would dispute the validity of the will? You would contest it, Mrs. Frederick Cargo?"

"But that should get us into Chancery, Mr. Hook, and speaking frankly, sir," said Fred, in a rush of candor, "it's on account of damned attorneys like yourself that we should never get out of it. Speaking frankly, sir."

"*Very* frankly, Mr. Frederick Cargo," said the damned attorney, gently smiling and nodding. "I see how it is. You would like your law from a lawyer as you would your waistcoat from a tailor."

"What I should like," broke in Susan, impatiently, "is to take this man Squailes by the nose, wherever he is, and shake him up, and shake him up some more, until a confession comes tumbling out of him. It's beastly, this influence he has exercised over Grandfather Cargo. It's blackmail!"

Again Pharaoh rose and took a thoughtful spin round his desk, to clear the dust and spices from body as well as brain, and again he resumed his seat.

"Let us put the case once more, Mrs. Frederick Cargo. You are worried that the bequest to Mr. Squailes may be the result of undue influence. You have never heard of Mr. Squailes and consider the bequest a cheat. You don't care a fig for Squailes, and for that matter neither do I. If he fails to turn up, let it be on his own head. An admirable sentiment! But you, Mrs. Frederick Cargo, and you, Mr. Frederick Cargo, and you, Miss Aspasia Veal, you do not care to place seven years between yourselves and the Squailes share. Is that not the case?"

"It is," declared Miss Veal, with great consciousness of the injury done them by Joseph Cargo.

"And an understandable one, for seven years in the span of a lifetime may be a very considerable impediment. Consider yourself, for instance, Miss Aspasia Veal, and your share of the bequest. You will permit me to observe that your advanced years make it unlikely you'll live long enough to see it."

Ensued a long, gaping pause on the part of Miss Veal. She blanched, her pale drab oblong of a face turning as white as a Malbury cheese. First shock, then indignation, then horror crossed it in following waves.

"*What!*" she cried, reaching first for her wig, and then for her reticule and her smelling-bottle. "This really is too much, sir, too much. What a terrible thing to say!"

"Ah, but a true thing to say, Miss Aspasia Veal, a true thing, its boldness notwithstanding. And as I look to be your professional adviser, your interests demand that I give you the truth. Truth, not false hopes; for I never give false hopes. I was made for unvarnished truth. But let us put another case. A considerable sum of money may be expended to find this man Squailes, yet he may never be found. The result? Money gone. Consider the case that there may be no Squailes to be found. Do we know for a certainty that he exists? No. Do we know for a certainty that he lives and breathes Nantle air? No. We have not a tittle of evidence, not a shadow of proof. For all any of us knows, Mr. Squailes may be long deceased. And as regards his heirs, we know even less."

"What you say is certainly true, Mr. Hook," Fred allowed.

"But neither can we be sure that he is *not* dead. If such be the case and he remains alive, why has he not responded to the advertisements or the publication of the will? Perhaps he has not seen them. Perhaps he is a criminal, and fears exposure. Perhaps he *cannot read.*"

"Not read!" said Susan, alarmed that such a low person could have any connection to the will of Grandfather Cargo, and by inference to her husband and herself as well.

"And so I present the case to you, Mrs. Frederick Cargo — why bother?"

"How do you mean, sir?"

"We shall disregard Mr. Squailes and his seven years, for they don't signify. We shall make no move to find him, for that right and duty belongs to the executor of the will, and you are not the executors. We shall instead bring an action in the courts against your Mr. Liffey for the share owed Squailes. We shall allege neglect of duty, nonfeasance, *magna culpa,* absence of steam — whatever you like. We shall extract the balance from this man Liffey" — this accompanied by a slow grasping and drawing motion of his hands, as though he were removing the imaginary pluck from an imaginary fowl — "and if Mr. Jerry Squailes should happen to declare himself, what care you? You shall have the balance notwithstanding — and should he fail to appear, you shall have doubled your money! Judgment rendered, suit wound up, justice done, my duty as your adviser prosperously concluded.

"Naturally, however," Mr. Hook went on, "there will be certain costs to be borne, such as may accrue in the normal discharge of my office, relating to some few small consultations and attendances, the copying of affidavits and warrants, and reports, and other like particulars as may arise touching the cause at issue. But in the broader perspective, when weighed against the successful winding-up of a suit, such costs, representing as they do mere legal formalities, may be so trifling as to be rendered nugatory."

It was a solution both simple and clear to Mr. Hook, sitting there with his eyes sharp and cold, and a faint smile on his lips, and his hands rubbing the one against the other, as if he had a client between them and was slowly and steadily grinding him to a powder.

The visitors proceeded to put their heads together in confidence. They had heard from Miss Trickle that the methods of this fellow Hook were innovative, but really! Very zealous the gentleman was in the pursuit of his duty; of that they had no doubt. Beyond this, however, there was little they could agree on. The upshot of it was that they failed to reach any agreement at all.

"My dear Susan, it's completely out of the question," Fred insisted. "We can't bring a suit against Mr. Liffey, regardless of what this crafty fellow says. It's preposterous! 'Pon my life, I'm afraid I don't trust this Mr. Hook. I believe he'd sell us anything from a shave to a shoehorn, as the saying is."

"But it's so very reasonable, Frederick," returned his wife. "You know very well that Mr. Liffey has money. You know for how long he has lawyered in the service of your grandfather and his other rich clients. In such capacity he has derived for himself a very considerable fortune, no doubt."

"But Mr. Liffey is our friend. Susan, dear, listen to what you're saying!"

"It seems reasonable to me," opined Miss Veal. "The thought of enduring another week in this city — another day — another hour — well, it's not for thinking on, thenk yaw!"

"And you may think on this, Frederick," said Susan. "Think of the suit as a form of insurance. If Mr. Squailes fails to reveal himself, we shall offer his share to Mr. Liffey. Will that satisfy your conscience?"

"This is how you would treat our good friend? This is how you would reward Mr. Liffey for his many favors to us? You would steal his money in the courts, and then return it to him in seven years?" Fred scoffed. "I suppose he should consider it a loan, one payable at no interest. Ah, that's a jolly good job!"

"That's his look-out," declared his wife.

"If Mr. Liffey's friendship counts for so little, in your view, what then of the bill of costs? How much do you suppose this pettifogger here means to extort from us? 'So trifling as to be rendered nugatory.' Shall we take him on trust? Ha! Will there be any money left at all, do you think? We might as well batter away in the High Court of Chancery as allow this damned lawyer to cozen us. We shall be lucky to be left with a roof over our heads."

Something in her husband's argument finally caught the attention of Susan — it was money, of course, and the threat of losing it. Money and its accumulation was the ruling passion of her life. It was a familiar argument, true, one she had heard before in the chambers of Mr. Liffey. As Chancery suitors contesting the will, they stood to lose everything — not just the money but Tiptop Grange as well — all of it vanishing down a drain-hole called *costs,* the farther end of which consisted of a kind of universal spigot dispensing comfort and emolument for the gentlemen of the law.

To her credit Susan reflected on these facts before she spoke again.

"Mr. Hook," said she, turning to Pharaoh, "are you quite certain we have a case here? What of its strength? Is it a strong case?"

"Ah, the strength of the case, Mrs. Frederick Cargo," said Mr. Hook, rubbing hands and smiling, "is very strong. Small doubt of it. And as you know, I am not a man to give false hopes. Absence of steam — neglect of duty — oh, yes, a very respectable case. Not a weak spot in it."

"And the chances against it?"

"So trifling as to be nugatory. There are ways and there are ways, Mrs. Frederick Cargo, to put a case. For instance, in drawing up the will, did your Mr. Liffey employ proper witnesses to subscribe it, none of them having a financial interest in the proceedings? None being creditors owed money, for example?"

"There was old Mr. Merripit, his neighbor," Susan replied, after a moment's thought. "And there was the notary."

"The notary is mere legal form. But this Mr. Merripit — he stood to gain no material advantage from witnessing the will?"

"None. And he himself has since died."

"Burst a vessel," Miss Veal informed him.

"And of course, there was Mr. Liffey himself —"

"Ah!" exclaimed Pharaoh, elevating his eyebrows. "Your Mr. Liffey, attorney-at-law — a solicitor, whose emolument is derived from those whom he advises — the very gentleman who executed the instrument — he has put himself down for a witness?"

"Yes. Is that so irregular, Mr. Hook? Have we another case?"

"What we have is another foothold, Mrs. Frederick Cargo. Not only absence of steam, but the possibility of undue influence."

Although the attorney's answers seemed to satisfy Susan, they did not satisfy her husband.

"I fail to see what influence Mr. Liffey could have exerted over my grandfather," he said. "He was a tight-fisted old potentate who knew his own mind and everybody else's."

"Did your Mr. Liffey not stand to be advanced materially by the drawing-up of the will? Did he not expect compensation for the service?"

"Of course."

"Well, there you are, then — improper witness. We have him, Mr. Frederick Cargo — *we have him!*"

The attorney began issuing a rapid flood of instructions to his clerk, all of them rife with the cabalistic language of the law, a tongue whose proper object among its disciples is the general obfuscation of the laity.

But Fred was not about to be obfuscated today. "I don't mean to give offense, Mr. Hook," he said, "but 'pon my life, sir, it won't do. Mr. Liffey is as valued a friend as the sun in winter. He was my grandfather's trusted legal adviser since both were young men."

"Ah! Another foothold, Mr. Frederick Cargo," enthused Pharaoh. "Do you know, I believe we may bring suit purely on grounds of age! How many of these winters has your Mr. Liffey seen?"

"Oh, round seventy, I suppose —"

"Eighty," corrected Susan.

"Ninety, if a day," declared Miss Veal, to draw attention from herself on this touchy subject.

"Ninety years!" exclaimed Mr. Hook, staring in disbelief. "Ninety years, and still in his practice!"

"Seventy years," Fred stated, to emend the record.

"Seventy, ninety, it's all the same to us, and all the more reason to bring an action. Generally speaking, the more decrepit the practitioner, the likelier the chance of error, failure to perform, absence of steam, et cetera. No Mr. Squailes in sight and no prospect of him in future — it's a plain case and a simple one. It's a straight road which lies before us to your Mr. Liffey. We shall baffle him, eh? We shall baffle the old buffer!"

The attorney, chuckling to himself, shook off some more dust and spices and erupted in another burst of instructions to his scribe.

"Now, Mr. Frederick Cargo, if you will oblige us with your autograph on certain papers we have here, to bring suit, and with your note for thirty pounds on account," he said. As he spoke, he patted each document fondly, as though it were some precious thing to be admired, before handing it across to Fred. "I tell you, we shall have this Mr. Liffey of yours. We shall not let him rest! You shall have your judgment, your due inheritance — minus the balance of the costs outstanding, naturally — and Mr. Squailes need not enter into it. Could anything be simpler?"

The clerk took up a pen and extended it to Fred, so that he might fill up the blanks in the documents; but despite the urgings of Susan and Miss Veal, he did not sign.

"Why do you hesitate, Frederick?" Susan asked, with an impatient rap of her hand upon the desk. "Really, there are times I cannot make you out. Do you not see how very simple is Mr. Hook's plan?"

"There is nothing simple in the law, dear," Fred replied.

Lords and ladies, readers near and far, high and low, we put the question — *Was truer statement ever made?*

"I'm not prepared at this juncture to sign. I must turn it over in my mind. I must sleep on it," Fred explained.

Pharaoh was clearly disappointed. Blinkin, his piratical scribe, was clearly disappointed. Susan and Miss Veal were clearly disappointed.

"Turn it over? Sleep on it? Mr. Frederick Cargo, what is there to sleep on?" Mr. Hook wanted to know. "It's a simple case — a strong case — a very respectable case. Have I not put it to you clearly? Why, I might offer you your judgment now, it's as good as won! What could be easier?"

Yes, Fred wondered, *what could be easier?* Still he hesitated, even after his wife had delivered a few loving cuffs to his arm, and Miss Veal accused him of siding with a nobody. But Fred was a persevering sportsman and stood his ground. He wouldn't be pitchforked into a decision, he declared; and when he left the grim, dark chambers of the attorney with the innovative methods, the interview at an end, it was a grim, dark wife and Miss Veal who left with him.

But time would show the wisdom of Fred's decision, and rather promptly, too. Meanwhile his thoughts had turned, as they often had of late, to the fine young woman from Crow's-end, so pretty of eye and dimpled of chin, and to the circumstances of her abduction in Jekyl Street. When he and the other gentleman giving chase had run upon the carriage and found it abandoned, they thought they would find the lady somewhere nearby; but they were wrong. So strange an incident to have drawn strangers together! The incident and the resulting fate of the young woman troubled him greatly. He wondered what had become of her, and why, and what business it was that had taken her so very far from home.

He wondered, too, what had become of the fellow Lanthorne, whom he had recognized that day in Jekyl Street, and who, according to the testimony of young John, had vanished mysteriously into air. *Vanished!* One moment there, the next moment not there; gone in the wink of an eye. How to explain it? For John was nothing if not a trustworthy fellow, and his witness more than credible.

And it was this same John, shortly after the interview on Gull's Wharf, whose testimony Fred found himself again taking on trust. No sooner had the party of three returned to the Crozier than John appeared at his door, bearing news that made Fred immeasurably glad he had filled in no blanks for the dubious Mr. Hook.

"Hallo! How goes it, John?"

"May I have a word with you, sir?"

"Of course, of course."

The servant entered with a hesitant step.

"Perhaps I should not have come, sir," he began, plainly unsure of himself. "Perhaps it's none of my affair. My master went out a short while ago and knows nothing of my errand here. I fear I shall be betraying his trust if I tell you — but if I do not tell you, sir, then I shall be betraying *your* trust. And so I'm at something of a loss what to do, as you may easily conceive, sir."

Fred was a trifle puzzled, but his natural good humor quickly asserted itself. "Well, in for a penny, in for a pound, as the saying is, John, and let us be the judges for ourselves. Mr. Liffey need not know, and no harm need be done. You have my word as a gentleman."

Whatever else Fred Cargo might have been, he was as even-handed and well-meaning a fellow as could be found in any neighborhood. So open and honest a man was he that young John, who had come to know him better these past weeks in their rambles about town, was put greatly at his ease. And as John accounted himself on the side of right, if there was something *not* so right in the actions of Mr. Liffey, then it was his bounden duty to speak of it. And if his master chose to dismiss him as a result, well, perhaps there might be a place for another servant at Tiptop Grange . . .

"It bears upon Mr. Squailes, sir," said John.

Fred's attention was instantly secured.

"Mr. Jerry Squailes?"

"Yes, sir. It would seem he's been found."

"Squailes found!" Fred exclaimed, jumping to his feet, his watch-chain and seals ringing out like the bells of Nantle Minster. He jumped high and

he jumped far, like a man who, having sat on lighted coals, feels a pressing need to launch himself out of his boots.

"Yes, sir. That is, sir, I believe that my master discovered him, some days ago now, but for purposes unknown has told no one of it."

Fred could hardly believe his ears. He looked closely at the servant.

"How do you know this, John? And when did you find it out?"

"I learned of it only this morning, sir, but my master would reprimand me if he knew. Asking pardon, sir, but might you refrain from telling him of this? Otherwise I must surely look out for another place."

"The soul of discretion, John, as the saying is. Now, what have you learned?" Fred asked eagerly.

"It was a pair of the scruffiest characters as ever I saw in this world, who showed their untidy faces this morning, sir, at this very door. They had come in search of you, with a message they said of some importance. I happened to be putting away your things at the time, and told them that you had gone out, but that perhaps Mr. Liffey might see them in your stead. I'm afraid it unnerved my master, sir, what they had to tell him. And I'm afraid as well that I listened at the door."

"It may be rather a good thing that you listened. What passed between them? Did you catch the names of these scruffy characters, as you term them?"

"There was one called Moeran, sir, with a face like a mule's, and a sneaking sort called Jones. Vagrants — wasters — common street-fellows by the look of them, sir. I should have given neither the time of day had they not said they were boon companions of yours."

"Moeran — Jones — boon companions — well, I'm hanged!" Fred blurted out in amazement. The vagrants in question passed before the eye of his memory; passing there, too, was the sight of himself dispensing cash to bail one of them out of the lock-up. Boon companions of Fred's they most certainly were not, but companions of Black Davy, yes! He began pacing to and fro with his hands in his pockets. He wasn't sure what it all meant yet, but he was sure it meant something.

The vagrants had proceeded to inform Mr. Liffey — a most prosperous-looking gentleman in their eyes, so John supposed, and as ripe for picking as Fred — that Mr. Jerry Squailes was known to them, and that he, too, was their boon companion; that his name was in fact not Squailes but Porter; that he was here in Nantle; and that for a liberal consideration they might go so far as to reveal where he could be found.

"This is astonishing — this is tremendous!" Fred exclaimed.

Was this not the very pair whom he and his wife had meant to employ in their search for Squailes, only to deem them unfit for the job? Was it not Comport's lock-up that had held them? And was it not the giant door-keeper from Comport's who had thrown the fine young woman from Crow's-end into the carriage?

"Once my master had heard them out, sir, his face went very red," John continued. "He gave them to understand he would pay them nothing, as the family knew already where Mr. Squailes was, and had held conversation with him, and so the offer was quite superfluous."

Fred, recovered from his initial surprise, stopped his pacing and gazed into the fire for a time, smoothing his mustaches and thinking.

"You're quite sure of all this, John?" he asked at length.

"Yes, sir. You'll not tell Mr. Liffey of my spying, will you, sir? Or that I revealed to you anything of his talk with the vagrants?"

"Rather not," Fred answered, "on both counts."

"I confess it's quite disheartened me. He's known all the while where this Mr. Squailes was but has told no one. I trusted him very much, sir, and have had nothing but the truest respect for him —"

"Not to worry, John," Fred assured him, clapping the poor downcast young man on the shoulder as any friend might have done. "The soul of discretion, as I've said. Mr. Liffey will hear nothing from my lips as regards your part in the affair. One capital thing has come of it already, at any rate — we'll need not waste so much as a groat on a low pettifogger named Hook. Yes, yes, capital!"

CHAPTER THIRTY-NINE

The Ladder in the Sky

There was a gigantic sea snail, and it was working its tedious way along the muddy ocean bottom, and she was perched atop it with the reins in hand. She was breathing water as well as any fish and paying the oddness of it no mind; it seemed as ordinary as breathing air. The shell of the snail was of the long, coiling, spiral kind, resembling those from which her earrings had been fashioned. Indeed, the giant could easily have served as the model: it was a kind of triton-shell, like that the priestess had sounded at the altar of Juktas to call the earth-shaker Poteidan.

The snail was crawling along by means of its muscular foot, but its progress was so very slow and the water so very thick and heavy. It was the water that was holding them back. *Faster! Faster!* If only it had been air through which they were moving instead of this briny syrup. If only the snail would put some speed on! Hadn't the creature heard of the sons of Poteidan, the cannibal Triametes? Didn't it know that the three-eyed giants even now were closing in on them? Away! She must get away!

Then her dream shifted from the ocean bottom to the valley she knew so well, where a little monkey was picking flowers in a field. It was a monkey very much like Juga, for it, too, was a pet and sported a leather harness. It was gathering crocuses into a pot. Yellow crocuses they were — saffron — plants of eternity — symbols of the hopes of mortal man for a happy life in the other world. Why hadn't she remembered this all those times before when she'd dreamed this same dream?

And the very name *Juga* — she remembered that, too. For wasn't it the name of another little monkey, who had brightened her short life all those centuries ago on Kaftor? No mystery now how the name had come to her — a memory from her childhood, true, but a childhood far more ancient than she could have imagined. In the lost tongue of Kaftor the word *juga* meant "the praising one." She hadn't remembered that either until her memories had been restored to her by Mr. Lanthorne.

Then the monkey picking crocuses hopped into her arms, without so much as a warning chirp, and the shock of it roused her from her doze. She awoke to find herself sunk in a chair by a hearth, with Juga stirring in her lap. There was an odd noise nearby, which she discovered was the sound of Lucy snoring in the chair next to hers. But what of that hearth and what of those chairs? They were not in her rooms in Chamomile Street, nor were they in her home in distant Pinewick, but in the marvelous flying coachhouse of Mr. Malachi Threadneedle.

A brilliant light was pouring in through the windows, revealing to Miss Wastefield and all aboard a kingdom of wonder where nothing but sun and sky reigned. The house had been running on steadily for some time now, but just how much time she couldn't say, for she'd lost track of it by falling asleep in the chair. She knew they were far above that world where the sons of Poteidan were on the hunt for her. She was safe from them up here, she thought, for the time being at least.

For the time being — and then what? Where was there for her to go in a sundered world? All this vast expanse around them stretching to the horizon, and yet no single place to hide! Even with Mr. Lanthorne's protection she could never rest, never again enjoy that blessed peace of mind that had been hers before her twenty-first birthday. Was there nowhere on earth to find sanctuary, no place where she would be truly safe from the agents of Poteidan?

For these cruel and selfish spirits have their agents everywhere, even in a sundered world, ready to do their bidding. So her grim-faced guardian had revealed to her, and such, she knew in her heart, was the truth of it.

"Look there!"

It was Tim Christmas. He was at his station before the bay window and pointing at something in the waters below. Although clouds had begun to gather in the channel far to the north, here they still had a clear view of the ocean on all sides. Nearly everyone came for a look — a cautious look, out and over the jut of the window — at whatever it was that had excited the lad's interest.

There, racing just beneath the water, were half-a-dozen gigantic forms — dark, serpent-like forms, swimming in loose formation — dusky leviathans with long, sinewy bodies, glossy backs, and arching spines, which could be seen breaking the surface here and there, and then plunging again in great bubbling rushes into the sea.

"What are they?" asked Mrs. Matchless, who had never before seen the like, either in her dreams or elsewhere, and most certainly never in Chamomile Street.

"Whales of a kind, I should say," opined Dr. Pinches. "Very large whales."

"Not whales of just any kind, Doctor," Mr. Threadneedle informed him, "but whales of a very special kind. Those are the zeugs of lore." The grocer had momentarily left his post at the gig-wheel to join the others and have a look for himself.

"Zeugs!" Tim exclaimed. "Are those the creatures described by Captain Barnaby? The great gliding monsters of the deep?"

"The very same. The serpent-behemoth, as Hicklebeep calls them," nodded the grocer.

"Predatory toothed whales," spoke up Mr. Frobisher. "The mariners refer to them as the sharks of the open seas. I have heard something of these creatures before, though I'd never seen one."

"We have seen their teeth — or rather we've seen one tooth," said Tim. "The trader, Mr. Hicklebeep, had one among his store."

"I am certainly glad we are up here, and they are down there," said Dottie, looking a trifle nervous.

"I should prefer they were not down there at all, Mrs. Matchless," returned Allan, "for their reputation is most unsavory. The greatest distance we can place between ourselves and a horde of zeugs would still be insufficient for me — that you may depend on!"

Mr. Somerset turned from the window at this point and, having observed that Miss Wastefield was sitting up, crossed to the hearth to see how she was feeling. Lucy, who had broken off her snoring long enough to wake up, was kneeling sleepy-eyed at her mistress's side.

"I am quite well now," Miss Wastefield assured them. "The brief rest has done me a power of good. Lucy — dash away those sleepers, girl! Martin, where are we?"

"Out at sea, somewhere," answered her *fiancé*. "Mr. Threadneedle — the gentleman who built this magnificent craft — thinks it wise to stay back from the coast for now."

"But how on earth can such a thing be? How can a house be made to fly?"

Overhearing these remarks, and thinking it as good a time as any to clarify certain matters for his guests, Mr. Threadneedle graciously obliged.

Achieving perfection was out of the question now. The proverbial cat, otherwise the coach-house, had escaped its bag, and everyone would know of his wondrous tinkering soon enough. The eye of the world was upon him, and the world might as well have the story from the tinkerer's own lips.

"Hoverstones," he explained, "those curious white stones you see there with the odd striations — a type of stone unique in the world. They're said to be remnants of the great meteor or comet that caused the sundering. They were discovered some years ago by the famous sailing captain, Wulf Clipperton. By applying a stack of magnets to them — those disks or 'coils' you see there — in a controlled fashion, they can be made to reflect the force of gravity. It's a general property inherent to the stones, and my apprentice and I have simply put it to practical use."

"This is a remarkable achievement, Mr. Threadneedle," said Dr. Pinches, for the idea had quite seized his imagination.

"Indeed, you have surpassed yourself, Mr. T.," Dottie beamed.

"But if you have magnets," Mr. Frobisher asked, "how do you prevent them from interfering with your compass there?"

Warming to his subject now, Mr. Threadneedle proceeded to enlarge at some length upon the construction of his ship's compass, or bittacle, and the ingenious means by which it had been shielded from the influence of the coils.

"Remarkable!" the doctor said again, shaking his grizzled head.

Having overcome his initial hesitation, Mr. Threadneedle was delighted to discover that his guests found his flying coach of a coach-house quite as extraordinary as he did, and he showed it. Miss Wastefield, knowing something about the sundering and its cause that Mr. Threadneedle did not, from all that Mr. Lanthorne had told her, was about to enlighten him when the grocer abruptly shifted the attention of himself and the others to her.

"But what of you, Miss Wastefield? We have had some troubling words from the doctor and Mr. Frobisher here as regards your difficulty. How may we be of help to you?"

"Truly, sir, I don't know what help either you or anyone else can be," she answered. "Those creatures whose path you were unfortunate enough to cross will not waver in their search for me. They serve under orders of a higher sort. I know of nothing that can rid me of them, no action that can avert their onslaught."

"My dear Miss W.," Dottie smiled, with all the ready sympathy at her disposal, "my dear, we are all of us here of one mind in this, I'm sure. But we had no idea — I had no idea — Mrs. J. had no idea! It was little Jilly, who has been so concerned for you, as have all of us in Chamomile Street, and who enlisted the aid of our Mr. F. We knew nothing of the nature of your difficulty. Is there nothing now we can do for you?"

"The coach-house is yours to command," Mr. Threadneedle offered gallantly.

"As are we," added Dr. Pinches.

"Allow us to help you, Jane," Martin entreated her, pressing her hand. It seemed that all his love for her, which had grown so much since they were first engaged, and which had only deepened in these past weeks they had been apart, was concentrated at that moment in his eyes. "It strikes to my heart to see you so. Surely something can be done! This is a civilized world, what remains of it. How can such a horror exist in a civilized world?"

Miss Wastefield looked round her at their inquiring faces, touched by their expressions of concern. Something in her own sweet eyes of hazel, in the set of her brow, her mouth, the pretty dimple in her chin, the very heart beating in her breast, wanted very much to be moved by them and accept their offers of help. She very nearly succumbed, too; but then the direness of her situation bore upon her once more, and as it did, the smile on her lips faded like a dying dream, and her resolve hardened anew.

"I am grateful to you, everyone," said she, gathering her cloak and furs about her, "but it would have been better if you hadn't become a party to this terrible business. It would have been better to have known nothing of it. Look at the trouble it has caused you!"

"Not to worry, dear," said Dottie. "It's been my experience that trouble is best taken face-on and dealt with, or it will most certainly prevail. As for myself it's no trouble, for I already was coming out to visit Mr. T. — he had the finest grocery in Chamomile Street once upon a time, you know — and was in hopes of a little excursion. Of course I'd no idea it would be in a flying coach-house! I'll admit it still leaves me a bit queasy. Knowing that Mr. T. had a jaunting-car, naturally I expected we should take the air round the island a time or two — but hardly in such a fashion as this!"

"Miss Wastefield," said Dr. Pinches, "since last we spoke, I have been cogitating upon the matter, and I wonder if there may not be a way to —"

The doctor's words were abruptly suspended in air, as the voice of Tim Christmas rang out again —

"Look here, sir!"

They thought at first he had spied another horde of zeugs; however, he was standing not at the window but at the rear of the coach-house, and with a puzzled expression on his face.

"What is it, young man?" Mr. Threadneedle asked, joining him.

"This large trunk, sir, with the chains and locks on it. How did it get here?"

Miss Wastefield gave vent to a long and weary sigh. She didn't need to walk across to know what trunk was meant. It was her own trunk, of course, with its vile contents of ancient polished bronze, with which the Triametes intended to hound her and hound her until she submitted.

"Who could have brought it aboard?" the grocer wondered.

"No one brought it," said Miss Wastefield. Her eyes were shut and she had one hand propped against her brow, as though her head ached. "I apologize for it, sir. I fear it has arrived of its own accord."

"Oh, sir," cried Lucy, "it's a wicked, unholy thing as abides there. It speaks to my mistress in the night, sir, in slitherous whisperings. I've heard it! And it was the cause of the late master's apoplopsy —"

"Hush! Be quiet, girl!" Miss Wastefield commanded her. "Do you understand now, Lucy, how it always comes back to me? Do you see now why I can never be rid of it?"

Miss Wastefield had resigned herself to the fact that all these people, from her *fiancé* and Lucy to strangers like Mr. Threadneedle and Tim Christmas, were privy now to something of her peculiar trouble. *But what was there to do?* Mr. Frobisher was not what he'd seemed to be — that is, he was not what her desperate mind had made him out to be. He hadn't relieved her of the burden of the mirror; indeed, he'd known nothing whatever of importance concerning it. And as for Martin, he still did not know all, because she had not seen fit to tell him all.

The Triametes, she understood, would never stop hunting for her wherever she might go. And what good was Mr. Lanthorne's offer of protection if she could never be free of them? It would serve only to delay the inevitable. Certainly this coach-house of Mr. Threadneedle's could take her most anywhere she wanted. But how long before the Triametes found her there? How long before the trunk and the mirror of ancient polished bronze found her there?

Not long, she realized, with a sinking heart — not long.

How much longer, then, to trouble Mr. Threadneedle and the other kind people who had offered her their assistance? How much longer to trouble poor Martin, and possibly endanger him? Again the answer was — *not long*.

The coach-house ran on for another hour or more, while the passengers — some of whom, like Dottie, had admitted to being a trifle squeam-

ish — watched from the windows and made observation of the world below. In time they became more comfortable, however, more secure in the
knowledge that the house was not about to plummet from the sky and sink,
as Captain Barnaby might have said, like a stone. Indeed, for Dr. Pinches
there was a certain exhilaration in it, a boldness and invigoration of the
spirit like that he felt high up in the towers of Nantle Minster. And what
he'd seen that one day from the belfry — the impossible object that had
dropped from the clouds and hovered there in space — it had of course
been the coach-house. How far from his tiresome, monotonous way of life
it all was!

To Mr. Frobisher, too, this invention of Mr. Threadneedle's was a first-
class marvel. He found himself admiring the little round inventor with the
curled-up mustaches and eyes that twinkled like a pixie's, and began to
imagine how his invention might be put to use in the making of money. As
for Mr. Somerset, he cared almost nothing about it, except so far as it was
a haven and a refuge for Miss Wastefield, and had saved her — and all of
them — from the three-eyed giants.

After a time, Mr. Threadneedle and Tim swung the coach-house round
to the north, where a fair-sized ship, very stout as to timbers and trim as to
rigging, had been observed bearing due southeasterly. To their joy they discovered it was the *Salty Sue*. So the lugger had not been sunk by the vengeful Triametes, which was something to be glad about; but of course neither
Captain Barnaby nor his vessel had been the object of their search. Likely
the captain had made sufficient repair of the damages as allowed him to sail
from the channel, and that in his eagerness to get clear of Truro he'd put off
his calls at the other islands.

Meanwhile an idea had occurred to Martin, one which he proceeded to
voice now to Mr. Threadneedle and the rest. Perhaps the Triametes could
be fooled, he suggested, if Miss Wastefield and he were returned to the lugger to resume their journey, and thereby make their way home to Crow's-
end. For wasn't the captain's ship, having already been searched by them,
the last place the Triametes would look for his *fiancée*?

"But how are you to be returned there?" Mr. Threadneedle asked him.
"For the ship is alow and we are aloft."

"Surely, sir, you'll not expect our host to bring his craft down on the
captain's head?" interjected Mr. Frobisher. It rubbed against the grain of
our friend Allan that this fellow Somerset might have the upper hand of
him in anything. Wasn't it bad enough he already had the hand of Miss
Wastefield?

"You've a rope-ladder there, I see," indicated Martin.

"Yes, it can be fastened to those cleats and unrolled from the door," Mr. Threadneedle told him.

"These creatures will have no interest in that ship knowing that Miss Wastefield is not aboard, and so it's only logical that she and I should return to it and be on our way. The rope-ladder can be of use in that regard. We can't remain aboard this coach-house of yours, sir — we can't further inconvenience you and the others here."

"Southwards of us, at Goforth, are any number of inns where you might hide yourselves for a time, or so I've heard from Captain Barnaby. Perhaps the captain can take you there, for I know he passes that way often. Once your road is clear, you may book passage for Crow's-end, when his ship or another sails that way again."

"If Crow's-end is what the lady wishes, of course," said Mr. Frobisher.

"It *is* what the lady wishes, sir," returned Martin, bristling.

"And how have you come by this knowledge, sir? Have you asked her of late what her wish might be?"

"By God, you are a bold and impertinent fellow, sir!" declared Martin, clenching his fists at his sides, in preparation perhaps for another ominous brushing-up of sleeves.

"Ah! I see she's told you of me," said Allan, with a cutting smile.

"And a fat lot of good an impertinent fellow will do her in her present situation. This lady is to be my wife, sir, and so you will have a care, for you are once again over the mark!"

"And this impertinent fellow for one, sir, is sorry for the lady," answered Mr. Frobisher, tit for tat.

"By God, sir —!"

"Couldn't we ourselves take the lady to Crow's-end, sir, in the coach-house?" Tim broke in, appealing to Mr. Threadneedle.

"I believe we could," the grocer answered, with a thoughtful rub of his chin. "Although it's a great long way to Crow's-end, and we've not traveled so far before at one jump. Moreover we have yet to put these newest modifications to the proof. But we shall never know the result if we don't try, eh? Of course, it needn't be a single jump. I dare say it'll be a fine test of the mechanism —"

"No!" said Miss Wastefield, speaking up for herself at last. There was that in her tone which made objection on the part of anyone a futile prospect. "No, sir — no. I thank you from the bottom of my heart, but no. I must encumber you no more."

"Encumber us? Not a jot!" returned Mr. Threadneedle. "My dear Miss Wastefield —"

"I thank you for your generosity, sir, but I must not further endanger you or these other good people. As Crow's-end is our home, I believe Martin's plan to be the correct one. We shall return there, but by means of our own resources; I'll not draw you any further into this trouble of mine. We shall, however, make avail of your suggestion and remain at Goforth, in some quiet house, until all is safe and passage can be secured for Crow's-end. This seems to me the best plan."

"Oh, but it seems to me a very dangerous plan, my dear," said Dottie. "And how will you inform the captain of it? For if you mean to entrust your life to a bit of rope swaying in the wind — high above the sea — oh, dear!"

"Ah, but she doesn't mean that at all, Mrs. Matchless," Martin assured her. "It is I myself who shall descend the ladder and make our request known to the captain. I shall ask him to put in at one of the small coves indenting the coast hereabouts. Miss Wastefield can go aboard there and the voyage to Goforth taken up without delay, if it meets with his approval."

"But he may not want you aboard his ship, sir," said Mr. Frobisher — it was a perfectly reasonable objection — "for the last time, you'll recall, it was nearly sunk by monsters from the sea."

"By your leave, Mr. Somerset, might I suggest another course of action?" said Mr. Threadneedle, who like Dottie was none too keen on the idea of the rope-ladder. "Let us instead attach a note to the foot of the ladder. That way the captain can be informed of your request without any harm coming to yourself. Sufficient unto the day is the danger thereof, eh, sir? Should the captain agree, you and Miss Wastefield can then go aboard in some lonely place out of the general view. For we haven't the least notion where these Triametes may be lurking."

The grocer's proposal being mooted, it met with broad approval; and so it was agreed. Materials for writing were procured from the little desk by the hearth, where Martin composed a letter to Captain Barnaby. The note was then placed in a canvas bag and tied to the lowermost rung of the ladder, and the ladder itself secured to the cleats on either side of the door.

"I'll confess, this maneuver may put a bit of a scare into the captain," said Mr. Threadneedle, although he couldn't resist a little chuckle at the thought of it. "He may have served aboard Wulf Clipperton's ship, but he's never beheld the power of the hoverstones. We're prepared for it, then, Tim?"

"We are, sir."

And so they took their stations, Tim drawing open the porthole so that he could keep a watch on the lugger and guide their actions at the mangles and gig-wheel.

"Coils up and easy, Tim!" said Mr. Threadneedle.

"Aye, sir!"

Slowly, carefully, with eyes glued to the window at his feet, Tim brought the coach-house down from the sky, at the same time calling out instructions to Mr. Threadneedle, until they had fetched a little ahead of the ship and lay directly athwart her course, at about the height of her swaying topsails.

From the windows the men of the lugger could be seen gathering on deck in open-mouthed astonishment. From the watch forward to the steersman aft, all were craning their necks and gesturing to skyward. There was lanky Bob Sly, and beside him the wide blue figure of the captain, staring from under crunched brows at the awful apparition. Mr. Threadneedle fancied he could hear the skipper voicing an oath at the sight and declaring himself a gooseneck barnacle.

The captain took up his spyglass and peered hard at the coach-house. To reassure him that the house was no emissary from the infernal regions, Mr. Threadneedle stepped to the bay window, which he knew the captain to be observing, and waved to him in a genial manner. Then he held the palms of both hands out, after which he pointed to the lugger, and then held his hands out again, to convey his wish that the vessel be brought to a stop in the water.

Shaken to see the figure of Mr. Malachi Threadneedle signaling him from the apparition, the captain removed the glass from his eye and declared himself a salted codfish. Then he began issuing orders to his men. Directly the halyards were eased and the sails trimmed. The seas through which the ship had been sailing were generally smooth and the winds light, and so she had little trouble in heaving to.

"Make yourselves fast, everyone," Mr. Threadneedle warned. "Miss Wastefield, pray watch your little pet there. We'll not want him scampering out!"

When all had prepared themselves as best they could, the grocer whisked open the door. In rushed the wind. It was salty, sweet, and chill, and though but light, still it was like a minor tempest in the close quarters of the coach-house. It raged and it puffed and generally tried to blow things about, but as most everything was fastened down, it achieved little save for a brisk ruffling-up of the travelers' hair.

Bracing himself, Mr. Threadneedle took hold of the rope-ladder and flung it out the door. Down and down it tumbled, unrolling as it went. The operation had placed the coach-house in some proximity to the lugger's masts and canvas — it was riding just above her foresail — and Captain

Barnaby, seeing what Mr. Threadneedle was about, exhorted his men to steady the ship further. The ladder came dancing down toward them, crossed the rail, and swung inboard midway twixt the fore and main masts, where Bob Sly seized hold of it and took charge of the canvas bag.

The captain unfolded Martin's letter and read it through. A deal of sailorly conversation with Mr. Sly followed. With the ship rocking to the gentle swell, her timbers creaking and her yards rattling, and the coach-house floating silently aloft, its wavy ladder like an umbilical joining the one craft to the other, it was a remarkable scene.

The reply was prepared by the skipper himself. After some further discussion with Mr. Sly it was agreed that they should put in at a spot called Sculpin Bight. It was a remote, unpeopled place with decent anchorage, though generally narrow and rock-walled, and with a small patch of ground for the coach-house to settle on. It was some distance yet down the coast, however, and would require another few hours to reach. The reply was then stuffed into the bag and tied to the ladder, which was on the point of being drawn up when a shout arose from the look-out, who had observed two objects surfacing to windward.

Came cry of *Monsters, ho!* at sight of the crested heads of the brother Triametes. Far from abandoning the lugger, the giants had been secretly trailing her, their presence all unsuspected by the captain and his men.

Or was it the coach-house they had been following?

A sailorly panic broke out aboard ship. Mr. Sly reached for the canvas bag, to take back the captain's reply, but at that moment the ladder swung outboard and he found himself nearly pitched into the sea. Meanwhile the captain was bellowing to his minions to away, away!

It was Mr. Frobisher who spotted two other dark forms in the water approaching side by side at a rapid pace. Their bodies were of such proportions as to dwarf the three-eyed giants, for whom they appeared to be making. Nearer and nearer they came, bearing down on the sons of Poteidan. How swiftly the gliding denizens of the deep gained on the unrecking Triametes! And of how little use were the third eyes of the gargoyles in spying their underwater foes.

Came a final surge forward as the zeugs closed in. The Triametes remained unaware of their presence until the last moment. Like monstrous saber-cats of the sea, the creatures pounced upon their victims, lunging at them from below. Their momentum carried them halfway out of the water, as they swept the gargoyles up into their mouths and crushed them with a vicious snapping motion. Roaring mightily, the sons of Poteidan disappeared amid a wild thrashing of limbs, a violent champing of jaws and teeth and crunching of bones, and a spreading wash of crimson. Then the leviathan zeugs, their hunger appeased, plunged back into the darksome depths from which they had risen, and were gone.

The *Salty Sue* lifted to the rising swell and took the buffets of the waters broadside on. Wave after mountainous wave broke against her and spilled aboard her decks. The captain and his men were thrown to the rails, clinging for dear life. Before the coming of the zeugs, the sea had been smooth enough; now it was a great tumbling mass of waters, and the bobbing lugger wholly at its mercy. The captain, douse him and bleed him, made orison to Davy Jones — and lo! his prayer was answered.

The waves gradually rolled themselves out, from that point where zeugs and Triametes had vanished in a white smother of foam. The seas gentled, the rocking subsided, until the *Salty Sue,* recovering herself, stood once more stout and trim in the water. Once again the captain's prime duck of a craft had stood what came her way and survived. So, too, the coach-house, which, in some peril itself, had been taken aloft to evade the lugger's reeling mast-heads.

Although the captain had been mightily impressed by the coach-house, he had been impressed even more by his latest glimpse of the leviathans of legend. The experience of seeing a pair of zeugs leaping out of the water had been enough to make his silvery hair stand on end. The creatures had very nearly capsized his ship, and although he'd been none too complimentary in the past as regards the hugeous fierce dragons of the deep, he saw fit now to offer thanks for their vanquishment of the giants. The captain's affairs might be in a parlous state, his wife a tartar, and his ship nearly drowned, but for the moment he had cheated sure death and sarten, damn it, or he was a jack mackerel.

For once it was Lord Zeug who had triumphed over Lord Poteidan. The Triametes had been condignly punished for their crimes, and sent to their rewards. And let Davy Jones take the measure of their worth!

"Wind's a-comin', and will be plenty on it, I rackon," said Bob Sly. He had cast his eyes to windward where the a massive army of clouds was gathering in the channel. The damage to the ship's timbers had yet to be fully attended to, and here now was the threat of an advancing storm on the horizon. The winds would not remain favorable for much longer. The waning sun, though it still shone clear, would soon plunge into those distant clouds and, dying, cast gloom and shadow over land and sea.

It was not unlike the shadow that had once again fallen across Miss Wastefield. All but she assumed that her trouble had been gotten over. But she knew better; and if she hadn't known it in her heart and soul, she would have known it from those words of her guardian.

For these spirits have their agents everywhere, ready to do their bidding.

She knew very well there were others of their kind — other Triametes, and other abominations even more horrid — prepared to take their place in the service of the lord Poteidan. They would stick at nothing in their pursuit of her. She would be driven from pillar to post, doomed to live out the balance of her existence on the watch. Always the days and nights would have their unseen eyes and ears. Every unknown sound, every quiet footfall, every knock at every door would possess its own measure of terror. And always there would be more, more!

Such was the bleak prospect called a life she saw stretching before her.

Where in the world could she go to escape them? Goforth? Nantle? Crow's-end? Hardly!

There was but one place where she would be safe; she knew that now.

And so she left the window and returned to her seat, and took some comfort in the presence of Martin and Lucy and little Juga. Weariness and indifference began to creep upon her, gradually easing her fears and leaving in their stead a magical calmness in the face of her fate, and resignation at the inevitability of it.

And at the *rightness* of it.

She saw that her journey's end was drawing near. The agents of the lord Poteidan were everywhere, and no matter where she went in a sundered world — whether by ship, carriage, mastodon train, or marvelous flying coach-house — there they would be.

Everywhere, but that one place where she had made up her mind now she must go.

CHAPTER FORTY

A Dream of Kaftor

Miss Wastefield lay in her small hutch of a stateroom aboard the *Salty Sue,* with Juga beside her and Lucy dozing in the berth above. The gentle swaying of the ship as it rode at anchor had made all of them drowsy. They had boarded the lugger in Sculpin Bight, after taking leave of Mr. Threadneedle and the rest, in particular Mr. Frobisher. It had been the aim of our impudent friend Allan to join her aboard the *Sue,* but to his disappointment he had been rebuffed. Miss Wastefield had instead urged him to abandon all thought of it and return with the others to Nantle. She had begged him in the name of charity, and in private, so that young Martin — already perilously close to brushing up his sleeves — should not catch word of his design; only then, and with a most grudging acquiescence, had he relented. Likely he never would see her again, and never would view the mirror of ancient polished bronze, nor have possession of either. We leave it to others to judge which would pain him more.

It was only Martin, then, he whose intent it was to be her husband, who had joined her aboard ship. The mystery-lady seemed much hove down since last he'd clapped eyes on her, the captain had remarked to Bob Sly. How pale and drawn she looked! Likely it was the shock of the three-eyed giants. She must lay her head well to the wind, he declared, and fight her way through it. But the captain and his first mate had more matters on their minds now than this. After due consideration, the captain had elected to remain for the present in their sheltered harborage and ride out the coming weather. They had doused sails and were anchored fast in the bight, with the high bluffs overhead to shield them from the worst of the gale. Once it had passed, they would heave up and lay a course for Goforth.

Like the coach-house, which had risen gently up and out of the narrow bight and floated off, a dream came floating through the mind of Miss Wastefield now as she lay on her pillow. And as she had so many times, she dreamed of Kaftor.

Keeping her company in her dream were other little children like herself, offspring of the temple hierocracy. There were robed priestesses, too, and temple elders, and temple servants. There were troops of noisy monkeys in red leather harnesses, and one little monkey in particular, sitting on a step. It was Juga — not the Juga of present day, but he of her earlier incarnation. Monkeys, she recalled, had been brought to Kaftor from Egypt of the Two Lands to serve as attendants of the deities — or rather, of those ascended beings who fancied themselves deities, and saw fit to hold the lesser spirits in thrall. So was her own lesser spirit, her bodied being, in thrall to Poteidan.

These other ascended ones — the lady Potnia of the temple-labyrinth, goddess supreme of Kaftor, and her son and consort Velchanos; sweet virgin Britomartis of the wild beasts; goddess Eleuthia of the caves; the warlord Enualios; Diktynna of the mountains — swelled full large in her mind's eye, and one by one bestrode the stage of her consciousness, as they had of old in her first childhood. Scenes and forms of an ancient past — *her* past — lay outspread before her. She saw fields bright with poppies and saffron crocuses, water lilies, fig trees and olive trees, butterflies, swallows, bluebirds. She saw greyhounds, and wild goats with their fleecy beards. She saw again the terraces, courtyards, and colonnades of the temple-labyrinth. Once more she climbed its staircases and viewed its glowing frescoes, its sanctuaries and shrines, its storerooms packed with offerings and tribute, its vestries and refectories. Everywhere around her were the images of bulls' horns, symbol of Poteidan, on altars here and altars there, and in long rows adorning the tops of walls, and sprouting from roofs, all in the days before the quaking-time. She saw again the boxing bouts and gymnastic displays in which all of Kaftor took pride. In the open courtyard of the labyrinth she thrilled again to the teams of acrobatic youths, male and female, the grapplers and vaulters engaged in the leaping of the bulls — the sacred and eternal rite of the bull dance, in which the participants were believed to dance with the lord Poteidan himself.

She closed her eyes and touched fist to forehead in the ritual pose of worship. She had been taught it by her parents and the temple servants. All praise, she called aloud in her dream, all praise to many-rayed Poteidan, the earth-shaker!

Then she awoke to the heaving of the ship, and to a very different vision of black clouds and a gray sea in a tiny porthole. The storm from the channel had arrived. The wind was blowing high. She could hear the harsh groaning of the ship's timbers, the call of voices from deck and passage, the sullen roar of waves breaking ashore. The captain's decision to remain within the narrow waters of the bight was, she dearly hoped, a wise one. Some of the clouds had hard, curdled edges to them, which bespoke little good, and the distant booming of the surf was like a kind of thunder.

An angry sea, empire of Poteidan, lord of earth and wave! But the calming sun, too, was a manifestation of Poteidan. Earth and earth-shaker he was, and the bull god as well. Was there no escape from him? No escape from a crafty overlord who demanded worship, and whose powers were beyond even those of such a being as Tom Lanthorne?

With such thoughts crowding her brain, she arose and, dislodging poor Lucy from her berth, sent her temporarily away. She claimed she wanted to be alone for a while, but of course it was pure deception. Nor would she be alone so long as Juga was with her.

Once her maid had gone, she took the mirror from her dressing-case — no longer had she need or want of a trunk now — and held it in her hand, with less distaste and apprehension than formerly. As she had before, she examined its ancient polished bronze, and the carved handle of ivory with its images of poppies and crocuses in bas-relief. Today, however, she seemed to be seeing the mirror clearly for the first time, and deemed it all in all not so foul or unholy an object as she'd thought. Instead it seemed like a comfortably familiar object. Although it had brought about the death of her father — Dr. James Wastefield, her father in this, her first and only rebodiment — she was no longer afraid of it. The feeling of nervous dread that had stalked her for so long had quite passed away.

She gazed into the mirror with an almost fearsome intensity, as if willing the image of the dark-haired woman to appear; and so it did. Wide, painted eyes, cherry-red lips, bountiful hair like spun coal — every aspect of the woman's countenance she examined minutely, no longer wondering why it had seemed familiar to her.

"*Tukatē*," said the woman, speaking in one of the lost tongues of Kaftor. It was a kind of Greek, so old it already was ancient when blind Homer sang; but Miss Wastefield found she understood it perfectly well.

Tukatē, the woman had said. *Daughter*.

Miss Wastefield held the mirror close and touched a quivering hand to it, as if reaching for the woman's face within it. It was the face of one she had very much loved, and who had loved her, a face her tiny fingers had explored with childish wonder all those long centuries ago.

"Mother," she whispered, her voice faltering. "Oh, my dear mother —"

"My little Djhana," the woman replied softly, "you have been from home for so very long. How changed you are! But you are still my little Djhana, my child, my dearest little one. Come back to us!"

In an instant her place was taken by the strong-faced man, he of the firm, steady features, and hair like the woman's worn in streaming braids and curls. He was a high priest of the temple-labyrinth. Seeing his face again called tears into the eyes of Miss Wastefield, a flow she was quite powerless to check, for she had loved him, too.

"Papa," she cried, as drop after warm salty drop slid down her cheeks. "I've missed you so, Papa!"

"Come back to us," her father called to her. "Leave this fleeting earthly existence of yours and return to us in Kaftor, where we abide for all eternity in the mind's eye of our god. We are forever young here. There is no earthly death here, there is no change; there is only life in the service of our lord. Here we serve in blessed peace forever — *here blessed Kaftor exists forever!* All praise to Poteidan, our master and great lord who sustains us."

Next there appeared the face of the beautiful dark priestess who had sounded the triton-shell — a high priestess of the labyrinth, she who had given little Djhana the honeyed wine laced with poppy juice, then throttled her with a cord and poured off her blood in obeisance to Poteidan. It had been a sacred libation made to spare Kaftor his wrath and avert disaster. But still disaster had come, and Kaftor was no more — not in this earthly world, at any rate.

All these things weighed heavily on the mind of Miss Wastefield, so that for a long time she did not notice her grim-faced guardian sitting patiently by in the cabin. When finally she looked up and saw him, she was not the least surprised, and did not start. Instead she turned to him at once and said —

"I should like to go home now, Mr. Lanthorne."

"You wish to return to Pinewick?"

"No, sir. I should like to return to Kaftor. I do not belong at Pinewick."

"I see."

"I had thought I was stronger than I find I am," she confessed. She looked at Juga, who had been observing her almost as closely as her guardian had. On impulse, she took the monkey into her arms and, settling him there, peered inquiringly into the two shiny black beads that served him for eyes.

"Who are you in there?" she asked. "Are you my old companion from childhood, full of all your old monkey-tricks? For I had a pet on Kaftor, once, when I was very small — a little monkey, and his name, too, was Juga. Are you my old friend — my own dear little one — come to watch over me? If you are, I thank heaven for you!"

She was rewarded with a soothing string of chirps and coos from Juga, his affectionate eyes just inches from her own.

A sudden ray of light came to illuminate the puzzle. Perhaps it came from Mr. Lanthorne, perhaps not; regardless she looked at him and said —

"Perhaps it is you I should thank, sir. You sent him to me, did you not?"

"Your little friend of old was most insistent," her guardian replied. He had removed his tall hat — for the staterooms of the *Salty Sue,* as we know, were rather cramped and low — and was sitting on a locker. It was of course but an image of himself sitting there, which he had projected into her thoughts.

"You were that friend of my father's at Strangeways so many years ago?" she said. "The friend of my second father, Dr. Wastefield? It was you who gave him Juga — to give to me?"

Mr. Lanthorne acknowledged the fact. "Your little friend was most eager to keep you company in your new life. He would not be dissuaded."

Her glance strayed to the mirror, and as she passed an idle finger over the inscription on the handle, she found to her surprise that she could read the mysterious characters rather easily. What had once been a line of unintelligible scratch-marks now meant something to her.

I am the mirror of — so the inscription ran in part, followed by a name, doubtless that of the woman to whom the mirror had belonged.

It was the name of her mother.

"It is my *wayward* new life you mean, sir," she said. "I was given in ritual sacrifice to the earth-shaker, so that Kaftor might be preserved forever in his mind's eye. It was my purpose in being, in living and dying. Kaftor may have passed from this transitory world, but it will live on in the realm of spirits for as long as Poteidan wills it. It was a mistake to come back. I must go home, Mr. Lanthorne; I don't belong here. I wanted so much to live again, to return to this earthly existence I had known so briefly, but I see now that it was very wrong. It was *selfish*!"

She looked into the mirror and saw the face of the little girl quietly watching her from the bronze. It was the same little girl who had died on the altar of Juktas.

"I know you now," said Miss Wastefield. "You are my own self, my past, my childhood self — my conscience — reproaching me for my transgression."

Miss O'Guppy had spoken of seeing two people when she looked at

Miss Wastefield — the one a young woman, the other, her former self, younger still, but at the same time immensely old. No morning time for so long a time! No further rebodiments now; but such had been her fate.

"Ritual murder — ritual *slaughter*," Mr. Lanthorne reminded her. "But it is your choice to make, Miss Wastefield. It was only fair you should know all that happened in that time. It was all I had within my power to do."

"He is remorseless," she said, "but he is the earth-shaker, the lord of earth and wave, and my ruling spirit. And as you have told me, sir, we poor bodied beings are ever in the grip of these ruling spirits." There was a change in her voice now; she spoke as one to whom all earthly things had lost their relish. Her guardian offered no reply, silently acknowledging her acceptance of a hard but universal truth.

From the ancient polished bronze she felt again that odd tugging sensation, as if her spirit were being drawn out of her through her forehead and sucked into the mirror-world. This time, however, it didn't frighten her, for it was showing her the way home. She knew how to return to Kaftor now, the one place where she would be safe. She needn't suffer at the hands of the Triametes or other dread abominations; it was the mirror — the vile, unholy mirror — that would be her salvation. Her way out of the thicket was the way *into* it, and it had been there all the time.

"You have helped me more than I have deserved, Mr. Lanthorne. You have helped me to understand myself, and I thank you for it," she said, conscious of being very much in his debt.

Her guardian rose and took her hand, and inclined his head slightly, and something like a smile softened his grim features.

"I wish you and your family every happiness," he said, in a voice of gentle benediction. "May the wise and ancient souls of Kaftor watch over you, Djhana, and care for you. Perhaps we shall meet again in another place and time, where the lord Poteidan holds no sway."

She felt the grip of his hand in hers, so warm, so firm, so reassuring. Then the feel of it slowly dissolved, like stone turning to sand; and when she looked again there was no one with her but Juga.

"And I thank you, too, my little one," she said, holding him close as she had done so long ago on Kaftor. Once more she was little Djhana, a child of the temple-labyrinth; once more he was her own little Juga, her dear one, snuggling in her arms and chirping in her ear; and the centuries that had intervened were as mere seconds.

In time she called Martin into her cabin, and for above an hour explained it all to him behind the shut door. His bewildered brain could scarce comprehend what she told him. By the time she had finished, he was brushing up his sleeves again, ready to take a cudgel to this villain Poteidan. But it was not to be, for what she told him next struck him with all the force of a thunderbolt. He responded in the most impassioned terms, beseeching her not to talk such folly, entreating her, pleading with her. He spoke from his deepest, his inmost heart, and a most generous devotion; but his efforts were fruitless. His undying love for her, it seemed, counted for nothing.

Now at last he knew all, but knowledge often is sorrow.

When he emerged from the interview, it was as a changed man — pale, stunned, sick. He leaned against a bulkhead to steady himself, and said not a word, not to Lucy, not to Bob Sly, not to anyone he encountered on his tottery way back to his cabin.

Poor Martin! Miss Wastefield's heart had wrung for him, truly it had; but, like Mr. Lanthorne, she hadn't the power to prevail.

When later he returned to comfort his *fiancée* — for the lugger had commenced another uneasy rolling from the storm passing over their heads — he found her cabin-door bolted, and no answer to his knock. When Lucy appeared in the passage, he was immediately concerned, as was Lucy herself, for he had presumed her to be in the cabin with her mistress.

He knocked again, and to the relief of both they heard the sound of the bolt being drawn back. But the door did not move; and so Martin pushed it open a little, and peeped inside.

"Jane? Jane, dear, are you there? Are you ill? The ship has been tossed about, I know — "

They entered, but found only Juga there. Evidently it was he who had responded, and with his clever fingers released the bolt. He was sitting on the lower of the two berths — the one that had been his mistress's — and gazing sadly down at the mirror on the floor. The ivory handle lay in several pieces beside it, as though the mirror had fallen and broken there. Overhead a lamp swinging to and fro was making an eerie creaking sound, and throwing weird shadows against the walls. Of Miss Wastefield there was no sign.

In the berth, wedged beneath her pillow, was an envelope inscribed with Martin's name. With a tremulous hand he tore it open. Out fell a small gold band — he recognized it at once as the ring of engagement he had given her. Inside the envelope was a single sheet of paper on which a few lines had been traced.

I hope you will not judge me harshly, were the last words, the conclusion of her simple farewell, which he read with a breaking heart.

"Oh, where is she, sir?" Lucy whimpered. "What's become of my mistress? She's gone overboard, Mr. Somerset, I know it — overboard, and in the dark! Oh, sir, I should never have left her!"

"She could not have gone anywhere, Lucy, for the door was secured on the inside — "

Something stirred at their feet. Young Martin dropped to his knees and took the mirror up by its bare stem. To his astonishment, he beheld in its polished surface the face of a small child. He reeled back, afraid, and nearly dropped the mirror himself, while Lucy began to cry.

Surely it was a trick played upon their senses! The image looked out at them from the bronze — impassive, improbable, unreachable — and Martin knew at once that it was she. He saw it in her eyes and the dimple in her chin.

"*Jane* — ?" he whispered, scarcely believing.

What a cruel enchantment it was had stolen his love from him! What a cruel judgment by the cruelest of ascended lords and masters! And what a cruel lesson to be learned.

In mute despair he watched as the child glanced aside, her attention drawn to some mysterious, unseen companion. A sudden rush of joy filled her face, her eyes, her lips. Enraptured, she turned from the mirror. As she did so her image faded from his sight, and the ancient polished bronze went forever dark and silent.

CHAPTER FORTY-ONE

In Which a Certain Account Is Squared

"Yes?"

Mr. Liffey was hardly surprised when, on answering a summons at the door of his chambers at the Crozier, he found Fred Cargo standing there with Susan and Miss Veal. But he was surprised to find them looking so serious, especially Fred, who in every other way was his usual smart and spiffish self.

"May we have a word with you, sir?" Fred asked crisply.

"Of course."

Mr. Liffey stood aside so they might enter. To his further surprise, and considerable consternation, a fourth member of the party, whom he hadn't seen in the passage, followed the others in. It was with some hesitation that this person followed them, edging his way through the door with his odd-shaped leathery hat in hand.

"Do you know this gentleman, sir?" Fred asked.

Mr. Liffey responded with a groan and staggered back. His face and ears flushed red behind his white hair and beard.

"Oh dear, oh dear," he said, "it's Mr. Porter!"

Mr. Jerry Porter the fish porter it was indeed, he of Musselgate Market, and he looked and smelled it, too.

"How?" Mr. Liffey stammered, sinking down into a chair.

"A chance bit of information has come our way," Fred explained, "which brought Mr. Porter to our notice."

The rest took seats, all but the aforementioned Mr. Porter, who, only too conscious of his fishy state amid the ancient and cloistered environs of the Crozier, preferred to remain standing, while turning the hat in his hands nervously round and round by its guttered brim.

"We found Mr. Porter on Nantle quay," Fred went on, closely watching the trusted family solicitor, "and to say truth, sir, he had rather an astonishing tale to relate."

"Ah," croaked Mr. Liffey, in a voice gone all dry and pinched.

"Beg indulgence, sir," said Mr. Porter, "but I don't means to be a bother. This gentleman here — Mr. Cargo — said you'd told him some as concerns the case. Very sorry I am, sir, if it's put a bungle in your plans."

"Mr. Liffey," said Susan, "be advised we have learned of your secret trysts with this man, and of your desire to keep the knowledge from us — which to my mind, sir, is nothing if not provoking."

"Not to say shocking!" added Miss Veal, the very picture of indignation under her wig.

"We know as well of Mr. Devenham's role in the matter," continued Fred, "and how he happened to lead you to Mr. Porter, and how you have held discussions with Mr. Porter in the interim regarding Grandfather's will. 'Pon my life, is it not all true, sir?"

The attorney croaked again. For once his lawyerly instincts had failed him, so overwhelmed was he by the suddenness of the *contretemps*. But he was nearly seventy years of age — or something to the back of it, if Susan and Miss Veal were to be believed — and so perhaps it can be forgiven him.

"It was your stated wish to travel alone to Nantle. You didn't solicit our company, or want it, because you wished to communicate with Mr. Interloper Squailes privately, in our absence," accused Susan. "You, who claimed not to know a person called Squailes. 'I know nothing of him,' or so you told us. It was a bald-faced lie, sir!"

"Mr. Porter informs us you were acquainted with his mother years past in Cargo," said Fred. "Her maiden name, as I understand it, was Rosemary Porter?"

"Yes," replied Mr. Liffey. A gleam of moisture had crept into his gentle blue eyes, and he seemed lost in the spell of some hazy, far-off remembrance. "Yes," he said again, "yes, that was the lady."

Silence.

"I think you'd best unburden yourself, sir," Fred advised him. "Not to worry, it will be better for all of us in the end. I needn't tell you we are tremendously disappointed, and more than a little puzzled."

"There is something beastly afoot here," said his wife, flashing her eyes. "We should like to know what has been going on behind our backs, sir, while you have been, as you have told us repeatedly, 'attending to the case.' You must explain yourself, sir, and explain who this man Squailes is here — or Porter, or whoever he is — and why Grandfather Cargo should have left him so much as a toothpick."

"The very idea — it's not to be thought on!" sniffed Miss Veal, barely able to hide her contempt for the fishy porter.

Mr. Liffey, trapped there in his ancient, dark-looking chambers with their saintly garnish of paintings and crucifixes — not a comfortable atmosphere for the guilty-minded — prepared himself for the task. He swallowed hard a couple of times, trying to loose the knot his throat had gotten itself into. Of course there was nothing for him to do now but to explain himself; and so he went about it the best he could.

"It was after your grandfather died, Fred, that this whole business began. As the executor of his estate, it had fallen to me to examine his papers after his decease. Unfortunately, in the course of my examination I discovered something that I found quite abhorrent."

"Pray, go on, sir," invited Fred.

"I ought to have told you of it at the time, that I see now, but it stands as a fact that I did not. I hadn't wanted to blacken the reputation of your grandfather in your eyes; I wanted you to remember him as you had known him in life. He was dead — why sully your memory of him? As a result, what I found there among his papers I kept to myself."

"And just what did you find, sir?" Susan asked, sternly.

"Secret evidence — from his personal accounts and other writings, all in his own hand — that years ago he had perpetrated a dire fraud on a man named Fred Drownder."

"That man was my father, sir," spoke up Mr. Porter, for the information of Fred and the others, "though o' course I never knew him, for I was raised a Squailes. There's but few round Nantle now as knows of it, I b'lieve, and o' course old Dermot O'Kilcoyne, afore he pegged out."

"Mr. Drownder was a sitting tenant on a plot of land adjoining Tiptop Grange, on the upper river. He had received assurances that the acreage would be granted him in fee simple — that is, as a freehold estate — upon the death of the landowner, one Mr. Edward Lavery, as per the dispositions of that gentleman's will. Mr. Lavery had no surviving issue and no heirs-at-law, and considered Mr. Drownder a good and worthy friend."

"Drownder — Drownder," Fred murmured to himself. "I've heard that name before. And Lavery, too!"

"Mr. Drownder you should recognize," said Mr. Liffey, "for he was a second cousin to your grandfather."

"Of course!" Fred exclaimed, snapping his fingers. "Remember it now. I recall hearing my parents speak of him, years ago, and not in very complimentary terms, either. 'That shameful absconder,' my mother called him, and 'Drownder the bounder,' and other things even worse. Oh, I'm tremendously sorry, Mr. Porter — I didn't mean to give offense."

"None taken, sir," smiled the fish porter, with a little nod and a turn round of the hat in his hands.

"As for Lavery, if I remember rightly, there was a family by that name living once in the area. There are inscriptions on the stones in the churchyard."

"What followed was all your grandfather's doing, I'm afraid," said Mr. Liffey, who was observed to hesitate, and steal an uneasy glance or two round his chambers before going on. "He coveted the acreage for himself. It was adjacent to Tiptop Grange, as I've said — the area known as Little Green Wood."

"That's a capital spot! There is a lovely old ruin there, and rather a nice farmhouse. A jolly fine situation," nodded Fred.

"It was the farmhouse that Mr. Drownder occupied as a tenant, he and his wife, and it is the house in which Mr. Porter was born."

"But no one in the family spoke of this Mr. Drownder in anything but the most opprobrious terms."

"That, too, was your grandfather's doing. When Mr. Lavery died, it was found he'd made a new will, one which disinherited Mr. Drownder and left the acreage instead to somebody else — namely to Mr. Joseph Cargo. The will was subsequently proved in the Court, and that is how Little Green Wood became annexed to Tiptop Grange."

"But why should this Mr. Lavery have changed his mind?"

"He hadn't. That is the secret I discovered among your grandfather's effects. For you see, Fred, this 'new' will of Lavery's had been very cleverly forged. It was all unbeknownst to me at the time, that I can assure you! Your grandfather himself had counterfeited the document, and bribed the witnesses, in effect denying Mr. Porter's father, and so Mr. Porter himself, the freehold of Little Green Wood. I'm afraid the evidence is only too clear there in his papers."

"It's unthinkable," Susan declared, meaning not the fraud but the persons defrauded. "Mr. Interloper Squailes — Mr. Porter — this man here in the stinking garb — a nobody — this man is a relation of ours? Heaven forfend, the world has gone lunatic! It's more than unthinkable — it's intolerable. Once again, Frederick, your grandfather has left us in a beastly state!"

"It was simply a matter of your grandfather being your grandfather, Fred," Mr. Liffey went on. "He was a friend of long standing, and a client, but in truth he was not the man you may have thought him to be. It was my aim to spare you the disappointment of it."

"I knew he was a tight-fisted old rascal, sir, and a cunning and a secretive one — that not all he did was completely above-board — but to cozen a poor fellow out of his inheritance!" Fred exclaimed.

"He was the most influential man in the county, lord of the manor of Tiptop and owner of a great part of the surrounding soil. There was very little he could say or do of which his neighbors did not approve, because they feared him. All desired to be in his good books, and as a result his imperfections were largely overlooked. He was a jealous man as well, and a greedy one. Unlike many another squire of goodly repute, he endowed no free school in his town or county. He made no improvements to the church of which he was the patron, and no provision for the distribution of bread among the needy. And Tiptop Grange one of the most fertile estates in the county! Of course he was the richer for it all, in the end."

"I suppose I didn't fully comprehend the extent of his greed, but 'pon my life I hardly ever saw him," Fred declared. His grandfather's hounds and horses, his sherry and port, his house and thousands in yearly land, indeed, nearly everything that Fred adored about Tiptop Grange, looked to be passing before his eyes in a kind of guilty parade. "It seems I had more illusions about dear old Grandfather than I had otherwise thought. What became of Mr. Drownder, then?"

"Died o' grog and a fever, sir," answered Mr. Porter, "and with such shame upon my mother as rushed her into the arms o' the brute Squailes, him as treated her murderous bad."

"I'm afraid I don't understand. What had your mother to be ashamed of?"

"It would appear that Mr. Drownder suspected a falsehood in the matter of the new will, although he could prove nothing," said Mr. Liffey, gaining a little strength as he went along. "Your grandfather, knowing this, had it worded about that a sum of money had gone missing from his counting-house, and that suspicion had fallen on Mr. Drownder, who as a sitting tenant under leasehold could not be removed from Little Green Wood save by non-payment of rent, or proof of criminality."

"Absconded with the squire's coin, that's how it was talked of," said Mr. Porter. "And o' course my father could say naught against the squire, for who would've believed him? And so he drank himself into his grave. O' course I never knew the man, but such be the honest truth as best I knows it."

"Mr. Porter's mother married again soon after, but this fellow Rodger Squailes, a merchant seaman, was, as Mr. Porter says, a brute, who cruelly misused her," said Mr. Liffey. It was noted that his voice shook a little, and that a gleam of moisture had crept into his eyes again at this mention of Rosemary and her sad life.

"So kind she was, sir, and so pretty, too — and dead so young!" said Mr. Porter, sighing and nodding. "I was myself a mere younker when Squailes was stabbed through the heart, and my mother returned to Falaise, where the last of her family abided. Porters they were, sir, and so Porter I became, in memory of her."

"This is rather astonishing," Fred declared.

For all these many years Mr. Porter had believed that his father had stolen money from Joseph Cargo, when in truth it had been a lie manufactured by Joseph Cargo himself, to relieve Mr. Drownder — his own cousin, distant though he might be — of his inheritance and thereby enlarge the boundaries of Tiptop Grange.

"It's a capital situation, Mr. Porter — Little Green Wood, I mean," said Fred, waxing museful, as he usually did when the topic was the Grange and Cargo and home. "I have ridden my hunter through its leafy arbors, and followed the river, and explored the farmhouse and the ancient ruin on many a summer's afternoon. Though as to the winters, those in Cargo I believe are rather more severe than yours here at Nantle."

"A fine place it must be, as you say, sir, though I've not laid eyes on it myself — comprehending eyes, at least, for in those days I was too young to note it," said Mr. Porter.

"Plainly my grandfather must have relented in the end. Dear old Grandfather! That's why he left you the money. Isn't that the case, Mr. Liffey? It was to atone for his grave misdeed."

Oddly, Mr. Liffey did not say that it was so; instead his face and ears flushed again, more deeply even than before.

"Well," said Fred. He rose and started to walk the room up and down, slowly and leisurely, with his hands in his pockets and his watch-chain a-jingle. "Well, well, well!"

He looked at Mr. Porter and smiled, and Mr. Porter smiled in return; then Susan and Miss Veal looked at Mr. Porter — no smiles there — and appealed first to Fred, then to Mr. Liffey.

"It's unthinkable," Susan insisted. "It can't be so. Tell us, Mr. Liffey, that it isn't so."

"I'm afraid it must be so, dear," her husband assured her, "and we shall simply have to accept it. But, dear — think of Grandfather, and how he reformed himself! 'Pon my life, I'm quite astounded by it. But it's a jolly fine thing the old potentate came round."

Here something like a shiver went through Mrs. Cargo, and Miss Veal too, although it had only partly to do with Fred's words and the revelations concerning the fishy porter.

"Do you feel a chill, Aspasia, or am I imagining it?" Susan asked, rubbing her hands to warm them.

"I do," said Miss Veal, "and you are not."

Most certainly it was not the imagination of Susan. Everyone felt it, even Mr. Porter, who, inured though he was to the elements from his life on the quay, instinctively raised his bobbing hat against it.

"It *is* rather cold in here," Fred admitted, glancing round. "Perhaps there is a window ajar —"

What brought him up short, however, when glancing round, was not an open window, but an open mouth — indeed a gaping mouth — and a look of fearful expectancy, both of them in the face of Mr. Liffey.

"Why, what is it, sir? Is something amiss?"

Came a sort of wrenching or cracking sound, as of timbers slowly giving way under a force of pressure. The eyes of Fred traced those of Mr. Liffey, and what he saw caused him great astonishment. The bare floor in one spot near the sitting-area, between the carpets, was slowly rising, as if something was forcing its way through from beneath.

Fascinated, he approached for a closer look. What he found was altogether wondrous and strange. What he found was that the stout oak boards, rather than being pushed up from below, were themselves rising up, seemingly of their own accord. It was as though the very substance of the wood had been altered, had become soft and malleable, and was in the process of assuming another shape.

The chill in the room appeared to emanate from that same spot between the carpets. While Fred, incredulous, stood observing the phenomenon, his wife and Miss Veal recoiled from it. Mr. Liffey, meanwhile, remained frozen in his chair, anxious and fearful, for he alone knew what the phenomenon portended. The attorney found, however, that he couldn't detach his eyes from the thing — so curious a thing it was, and so curious, too, its manner of growth. It was as if the floor itself in that spot was rearing up, like a sinister wood-monster sprung from the planks. As the thing emerged, it was seen to be turning slowly round and round like a screw. Higher and higher it rose, still turning round; and yet, still in its essence it was a part of the floor, the same material as the boards but weirdly transformed.

The thing continued to rise until it was as high as a full-sized person. As it grew, it slowly ceased its revolving and assumed a man-like shape, like a human tree — gnarled, gaunt, craggy, with two limbs and something like a head, but bare and leafless, its bark studded with knotty protuberances. It was the very suggestion of something *human* in the thing, abiding within and informing its woody texture, that made it horrible.

All at once the apparition exploded in a burst of rage.

"No-o-o-o-o-o!" it cried, in a loud and vengeful tone.

Instinctively Fred placed himself between the thing and his wife. Mr. Liffey remained buried in his chair, while a frightened Mr. Porter looked on from behind his hat.

The creature threw out one grotesquely long and woody limb that was like a branch, with an accusing hand at the end of it that was like a knot of twigs, and aimed it at Mr. Liffey.

"You — ungrateful old wretch!" it snarled, in a voice both caustic and cold. "Traitor! Foul *trusted* traitor!"

"How now!" exclaimed Fred, leaping back and jingling. "What in heaven are you?"

"It's naught to do with heaven, I don't b'lieve, sir, whatever it be," opined the fish porter from behind his hat — "but certain sure, it's very cross!"

"What is it, Mr. Liffey? Have you some knowledge of this thing? For 'pon my life, sir, your face betrays you."

The attorney was trying very hard not to look at the creature and its accusing knot of twigs.

"My duty," he groaned, writhing uncomfortably in his seat. "It was my duty, none but mine. If I've done but one right and proper thing in my life — then it was this!"

"What is it, sir?" Fred asked again.

Still there was no answer from Mr. Liffey; and so Fred stepped boldly forward, approaching the thing with its limb like a branch outthrust, deep within the sphere of its chilling influence. As it swung round to confront him, Fred shuddered, not from the cold but from the shock of recognition — for in the gaunt and craggy thing that was like a human head, something familiar lurked. Fred started as he saw two eyes there — two death-cold eyes — couched amidst the bark, both shining with a weird, unearthly light, and both locked upon him; and between them an ugly protuberance like a nose, and beneath that a grin at once fiendish and sly. To his dismay Fred thought he recognized the outlines of each, and his skin crawled at the knowledge.

"'Pon my life!" he gasped. "Are you not — ?"

"Once," said the woody apparition, "before the silence of the tomb closed about me, I was your grandfather — Joseph Cargo. Don't you know me, Fred?"

An hysteric shriek, a piercing scream, and expressions of the most dreadful horror from Susan and Miss Veal. They stared, they gaped; Miss Veal clutched at her wig and then at her heart, as if to prevent either from taking leave. The shock of gazing again on the features of the corpse they had seen planted in its tomb at St. Loope's; of seeing that corpse reanimated now, by whatever unholy means, and transformed in so bizarre a fashion, and of hearing again that well-remembered voice — well, it was nearly too much to be borne!

Even Fred was mightily shaken by it, and temporarily bereft of words. It was quite enough to make one's hair (or wig) stand on end. But Fred was a sportsman and well-used to danger in the field, unlike the ladies, and as a consequence recovered his self-possession in shorter order than they.

"You say you are my grandfather?" he asked.

"Say that I *was,*" growled the thing, a trifle testily.

"But I hardly ever saw you."

"It is I, Fred. Believe it!"

"So what are you telling me? That my grandfather was dead, but now he's come back — *as a tree?*"

Another outburst from the fiend. All could hear the floor straining and cracking, and feel it, too. In the dark and woody thing that was like a head, the features of old Joseph Cargo loomed large. It was undeniably he, the former master of Tiptop Grange, risen from the earth like one of the ancient oaks that guarded his grave in far-away Cargo.

"If you are my grandfather, sir, then I'm jolly glad to see you reformed yourself in the matter of Mr. Porter here," Fred declared.

Another cry from the fiend, wholly as dreadful as the one before, but with more than a suggestion of mockery in it.

"Reformed?" The accusing limb was pointing again at Mr. Liffey. "Ha! Ask the old wretch there — ask the traitor!"

All eyes turned to Mr. Liffey; all ears awaited his response.

"What does he mean, Mr. Liffey?" Fred asked. "Why are you a traitor?"

Again the attorney wriggled uncomfortably.

"No bequest!" growled the creature, swinging its arm round in the direction of Jerry Porter. "No bequest for *that* one!"

So staggered was the poor untidy porter that he dropped his hat.

"Sir?" said Fred, turning again to Mr. Liffey.

"Tell 'em, wretch!" thundered the apparition, doing the like. "Tell 'em!"

"No bequest," cried the attorney, giving in. He was shaking so much from the strain, it seemed he must shake himself apart there in the chair. "Yes, Fred, it's — it's true. There was no bequest. I'm very sorry, Mr. Porter, for deceiving you. I'm sorry for deceiving all of you! I'm afraid the truth must come out."

"Tell 'em, traitor!" commanded the thing that had been Joseph Cargo.

"It was for her," said Mr. Liffey; and taking from his blue bag the picture of the lambent beauty — she of the almond-colored hair and laughing face — which he had brought with him from Cargo, he passed it tremblingly to Fred. "It was for her — *dear girl!*"

"Should I know this young lady, sir?" Fred asked.

"It's my mother, sir," said Mr. Porter. "Rosemary Porter, as then was Drownder, and last was Squailes. The daintiest thing under a bonnet she was — God bless her immortal soul."

"Dear Rosemary!" Mr. Liffey was heard to murmur. Strangely, in speaking of her, his voice seemed to regain something of its normal tone; or perhaps it was merely the softness with which he spoke, as set against the harsh thunderings of the fiend. "I must confess it — I loved her, dearly. I, who had never loved anyone, loved *her*! Can you believe it? Forgive me, Mr. Porter — this you didn't know. I loved your mother all those years ago, but she, like yourself now, knew little of it. Oh dear, oh dear!"

"Mr. Liffey?" said Fred, wrinkling up his brow. Clearly he was taken aback by Mr. Liffey's admission; equally clear was the fact that he did not immediately grasp the relevance of it.

"It was partly my profession, you see," the attorney went on. He spoke slowly, his every word tinged with a deep and sincere regret. "I was such a dogged, determined young fellow in those years. After my brief time out in the world on one of my father's ships, I returned home fired for the study of the law. And with what single-minded industry I pursued it! Even years on, in practice, I cared more for lawyering than for a woman's tender regard — that is until the day I met Miss Porter, and my world was forever changed.

"She was the daughter of a small client of our firm. Dear Rosemary! My heart was stricken at once. But in her eyes I was merely an acquaintance of the family — her father's solicitor, not an aspirant to her favor. Already she was attached to Mr. Drownder; she always had loved him, I suppose. But in spite of this, my affection for her grew; it could hardly do otherwise. It was this doggedness of mine, you see, this ever holding to one's course in the face of opposition. It has served me well in the practice of the law, but in the practice of life I'm afraid it is not always a blessing. So my dear Rosemary was wedded to Fred Drownder, and I was left to admire from the position of a generous and disinterested friendship. But through all these many years the ache in my heart has never left me. This picture of her I have cherished, since acquiring it after her father's death."

"And it's on this account that you never married, sir?" Fred asked.

The attorney nodded, his kindly gaze half on Fred and half on the portrait. "There was none to compare with her; she was incapable of inspiring anything but the most affectionate devotion. When she married that fellow Squailes, I could do little but observe from afar, in horror. I pledged to myself then that I should help her by whatever means possible. But she would accept nothing from me, not even after Rodger Squailes was killed."

"Stabbed through the heart," said Mr. Porter.

"Afterwards she returned to Falaise with her son to join what remained of her family. I kept myself informed of her situation over the years, through the good offices of some friends in that city. And I mourned the day that the news of her death reached me." Here he paused for a moment to stare, and to wring his head in a faint, helpless sort of way. "The last knowledge I had of Mr. Porter was that he'd removed to Nantle, after which I lost track of him — it was when he renounced his name. I didn't think to look for a man called Porter! Then your grandfather died, Fred" — an uneasy glance toward the creature looming over him — "and the evidence I have related came to light among his papers. My duty was clear; I was resolved that something should be done. Perhaps I had no means to help poor Rosemary, but at the very least I could help her son."

Here the creature began to tremble — not from fear but from a corked-up rage, which was threatening to erupt at any moment.

"And what do you mean, sir, that there was no bequest?" Fred asked, with a side-glance of his own at the thing that had been his grandfather. How appropriate, the thought flashed into his mind then, for his grandfather to have manifested himself in such wise. For hadn't the old tyrant spent the whole of his earthly existence in the pursuit of land and timber?

"It's just as I told you, Fred. Your grandfather left nothing to Mr. Porter. It was I who left it," said Mr. Liffey.

The admission seemed to ease the attorney of a mighty load. "It must all come to light now," he sighed. "Oh dear, oh dear! So stupid I've been. So damnably stupid!"

But Fred remained puzzled. "You gave Mr. Porter some of your own money, then, sir? That is why you've met with him secretly?"

Mr. Liffey answered with a tolerant smile and shook his head gently.

"It was *your* money, Fred — or, more correctly, it was your grandfather's money, left to you. He had cheated Mr. Drownder by counterfeiting a will, and so I returned the favor by counterfeiting a will of my own — your grandfather's. In my mind, turnabout seemed to be rather fair play."

"As the saying jolly well is, sir!" Fred cried, with indignation and astonishment vying for dominance in his eyes.

"Ungrateful wretch!" roared the fiend. "No bequest! All for Fred — none for Drownder! All for Tiptop Grange!"

"Then my grandfather never did reform himself?" Fred asked.

Mr. Liffey shook his head. "No. The bequest I myself appended to the will as a codicil, in order to recompense Mr. Porter for your grandfather's misdeed. The case was not actionable against the estate, you see — it had been too many years — and it was simpler in law to give him the money rather than the land. Forgive me, Mr. Porter! I very nearly told you everything, several times, but on each occasion my courage failed me. And so I delayed — and I delayed . . ."

His voice trailed off and he retreated again into the depths of his chair, shamefaced, his head sunk upon his breast in contemplation of his own grave misdeed and his weakness and his folly. A smile flickered with a wintry light in his face, briefly, as if he were seeing his ill-fated scheme blown to atoms before his eyes, and taking a just delight in it.

"I can scarcely believe it," Fred declared. "Is it all true, Grandfather? Did you indeed cozen Mr. Drownder?"

"Believe it!" answered the fiend, throwing out a wrathful limb at poor downcast Mr. Liffey. "Perjured wretch! Your very countenance hangs you. Foul cringing traitor! Consider all I gave you — employment for life in attending to the interests of Tiptop Grange — and you thank me by cheating me out of my own money — *by cheating my grandson!*"

In the midst of this tirade there came a polite knocking at the room-door, and a voice in the passage inquiring whether anything was amiss? It was the landlord of the Crozier, Mr. Blackshaw, come to investigate the raised voices and harsh thunderings issuing from a corner of his otherwise sober and respectable establishment.

But all in the room ignored the interruption, and for good reason. It was hard to know if Susan and Miss Veal were more distressed by the sight of a dead Joseph Cargo or the confession of a live Mr. Liffey; nevertheless, both they and the fish porter, and indeed Mr. Liffey himself, were looking to Fred now for his reaction. It was a crucial juncture.

Fred glanced at the portrait of the fair Rosemary in its gilded frame, and considered. His gaze shifted to Mr. Porter — Mr. Jerry Porter, distant relation of the family Cargo — *distant relation!* — and then to Mr. Liffey, looking rather too much his age as he sat there slumped in his chair, limp and defeated — the trusted family solicitor, who over the course of the past months had foisted on the family an utter humbug —

"Well," Fred concluded, jingling a little, "turnabout may indeed be fair play, I suppose, as the saying is." He returned the portrait to Mr. Liffey, who accepted it as he might have the forged will of Joseph Cargo — painfully, reluctantly — for the picture seemed to remind him now of that and nothing more. No longer did it put him in mind again of his youth. Instead he looked at it as though he were gazing at his crime, and at every other crime he had been guilty of in his life, and judging himself accordingly.

"Mr. Liffey, I have always thought of you as the best and kindest friend of our family, and I shall not veer from that opinion one jot," Fred declared. "I've known you since I was no higher than my father's top-boots. You have been ever vigilant in guarding the interests of our family, and so have you been now. Though to be blunt, sir, I can't myself conceive of that dogged devotion to a woman such as you've confessed to. It's one thing to admire a pretty face, but it's quite another thing to dedicate one's life to the memory of it."

"Frederick!" his wife cried out, in disappointed amazement.

"Hush, Susan," said Fred, restraining her with a look — albeit an affectionate look, but a firm one nonetheless. *Hush* he had said, and *hush* he meant; and for once his quick-spoken little wife dared not contest his authority. "Not to worry, dear. Mr. Liffey risked all to see that a tremendous wrong was put right. It's true, he may have taken matters into his hands rather liberally, but they have always been, to my mind at least, most capable hands. It would seem that a grave injustice was perpetrated by my grandfather, and like Mr. Liffey, I mean to correct it."

"*Fred!*" cried the apparition, brandishing a gnarled and woody arm. But Fred, standing his ground, thrust out an arm of his own, in a warning gesture that forestalled any action.

Came then another knocking at the door, more insistent this time, and another inquiry from Mr. Blackshaw as to the nature of the disturbance within. Again both were ignored.

"You've admitted your chicanery, Grandfather, and that's jolly sufficient for the day," said Fred. "We have Tiptop Grange, we need no more. You have left us well-provided and we thank you for that. No harm shall come to the Grange, or to Little Green Wood, save that the lawful freehold of that beautiful small property shall be restored. I see no harm in that. I'll not approve of what Mr. Liffey has done, but at any rate I understand his

motives. Although I do wish you would have come to me, sir, the moment
this treachery was uncovered, and explained the matter!"

Mr. Liffey, his old hands folded in his lap, nodded regretfully. "Oh dear,
oh dear," he sighed.

"Turn the wretch out!" growled the fiend. "Dry old cake — *baugh!*"

"It appears such a simple thing now. It was my own sad, silly fault —
forgive me, Fred! The choice was mine, and so the disgrace shall be mine.
Once we've returned to Cargo, I shall submit myself to every proper
penalty for my unlawful acts. My name shall be struck from the honorable
roll of attorneys at Common Law, and worse besides. I shall accept whatever severe measures the Court may impose, and shall expect nothing less."

"Penalty? Severe measures?" returned Fred. "Do not berate yourself
unnecessarily, sir. I shall certainly push for no penalty. Your admission and
disclosure of the facts are quite enough for me in the way of amends. No
one has been harmed here; rather, a great harm has been undone. Now, sir,
please — you must leave this melancholy mood of yours. If a man can't be
pardoned for seeing justice served, whatever can he be pardoned for?"

"Fred!" protested the apparition, with its arms outstretched as though
pleading its case to earth, heaven, and possibly elsewhere. "Fred! Fred! *Tiptop Grange!*"

"Grandfather," said the heir of Tiptop, squaring himself like the sportsman he was against the thing that had been Joseph Cargo, "you were a hard
man in this life, and a sharp one, and a cross-tempered old rascal. You were
not a man for sentiment. But Mr. Porter there and his late parents were
greatly wronged by you and by our family. To be turned out neck and crop
from one's own home, as the saying is — I can't imagine it. If Mr. Lavery had
intended Little Green Wood for the Drownders, then I mean to see it done."

"Frederick!" cried his wife.

"But dear —"

"It's a b-blight!" stammered Miss Veal, haughty of face, but pale and
trembling, too.

Then Susan, gaining courage enough to conquer her fright, boldly exclaimed —

"Not Little Green Wood! Not Mr. Interloper Squailes! Was it Mr.
Squailes who cared for your grandfather in his last days? Was it Mr.
Squailes who saw that his meals were given him? That his bedchamber was
tidied? That the doctor was sent for? Who was it who acceded to his every
wish? The money is owed to us, Frederick, to *us* — not to Mr. Interloper
Squailes — for hours and effort expended."

"*WHAT!*" exploded the horrid woody thing, turning suddenly upon her.

The face of Susan blanched, her heart missed a whole run of beats, and her hair, had it not been curly, most certainly would have curled itself.

"Not for you — only for Fred!" the apparition roared, throwing one arm and its knot of twigs in her direction. "What did you do? Order servants about? A fig for your care! What hours? What effort? Ingrate you are! Pampered little schemer! All you wanted was money — *my* money — and you not even a Cargo!"

Thus scorned, Susan beat a hasty retreat, her defiance crushed, her courage defeated; at which point the fiend trained its menacing limb on Miss Veal.

"*And you even worse!*" it thundered.

Appalled by these denunciations, the ladies were rendered too shocked for words, for the moment at least. They quailed beneath the fiend's wrathful glance, from fear as much as from the indignity of being seen to be fearful, and from the slanders delivered in so callous a fashion, in Miss Veal's mind at least, by so unthankful and uncaring a person for a deceased person as Mr. Joseph Cargo.

"Grandfather!" rang out the voice of Fred. It was so clear and commanding a voice, it was like the voice of Joseph Cargo himself in life; so clear and commanding it gave the fiend pause for a moment, as it twisted itself round to confront its grandson again — the son of its son, and the last left to carry on the noble name of Cargo. And the fiend knew it very well, too.

"I've made my mind up, Grandfather," Fred stated, drawing his neat, trim figure up a notch, "and so there is nothing more for you to rail against."

But apparently there was, as evidenced by yet another outburst, the words unintelligible but their meaning plain; but again a raised hand from Fred contained it. It was the horseman in Fred come to the fore, that authority of voice and gesture that was so useful for controlling an unruly nag, or in this case an unruly, horrid, knotty tree–like thing of a dead grandfather.

Came again the sound of Mr. Blackshaw at the door, and now a jiggling of the latch as well.

"You are the rascally side of my grandfather," Fred went on. "The good side of him, what there was of it, never would have treated Mr. Drownder so. I hold in my mind the memory only of that good side, although I hardly ever saw it. Well, sir," he said in conclusion, with a few brisk strokes of his mustaches, and a finishing tug at his waistcoat, "I am the master of Tiptop Grange now, by your choice and lawful succession. We thank you again for your generosity towards us. You've lived a long life entirely as you wished;

permit us the courtesy to do the same. And so, Grandfather, I believe it's time for you to go."

The eyes of the apparition glared at Fred from their woody setting, and at Susan and Miss Veal, who had voiced no objections to Fred's plan; for they, too, longed to see Mr. Joseph Cargo depart, and as speedily as possible. The eyes then swung round to Mr. Liffey, whose spare frame looked so much the worse for his experience, like a piece of worn drapery thrown on a chair. The apparition glared a single full look upon him, and held it.

"*Wretch!*" was its only remark, delivered in a little, low, peevish, disgusted sort of mutter.

It saw how the land lay, and however fierce its zeal for revenge, its zeal for Fred and the Grange and the sanctity of the family line trumped it; and so it yielded at last. Without further comment, the apparition shut its eyes, pulled in its limbs, and began turning slowly round and round. Its knotty face and figure began to dissolve; the wood cracked and groaned as the thing that had been Joseph Cargo proceeded to dwindle down and down, revolving as it went, getting shorter and shorter, and smaller and smaller, until it disappeared into the floor. With it went the chill that had pervaded the apartment; and so the boards of the floor were boards once more.

There was a dead pause in the room. No none stirred; no one spoke — certainly no one made a move to traverse the haunted flooring where the apparition had decamped.

It was the voice of Susan that broke the stillness at last.

"That," she declared, tossing up her chin, "is gratitude for you. He always was a frightful old screw, and an insufferable one. Get along with you, then, old brute! Frederick, your grandfather has left us in a beastly state."

"Well, dear," said her husband, smiling, "for a state it's not so bad, in my view. In fact, I find it tremendously capital!"

So easy a fellow was Fred, so affable, so generous of spirit — and so very much the opposite of his grandfather — that his natural good humor would have been proof against damnation itself. And so he extended a hand and grasped the grimy, fishy one of Mr. Porter, and wrung it heartily — wrung the hand of Mr. Jerry Porter, he who had once been Squailes, and before that Drownder, and thereby was kin to the illustrious Cargoes of Cargo.

"Well, I for one am glad to welcome you back into the family, Mr. Porter," said the master of Tiptop Grange.

"Frederick!" snapped his wife, dealing him a loving cuff upon the arm.

"The farmhouse of Little Green Wood has been long vacant, and is in some need of living in. Might you have an interest in it, Mr. Porter?"

The sum total of the horror was simply too much for Miss Veal.

"Oh, no, thenk yaw!" she cried; then she groaned, her eyes rolled back and, losing hold of her wig, she fell down in a swoon on the sofa.

It was at this moment that the door of the room opened a crack, and the sober countenance of Mr. Blackshaw came sliding round its edge. He observed Miss Veal in a stupendous faint with her wig off, and Mrs. Susan Cargo in a pet, and old Mr. Liffey buried alive in the back of his chair, and a smelly dockside creature littered with fish-scales shaking the gentlemanly hand of Fred Cargo.

"I trust I am not interrupting?" the landlord said.

CHAPTER FORTY-TWO

Another Wizard Notion

The storm that had been moving down-channel had struck fast and with a fury, and at just the wrong time. The *Salty Sue* had been left behind not long ago in Sculpin Bight, and already Mr. Threadneedle was calling for more altitude, the better to see by, and an easing of his ship's velocity, the safer to travel by. Ranged forward of the coach-house was an army of thunderclouds, their towering heads looming monstrous and phantomlike against the sky. Now and again a flash of lightning would burst from them and illuminate the heavens like another sun.

Down below the seas were running high. A few hardy ships could be glimpsed here and there, making for whatever bit of anchorage might be had amid a field of dangerous reefs and shoals. As for the grocer's own hardy ship of a flying coach-house, she, too, was struggling. Huge raging gusts of wind were lashing at her walls and roof, sending eerie, droning wails round corners and eaves. Even the chimney was howling. It was a much stiffer gale than Mr. Threadneedle had anticipated, more blusterous even than that they had weathered on the return from Deeping St. Magma. And they were battling not just wind and rain but hailstones, too, which were pounding the roof with bird-bolts and threatening the windows. It wasn't long before Mr. Threadneedle decided they must find some shelter until conditions moderated.

But where to take the house down? The mainland roundabout was rugged and high, with sheer cliffs dropping straight down into the sea. Moreover the mountains were known to extend for a considerable distance eastwards — no harborage there. A flat stretch of earth — indeed safe harborage of any kind — was in short supply along this particular coast. It rapidly became clear, however, that they had little choice, for flying on into the teeth of the gale was not only imprudent, it was downright foolhardy. Already there had been some odd little jerks and shudders of the wheel, and ominous groanings from the walls, of a sort Mr. Threadneedle had no experience of, and which an uneasy presentiment urged him to heed.

"We shall need to set her down, I think," he announced to the others from his station at the helm. "I dare say it'll be far the wiser course to allow this storm to pass us by."

"Hallo! And where do you propose to set her down, sir?" returned Mr. Frobisher. He had been examining the way ahead from the front bay window along with Tim Christmas. The grocer's apprentice-of-sorts had just eased the speed-coils to one-tenth, slowing the house to a relative snail's pace across the sky.

"Will it be safe, do you think, Mr. T., setting her down in these conditions?" asked Mrs. Matchless.

"It will be safer than holding to our present course," the grocer replied. "This storm is growing too violent; I shouldn't care to tangle with it further. And the clouds themselves are of such proportions that —"

"There's a small island, sir, dead straight ahead, with what looks to be a strip of beach!" Tim called out.

"I see it there," said Dr. Pinches, peering with hooded hands through the glass. "It appears promising — if tiny!"

"It looks to be Soar," said Mr. Frobisher. "Yes, that's just what it is. I've seen it before in my travels. That arching bridge of rock there is distinctive."

"I know of Soar," said Mr. Threadneedle. "Tim, you'll remember — we passed it on the journey home from Magma. By my recollection it should suit our needs. We shall make for Soar. Prepare to go alow."

"Aye, sir," said the boy, returning at once to the mangles. He kicked open the panel in the floor, to uncover the porthole, and seized a crank-handle in each hand.

"Coils up! Bring her down, lad, steadily, and slow us as we go."

Tim swung the mangles in reverse, sending the coach-house down toward the approaching bit of shore. At the same time a touch on one of the pedals dampened her forward velocity.

"It does seem rather a small place," Dottie observed, "but it is coming up on us frightfully fast!"

"Tim will guide her," Mr. Threadneedle said, trusting as always to the keen eye and steady hand of his apprentice. His own hands, steady as they were, he kept on the helm. The rather small place began growing rather large in the windows as the coach-house plunged down towards it.

On a sudden there was a vivid burst of light, followed by a clap of thunder. Once, twice, three times a burst and then a boom. Came then an utterly blinding flash, and what sounded more like an explosion than thunder, and something that looked and smelled like smoke began filling the coach-house.

A fire had broken out in the ceiling. At the same time the house lurched violently to one side, and then abruptly swung about. The weather-vane came crashing down through the roof, narrowly missing Mr. Threadneedle at his station on the platform. A shower of rain poured in through the opening left behind — a black, smoking hole — as yellow flames licked at the belts and pulleys around it.

"We've been hit by lightning!" Mr. Frobisher exclaimed.

"The rudder, sir!" Tim cried out, staring in alarm at the charred corpse of the weather-vane, and then at Mr. Threadneedle, who was undergoing as thorough a drenching as if he were standing under a pump.

"Oh, gracious goodness!" said Dottie, as the water jetting off the grocer spilled over her. Dr. Pinches stumbled backwards, the rain in an instant soaking his hat and transforming his suit into a makeshift mack.

Shouts of warning, exclamations of dismay. All at once the coach-house pitched forward, and for a horrid moment Mr. Threadneedle thought she was about to lose her lift. The cage-coil in one corner had been damaged, and now the fire was threatening the apparatus of another.

The electric fluid apparently had struck the weather-vane and shot down through its controlling rod and wheel. Fortunately Mr. Threadneedle's hand had *not* been upon that small wheel the moment the lightning hit; fortunately, too, the hole in the roof was allowing much of the smoke to escape. Now if only the rain, which was pelting Mr. Threadneedle with such efficiency, could put out the fire!

Nonetheless the mangles still turned in the capable hands of Tim, and most of the wheels and pulleys still went round, and the belts and chains still rolled. Owing to the damaged coil, all aboard had been forced to grab at whatever was handy to preserve their balance. As for Mr. Threadneedle, he had no choice; he had to remain at the helm gripping the wheel and taking the rain.

"We're coming over land now, sir," Tim announced. "The strip of beach is dead straight below. Just a bit more on the steering-coil to larboard — gently, sir!"

Down the house plummeted through the mist and rain. The hole in the roof was growing as the wind stripped more of the tiles away. By now the rain was having an effect on everyone — not only was it disagreeably wet, it was disagreeably cold. Great blown sheets of it were lashing the house on all sides, but were serving the hoped-for purpose: they were drenching the flames almost as effectively as they were Mr. Threadneedle.

"We're very nearly there!" came the call from Tim.

"Prepare yourselves, everyone!" the grocer warned, straining to make his voice heard above the droning of the wind. "There is liable to be a considerable jolt!"

Suiting the action to the word, Dr. Pinches braced himself against the nearest bulkhead, and Dottie the nearest locker, and Mr. Frobisher the carpenter's-bench.

Down and down the coach-house plunged toward the strip of beach. Tim had fixed his eye on an area of higher ground far back of the seething breakers, and was endeavoring to guide the house towards it. At the last moment, however, a tremendous gust of wind blew up that tossed his calculations out of window. It was followed almost at once by a rending crash as the coach-house made acquaintance with the island of Soar.

Sounds of timbers splintering, masonry cracking, and glass shattering erupted on every side. Mr. Threadneedle lost his hold on the wheel and toppled from the platform into the arms of Mr. Frobisher, whose action saved him no doubt from a very nasty injury. Dottie was sent reeling towards one of the well-stuffed chairs by the hearth, where she came to rest, comfortably enough, in a sitting posture on its cushioned seat. Dr. Pinches, having collided with a locker, tumbled over it like an acrobat, as cleanly as any reverend gentleman ever tumbled over an inconvenient point of Scripture.

"Are you damaged? Mrs. Matchless? Dr. Pinches?" cried the grocer, as he rushed from one to another of his friends to ascertain their condition. Poor Mr. Threadneedle! Oblivious to his own sorry state, he was looking more like a drowned duck than an island squire as he attended to them.

"Not to worry, Mr. T., I'm quite unharmed," said Dottie, rising from her chair, with both her sprightliness and her good sense reasonably intact. "And what of you, Doctor? Have you survived?"

"I have, thank you, Mrs. Matchless," said Dr. Pinches, with rather more confidence perhaps than his soggy appearance justified. "But I'm afraid, Mr. Threadneedle, that your coach-house is something of a sight, as are you — as are all of us, I fear!" he added, and taking up his hat, proceeded to wring an amazing amount of water from it.

The doctor was correct on every count. Much of the roof, from the helm right across to the farther side of the house, had gone missing, as had much of the glass and many of the lattice frames in the windows. Moreover on setting down — or crashing — one entire corner, that with the damaged cage-coil, had partially separated from the main fabric. Gaps in the timbers and plasterwork had been created through which more rain was seeping. The fire in the ceiling had gone out, but a part of the apparatus round it had been damaged, some of it dismembered, some melted, some mangled. And as for the mangles themselves —

They were unoccupied.

"Tim!" Mr. Threadneedle called out. A sudden stab of fear, more chilling than any he had encountered in his life — worse even than the fear of saber-cats in Chamomile Street, or Mistress Scimitar prowling the church of Deeping St. Magma — pierced his heart. "Tim! Tim! Where are you, young man?"

No reply.

They discovered the boy lying unconscious on the floor not far from his station. He had a sorely bruised cheek, and a wound in the side of his head was oozing crimson.

"Oh, my Lord — *Tim!*" the grocer exclaimed, horrified, and dashing to the lad's aid, attempted as best he knew how to revive him. It was Dottie, however, the experienced boarding-house-keeper, who adroitly took charge of the crisis. The good landlady directed that Tim be moved to a chair by the hearth — the one area of the house still protected from the weather — and there commenced tending to his injuries with a handkerchief.

"Have you any medicines, Mr. T.? Have you some soap, perhaps? Lavender-water? Have you any plasters?" she asked, while stopping a moment to fit on her silver spectacles, so as to view her patient better.

Mr. Threadneedle went quickly to one of the lockers where a small store of medical items was kept, and returned with some washballs and a bar of soap, some extract of witch hazel, and a piece of court plaster. He watched in admiration of the widow Matchless — dear Dottie from Chamomile Street days! — as she skillfully dressed the wound in the side of Tim's head, and soothed the bruise on his cheek. The doctor and Mr. Frobisher looked on with expressions of concern. Mr. Threadneedle, feeling suddenly helpless and chicken-hearted, turned briefly away. One might have supposed those were tears dripping down his face, but of course they were only raindrops leaking from his hair.

Or were they?

The coach-house — his workshop, his sanctuary, his place of glorious retreat from Plush and Kimber, and the best and finest jewel of his fancy — was a hopeless ruin, impossible to be mended. A sad and broken wreck it had become, all in an instant — a shattered dream, a vanished wonder of the world. How staunch and skyworthy she had been, but how fragile, too!

His marvelous flying coach of a coach-house lay a shambles, and Tim unconscious and who knew what else besides.

"Tinkering! All on account of tinkering!" he was heard to say, in an agony of self-approach. "If Mrs. Matchless can't restore him — if the lad should sink — I shall never be forgiven it, and justly so. *Justly so!* And as I am an honest man and a true Christian grocer, never shall I forgive myself in this life — never, never!"

Dr. Giddeus Pinches — he who longed to be shorn of his priestly duties and immerse himself in his retirement and his Greenshields — stepped in now to aid Mrs. Matchless in attending to the lad, and together they worked to coax him back to wakefulness. Dr. Giddeus Pinches, he who had grown so impatient with his life of ministering to the noisy denizens of the quay, now found himself ministering to a poor village lad from far-off Truro whom he hardly knew. To his surprise, all thought of ancient polished bronze and Nantle Minster and his Greenshields went right out of his head, so many miles away they seemed now — and which, of course, they were.

At length there arose a sigh from the lips of Tim, and he opened those keen eyes of his — eyes that remained albeit a trifle muddied — and glanced about him. At once Mr. Threadneedle placed a comforting hand on his arm.

"How are you, lad?" he inquired, eagerly. "How are you, Tim? No serious damage, eh?" (This last he added, as much perhaps for his own comfort of mind as for Tim's.)

Dazed and shaken, the boy drew himself up a little in his chair and looked about him. Then he touched a hand to the plaster on his temple and groaned. The feel of the plaster, and the sting of the wound it concealed, jarred loose his thoughts and sent his memory rushing back to him.

"I'm quite all right, sir," he answered. "No serious damage, I — I don't think."

"Good lad! Excellent!"

"Not to worry," Dottie told the boy, smiling at him through her spectacles. "It will mend in time. We are certainly glad your injuries were no worse."

"Chin up," Mr. Frobisher encouraged him.

"You must rest awhile," said the grocer.

"And you, sir? And all of you?" Tim asked, glancing round again. "You are well?"

"No other injuries of note," said Mr. Frobisher.

"How fares your recollection?" Dr. Pinches asked.

"It's returning to me, sir, slowly," the lad replied. "When we collided with the earth, I lost my grip on the mangles and was thrown down. My head must have struck against one of the crank-handles. It quite knocked me out, I'm afraid."

"Is your sight affected? Can you see clearly?" Dottie asked, with an inquiring peer into his eyes.

"Yes, ma'am, I can see quite well."

"There is no ringing of the ears?"

"No, ma'am. There is something of an ache in my neck, though, but apart from that —"

Here Tim stopped and looked about him a third time, not at the anxious faces of his companions, but at the dripping ruin that surrounded them. "It looks to be raining in the coach-house," he observed. "The roof — the lightning —"

"It *is* very wet," Mr. Threadneedle admitted, "and very cold. This storm has soaked us thoroughly, and I dare say it isn't finished with us yet. It'll be dark soon. We must make ourselves a shelter here, where the roof is still in place, and build a nice little fire, or we'll surely freeze."

"It seems we have run ourselves into another scrape, sir."

"A scrape it is indeed," the grocer admitted with a frown, "but sufficient unto the day are the vicissitudes thereof. Eh, young man?"

Before getting to the aforesaid task, however, Mr. Threadneedle paid a visit to the window for a brief examination of the neighborhood.

The house had set down nearly as Tim had intended it, on some relatively smooth ground at the hinder end of the beach. The breakers lay half a furlong or more below them, and if high water on Soar were not too high, they should remain comfortably distant. The sky still flashed on occasion, and the thunder still boomed, but with greater intervals now between the two. The storm was moving off, although it was unlikely to be gone until well after nightfall.

Of the island and its inhabitants, Mr. Threadneedle knew next to nothing, nor did Mr. Frobisher seem to know much more; and so the thought of being marooned here with smashed windows open to the air and the night coming on was making him a trifle uneasy. Aside from the iron crow and a light hatchet, the fire shovel and poker, and a hammer and chisel or two, they had no weapons, not so much as a rusty cutlass. The grocer had been meaning to correct this deficiency since the return from Deeping St. Magma, but, like many another thing, he had yet to get around to it.

It was Mr. Frobisher who joined him now at the window. Having found an umbrella in one of the lockers, he had put it to immediate use, in view of the rain that *would* persist in dripping through the roof.

"Look here," said Allan, striding up under cover of twilled silk, "you say you have some kindling and turf hidden round this house of yours? Well, we should like to get a fire blazing in the chimney now, crave your pardon, sir, or as soon as feasible."

The grocer, who had been thinking so hard at the window he had lost track of the minutes, hurriedly replied in the affirmative, having taken this broad hint of Mr. Frobisher's that they should be getting on with the task at hand.

The area round the chimney remained the best preserved, although the hearth-rug had been soaked through and through, and so some dry tarpauling was procured from a locker and laid over it as a temporary measure. Some old curtains of the damask variety, which were to have been hung at the windows — another thing Mr. Threadneedle hadn't gotten around to — were taken from storage and hung instead from the apparatus above, to form a kind of screen round the area. Some tapers and kindling, a tinderbox, and some pieces of turf and cordwood — all thankfully dry — were brought out as well and pressed into service.

"Unfortunately we can't shift the furniture, as it's fastened rather solidly in place," Mr. Threadneedle said. "But with the damask hung round us here, like a stage-curtain, a good shelter may be had while we await some improvement in the weather."

Some blankets had been hunted up as well, and an old boat-cloak, and a jacket, and a muffler or two, and a couple of hats. A pleasant bit of fire was soon burning in the grate, and some progress was made in drying articles of their clothing round the fender. Tim, who looked to be regaining his spirits in the fire's cheery blaze, sat across from Mrs. Matchless, who had been accorded the chair opposite, while the doctor, Mr. Threadneedle, and Allan Frobisher disposed themselves about the tarpauling. The warmth of the fire soon filled the space where they were ensconced and did much to alleviate their discomfort. And despite the darkening scene without, the combined glow of the chimney and the wax-lights kept their little world inside the curtains lively and bright.

To be on the safe side, they had double-latched the door, and drawn the shutters across what remained of the windows, being careful about the fragments of glass that lay strewn about. None knew what manner of beasts might be afoot on this island of Soar, but apart from these few measures there was little available to the travelers in the way of security. Still, things could have been worse. The coach-house could have broken apart in the sky after the lightning-strike; and so Mr. Threadneedle, after some careful reflection, was moved to offer thanks for their having arrived safe and whole upon the island, marooned though they might be.

There was little food in the house, only half a brown loaf and some cheese, a few tea-cakes and some tea, a bag of walnuts, and a couple of biffins that Mustard had *not* plundered. Some rainwater was collected — it was one item they had in quantity — and was set to boiling on the hob for making the tea, which they drank from pewter goblets. Both the doctor and Mr. Threadneedle were soon yearning for their pipes, inspired perhaps by Mr. Frobisher's taking his ease upon an elbow while smoking out his one and only cigar.

In time the thunder was reduced to the occasional distant grumble, and the lightning to vague flickerings, until both ceased altogether; and so the storm moved on and over the mountains and departed the coast.

The morning dawned crisp and pink. Instead of rain, it was a shower of sunbeams that greeted their eyes, streaming through huge rifts in the remnant overcast. Blessedly welcome as it was, the day brought with it a fresh and even more sobering view of the ruin that had been the coach-house. The curtains had been opened and the shutters drawn back, to let in whatever light was not already streaming in through the roof. And so there it all was around them.

"It really is a mess, sir," Tim declared.

The grocer nodded sadly. *"Tinkering!"* he was heard again to mutter, before turning away from the sight, the dismal, charred, waterlogged reality of it simply too much for him to bear. "Rather a jumble. And so there's an end to it, I suppose . . ." And his voice trailed off.

"A difficult problem, sir, how we're to get out of this."

"A skull-cruncher, lad, and I for one am quite at a loss for a solution. Our coach, Tim," the grocer sighed, with a mournful shake of his head, "will, I fear, never again carry us joyfully through the cloud-tops. We have had our day and must be satisfied with that. I'm afraid there's no such thing as perfection in this world. Do you know, I believe I've quite gone off the idea of flying coach-houses altogether. Still, I'm grateful for our good fortune, for we have had the narrowest of squeaks and are here to talk of it!"

Mr. Threadneedle was feeling a trifle sorry for himself this morning, and Tim recognized it; but of course the feeling was understandable, even in one of the best-hearted men in existence.

"What you say is very true, sir," the lad acknowledged.

The grocer picked up the fused and blackened mass that had been a gleaming weather-vane, looked at it, shook his head sadly, and laid the object by. Then he turned and his glance fell on Tim, his young charge, his apprentice-of-sorts, and his solemn responsibility — intelligent, well-mannered, unfailingly cheerful Tim, so bruised now of cheek and plastered of temple. Instantly the self-pity that had sunk his spirits took its leave of him, like a bad dream fleeing the sunshine, and his face beamed again with its customary radiance. His gray eyes twinkled again, his meek little mustaches curled themselves up again, and all was right once more with a sundered world — or very nearly.

"Yes, Tim, it is true. And what is true as well is that *you* are well — and for that I am most grateful of all."

"And Mrs. Matchless is well, too, sir."

"Of course, of course!"

"And the doctor and Mr. Frobisher."

"Just so, lad! Isn't it a wonder, and a miracle? Let us venture outside then, and see what surprises this place may have in store."

The place did indeed have a surprise in store, but it was not until the next day that it saw fit to deliver it. The morning was spent inspecting the damage to the coach-house — the charred beams and splintered timbers, the heaps of red brick that had tumbled from the chimney-top, the tiles loosed from the high roof and eaves, and the roof itself with its gaping cavity — and exploring round the general area. The house had settled in the crook of an earthy slope. Below it lay the sand beach and the waves curling ashore; above it some open ground rose toward a dark forest. Above the vast watery expanse to the east the sun shone clear. Through the haze an outline of the mainland could be glimpsed, dim and vague in the distance.

It was a wild scene, and a solitary one. No one and no thing came to disturb them as they pursued their activities; if there were inhabitants in the neighborhood, they offered no sign of their presence. Nonetheless everyone remained vigilant, casting regular glances here and there for a hint of anything suspicious, particularly in the direction of the dark wood. A freshwater spring was discovered nearby, and a cache of mussels at the shore, both by Dr. Pinches. Meanwhile Mrs. Matchless and Tim spent some time tidying up inside the house, putting the contents of the lockers in order, and sweeping the glass and other debris from the floor.

It was in the afternoon of their second day on the island that Mr. Threadneedle, standing on a little point of ground before the house, spied what he thought to be a sail on the horizon. Taking out his pocket-telescope, he trained it on the spot, and beheld there the sheen of distant canvas. It was a coasting-vessel, and as he tracked her, it became apparent that she was making for Soar. As the ship grew large in his glass, Mr. Threadneedle could see that she was a three-master, one hung with a lug-rig rather than square, and carrying both main-and mizzen-topsails. Near and nearer she came, and as she did, the grocer's heart leaped; a shout escaping his lips brought the others to his side. He knew that three-master in the eye of his telescope only too well — she was the *Salty Sue*.

As the lugger drew in, it was observed that her progress was something labored, with more than a hint of a roll to her starboard beam. She dropped her hook in the waters offshore — heavy waters they were still, so that it required some little effort for the anchorage to be made secure. Mr. Threadneedle and his companions strode down to the water's edge and began waving their arms above their heads, to gain the attention of those on deck. It was not long before the ship's surf-boat was lowered and begin pulling briskly for the shore. First of the two aboard to plant sea-boot to strand was Captain Barnaby, who with one of his primest sailormen had come to learn what assistance they might render, for he had observed the castaways and their plight in his spyglass.

"Smite me dumb and split me!" was his reaction on viewing the ruin of the coach-house at close range. The eyes in his hatchet-face were filled with sorrow. Knitting his brows and crunching them down tight, he threw out his chin and took a skipperly turn round the house, demanding to know what could be done to save her. Mr. Threadneedle had to inform him that nothing could be done, that the house had become a casualty of the gale. On hearing this, the captain became so disheartened, one might have thought it was his own marvelous flying coach rather than the grocer's that had been wrecked. In his view, a ship that sailed the skies was every bit the equal of a ship that sailed the seas, soak him and bleed him, and deserving of all due reverence and admiration.

As for the captain's own vessel, it turned out that the *Salty Sue* had begun taking on water again after departing Sculpin Bight, and so he'd decided to haul his wind and stand away northeasterly, having no longer pressing cause to make for Goforth. The three-eyed giants having been dispatched by the great gliding demons of the deep, he intended to hug the coast and make his slow way back to channel waters. The hurried repairs to his ship had been insufficient, and the rough seas left in the wake of the storm had further weakened her planking. Then other seams had opened up at her starboard waterline, causing the men even heavier labor at the pumps. Knowing that this island of Soar boasted small but safe harborage, the captain had laid his course for its tiny bit of shore, there to bide awhile and repair damages. On drawing in, he had been attracted by the signals from Mr. Threadneedle and the others, and so the rest we know.

It was clear that the injuries to the lugger were nothing so extensive as those to the coach-house, which never more would be skyworthy; nonetheless, it would be some little while before the *Salty Sue* was plying channel seas again. But she had provisions aboard her to last for a spell, and her small hutches for the (purported) comfort of passengers, and a skipper who was only too glad to welcome the travelers aboard — even the reverend doctor, the self-professed fisher of men — once repairs were complete. As if this were not enough, her captain steadfastly refused any offer of money for their rescue, refuge, or even their victuals.

"Belly-timber," he called it, speaking of his galley-cook's daily board — his ship's biscuit, dried neat's tongue, and pickles — "spiced," he hinted, "with salt pork fried and prime ale." Moreover there were fish in the sea to be hooked, and a good store of mussels roundabout to plenish supplies. And so there they all were now, the captain and his company, and the grocer and *his* company, all marooned together for a time on the island of Soar, and casting about how best to improve their lots.

"For look 'ee now," the captain reminded them, "how this life of ours may go foul and a-wrack. Still ye must keep bold hearts. Ye must keep yer bearings secure and yer sails trimmed. Ye must lay yer head to the wind and fight through it, though ye be kicked into the scuppers for it!"

And while neither Mr. Threadneedle nor any of his companions had the least intention of being kicked into the scuppers of life, or sunk fathoms deep like a stone to bunk with Davy Jones, none saw fit to raise an objecting voice, for they understood the sentiment.

When Dottie Matchless learned that the captain had abandoned his plans to sail for Goforth, she naturally inquired after the lady lodger of her friend Mrs. J.; and so the puzzling and tragic events concerning the loss of Miss Wastefield were made known to her and the others. In conclusion it was the captain's opinion that his pretty-timbered passenger, in despair at her troubles, had flung herself overboard, to the considerable sorrow of both her young gentleman and her maid. A mystery-lady she had been, sarten sure! And he shook his great silvery head at the tragedy of it.

The reaction of Mr. Frobisher on hearing this was not difficult to judge. Ancient polished bronze be hanged, it was clear he had suffered a shock. He had parted from Miss Wastefield knowing it unlikely he would ever set eyes on her again — but such an outcome as this he had hardly foreseen! A vision of her loveliness seemed to drift before those eyes now, filling him with sadness and regret. Though he strove to hide it, he remained in his shocked state for some while after. It was a state not so different in its way, perhaps, from that of young Martin, a man grieving for a woman he had known so long, and loved, and ultimately lost, and Mr. Frobisher for a woman he'd hardly known at all.

Dr. Pinches, too, was saddened to hear of Miss Wastefield's disappearance, and the manner of it, and was driven to reflect on his own conduct in respect of her. It seemed not that long ago that she had come to the rectory seeking his help, and indeed it hadn't been long; it was merely that so much had happened in the interval. What he had given more thought to, it struck him now, was the treasure he'd never seen — priceless relic from glorious Aegean days! — more thought perhaps than to the young lady herself and her troubles. He even went so far as to blame himself for her loss, for not having aided her sufficiently in her time of crisis. In truth he'd scarcely credited her story at first hearing, and who could have condemned him for that? But the sight of three-eyed pincered giants from ancient Kaftor had quite altered his opinion.

He had been more concerned for an ancient treasure than for her. How paltry it seemed to him now! Still, even in his present mood he found he couldn't restrain his curiosity, and soon found himself inquiring of Captain Barnaby as to the fate of a certain hand-mirror. To this the skipper replied he'd gotten it second-hand (as it were) that Mr. Somerset had cast it over the rail, never wanting to see it again; though what a hand-mirror might have had to do with the mystery-lady's disappearance the captain had no notion. The heart of Dr. Pinches promptly sank with the mirror, and so he left off his melancholy ponderings, resolved never again to place ancient polished bronze above priestly duty.

Subsequent to this, Captain Barnaby, still very much fascinated by the coach-house, resumed his walk round its dreary, storm-battered front. Shortly he came upon Mr. Threadneedle, who was at the moment inspecting that part of the house and its cage-coil that had separated from the main fabric. The hoverstone of the coil had been torn free of its restraints in the crash and broken into two halves. Now, as the grocer examined that fractured stone with its mysterious gridwork of colors, he was for the first time granted a view of its interior. It was then that a revelation flashed upon him, so abruptly and so momentously it caused his quizzing-glass to pop from his eye.

"Why, this isn't so much a stone as it is a manufactured article of some kind — a part of a mechanism," he murmured, thinking himself alone.

"A mechanism, sir?" repeated the captain, crouching for a peer across his shoulder. "Sink me for a grunion and roast me — so it looks!"

"These bands here of the many colors — their arrangement is far too extensive and regular to be natural. I had thought them a mere curiosity of the rock face, but as you can see, they extend right through the stone. But they're not veins; what's more, they are not even of mineral composition. I am quite at a loss to know what they are! And these other structures here, these thin plates at the very heart of the stone — they are not natural either. What can they be? They are like nothing I've ever seen."

"Aye, so it be — Clipperton's stones!" nodded the captain.

"But they *are* only stones, sir — bits of the shooting star that caused the sundering. How can there be a mechanism in them?" asked Tim, who had joined them now, as had Mr. Frobisher, the latter in an effort to put off his mood.

"Mayhap," suggested the captain, pushing back his mariner's bonnet — "mayhap they bean't bits of a shooting star at all? Leastwise none as any alive has knowledge of."

So what might they be, then, Tim wondered? For surely these *were* the hoverstones of Captain Clipperton, were they not? Or so Mr. Threadnee-dle had been told by the trader Hicklebeep.

"If Clipperton laid 'em to blame for the sundering, then so it likely was," opined the captain. "But what business a mechanism has in a shooting star be a plaguy, perplexable question, one beyond any answering at present, or I'm a shotten tomcod. Well, sirs and boy, to yarn with ye be fair and pleasant diversion, that's sure, but I've a need to give run again to these sea-legs and make inspection o' the *Sue*. Much there is to be 'complished aboard her, and I'd best see how Mr. Sly and the men be getting about it."

Mr. Threadneedle, rapt in thought at this latest riddle of the stones, on a sudden glanced up, looking first at the captain, and then at the captain's vessel lying wounded offshore. In a single instant he had been struck with the most wondrous, the most marvelous of ideas; it was like a thunderbolt of the imagination. With every second that passed, the idea grew in his mind's eye, like the lugger in his glass — luminous, expansive, triumphant. It was an idea, indeed, so very marvelous, it would cause him to put off his renouncement of tinkering for some long time to come. It was, simply put, a staggerer.

"Captain Barnaby?" he said, rising.

"Sir?" returned the captain, delaying.

"By your leave, Captain Barnaby, that ship of yours — the *Salty Sue*. Though presently damaged, she is otherwise a right seaworthy craft, is she not, all things considered?"

"Sink me, sir, if she bean't! And the primest."

"And built to withstand much buffeting from the weather? Apart from those few occasions, of course, when her seams stand in need of oakum?"

"Aye, sir," the captain replied, only too conscious of his ship's present indisposition. "But she's stout-built and trim, and will take many a heavy lashing of sea and cankering of brine, or I'm a spiced jurket."

"So she is very sturdily built?"

"Aye, sir, and she rides well."

Mr. Threadneedle shifted his attention again to the coach-house. So sadly drooping she looked now! Certainly she would never sail the skies again; however —

"I have had an idea," he said, drawing the captain a little aside, the better to speak with him in confidence. It was plain this marvelous new fancy of his had quite captured his fancy.

"You have stood in some need of funds of late, I think, Captain?"

The question he posed in this delicate way, so as not to cause the captain undue embarrassment, for the skipper, he knew, was a proud man.

"Aye, sir, perish and plague me," the captain admitted, with a fierce crunching of his brows. He rolled the huge quid in his mouth to his other cheek. "Sarten sure it is that the bailiff's men await at Nantle. Nuthooks, sir! Likely yon duck shall be taken as soon as she hoves in sight o' the quay. So we've a need to keep her clear of the city and rove 'mongst these islands for a spell, with eyes and ears on the stretch, till my wife sends word she can be taken safe inshore."

"Then my idea should serve, and admirably, too. You have a vessel with an otherwise sturdy frame. You have sailorly men in your company to effect improvements. The coach-house will never move from this spot; I fear she has seen Smithy Bank for the last time. But," said the grocer, laying his hand on the fractured hoverstone — "we have here six stones of gravitite remaining, and a seventh if pressed, and cage-coils, too, and most of the apparatus."

Captain Barnaby stroked his long chin in thought as he listened. Then he pulled off his mariner's bonnet and ran a fist through his silvery hair. His eyes, as sharp and piercing as a frigate bird's, traded glances with the grocer's twinkling dittoes.

"So-ho — cherish my guts, sir!" he cried, as understanding dawned.

"And your own ship, although damaged and not so seaworthy at present, is *not* hopelessly marooned."

"Nor she is."

"It seems to me rather a natural progression. It will broaden the range and services of your craft considerably, this idea I have in mind. Why, there are a thousand and one advantages I could name."

"A thousand and one, sir?"

"Not least of which it should put her quite out of reach of the bailiff's men."

"Aye, that it will!" said the skipper, nodding vigorously.

"Then my idea is of some interest to you, Captain?"

"Aye, sir!"

"Some space will need to be cleared in your hold, of course — in the area of the ship's waist, I should think — once your repairs have been completed."

"Aye, it can be done, sir, for she be fair and capacious craft."

"The surf-boat can be used for the transport of materials from the coach-house, with the heavier apparatus hauled aboard by lever and tackle —"

Tim Christmas, who had overheard much of this exchange — he had been stretching his own eyes and ears considerably to make it all out — comprehended the grocer's plan at once and, before the captain could make further answer, exclaimed —

"That's the *wizardest* notion, sir!"

Mr. Frobisher, too, had heard sufficient to enlighten him. He and the others then glanced at one another, as though to confirm that each was thinking along the same lines, and that each believed this latest and most marvelous notion of Mr. Threadneedle's was a feasible one.

"What say you, then, Captain?" said the grocer, folding his arms and smiling. "It will get us safely clear of this island, and home and dry before too many days have passed."

Captain Barnaby thought it over some few moments more. He crunched his brows, and shifted his quid, and ruffled up his hair. His gaze strayed numerous times from the coach-house to his ship yonder and back again. He tugged a little at his coat, and at the shawls and mufflers slung round his neck, and stamped his old sea-boots on the ground. Then he cleared his voice, and in loud and right sailorly fashion declared —

"Love my limbs, sir, but these stones o' Clipperton's mustn't be left to languish on this island o' Soar. They must be put to their proper use, sarten sure. Smite me dumb, what's the worst as could happen? The worst I bleeve is that she could sink, sir — like *six* stones!"

"And a seventh, if pressed," said Tim.